The Best Novels and Stories of Eugene Manlove Rhodes

The Best Novels and Stories of

EUGENE MANLOVE RHODES

Edited by Frank V. Dearing

Introduction by J. Frank Dobie

Foreword to the Bison Book Edition
by W. H. Hutchinson

University of Nebraska Press
Lincoln and London

First Bison Book printing: 1987
Most recent printing indicated by the first digit below:
1   2   3   4   5   6   7   8   9   10

Library of Congress Cataloging-in-Publication Data
Rhodes, Eugene Manlove, 1869–1934.
The best novels and stories of Eugene Manlove Rhodes.
1. Western stories. 2. New Mexico—Literary
collections. 3. Frontier and pioneer life—Literary
collections. I. Dearing, Frank V.   II. Title.
PS3535.H68A6   1987   818'.5209   87-12466
ISBN 0-8032-3885-1
ISBN 0-8032-8928-6 (pbk.)

Reprinted by arrangement with W. H. Hutchinson, Literary Executor of
the Estate of Eugene Manlove Rhodes.

"Pasó Por Aquí" and "Bransford of Rainbow Range" are reprinted
by permission of the University of Oklahoma Press.

"Good Men and True," "Say Now Shibboleth," "Bransford of Rainbow
Range," ("The Little Eohippus"), "Consider the Lizard," "Hit the Line
Hard," "The Desire of the Moth," "Pasó Por Aquí," "Maid Most Dear" and
"The Trusty Knaves" originally appeared in the Saturday Evening Post.

To
MAY DAVISON RHODES
without whose encouragement
and help none of the stories
in this volume would likely
have been written

CONTENTS

FOREWORD TO THE
BISON BOOK EDITION

BY W. H. HUTCHINSON

People who approach these stories expecting them to come from the realm of thud-and-blunder, the domain of horse opera, are apt to be as surprised as is a pup with its first porcupine. The land, the people, the flora and fauna in Rhodes's stories are drawn from the life he had known and loved and had written about with the longing of an exile for his "ain countree."

Rhodes came to Engle, New Mexico, on the *Jornada del Muerto* in 1881, "the year that Billy the Kid was killed" and he began his teens. He lived the next twenty-five years on the frontier that was southern New Mexico—from the White Sands of the Tularosa Basin to the Arizona line, from El Paso northward to the plains of San Augustine—and lived each of those years like a colt that keeps fishing for the bit.

Every major tile in the whole mosaic of frontier development between the Front Range and the Sierra Nevada–Cascade crests was laid down at Engle—so compressed in time that one boy growing into manhood could see and be a part of it all. It was the supply point for the mining boom in the Black Range across the Rio Grande that saw at least a half-dozen prospect holes blossom into towns of two thousand or more people within six months and smaller settlements that Rhodes once described as "too humorous to mention."

Coincidental with this excitement, the Santa Fe Railway, building down from Albuquerque to meet the Southern Pacific at Deming, made Engle a division point, with sidings, roundhouse, and a pumping plant that brought water from the Rio Grande. The craze for cattle that swept the West after the Civil War came to the *Jornada* when Rhodes did, the cattle in Socorro County jumping from nine thousand to seventy thousand head between 1882 and 1884.

Engle inevitably became the shipping and supply point for a vast range area, as well as the operational center for outfits that used the unfenced grama grasslands of the *Jornada* proper. There both the Bar Cross and the 7TX ran between fifteen and twenty thousand head, *poco más o menos,* while across the Rio Grande the J-Half Circle-Cross, the "John Cross" in the land's lingo, tallied forty thousand head at its peak.

The pattern of Rhodes's frontier years was work—hard, physical, dangerous, sweaty, grimy toil. Mining, jerk line freighting, horse wrangling, bronc riding, cowboying, road building, ditch and well digging—he did them all and anything else at hand to be done and did them with everything he had to offer. Work became and remained the hard core of the importunate spirit with which he confronted life as a "Ragged Individualist." So you will find that his characters are humanists enough to find joy in what they do, even as did Rhodes himself.

In the work equality of the oasis land in which he spent memorable years, he learned that a man's color, race, creed, or tongue mattered not when it came down to the nitty-gritty. What mattered is what he did when he stood in a dark place with a chill wind blowing. You will find no ethnocentrism in Rhodes's stories, although he stemmed from English-Welsh stock that had been in this country since 1665. "When you ride up to that camp," he wrote, "you ride a'whistlin, real loud and pleasant. That Charlie Bird's half-Cherokee and half white and them's two bad breeds." Among his idols was Francisco Bojórquez, Baja California–born, who bossed the Texan crew that worked the John Cross cattle.

These years gave Rhodes a carefree fatalism, never voiced as such but implicit in the life of the land. He and three friends were riding the *Jornada* one day, laughing and joking, "hoorawin'" one another, when a thunderstorm came up. Lightning killed Warren Carpenter and his horse; the others were only stunned. When they rolled the horse off, they saw that he had died with laughter on his lips. Rhodes and two friends—three sixteen-year-olds—were building a stone house for a homesteader on Animas Creek. When they finished up at noon one day, Gene rode east; his friends rode west. An Apache got them the next day, killing one outright because he had a gun, and driving a crowbar through the other's skull. Besides these natural hazards of his frontier years, Rhodes had known flaring violence—"I have seen thirteen men killed and I prefer peace."

Unless the women in his stories—and the best of them have no feminine interest at all—are road-weary from the hammering of their years, they are "infrangibly virginal" and often creak when they move. This is the way the lonely lad with the cleft palate had pedestaled the *correctas* of his youth. He had known the other kind, *seguramente que sí,* but he did not commemorate them in his prose.

He used easterners in his stories as an explicatory device, and also to show that his beloved West had not been inhabited by tawny, unlettered Visigothic barbarians. His villains, those of deepest dye, are those who profit, yea grow swollen and fat, from the labors of other men, and the worst are those who also betray their trust. Should you think that the protagonists in his stories are improbable, you must remember that many of the men he had known in his frontier years were not improbable, they were incredible.

Fidelity to the land and to the people of his frontier years, fidelity to the *ethos* of the oasis society that he loved until he died—these are the hallmarks of Rhodes's writings. Add to these his poet's soul and a scholar's respect for the language he used and it can be said of Rhodes what once was said of De Maupassant: "He was almost irreproachable in a genre which was not."

A SALUTE TO GENE RHODES

"CAN YOU TELL ME why the work of Eugene Manlove Rhodes is not better known?" asked a contributor to the second issue of *The Saturday Review of Literature*, August 2, 1924. "As to literature, this man's writings have a variety of charms; in sensitive, vivid description; in clear characterizations: in an easy, light-running style, warm with humor and brilliant with wit. In time, place and character, he is American of the Americans. . . . His stories are fresh and original. . . . He is himself a reader; his work is continuously pricked and sparkling with allusion and lightly touched quotation, filling the mind with a sense of old friendships close at hand. There ought to be a good library edition of the works of Mr. Rhodes."

The writer of this appraisal belonged to the "passionate few" who, according to Arnold Bennett, make and maintain the fame of classical authors. The critical passion of the few that keeps many classics alive resulted, in 1946, in the private publication of a collection of stray stories and verses by Eugene Manlove Rhodes under the title of *The Little World Waddies*.

The readers of it were not confined to the "passionate few" any more than were the readers of Rhodes novels serialized for years in the *Saturday Evening Post* and then of the same novels in book form. On the author known familiarly as Gene Rhodes, I ask for no better judges than the waddies themselves — the ones who read. During World War II, Captain Tom Hickman, who used to ride as cowboy and Texas ranger, came to see me. We talked about R. B. Cunninghame Graham — who wrote so well of South American gauchos and Spanish horses — and about Gene Rhodes.

Back in 1924 while Tom Hickman was on his way to England with Tex Austin's rodeo, he stayed in New York a few days and went up to Apalachin to call on his favorite writer of the West. There May Rhodes told him something only lightly intimated in her very human book about her husband. She said that a passion for playing poker kept Gene poor even while he was selling stories at a good rate. Gene "didn't care for money." May Rhodes showed the cowboy from Texas a file of correspondence between Gene and some individual in New York who also liked to play poker. The five letters read as follows:

"Come down."

"Can't come."

"Why?"

"Broke."

"Sad."

Eugene Manlove Rhodes put Cole Railston into more than one of his stories. Cole Railston was range foreman for the Bar N Cross when, about 1889, Gene came to work for it. Cole was a very young boss then; now he lives on his own modest ranch out from Magdalena, New Mexico, and reads and remembers and reflects. Perhaps no other man so combines knowledge of Gene Rhodes's life as a cowboy with appreciation of him as a writer.

"Gene grew and spread after leaving our Bar Cross outfit at Engle," Cole Railston wrote me in a letter. "He was a remarkable character. About 1905 he put out a little story called 'The Last Guard.' I liked it best of all his writings. Should you know of any way to find it, I wish you would get one or a dozen copies for me.

"As to the kind of cowboy he made, while Gene worked for me on summer roundups some three seasons, his job was mostly to care for the saddle horses, but the last summer he was a cowhand. Gene never claimed to be a top hand, but he was an all-around good hand. On day herd, night guard, or in the branding pen, he was loyal, tireless and fearless. There is no question about Gene's courage in the wild work of duty and danger. They used to say jokingly that young Rhodes carried a book instead of a gun. I never knew him to carry a pistol. I believe he liked to herd the saddle horses because that work gave him more time for reading. The boys all liked him. Next to cowboying and reading, he liked poker and a fight. He was not a trouble-maker, far from it, but no one stepped on his toes or rode his pet horse. I never knew any man to throw Gene in a wrestling match. He feared no bad man or bad horse. He was a real good rough bronc rider. Send him anywhere to be gone from the roundup wagon for a day or so, and he made no fuss about bed or food. He simply went, did the job, and came back smiling."

The first novel of any consequence to be published about the range, *The Virginian*, in 1902, is deft on situations and the code of men of spurs, but Owen Wister was not looking at range life from the inside. His cowboys do not work with cows. In *The Log of a Cowboy*, by Andy Adams, published in 1903, the men — and no women belong here — are never away from cows and horses. If all literature on whales and whalers were destroyed with the exception of *Moby-Dick*, we could still get from that novel a just conception of the occupation of whaling. If, excepting *The Log of a Cowboy*, all literature pertaining to trail herds, to the seas of unfenced grass and to the sinewy men who "rattled their hocks" behind Longhorn cattle from the Rio Grande to the Plains of Alberta were destroyed, we could still get from the homemade classic that Andy Adams wrote a just conception of range-riding and trail-driving.

The riders that ride so free through Rhodes's fiction are usually separated from their cows, but they are infused by the fact — including the code — of their occupation. Their eyes are used to looking through heat devils shimmering over drouth-browned mesas and at mountains a look and a half away. Without their knowing it, something of the tonic of sagebrush aroma has passed into the very corpuscles of their blood and something of the assurance belonging to the quietness of sky and earth has entered into their mental attitudes. They cannot be called earthy characters; the created components of their nature are sometimes too apparent; but they always belong to the Land of Little Rain.

Aside from their inherent decency, their most distinguishing characteristic is the vivacity of their talk. It is never glib; it is often witty; it is uniformly natural. The culmination of the art of writing as Eugene Manlove Rhodes practiced it, so it seems to me, is in this talk. It constantly fulfills Stevenson's direction — Stevenson, who in Rhodes's opinion, "used the English tongue more skilfully than any other man" — to have characters talk "not as men talk in parlors, but as they might talk." This talk may be homely and earthy: "We'll wash our hands and faces right good, catch us up some fresh horses out of the pasture, and terrapin up the road a stretch." It may be, and often is, as lightsome as the white smoke from mesquite coals in a serene campfire; it may occasionally be dark with human destiny; it repeatedly glints and gleams with literary allusions. Yet no bright speaker ever sacrifices fidelity to his own naturalness or to the flavor of the earth to which he belongs in order to say a good thing.

" 'You give me that gun,' " thundered Marshall Yewell, of *The Trusty Knaves*.

"Pres Lewis took a square of plug tobacco from his pocket, scrutinized it, selected a corner, and gnawed a segment from it. 'You keep your voice down, brother,' he said, restoring the mutilated plug to its pocket. 'If you bellow at me any more, I'm liable to prophesy against you. You just turn your mind back and see what happened when people crowded me into foretelling. When you got any communications for me, I want 'em sweet and low, like the wind of the western sea.' "

The girl in *Bransford of Rainbow Range* considered, "What manner of cowboy was this, from whose tongue a learned scientific term tripped spontaneously in so stressful a moment — who quoted scraps of The Litany unaware?" It is the Eugene Manlove Rhodes "manner of cowboy." And the manner belonged to the Rhodes who night-herded and day-herded too, as well as to the Rhodes who wove out of experience and imagination those gay riders named John Wesley Pringle, Johnny Dines, Jeff Bransford, Ross McEwen, Ptomaine Tommy and a cavalcade of others. Their individualism goes deeper than bowlegs and the you-all drawl. They can all read, write and recollect. They have read; they combine in themselves generosity with that you-be-damned air; they are utterly at ease on the planet that their author "recommended" as being "a good place to spend a life-time"; they carry "bottles of salvation" filled with uncorked champagne-natured mother wit.

" 'Thanks, but you are a tee-totaler?' said Jeff Bransford.

" 'A — well — not exactly,' stammered Aughinbaugh. 'But I have to be very careful. I — I only take one drink at a time!' He fumbled out another glass.

" 'I stumble, I stumble!' said Bransford gravely. He poured out a small drink and passed the bottle. 'I fill this cup to one made up!' He held the glass up to the light.

" 'Well?' said Aughinbaugh expectantly. 'Go on!'

" 'That description can't be bettered,' said Bransford."

Now it's John Wesley Pringle speaking. " 'You had all the material to build a nice plump hunch. It all went over your head. You put me in mind of the lightning bug.

> " 'The lightning bug is brilliant,
> But it hasn't any mind;
> It wanders through creation
> With its headlight on behind.' "

The Bernheimer Oriental Gardens at Pacific Palisades, California, no longer exist, but what was their chief adornment will always exist for me. There among the flowers, a bronze figure of a Chinese philosopher sits at ease on a water buffalo, absorbed in a book, while the understanding beast carries him to whatever may be his destination. It is an exquisite piece of work, both joyful and placid. I want to contribute to a fund for erecting a bronze figure of Eugene Manlove

Rhodes, at whatever may be the most appropriate spot in New Mexico. I want the figure to be of Gene reading a book on a gentle cow horse manifestly in harmony with the philosophy of his rider. As horse wrangler he used to snake up wood for the camp cook. He would rope some poles, wrap the rope around the horn of his saddle, head his horse for camp, take out one of the books he habitually carried in saddle pocket or coat pocket, and lose himself in the pages as the horse walked along. A woman on a lone, lone ranch in New Mexico told me how she looked out the window one day and saw Gene Rhodes reading a book on his horse, which had stopped at the yard gate. She saw that he was oblivious to everything but the imagined world and went on about her work until, about half an hour later, seeing that Gene had not moved except to turn the page, she called to him to get down and come in. "I guess I will," he replied. "That's what I rode over here for."

He once complained that the ranch people seemed to be remembering him more for reading than for riding. In his cowboy days he gloried in hanging with the highest pitchers and the crookedest twisters, but his idea of a "broke" horse was one broken to the sound of paper-rustling as well as to the saddle. One bronc he rode would rear over backward upon hearing a page turned; Gene always stepped clear, holding to the bridle reins. Once, after stepping clear, he grabbed the horse's head while the horse was still down and sat on it reading a volume of Browning's poetry until, presumably, the bronc had absorbed something of literary usage.

The memorable time I visited Cole Railston on his ranch, I asked him if Gene Rhodes had a model for the extraordinary facility with which certain cowboys in his fiction make literary allusions, generally obliquely, and quote verse, both doggerel and classic.

"It might have been Bill Barbee," Cole Railston answered, and then, in his rich way, he went ahead to sketch Bill Barbee.

When Bill Barbee rode into Marfa that time to catch a westbound train, he and his ga'nted horse both looked suspicious to some Texas rangers stationed there. They arrested him, searched him, questioned him. They consulted their book of "wanted men." Then they reported to Captain Hughes that, although they felt certain this stranger was "wanted," they could not find a single identifying clue.

"Anything in his vest pocket?" the Captain asked.

"Yes, a little notebook with some pages torn out and not a name, date, or place in it."

"Let's see the notebook."

The prisoner was present and he handed out his notebook. The

Captain opened it. On the inside of the front cover he saw a B with a horizontal line — a bar — under it, and, under the bar, another B. Cowboys have brands even if they own nothing but spur-leathers to put the brand on. A favorite form of brand is a rebus. The Captain looked at the B combined with bar and B. He looked at the prisoner.

"Bill Bar-bee," he said.

"I always heard you were a dictionary on brands," Bill Barbee answered.

The rangers had him on their list. He was wanted for what he considered a killing of honor — not a murder. He had ordered his sister not to marry a certain man; she persisted; he made the man unmarriageable. Not long after the arrest a jury decided that Bill Barbee's interpretation of honor was too liberal and detained him at Huntsville two years before he went to work for the Bar Cross in New Mexico, under Cole Railston. Gene Rhodes was working for the outfit at the time. He told Cole Railston how he first met Barbee.

Along late one evening, alone in camp and standing beside his cabin, he saw a strange cowboy riding up. The stranger fulfilled all of Gene's dreams of the gallant cow-boy-ee. He was dressed cap-à-pie just right, not a mite overdressed, the crease in his Stetson both distinguished and careless. He rode as "active-valiant" as Hotspur. After he had dismounted, he walked with a walk marked but not marred by times in the saddle. He was as alert as his spur jingle; he had the reserve that belongs to nature's modesty. Inside the cabin his eye fell on the table of books that his host kept, a volume of Shakespeare dominant among them.

"Now there's something about that second soliloquy in *Richard the Third*," Bill Barbee said.

But Gene Rhodes had been putting this ideal cowboy into another kind of story. Right at this point, he wanted to get a bit of horse lore from him. Three times he shifted the subject, and each time the visitor came back to Richard the Third. He quoted all of the soliloquy. He could quote Shakespeare like Leviticus quoting the Good Book itself.

I have spruced Bill Barbee up. Yet he may well have served for one model. "I cribbed that remark from Billy Beebe," says John Wesley Also-Ran Pringle in *The Desire of the Moth*. Rhodes often transmuted real people into book characters. If a writer does not steal, he naturally has to borrow. John Wesley Pringle would have talked in his way, however, had Bill Barbee never existed. He came out of Gene Rhodes himself. "I have a woodshed where I can retire to split an infinitive with a friend," he wrote. He proposed to an editor a column for letter-writers, "where the liar and the lamb can lie down together."

He seems to have felt under compulsion to justify his literary-allusioning cowboys. "They all smoked," he explains in *Bransford of Rainbow Range* — smoked Bull Durham tobacco. "A certain soulless corporation placed in each package of the tobacco a coupon, each coupon redeemable by one paper-bound book. . . . There were three hundred and three volumes on that list, mostly — but not altogether — fiction. And each one was a classic. Classics are cheap. They are not copy-righted. . . . Cowboys all smoked: and the most deep-seated instinct of the human race is to get something for nothing. They got those books. In due course of time they read those books. Some were slow to take to it; but when you stay at lonely ranches, when you are left afoot until the waterholes dry up, so you may catch a horse in the waterpen — why, you must do something. The books were read. Then, having acquired the habit, they bought more books. Since the three hundred and three were all real books, and since the cowboys had been previously uncorrupted of predigested or sterilized fiction, or by 'gift,' 'uplift' and 'helpful' books, their composite taste had become surprisingly good, and they bought with discriminating care."

This account of literary pursuits in the cow camps varies slightly from that given by Gene Rhodes's admired friend, Charlie Siringo, in the Preface to *A Texas Cowboy, or, Fifteen Years on the Hurricane Deck of a Spanish Pony*. In this first-published of all cowboy auto-biographies, rollicky Charlie Siringo recollected:

"While ranching on the Indian Territory line, close to Caldwell, Kansas, in the winter of '82 and '83, we boys — there being nine of us — made an ironclad rule that whoever was heard swearing or caught picking grey backs off and throwing them on the floor without first killing them, should pay a fine of ten cents for each and every offense. The proceeds to be used for buying choice literature — something that would have a tendency to raise us above the average cow-puncher. Just twenty-four hours after making this rule we had three dollars in the pot — or at least in my pocket, I having been appointed treasurer.

"As I was going to town that night to see my Sunday girl, I proposed to the boys that, while up there, I send the money off for a year's subscription to some good newspaper. The question came up, what paper shall it be? We finally agreed to leave it to a vote — each man to write the one of his choice on a slip of paper and drop it in a hat. There being two young Texans present who could neither read nor write, we let them speak their choice after the rest of us got our votes deposited. At the word given them to cut loose they both yelled 'Police Gazette,' and on asking why they voted for that wicked sheet, they both replied as though with one voice: 'Cause we can read the pictures.' We found, on counting the votes, that the *Police Gazette* had won, so it was subscribed for."

But Charlie Siringo's cowboys were from southern Texas, where to this day many of their descendants suspect literature that rises to the plane of having ideas as being "subversive," and, therefore, as not to be trusted; also, where boiled frijoles have for generations been much more common than canned goods. New Mexico cowboys, even those "who could not read at all," became letter perfect in finishing off "any sudden quotation from the labels of such cans, bags, sacks or other containers as were used for standard brands of coffee, sugar, flour, condensed milk, pears, peaches and other such." Rhodes might have added to what he thus wrote, in *Beyond the Desert*, that it never was settled whether "ozs." was to be recited as "ozzes" or "ounces." Anyway, the exercise is supposed to have induced excellence of memories in quoting literature.

Despite the pretenses of advertisements of the classics and despite the practices of book review clubs, nobody ever read seriously for the purpose of displaying familiarity with literature; least of all, Eugene Manlove Rhodes. In *Say Now Shibboleth*, he rejects the idea that a writer should read the great writers "for style." He says: "Read the great dead masters for ideas. Devour them, Fletcherize them, digest, assimilate, make them part of your blood; let the enriched blood visit your brain. The resultant activities will be fairly your own, and the little kinks and convolutions of your brain, which are entirely different from the kinks of any other brain, will furnish you all the style you will ever get."

A newspaper article about Eugene Manlove Rhodes by a very thoughtful historian of the West characterizes him as "a bold, gallant, card-playing, pool-playing, cowpunching natural son of the American West." It is this philistine conception of what constitutes natural sons that makes the civilized pursuit of art and ideas so difficult everywhere in America and especially in the Southwest. The passionate few are not passionate in their regard for Eugene Manlove Rhodes because he was a card-playing cowpuncher; they are passionate towards him because of the way his cultivated mind played upon the cowpuncher world. One part of him was a part of this world, but the "immortal residue" of him was beyond it — the part that justified Bernard De Voto in calling his fiction the only fiction of the cattle country "that reaches a level which it is intelligent to call art." Being a good hand on horseback did not make Gene Rhodes a good writer, though pride and vitality are common denominators of both.

True art always transcends the provincial. Gene Rhodes loved his waddie land and its people passionately. He made that land more interesting, gave it significance, added something of the spirit to its expanses. We dwellers upon it must feel an abiding gratitude to him. His art, however, is to be judged not by what he translated into books, but by how he translated it. He died before the basic fact — along with oceans of jargon — of our One World had sunk into the minds of the thinking minority of this country; but the assimilation of ideas from the earth's great thinkers and writers had made him conscious of the harmony between loyalty to one province and indebtedness to provinces beyond. In *The Proud Sheriff*, Andy Hinkle reports to Spinal Maginnis on the people "hither," whence he has just returned. "Fine people. Just like here. Nine decent men for every skunk. Nine that hate treachery and lies and hoggishness and dirt. They got different ways."

"But you think our ways are best?"

"I would never say so. I think our ways are different."

The people foreign to Rhodes were what he called "The Tumble-bug People." He was sensitive to injustice anywhere. He wrote "In Defense of Pat Garrett," who had been maligned by Walter Noble Burns in a jingoistic attempt to Robin Hood that cold-blooded murderer and horse thief known as Billy the Kid. He would not linger in Socorro because he "had seen a man stamped to death in front of the post office." He wanted to organize the whole West into resenting aspersions on its manhood and womanhood by Stuart Henry — aspersions hardly worth noticing. He never attained to the amplitude of Mark Twain, but inside his own confining range he was blood brother to that genius who wrote books out of righteous wrath to defend Joan of Arc and Harriet Shelley and to expose hypocrisies in at least three religions. More than two hundred years after Don Diego Dionisio de Peñalosa had ridden in the land of the Apache and espoused the cause of the "copper-colored children of the New World" against their Christianizing enslavers and, for reward, been indicted as *embustero* (liar) by the Spanish Inquisition, Eugene Manlove Rhodes flamed to salute him as "first in America to strike a blow for freedom, first to dare the Inquisition."

He stood for "the little people" against important oppressors.

Lo, we have dreamed down slavery, and we have dreamed down kings,
And still we dream of decency and the end of evil things.

A Mexican sheepherder is saved from being lynched by greed, and a poor squatter from being ousted by more greed. The savior, in Rhodes's stories, is always witty as well as decent, debonair as well as just. The hero's being a cowboy is secondary to his believing in something. Rhodes was not a sociological righter of a system's wrongs in the manner of Upton Sinclair. He did not understand systems, and being a man of intellectual integrity, he did not pretend to understand them. He more or less accepted them — as systems. He stood on the principle of applied democracy. For him, "a man's a man for a' that" was poetry only incidentally; primarily it was eternal verity. His nearest kinsman was Cyrano de Bergerac — with whom he would have uncovered to "that divine madman," Don Quixote.

"And what should a man do? Attain to height by craft instead of by strength? No, I thank you. Push himself from lap to lap, become a little great man in a great little circle? No, I thank you. But . . . sing, dream, laugh, loaf, be free, have eyes that look squarely, a voice with a ring; wear, if he chooses, his hat hindside afore; for a yes, for a no, fight a duel or turn a ditty! Work, without concern of fortune or of glory, to accomplish the heart's desired journey to the moon! Put forth nothing that has not its spring in the very heart, yet, modest, say to himself, 'Old man, be satisfied with blossoms, fruits, yea, leaves alone, so they be gathered in your garden and no other man's!' "

It was righteous indignation against an ignorant definition of the cowboy as "never anything more than a hired hand on horseback" that produced — despite a dead tree's "lashing fate" — not only the finest poem yet written on any range subject but the strongest, noblest and most moving poem that the Southwest can claim.

> Merry eyes and tender eyes, dark head and bright . . .
> Doggerel upon his lips and valor in his heart . . .
> The hired man on horseback goes laughing to his work . . .
> The hired man on horseback has raised the rebel yell.

"No better description of Gene's romantic years will ever be written" than these lines give, May Rhodes well says. He was about to be sixty when he wrote them. His best years were the romantic years; he was still amid the romantic years when he died. His best characters are constitutionally generous, gay and gallant because he himself was constitutionally generous, gay and gallant. I do not mean gallant in the self-esteeming *caballero* sense, but gallant in prodigal selflessness, in upholding a principle, in being ready to charge hell with a bucket of water, to take the side of the wronged, "to find quarrel in a straw when honour's at the stake." As he has Jeff Bransford put it, "Speaking the truth comes easier for them than for some folks, 'cause if speaking the aforesaid truth displeases anyone, they mostly don't give a damn."

Whoever wants the full and flavored facts about the life of Gene Rhodes will find them in *The Hired Man on Horseback* by May Rhodes. He was born in Nebraska, January 19, 1869, to a family of homesteaders. Prairie fires, grasshoppers and cyclones drove them to Kansas, where they homesteaded and suffered plagues again. Then in 1881 they came to New Mexico and filed on another homestead. There were always some good books for the children to read and scanty schooling. When he was thirteen, riding a saddle bought with soap coupons, Gene got a job with a cow outfit. For seven years he drew cowboy wages. Then he borrowed fifty dollars from his father and for two years, living mainly on oatmeal, attended a college at San Jose, California. Here a wider choice of literature fertilized him and he practised writing.

Now he was back in the saddle, though he taught a country school for a spell. He had a little ranch of his own in the San Andrés Mountains. He was better at riding horses and driving cows than he was at ownership; he valued other things higher than he valued property. A young widow named May Davison Purple in a faraway village called Apalachin, in the state of New York, read one of his poems and wrote him of her appreciation. He was thirty when, riding a cattle train, he followed his letters to her home and married her. After three years of ranch life, Mrs. Rhodes went back to Apalachin; Gene soon followed and stayed for twenty years, developing as a story writer, also as poker player. In 1926 the two returned with their son Alan to New Mexico, lingered a few years, and then moved to California, where, still writing, Gene died, June 27, 1934.

Towards sundown one September day in 1940, I headed west out of Tularosa, New Mexico, with the intention of camping at the water beside which Gene Rhodes used to live. I was alone and had my camping outfit in the car. During the twenty-five-mile drive across the sands and alkali flats I did not meet or see a soul. It was away after dark when I got among the boulders of Rhodes Canyon. I stopped to eat a supper of bread, cheese and an apple. Soon after I got out of the car I saw headlights coming the way I had come. I had finished eating and, standing against my car door, was filling my pipe when the oncomer halted beside me.

"Having trouble?" a hearty voice asked.

"No, I thank you."

"What part of Texas you from?"

"Austin."

"Let's drink to Old Texas." The stranger was already dangling a pint bottle out the car window.

"I've come to this canyon to spend the night on the ground where Gene Rhodes used to rattle his spurs," I said. "Let's drink to his cheerful soul."

"I helped bury him. Here's to Gene. Follow me and I'll show you where to spread your bedroll."

We rode on a good while. My guide knew the gullies, boulders and sharp curves and was more strongly fortified against all tame considerations of security than I was. Finally I caught up with him where he had halted. "Gene's cabin used to be over there," he said. "You can drive down close to the water and have a level place to camp on."

I never slept a more freeing sleep. I washed in the cool, fresh water, boiled coffee in it and filled a jug. I gathered some wild verbena next to Gene's old corral. "Gene was considered wild," they say — wild like the free flowers. I felt freer and gladder and richer because he had lived and said what he said. May Rhodes tells me that she still has the pressed wild flowers.

On up the slope, I stopped in the New Mexico sunshine and walked to the grave. It is where Gene Rhodes wanted it, alone in the San Andrés Mountains, overlooking the Pass that bears his name. A bronze plaque on a great boulder bears the epitaph of supreme fitness.

"PASO POR AQUI"
EUGENE MANLOVE RHODES
JAN. 19, 1869 — JUNE 27, 1934

Had he written nothing else but *Pasó por Aquí*, the passion of the few would persist. My copy of this story, bound with *Once in the Saddle*, is inscribed with black ink, and on pages that follow, Monte's Spanished-English is corrected with red lead. What artist with words — in a phrase from Eddy Orcutt's fine essay on Rhodes — conscious of "the salt and glory of our language," ever escaped the gross luminosity given by print to his own imperfections? There is nothing to change in the story's finality on human dignity, decency and gallantry. On the fly leaf of my copy of *Pasó por Aquí* Gene Rhodes wrote, "Why is joy not considered a fit subject for an artist?" He never wrote the last book he wanted to write. He did write the concluding sentence for it — a farewell salute to the "gay, kind and fearless." That salute is for you also, one of the "Masterless Men," you, Eugene Cyrano de Bergerac Manlove Gene Rhodes!

J. FRANK DOBIE

Pasó Por Aquí

PASO POR AQUI

Chapter I

EXCEPTIONS are so inevitable that no rule is without them — except the one just stated. Neglecting fractions, then, not to insult intelligence by specifying the obvious, trained nurses are efficient, skillful, devoted. It is a noble calling.

Nevertheless, it is notorious that the official uniform is of reprehensible charm. This regulation is variously explained by men, women and doctors. "No fripperies, curlicues and didos — bully!" say the men. "Ah! Yes! But why? Artful minxes!" say the women, who should know best. "Cheerful influence in the sickroom," say the doctors.

Be that as it may, such uniform Jay wore, spotless and starched, crisp and cool; Jay Hollister, now seated on the wide portico of the Alamogordo Hospital; not chief nurse, but chief ornament, according to many, not only of that hospital but of the great railroad which maintained it. Alamogordo was a railroad town, a new town, a ready-made and highly painted town, direct from Toyland.

Ben Griggs was also a study in white — flannels, oxfords and panama; a privileged visitor who rather overstepped his privileges; almost a fixture in that pleasant colonnade.

"Lamp of life," said Ben, "let's get down to brass tacks. You're homesick!"

"Homesick!" said Jay scornfully. "Homesick! I'm heartsick, bankrupt, shipwrecked, lost, forlorn — here in this terrible country, among these dreadful people. Homesick? Why, Ben, I'm just damned!"

"Never mind, heart's delight," said Ben the privileged. "You've got me."

Miss Hollister seemed in no way soothed by this reassuring statement. "Your precious New Mexico! Sand!" she said. "Sand, snakes, scorpions; wind, dust, glare and heat; lonely, desolate and forlorn!"

"Under the circumstances," said Ben, "you could hardly pay me a greater compliment. 'Whither thou goest, I will go,' and all that. Good girl! This unsolicited tribute — "

"Don't be a poor simpleton," advised the good girl. "I shall stick it out for my year, of course, since I was foolish enough to undertake it. That is all. Don't you make any mistakes. These people shall never be my people."

"No better people on earth. In all the essentials — "

"Oh, who cares anything about essentials?" cried Jay impatiently — voicing, perhaps, more than she knew. "A tin plate will do well enough to eat out of, certainly, if that is what you mean. I prefer china, myself. I'm going back where I can see flowers and green grass, old gardens and sundials."

"I know not what others may say," observed Ben grandly, "but as for me, you take the sundials and give me the sun. Right here, too, where they climb for water and dig for wood. Peevish, my fellow townsman, peevish, waspy, crabbed. You haven't half enough to do. In this beastly climate people simply will not stay sick. They take up their bed and beat it, and you can't help yourself. Nursing is a mere sinecure." His hands were clasped behind his head, his slim length reclined in a steamer chair, feet crossed, eyes half closed, luxurious. "Ah, idleness!" he murmured. "Too bad, too bad! You never were a grouch back home. Rather good company, if anything."

Ben's eyes were blue and dreamy. They opened a trifle wider now, and rolled slowly till they fell upon Miss Hollister, bolt upright and haughty in her chair, her lips pressed in a straight line. She regarded him sternly. He blinked, his hands came from behind his head, he straightened up and adjusted his finger tips to meet with delicate precision. "But the main trouble, the fount and origin of your disappointing conduct is, as hereinbefore said, homesickness. It is, as has been observed, a nobler pang than indigestion, though the symptoms are of striking similarity. But nostalgia, more than any other feeling, is fatal to the judicial faculties, and I think, my dear towny, that when you look at this fair land, your future home, you regard all things with a jaundiced eye."

"Oh-h!" gasped Jay, hotly indignant. "Look at it yourself! Look at it!"

The hospital was guarded and overhung by an outer colonnade of cottonwoods; she looked through a green archway across the leagues of shimmering desert, somber, wavering and dim; she saw the long bleak range beyond, saw-toothed and gray; saw in the midway levels the unbearable brilliance of the White Sands, a wild dazzle and tumult of light, a blinding mirror with two score miles for diameter.

But Ben's eyes widened with delight, their blue darkened to a deeper blue of exultation, not to be feigned.

"More than beautiful — fascinating," he said.

"Repulsive, hateful, malignant, appalling!" cried Jay Hollister bitterly. "The starved, withered grass, the parched earth, the stunted bushes — miserable, hideous — the abomination of desolation!"

"Girl, by all good rights I ought to shut your wild, wild mouth with kisses four — that's what I orter do — elocutin' that way. But you mean it, I guess." Ben nodded his head sagely. "I get your idea. Blotched and leprous, eh? Thin, starved soil, poisoned and mildewed patches — thorns and dwarfed scrub, red leer of the sun. Oh, *sí!* Like that bird in Browning? Hills like giants at a huntin' lay — the round squat turret — all the lost adventures, my peers — the Dark Tower, weird noises just offstage, increasin' like a bill, I mean a bell — increasin' like a bell, fiddles a-moanin', 'O-o-o-h-h-h! What did you do-o-o with your summer's wa-a-a-ges? So this is Paris!' Yes, yes, but why not shed the second-hand stuff and come down to workaday?"

"Ben Griggs," said Miss Hollister with quiet and deadly conviction, "you are absolutely the most blasphemous wretch that ever walked in shoe leather. You haven't anything even remotely corresponding to a soul."

"When we are married," said Ben, and paused, reflecting. "That is, if I don't change my mind — "

"Married!" said Miss Hollister derisively. "When! You!" Her eyes scorned him.

"Woman," said Ben, "beware! You make utter confusion with the parts of speech. You make mere interjections of pronouns, prepositions and verbs and everything. You use too many shockers. More than that — mark me, my lass — isn't it curious that no one has ever thought to furnish printed words with every phonograph record of a song? Just a little sheet of paper — why, it needn't cost more than a penny apiece at the outside. Then we could know what it was all about."

"The way you hop from conversational crag to crag," said Jay, "is beyond all praise."

"Oh, well, if you insist, we can go back to our marriage again."

"My poor misguided young friend," said Jay, "make no mistakes. I put up with you because we played together when we were kids,

and because we are strangers here in a strange land, townies together — "

Ben interrupted her. "Two tawny townies twisting twill together!"
he chanted happily, beating slow time with a gentle finger. "Twin
turtles twitter tender twilight twaddle. Twice twenty travelers — "

"Preposterous imbecile!" said Jay, dimpling nevertheless adorably.
"Here is something to put in your little book. Jay Hollister will never
marry an idler and a wastrel. Why, you're not even a ne'er-do-well.
You're a do-nothing, net."

"All the world loves a loafer," Ben protested. "Still, as Alice remarked, if circumstances were different they would be quite otherwise. If frugal industry — "

"There comes your gambler friend," said Jay coldly.

"Who, Monte? Where?" Ben turned eagerly.

"Across the street. No, the other way." Though she fervently dis-
approved of Monte, Jay was not sorry for the diversion. It was daily
more difficult to keep Ben in his proper place, and she had no desire to
discuss frugal industry.

"Picturesque rascal, what? Looking real pleased about something
too. Say, girl, you've made me forget something I was going to tell
you."

"He is laughing to himself," said Jay.

"I believe he is, at that." Ben raised his voice. "Hi, Monte! Come
over and tell us the joke."

2

Monte's mother had known him as Rosalio Marquez. The overname
was professional. He dealt monte wisely but not too well. He was
nearing thirty-five, the easiest age of all; he was slender and graceful;
he wore blue serge and a soft black hat, low crowned and wide
brimmed. He carried this hat in his hand as he came up the steps.
He bowed courteously to Jay, with murmured greetings in Spanish,
soft syllables of lingering caress; he waved a friendly salute to Ben.

"Yes, indeed," said Ben. "With all my heart. Your statement as to
the beauty of the day is correct in every particular, and it affords me
great pleasure to indorse an opinion so just. But, after all, dear heart,
that is hardly the point, is it? The giddy jest, the merry chuckles —
those are the points on which we greatly desire information.

Monte hesitated, almost imperceptibly, a shrewd questioning in
his eyes.

"Yes, have a chair," said Jay, "and tell us the joke."

"Thees is good, here, thank you," said Monte. He sat on the top
step and hung the black hat on his knee; his face lit up with soft

low laughter. "The joke? Oh, eet ees upon the sheriff, Jeem Hunter. I weel tell eet."

He paused to consider. In his own tongue Monte's speech sounded uncommonly like a pack of firecrackers lit at both ends. In English it was leisured, low and thoughtful. The unslurred vowels, stressed and piquant, the crisp consonants, the tongue-tip accents — these things combined to make the slow caressing words into something rich and colorful and strange, all unlike our own smudged and neutral speech. The customary medium of the Southwest between the two races is a weird and lawless hodge-podge of the two tongues — a barbarous lingua franca.

As Miss Hollister had no Spanish, Monte drew only from his slender stock of English; and all unconsciously he acted the story as he told it.

"When Jeem was a leetle, small boy," said Monte, his hand knee-high to show the size in question, "he dream manee times that he find thoss marbles — oh, many marbles! That mek heem ver' glad, thees nize dream. Then he get older" — Monte's hand rose with the sheriff's maturity — "and sometime he dream of find money lak thoss marble. And now Jeem ees grown and sheriff — an' las' night he come home, ver' late, ver' esleepy. I weel tell you now how eet ees, but Jeem he did not know eet. You see, Melquiades, he have a leetle, litla game." He glanced obliquely at Miss Hollister, his shoulders and down-drawn lips expressed apology for the little game, and tolerance for it. "Just neeckels and dimes. An' some fellow he go home weener, and there ees hole een hees pocket. But Jeem he do not know. *Bueno*, Jeem has been to Tularosa, Mescalero, Fresnal, all places, to leef word to look out for thees fellow las' week what rob the bank at Belen, and he arrive back on a freight train las' night, mebbe so about three in the morning — oh, veree tired, ver' esleepy. So when he go up the street een the moonlight he see there a long streeng of neeckels and dimes under hees feet." Without moving, Monte showed the homeward progress of that drowsy man and his faint surprise. "So Jeem, he laugh and say, 'There ees that dream again.' And he go on. But bimeby he steel see thoss neeckels, and he peench heemself, so — and he feel eet." Monte's eyes grew round with astonishment. "And he bend heemself to peek eet, and eet ees true money, and not dreaming at all! Yais. He go not back, but on ahead he peek up one dollar seexty-five cents of thees neeckels and dimes."

"I hadn't heard of any robbery Monte," said Ben. "What about it?"

"Yes, and where is Belen?" said Jay. "Not around here, surely. I've never heard of the place."

"Oh, no — *muy lejos* — a long ways. Belen, what you call Bethlehem, ees yonder this side of Albuquerque, a leetle. I have been there manee times, but not estraight — round about." He made a looping motion of his hand to illustrate. "Las Vegas, and then down, or by Las Cruces, and then up. Eet is hundred feefty, two hundred miles in estraight line — I do not know."

"Anybody hurt?" asked Ben.

"Oh, no — no fuss! Eet ees veree funnee. Don Numa Frenger and Don Nestor Trujillo, they have there beeg estore to sell all theengs, leetle bank, farms, esheep ranch, freighting for thoss mines, buy wool and hides — all theengs for get the monee what ees there een thees place. And las' week, maybe Friday, Saturday, Nestor he ees go to deenair, and Numa Frenger ees in the estore, *solito*.

"Comes een a customer, *un colorado* — es-scusa me, a redhead. He buy tomatoes, cheese, crackers, sardines, sooch things, and a nose bag, and he ask to see shotgun. Don Numa, he exheebit two, three, and thees red he peek out nize shotgun. So he ask for shells, bird-eshot, buck-eshot, and he open the buck-eshot and sleep two shells een barrel, and break eet to throw out thoss shell weeth extractor, and sleep them een again. 'Eet work fine!' he say. 'Have you canteen?'

"Then Numa Frenger he tek long pole weeth hook to get thoss canteen where eet hang from the *viga*, the r-rafter, the beams. And when he get eet, he turn around an' thees estranger ees present thees shotgun at hees meedle.

"'Have you money een your esafe?' say the *estranjero*, the estr-ranger. And Numa ees bite hees mouth. 'Of your kindness,' say the customer, 'weel you get heem? I weel go weeth you.'

"So they get thees money from the esafe. And thees one weel not tek onlee the paper money. 'Thees gold an' seelver ees so heav-ee,' he tell Numa Frenger. 'I weel not bozzer.' Then he pay for those theengs of which he mek purchase an' correc' Don Numa when he mek meestake in the *adición*, and get hees change back. And then he say to Numa, 'Weel you not be so good to come to eshow me wheech ees best road out from thees town to the ford of the reever?' And Numa, he ees ge-nash hees teeth, but there ees no *remedio*.

"And so they go walking along thees lane between the orchards, these two togezzer, and the leetle bir-rds esing een the *árboles* — thees red fellow laughing and talkin' weeth Numa, ver' gay — leading hees horse by the bridle, and weeth the shotgun een the crook of hees arm. So the people loog out from the doors of their house and say, 'Ah! Don Numa ees diverrt heemself weeth hees friend.'

"And when they have come beyond the town, thees fellow ees mount hees horse. 'For your courtesy,' he say, 'I thank you. At your feet,' he say. 'Weeth God!' And he ride off laughing, and een a leetle way he toss hees shotgun een a bush, and he ride on to cross the reever eslow. But when Numa Frenger sees thees, he run queeckly, although he ees a ver' fat man, an' not young; he grab thees gun, he point heem, he pull the triggle — Nozzing! He break open the gun to look wizzen side — Nozzing! *O caballeros y conciudadanos!*" Monte threw down the gun; both hands grabbed his black locks and tugged with the ferocity of despair.

"Ah-h! What a lovely cuss word," cried Jay. "How trippingly it goes upon the tongue. I must learn that. Say it again!"

"But eet ees not a bad word, that," said Monte sheepishly. "Eet ees onlee idle word, to feel up. When thees politicos go up an' down, talking nonsense een the nose, when they weesh to theenk of more, then they say with *emoción*, 'O caballeros y conciudadanos'; that ees, 'gentlemen and fellow ceetizens.' No more."

"Well, now, the story?" said Ben. "He crossed the river, going east — was that it?"

"Oh, yes. Well, when Numa Frenger see that thees gun ees emptee, he ees ver' angree man. He ees more enr-rage heemself for that than for all what gone befor-re. He ees arrouse all Belen, he ees send telegraph to Sabinal, La Joya, Socorro, San Marcial, ever wheech way, to mek queek the posse, to send queek to the mesa to catch thees man, to mek *proclamación* to pay for heem three thousand dollar of rewar-rd. 'Do not keel heem, I entr-reat you,' say Don Numa. 'Breeng heem back. I want to fry heem.' "

"Now isn't that New Mexico for you?" demanded Jay "A man commits a barefaced robbery, and you make a joke of it."

Monte pressed the middle finger of his right hand firmly into the palm of his left, pressed as if to hold something there, and looked up under his brows at Miss Hollister.

"Then why do you laugh?" said Monte.

"You win," said Jay. "Go on with the story."

"Well, then," said Monte, "thees fellow he go up on the high plain on thees side of the reever, and he ride east and south by Sierra Montoso, and over the mountains of Los Pinos, and he mek to go over Chupadero Mesa to thoss ruins of Gran Quivira. But he ride onlee *poco á poco*, easalee. And already a posse from La Joya, San Acacia is ride up the Alamillo Cañon, and across the plain." His swift hands fashioned horseman, mountain, mesa and plain. "Page Otero and six, five other men. And they ride veree fast so that already they pass in front of him to the south, and are now before heem on Chupadero, and there they see heem. Eet ees almost sundown.

"*Immediatamente* he turn and go back. And their horses are not so tired lak hees horse, and they spread out and ride fast, and soon they are about to come weethen gunshot weeth the rifle. And when he see eet, thees *colorado* ees ride oopon a reedge that all may see, and he tek that paper money from the nose bag at the head of the saddle and he toss eet up — pouf! The weend is blow gentle and thees money it go joomp, joomp, here, there, een the booshes. Again he ride a leetle way, and again he scatter thees money lak a man to feed the hen een hees yard. So then he go on away, thees red one. And when thees posse come to that place, thees nize money is go hop, hop, along the ground and over the booshes. There ees feefty-dollar beel een the mesquite, there ees twenty-dollar beel een the tar-bush, there ees beels blow by, roll by, slide by. So thees posse ees deesmount heemself to peek heem, *muy enérgico* — lively. And the weend ess come up faster at sundown, *como siempre.* 'Come on!' says Page Otero. 'Come on, thees fellow weel to escape!' Then the posse loog up surprise, and say, 'Who, me?' and they go on to peek up thees monee. So that redhead get clear away thees time."

"Did they get all the money?" asked Ben.

"Numa he say yes. He do not know just how mooch thees bandit ees take, but he theenk they breeng back all, or most nearly all."

"Do they know who he was?" asked Jay.

"*Por cierto,* no. But from the deescreepcion and hees horse and saddle, they theenk eet ees a cowboy from Quemado, name — I cannot to pr-ronounce thees name, Meester Ben. You say heem. I have eet here een La Voz del Pueblo." From a hip pocket he produced a folded newspaper printed in Spanish, and showed Ben the place.

"Ross McEwen — about twenty-five or older, red hair, gray eyes, five feet nine inches — humph!" he returned the paper. "Will they catch him, do you think?"

Monte considered. He looked slowly at the far dim hills; he bent over to watch an inch-high horseman at his feet, toiling through painful immensities.

"The world ees ver' beeg een thees country," he said at last. "I theenk most mebbe not. *Quién sabe?* Onlee thees fellow must have water — and there ees not much water. Numa Frenger ees send now to all places, to Leencoln County, to Jeem Hunter here, and he meks everyone to loog out, to Pat Garrett in Doña Ana Countee, and Pat watches by Parker Lake and the pass of San Agustin; to El Paso, and they watch there most of all that he pass not to Mexico Viejo. Eet may be at some water place they get heem. Or that he get them. He seem lak a man of some enterpr-rize, no?" He rose to go. "But I have talk too much. I mus' go now to my beesness."

"A poor business for a man as bright as you are," said Jay, and sniffed.

"But I geeve a square deal," said Monte serenely. "At your feet, señorita! Unteel then, Meester Ben."

"Isn't he a duck? I declare, it's a shame to laugh at his English," said Jay.

"Don't worry. He gets to hear our Spanish, even if he is too polite to laugh."

"I hate to think of that man being chased for blood money," said Jay. "Hunter and that Pat Garrett you think so much of are keen after that reward, it seems. It is dreadful the way these people here make heroes out of their killers and man hunters."

"Let's get this straight," said Ben. "You're down on the criminal for robbing and down on the sheriff for catching him. Does that sound like sense? If there was no reward offered, it's the sheriff's duty to catch him, isn't it? And if there is a reward, it's still his duty. The reward doesn't make him a man hunter. Woman, you ain't right in your head. And as for Pat Garrett and some of these other old-timers — they're enjoying temporary immortality right now. They've become a tradition while they still live. Do you notice how all these honest-to-goodness old-timers talk? All the world is divided into three parts. One part is old-timers and the other two are not. The most clannish people on earth. And that brings us, by graceful and easy stages, to the main consideration, which I want to have settled before I go. And when I say settled I mean that nothing is ever settled till it is settled right — get me?" He stood up; as Jay rose he took her hands. "If circumstances were otherwise, Jay?"

She avoided his eyes. "Don't ask me now. I don't know, Ben — honest, I don't. You mustn't pester me now. It isn't fair when I'm so miserable." She pulled her hands away.

"Gawd help all poor sailors on a night like this!" said Ben fervently. "Listen, sister, I'm going to work, see? Goin' to fill your plans and specifications, every one, or bust a tug."

"I see you at it," jeered Jay, with an unpleasant laugh. "Work? You?"

"Me. I, myself. A faint heart never filled a spade flush," said Ben. "Going to get me a job and keep it. Lick any man that tries to fire me. Put that in your hope chest. Bye-bye. At your feet!"

As he went down the street his voice floated back to her:

But now my hair is falling out,
And down the hill we'll go,
And sleep together at the foot —
John Barleycorn, my Jo!

3

A high broad tableland lies east of the Rio Grande, and mountains make a long unbroken wall to it, with cliffs that front the west. This mesa is known locally as El Corredor. It is a pleasing and wholesome country. Zacatón and salt grass are gray green upon the level plain, checkered with patches of bare ground, white and glaring. On those bare patches, when the last rains fell, weeks, months or years ago, an oozy paste filmed over the glossy levels, glazed by later suns, cracking at last to shards like pottery. But in broken country, on ridges and slopes, was a thin turf of buffalo and mesquite grass, curly, yellow and low. There was iron beneath this place and the sand of it was red, the soil was ruddy white, the ridges and the lower hill slopes were granite red, yellowed over with grass. Even the high crowning cliffs were faintly cream, not gray, as limestone is elsewhere. Sunlight was soft and mellow there, sunset was red upon these cliffs. And Ross McEwen fled down that golden corridor.

If he had ridden straight south he might have been far ahead by this time, well on the road to Mexico. But his plan had been to reach the Panhandle of Texas; he had tried for easting and failed. Three times he had sought to work through the mountain barrier to the salt plains — a bitter country of lava flow and sinks, of alkali springs, salt springs, magnesia springs, soda springs; of soda lakes, salt lakes, salt marshes, salt creeks; of rotten and crumbling ground, of greasy sand, of chalk that powdered and rose on the lightest airs, to leave no trace that a fugitive had passed this way.

He had been driven back once by posse on Chupadero. Again at night he had been forced back by men who did not see him. He had tried to steal through by the old stage road over the Oscuro, and found the pass guarded; and the last time, today, had been turned back by men that he did not even see. In the mouth of Mockingbird Pass he had found fresh-shod tracks of many horses going east. Mockingbird was held against him.

He could see distinctly, and in one eye-flight, every feature of a country larger than all England. He could look north to beyond Albuquerque, past the long ranges of Manzano, Montoso, Sandia, Oscuro; southward, between his horse's ears, the northern end of the San Andrés was high and startling before him, blue black with cedar brake and piñon, except for the granite-gold top of Salinas Peak, the great valley of the Jornado del Muerto, the Journey of the Dead, which lay between the San Andrés and the Rio Grande.

And beyond the river was a bright enormous expanse, bounded only by the crest of the dozen ranges that made the crest of the Continental Divide — Dátil, Magdalena, San Mateo, the Black Range, the Mimbres, Florida.

Between, bordering the midway river, other mountain ranges lay tangled: Cuchillo Negro, Cristobál, Sierra de los Caballos, Doña Ana, Robelero. It was over the summits of these ranges that he saw the Continental Divide.

Here was irony indeed. With that stupendous panorama outspread before him, he was being headed off, driven, herded! He cocked an eyebrow aslant at the thought, and spoke of it to his horse, who pricked back an ear in attention. He was a honey-colored horse, and his name was Miél; which is, by interpretation, Honey.

"Wouldn't you almost think, sweetness," said Ross McEwen in a plaintive drawl, "that there was enough elbowroom here to satisfy every reasonable man? And yet these lads are crowdin' me like a cop after an alley cat."

He sensed that an unusual effort was being made to take him, and he smiled — a little ruefully — at the reflection that the people at Mockingbird might well have been mere chance comers upon their lawful occasions, and with no designs upon him, no knowledge of him. Every man was a possible enemy. He was out of law.

This was the third day of his flight. The man was still brisk and bold, the honey-colored horse was still sturdy, but both lacked something of the sprightly resilience they had brought to the fords of Belen. There had been brief grazing and scant sleep, night riding, doubling and twisting to slip into lonely water holes. McEwen had chosen, as the lesser risk, to ride openly to Prairie Springs. He had found no one there and had borrowed grub for himself and several feeds of corn for the Honey horse. There had been no fast riding, except for the one brief spurt with the posse at Chupadero. But it had been a steady grind, doubly tiresome that they might not keep to the beaten trails. Cross-country traveling on soft ground is rough on horseflesh.

And now they left the plain and turned through tar-bush up the long slope to the San Andrés. A thousand ridges and hollows came plunging and headlong against them. And suddenly the tough little horse was tiring, failing.

Halfway to the hill foot they paused for a brief rest. High on their slim lances, banners of yucca blossoms were white and waxen, and wild bees hummed to their homes in the flower stalks of last

year; flaunting afar, cactus flowers flamed crimson or scarlet through
the black tar-bush.

Long since, McEwen had given up the Panhandle. He planned
now to bear far to the southeast, crossing the salt plains below the
White Sands to the Guadalupe Mountains, straddling the boundary
between the territory and Texas, and so east to the Staked Plains.
He knew the country ahead, or had known it ten years before. But
there would be changes. There was a new railroad, so he had heard,
from El Paso to Tularosa, and so working north toward the states.
There would be other things, too — new ranches, and all that. For
sample, behind him, just where this long slope merged with the flats,
three unexpected windmills, each five miles from the other, had made
a line across his path; he had made a weary detour to pass unseen.

The San Andrés made here a twenty-mile offset where they joined
the Oscuro, with the huge round mass of Salinas Peak as their mutual
corner. Lava Gap, the meeting place of the two ranges, was now
directly at his left and ten miles away. The bleak and mile-high
walls of it made a frame for the tremendous picture of Sierra Blanca,
sixty long miles to the east, with a gulf of nothingness between.
Below that nothingness, as McEwen knew, lay the black lava river of
the Mal Pais. But Lava Gap was not for him. Unless pursuit was
quite abandoned, Lava Gap and Dripping Springs would be watched
and guarded. He was fenced in by probabilities.

But the fugitive was confident yet, and by no means at the end of
his resources. He knew a dim old Indian trail over a high pass beyond
Salinas Peak. It started at Grapevine Spring, Captain Jack Crawford's
ranch.

"And at Grapevine," said Ross aloud, "I'll have to buy, beg, borrow
or get me a horse. Hope there's nobody at home. If there's anyone
there I'll have to get his gun first and trade afterwards. Borrowing
horses is not highly recommended, but it beats killing 'em."

To the right and before him the Jornado was hazy, vast and mysterious. To the right and behind him, the lava flow of Pascual
sprawled black and sinister in the lowlands; and behind him — far
behind him, far below him, a low line of dust was just leaving the
central windmill of those three new ranches, a dozen miles away.
McEwen watched this dust with some interest while he rolled and
lit a cigarette. He drank the last water from his canteen.

"Come on, me bold outlaw," he said, "keep moving. You've done
made your bed, but these hellhounds won't let you sleep in it." He
put foot to stirrup; he stroked the Honey horse.

"Miél, old man, you tough it out four or five miles more, and your

troubles will be over. Me for a fresh horse at Grapevine, come hell
or high water. Take it easy. No hurry. Just shuffle along."

The pursuing dust did not come fast, but it came straight his way.
"I'll bet a cooky," said Ross sagely, "that some of these gay bucks
have got a spyglass. I wonder if that ain't against the rules? And
new men throwin' in with them at every ranch. I reckon I would,
too, if it wasn't for this red topknot of mine. Why couldn't they
meet up with some other redheaded hellion and take him back?
Wouldn't that be just spiffin'? One good thing, anyway—I didn't
go back to the Quemado country. Some of the boys would sure
have got in Dutch, hidin' me out. This is better."

He crossed the old military road that had once gone through Lava
Gap to Fort Stanton; he smiled at the shod tracks there; he came to
the first hills, pleasingly decorated with bunches of mares—American
mares, gentle mares—Corporal Tanner's mares. He picked a bunch
with four or five saddle horses in it and drove them slowly up Grapevine Cañon. The Miél horse held up his head and freshened visibly.
He knew what this meant. The sun dropped behind the hills. It
was cool and fresh in Grapevine. The outlaw took his time. He had
an hour or more. He turned for a last look at the north and the
cliffs of Oscuro Mountain blazing in the low sun to fiery streamers
of red light. You would have seen, perhaps, only a howling wilderness, but this man was to look back, waking and in dream, and to
remember that brooding and sunlit silence as the glowing heart of
the world. From this place alone he was to be an exile.

"Nice a piece of country as ever laid outdoors," said Ross McEwen.
"I've seen some several places where it would be right pleasant to
have a job along with a bunch of decent punchers—good grub and
all that, mouth organ by the firelight after supper— Or herding
sheep."

Grapevine Spring is at the very head of the cañon. To east, south
and west the hills rise directly from the corral fences. McEwen
drove the mares into the water pen and called loudly to the house.
The hail went unanswered. Eagles screamed back from a cliff above
him.

"A fool for luck," said McEwen.

He closed the bars, he gave Miél his first installment of water.
Then he went to the house. It was unlocked and there was no one
there. The ashes on the hearth were cold. He borrowed two cans
of beans and some bacon. There was a slender store of corn, and
he borrowed one feed of this to make tomorrow's breakfast for the
new horse he was soon to acquire. He found an old saddle and he

borrowed that, with an old bridle as well; he brought his own to replace them; he lit the little lamp on the table and grinned happily.

"They'll find Miél and my saddle and the light," he said, "and they'll make sure I've taken to the brush."

He went back to the pen, he roped and saddled a saddle-marked brown, broad chested and short coupled, unshod. Shod tracks are too easily followed. Then he scratched his red head and grinned again. The pen was built of poles laid in panels, except at the front; the cedar brake grew to the very sides of it. He went to the back and took down two panels, laying the poles aside; he let the mares drift out there, seeing to it that some of them went around by the house, and the rest on the other side of the pen. It was almost dark by now.

"There," he said triumphantly. "The boys will drive in a bunch of stock when they come, for remounts, and they'll go right on through. Fine mess in the dark. And it'll puzzle them to find which way I went with all these tracks. Time I was gone."

He came back to the watering trough; he washed his hands and face and filled his canteen; he went on where Miél stood weary and huddled in the dusk. His hand was gentle on that drooping neck.

"Miél, old fellow," he said, "you've been one good little horse. *Bueno suerte.*" He led the brown to the bars. "I hate a fool," said Ross McEwen.

He took down the bars and rode into the cedar brush at right angles to the cañon, climbing steadily from the first. It was a high and desperate pass, and branches had grown across the unused trail; long before he had won halfway to the summit he heard, far below him, the crashing of horses in the brush, the sound of curses and laughter. The pursuit had arrived at Grapevine.

He topped the summit of that nameless pass an hour later, and turned down the dark cañon to the east — to meet grief at once. Since his time a cloud-burst had been this way. Where there had once been fair footing the flood had cut deep and wide, and every semblance of soil had washed away, leaving only a wild moraine, a loose rubble of rocks and tumbled boulders. But it was the only way. The hillsides were impossibly steep and sidelong, glassy granite and gneiss, or treacherous slides of porphyry. Ross led his horse. Every step was a hazard in that narrow and darkened place, with crumbling ridge and pit and jump off, with windrows of smooth round rock to roll and turn under their feet. It took the better part of two hours to win through the narrows, perhaps two miles. The cañon widened then, the hillsides were lower and Ross could ride again, picking his doubtful way in the starlight. He turned on a stepladder of hills to the north, and came about midnight to Dripstone, high in a secret hollow of the hills. The prodigious bulk of Salinas loomed mysterious and incredible above him in the starlight.

He tied the brown horse securely and named him Porch Climber. He built a tiny fire and toasted strips of bacon on the coals. Then he spread out his saddle blankets with hat and saddle for pillow, and so lay down to untroubled sleep.

4

He awoke in that quiet place before the first stirring of dawn. A low thin moon was in the sky and the mountains were dim across the east. He washed his eyes out with water from the canteen. He made a nose bag from the corn sack and hung it on Porch Climber's brown head. The Belen nose bag had gone into the discard days before. He built a fire of twigs and hovered over it while his precious coffee came to a boil; his coat was thin and the night air was fresh, almost chilly. He smacked his lips over the coffee, he saddled and watered Porch Climber at Dripstone and refilled his canteen there. The horse drank sparingly.

"Better fill up, old-timer," Ross advised him. "You're sure going to need it."

Knuckled ridges led away from Salinas like fingers of a hand. The eastern flat was some large fraction of a mile nearer to sea level than the high plain west of the mountain, and these ridges were massive and steep accordingly. He made his way down one of them. The plain was dark and cold below him; the mountains took shape and grew, the front range of the Rockies — Capitán, Carrizo, Sierra Blanca, Sacramento, with Guadalupe low and dim in the south; the White Sands were dull and lifeless in the midway plain. Bird twitter was in the air. Rabbits scurried through the brush, a quail whirred by and sent back a startled call; crimson streaks shot up the sky, and day grew broad across the silent levels. The cut banks of Salt Creek appeared, wandering away southwest toward the marshes. Low and far against the black base of the Sacramento, white feathers lifted and fluffed, the smoke of the first fires at Tularosa, fifty miles away. Flame tipped the far-off crests, the sun leaped up from behind the mountain wall, the level light struck on the White Sands, glanced from those burnished bevels and splashed on the western cliffs; the desert day blazed over this new half-world.

He had passed a few cows on the ridges, but now, as he came close to the flats, he was suddenly aware of many cattle before him, midges upon the vast plain; more cattle than he had found on the western side of the mountains. He drew rein, instantly on the alert, and began to quarter the scene with a keen scrutiny. At once a silver twinkling showed to northward — the steel fans of a windmill, perhaps six miles out from the foot of the main mountain. His eye moved slowly across the plain. He was shocked to find a second windmill tower some six or eight miles south of the first, keeping at the same distance from the hills, and when he made out the faint glimmer of a third, far in the south, he gave way to indignation. It was a bald plain with no cover for the quietly disposed, except a few clumps of soapweed here and there. And this line of windmills was precisely the line of the road to El Paso. Where he had expected smooth going he would have to keep to the roughs; to venture into the open was to court discovery. He turned south across the ridges.

He had talked freely to Miél, but until now he had been reticent with Porch Climber, who had not yet won his confidence. At this unexpected reverse he opened his heart.

"Another good land gone wrong," he said. "I might have known it. This side of Salt Creek is only half-bad cow country, so of course it's all settled up, right where we want to go. No one lives east of Salt Creek, not even sheep herders. And we couldn't possibly make it, goin' on the other side of Salt Creek with all that marsh country and the hell of the White Sands. Why, this is plumb ridiculous!"

He meditated for a while upon his wrongs and then broke out afresh: "When I was here, the only water east of the mountains was the Wildy Well at the corner of the damn White Sands. Folks drove along the road, and when they wanted water they went up in the hills. It's no use to cross over to Tularosa. They'll be waiting for us there. No, sir, we've pointedly got to skulk down through the brush. And you'll find it heavy going, up one ridge and down another, like a flea on a washboard."

Topping the next ridge, he reined back swiftly into a hollow place. He dismounted and peered through a mesquite bush, putting the branches aside to look. A mile to the south two horsemen paced soberly down a ridge — and it was a ridge which came directly from the pass to Grapevine.

"Now ain't them the bright lads?" said the runaway, divided between chagrin and admiration. "What are you going to do with fellows like that? I ask you. I left plain word that I done took to the hills afoot, without the shadow of a doubt. Therefore they reasoned I hadn't. They've coppered every bet. Now that's what I call clear thinkin'. I reckon some of 'em did stay there, but these two crossed over that hell gate at night, just in case.

"I'll tell a man they had a ride where that cloud-burst was. Say, they'll tell their grandchildren about that — if they live that long, which I misdoubt, the way they're carryin' on. This gives me what is technically known as the willies. Hawse," said McEwen, "let's us tarry a spell and see what these hirelin' bandogs are goin' to do now."

He took off the bridle and saddle, he staked Porch Climber to rest and graze while he watched. What the bandogs did was to ride straight to the central windmill, where smoke showed from the house. McEwen awaited developments. Purely from a sense of duty he ate the other can of beans while he waited.

"They'll take word to every ranch," he prophesied gloomily. "Leave a man to watch where there isn't anyone there — take more men along when they find more than one at a well. Wish I was a drummer."

His prognostications were verified. After a long wait, which meant breakfast, a midget horseman rode slowly north towards the first windmill. A little later two men rode slowly south towards the third ranch.

"That's right, spread the news, dammit, and make everybody hate you," said Ross. He saddled and followed them, paralleling their course, but keeping to the cover of the brush.

It was heavy and toilsome going, boulders and rocks alternating with soft ground where Porch Climber's feet went through; gravel, coarse sand or piled rocks in the washes; tedious twisting in the brush and wearisome windings where a bay of open country forced a detour. He passed by the mouths of Good Fortune, Antelope and Cottonwood cañons, struggling through their dry deltas; he drew abreast of the northern corner of the White Sands. The reflection of it was blinding, yet he found it hard to hold his eyes away. The sun rode high and hot. McEwen consulted his canteen.

More than once or twice came the unwelcome thought that he might take to the hill country, discard Porch Climber and hide by some inaccessible seep or pothole until pursuit died down. But he was a stubborn man, and his heart was set upon Guadalupe; he had an inborn distaste for a diet of chance rabbit and tuna fruit — or, perhaps, slow deer without salt. A stronger factor in his decision — although he hardly realized it — was the horseman's hatred for being set afoot. He could hole in safely; there was little doubt of that. But when he came out of the hole, how then? A man from nowhere, on foot, with no past and no name and a long red beard — that would excite remark. He fingered the stubble on his cheeks with that reflection. Yes, such a man would be put to it to account for himself — and he would have to show up sometime, somewhere. The green cottonwood of Independent Spring showed high on the hill to his right. He held on to the south.

And now he came to the mouth of Sulphur Springs Cañon. Beyond here a great bay of open plain flowed into the hill foot under Kaylor Mountain; and midmost of that bay was another windmill, a long low house, spacious corrals. McEwen was sick of windmills. But this one was close under the mountain, far west of the line of the other ranches and of the El Paso road; McEwen saw with lively interest that his pursuers left the road and angled across the open to this ranch. That meant dinner.

"Honesty," said McEwen with conviction, "is the best policy. Dinnertime for some people, but only noon for me. Early for grub too. . . . And how can these enterprisin' chaps be pursuin' me when they're in front? That isn't reasonable. Who ever heard of deputies goin' ahead and the bandit taggin' along behind? That's not right. It's not moral. I'm goin' around Besides, if I don't this thing is liable to go on always, just windmills and windmills — to Mexico City — Peru — Chile. I'm plumb tired of windmills. Porch Climber," said McEwen, "have you got any gift of speed? Because, just as soon as these two sheriff men get to that ranch and have time to go in the house, you and me are going to drift out quiet and unostentatious across the open country till we hit the banks of the Salt Marsh. And if these fellows look out and see us you've just got to run for it. And they can maybe get fresh horses too. But if they don't see us we'll be right. We'll drift south under cover of the bank and get ahead of 'em while they stuff their paunches."

Half an hour later he turned Porch Climber's head to the east, and rode sedately across the smooth plain, desiring to raise no dust. Some three miles away, near where he crossed the El Paso road, grew a vigorous motte of mesquite trees. Once beyond that motte, he kept it lined up between him and the ranch; and so came unseen to where the plain broke away to the great marsh which rimmed the basin of the White Sands.

In the east the White Sands billowed in great dry dunes above the level of the plain, but the western half was far below that level, and waterbound. This was the home of mirages; they spread now all their pomp of palm and crystal lake and fairy hill. McEwen turned south along the margin. Here, just under the bank, the ground was moist, almost wet, and yet firm footing, like a road of hard rubber. He brought Porch Climber to a long-reaching trot, steady and smooth; he leaned forward in his stirrups and an old song came to his lips, unsummoned. He sang it with loving mockery, in a nasal but not unpleasing baritone:

> *They give him his orders at Monroe, Virginia,*
> *Sayin', "Pete, you're way behind ti-ime"* —

"Gosh, it does seem natural to sing when a good horse is putting the miles behind him," said McEwen. "This little old brown pony is holdin' up right well, too, after all that grief in the roughs this mawnin'.

> He looked round then to his black, greasy fireman,
> "Just shovel in a little more co-o-oal,
> And when we cross that wide old maounting,
> You can watch old Ninety-Seven roll!"

"Hey, Porch Climber! You ain't hardly keepin' time. Peart up a little! Now, lemme see. Must be about twenty mile to the old Wildy Well. Wonder if I'll find any more new ranches between here and there? Likely. Hell of a country, all cluttered up like this!

> It's a mighty rough road from Lynchburg to Danville,
> And a line on a three-mile gra-ade;
> It was on that grade that he lo-ost his av'rage,
> And you see what a jump he made!

He rejoined the wagon road where the White Sands thrust a long and narrow arm far to the west. The old road crossed this arm at the shoulder, a three-mile speedway. Out on the sands magic islands came and went and rose and sank in a misty sea. But in the south, where the road climbed again to the plain, was the inevitable windmill — reality and no mirage.

McEwen followed the road in the posture of a man who had nothing to fear. He had outridden the rumor of his flight; he could come to this ranch with a good face. But he reined down to a comfortable jog. Those behind might overtake him close enough to spy him here in this naked place. Jaunting easily, nearing the ranch where he belonged, a horseman was no object of suspicion, but a man in haste was a different matter.

There was no one at the ranch. The water was brackish and flat, but the two wayfarers drank thankfully. He could see no signs that any horses were watering there; he made a shrewd guess that the boys had taken the horses and gone up into the mountains for better grass and sweet water, or perhaps to get out of sight of the White Sands, leaving the flats to the cattle.

"Probably they just ride down every so often to oil the windmill," he said. "Leastways, I would. Four hundred square miles of lookin'-glass, three hundred and sixty-four days a year — no, thank you! My eyes are most out now."

J. B. was branded on the gate posts of the corral, and on the door. There was canned stuff on a shelf and a few baking-powder biscuits, old and dry. He took a can of salmon and filed it for future reference.

"No time for gormandizin' now," he said. He stuffed the stale biscuits into his pocket to eat on the road. "There's this much about bread," said McEwen, "I can take it or I can leave it alone. And I've been leaving it alone for several days now."

A pencil and a tablet lay on the table. His gray eyes went suddenly a-dance with impish light. He tore out a page and wrote a few words of counsel and advice.

Hey, you J. B. waddies: Look out for a fellow with red hair and gray eyes. Medium-sized man. He robbed the bank at Belen, and they think he came this way. Big reward offered for him. Two thousand, I hear. But I don't know for certain. Send word to the ranches up north. I will tell them as far south as Organ.

JIM HUNTLEY.

He hung this news-letter on a nail above the stove.

"There!" he said. "If them gay jaspers that are after me had any sense at all, they'd see it was no use to go any further, and they'd stay right here and rest up. But they won't. They'll say, 'Hey, this is the way he went — here's some more of the same old guff! But how ever did that feller get down here without us finding any tracks? You can see what a jump he made.' I don't want to be ugly," said McEwen, "but I've got to cipher up some way to shake loose from these fellows. I want to go to sleep. Now who in hell is Jim Huntley?"

Time for concealment was past. From now on he must set his hope on speed. He rode down the big road boldly and, for a time, at a brisk pace; he munched the dry biscuits and washed them down with warm and salty water from his canteen.

There was no room for another ranch between here and Wildy's Well. Wildy's was an old established ranch. It was among the possibilities that he might hit here upon some old acquaintance whose failing sight would not note his passing, and who would give him a fresh horse. He was now needing urge of voice and spur for Porch Climber's lagging feet. It sat in his mind that Wildy was dead. His brows knitted with the effort to remember. Yes, Wildy had been killed by a falling horse. Most likely, though, he would find no one living at the well. Not too bad, the water of Wildy's Well — but they would be in the hills with the good grass.

The brown horse was streaked with salt and sweat; he dragged in the slow sand. Here was a narrow broken country of rushing slopes, pinched between the White Sands and the mountains. The road wound up and down in the crowding brush; the footing was a coarse pebbly sand of broken granite from the crumbling hills. Heat waves rose quivering, the White Sands lifted and shuddered to a blinding shimmer, the dream islands were wavering, shifting and indistinct, astir with rumor. McEwen's eyes were dull for sleep, red rimmed and swollen from glare and alkali dust. The salt water was bitter in his belly. The stubble on his face was gray with powdered dust and furrowed with sweat stains; dust was in his nostrils and his ears, and the taste of dust was in his mouth. Porch Climber plowed heavily. And all at once McEwen felt a sudden distaste for his affair.

He had a searching mind and it was not long before he found a cause. That damn song! Dance music. There were places where people danced, where they would dance tonight. There was a garden in Rutherford —

5

There was no one at Wildy's Well, no horses there and no sign that any horses were using there. McEwen drank deep of the cool sweet water. When Porch Climber had his fill, McEwen plunged arms and head into the trough. Horse and man sighed together; their eyes met in comfortable understanding.

"Feller," said McEwen, "it was that salt water, much as anything else, that slowed you up, I reckon. Yuh was sure sluggish. And yuh just ought to see yourself now! Nemmine, that's over." He took down his rope, and cut off a length, the spread of his arms. He untwisted this length to three strands, soaked these strands in the trough, wrung them out and knotted them around his waist. He eyed the cattle that had been watering here. They had retreated to the far side at his coming and were now waiting impatiently. "Been many a long year since I've seen any Durham cattle," said McEwen. "Everybody's got white-face stuff now. Reckon they raise these for El Paso market. No feeder will buy 'em, unless with a heavy cut in the price."

He hobbled over and closed the corral gate. Every bone of him was a separate ache. A faint breeze stirred; the mill sails turned lazily; the gears squeaked a protest. Ross looked up with interest.

"That was right good water," he said. "Guess you've earned a greasing." He climbed the tall tower. Wildy's Well dated from before the steel windmill; this was massive and cumbersome, a wooden tower, and the wheel itself was of wood. After his oiling Ross scanned the north with an anxious eye. There was no dust. South by east, far in the central plain, dim hills swam indeterminate through the heat haze — Las Cornudas and Heuco. South by west, gold and rose, the peaks of the Organs peered from behind the last corner of the San

Andrés. He searched the north again. He could see no dust — but he could almost see a dust.

He shook his head. "Them guys are real intelligent," he said. "I'm losin' my av'rage." He clambered down with some celerity, and set about what he had to do.

He tied the severed end of his rope to the saddle horn, tightened the cinches, swung into the saddle and shook out a loop. Hugging the fence, the cattle tore madly around the corral in a wild cloud of dust. McEwen rode with them on an inner circle, his eye on a big roan steer, his rope whirling in slow and measured rhythms. For a moment the roan steer darted to the lead; the loop shot out, curled over and tightened on both forefeet; Porch Climber whirled smartly to the left; the steer fell heavily. Ross swung off; as he ran, he tugged at the hogging string around his waist. Porch Climber dragged valiantly, Ross ran down the rope, pounced on the struggling steer, gathered three feet together and tied them with the hogging string. These events were practically simultaneous.

McEwen unsaddled the horse. "I guess you can call it a day," he said. He opened the gate and let the frightened cattle run out. "Here," he said, "is where I make a spoon or spoil a horn." He cut a thong from a saddle string and tied his old plow-handle .45 so that it should not jolt from the scabbard. He made a tight roll of the folded bridle, that lonely can of salmon and his coat, with his saddle blanket wrapped around all; he tied these worldly goods securely behind the cantle. He uncoupled the cinches and let out the quarter straps to the last hole.

The tied steer threshed his head madly, bellowing wild threats of vengeance. McEwen carried the saddle and placed it at the steer's back, where he lay. He found a short and narrow strip of board, like a batten, under the tower; and with this, as the frantic roan steer heaved and threshed in vain efforts to rise, he poked the front cinch under the struggling body, inches at a time, until at last he could reach over and hook his fingers into the cinch ring. Before he could do this he was forced to tie the free foot to the three that were first tied; it had been kicking with so much fury and determination that the task could not be accomplished. Into the cinch ring he tied the free end of his rope, bringing it up between body and tied feet; he took a double of loose rope around his hips, dug his heels into the sand and pulled manfully every time the steer floundered; and so, at last and painfully, drew the cinch under until the saddle was on the steer's back and approximately where it should be. Then he put in the latigo strap, taking two turns, and tugged at the latigo till the saddle was pulled to its rightful place. At every tug the roan steer let out an agonized bawl. Then he passed the hind cinch behind the steer's hips and under the tail, drawing it up tightly so that the saddle could not slip over the steer's withers during the subsequent proceedings.

McEwen stood up and mopped the muddy sweat from his face; he rubbed his aching back. He filled his canteen at the trough, drank again and washed himself. He rolled a smoke; he lashed the canteen firmly to the saddle forks. Porch Climber was rolling in the sand. McEwen took him by the forelock and led him through the open gate.

"If you should ask me," he said, "this corral is a spot where there is going to be trouble, and no place at all for you." He looked up the north road. Nothing in sight.

He went back to the steer. He hitched up his faded blue overalls, tightened his belt and squinted at the sun; he loosened the last-tied foot and coiled the rope at the saddle horn. Then he eased gingerly into the saddle. The steer made lamentable outcry, twisting his neck in a creditable attempt to hook his tormentor; the free foot lashed out madly. But McEwen flattened himself and crouched safely, with a full inch of margin; the steer was near to hooking his own leg and kicking his own face and he subsided with a groan. McEwen settled himself in the saddle.

"Are ye ready?" said McEwen.

"Oi am!" said McEwen.

"Thin go!" said McEwen, and pulled the hogging string.

The steer lurched sideways to his feet, paused for one second of amazement, and left the ground. He pitched, he plunged, he kicked at the stirrups, he hooked at the rider's legs, he leaped, he ran, bawling his terror and fury to the sky; weaving, lunging, twisting he crashed sidelong into the fence, fell, scrambled up in an instant. The shimmy was not yet invented. But the roan steer shimmied, and he did it nobly; man and saddle rocked and reeled. Then, for the first time, he saw the open gate and thundered through it, abandoning all thought except flight.

Shaken and battered, McEwen was master. The man was a rider. To use the words of a later day, he was "a little warm, but not at all astonished." Yet he had not come off scot-free. When they crashed into the fence he had pulled up his leg, but had taken an ugly bruise upon the hip. The whole performance, and more particularly the shimmy feature, had been a poor poultice for aching bones.

Worse than all, the canteen had been crushed between fence and saddle. The priceless water was lost.

His hand still clutched the hogging string; he had no wish to leave that behind for curious minds to ponder upon. Until his mount slowed from a run to a pounding trot, he made no effort to guide him, the more because the steer's chosen course was not far from the direction in which McEwen wished to go. Wildy's Well lay at the extreme southwestern corner of the White Sands, and McEwen's thought was to turn eastward. He meant to try for Luna's Wells, the old stage station in the middle of the desert, on the road which ran obliquely from Organ to Tularosa.

When time was ripe McEwen leaned over and slapped his hat into the steer's face, on the right side, to turn him to the left and to the east.

The first attempt at guidance, and the fourth attempt, brought on new bucking spells. McEwen gave him time between lessons; what he most feared was that the roan would "sull," or balk, refusing to go farther. When the steer stopped, McEwen waited until he went on of his own accord; when his progress led approximately toward McEwen's goal, he was allowed to go his own way unmolested. McEwen was bethorned, dragged through mesquite bushes, raked under branches; his shirt was ribboned and torn. But he had his way at last. With danger, with infinite patience and with good judgment, he forced his refractory mount to the left and ever to the left, and so came at last into a deep trail which led due east. Muttering and grumbling, the steer followed the trail.

All this had taken time, but speed had also been a factor. When McEwen felt free to turn his head only a half circle of the windmill fans showed above the brush. Wildy's Well was miles behind them.

"Boys," said McEwen, "if you follow me this time, I'll say you're good!"

The steer scuffed and shambled, taking his own gait; he stopped often to rest, his tongue hung out, foam dripped from his mouth. McEwen did not urge him. The way led now through rotten ground and alkali, now through chalk that powdered and billowed in dust; deep trails, channeled by winds at war. As old trails grew too deep for comfort the stock had made new ones to parallel the old; a hundred paths lay side by side.

McEwen was a hard case. A smother of dust was about him, thirst tormented him, his lips were cracked and bleeding, his eyes sunken, his face fallen in; and weariness folded him like a garment.

"Slate water is the best water," said McEwen.

They came from chalk and brush into a better country; poor indeed, and starved, but the air of it was breathable. The sun was low and the long shadows of the hills reached out into the plain. And now he saw, dead in front, the gleaming vane and sails of a windmill. Only the top — the fans seemed to touch the ground — and yet it was clear to see. McEwen plucked up heart. This was not Luna's. Luna's was far beyond. This was a new one. If it stood in a hollow place — and it did — it could not be far away. Water!

For the first time McEwen urged his mount, gently, and only with the loose and raveled tie string. Once was enough. The roan steer stopped, pawed the ground and proclaimed flat rebellion. For ten minutes, perhaps, McEwen sought to overrule him. It was no use. The roan steer was done. He took down his rope. With a little loop he snared a pawing and rebellious forefoot. He pulled up rope and foot with all his failing strength, and took a quick turn on the saddle horn. The roan made one hop and fell flat-long. McEwen tied three feet, though there was scant need for it. He took off the saddle, carried it to the nearest thicket and raised it, with pain, into the forks of a high soapweed, tucking up latigos and cinches. With pain; McEwen, also, was nearly done.

"My horse gave out on me. I toted my saddle a ways, but it was too heavy, and I hung it up so the cows couldn't eat it," he said, in the tone of one who recites a lesson.

He untied the steer, then came back hotfoot to his soapweed, thinking that the roan might be in a fighting humor. But the roan was done. He got unsteadily to his feet, with hanging head and slavering jaws; he waited for a little and moved slowly away.

"Glad he didn't get on the prod," said McEwen. "I sure expected it. That was one tired steer. He sure done me a good turn. Guess I'd better be strollin' into camp."

It was a sorry strolling. A hundred yards — a quarter — a half — a mile. The windmill grew taller; the first night breeze was stirring, he could see the fans whirl in the sun. A hundred yards — a quarter — a mile! An hour was gone. The shadows overtook him, passed him; the hills were suddenly very close and near, notched black against a crimson sky. Thirst tortured him, the windmill beckoned, sunset winds urged him on. He came to the brow of the shallow dip in which the ranch lay, he saw a little corral, a water pen, a long dark house beyond; he climbed into the water pen and plunged his face into the trough.

The windmill groaned and whined with a dismal clank and grinding of dry gears. Yet there was a low smoke over the chimney. How was this? The door stood open. Except for the creaking plaint of the windmill, a dead quiet hung about the place, a hint of something

ominous and sinister. Stumbling, bruised and outworn, McEwen came
to that low dark door. He heard a choking cough, a child's wailing
cry. His foot was on the threshold.

"What's wrong? *Qué es?*" he called.

A cracked and feeble voice made an answer that he could not hear.
Then a man appeared at the inner door; an old man, a Mexican,
clutching at the wall for support.

"*El garrotillo*," said the cracked voice. "The strangler — diphtheria."

"I am here to help you," said McEwen.

6

Of what took place that night McEwen had never afterward any
clear remembrance, except of the first hour or two. The drone of
bees was in his ears, and a whir of wings. He moved in a thin, unreal
mist, giddy and light-headed, undone by thirst, weariness, loss of sleep
— most of all by alkaline and poisonous dust, deep in his lungs. In the
weary time that followed, though he daily fell more and more behind
on sleep and rest, he was never so near to utter collapse as on this first
interminable night. It remained for him a blurred and distorted vision
of the dreadful offices of the sickroom; of sickening odors; of stumbling from bed to bed as one sufferer or another shook with paroxysms
of choking.

Of a voice, now far off and now clear, insistent with counsel and
question, direction and appeal; of lamplight that waned and flared and
dwindled again; of creak and clank and pounding of iron on iron in
horrible rhythm, endless, slow, intolerable. That would be the windmill. Yes, but where? And what windmill?

Of terror, and weeping, and a young child that screamed. That
woman — why, they had always told him grown people didn't take
diphtheria. But she had it, all right. Had it as bad as the two youngsters, too. She was the mother, it seemed. Yes, Florencio had told him
that. Too bad for the children to die. . . . But who the devil was
Florencio? The windmill turned dismally — clank and rattle and
groan.

That was the least one choking now — Felix. Swab out his throat
again. Hold the light. Careful. That's it. Burn it up. More cloth,
old man. Hold the light this way. There, there, *pobrecito!* All
right now. . . . Something was lurking in the corners, in the shadows.
Must go see. Drive it away. What's that? What say? Make coffee?
Sure. Coffee. Good idea. Salty coffee. Windmill pumpin' salt water.
Batter and pound and squeal. Round and round. Round and round.
Round and round. . . . Tell you what. Goin' to grease that damn

windmill. Right now. . . . Huh? What's that? Wait till morning? All right. All ri'. Sure.

His feet were leaden. His arms minded well enough, but his hands were simply wonderful. Surprisin' skillful, those hands. How steady they were to clean membranes from little throats. Clever hands! They could bring water to these people, too, lift them up and hold the cup and not spill a drop. They could sponge off hot little bodies when the children cried out in delirium. Wring out rag, too! Wonnerful hands! Mus' call people's 'tention to these hands sometime. There, there, let me wash you some more with the nice cool water. Now, now — nothing will hurt you. Uncle Happy's goin' to be right here, takin' care of you. Now, now — go to sleep — go-o to sleep!

But his feet were so big, so heavy and so clumsy, and his legs were insubordinate. Specially the calves. The calf of each leg, where there had once been good muscles of braided steel, was now filled with sluggish water of inferior quality. That wasn't the worst either. There was a distinct blank place, a vacuum, something like the bead in a spirit level, and it shifted here and there as the water sloshed about. Wonder nobody had ever noticed that.

Must be edgin' on toward morning. Sick people are worst between two and four, they say. And they're all easier now, every one. Both kids asleep — tossin' about! And now the mother was droppin' off. Yes, sir — she's goin' to sleep. What did the old man call her? Estefanía. Yes — Est'fa' —

He woke with sunlight in his eyes. His arm sprawled before him on a pine table and his head lay on his arm. He raised up, blinking, and looked around. This was the kitchen, a sorry spectacle. The sickroom lay beyond an open door. He sat by that door, where he could see into the sickroom.

They were all asleep. The woman stirred uneasily and threw out an arm. The old man lay huddled on a couch beyond the table.

McEwen stared. The fever had passed and his head was reasonably clear. He frowned, piecing together remembered scraps from the night before. The old man was Florencio Telles, the woman was the wife of his dead son, these were his grandchildren. Felix was one. Forget the other name. They had come back from a trip to El Paso a week ago, or some such matter, and must have brought the contagion with them. First one came down with the strangler, then another. Well poisoned with it, likely. Have to boil the drinking water. This was called Rancho Perdido — the Lost Ranch. Well named. The old fellow spoke good English.

McEwen was at home in Spanish, and, from what he remembered

of last night, the talk had been carried on in either tongue indifferently. What a night!

He rose and tiptoed out with infinite precaution. The wind was dead. He went to the well and found the oil; he climbed up and drenched the bearings and gears. He was surprised to see how weak he was and how sore; and for the first time in his life he knew the feeling of giddiness and was forced to keep one hand clutched tightly to some support as he moved around the platform — he, Ross McEwen.

When he came back the old man met him with finger on lip. They sat on the warm ground, where they could keep watch upon the sickroom, obliquely, through two doors; just far enough away for quiet speech to be unheard.

"Let them sleep. Every minute of sleep for them is so much coined gold. We won't make a move to wake them. And how is it with you, my son, how is it with you?"

"Fine and fancy. When I came here last night I had a thousand aches, and now I've only got one."

"And that one is all over?"

"That's the place. Never mind me. I'll be all right. How long has this been going on?"

"This is the fifth day for the oldest boy, I think. He came down with it first, Demetrio. We thought it was only a sore throat at first. Maybe six days. I am a little mixed up."

"Should think you would be. Now listen. I know something about diphtheria. Not much, but this for certain. Here's what you've got to do, old man: Quick as they wake up in there, you go to bed and stay in bed. You totter around much more and you're going to die. There's your fortune told, and no charge for it."

"Oh, I'm not bad. I do not cough hard. The strangler never hurts old people much." So he said, but every word was an effort.

"Hell, no, you're not bad. Just a walkin' corpse, tha's all. You get to bed and save your strength. When any two of 'em are chokin' to death at once that'll be time enough for you to hobble out and take one of them off my hands. Do they sleep this long, often?"

"Oh, no. This is the first time. They are always better when morning comes, but they have not all slept at the same time, never before. My daughter, you might say, has not slept at all. It has been grief and anxiety with her as much as the sickness. They will all feel encouraged now, since you've come. If it please God, we'll pull them all through."

"Look here!" said McEwen. "It can't be far to Luna's Well. Can't

I catch up a horse and lope over there after while — bring help and send for a doctor?"

"There's no one there. Francisco Luna and Casimiro both have driven their stock to the Guadalupe Mountains, weeks ago. It has been too dry. And no one uses the old road now. All travel goes by the new way, beyond the new railroad."

"I found no one at the western ranches yesterday," said McEwen.

"No. Everyone is in the hills. The drought is too bad. There is no one but you. The nearest help is Alamogordo — thirty-five miles. And if you go there some will surely die before you get back. I have no more strength. I will be flat on my back this day."

"That's where you belong. I'll be nurse and cook for this family. Got anything to cook?"

"Not much. Frijoles, jerky, bacon, flour, a little canned stuff and dried peaches."

McEwen frowned. "It is in my mind they ought to have eggs and milk."

"When the cattle come to water you can shut up a cow and a calf — or two of them — and we can have a little milk tonight. I'll show you which ones. As I told you last night, I turned out the cow I was keeping up, for fear I'd get down and she would die here in the pen."

"Don Florencio, I'm afraid I didn't get all you told me last night," said McEwen thoughtfully. "I was wild as a hawk, I reckon. Thought that windmill would certainly drive me crazy. Fever."

The old man nodded. "I knew, my son. It galled my heart to make demands on you, but there was no remedy. It had to be done. I was at the end of my strength. Little Felix, if not the other, would surely have been dead by now except for the mercy of God which sent you here."

McEwen seemed much struck by this last remark. He cocked his head a little to one side painfully, for his neck was stiff; he pursed his lip and held it between finger and thumb for a moment of meditation.

"So that was it!" he said. "I see! Always heard tell that God moves in a mysterious way His wonders to perform. I'll tell a man He does!"

A scanty breakfast, not without gratitude; a pitiful attempt at redding up the hopeless confusion and disorder. The sick woman's eyes followed McEwen as he worked. A good strangling spell all around, including the old man, then a period of respite. McEwen buckled on his gun and brought a hammer and a lard pail to Florencio's bed.

"If you need me, hammer on this, and I'll come a-running. I'm going out to the corral and shoot some beef tea. You tell me about what milk cows to shut up."

Don Florencio described several milk cows. "Any of them. Not all are in to water any one day. Stock generally come in every other day, because they get better grass at a distance. And my brand is T T—for my son Timoteo, who is dead. You will find the cattle in poor shape, but if you wait awhile you may get a smooth one."

McEwen nodded. "I was thinking that," he said. "I want some flour sacks. I'll hang some of the best up under the platform on the windmill tower, where the flies won't bother it."

They heard a shot later. A long time afterward he came in with a good chunk of meat, and set about preparing beef tea. "I shut up a cow to milk," he said. "A lot of saddle horses came in and I shut them up. Not any too much water in the tank. After while the cattle will begin bawling and milling around if the water's low. That will distress our family. Can't have that. So I'll just harness one onto the sweep of the horse power, slip on a blindfold and let him pump. You tell me which ones will work."

The old man described several horses.

"That's O. K." said McEwen. "I've got two of them in the pen. Your woodpile is played out. Had to chop down some of your back pen for firewood."

He departed to start the horse power. Later, when beef tea had been served all around, he came over and sat by Florencio's bed.

"You have no drop or grain of medicine of any kind," he said, "and our milk won't be very good when we get it, from the looks of the cows—not for sick people. So, everything being just as it is, I didn't look for brands. I beefed the best one I could find, and hung the hide on the fence. Beef tea, right this very now, may make all the difference with our family. Me, I don't believe there's a man in New Mexico mean enough to make a fuss about it under the circumstances. But if there's any kick, there's the hide and I stand back of it. So that'll be all right. The brand was D W."

"It is my very good friend, Dave Woods, at San Nicolas. That will be all right. Don David is *muy simpático.* Sleep now, my son, sleep a little while you may. It will not be long. You have a hard night before you."

"I'm going up on the rising ground and set a couple of soapweeds afire," said McEwen at dark. "They'll make a big blaze and somebody might take notice. I'll hurry right back. Then I'll light some more about ten o'clock and do it again tomorrow night. Someone will be sure to see it. Just once, they might not think anything. But if they see a light in the same place three or four times, they might look down their nose and scratch their old hard heads — a smart man might. Don't you think so?"

"Why, yes," said Florencio; "it's worth trying."

"Those boys are not a bit better than they was. And your daughter is worse. We don't want to miss a bet. Yes, and I'll hold a blanket before the fire and take it away and put it back, over and over. That ought to help people guess that it is a signal. Only — they may guess that it was meant for someone else."

"Try it," said Florencio. "It may work. But I am not sure that our sick people are not holding their own. They are no better, certainly, even with your beef-tea medicine. But we can't expect to see a gain, if there is a gain, for days yet. And so far, they seem worse every night and then better every morning. The sunlight cheers them up at first, and then the day gets hot and they seem worse again. Try your signals, by all means. We need all the help there is. But if you could only guess how much less alone I feel now than before you came, good friend!"

"It must have been plain hell!" said the good friend.

"Isn't there any other one thing we can do?" demanded McEwen the next day, cudgeling his brains. It had been a terrible night. The little lives fluttered up and down; Estefanía was certainly worse; Florencio, though he had but few strangling spells, was very weak — the aftermath of his earlier labors.

"Not one thing. My poor ghost, no man could have done more. There is no more to do."

"But there is!" McEwen fairly sprang up, wearied as he was. "We have every handicap in the world, and only one advantage. And we don't use that one advantage. The sun has a feud with all the damn germs there is; your house is built for shade in this hot country. I'm going to tote all of you out in the sun with your bedding, and keep you there a spell. And while you're there I'll tear out a hole in the south end of your little old adobe wall and let more sunlight in. After the dust settles enough I'll bring you back. Then we'll shovel on a little more coal, and study up something else. And tonight we'll light up our signal fires again. Surely someone will be just fool enough to come out and see what the hell it's all about."

Hours later, after this program had been carried out, McEwen roused from a ten-minute sleep and rubbed his fists in his eyes.

"Are you awake, Don Florencio?" he called softly.

"Yes, my son. What is it?"

"It runs in my mind," said McEwen, "that they burn sulphur in diphtheria cases. Now, if I was to take the powder out of my cartridges and wet it down, let it get partly dry and make a smudge with it — a little at a time — There's sulphur in gunpowder. We'll try that little thing." He was already at work with horseshoe pinchers, twisting out the bullet. He looked up eagerly. "Haven't any tar, have you? To stop holes in your water troughs."

"*Hijo,* you shame me. There is a can of piñon pitch, that I use for my troughs, under the second trough at the upper end. I never once thought of that."

"We're getting better every day," said McEwen joyfully. "We'll make a smoke with some of that piñon wax, and we'll steep some of it in boiling water and breathe the steam of it; we'll burn my wet powder, and when that's done, we'll think of something else; and we'll make old bones yet, every damn one of us! By gollies, tomorrow between times I'm goin' to take your little old rifle and shoot some quail."

"Between times? Oh, Happy!"

"Oh, well, you know what I mean — just shovel on a little more coal — better brag than whine. Hi, Estefanía — hear that? We've dug up some medicine. Yes, we have. Ask Don Florencio if we haven't. I'm going after it."

But as he limped past the window on his way to the corral he heard the sound of a sob. He paused midstep, thinking it was little Felix. But it was Estefanía.

"*Madre de Dios, ayudale su enviado!*"

He tiptoed away, shamefaced.

7

Sleeping on a very thin bed behind a very large boulder, two men camped at the pass of San Agustin; a tall young man and a taller man who was not so young. The very tall man was Pat Garrett, sheriff of Doña Ana, sometime sheriff of other counties.

The younger man was Clint Llewellyn, his deputy, and their camp was official in character. They were keeping an eye out for that Belen bandit, after prolonged search elsewhere.

"Not but what he's got away long ago," said Pat, in his quiet drawling speech, "but just in case he might possibly double back this way."

It was near ten at night when Pat saw the light on the desert. He pointed it out to Clint. "See that fire out there? Your eyes are younger than mine. Isn't it sinking down and then flaring up again?"

"Looks like it is," said Clint. "I saw a fire there — or two of 'em, rather — just about dark, while you took the horses down to water."

"Did you?" said Pat. He stroked his mustache with a large slow hand. "Looks to me like someone was trying to attract attention."

"It does, at that," said Clint. "Don't suppose somebody's had a horse fall with him and got smashed, do you?"

"Do you know," said Pat slowly, "that idea makes me ache, sort of? One thing pretty clear. Somebody wants someone to do something for somebody. Reckon that's us. Looks like a long ride, and maybe for nothing. Yes. But then we're two long men. Where do you place that fire, Clint?"

"Hard to tell. Close to Luna's Wells, maybe."

"Too far west for that," said Garrett. "I'd say it was Lost Ranch. We'll go ask questions anyway. If we was layin' out there with our ribs caved in or our leg broke — Let's go!"

That is how they came to Lost Ranch between three and four the next morning. A feeble light shone in the window. Clint took the horses to water, while Garrett went on to the house. He stopped at the outer door. A man lay on a couch within, a man Garrett knew — old Florencio. Folded quilts made a pallet on the floor, and on the quilts lay another man, a man with red hair and a red stubble of beard. Both were asleep. Florencio's hand hung over the couch, and the stranger's hand held to it in a tight straining clasp. Garrett stroked his chin, frowning.

Sudden and startling, a burst of strangled coughing came from the room beyond and a woman's sharp call.

"*Hijo!*" cried Florencio feebly, and pulled the hand he held. "Happy! Wake up!" The stranger lurched to his feet and staggered through the door. "Yes, Felix, I'm coming. All right, boy! All right now! Let me see. It won't hurt. Just a minute, now."

Garrett went into the house.

"Clint," said Pat Garrett, "there's folks dyin' in there, and a dead man doin' for them. You take both horses and light a rag for the Alamogordo Hospital. Diphtheria. Get a doctor and nurses out here just as quick as God will let them come." Garrett was pulling the saddle from his horse as he spoke. "Have 'em bring grub and everything. Ridin' turn about, you ought to make it tolerable quick. I'm stayin' here, but there's no use of your comin' back. You might take a look around Jarilla if you want to, but use your own judgment. Drag it, now. Every minute counts."

A specter came to the doorway. "Better send a wagonload of water," it said as Clint turned to go. "This well is maybe poisoned. Germs and such."

"Yes, and bedding, too," said Clint. "I'll get everything and tobacco. So long!"

"Friend," said Pat, "you get yourself to bed. I'm takin' on your job. Your part is to sleep."

"Yes, son," Florencio's thin voice quavered joyously. "*Duerme y descansa.* Sleep and rest. Don Patricio will do everything."

McEwen swayed uncertainly. He looked at Garrett with stupid and heavy eyes. "He called you Patricio. You're not Pat Nunn, by any chance?"

"Why not?" said Garrett.

McEwen's voice was lifeless. "My father used to know you," he said drowsily. He slumped over on his bed.

"Who was your father?" said Garrett.

McEwen's dull and glassy eyes opened to look at his questioner. "I'm no credit to him," he said. His eyes closed again.

"Boil the water!" said McEwen.

"He's asleep already!" said Pat Garrett. "The man's dead on his feet."

"Oh, Pat, there was never one like him!" said Florencio. He struggled to his elbow, and looked down with pride and affection at the sprawling shape on the pallet. "Don Patricio, I have a son in my old age, like Abrahán!"

"I'll pull off his boots," said Pat Garrett.

Garrett knelt over McEwen and shook him vigorously. "Hey, fellow, wake up! You, Happy — come alive! Snap out of it! Most sundown, and time you undressed and went to bed."

McEwen set up at last, rubbing his eyes. He looked at the big, kindly face for a little in some puzzlement. Then he nodded.

"I remember you now. You sent your pardner for the doctor. How's the sick folks?"

"I do believe," said Pat, "that we're going to pull 'em through — every one. You sure had a tough lay."

"Yes. Doctor come?"

"He's in sight now — him and the nurses. That's how come me to rouse you up. Fellow, I hated to wake you when you was going so good. But with the ladies comin', you want to spruce yourself up a bit. You look like the wrath of God!"

McEwen got painfully to his feet and wriggled his arms experimentally.

"I'm just one big ache," he admitted. "Who's them fellows?" he demanded. Two men were industriously cleaning up the house; two men that he had never seen.

"Them boys? Monte, the Mexican, he's old Florencio's nephew. Heard the news this mawnin', and comes boilin' out here hell-for-leather. Been here for hours. The other young fellow came with him. Eastern lad. Don't know him, or why he came. Say, Mr. Happy, you want to bathe those two eyes of yours with cold water, or hot water, or both. They look like two holes burned in a blanket. Doc will have to give you a good jolt of whisky too. Man, you're pretty nigh ruined!"

"I knew there was something," said Mr. Happy. "Got to get me a name. And gosh, I'm tired! I'm a good plausible liar, most times, but I'll have to ask you to help out. Andy Hightower — how'd that do? Knew a man named Alan Hightower once, over on the Mangas."

"Does he run cattle over there now somewhere about Quemado?"

"Yes," said McEwen.

"I wouldn't advise Hightower," said Garrett.

"My name," said McEwen, "is Henry Clay."

Doctor Lamb, himself the driver of the covered spring wagon, reached Lost Ranch at sundown. He brought with him two nurses, Miss Mason and Miss Hollister, with Lida Hopper, who was to be cook; also, many hampers and much bedding. Dad Lucas was coming behind, the doctor explained, with a heavy wagon loaded with water and necessaries. Garrett led the way to the sickroom.

Monte helped Garrett unload the wagon and care for the team; Lida Hopper prepared supper in the kitchen.

Mr. Clay had discreetly withdrawn, together with the other man. They were out in the corral now, getting acquainted. The other man, it may be mentioned, was none other than Ben Griggs; and his discretion was such that Miss Hollister knew nothing of his presence until the next morning.

Mr. Clay, still wearied, bedded down under the stars, Monte rustling the credentials for him. When Dad Lucas rolled in, the men made camp by the wagon.

"Well, doctor," said Garrett, "how about the sick? They going to make it?"

"I think the chances are excellent," said the doctor. "Barring relapse, we should save every one. But it was a narrow squeak. That young man who nursed them through — why, Mr. Garrett, no one on earth could have done better, considering what he had to do with. Nothing, practically, but his two hands."

"You're all wrong there, doc. He had a backbone all the way from his neck to the seat of his pants. That man," said Garrett, "will do to take along."

"Where is he, Mr. Garrett? And what's his name? The old man calls him 'son,' all the boys call him 'Uncle Happy.' What's his right name?"

"Clay," said Garrett. "He's dead to the world. You won't see much of him. A week of sleep is what he needs. But you remind me of something. If you will allow it I would like to speak to all of you together. Just a second. Would you mind asking the nurses to step in for a minute or two, while I bring the cook?"

"Certainly," said Doctor Lamb.

"I want to ask a favor of all of you," said Garrett, when the doctor had ushered in the nurses. "I won't keep you. I just want to declare myself. Some of you know me, and some don't. My name is Pat Garrett, and I am the sheriff of Doña Ana County, over west. But for reasons that are entirely satisfactory to myself, I would like to be known as Pat Nunn, for the present. That's all. I thank you."

"Of course," said Doctor Lamb, "if it is to serve the purpose of the law — "

"I would not go so far," said Garrett. "If you put it that my purpose is served, you will be quite within the truth. Besides, this is not official. I am not sheriff here. This ranch is just cleverly over the line and in Otero County. Old Florencio pays taxes in Otero. I am asking this as a personal favor, and only for a few days. Perfectly simple. That's all. Thank you."

"Did you ask the men outside?"

"No. I just told them," said Mr. Pat Nunn. "It would be dishonorable for a lady to tip my hand; for a man it would be plumb indiscreet."

"Dad Lucas," said the doctor, "is a cynical old scoundrel, and a man without principle, and swivel tongued besides."

"He is all that you say, and a lot more that you would never guess," said Garrett, "but if I claimed to be Humpty Dumpty, Dad Lucas would swear that he saw me fall off of the wall." He held up his two index fingers, side by side. "Dad and me, we're like that. We've seen trouble together — and there is no bond so close. Again, one and all, I thank you. Meetin's adjourned."

Lost Ranch was a busy scene on the following day. A cheerful scene, too, despite the blazing sun, the parched desert and the scarred old house. Reports from the sickroom were hopeful. The men had spread a tarpaulin by the wagon, electing Dad Lucas for cook. They had salvaged a razor of Florencio's and were now doing mightily with it. Monte and Ben Griggs, after dinner, were to take Dad's team and Florencio's wagon to draw up a jag of mesquite roots. In the meantime Monte dragged up stop-gap firewood by the saddle horn, and Ben kept the horse power running in the water pen. Keeping him company, Pat Garrett washed Henry Clay's clothes. More accurately, it was Pat Nunn who did this needed work with grave and conscientious thoroughness.

"Henry Clay and me, after bein' in the house so long," said Mr. Nunn, "why, we'll have to boil up our clothes before we leave, or we might go scattering diphtheria hither and yonder and elsewhere."

"But how if you take it yourselves?"

"Then we'll either die or get well," said Mr. Nunn slowly. "In either case, things will keep juneing along just the same. Henry Clay ain't going to take it, or he'd have it now. It takes three days after you're exposed. Something like that. We'll stick around a little before we go, just in case."

"Which way are you going, Mr. Nunn?" asked Ben.

"Well, I'm going to Tularosa. Old Florencio will have to loan me a horse. Clay too. He's afoot. Don't know where he's going. Haven't asked him. He's too worn out to talk much. His horse played out on him out on the flat somewheres and he had to hang up his saddle and walk in. So Florencio told me. He's goin' back and get his saddle tomorrow."

Miss Mason being on duty, Jay Hollister, having picked up a bite of breakfast, was minded to get a breath of fresh air; and at this juncture she tripped into the water pen where Mr. Nunn and Ben plied their labors.

"And how is the workingman's bride this morning?" asked Ben brightly.

"Great Cæsar's ghost! Ben Griggs, what in the world are you doing here?" demanded Jay with a heightened color.

"Workin'," said Ben, and fingered his blue overalls proudly. "Told you I was goin' to work. Right here is where I'm needed. Why, there are only four of us, not counting you three girls and the doctor, to do what Clay was doing. You should have seen Monte and me cleaning house yesterday."

"Yes?" Jay smiled sweetly. "What house was that?"

"Woman!" said Ben, touched in his workman's pride. "If you feel that way now, you should have seen this house when we got here."

"You're part fool. You'll catch diphtheria."

"Well, what about you? The diphtheria part, I mean. What's the matter with your gettin' diphtheria?"

"That's different. That's a trade risk. That's my business."

"You're my business," said Ben.

Jay shot a startled glance at Mr. Nunn, and shook her head.

"Oh, yes!" said Ben. "Young woman, have you met Mr. Nunn?"

Soap in hand, Mr. Nunn looked up from his task. "Good morning, miss. Don't mind me," he said. "Go right on with the butchery."

"Good morning, Mr. Nunn. Please excuse us. I was startled at finding this poor simpleton out here where he has no business to be. Have I met Mr. Nunn? Oh, yes, I've met him twice. The doctor introduced him once, and he introduced himself once."

Mr. Nunn acknowledged this gibe with twinkling eye. Miss Hollister looked around her, and shivered in the sun. "What a ghastly place!" she cried. "I can't for the life of me understand why anybody should live here. We came through some horrible country yesterday, but this is the worst yet. Honestly, Mr. Nunn, isn't this absolutely the most God-forsaken spot on earth?"

Mr. Nunn abandoned his work for the moment and stood up, smiling. So this was Pat Garrett of whom she had heard so much; the man who killed Billy the Kid. Well, he had a way with him. Jay could not but admire the big square head, the broad spread of his shoulders and a certain untroubled serenity in his quiet face.

"Oh, I don't know," said Mr. Nunn. "Look there!"

"Where? I don't see anything," said Jay. "Look at what?"

"Why, the bees," said Pat. "The wild bees. They make honey here. Little family of 'em in every sotol stalk; and that old house up there with the end broken in — No, Miss Hollister, I've seen worse places than this."

8

The patients were improving. Old Florencio, who had been but lightly touched, mended apace. He had suffered from exhaustion and distress quite as much as from disease itself. Demetrio and little Felix gained more slowly, and Estefanía was weakest of all.

The last was contrary to expectation. As a usual thing, diphtheria goes hardest with the young. But all were in a fair way to recover. Doctor Lamb and Dad Lucas had gone back to town. Dad had returned with certain comforts and luxuries for the convalescents.

Jay Hollister, on the morning watch, was slightly annoyed. Mr. Pat Garrett and the man Clay were leaving, it seemed, and nothing would do but that Clay must come to the sickroom for leave-taking. Quite naturally, Jay had not wished her charges disturbed. Peace and quiet were what they needed. But Garrett had been insistent, and he had a way with him. Oh, well! The farewell was quiet enough and brief enough on Clay's part, goodness knows, but rather fervent from old Florencio and his daughter-in-law. That was the Spanish of it, Jay supposed. Anyhow, that was all over and the disturbers were on their way to Tularosa.

Relieved by Miss Mason, Jay went in search of Ben Griggs to impart her grievance, conscious that she would get no sympathy there, and queerly unresentful of that lack. He was not to be seen. She went to the kitchen.

"Where's that trifling Ben, Lida?"

"Him? I'm sure I don't know, Miss Jay. That Mexican went up on top of the house just now. He'll know, likely."

Jay climbed the rickety ladder, stepped on the adobe parapet and so down to the flat roof. Monte sat on the farther wall, looking out across the plain so intently that he did not hear her coming.

"Do you know where Ben is?" said Jay.

Monte came to his feet. "Oh, yais! He is weeth the Señor Lucas to haul wood, Mees Hollister. Is there what I can do?"

"What are we going to do about water?" said Jay. "There's only one barrel left. Of course we can boil the well water, but it's horrible stuff."

"*Prontamente* — queekly. All set. Ben weel be soon back, and here we go, Ben and me, to the spreeng of San Nicolas." He pointed to a granite peak of the San Andrés. "There at thees peenk hill yonder."

"What, from way over there?"

"Eet ees closest, an' ver' sweet water, ver' good."

Jay looked and wondered, tried to estimate the void that lay between, and could not even guess. "What a dreadful country! How far is it?"

"Oh, twent-ee miles. *Es nada.* We feel up by sundown and come back in the cool stars."

"Oh, do sit down," said Jay, "and put on your hat. You're so polite you make me nervous. I shouldn't think you'd care much about the cool," said Jay, "the way you sit up here, for pleasure, in the broiling sun."

"Plezzer? Oh, no!" said Monte. "Look!" He turned and pointed. "No, not here, not close by. Mebbe four, three miles. Look across thees bare spot an' thees streep of mesquite to thees long chalk reedge; and now, beyond thees row and bunches of yuccas. You see them now?"

Jay followed his hand and saw, small and remote, two horsemen creeping black and small against the infinite recession of desert. She nodded.

"Eet ees with no joy," said Monte, "that I am to see the las' of *un caballero valiente* — how do you say heem? — of a gallan' gentleman — thees redhead."

"You are not very complimentary to Mr. Garrett," said Jay.

"Oh, no, no, no — you do not unnerstand!" Monte's eyes narrowed with both pity and puzzlement. He groped visibly for words. "*Seguramente, siempre*, een all ways Pat Garrett ees a man complete. Eet is known. But thees young fellow — he ees play out the streeng — *pobrecito!* Oh, Mees Jay, eet ees a bad spread! Es-scusame, please, Mees Hollister. I have not the good words — onlee the man talk."

"Oh, he did well enough — but why not?" said Jay. "What else could he do? There has been something all the time that I don't understand. Danger from diphtheria? Nonsense. I am not a bit partial to you people out here. Perhaps you know that. But I must admit that danger doesn't turn you from anything you have set your silly heads to do. Of course Mr. Clay had to work uncommonly hard, all alone here. But he had no choice. No; it's something else, something you have kept hidden from me all along. Why all the conspiracy and the pussyfoot mystery?"

"Eet was not jus' lak that, mees. Not *conjuración* exactlee. But everee man feel for heemself eet ees ver' good to mek no talk of thees theeng." For once Monte's hands were still. He looked off silently at the great bare plain and the little horsemen dwindling in the distance. "I weel tell you, then," he said at last. "Thees *cosa* are bes' not spoken, and yet eet ees right for you shall know. Onlee I have not those right words. Ben, he shall tell you when he come.

"Eet ees lak thees, Mees Jay. Ver' long ago — yais, before not any of your people is cross over the Atlantic Ocean — my people they are here een thees country and they go up and down to all places —yais, to *las playas de mar*, to the shores of the sea by California. And when they go by Zuñi and by thees rock El Morro, wheech your people call — I have forget that name. You have heard heem?"

"Yes," said Jay. "Inscription Rock. I've read about it."

"*Sí, sí!*" That ees the name. Well, eet ees good camp ground, El Morro, wood and water, and thees gr-reat cleef for shade and for shelter een estr-rong winds. And here some fellow he come and he cry out, '*Adiós, el mundo!* What lar-rge weelderness ees thees! And me, I go now eento thees beeg lonesome, and perhaps I shall not to r-return! *Bueno, pues,* I mek now for me a gravestone!' And so he mek on that beeg rock weeth hees dagger, '*Pasó por aquí, Don Fulano de Tal*' — passed by here, Meester So-and-So — weeth the year of eet. And after heem come others to El Morro — so few, so far from Spain! They see what he ees write there, and they say, '*Con razón!*' — eet ees weeth reason to do thees. An' they also mek een-screepción, '*Pasó por aquí*' — and their names, and the year of eet."

His hand carved slow letters in the air. His eye was proud.

"I would not push my leetleness upon thees so lar-rge world, but one of thees, Mees Hollister — oh, not of the great, not of the first — he was of mine, my ver' great, great papa. So long ago! And he mek also '*Pasó por aquí*, Salvador Holguin.' I hear thees een the firelight when I am small fellow. And when I am man-high I mek veesit to thees place and see heem."

His eyes followed the far horsemen, now barely to be seen, a faint moving blur along the north.

"And thees fellow, too, thees redhead, he pass this way, *Pasó por aquí*" — again the brown hand wrote in the air — "and he mek here good and not weeked. But, before that — I am not God!" Lips, shoulders, hands, every line of his face disclaimed that responsibility. "But he is thief, I theenk," said Monte. "Yais, he ees thees one — Mack-Yune? — who rob the bank of Numa Frenger las' week at Belen. I theenk so."

Jay's eyes grew round with horror, her hand went to her throat. "Not arrested?"

For once Monte's serene composure was shaken. His eyes narrowed, his words came headlong.

"Oh, no, no, no! You do not unnerstan'. Ees eemposevilly, what you say! Pat Garrett ees know nozzing, he ees fir-rm r-resolve to know nozzing. An' thees Mack-Yune, he ees theenk *por verdad* eet ees Pat Nunn who ride weeth heem to Tularosa. He guess not one theeng that eet ees the sheriff. Pat Garrett he go that none may dees-turb or moless' heem. Becows, thees young fellow ees tek eshame for thees bad life, an' he say to heemself, 'I weel arize and go to my papa.' "

She began to understand. She looked out across the desert and the thorn, the white chalk and the sand. Sun dazzle was in her eyes. These people! Peasant, gambler, killer, thief — She felt the pulse pound in her throat.

"And een Tularosa, all old-timers, everee man he know Pat Garrett.

Not lak thees Alamogordo, new peoples. And when thees old ones een Tularosa see Meester Pat Garrett mek good-by weeth hees friend at the tr-rain, they will theenk nozzing, say nozzing. *Adiós!*"

He sat sidewise upon the parapet and waved his hand to the nothingness where the two horsemen had been swallowed up at last.

"And him the sheriff!" said Jay. "Why, they could impeach him for that. They could throw him out of office."

He looked up, smiling. "But who weel tell?" said Monte. His outspread hands were triumphant. "We are all decent people."

Good Men
and True

GOOD MEN AND TRUE

CHAPTER I

I always thought they were fabulous monsters. Is it alive?
— *The Unicorn*

SUN AND WIND of thirty-six out-of-door years had tanned Mr. Jeff Bransford's cheek to a rosy-brown, contrasting sharply with the whiteness of the upper part of his forehead, when exposed — as now — by the pushing up of his sombrero. These same suns and winds had drawn at the corners of his eyes a network of fine lines: but the brown eyes were undimmed, and his face had a light, sure look of unquenchable boyishness; sure mark of the unattached, and therefore carefree and irresponsible man, who, as the saying goes, "is at home wherever his hat is hung."

The hat in question was a soft gray one, the crown deeply creased down the middle, the wide brim of it joyously atilt, merging insensibly from one wavy curve into another and on to yet a third, like Hogarth's line of beauty.

Mr. Bransford's step was alert and springy: perhaps it had even a slight, unconscious approach to a swagger, as of one not unsatisfied with himself. He turned at the corner of Temple Street, skipped lightsome up a stairway and opened an office door, bearing on its glass front the inscription:

SIMON HIBLER

ATTORNEY-AT-LAW

"Is Mr. Hibler in?"

The only occupant of the room — a smooth-faced and frank-eyed young man — rose from his desk and came forward.

"Mr. Hibler is not in town."

"Dee-lightful! And when will he be back?" The rising inflection on the last word conveyed a resolute vivacity proof against small annoyances.

"To tell you the truth, I do not know. He is over in Arizona, near San Simon — for change and rest."

"H'm!" The tip of the visitor's nose twitched slightly, the brown eyes widened reflectively; the capable mouth under the brown mustache puckered as if to emit a gentle whistle. "He'll bring back the change. I'll take all bets on that. San Simon! H'm!" He shrugged his shoulders, one corner of his mouth pulled down in whimsical fashion, while the opposite eyebrow arched, so giving his face an appearance indescribably odd: the drooping side expressive of profound melancholy, while the rest of his face retained its habitual look of invincible cheerfulness. "San Simon! Dear, oh dear! And I may just nicely contemplate my two thumbs till he gets back with the change — and maybe so the rest!" He elevated the thumbs and cast vigilant glances at each in turn: half-chanting, dreamily:

> " 'O, she left her Tombstone home
> For to dwell in San Simon,
> And she run off with a prairie-navigator.'

— Ran off, I should say." His nose tweaked again.

The clerk was a newcomer in El Paso, hardly yet wonted to the freakish humor and high spirits that there flourish unrebuked — and indeed, unnoticed. But he entered into the spirit of the occasion. "Is there anything I can do?" he inquired. "I am Mr. Hibler's chief — and only — clerk."

"No-o," said the visitor doubtfully, letting his eyes wander from his thumbs to the view of white-walled Juárez beyond the river. "No-o — That is, not unless you can sell me his Rainbow ranch and brand for less than they're worth. Such is my errand — on behalf of Pringle, Beebe, Ballinger and Bransford. I'm Bransford — me."

"Jeff Bransford? Mr. Hibler's foreman?" asked the young man eagerly.

"*Mr.* Jeff Bransford — foreman *for* Hibler — not of," amended Bransford gently. His thumbs were still upreared. Becoming suddenly aware of this, he fixed them with a startled gaze.

"Say! Take supper with me!" The young man blurted out the words. "Mr. Hibler's always talking about you and I want to get acquainted with you. Aughinbaugh's my name."

Bransford sat down heavily, thumbs still erect, elbows well out from his side, and transferred his gaze, with marked respect, to the clerk's boyish face, now very rosy indeed.

Jeff's eyes grew big and round; his lips were slightly parted; the thumbs drooped, the fingers spread wide apart in mutual dismay.

Holding Aughinbaugh's eyes with his own, he pressed one outspread hand over his heart. Slowly, cautiously, the other hand fumbled in a vest pocket, produced notebook and pencil, spread the book stealthily on his knee and began to write. " 'A good name,' " he murmured, " 'is rather to be chosen than great riches.' "

But the owner of the good name was a lad of spirit, and had no mind to submit tamely to such hazing. "See here! What does a cowboy know about the Bible, anyway?" he demanded, glaring indignantly. "I believe you're a sheep in wolves' clothing! You don't talk like a cowboy — or look like a cowboy."

Jeff glanced down at his writing, and back to his questioner. Then he made an alteration, closed the book and looked up again. He had a merry eye.

"Exactly how does a cowboy look? And how does it talk?" he asked mildly. He glanced with much interest over as much of his own person as he could see; turning and twisting to aid the process. "I don't see anything wrong. Is my hair on straight?"

"Wrong!" echoed Aughinbaugh severely, shaking an accusing finger. "Why, you're *all* wrong. What the public expects — "

Mr. Bransford's interruption may be omitted. It was profane. Also, it was plagiarized from Commodore Vanderbilt.

"You a cowboy! Yah!" said Aughinbaugh in vigorous scorn. "With a silk necktie! Everybody knows that the typical cowboy wears a red cotton handkerchief."

"How long since you left New York?"

"Me? I'm from Kansas City."

"Same thing," said Bransford coldly. "I mean, how long since you came to El Paso? And have you been out of town since?"

"About eight months. And I confess that my duties — at first in the bank and afterwards here, have kept me pretty close, except for a trip or two to Juárez. But why?"

"Why enough!" returned Jeff. "Young man, young man! I see the finger of fate in this. It is no blind chance that brought me here while Hibler was away. It was predestined from the foundations of earth that I was to come here at this very now to explain to you about cowboys. I have the concentrated venom of about twenty-one years stored away to work off on somebody, and I feel it in my bones that you are the man. Come with me and I will do you good — as it says in mournful Numbers. You've been led astray. You shouldn't believe all you read and only half what you see.

"In the first place, take the typical cowboy. There positively ain't no sich person! Maybe so half of 'em's from Texas and the other half from anywhere and everywhere else. But they're all alike in just one thing — and that is that every last one of them is entirely different from all the others. Each one talks as he pleases, acts as he pleases and — when not at work — dresses as he pleases. On the range though, they all dress pretty much alike. Because, the things they wear there have been tried out and they've kept only the best of each kind — the best for that particular kind of work."

"They 'proved all things and held fast that which was good,'" suggested Aughinbaugh.

"Exactly. For instance, that handkerchief business. That isn't meant as a substitute for a necktie. Ever see a drought? If you did, you probably remember that it was some dusty. Well — there's been a steady drought out here for two hundred and eight million years come August. And when you drive two, three thousand head of cattle, with four feet apiece, to the round-up ground and chouse 'em 'round half a day, cutting out steers, the dust is so thick a horse can't fall down when he stumbles. Then mister cowboy folds his little hankie, like them other triangles that the ladies, God bless 'em with their usual perversity, call 'squares,' ties the ends, puts the knot at the back of his neck, pulls the wide part *over* his mouth and up over the bridge of his nose, *and breathes through it!* Got that? By heavens, it's a filter to keep the dust out of your lungs, and not an ornament! It's usually silk — not because silk is booful but because it's better to breathe through."

"Really, I never dreamed —" began Aughinbaugh. But Jeff waved him down.

"Don't speak to the man at the wheel, my son. And everything a cowboy uses, at work, from hats to boots, from saddle to bed, has just as good a reason for being exactly what it is as that handkerchief. Take the high-heeled boots, now —"

"Dad," said Aughinbaugh firmly. "I am faint. Break it to me easy. I was once an interior decorator of some promise, though not a professional. Let me lead you to a restaurant and show you a sample of my skill. Then come round to my rooms and tell me your troubles at leisure. Maybe you'll feel better. But before you explain your wardrobe I want to know why you don't say "You all' and 'that-a-way,' 'plumb' and 'done gone,' and the rest of it."

"I do, my dear, when I want to," said Bransford affectionately. "Them's all useful words, easy and comfortable, like old clothes and old shoes. I like 'em. But they go with the old clothes. And now, as you see, I am — to use the metropolitan idiom — in my 'glad rags' and my speech naturally rises in dignity to meet the occasion. Besides, associating with Beebe — he's one of them siss-boom-ah! boys — has mitigated me a heap. Then I read the signs, and the brands on the freight cars. And I'll tell you one more thing, my son. A large proportion — I mean, of course, a right smart chance — of the cowboys are illiterate, and some of them are grand rascals, but they ain't none of 'em plumb imbeciles. They couldn't stay on the job. If their brains don't naturally work pretty spry, things happen to 'em — the chuck-wagon bunts 'em or something. And they all have a chance at 'the education of a gentleman' — 'to ride, to shoot and to speak the truth.' They have to ride and shoot — and speakin' the truth comes easier for them than for some folks, 'cause if speaking the aforesaid truth displeases anyone they mostly don't give a damn."

"Stop! Spare me!" cried Aughinbaugh. He collapsed in his chair, sliding together in an attitude of extreme dejection. "My spirits are very low, but — " He rose, tottered feebly to his desk and took therefrom a small bottle, which, with a glass, he handed to Bransford.

"Thanks. But you — you're a tee-totaler?" said Jeff.

"A — well — not exactly," stammered Aughinbaugh. "But I have to be very careful. I — I only take one drink at a time!" He fumbled out another glass.

"I stumble, I stumble!" said Bransford gravely. He poured out a small drink and passed the bottle. " 'I fill this cup to one made up!' " — He held the glass up to the light.

"Well?" said Aughinbaugh, expectantly. "Go on!"

"That description can't be bettered," said Bransford.

"Never will I drink such a toast as that," cried Aughinbaugh, laughing. "Let me substitute, Here's to our better acquaintance!"

CHAPTER II

Life is just one damn thing after another.
                              — A Nameless Philosopher

AUGHINBAUGH CLOSED THE DOOR behind him and paused, vastly diverted. His entrance had passed unnoted, muffled by the jerky click-click of the typewriter on which Jeff Bransford toiled with painful absorption. On Jeff's forehead little beads of sweat stood out, glistening in the lamp-light. He scanned the last line, scowled ferociously, and snapped the platen back. His uncertain fingers twitched solicitously above the keys. Aughinbaugh chuckled offensively:

" 'Yond Cassius has a lean and hungry look;
   He thinks too much: such men are dangerous,' "

he declaimed.

Jeff whirled around. "Hello, here you are! Any news from our em-

ployer?" He rose with a sigh of relief and mopped his brow. "Gee!
I've got to work the Jimfidgets out of my fingers."

Ignoring the query, Aughinbaugh took a step forward, drew up his
slender frame, inflated his chest, spread one hand upon it, and threw
up his other hand with a flourish of limber fingers. " 'Now is the
time,' " he spouted forth at Bransford, mouthing the well-known
words, " 'for all good men and true to come to the aid of the party!' "

Jeff grinned sheepishly. "I'll dream that cussed thing tonight. How
long did it take you to learn to play a tune on this fool contraption,
anyhow?"

"It took me three months — to play on it anyhow. But then I
already knew how to spell. I've been at it two years since and am still
improving. I should estimate that you would need about eight years.
Better give it up. Try a maul or a piledriver. More suited to your
capabilities. Why, Jeff, a really good stenographer can do first-class
work in the dark."

"Eight years? George, you're an optimist. I've worked two solid
hours on this one 'simple little sentence,' as you call it, and I've never
got it right once. Sometimes I've come within one letter of it. Once I
made a mighty effort and got all the letters right, but I forgot to space
and ran the words together. And say — that simple little sentence
hasn't got near all the letters in it. B, j, k, q, v, x and z are left out."

"Here, then — here's one that contains every letter: 'A quick move
by the enemy will jeopardize six fine gunboats.' "

Jeff pulled pad and pencil to him. "Give me that again and I'll take
it down." Repeating the alphabet slowly, he canceled each letter as he
went. "Right you are! Say, the fellow that got that up was on the
job, wasn't he? Why didn't you give me this one in the first place?
Wonder if it's possible to get 'em all in another sentence as short?"

"I think not," said Aughinbaugh. "It's been tried. But I don't share
your admiration for the last one. Besides reeking of militarism abhor-
rent to my peaceful disposition, it is stiff, labored, artificial and insincere. Compare it with the spontaneity, the beauty, the stately cadences,
the sonorous fire, the sweep and swing of the simple, natural appeal:
'Now is the time for all good men and true to come to the aid of the
party!' "

If it has ever been your privilege to observe a wise old she-bear
watching her cubs at play and to note the expression of her face —
half patience, tolerance, resignation; the remainder pride and approval — you will know exactly how Jeff looked. As for Aughinbaugh, he bore himself grandly, chin up. His voice was vibrant, resonant, purposeful; his eyes glowed with serious and lofty enthusiasm:
no muscle quivered to a smile.

"Why, there is philosophy in it! The one unvarying factor of the human mind," he went on, "is the firm, unbiased conviction that I am right, and all opposition necessarily, consciously and wilfully wrong. This belief is the base and foundation of all human institutions, of sectionalism, caste, creeds, parties, states, of patriotism itself. It is the premise on which all wars are based. Mark, now, how human nature speaks from its elemental depths in the calm, complacent, but entirely sincere assumption that all good men and true will be unconditionally with the party!"

He warmed to his subject; he strode back and forth; he smote open palm with clenched fist in vehement gesture. Jeff snickered. George rebuked him with a stern and withering glance.

"I grant you that b, j, k, q, v, x and z are omitted. But what are b, j, k, q, v, x and z in comparison to the chaste perfection of this immortal line? Let them fitly typify the bad men and false who do not come to the aid of the party. Injustice is only what they deserve!"

Consigning b, j, k, q, v, x and z to outer darkness with scornful, snapping fingers, he poured a glass of water, sipped it slowly, with resolute suppression of his Adam's apple, fixed Jeff with another severe glance, paused impressively, rose to his tiptoes with both hands outspread, and continued:

"Why, sir, this is the grandest line in literature! It should hang on every wall, a text worked on a sampler by tender, loving hands! It is a ready-made watchword, a rallying cry for any great cause! It might be sung by marching thousands. When, in a great crisis, the mighty statesman, the intellectual giant between whose puny legs we petty men do creep and peer about, has proclaimed the Fla-ag in Danger; has led us to stand at the parting of the ways; has shown that the nation must make irrevocable choice of good or evil; when our hearts are thrilled with the consciousness of our own virtue" — he sprang to a chair and flaunted his handkerchief in rhythmical waves — "this, then, is his crashing peroration: 'Now is the time for all good men and true to come to the aid of the party!' "

Bowing gracefully, he carefully parted imaginary coat-tails and seated himself, beaming.

Jeff lolled contentedly back in his chair, puffing out clouds of smoke. "That's a fine line of talk you get out. You sure did a wise thing when you quit the bank and took to studying law. You have all the qualifications for a successful lawyer — or a barker for a side-show." He tapped out his pipe and yawned lazily. "I infer from your slurring remarks about solemn, silly twaddle that you are not permanently tagged, classified, labeled and catalogued, politically?"

"I am a consistent and humble follower," replied George, "of the

wise Democritus, who, as I will explain for the benefit of your benighted ignorance, is known as the Laughing Philosopher. I laugh.
Therefore I can truthfully say, to paraphrase the words of a famous
leader, 'I am a Democrit!' "

Jeff showed his teeth. "I guess I am, too — but I didn't know what
it was till you told me. Now I have a party, at last — and now is the
time for all good men and true — and that reminds me, my young and
exuberant friend, that you have not yet told me when our esteemed
and respected employer intends to return."

"I do not quite like the tone you adopt in speaking of Mr. Simon
Hibler," said George icily. "It smacks of irreverence and presumption.
Still less do I relish your persistent reference to him as 'our' employer.
It amounts to an assumption of a certain equality in our respective
positions that I cannot for an instant tolerate." He strutted to the
hearthrug and turned his back to the fire; he fiddled with his watch-
chain; tone and manner were heavily pompous. "In a way, of course,
Mr. Hibler might be said to employ us both. But I would have you
realize that a vast gulf separates the social status of a lowly cow-
servant, stolid and stunned, a brother to the ox, from that of an embryo
Blackstone — like myself. I accept a position and receive a salary. You
take a job and draw wages. Moreover, a lawyer's clerk marries the
youngest daughter and is taken into the firm. By the way, Hibler
has no daughter. I must remind him of this. 'Hibler & Aughinbaugh,
Counselors at Law.' That'll look good in silver letters on a sanded,
dark-blue background, eh, Jefferson? But soft! methinks my natural
indignation has diverted me from your question. No, my good fellow, I do not know when Mr. Hibler is returning to El Paso. Are you
already tired of urban delights, Mr. Bransford?"

"I was tired of urban delights," remarked Mr. Bransford, "before
you were out of short dresses. However, I've waited this long and
I'll stay right here in El Paso till he comes. I bore myself some, day-
times, but we have bully good times of nights. You're as good as a
show — better. Tune up your Julius Caesar!"

"Your attitude — if you will overlook the involuntary rhyme," said
George, "is one of base ingratitude. I endeavor to instruct and uplift
you. You might be absorbing sweetness and light at every pore, ac-
quiring a love for the true, the good and the beautiful — and you are
merely amused! It is disheartening. As for this golden volume, this
masterpiece of William Shakespere's genius — 'which, pardon me, I do
not mean to read.' "

"Oh, go on! Of course you're going to read it. We've got almost
through it. You left off just beyond 'the-will-give-us-the-will, we-will-
have-the-will.' "

"Why, you lazy pup, why didn't you read it yourself? You have nothing to do. I have to work."

"I did read it through today. And began at the first again. But," said Jeff admiringly, "I like to hear you read it. You have such a lovely voice, Mr. Crow."

Aughinbaugh bowed. "Thank you, Mr. Bransford, thank you! But I am proof against even such subtle and insidious flattery as yours. Hereafter, sir, I shall read no book through to you. I shall select works suited to your parts and your station in life and read barely enough to stimulate your sluggish mind. Then you can shell corn or be buried alive. Tonight, for instance, I shall read some salient extracts from Carlyle's *French Revolution*. You will not in the least understand it, but your interest and curiosity will be aroused. You will then finish it, with such collateral reading as I shall direct."

"Sure you got all those 'shalls' and 'wills' just right?" suggested Jeff. "It's mighty easy to get 'em tangled up."

"That is the only proper way to study history," George went on, wisely ignoring the interruption. "Read history lightly, about some period, then read the best works of poetry or fiction dealing with the same events. Then came back to history again. The characters will be real people to you and not mere names. You will eagerly extend your researches to details about these familiar acquaintances and friends, and learn particulars that you would else have shirked as dull and laborious." He took a book from the shelf. "I will now read to you — after you replenish the fire — a few chapters here and there, especially there, dealing with the taking of the Bastille."

Without, a wild March wind shrilled and moaned at the trembling casements; within, firelight's cozy cheer, Aughinbaugh's slim youth lit by the glowing circle of the shaded lamp, the dusky corners beyond. The flexible voice sank with pity or swelled with hot indignation. And Bransford, as he listened to that stupendous, chaotic drama of incoherent clangorous World Bedlam, saw, in the glowing coals, tumultuous, dim-confused figures come and go, passionate, terrible and grim; the young, the gay, the beautiful, the brave, the brave in vain; fire-hearted, vehement, proud, swallowed up by delirium. Newer shapes, wild, portentous, spluttering, flashing, whirling, leaping in wild dervish dance. In the black shadows, in the eddying thick smoke, lurked crowding shapes more terrible still, abominable, malignant, demoniacal, imbecile — Proteus shapes that changed, dwindled, leaped and roared to an indistinguishable sulphurous whirlpool, sport of all the winds. Brief flashes of clearer light there were, as the smoke billowed aside; faces gleamed a moment distinct, resolute, indomitable, bright-sparkling; blazed high — and fell, trampled down by fresh legion-changing apparitions. Sad visions, some monstrous, some heroic, all pitiful; thronging innumerable, consuming and consumed.

.   .   .   .

"Likewise ashlar stones of the Bastille continue thundering through the dusk; its paper archives shall fly white. Old secrets come to view; and long buried despair finds voice. Read this portion of an old letter: 'If for my consolation monseigneur would grant me, for the sake of God and the most blessed Trinity, that I should have news of my dear wife; were it only her name on a card to show that she is alive! It were the greatest consolation I could receive; and I should forever bless the greatness of monseigneur.' Poor prisoner, who signest thyself Queret-Demery, and hast no other history, she is dead, that dear wife of thine, and thou art dead! 'Tis fifty years since thy breaking heart put this question; to be heard now first, and long heard, in the hearts of men."

.   .   .   .

A long silence. The fire was low. One dim, blurred form was there — an old man, writing, in a stone cell.

Aughinbaugh closed the book. His eyes were moist. "One of the greatest novels ever written, *A Tale of Two Cities,* is based entirely upon and turns upon this last paragraph. Read that tomorrow and then come back to the *French Revolution.* You'll be around tomorrow night?"

Jeff rose, laughing. "You remind me of my roommate at school."

"Your — what? Where?" said George in astonishment.

"Oh, yes, I've been to school, but not very long. When the boys used to stay too late he'd yawn and say to me: 'Jeff, perhaps we'd better go to bed. These people may want to go home!' "

"Oh, well, it's nearly twelve o'clock," said George, unabashed. "And I have to work if you don't. Bless you, my children, bless you! Be happy and you will be good! *Buenas noches!*"

"*Buenas noches!*"

.   .   .   .

A trolley car whirred by, with scintillation of blue-crackling sparks. Jeff elected to walk, companied by his storied ghosts — their footsteps sounded through the rustling leaves. The wind was dead; the night was overcast, dark and chill. Aughinbaugh's lodgings were in the outskirts of the residence section; the streets at this hour were deserted. Jeff had walked briskly for ten minutes when, as he neared a corner in a quiet neighborhood, he saw a tall man in gray come from the farther side of the intersection street just ahead. The gray man paused under the electric light to let a recklessly driven cab overtake and pass him, and then turned diagonally over toward Jeff, whistling as he came. He was halfway across, and Jeff was within a yard of the corner, when another man, short and squat, hurried from the street to the left, brushing by so close that Jeff might have touched him. So unexpected was his appearance — for his footsteps had been drowned by the clattering cab — that Jeff was startled. He paused, midstep, for the merest fraction of a second. The town clock boomed midnight.

Thereafter, events moved with all the breathless unreality of dream. The second man turned across to meet the first. A revolver leaped up, shining in the light; he fired pointblank. The gray man staggered back. Yet, taken all unaware, so deadly swift he was that both men fired now together.

Nor was Jeff imprudently idle. He was in the line of fire, directly behind the short man. To the left, across the sidewalk, the bole of a tree was just visible beyond the house corner. Jeff leaped for this friendly shelter — and butted headlong into human ribs.

A one-hundred-and-sixty-pound projectile deals no light blow, and Jeff's initial velocity was the highest he could command at such slight notice. The owner of the ribs reeled out into the street, beyond the shadows. A huge man, breathless, gasping, with a revolver drawn; his thumb was on the hammer. So much Jeff knew and closed on him, his left hand clutched the gun, the hammer was through his finger. They wrenched and tore at the gun; and had the bigger man grappled now he might have crushed Jeff at once, broken him by main strength. But he was a man of one idea — and he had a second gun. A violent jerk threw Jeff to his knee, but he kept his desperate grip. The second gun flashed in the giant's left hand, rising and falling with the frontier firing motion; but Jeff's own gun was out, he struck up the falling death, the bullet sang above him. He was on his feet, in trampling, unreal struggle; again he struck the gun aside as it belched fire. Turning, whirling, straining, Jeff was dizzily conscious that the men beneath the light were down, both still shooting, the cab had stopped, men were running toward him shouting. The giant's dreadful strength was undirected, heaving and thrusting purposeless; time for order and response would be time for crashing death to find him; his one frantic thought was to shoot first, to shoot fast. Shaken, tossed and thrown, Jeff kept his feet, kept his head, kept close in; as the great man's gun rose and fell he parried with his own. Three shots, four — the others fired no longer; five — one more — Six! It was warded, Jeff drew back, fired his first shot from his hip;

the giant dragged at him, heaved forward, and struck out mightily, hammerwise. Jeff saw the blow gleaming down as he fired again. Glint of myriad lights streamed sparkwise across an infinite blackness; he knew no more.

The clock was still striking.

CHAPTER III

Please go 'way and let me sleep,
I would rather sleep than eat!
— *The Sluggard*

"He's coming round. That man's suhtenly got a cast-iron skull. Such a blow with a .45 would 'a' killed most fellers. What you goin' to do with him, Judge?"

"I don't know. It strikes me that he would be a valuable man for us. That was the nerviest performance I ever saw. Had I been told that anyone could mix it that way with Oily Broderick and two guns, and get off with it scot-free except for this little love tap, I should never have believed it." The voice was rich, clear, slow, well-modulated. "Perhaps he may be induced to join us. If not —"

The words reached Jeff from immeasurable distances. He was floating on a particularly soft and billowy cloud at the time: a cloud with a buoyant and undulant motion, very soothing. Jeff noted it with approval. Underneath and a little ahead, a high and exceedingly steep mountain rose abruptly from the sea. It was built entirely of piled, roundish boulders. The contour seemed familiar. Madagascar, of course! How clever of him to remember! Jeff turned the cloud. It sank in slow and graceful spirals to the peak. Doubtless the voices came from there. The words seemed to have an unexplained connection with some circumstance that he could not quite recall. He felt the elusive memory slipping away. However, it made no difference. He drifted into a delicious vagueness.

Something hard was forced between his teeth; a fiery liquid trickled down his throat. He gasped and struggled; his eyes fluttered open. To his intense disappointment the cloud was gone. An arm was propping him up. Mysterious blankets appeared before him from somewhere or other. On them lay an arm and a bandaged hand. The hand was hurting someone very much. Jeff wondered whose it was. He looked at the hand fixedly for a long time and, on further examination, found it to be his own. Here was a pretty state of affairs!

A pillow was thrust behind him and the supporting arm withdrawn. At once he felt a throbbing pain in his head. He put his hand up and lo! his head was also heavily bandaged! He regretted Madagascar more than ever. He settled back for reflection. Looking up, after a little, he saw a chair with the back turned toward him; astride the chair, a middle-aged man, large, clean-shaven, rosy, well-dressed, and, as it seemed to Jeff, unnecessarily cheerful. His eyes twinkled; his hands, which were white and plump and well kept, played a little ditty on the chairback. There was a ruby on one finger. Beyond him sat a gross, fat man with a stubbly beard, a coarse, flat nose and little, piggish, red eyes. His legs were crossed and he smoked a villainous pipe. There were other men behind these two. Jeff was just turning to look at them when his attention was recalled by a voice from the man astride the chair.

"And how are we now, my young friend? A trifle dazed, I fancy? Something of a headache?" He showed his white teeth in a friendly smile; his voice was soft and playful. "Are we well enough to eat something? What with our recent disagreeable shock and our long abstinence from food, we must find ourself rather feeble."

Jeff stared at the man while he digested this communication. "A little coffee," he said at last. "I can't eat anything now. I am dizzy and most everlasting sick at my stomach. Put out that damned pipe!"

The soft-voiced man chuckled delightedly, as if he found this peremptory command exquisitely humorous. "You hear, Borrowman? Evidently Mr. Bransford is of those who want what they want when they want it. Bring a little soup, too. He'll feel better after he drinks his coffee."

The man addressed as Borrowman disappeared with a shuffling gait. Jeff lay back and considered. His half-shut eyes wandered around. Whitewashed stone walls, a heavily ironed door, no window — that was queer, too! — floor and ceiling of rough boards, a small fireplace, two chairs, a pine table, a lighted lamp. That was all. His gaze came back to the man in the chair, to find the gentleman's large blue eyes watching him with a quizzical and humorous look — a look highly suggestive of a cat enjoying a little casual entertainment with a mouse. In his weakened condition, Jeff found this feline regard disconcerting.

The coffee came, and the soup. After Jeff's refreshment the man in the chair rose. "We will leave you to the care of our good Borrowman," he said, baring his white, even teeth. "I will be back this evening and, if you are stronger, we will then discuss some rather momentous affairs. Go to sleep now."

The caressing advice seemed good. Jeff was just dropping off when a disturbing thought intruded itself.

This evening? Then it must be day now. Why did they burn a lamp in daytime? The problem was too much for Jeff. Still pondering it, he dozed off.

When he woke the lamp was yet burning; the objectionable fat man sat by the fire. When he turned his head, presently, Jeff was startled to observe that this man had got hold of an entirely new set of features. Here was an extraordinary thing! Hard features, and unprepossessing still, but clean at least. How very curious!

After a while a simple solution presented itself. It was not the same man at all! Jeff wondered why he had not hit upon that at first. It seemed that he had now become a body entirely surrounded by fat men — no — that wasn't right. "Let me — let me name the Supreme Court of a nation and I care not who makes the laws." No, that was John Wesley Pringle's gag. Good old Wes! Wonder where he is? He wasn't fat. How did that go? Oh, yes! "Let me have men about me that are fat!" — Something snapped — and Jeff remembered.

Not all at once. He lay silent, with closed eyes, and pieced together scraps of recollection, here and there, bit by bit. It was like a picture puzzle; so much so that Jeff quite identified each random memory with some definite shape, eagerly fitting them together in a frame; and, when he had adjusted them satisfactorily to a perfect square, fell peacefully asleep.

CHAPTER IV

Good fellow, thy shooting is good,
  An' if thy heart be as good as thy hand,
Thou art better than Robin Hood.
                              — *Guy of Gisborne*

WHEN HE WOKE the soft-voiced, white-handed man again sat beside the bed, again in the same equestrian attitude, clasping the back of the chair, beaming with good humor.

"And how is our young friend now? Much better, I trust. We have had a long and refreshing sleep. Is our brain quite clear?"

Here the fat man — the less ill-favored one — rose silently from beside the fire and left them.

"Our young friend is extremely hungry," said Jeff. "Our young friend's brain is clear, but our young friend's head is rather sore. Where am I? In jail?" He sat up and pushed back the bandage for clearer vision.

The jovial gentleman laughed — a merry and mellow peal. "What a spirited fellow you are! And what an extremely durable headpiece you have! A jail? Well, not exactly, my dear fellow, not exactly. Let us say, in a cache, in a retreat, sometimes used by gentlemen wishing temporary retirement from society. You are also, though I grieve to say it, in a jackpot — to use a phrase the precise meaning and origin of which I do not comprehend, but which seems to be, in the vernacular, a synonym for the more common word predicament." He shook his head sorrowfully. "A very sad predicament, indeed! Quite unintentionally, and in obedience to a chivalrous impulse — which does you great credit, I assure you — you have had the misfortune to mar a very well-laid plan of mine. Had I not been a quick thinker, marvelously fertile in expedients, your officiousness would have placed me in an awkward quandary. However, in the very brief time at my disposal I was able to hit upon a device equally satisfactory — I may say even more satisfactory than the original."

"Hold on!" said Jeff. "I don't quite keep up. You planned a midnight assassination which did not go off smoothly. I've got that. You were one of the men in the cab. There was a fight — "

"There was, indeed!" interrupted the genial gentleman. His eyes lit up with enthusiasm; his shapely fingers tapped the chair back. "Such a fight! It was magnificent! Believe me, my dear Bransford, it inspired me with an almost affectionate admiration for you! And your opponent was a most redoubtable person, with a sensitive trigger finger — "

"Excuse the interruption," said Jeff. "But you seem to have the advantage of me in the matter of names."

"So I have, so I have! As you will infer, I looked through your pockets. Thorpe is my name — S. S. Thorpe. Stay — here is my card. You will see that I am entitled to the prefix 'Hon.,' having been sometime State Senator. Call me Judge. I have never occupied that exalted position, but all the boys call me Judge. To go back — we were speaking of your opponent. Perhaps you knew him? No? Mr. Broderick, Mr. Oily Broderick, once of San Antonio, a man of some renown. We shall miss him, Mr. Bransford, we shall miss him! A very useful fellow! But your eyes ask the question — Dead? Dear me, yes! Dead and buried these many hours. He never knew what ailed him. Both of your bullets found a vital spot. A sad loss! But I interrupt. I am much interested to see how nearly accurate your analysis of the situation will be."

"The short man — was he killed, too?" asked Jeff.

"The worthy Krouse was killed as well," said Judge Thorpe, sighing with comfortable resignation. "But Krouse was a negligible quantity. Amiable, but a bungler. Go on!"

"Your intended victim seems to have escaped — "

"Survived," corrected Judge Thorpe gently, with complacent inspection of his shapely hands. "Survived is the better word, believe me. Captain Charles Tillotson, Captain of the Rangers. An estimable gentleman, with whom, I grieve to say, I was not on the best of terms. To our political enmity, of long standing — and you perhaps know that Southwestern politics are extremely bitter — has been added of late a certain social rivalry. But I digress. You were saying — "

"But you are prompting me," said Jeff testily. "It is hardly necessary. Your enemy not being killed outright, you choose to assassinate his good name, juggling appearances to make it seem that he was the murderer — and to that end you have spirited me away."

"Exactly! You are a man after my own heart — a man of acumen and discernment," said Judge Thorpe, beaming, "although I did, as you suggest, prompt you at some points — knowing that you were not familiar with all the premises. Really, Mr. Bransford, though I would not unduly exalt myself, I cannot help but think my little device showed more than mere talent. It was, considering the agitating circumstances, considering that both conception and execution had to be instantaneous, little less than Napoleonic! I feel sure that when I tell you the details you will share my enthusiasm."

Jeff was doing some quick thinking. He recalled what he had heard of Thorpe. He was best known as a powerful and wealthy politician of El Paso, who in his younger days had been a dangerous gunfighter. Of late years, however, he had become respected and reputable, his youthful foibles forgotten.

The appalling frankness of this avowal could bode no good to Jeff. Evidently he was helplessly in this man's power, and his life had been spared for some sinister and shameful purpose.

"Before you favor me with any more details, Judge," said Jeff, "can't you give me an old boot to chew on?"

"What wonderful spirits, what splendid nerves! I compliment you!" said the Judge. "Our good Mac went, when you first awoke, to prepare steak, eggs and coffee for you. You will pardon us if we do not have your meals brought in from a restaurant. It would not do. We are quiet here, we do not court observation. For the same reason we have been forced to abstain from medical attendance for you, otherwise so desirable. I, myself, have filled that office to the best of my ability. Now as to the replenishing of the inner man. Mac is an excellent cook."

"Cleaner than Borrowman," said Jeff.

"And is, as you observe, much cleaner than Borrowman. He will prepare whatever the market affords. You have only to ask. And, while we are waiting, I will return to my story.

"I was, as you so readily surmised, in the cab, together with my good friend, colleague and lieutenant, Mr. Sam Patterson. We had telephoned ahead to Krouse and Broderick that Tillotson was on his way. We were to be witnesses that Krouse acted purely in self-defense, you know — as, indeed, were also the cab driver and Broderick. Broderick was to hold himself in reserve and not to assist, except in case of mishap. We supposed that Krouse would kill Tillotson without difficulty. Krouse bungled. He inflicted three wounds, painful but not dangerous; including one which creased the scalp and produced unconsciousness."

The man took such shameless delight in parading his wickedness that Jeff began to wonder if, after all, it would not have saved himself much difficulty if Broderick had killed him. But he set his mind like a flint to thwart this smiling monster at any cost.

The Judge went on: "Such was the distressing situation when I came up. Some men would have finished Tillotson on the spot. But I kept my presence of mind; I exercised admirable self-restraint. It would be but an instant before the aroused neighborhood would be on the street. We bundled you and your gun into the cab and the driver hurried you away to a certain rendezvous of ours. To have done with the driver, I will say at this time that he came in and gave his testimony the next day very effectively, fully confirming ours; accounting for his conduct by the very natural excuse that he was scared and so ran away lest he should be shot.

"The gun in Broderick's right hand, you may remember, had not been fired. His stiffening fingers still held it. I picked up his other gun, unbuckled his belt, buckled it around Tillotson, and dropped Broderick's empty gun by him. No more was needed. The populace found me caring for Captain Tillotson like a brother, pouring whisky down him — and thereby heaping coals of fire on his head.

"Now, as to our evidence. As you may readily guess, we were driving by when the trouble began. We saw Captain Tillotson when he fired the first shot, killing Broderick with it. He continued to shoot after Broderick dropped; Krouse, defending his friend, was killed also, wounding Tillotson, who kept on shooting blindly after he fell. The circumstantial evidence, too, was damning, and bore us out in every respect. Broderick, a man of deadly quickness, had been killed before he could shoot. Tillotson had emptied one gun and fired four shots from the other; his carrying two guns pointed toward deliberate, fore-planned murder. The marks on the houses, made by a number of his wild bullets, were in a line directly beyond Broderick's body from where Tillotson lay. Broderick was between you and the others, you know," explained the Judge parenthetically. "But as nothing is known of you, the marks of Broderick's bullets are supposed to be made by Tillotson's — incontrovertible evidence that he began the fighting."

Nothing could have been more hateful, more revolting, than this bland, smiling complacency: Jeff's fingers itched to be at his throat. It became clear to him that either this man would be his death, or, which was highly improbable, the other way about. His resolution hardened; he began to have visions of this smiling face above a noose.

"When Tillotson regained consciousness he told a most amazing story, obviously conflicting with the facts. He had carried but one gun; Krouse had made a wanton attack upon him, without warning; he had returned the fire. Simultaneously Broderick had been killed by some fourth man, a stranger, whom Tillotson did not know, and who had mysteriously disappeared when the people of the neighborhood arrived. It looks very black for Captain Tillotson," purred the Judge, shaking his hands and head sorrowfully. "Even those who uphold him do not credit this wildly improbable tale. It is universally thought that his wealth and position will not save him from the noose. El Paso is reforming; El Paso is weary of two-gun men.

"And now, my dear Bransford, comes the crucial point, a matter so delicate that I hesitate to touch upon it. All of my ingenious little impromptu was built and founded on the natural hypothesis of your demise, which, in my haste, I did not stop to verify. It did not occur to me as among the possibilities that any man — even myself — could weather six shots, at hand-grips, from Oily Broderick. Imagine, then, my surprise and chagrin when I learned that you were not even seriously hurt! It was a shock, I assure you! But here comes Mac with the tray. I will bathe your hands, Mr. Bransford. Then I beg that you will fall to at once. We will discourse while you break your fast."

"Oh, I can get up," said Jeff. "I'm not hurt. Put it on the table."

CHAPTER V

Quoth Robin, "I dwell by dale and down
By thee I set right naught."
— *Guy of Gisborne*

"I PERCEIVE," said the Judge, surveying the tempting viands, "that Mac has thoughtfully cut your meat for you. You are provided with many spoons, but neither knife nor fork. A wise and wholesome precaution, I may remark. After your recent exploit we stand quite in awe of you. Pray be seated. I will take a cup of coffee with you — if you will allow me?

"It will not have escaped a man of your penetration that an obvious course was open to me. But your gallantry had quite won my heart, and I refrained from that obvious course, though strongly urged to it. Mac, tell Mr. Bransford what your advice was."

"I said: 'Dead men tell no tales!'" replied Mac sturdily. "And I say it again. Yon is a fearsome man."

"You are a dangerous man yourself, Mac. Yet I trust you. And why? Because," said the Judge cooingly, "I am more dangerous still — leader by right of the strongest. I admire you, Mr. Bransford; I needed such a man as you seem to be. Moreover, singular as it may seem, I boggled at cutting you off in cold blood. I have as good a heart as can be made out of brains. You had not intentionally harmed me; I bore you no grudge; it seemed a pity. I decided to give you a chance. I refused this advice. If you but knew it, Mr. Bransford, you owe me a heavy debt of gratitude. So we brought you across quite unostentatiously. That brings us up to date.

"You see the logic of the situation, my dear fellow? Your silence must be insured. Either you must throw in your lot with us, commit yourself entirely and irrevocably to us, or suffer the consequences of — shall we say, your indiscretion?"

The Judge sipped his coffee daintily. "It is distressing even to mention the alternative; it is needless to lay undue emphasis upon it; circumstances have already done that. You see for yourself that it must be thus, and not otherwise."

Jeff took a toothpick, pushed his chair back and crossed his legs comfortably. "I must have time to consider the matter and look at it from all sides," he said meditatively. "But I can tell you now how it strikes me at first blush. Do you believe in presentiments, Judge?"

The Judge shook his head. "I am singularly free from all superstition."

"Now, I do," said Jeff steadily, his face wearing as engaging an expression as its damaged condition would permit. "And I have a very strong presentiment that I shall see you hung, or perhaps I should say, hanged."

The Judge went off in another peal of laughter. Even the saturnine Mac relaxed to a grim smile. The Judge pounded on the table. "But what a droll dog it is!" he cried. "Positively, I like you better every moment. Such high spirits! Such hardihood! Really, we need you, we must have you. I cannot imagine anyone better fitted to fill the place of the departed brother whom you — as the instrument of an inscrutable and all-wise Providence — have removed from our midst."

At this disloyalty to the dead, Jeff's gorge rose at the man; treacherous, heartless, revolting. But he kept a tranquil, untroubled face. The Judge went on: "Your resolution may change. You will suffer from ennui. I may mention that, should you join us, the pecuniary reward will be great. I am wealthy and powerful, and our little organization — informal, but very select — shares my fortunes. They push me up from below and I pull them up from above. I will add that we seldom find it necessary to resort to such extreme measures as we did in the Tillotson case. He was a very troublesome man; he has been a thorn in my side for years.

"On the contrary, we conduct many open and perfectly legitimate enterprises, political, legal, financial. We are interested in mining propositions; we have cattle ranches in Texas and Old Mexico; we handle real estate. As side lines, we do a miscellaneous business — smuggle a vast amount of opium and a few Chinamen, keep sanctuary for unhappy fugitives, jump good mines and sell poor ones, furnish or remove witnesses — Oh, many things! But perhaps, our greatest activity is simply to exert moral pressure in aid of our strictly legitimate enterprises.

"Tut, tut! I have been so charmed that I have overstayed my time. Think this matter over carefully, my dear fellow. There is much to gain or to lose. You shall have ample time for consideration. Mac and Borrowman will get you anything you want, within the bounds of reason — clothes, books, tobacco, such knickknacks. And, by the way, here are yesterday's papers. You may care to read the Tillotson case. The editorials, both those that condemn him and those that defend, are particularly amusing."

"Mac and Borrowman are to be my jailers?" said Jeff.

The Judge raised his hands in expostulation. "Jailers?" he repeated. "What a harsh term! Let us say, companions. You might break out of jail," said the Judge, tapping Jeff's breast with his strong fingers, "but you will not get away from me. They will tell you their instructions. I will attend to your hurts, now, and then I must go."

"I would like clean clothes," said Jeff, while the Judge dressed his wounds skilfully. "A safety razor — they can keep it when I'm not using it — the daily papers, cigars, tobacco — let me see, what else? Oh yes — I was trying to learn the typewriter. I'd like to try it again when my finger gets better. For books, send in Shakespeare's works and Carlyle's *French Revolution*, for the present."

"You're quite sure that's all?" said the Judge, entertained and delighted. "You must intend to take your time about making up your mind."

"My mind is entirely made up now. I would insure you against a watery death," said Jeff with utmost calmness, "for a dime!"

"We shall see, we shall see!" said the Judge skeptically. "Time works many wonders. You will be ennuied! I prophesy it. Besides, I count upon your gratitude. Good night!"

"Good night!"

.   .   .   .

So you "brought me unostentatiously across," did you? You made a slip that time. You talk well, Judge, but you talk too much. Across? Across the Rio Grande. I am in Juárez. I had already guessed it, for I hear the sounds of many whistling engines from far off, and but few from near at hand. My prison is underground, since those whistles are the only sounds that reach me, and they muffled and indistinct; coming by the fireplace.

That chimney goes through a house above, since they keep up a fire. What to do?

Through the long hours he lay on his bed, sleepless. When he opened his eyes, at intervals, it was always to find the guard's face toward him, watching him intently. They were taking no chances.

His vigorous brain was busy with the possibilities; contriving, hopeless as the situation might seem, more than one scheme, feasible only to desperation, and with terrible odds against success. These he put by to be used only as a last recourse, and fell to his Sisyphean task again with such concentration of all his powers upon the work in hand as few men have ever dreadful need to attain — such focused concentration that, had his mind been an actual searchlight, capable, in its turning, to throw a shining circle upon actual, living, moving men, in all places, far or near, in time past, present or to come — where it paused, the places, men and events could not have been more real, more clear, more brightly illumined. When this inner light wearied and grew faint he turned it back till it pierced the thick walls to another prison, dwelt on another prisoner there: a tall, gray figure, whose face was turned away, ringed round with hate, with ignominy, shame, despair and death; not friendless. And the light rose again, strong and unwavering, ranging the earth for what help was there; so fell at last upon a plan, not after to be altered. A rough plan only — the details to be worked out — tomorrow and tomorrow. So thinking, utter exhaustion came upon him and he fell asleep.

CHAPTER VI

The bosun's mate was very sedate, but fond of
amusement too,
So he played hop-scotch with the larboard watch,
while the Captain tickled the crew.
— *Ballad of The Walloping Window Blind*

"AND WHAT ARE these famous instructions of yours, Mac?"

"They are verra precise, Mr. Bransford. One of us will be always in the room. That one will keep close and constant watch upon you, even when you are asleep. Your wound will be dressed only when we are both here. Coal and water, your meals, the things you send for, will be brought in only when we are both here. And on any slightest eendication of an attempted rescue or escape we are to kill you without hesitation!"

It was plain that Mac was following the manner as well as the matter of his instructions. He gave this information slowly, with dour satisfaction, checking each item by forcibly doubling down, with his right hand, the fingers of his left. Having now doubled them all down, he undoubled them and began again.

"If you attempt to give any alarm, if you attempt to make any attack, if on any pretext you try to get near enough for a possible attack, we will kill you without hesitation." He rolled the phrase under his tongue with great relish.

"Your precautions are most flattering, I'm sure," said Jeff idly. "I must be very careful. The room is large, but I might inadvertently break your last rule at any time. If I understand you correctly, should I so much as drop my pencil and, picking it up, forgetfully come too close —"

"I will shoot you," repeated this uncompromising person, "without any hesitation. I have a verra high opeenion of your powers, Mr. Bransford, and have no mind to come to grips wi' you. You will keep your distance, and we will agree fine."

"All this is like to be very tiresome to you." Jeff's tones were level and cheerful; he leaned back in his chair, yawning; his hands were clasped behind his head. "Such constant vigilance will be a strain upon you; your nerves will be affected. I will have by far the best of it. I can sleep, read, think. But if you turn your head, if you close your eyes, if you so much as falter in your attention," said Jeff dispassionately, "my fingers will be at your throat to tear your life out for the dog that you are!"

"Why, now we understand each other perfectly," returned Mac, in nowise discomposed. "But I would have ye to observe that your last remark was highly discourteous. My instructions are not yet ended. Look now!" He held up his hand, with three fingers still tightly closed to indicate three several unhesitancies. "Our last instruction was to treat you with ceeveelity and consideration, to give you any indulgence which would not endanger your safe keeping, to subject you to no indignity or abuse." He folded down the fourth finger and extended his closed hand, thrusting out his thumb reproachfully. "To no abuse!" he repeated.

"I am properly rebuked," said Jeff. "I withdraw the 'dog.' Let me amend the offending remark to read thus: 'to tear out your life without any hesitation.' But even the remarkable foresight of Judge Thorpe seems to have overlooked one important thing. I refer to the possible corruption of my jailers. Do I likewise forfeit my life if I tamper with your integrity?"

His grim guardian chose to consider this query as extremely facetious. His leathern face wrinkled to cavernous gashes, indicative of mirth of a rather appalling sort; he emitted a low rumble that might be construed, in a liberal translation, as laughter; his words took on a more Scottish twist. "You might try it on Borrowman," he said. "Man, you've a taking way with you! 'Tis fair against my advice and sober judgment that ye are here at all — but I am begeening to feel your fasceenations! Now that ye'er here I e'en have the hope that ye will be weel advisit. I own it, I would be but loath to feed so gay and so plain-dealing a man to the feeshes!"

These two had many such skirmishes as the days went by: slow, dragging days, perpetually lamp-lit, their passage measured only by the irregularly changing guards and the regular bringing in of the daily papers.

Jeff timed his sleeping hours to come on Borrowman's trick; finding that jailer dull, ferocious and unendurable. His plan was long since perfected, and now he awaited but the opportunity of putting it into execution.

The Judge had called — as a medical adviser, he said — pronounced Jeff's progress all that could be desired, and touched upon their affair with argument, cajolery and airy badinage. Jeff had asked permission to write to his wife, to send some message, which the Judge might dictate; any sort of a story, he implored, to keep her from alarm and anxiety; which petition the Judge put merrily by, smiling at the absurdity of such request.

In his waking hours Jeff read the papers. Tillotson was mending, his trial would be soon. He read his books, sometimes aloud; he chaffed his jailer; he practised on the typewriter, but never, in his practice, wrote off any appeal for aid to good men and true, or even the faintest suggestion that a quick move by the enemy would jeopardize any possible number of gunboats. Instead, Jeff undertook to produce another "speed sentence." He called Mac to his assistance, explaining his wants; and between them, with great glee, they concocted the following gem:

He kept vexing me with frantic journeys hidden by quiet zeal.

They showed this effusion to the Judge with much pride, defying him to better it. Jeff pounded it off by the hour; he mingled fragments of it with his remarks in season and out.

There were long visits from the Judge. In his own despite Jeff grew to enjoy them and to look forward to them — so strange a thing is man! The Judge was witty, cynical, informed, polished, keen, satirical. At times Jeff almost forgot what thing he was besides. Their talk ranged on many things, always in the end coming back to the same smiling query, the same unfaltering reply. Once, Patterson came with him — a younger man, with a brutal and bloated face — and urged the closing of the incident in clear and unmistakable terms.

And, as day followed day, Jeff let it appear — as a vital part of his plan — in his speech, his manner, his haggard looks, that danger, suspense and confinement were telling upon him, that he was worried and harassed, that he was losing his nerve. These things appeared slowly, lest he should seem to weaken too soon and too easily.

CHAPTER VII

And when 'e downs 'is 'ead and 'umps 'is back,
ye cawn't remain, y'know!
　　　　　　　　　—*Beresford on the Bronco*

"My iron-headed friend," said the Judge — "and I use the word in more senses than one — you have now had ample time for deliberation. I have given you the opportunity to choose — life —"

No menace, no violence, could have left an impression so strong, so dreadful in its finality, as this brief ellipsis, the casual, light-hearted manner.

" — at no slight risk to myself. Because, the admiration, the liking which I have professed to you is real and sincere enough, though, perhaps, none of the deepest. I will be quite frank with you, Mr. Bransford; that liking, that admiration has grown with our acquaintance. A weakness; I admit it; it would be with a real regret that I should speak the word to cut that acquaintance short. I will be so much further frank with you as to say that I fancy I can sufficiently steel myself to speak that word should you again refuse good counsel. This may be the last of our pleasant meetings. For the last time, in the words of your favorite writer: 'Under which king, Bezonian? Speak, or die!' "

Jeff's hands gripped visibly at his chair-arms, so that the Judge observed it — as was intended — and smiled. But Jeff gave his answer quietly: "I can't do it. If you had killed Tillotson outright I might, to save my life, keep silence and let you go unpunished. But I can't do this."

"You mean you won't," said the Judge acidly.

"I mean that I can't," said Jeff. "I would if I could, but I can't."

"By Heavens, I believe you will stick to it!" said the Judge, greatly disappointed. "Had you couched your refusal in some swelling phrase — and I can think of a dozen sonorous platitudes to fit the case — I might yet have hopes of you. I believe, sir, that you are a stubborn fellow. The man is nothing to you!"

"The man is much to me," returned Jeff. "He is innocent."

"So, I believe, are you. How will it help him for you to die? And so obscurely, too! I think," said the Judge gently, flicking at his cuff, "that you mentioned a wife? Yes? And children? Two, I think. Two boys?"

His elbows were upon the table, his white hands were extended upon the table, he held his head a little to one side and contemplated his fingers as they played a little tune there, quite as if it were a piano.

Jeff's face worked; he rose and paced the floor. Mac, by the door, regarded him with something very like compassion in his hard face. The Judge watched him with feline amusement.

When he came back he passed by his chair; he stood beside the table, resting his fingers lightly on the typewriter frame. "Life is dear to me," he said, with a slight break in his voice. "I will make this one concession. More I will not do. Tillotson's trial is half over; the verdict is certain; there are powerful influences at work to insure the denial of an appeal and to hasten his execution. If you can keep me here until after his execution I will then — to save my life, for my wife's sake, for my children's sake — keep silence. And may God forgive me for a compromiser and a coward!" he added with a groan.

"But if, before that, I can make my escape; if, before that, I can in any way communicate with the outside world, I will denounce you, at any cost to myself."

The Judge would have spoken, but Jeff held up his hand. "Wait! I have listened to you — listen now to me. You have forgotten that there are two sides to every bargain. You sit directly between me and Mac, your hands are upon the table, your feet are beneath the table, the typewriter is at my hand. Do not move! If Mac stirs but an inch, if you dare raise a finger, until you have agreed to my proposition, by the God that made me, I will crush your skull like an egg!"

"Had ye wrung his neck off-hand, as I urgit upon ye frae the first — " The words came bitterly from Mac, sitting rigid in his corner — "this wadna have chancit." His tones conveyed a singular mixture of melancholy and triumph; the thickening of his Scotch burr betrayed his agitation. "Be guidit by me noo at the last, Judge, and tak the daft body's terms. In my opeenion the project of smashin' your head wi' the machine is enteerly pract'ecable, and I think Mr. Bransford will e'en do it. Why should he no? A dead man has naught to fear. My gude word is, mak treaty wi' him and save your — "

"Neck. For this time," hinted Jeff delicately.

The Judge did not shrink, he did not pale; but neither did he move. "And your presentiment that you would see me hanged? You have abandoned that, it seems?"

"Not at all, not at all," said Jeff, cheerily. "You are going to do just what I propose. You'd rather take the chance of having your neck broken legally than the certainty that I'll break it now."

"With that thing? Humph! You couldn't hurt me much with that. I think I could get up and away before you could hit me with it. And Mac would certainly shoot you before you could hit me a second time."

"Once will be a-plenty." Bransford laughed. "You go first, I beseech you, my dear Alphonse! Oh no, Judge — you don't think anything of the kind. If you did you'd try it. Your legs — limbs, I mean of course — are too far under the table. And I've been practising for speed with this machine every day. What Mac does to me afterward won't help you any. You'll be done dead, damned and delivered. If he could shoot me now without shooting through you, it would be a different proposition. Your mistake was in ever letting me line you up. 'Tit, tat, toe — Three in a row!' Well, what are you going to do about it?"

"Oh, man, ye chargit me streectly to keep this wild cat-a-mountain at his distance," interrupted Mac in mournful reproach, "and then pop ye down cheek by jowl wi' the deil's buckie your ainsel'. I'd as lief seat me to sup wi' the black devil and his muckle pitchfork!"

As often happens in such cases, the man who was in no immediate danger was more agitated than the one imperiled; who, after a moment's reflection, looked up at Bransford with a smile in his eyes.

"And how am I to know you will not denounce me if I let you go after this unfortunate Tillotson is hanged?" he demanded. "Or, for that matter, how are you to know that I will not kill you as soon as I am beyond the reach of your extremely novel weapon — which, I grant you, might be effective at such close quarters and in such capable hands — or that I will not have you killed at any time hereafter? This," said the Judge, picking his words leisurely and contemplating his fine fingers with unreserved approval, "is the crux of the very interesting situation. Rigid moralists, scrutinizing the varied actions of my life, might find passages not altogether blameless. But I have always held and maintained that a man should keep faith where it is expressly pledged. This is the bedrock upon which is based all relations of man with man, and to no class is it so needful as to those who are at variance with society. If a man will not hold by his plighted word, even to his hurt, he has lost all contact with reality and is become henceforth no actuality, but a vain and empty simulacrum, not to be dealt with, useless either for good or evil. Here, for instance, are we, two intelligent men, confronting mutual instant annihilation; which might be avoided could each be perfectly sure the other would keep his word! It is quite amusing!"

"I will take your word if you will take mine," said Jeff. "You should know who runs the greater risk. But I have a stipulation to make."

The Judge arched his brows. "A stipulation? Another? My volatile and resourceful friend, do not ask too much. It is by no means certain that your extraordinary missile — or was it to be a war-club? — might not fail of the desired effect. You have already stipulated for your life, and I think," said the Judge dryly, "that if you have any other demand to make, it had best be a modest one."

"I do not choose," said Jeff steadily, "that my wife shall suffer needless anxiety — unneeded if you set me free at last. Still less do I choose, if I meet with foul play at your hands, or if I should be killed attempting an escape, to have her haunted by any doubt of me. I shall write to her that I am in Old Mexico, in some part known to be dangerous, tempted by high pay. You will send it to be mailed down there. Then, if I do not come back, she will think of me as honorably dead, and be at peace."

It came into the Judge's active mind that such a letter — dated and signed from some far-off Mexican town — might, in some contingencies, be useful to him; his bold, blue eyes, which had faced an imminent death firmly enough, dropped now to hide the treacherous thought. And upon this thought, and its influence upon sending the letter, Jeff had counted from the first.

"There are other reasons," said Jeff. "You have been pleased to speak well of me. You have boasted, both for yourself and for me, enough and more than enough. Let me now boast for myself. Has it never occurred to you that such a man as I am would have friends — formidable friends? That they are wondering what has become of me? If you agree to my arrangement, I have a chance of saving both my life and some shreds of decency. I do not now want my friends to come in search of me and get me killed in trying to rescue me — for you will, of course, redouble your precautions after this. This letter will put my friends at ease. I will have to trust you to mail it. That is the weakness of my position. But I think that there is a chance that you will mail it — and that chance will help me to keep a quiet mind. That much, at least, will be a clear gain. Do this, and I will yield a point to you. If you would rather I didn't, I will not go to see you hanged!"

The amazing effrontery of this last coaxing touch so appealed to Judge Thorpe's sense of humor that he quite recovered his good nature. "My dear boy," he said, "if I should ever be hanged, I wouldn't miss having you there for worlds. It would add a zest to the occasion that I should grieve to lose. I will agree unconditionally to your proposed *modus vivendi*. As I understand it, if I can hang Tillotson you are to keep silence and go free. But if you can contrive to get me hanged you are to attend the festivity in person? It is a wager. Write your letter and I'll mail it. Of course, I'll have to read it and edit it if needed. And say — Bransford! I'll mail it, too! You can be at rest on that point. In the meantime, I presume, I may move without bringing the typewriter about my ears?"

"You may," said Jeff. "It's a bet. I wish you'd wait and I'll write the letter now. She'll be anxious about me. It'll take some time. I always write her long letters. Let me have your fountain-pen, will you?"

"Why don't you use your typewriter?" said the Judge. "And, by the way, I fear we shall have to deprive you of your typewriter in the future."

"A typewritten letter wouldn't be consistent at all," said Jeff. "I am supposed to be writing from darkest Old Mexico. No typewriters there. Besides, I can't write with the damn thing to do any good. Say, don't take it away from me, Judge; there's a good fellow. I want to master it. I do hate to be beaten."

"The elasticity with which you adjust yourself to changing conditions is beyond all praise," said the Judge, smiling. "Like the other Judge, in the Bible, I yield to importunity. I can deny you nothing. Keep your typewriter, then, with the express understanding that its use as a deadly weapon is barred. Here's the pen."

CHAPTER VIII

Alice's Right Foot, Esq.,
   Hearthrug,
      Near the Fender,
      (With Alice's love).

. . . .

O, there be many systems
But only one that wins —
When leading from your strongest suit,
Just kick your partner's shins.

— Hoyle

JEFF PULLED the paper over and began to scribble madly; pausing from time to time to glance around for inspiration: at the Judge, at Mac, at the papers, the books, the typewriter. "I'll slip in a note for the kids," said Jeff. His lips moved, his eyes kindled in his eager absorption; his face took on a softer and tenderer look. The Judge, watching him, beamed with almost paternal indulgence.

On the whole Jeff wrote with amazing swiftness for a man who professed to be unaccustomed to lying. For this communication, apparently so spontaneous, dashed off by a man hardly yet clear of the shadow of death, was learned by rote, no syllable unpremeditated, the very blots of it designed.

This is what he handed the Judge at last:

SAN MIGUEL, Chihuahua, March 24

My dear Wife:

Since I last wrote you I have been on a long trip into the Yaqui country as guide, interpreter and friend to a timid tenderfoot — an all-round sharp from the Smithsonian. His main lay is Cliff-Dweller-ology, but he does other stunts — rocks and bugs and Indian languages, and early Spanish relics.

I get big pay. I enclose you $100 —

"A hundred dollars! Why, this is blackmail!" remonstrated the Judge, grinning nevertheless.

"But," said Jeff, "I've got to send it. She knows I wouldn't stay away except for good big pay, and she knows I'll send the big pay to her. I didn't think you were a piker. Why, I had thirty dollars in my pocket. You won't be out but seventy. And if you don't send it she'll know the letter is a fake. Besides, she needs the money."

"I surrender! I'll send it," said the Judge, and resumed his reading:

— and will send you more when I get back from next trip. Going way down in the Sierra Madre this time. Don't know when we will hit civilization again, so you needn't write till you hear from me.

The Cliff-Dweller-ologist had the El Paso papers sent on here to him and I am reading them all through while he writes letters and reports and things. I am reading some of his books, too.

Mary, I always hated it because I didn't have a better education. I used to wonder if you wasn't sometimes ashamed of me when we was first married. But I've learned a heap from you and I've picked up considerable, reading these last few years — and I begin to see that there are compensations in all things. I see a good deal in things I read now that I would have missed if I'd just skimmed over the surface when I was younger. For instance, I've just made the acquaintance of Julius Caesar — introduced by my chief.

Say, that's a great book! And I just know I'm getting more out of it than if I'd been familiar with it ever since I was a boy, with stone-bruises on my hoofs. I've read it over two or three times now, and find things every time that I didn't quite get before.

It ought to be called Yond Caius Cassius, though. Shakespere makes Julius out to be a superstitious old wretch. But Julius had some pretty good hunches at that.

Of course Mark Antony's wonderful speech at the funeral was fine business. Gee! how he skinned the "Honorable men!" Some of the things he said after that will stand reading, too.

But Yond Cassius, he was the man for my money. He was a regular go-getter. If Brutus had only hearkened to Cassius once in a while they'd have made a different play of it. I didn't like Brutus near so well. He was a four-flusher. Said he wouldn't kill himself and sure enough he did. He was set up and heady and touchy. I shouldn't wonder if he was better than Cassius, just morally. I guess maybe that's why Cassius knuckled down to him and humored him so. But intellectually, and as a man of action, he wasn't ace-high to Cassius.

Still there's no denying that Brutus had a fine line of talk. There was his farewell to Cassius — you remember that — and his parting with his other friends.

I've been reading Carlyle's *French Revolution* too. It's a little too deep for me, so I take it in small doses. It looks to me like a great writer could take a page of it and build a book on it.

Well, that's all I know. Oh, yes! I tried to learn typewriting when I was in El Paso — I mustn't forget that. I made up a sentence with all the letters in it — he kept vexing me by frantic journeys hidden with quiet zeal — I got so I could rattle that off pretty well, but when I tried new stuff I got balled up.

Will write you when I can. George will know what to do with the work. Have the boys help him.

Your loving husband,

JEFF

Dear Kids:

I wish you could see some of the places I saw in the mountains. We took the train to Casas Grandes and went with a pack outfit to Durasno and Tarachi, just over the line into Sonora. That's one fine country. Had a good time going and coming, but when we got there and my chief was snooping around in those musty old underground cave houses I was bored a-plenty. One day I remember I lay in camp with nothing to do and read every line of an old El Paso paper, ads and all.

Leo, you're getting to be a big boy now. I want you to get into something better than punching cows. When you get time you ought to go down to your Uncle Sim's and make a start on learning to use a typewriter. I've been trying it myself, but it's hard for an old dog to learn new tricks.

You and Wesley must both help your mother, and help George. Do what George tells you — he knows more about things than you do. Be good kids. I'll be home just as soon as I can.

DAD

"There," said Jeff, "if there's anything you want to blue-pencil I'll write it over. Anything you want to say suits me so long as it goes."

"Why, this seems all right," said the Judge, after reading it. "I have an envelope in my billbook. Address it, but don't seal it. You might attempt to put in some inclosure by sleight-of-hand. If you try any such trick I shall consider myself absolved from any promise. If you don't, I'll mail it. I always prefer not to lie when I have nothing to gain by lying. Bless my soul, how you have blotted it!"

"Yes. I'm getting nervous," said Jeff.

The envelope bore the address:

MRS. JEFF BRANSFORD
Rainbow South
Escondido, N. M.

c/o WILLIAM BEEBE.

"Of course you will do as you like," remonstrated Patterson, later. "But I shouldn't send that letter, and I should, without any further delay, erase Mr. Bransford's name from the list of living men."

"Tush!" said the Judge. "The letter is harmless. The man is a splendid fighter, and has some practical notion of psychology, but the poor fellow has no imagination. In his eagerness, he made his letter up on the spur of the moment. There is scarcely a line in it but was suggested by his surroundings. His haste and affection made him transparent; I followed the workings of his mind and, except for personalities, anticipated practically all of it.

"As for killing him, I shall do nothing of the kind. I made a bargain with him in the very article of death and I shall keep to it. He cannot escape; it is not possible. Besides, I like the man. Hang it, Patterson, he is what I would wish my son to be, if I had one. I'll not kill him and I'll send his letter."

He did send it. It reached Billy Beebe some days later, to his no small mystification — Jeff Bransford was unmarried. Yet the address was indubitably in Jeff's handwriting. Taking Leo Ballinger into consultation, he carried it unopened to John Wesley Pringle; taking also a letter for that person, bearing an El Paso postmark many days earlier than the one for the mysterious Mrs. Bransford. Both had lain long in the Escondido office before anyone passed going to Rainbow, so the two letters reached there together.

Pringle's letter was brief:

EL PASO, TEXAS, March 20

MR. JOHN WESLEY PRINGLE,
Rainbow, N. M.

Dear Sir:

Your friend, Mr. Jeff Bransford, came here some time since on some business with Mr. Simon Hibler — whose clerk I am. Mr. Hibler was on a trip to San Simon, Arizona, and I did not know exactly when he would return. Mr. Bransford decided to wait for him. We became great friends and he rather made his headquarters with me. He told me a great deal about you.

On the night of March 16th, Mr. Bransford was with me until almost midnight, when he started for his rooms. So far as I can learn he has not been seen or heard of since; his effects are still at his lodgings. He did not take the street car home. I inquired carefully of all the men.

It is now the fourth day since his disappearance and I am much distressed. I have lodged information with the police — but, between you and me, I don't feel any enthusiasm about the police.

If you have knowledge of his whereabouts I wish you would be so kind as to drop me a line. If you know nothing I hope that you and the other friends he spoke of so often would come down, and I will put myself at your orders. I am uneasy. As you doubtless know, this is one awful tough town.

Trusting to hear good news at an early date, I remain,

Yours truly,

GEO. T. AUGHINBAUGH

112 Temple Street

On reading this John Wesley took it upon himself to open the letter for the non-existent Mrs. Bransford. From that cryptic document they gathered three things only. First, Jeff was under duress, his letter was written to pass inspection by hostile eyes. Second, Leo Ballinger was to visit Uncle Sim and to learn typewriting. Third, George would tell them what to do. There was no George at Rainbow; Leo's only uncle, Simon Hibler, lived in El Paso, his clerk's name was George. The inference was plain.

The next day the three friends presented themselves at 112 Temple Street.

CHAPTER IX

And so these men of Indostan
Disputed loud and long,
Each in his own opinion
Exceeding stiff and strong.

SO SINGULAR AN EFFECT did Mrs. Bransford's letter have upon Mr. George Aughinbaugh that he went red and white by turns, and became incoherent in excited endeavor to say a number of different things at one and the same time; so that Mr. John Wesley Pringle was moved to break off in his reading, to push Mr. Aughinbaugh into a chair, and to administer first aid to the distracted from a leather-covered bottle.

"Take a sip o' this. One swallow will make you simmer," he said earnestly. "Old Doctor Pringle's Priceless Prescription, a sovereign remedy for rattlesnake bites, burns, boils, sprains and bruises, fits, freckles and housemaid's sore knee; excellent for chilblains, sunburn, congestion of the currency, inflammation of the ego, corns, verbosity, insomnia, sleeplessness, lying awake and bad dreams, punctuality, fracture of the Decalogue, forgetfulness, painful memory, congenital pip, the pangs of requited affection, mange, vivacity, rush of words to the head, old age and lockjaw.

"I know that Jeff is in one big difficulty, and I see that you understand what his letter means, which is more than I do. Speak up! Say, state and declare what lies heavy on your mind. Tell us about it. If you can't talk make signs."

Neither this speech nor the restorative served wholly to dispel Aughinbaugh's bewilderment. He looked at Mr. Pringle in foggy confusion, holding fast to the panacea, as if that were the one point on which he was quite clear. Seeing which, Mr. Pringle, somewhat exasperated, renewed his eulogy with increased energy and eloquence. "It is also much used in cases of total depravity, contributory negligence, propinquities, clergyman's sore throat, equilateral strangulation and collar galls, veracity, pessimism, Scylla and Charybdis, stuttering, processions of equine oxen and similar phenomena, insubordination, altitude, consanguinity, chalcedony, irritation of the Ephemeridae, symmetry, vocalization, mammalia, clairvoyance, inertia, acrimony, persecution, paresis, paraphernalia, perspective, perspiration, tyranny, architecture and entire absence of mind — take another dose!" He cast an appealing glance around. "I can't get at what Jeff's trying to say," declared Mr. Pringle with some asperity, "but if I could, I'm damned if I couldn't tell it! Speak up! Play it out on the typewriter."

Acting upon this hit, Aughinbaugh turned to the typewriter and clattered furiously on the keys. He took off two sheets and spread them on the table, face to face, so that one sheet covered all of the other but the first two lines. "There!" he said, pointing. Beebe read aloud:

"'Now is the time for all good men and true to come to the aid of the party.
A quick move by the enemy will jeopardize six fine gunboats.'"

"He spoke twice — once in each letter," said George Aughinbaugh, "of learning to use the typewriter. He gave a speed sentence that he had made up, containing the entire alphabet. These are similar sentences, used by nearly every one who learns to typewrite. Jeff was familiar with them. He practised the first one by the hour. I gave him the second one the last night he was here. He is calling on us to come to his help; he is warning us to be careful, that one unconsidered move on our part, 'a quick move,' will be dangerous to him. Taken in connection with the other allusions in his letter, and to things that I know outside of his letter, it probably means that such a quick move might be fatal to him. He is imprisoned — not legally; secretly — and in great danger. Of course, parts of his letter are only padding to introduce and join plausibly the vital allusions so that his captors would allow the letter to go. The allusions are not consecutive. When he speaks of — "

"Hold on, old man; you're getting all balled up again," said Pringle. "Suppose, first of all, you tell us, as clearly as you can, exactly what you understand him to mean, just as if he had written it to you direct, without any parables. Then you can explain to us how you got at it, afterwards."

George walked the room, rearranged his thoughts and, in the process, mastered his agitation.

Finally he faced the three friends and said: "He is in prison in Juárez, the victim of a conspiracy. He is in utmost danger; he is closely guarded; the persons involved have such powerful reasons for holding him that they would kill him rather than allow him to be rescued. What we do must be done with the greatest caution; his guards must not have the slightest suspicion that a rescue is attempted, or planned, or possible, till it is carried out. In addition to this he tells us that we are to communicate with him by means of the personal columns of the El Paso papers — "

"I got that," said Pringle, "but that is about all I did get. Of course, we all figured it out that we were to come to you for instructions, and that there was something about a typewriter we wanted to look into. That was plain enough. There, I'm talking with my mouth. Go on!"

"And, in his great danger and distress, he sends you — to Mr. Pringle first, and then to all of you — a last and tenderest farewell, and the strong assurance of his faith that you will do for him all that men can do."

"Good God!" exclaimed Leo. "And was there no hint of who it was that had done this?"

"There was!" said Aughinbaugh, with sparkling eyes. "It was two

well-known, wealthy and influential El Paso men — the Honorable
S. S. Thorpe and Sam Patterson."

"Show me!" said Pringle — "though I begin to see."

"Half the letter is taken up by comment on the play of Julius
Caesar, which he and I had been reading together," said George. "He
tells us plainly, over and over, in different words, to look in it for
meanings beneath the surface. You remember that?"

"Yes," said Billy.

"Well, the play hinges upon the conspiracy of Brutus and Cassius
— a conspiracy carried out on the Ides of March. Look!" He moved
the paper to expose another line:

Remember March, the Ides of March remember!

"Not till then did I remember that the sixteenth of March, the day
on which Jeff disappeared, was — not indeed the Ides of March, the
fifteenth, but devilish close to it, close enough. So what he says is:
'George, remember — think carefully — remember exactly what took
place the day you saw me last.'

"He left my rooms just before midnight. And at midnight exactly,
as sworn to by many people, at a spot about a mile from here — at a
spot which Jeff might have reached at just that time — something
happened: a street fight in which two men were killed, and the survivor, Captain Charles Tillotson, was wounded. Have you, by any
chance, read the evidence in the Tillotson case?"

"Every word of it," said Billy. "We read the full account of the
trial at Escondido yesterday, while we were waiting for the train."

"Good! Good! That simplified matters. Think closely — keep in
your minds the evidence given at the trial — while I follow Jeff up
after he left my door. He must have gone somewhere, you know —
and he said he was going home. He usually took the car, but I have
already told you that he didn't that night.

"Now, my rooms are two blocks north of the streetcar line; Jeff's
were three blocks south, and a long way up toward town. The corner of Colorado and Franklin, where the fight took place, was on one
of the several routes he might have taken. And, if he had chosen that
particular way, he would have reached the scene of the shooting precisely in time to get mixed up in it. I ought, by all means, to have
thought of that before, but I didn't — till my wits were sharpened
trying to make out Jeff's letter.

"Tillotson, you remember, claims that Krouse shot him without
cause or warning; that he, himself, only fired in self-defense; that a

fourth man killed Broderick — a fourth man who mysteriously disappeared, as Jeff did.

"Thorpe and Patterson, on the contrary, swore that Tillotson made the attack, not upon Krouse but upon Broderick. Few have ever doubted that evidence, because it was not likely that a man of Broderick's known and deadly quickness could be shot twice without firing a shot himself, except by a man who took him by surprise.

"But, if Tillotson tells the truth, Thorpe and Patterson lied; and there is a conspiracy for you. And if Tillotson tells the truth, a fourth man did kill Broderick — who more likely than Jeff Bransford, who disappeared, due at that time and place?"

"You mean, possibly due at that time and place," interrupted Billy. "And how do you account for Jeff's taking Broderick at a disadvantage? It seems to me you are giving him a poor character."

"Possibly due at that time and place," corrected Aughinbaugh, "but certainly disappeared — like Tillotson's fourth man. As to taking Broderick unawares — wait till you hear Jeff's story. I can suggest one solution, however — which holds only if there was a conspiracy to murder Tillotson, which, failing, took the turn of hanging him instead. Assassins in ambush are not entitled to the usual courtesies. If Jeff happened along and observed an ambuscade, he would be likely to waive ceremony."

"But Thorpe and Patterson have good characters, haven't they?" asked Pringle.

"Good reputations," said George tartly. "Though it is whispered that Thorpe, as a young man, was habitually careless with firearms. But Tillotson also bore an excellent reputation, minus the whispering. It is at least half as probable that two men of good repute should turn perjurers overnight, as that one should. Broderick had a very bad reputation and Krouse had no reputation at all. In fact, that is the only reason a few cling to their belief in Tillotson's innocence. No motive or reason of any kind is assigned for Tillotson's unprovoked attack upon Krouse, as alleged. But the enmity of Thorpe and Tillotson was of common knowledge. It is also rumored that both had been paying marked attention to the same lady. Here are two possible motives for a conspiracy: hatred and jealousy. Of the two dead men, Broderick was a led captain, a bravo, a proven tool for any man who had a handle to him; the other man was unknown."

"The cab driver told the same story," said Pringle. "Was he an enemy of Tillotson?"

"He did," agreed George. "He also ran away. When he came back, the next day, he accounted for himself by saying that he was scared.

That sounds queer to me. Timid people may drive cabs, but timid people do not drive cabs in El Paso. The life is too hilarious. But, if he wasn't scared, why did he run away? But again, Jeff Bransford wouldn't get scared — "

"You're all wrong there," said Pringle. "Me — I've been scared stiff, lots of times. And anyhow — how could any fourth man get away? The neighborhood turned out at once — and they didn't see him."

"Jeff Bransford wouldn't be scared enough to run away, nor you either," amended George. "If you did that, you wouldn't want anybody to believe you under oath. Come back now. How did the fourth man get away, if he was Jeff Bransford and wouldn't run away, no matter what he had done? To figure it out, suppose you knew it was Jeff, but didn't know how he got away — you see? He went into that cab! If the driver was really so timid, why did he come back to mix in the trouble of a murder trial? To help hang Tillotson. And his evidence was needed because Thorpe and Patterson were known foes to Tillotson — while he was not.

"If they lied, if the whole thing was a put-up job, if they carried Jeff off in the cab, probably wounded — "

"It strikes me," said Leo, "that there are a fatal number of 'ifs' and 'buts' in your theory. Given a series of four even chances, each of which you are to win, and each of which, to count for you, is contingent upon your winning each of the other three, and your chances are not one in eight but one in two hundred and fifty-six."

"This is not a game of dice, Mr. Ballinger," retorted Aughinbaugh. "This letter is not the result of chance, but purposed and planned by an unusual man — who had ten days in which to study it out. I have only touched on a few of his significant allusions and stopped to put forward the complete theory based on them all. If you will be patient I will now show you how he unmistakably denounces these men."

"I'm sorry," said Billy, "but I have to acknowledge that I agree with Leo. A theory based upon too many probabilities becomes improbable for that very reason. Too many 'ifs'!"

"There is no 'if' about Jeff's disappearance," rejoined George hotly. "That we know. There is no 'if' about this letter, written in his own hand long after, written to a non-existent wife, in care of Billy Beebe; written under no conceivable conditions and for no conceivable purpose except to convey information under the very eyes of a vigilant jailer; a wanton and senseless folly, that could serve no purpose but to stir us to cruel and useless alarm, if it does not carry to us this information. When two hundred and fifty-six grossly improbable things point each to a common center, the grossness of each separate improbability makes the designed pointing just so much more convincing. You won't let me go on. By Heavens, we are discussing the laws of evidence and lower mathematics, instead of deciphering this letter!"

"Let Mr. Aughinbaugh be!" said Pringle. "Jeff said, once and again, that George would tell us what to do. We know two very significant truths, and only two: Jeff left Mr. Aughinbaugh's rooms a few minutes before midnight. He should have reached his own rooms just after midnight; he didn't. There are the contradicting events, apparently giving each other the lie; there, and not at another time. If Thorpe and his striker lied — and men do lie, even politicians — Jeff is accounted for. And it is the weakness of a lie that it is no real thing, but an appearance botched upon the very truth. When in doubt, search for the joint. The lie is compressed by hard facts into these few minutes. George is looking in the right place, George knows what to do; go on, George! That will be all from the Great Objectors."

CHAPTER X

And then he will say to himsel', The son of Duncan is in the heather and has need of me.

— Alan Breck

So George went on: "As Mr. Pringle says, the fact of Jeff's disappearance at this exact time and possible place strengthened all of the otherwise far-fetched 'ifs' twenty-fold. For that reason I stopped any translation of Jeff's letter, though I had barely begun it, to state in full my theory, or rather my hypothesis, based on the remarkable conjunction of a hinted conspiracy, the occasion and motive of a conspiracy, and what was in all likelihood the consummation of that conspiracy, with both Jeff and Tillotson as victims.

"We will now take up the consideration of the letter. See if it does not reinforce my hypothesis on every point, until, as block after block falls inevitably into place, ordered and measured, it becomes a demonstration.

"To begin with, the reference to the *French Revolution* is to the paragraph that I finished reading to him a few minutes before he left me, telling of a man secretly and falsely imprisoned in the Bastille by a *lettre de cachet*, a letter of hiding, procured by some powerful personage; a man whose one vain thought and hope and prayer was to have some word of his wife — of his dear wife. And there, I have no doubt, is where Jeff got the idea for this dear, sudden wife of his. Shall I read the paragraph for you?"

He should; and did.

"And from that paragraph — as I told Jeff in the very last words I spoke to him — Dickens got the inspiration for his novel, *A Tale of Two Cities*. What did Jeff say? In effect, that a great writer could find material for a novel from any page. *A Tale of Two Cities!* And here are the two cities, El Paso and Juárez, side by side — as closely associated as Sodom and Gomorrah, of which, indeed, they remind me at times. Could he, under the circumstances, say any plainer: 'I am in Juárez, in a strong and secret prison'?"

"That seems likely enough," admitted Leo grudgingly.

"It is plain," said Billy. "It is there; it must mean something; it means that."

"Keep that in mind, then, and consider all the other hints in the light of that admitted message. Weigh them and their probable meaning in connection with this plain warning.

"He speaks of Antony's great oration. He actually quotes two words of it: 'Honorable men!' Therefore, it was important; he wished to put unusual emphasis on it. Three other important things were called to our attention by being mentioned twice: one vital point, which I will take up later — in fact, the last of all — was distinctly referred to no less than four times. But this is the only direct quotation in the letter.

"Yet of all the words in the play, these two are precisely the two that least need quoting to bring them to remembrance. No one who has read Antony's speech will ever forget them. Jeff had no need to reiterate here; Antony has done it for him. They were the very heart and blood of it; the master of magic freighted those two words, in their successive differing expression, with praise, uncertainty, doubt, suspicion, invective, certainty, hate, fury, denunciation and revenge. 'Honorable men!' and Thorpe, too, is an honorable man! The Honorable S. S. Thorpe! Is that chance?

"More yet! Jeff went out of the way to drag in the wholly superfluous statement that Antony said some things after that which would bear reading. As a literary criticism that is beneath contempt. The words of Antony, as reported by William Shakespeare, would be all that without the seal of his approval. But let us see! He says 'after' Caesar's funeral oration. Look at the words, Mr. Ballinger. Do you observe anything unusual?"

"I see a blot," said Leo.

"You see a blot—and you speak of it, unhesitatingly, as unusual. Why? Because Jeff was a man of scrupulous neatness, over-particular, old-maidish. If that blot had been made by accident he would have written the page over again. It was made purposely. And so anxious was he that we should not overlook it, that he has fairly sprinkled the blank half-page below his signature with blots, trusting that we would then notice and study out the other one. Let us do it. 'After' the funeral oration, he said—but wait. You look, Mr. Beebe; look closely. Do you see anything else there? Pass your finger over it."

"I see and feel where he has twice thrust the pen through the paper," said Billy, changing color. "And I begin to see, and feel, and believe."

"You mean, doubtless, that you begin to believe and tremble," said George spitefully. "Now we will find what Antony says 'after' the oration, so well worth looking into. Gentlemen, the first words Shakespeare puts into Antony's mouth after the funeral scene are these—and remember it is where the Triumvirs are proscribing senators to death, and that Thorpe was formerly a senator, if only a state senator—here Mark Antony:

These many, then, shall die; their names are prick'd.

"Pricked!" echoed George triumphantly. "He has denounced them—two of them—the two we know! Thorpe and Patterson. But perhaps that is a gross improbability—a mere coincidence. If anything is lacking to make the denunciation complete, terrible and compelling, it is now supplied. The next words Antony speaks—"

"Wait a minute," said Pringle, eyeing Beebe. "Let's see if Billy can carry on your argument. Can you, Billy?"

Billy put a shaky finger on the blot. His voice was hoarse with passion.

He shall not live; look, with a spot I damn him!

"He shall not live," repeated Pringle, "this honorable senator—not if I have to strangle him with my bare hands!"

"I—I suppose you are right," gasped Leo, aghast. "But, suffering saints, he must think we are remarkable men to study out anything so obscure as all that. Why, there isn't one chance in a million for it!"

"Well—so we all are, just that kind of men," said George modestly, "even if some of us are chiefly remarkable for incredulity and—firmness. Obscure? Why, dear man, it had to be obscure! If it hadn't been obscure it would never have been allowed to reach us — I mean, of course, to reach Mrs. Bransford. And yet, in a way, it was neither so obscure nor so remarkable. In the first place, this is not a case of solving puzzles, with a nickel-plated Barlow knife for a prize, or a book for good little girls. This letter means something; it is the urgent call of a friend in need; we are friends indeed, grown-up men, and it is our business to find out what it means. We have to find out; a man's life is the prize — and more than that, as it turns out. He sent you to me as interpreter, not because he wanted Mr. Pringle to take orders from me, but for the one only reason that it was not obscure to me, and that he knew it would not be obscure to me. Do you notice that I did not have to turn to the play to verify the quotations? It is fresh in my mind and in his: we read it aloud together, we spouted it at each other, we used phrases of it instead of words to carry on ordinary conversation. Mr. Beebe here, when once he was on the right track, could supply the words for the most difficult of all the allusions, though he had probably not read the book for years."

"I ain't never read this Mr. Shakespeare much, myself," said Pringle meditatively. "But oncet — 'twas the first time I was ever in love — I read all that stuff of Tennyson's about King Arthur's 'Ten Knights in a Bar Room,' and I want to tell you that I couldn't even think of anything else for a month. So it seems mighty natural that Jeff, with his head full of this Shakespeare party, would try that particular way of getting word to us, and no other. You spoke of a message for me, Mr. Aughinbaugh?"

"I did. Of a message sent in the knowledge that for all your daring, for all your devotedness, you may not be able to avert the threatened danger. In his desperate pass he sends to you, as if he spoke with you face to face for the last time, the words of Brutus to his friend:

> *Therefore, our everlasting farewell take:*
> *Forever, and forever, farewell, Cassius!*
> *If we do meet again, why, we shall smile;*
> *If not, why then, this parting was well*
> *made.*

Silence fell upon them. Pringle went to the window and stood looking out at the night; the clock ticked loudly. Aughinbaugh, keeping his eyes on the blurred typewritten lines, went on:

"And the other message, of hope, and confidence, and trust, is this:

> *My heart doth joy that yet, in all my life,*
> *I found no man but he was true to me.*

"All of which adds force to his injunction that when the society of good men and true come to his aid, they shall be careful to make no move so quick as to jeopardize Jeff. Q.E.D."

"Since the majority is plainly against me, and also since I am convinced myself, I'll give up," said Ballinger. "And the next thing plainly is, what are we going to do — or who are we going to do?"

CHAPTER XI

I will advertise thee what this people shall do.

— *Balaam*

"Jeff tells us that too," said George. "In both letters he speaks of the El Paso papers. In the letter to 'the kids' he says that he read every line of one of them. Knowing what we do, it is easy to see that they are brought in to him and that he expects us to communicate with him by means of personals worded for his eye alone. He is looking for them now. As he is so certain of seeing personals, it seems sure that the papers are brought in regularly to him. You know he said his Chief had all the El Paso papers sent on. And since they allow him this indulgence, it is probable and consistent that they do not otherwise ill-treat him. I suppose they are trying to extort a promise of silence from him under threat of death. But what I don't see is why they didn't kill him right away."

"I understand that well enough," said Pringle. "Jeff has talked 'em out of it! And did he give any hint about what to do?"

"That is the thing I put off till the last," George responded. "It is the most ambiguous of all the allusions. When he twice spoke of Cassius as 'Yond Cassius,' when he mentioned Caesar's superstitions, and afterward said that some of his hunches were pretty good at that, he might have been referring me to either 'Yond Cassius has a lean and hungry look' or to the line immediately above: 'Let me have men about me that are fat.' I am reasonably sure that he meant the last. Because he knew that we would get this far — to the big question of what we were going to do about it. We are clear as to Thorpe's guilt; but that isn't going to help Jeff — or Tillotson.

"Under the circumstances it would have been imprudent for him to give his street and number; they might not have liked it — "

"By Jove!" said Leo, "don't you see? He tells us, in so many words: 'That's all I know.' He didn't know just where he was. It wasn't likely that he would know."

"So he does! I hadn't seen through that at all," said George. "Thank you. That makes it almost a certainty that he meant 'the men about him,' his jailers, were fat. We have to find his jail, and our best chance is to find his jailers. To tell us to look for 'lean and hungry' men in this country of hard-riding, thin, slim, slender, lean, lank, scrawny men, would serve no purpose. But fat men are scarce enough to be noticeable. Besides, Patterson is a mere mountain of flesh; Thorpe himself is not actually fat, but is dangerously near it. He laid so much stress on this, coming back to it four times, that he must have meant it for a big, plain signpost for our guidance. That settles it. He has men about him that are fat. And we'd better look for them. Mr. Pringle, will you take the lines?"

"The head of the table is wherever Wes' sits down, anyway," remarked Beebe loyally.

"It is moved and seconded that Mr. John Wesley Pringle be elected — er — Sole Electee of the•Most Ancient Society of Good Men and True," said Leo. "All in favor will rise or remain seated. Contrary-minded are not members and will kindly leave the room. It is unanimously carried and so ordered. Gentlemen, Mr. Pringle!"

"The Society will come to order," said the Sole Electee severely. "Some good man and true will please state the object of the permanent session and, also, how and why and what he proposes to do first."

"Hadn't we better get some detectives to work," ventured Billy, "and join forces with Tillotson's lawyers?"

"No detectives," said Pringle hastily and decidedly. And "No lawyers," echoed George with equal decision, adding: "Please excuse Mr. Pringle and myself from giving the reasons for our respective vetoes. But they are good ones."

"Then we are to depend on our own resources alone?" demanded Leo.

"Exactly. That's the way the farmer in the second reader got in his wheat. Let us by all means have Fools for Clients and Every Man His Own Detective; that's what makes the guilty quail," said Pringle darkly. "If we four can't do the trick for love, no man can do it for hire. And there will be no defalcation or failure for fear, favor or funds or through any fatal half-heartedness. We four friends for our friend unconditionally, without regard for law or the profits, man or devil, death, debt, disgrace or damnation! To the last ditch — and then some!"

Pringle reflected a little. "Gentlemen," he said, "we will put our little ad. in the papers tonight, at once, *muy pronto* and *immediata-*

mente. After which I should think a good sleep would be the one first wise move. We will then sally forth, or Sarah forth, in pursuit of knowledge in general, both in El Paso and in Juárez — vulgarly called Whereas — and, more especially, knowledge of Messrs. Thorpe and Patterson and all fat men with whom they do consort. To avoid giving any slightest ground for suspicion — which must be avoided at all hazards — I will disguise myself as a bald-headed, elderly cattleman from Rainbow. Mr. Aughinbaugh — "

"Mister? George, you mean," said that person.

"George, then. George, you will masquerade as a lawyer's clerk. Billy, you'd better buy a haircut and canvas leggings and get yourself up as a reformed Easterner in the act of backsliding. And you, Leo" — he paused and regarded Ballinger doubtfully — "You," he said, and stopped again, with a puzzled frown. The unhappy victim writhed and twisted, thus held up to public scorn and derision as neither fish, flesh, nor herring.

"I have it," said the poor nondescript with a brave attempt at a smile. "I'll buy some clothes, some booze and a stack of blues — and pass myself off for a Remittance Man."

Pringle heaved a sigh of relief. "I hated to name it to you," he said. "Say, when Jeff first rescued you, exhumed you, resuscitated you, or whatever it was, he told me a little quotation the first time you went out and left us. His explanation went some like this:

" *'I traced my son through a street of broken windows, and found him dead of old age at five-and-twenty.'*

"So, my boy, it's back to the husks and the hogs for yours. You are assigned to cover the Street of Broken Windows. And that's a pretty big order — in El Paso."

The next morning Jeff found what he had been looking for these many days. In both the *Times* and the *Herald* was an inconspicuous personal in the modest retirement of the advertising section, of obscure wording and small type:

Now is the time for all good men and true to get a cautious move on the trail sit tight coming up.

It was the twenty-fourth day of his imprisonment.

CHAPTER XII

No, no! the adventures first: explanations take such a dreadful time.
— *The Gryphon*

BILLY TOOK UP his quarters at the leading hotel and permeated both El Paso and Juárez with much abandon. He wired Cleveland, Ohio, for funds, and Cleveland responded generously, sending him, without delay or demur, a noble wad for the emergency.

George frequented the real-estate section on legitimate, if trivial, pretexts connected with Hibler's business; demanding vacation from that legal luminary on his arrival. Pringle waxed talkative with visiting and resident cowmen, among whom exists a curious freemasonry, informal but highly effective.

Moreover, Pringle disregarded his own explicit instructions. Such cowmen as he knew well — and trusted — began to infest Juárez. Their mere orders — for he gave them no reasons — were to watch either Thorpe or Patterson if they visited the Mexican city; also any obnoxiously fat men with whom they should hold conference; and to report progress.

The four friends between them watched Thorpe in all his doings, dogged his footsteps by night and by day — passed him from one to the other like the button in the game — with such vigilance that at the end of the week they had discovered no single thing to their help.

Thorpe loitered through life in sybaritic fashion; rose late, fared sumptuously; gave a little time to the real-estate office in which he was investing partner; more to political conferences. In the afternoons he rode or motored; sometimes he dropped in to the Fire Company's bowling alley instead, combating a certain tendency to corpulence.

For the rest there was dinner at his club; bridge with a select coterie, or perhaps the theater; occasionally, a social function. And the day usually ended with a visit to the big Turkish Baths on Franklin Street, another precaution against fatness. Nothing could be more open and aboveboard than this respectable gentleman's walk and auto.

Patterson's doings were much the same, save that he shunned the little entertainments where the Judge shone with a warm and mellow splendor, and ventured often into that quarter of the town that was Leo's particular care, breaking rather more than his full quota of windows. He made also a brief trip to Silver City, on which occasion Pringle again violated his own orders by sending red-headed Joe Cowan, cowboy, of Organ, as an observer for the G.M.A.T. — to no benefit to the society.

Patterson had gone to look over a mining proposition for a client.

This unavailing search had one curious and unexpected result. Noticing many people closely, perforce, they observed that a surprising number of these had done those things that they really ought not to have done. Also, they kept on doing them; confident that no man saw them; so cunning were they. So that Ballinger gloomily avowed his intention of turning blackmailer, rather than again to appeal to what he was pleased to term the "unremitting kindness" of his family.

Only one thing had occurred so far which the most besotted optimist could interpret as even a possible confirmation of their suspicions.

One night, the fourth of their surveillance, Judge Thorpe took a late streetcar for Juárez, foregoing the baths. When he alighted from it, at Calle San Rafael, John Wesley Pringle also left the car on the farther side and walked smartly away.

Thorpe having turned eastward, Pringle came back and trailed along far behind. He dared not follow closely; if Thorpe's suspicions should be aroused it would go hard with Jeff. He preferred to risk losing his man rather than to risk the consequences of an alarm.

And lose him he did. The Judge turned to the left at Terrazas Street. Pringle was just a little too far behind. He made haste to come up, but when he reached the corner the Judge was out of sight; nor could he catch the trail again. And the Judge returned to El Paso without being seen again.

Of the other labors of the four friends during this weary time; of myriad casual questions that came to naught; of unnumbered fat men traced, unsuspecting, to their blameless homes; of hope deferred, disappointments, fastings, vain vigils, and all their acts — behold! are they not written in the book of Lost Endeavor?

. . . .

Meanwhile Jeff read many books, he practised his typewriting, he baited Mac mercilessly, he experimented with new dishes procured by that trusty henchman; and day by day he noted in the papers little personals: "Understand situation perfectly that quick move will jeopardize"; "Making haste slowly to come to aid of party, whereabouts unknown sit steady"; and others, variously worded to report no progress, to extol the difficult virtue of patience and to recommend its practice — always with a fragment from one of the catchword sentences for an identification tag. One of them gave no news at all. It read: "Pack my box with five dozen liquor jugs. Practise that for quick movement. Lots of time."

But as John Wesley sagely remarked, "The end doesn't come till along towards the last."

CHAPTER XIII

You've been listening at doors — and behind trees — and down chimneys — or you couldn't have known it!

— *Humpty-Dumpty*

At last, on a happy day, there came to the Judge's office, demanding and receiving brief audience, a fat man with an indictable face; a man disreputable, vast and unkempt, with a sloven's shoebrush for beard. Him, so propitiously ill-favored, Aughinbaugh dogged to Leo's satrapy. There Leo took cognizance of him and, after a window-breaking progress, accompanied him to Juárez.

Mindful of Pringle's adventure and mishap with the Judge he took a long chance. Reasoning that, if their theories held good, this man would take the same route the Judge did, Leo left the car at the first street before San Rafael and followed it eastward till he came to Calle Terrazas. After heartbreaking delay he had the satisfaction of seeing his man turn the corner above and come lurching on his way. Apparently the delay had not been totally unconnected with the wineshops en route.

Leo took refuge in a curio store, buying things he did not in the least want. Emerging with his compulsory parcels, he followed in the wake of the unwieldy leviathan to the International Hotel. Leo entered shortly after him, ordered supper, and went into eclipse behind a paper. The big man took another at the bar, called for his key and stumbled upstairs.

Supper over, Leo loafed aimlessly; and so became involved in many games of pool with a person in a voluble plaid vest — who beat him shamefully. After this hanger-on had been encouraged a few times, a careless mention of the big man 'on the bat' elicited the information that the big man's name was Borrowman, that he was off his schedule by reason of his hilarity, since he usually did night work — running a stationary engine, the pool shark thought, or something like that — that he was a sulky swine and several other things.

Ballinger lost enough games and departed to 'phone Aughinbaugh.

Not getting him, he next sent urgent summons to Billy Beebe's hotel, the whereabouts of John Wesley being problematical in the extreme. Mr. Beebe was not in; but the clerk would deliver any message when he came. So Leo made an appointment, naming a hostelry in the block adjacent to the International, whither he repaired, engaged a room and kept sharp watch till Billy came.

After consultation, Billy registered at the International. Borrowman had not seen him before, whereas he might easily remember Ballinger's face and become suspicious. This was no ordinary chase: an alarm meant, in this case, not a mere temporary setback, but irremediable disaster. Leo went to El Paso, left an ad. with the papers, the purport of the same being that the search was "getting warm for enemy of good men and true," and then hunted up Pringle and Aughinbaugh. They returned to Juárez and there separated, to a loitering patrol of the streets east, south and north of the International House.

Billy passed a tedious evening in the office and barroom of the International. At midnight Borrowman had not shown up as expected; it began to look as though his work had gone by the board for that night. But he came down shortly before one, little the worse for his liquor, and set forth at once.

When Borrowman came out he turned east at the first corner. A little in front of him was a slim and sauntering youth — Aughinbaugh by name — who presently quickened his pace and drew ahead, keeping straight on. Far behind, Beebe brought up the rear, and on the next streets, paralleling the quarry's course, came Pringle on the north and Ballinger on the south, with varying gaits; one or the other waiting at each corner till the chase had crossed between them.

So pursuit drew on for blocks. Aughinbaugh was far ahead, when, near the town's edge, Borrowman turned to the left again, northward to the river. The chase wheeled with him — Pringle, a block to the north, crossed the street openly and walked briskly ahead; Billy turned riverward on the street west of him; Aughinbaugh brought up the east side, and Ballinger fell in behind.

There was no more doubling. Pringle, in front, saw the river close ahead. The end must be near; he turned east into a side street and disappeared. Borrowman kept straight on; Ballinger, hidden in a doorway, close behind, saw him enter an adobe house on the river bank. It was a dark and shuttered house; no light appeared from within, but smoke was rising from the chimney.

Ballinger turned back, rounded the block and so foregathered with Aughinbaugh and Pringle. After a long wait Beebe joined them, guided at the last by sundry guarded whistlings; slowly, stealthily, tiptoe, they glided through the rustling shadows to reconnoiter.

The old adobe was flat-roofed and one-storied, as usual. They found chinks in the shuttered windows. No fire was to be seen; the smoke came from an underground room; the hunt was over.

Billy plucked Pringle by the sleeve and bent over, clasping Leo in a fond embrace. After wordless investigation of this human stairway, by sense of touch, Pringle stepped from Billy's back to Ballinger's broad shoulders, and so wriggled to the roof with noiseless caution.

After an hour-long infinity he reappeared, bulked black and startling against the starlight; descended, led his little flock to the safety of the open *playa* by the river bank and made exultant oration:

"Jeff's there! Having the time of his life! Chimney goes straight down; I could hear every word they said. They're a clever gang of all-round crooks, counterfeiters, smugglers and what-not. Thorpe is the brains. They have a stand-in with some of the police and officials. This cellar was used as a warehouse for storing Chinamen, to be smuggled across in boatload lots. The other man on guard is fat, as we expected, and better looking than Borrowman. He was hopping mad at Borrowman for getting full and leaving him on guard overtime; threatened him with discipline, gave him a tongue-lashing — Jeff egging him on, enjoying himself very much and urging Borrowman not to stand such abuse. He wouldn't trust Jeff to Borrowman till he was comparatively sober; cussed him again and made him turn in to sleep it off. So of course they'll both be here all night."

"Why, how can you tell that this other man is better looking than Borrowman?" asked George, puzzled. "You couldn't possibly see him."

"Suppose I didn't — I've seen Borrowman, haven't I?" retorted Pringle triumphantly.

"What else did you gather?" asked Billy.

"Well, not much except that we had it all figured out about right. They kept him there at first to make him join 'em. He wouldn't, and what they are keeping him for instead of wiping him out I don't just see. I'd sure hate to have to keep him. And now, boys, us for El Paso, U.S.A. No more to be done here tonight."

"How are we going to get him out without getting him slightly killed?" demanded George. "I can sit down in an office and study things out, all right — I learned deduction from observing Hibler's methods of settling up estates. But when it comes to violent action I don't know which foot goes first."

"Easiest thing there is," said Pringle. "We'll put him wise by a personal. Tomorrow we'll keep out of sight for a day to give him time to see it. We'll get a hook, a line and a gun, wait till only one man is with Jeff, till Jeff is standing by the fire, and till he gives us the signal we mention in our little ad. Then we let the gun down the chimney to him and he'll do the rest. Why, it's the only way! There ain't no other way, and couldn't be. Two days more and the jig is strictly up. Let's go home and sleep those two days."

CHAPTER XIV

It's a long worm that has no turning.
— J. W. PRINGLE

THE TRACKING of Borrowman had ended on Wednesday in the wee sma' hours. On Friday Jeff found this communication in his morning paper:

Run to earth hear everything by hot air now is the time for party to aid himself tonight at nine sharp be at fire signal when ready by cowboy's lament hold fast all six fine friends I give you.

Jeff was pleased. Yet this was the hardest day of his captivity. He made things very unpleasant for Borrowman, who was on guard, his drunk having disarranged the previous schedule. The day dragged slowly on. Mac came at seven and Borrowman left as soon as supper was cooked.

Jeff had let the fire run low. He stood with his back to it, carrying on an earnest conversation with Mac, who sat on the bed.

"What time is it, Mac?"

"Eight-feefty."

"Most bedtime," said Jeff, yawning. "Can't you manage to stick it out till this time tomorrow night?" he demanded querulously. "That'll put it back the way it was, so Borrowman'll be on while I'm asleep. That filthy brute isn't fit for a gentleman to associate with. Besides, he'll be letting me get away."

"He's all that and worse," said Mac, grinning toothsomely, "but he'll na let ye get away. Man, I jalouse he fair aches to kill ye. Ye treat him with much disrespect. Ye'll na get away from him or me, neither. We'll hold you here till crack o' doom, if need be."

"Oh, yes, I'll escape sooner or later, of course," said Jeff pleasantly. "And that reminds me — I'll be wanting a hat before long. I wish

you'd get me a good one. You didn't fetch mine here, you know. I
suppose the barrel of Broderick's gun cut it. Certainly it did. How
else could it have cut my head open so? Get a J. B., 7⅛, four-inch
brim, pearl gray. It'll supply a long-wanted felt."

"Ye'll need no hat. Man, ye vex me wi' your frantic journeys. Ye
canna escape. It is na possible. If ye do, ye may e'en take my hat,
for I'll no be needin' it mair."

"Oh, well, I'll not argue with you. It just ruffles you up, without
convincing you of your error," said Jeff. "But you're wrong." He
turned his face to the fire and lightly hummed the first line of the
Cowboy's Lament:

"As I rode down to Latern in Barin — "

Immediately the long, blue barrel of a .45 nosed inquiringly down
the chimney. Jeff disengaged the gun from the hook and slipped it
under his coat. He jerked the line slightly: it was drawn up. Jeff
left the fire and sat down, facing Mac across the table.

"Mac what?" he demanded. "We've spent a good many pleasant
days together, but I don't know your name till this very yet. Mac
what?"

"It is no new thing for men of my blood to be nameless," said
Mac composedly. His voice took on a tone of pride; his bearing was
not without a certain dignity. "For generations we were a race pro-
scribit, outlawed, homeless and nameless. The curse of yon wild
man Ishmael was ours, and the portion of unblessed Esau — to live
by the sword alone, wi' the dews of heaven for dwellingplace. Who
hasna heard of the Gregara?"

"Oh! So you're a MacGregor? Well, Mr. MacGregor, it is likewise said in that same book that they who take up the sword shall
perish by the sword," said Jeff, holding the gun handle beneath the
table. "It seems almost a pity that an exception should be made in
your case. For you have your points; I'll not deny it. Of course,
you richly deserve to be hung on the same scaffold with Thorpe.
But you are so much the more wholesome scoundrel of the two, so
straightforward and thoroughgoing in your villainy, that I must admit
that I shall feel a certain regret at seeing you make such an unsatisfactory end. Besides, you don't deserve it from me. If Thorpe had
listened to you I would never have escaped to hang you both."

"Let me tell you then," said MacGregor with spirit, "that I could
hang in no better company. And I shall na stumble on the gallow-
steps. Dinna trouble yourself. If I could hang for him it would be
na mair than he has deservit at my hands. He has been staunch wi'

me. Wi' wealth and name to lose, he broke me out of San Saba prison wi' his own hands, where else I had been rotting now. But we talk foolishness." He tamped tobacco into his pipe, struck a match and held it over the bowl.

"I assure you that I do not," said Jeff earnestly. "But I'll change the subject. Did you know there was a much shorter sentence with all the letters in it than we've been using? There is. 'Pack my box with five dozen liquor jugs.' It reached me by R.F.D. So did this!"

He rose; the long barrel leaped to level with sinister exultance. "Hold your hands there, Mr. MacGregor — it'll warm your fingers."

The MacGregor held his fingers there, eyeing the unwavering blue barrel steadily. He kept his pipe going. Bransford could not withhold his admiration for such surly, indomitable courage. Making a wary circuit to the rear of the defeated warrior, and keeping him covered, he gingerly reached forth to take the MacGregor gun. "Now you can take 'em down. Come on, boys — all clear!" he said, raising his voice.

Sound of running feet from above; the outer door smashed open. Mac flung his hat over to Jeff and sat glowering in wordless rage. Footsteps hurried down the stairs and the passageway. An ax hewed at the door. It crashed in; Pringle, gun in hand, burst through the splintered woodwork; the others pressed behind. John Wesley leaned upon his ax, fumbled at his coat pocket, and extended the famous leather bottle:

"Well, Brutus, old pal, we meet again! Shall we smile?"

CHAPTER XV

If the rascal have not given me medicines to make me love him, I'll be hanged.

— Falstaff

At the envoy's end, I touch!

— Cyrano

"Now, WE MUST GET TO WORK," said Jeff, after hurried mutual explanations. "The natural impulse is to throw the customs house into the river, link arms and walk up Main Street, five abreast, pushing the policemen off the curb, raising our feet high and bringing them down ker-smack — hay-foot, straw-foot, right foot, left: now is the time for all good men — and the rest of it. But, perhaps, it wouldn't be wise. We've got to catch Thorpe off his guard — and that may be hard to do — "

Wes' pulled him down and whispered in his ear. Jeff's face became radiant.

"And after we have him safe we'll get the others. Let's go down to the bank and steal a boat. Boys, this is Mr. MacGregor. We'll take him with us. Mac, you'd better tie a handkerchief around your head. You'll take cold."

"Ye canna take a man from Mexico without extradeetion papers. It's fair keednappin'," said Mac with a leer.

"So we can't, so we can't," said Jeff pleasantly. "Not live men. Go first. If you don't come quietly — "

"Dinna tell me," said the MacGregor scornfully. "Would I no have done as much for you? But let me tell you one thing — and that is that ye are showing small thanks to Thorpe for sparing your life."

"Heck! I didn't ask him for my life and I owe him no gratitude," said Jeff. "It was a square contract. I was to hang him if I could escape — and I had practically escaped when he agreed to it, except for the mere detail of time. I am doing nothing unfair. Go on!"

"You're right, 'twas a contract — I'll say nae mair," admitted Mac grudgingly, and went up the stair.

Once on the street, however, he paused. "Mr. Bransford, there have been kindly passages atween us. Let me have a word more."

"Well?" said Jeff.

The outlaw sat him down on a crumbling wall. "I value your good opeenion, Mr. Bransford, and I would not have ye judge that fear held me from fightin' ye, drop or no drop. 'Twould have done no good to any one and I should certainly have been killed. Men, ye've a grand idee of strategy yourself. I wouldna hae ye think I'm daft enough to throw away my life to no good purpose. But there the case is verra diff'rent. There are no thick walls now to muffle the noise: ye canna keel me wi'oot muckle deesturbance, bringin' the police on ye. Thorpe has friends here, verra alert folk — and 'gin he gets wind o' any deesturbance at just this place — ye see!" He wagged his head in slow cunning; he drew in a long breath. "*Ho!*" he bellowed. "*Ho! Murder!*"

"Damnation!" said Jeff, and sprang at his throat. The others had his arms: they pulled him down, fighting savagely, turned him over, piled on his back, and gagged him. But it was too late. Two policemen were already running down the street. The neighbors, however, kept prudently within doors.

"Jeff, you and Pringle hike for the U.S.A.," gasped Leo. "Get

Thorpe, anyhow. I'll tap this devil dumb, and stay here and stand the gaff, to give you a start."

"Hold on! Don't do it," said Beebe. "Let me talk to the policemen. Do you tie Mr. MacGregor up."

"Talk to — why, you can't even speak Spanish!" said Pringle.

"You don't know me. Watch!" said Billy.

Without waiting for further remonstrance he went to meet the advancing officers. They halted; there was a short colloquy and, to the amazement of the three friends, they turned amicably back together and passed from sight at the next corner.

"Let me make a suggestion," said Aughinbaugh. "Lug this gentleman back to Jeff's quarters, tie him up tight, and I think I can undertake to keep him while you get your man. As soon as you have Thorpe, see Tillotson's lawyers and let them swear out warrants for the arrest of Patterson and the cab driver, and then take steps to secure Borrowman and Mr. MacGregor legally. You can have them arrested for kidnapping or illegal detention, and held here until we can get extradition papers. You might send some one — or two, or three — over right away, in case Mr. Borrowman drops in. He might eat me if he found me there alone. For myself, I am not sorry to remain in the background. I have no desire for prominence. You fellows are going back to Rainbow — and you're used to trouble anyway, so it's all very well for you. But I have to stay here and I'm a legal-minded person. This will be a hanging matter for some of 'em before they get done with it. They'll talk like the parrot. I've no desire to make a lot of enemies. There's no knowing how many leading lights may be implicated in this thing when they go to turning state's evidence."

Here he was interrupted by a kick from the gagged prisoner. It was not a vicious kick and evidently meant only to attract attention. They bent over him. He was shaking his head; in the starlight his eyes blazed denial.

"I didn't mean you," said George, respectfully and apologetically. "I'm sure you wouldn't do such a thing. But Borrowman might, and Patterson will be even more likely to betray the others to save his own neck."

The eyes expressed gloomy agreement. At Pringle's urging, Mac consented to walk back down to the underground room. That wily veteran evidently reserved his stubbornness till there was a chance to accomplish something by it. They were binding him to the bed when Billy rejoined them. "Well! Wherever did you learn Spanish, Billy?" said Pringle curiously.

"It wasn't Spanish — not exactly," said that accomplished linguist modestly. "It was a sort of Esperanto. I met them with a cocked revolver in one hand and a roll of bills in the other. They took the bills."

Jeff's sprightly spirits were somewhat dampened. "Whoever would have looked for such stubborn loyalty from this battered old rascal?" he demanded, sighing. "Even Thorpe is not altogether to be despised — or pitied. He had a friend. By Heavens, Mac! I'll take every precaution to hold fast to you — but I find it in my heart to hope you get away in spite of me." He bent over and met the dauntless eyes; he laid his fingers on Mac's hair, almost tenderly. "I'll tell him, old man," he whispered.

He turned away, but after a step or two paused and looked back with an irresolution foreign to his character. He finally came back and sat on the edge of the bed, with his back to the MacGregor. He squeezed his hands between his knees, idly clicking his heels together. His eyes were intent on a crack in the floor: he recited in a dull monotone:

> "'And often after sunset, sir,
>   When it is bright and fair,
> I take my little derringer
>   And eat my supper there!'"

The others waited by the door. John Wesley posted George with a sedate and knowing wink. George eyed these movements of Jeff's with grave disapproval.

"How often have I heard you denounce precisely such proceedings as these, as the fatal vice of Hamleting!" he jeered. "Flip up a dollar! Or are you going to favor us with a soliloquy?"

Jeff raised his eyes. "I was just trying to remember an old story," he explained innocently. "My grandfather was a Hudson Bay man, and this story was a John Company tradition when he was a boy. It's about two canny Scots. That's what put me in mind of it, Mac being a Scotchman — and in trouble.

"Their names were Kerr and McKensie. One day Kerr upset his canoe in some rapids and lost everything he had but his clothes and his sheath-knife. But at dark he happened on McKensie's camp, and stayed the night with him. McKensie had a good outfit — canoe, rifle, grub, traps, and a big bundle of furs. He had also a deserved reputation for shrewdness and thrift. And in the night they got to trading.

"When morning came McKensie had the sheath-knife and Kerr had everything else. McKensie would never explain what happened.

When asked about it he looked a little dazed. He said, with marked emphasis:

" 'Yon is a verra intelligent pairson!'

The moral is, You've got to be careful with a Scotchman."

"You get out!" said George indignantly. "Go gather the Judge. I'll 'tend to Mac."

"All right," said Jeff. "We'll go. But don't say I didn't warn you."

· · · · · · ·

Judge Thorpe was particularly well pleased with himself. After a prosperous and profitable day and a pleasant evening at his club, he bethought himself of his old relentless enemy, obesity, and made his way to the Turkish baths.

He had been boiled, baked and basted, and now lay swathed in linen on a marble slab, blissfully drowsy, waiting to be curried. He was more than half asleep when the operator came.

When the currying process began, however, the Judge noticed that the hostler seemed anything but an expert. Why had they not sent Gibbons as usual? He opened his eyes, intending remonstrance, but closed them immediately; they were playing tricks on him. A curious thing! The white-tunicked attendant, seen through the curling spirals of steam, looked startlingly like his prisoner in Juárez. The Judge's heart skipped a beat or two and then started with a fearful thumping.

The rubber plied his mitten briskly; the Judge opened his eyes again. Of course the prisoner was safe; the illusion was doubtless the effect of the perspiration on his eyelashes. The billowy vapor parted, the industrious attendant bent impersonally over him with a serene, benevolent look — Good Heavens!

The Judge's heart died horribly within him, his tongue was dry, his bones turned to water and his flesh to a quivering jelly. He cast a beseeching look to the open door. Beyond it, looking idly in, were three men in street clothes. They entered, ranging themselves silently against the wall. They looked amused. Thorpe's lips moved, but no words came.

Jeff Bransford rubbed away assiduously; there was a quizzical glint in his pleasant brown eyes. "My wife, Judge," he said cheerfully, jerking his head to introduce Beebe, "and my two boys, Wes' and Leo. Fine, well-grown boys, aren't they?" He prodded the Judge's ribs with a jocular thumb. "Say, Judge — how about that presentiment now?"

· · · · · · ·

After personally attending the Judge and Patterson to jail, the G. M. A. T. felt that the capture of minor offenders might safely be left to the government. So they routed out Tillotson's lawyers at the unseemly hour of 4 A.M., broke the news gently, and haled them off to jail for consultation with Tillotson.

Congratulation and explanation were over: the cumbrous machinery of the law was fairly under way (creakingly, despite liberal oiling), and a gorgeous breakfast for all hands was being brought into the jail from a near-by restaurant, when the jailer ushered Aughinbaugh into the presence of the friends in council.

He sauntered in with the most insouciant and complacent air imaginable. El Paso's best cigar was perked up at a jaunty angle from the corner of his mouth; it was plain he was particularly well pleased with himself.

"Hello! where's your prisoner?" said the firm in chorus.

Aughinbaugh removed the cigar and flicked the ash. "Mac? He got away," he said indifferently.

"Got away!" shrieked the senior lawyer. "Gagged, bound hand and foot, tied to the bed — and got away!"

Aughinbaugh surveyed him placidly, and waved his cigar in graceful explanation.

"Yon was a verra intelligent pairson!" said he.

THE END

Bransford
of Rainbow Range

(*The Little Eohippus*)

BRANSFORD OF RAINBOW RANGE

(The Little Eohippus)

CHAPTER I

The Pitcher That Went to the Well

When I bend my head low and listen at the ground,
I can hear vague voices that I used to know,
Stirring in dim places, faint and restless sound;
I remember how it was when the grass began to grow.
Song of The Wandering Dust
ANNA HEMPSTEAD BRANCH

THE PINES THINNED as she neared Rainbow Rim, the turfy glades grew wider; she had glimpses of open country beyond — until, at last, crossing a little spit of high ground, she came to the fairest spot in all her voyage of exploration and discovery. She sank down on a fallen log with a little sigh of delight.

The steep bank of a little cañon broke away at her feet — a cañon which here marked the frontier of the pines, its farther side overgrown with mahogany bush and chaparral — a cañon that fell in long, sinuous curves from the silent mystery of forest on Rainbow Crest behind her, to widen just below into a rolling land, parked with green-black powderpuffs of juniper and cedar; and so passed on to mystery again, twisting away through the folds of the low and bare gray hills to the westward, ere the last stupendous plunge over the Rim to the low desert, a mile toward the level of the waiting sea.

Facing the explorer, across the little cañon, a clear spring bubbled from the hillside and fell with pleasant murmur and tinkle to a pool below, fringed with lush emerald — a spring massed about with wild grapevine, shining reeds of arrow-weed; a tangle of grateful greenery, jostling eagerly for the life-giving water. Draped in clinging

vines, slim acacias struggled up through the jungle; the exquisite
fragrance of their purple bells gave a final charm to the fairy chasm.

But the larger vision! The nearer elfin beauty dwindled, was lost,
forgotten. Afar, through a narrow cleft in the gray westward hills,
the explorer's eye leaped out over a bottomless gulf to a glimpse of
shining leagues midway of the desert greatness — an ever-widening
triangle that rose against the peaceful west to long foothill reaches,
to a misty mountain parapet, far-beckoning, whispering of secrets,
things dreamed of, unseen, beyond the framed and slender arc of
vision. A land of enchantment and mystery, decked with strong barbaric colors, blue and red and yellow, brown and green and gray;
whose changing ebb and flow, by some potent sorcery of atmosphere, distance and angle, altered, daily, hourly; deepening, fading,
combining into new and fantastic lines and shapes, to melt again as
swiftly to others yet more bewildering.

The explorer? It may be mentioned in passing that any other
would have found that fairest prospect even more wonderful than
did the explorer, Miss Ellinor Hoffman. We will attempt no clear
description of Miss Ellinor Hoffman. Dusky-beautiful she was; crisp,
fresh and sparkling; tall, vigorous, active, strong. Yet she was more
than merely beautiful — warm and frank and young; brave and kind
and true. Perhaps, even more than soft curves, lips, glory of hair or
bewildering eyes, or all together, her chiefest charm was her manner,
her frank friendliness. Earth was sweet to her, sweeter for her.

This by way of aside and all to no manner of good. You have no
picture of her in your mind. Remember only that she was young —

> The stars to drink from and the sky to dance on

— young and happy, and therefore beautiful; that the sun was shining
in a cloudless sky, the south wind sweet and fresh, buds in the willow.

. . . .

The peace was rent and shivered by strange sounds, as of a giant
falling downstairs. There was a crash of breaking boughs beyond the
cañon, a glint of color, a swift black body hurtling madly through
the shrubbery. The girl shrank back. There was no time for thought,
hardly for alarm. On the farther verge the bushes parted; an appari-
tion hurtled arching through the sunshine, down the sheer hill — a
glorious and acrobatic horse, his black head low between his flashing
feet; red nostrils wide with rage and fear; foam flecks white on the
black shoulders; a tossing mane; a rider, straight and tall, superb — to
all seeming an integral part of the horse, pitch he ever so wildly.

The girl held her breath through the splintered seconds. She thrilled at the shock and storm of them, straining muscles and white hoofs, lurching, stumbling, sliding, lunging, careening in perilous arcs. She saw stones that rolled with them or bounded after; a sombrero whirled above the dust and tumult like a dilatory parachute; a six-shooter jolted up into the air. Through the dust clouds there were glimpses of a watchful face, hair blown back above it; a broken rein snapped beside it, saddle-strings streamed out behind; a supple body that swung from curve to easy curve against shock and plunge, that swayed and poised and clung, and held its desperate dominion still. The saddle slipped forward; with a motion incredibly swift, as a hat is whipped off in a gust of wind, it whisked over withers and neck and was under the furious feet. Swifter, the rider! Cat-quick, he swerved, lit on his feet, leaped aside.

Alas, oh, rider beyond compare, undefeated champion, Pride of Rainbow! Alas, that such thing should be recorded! He leaped aside to shun the black frantic death at his shoulder; his feet were in the treacherous vines: he toppled, grasped vainly at an acacia, catapulted out and down, head first; so lit, crumpled and fell with a prodigious splash into the waters of the pool! *Ay di mi, Alhama!*

The blankets lay strewn along the hill; but observe that the long lead rope of the hackamore (a "hackamore," properly *jaquima*, is, for your better understanding, merely a rope halter) was coiled at the saddle horn, held there by a stout hornstring. As the black reached the level the saddle was at his heels. To kick was obvious, to go away not less so; but this new terror clung to the maddened creature in his frenzied flight — between his legs, in the air, at his heels, his hip, his neck. A low tree leaned from the hillside; the aerial saddle caught in the forks of it, the bronco's head was jerked round, he was pulled to his haunches, overthrown; but the tough hornstring broke, the freed coil snapped out at him; he scrambled up and bunched his glorious muscles in a vain and furious effort to outrun the rope that dragged at his heels, and so passed from sight beyond the next curve.

Waist-deep in the pool sat the hatless horseman or perhaps horse-less horseman were the juster term, steeped in a profound calm. That last phrase has a familiar sound; Mark Twain's, doubtless — but, all things considered, steeped is decidedly the word. One gloved hand was in the water, the other in the muddy margin of the pool: he watched the final evolution of his late mount with meditative interest. The saddle was freed at last, but its ex-occupant still sat there, lost in thought. Blood trickled, unnoted, down his forehead.

The last stone followed him into the pool; the echoes died on the hills. The spring resumed its pleasant murmur, but the tinkle of its

fall was broken by the mimic waves of the pool. Save for this
troubled sloshing against the banks, the slow-settling dust, and the
contemplative bust of the one-time centaur, no trace was left to mark
the late disastrous invasion.

The invader's dreamy and speculative gaze followed the dust of the
trailing rope. He opened his lips twice or thrice, and spoke, after
several futile attempts, in a voice mild, but clearly earnest:

"Oh, you little eohippus!"

The spellbound girl rose. Her hand was at her throat; her eyes
were big and round, and her astonished lips were drawn to a round,
red O.

Sharp ears heard the rustle of her skirts, her soft gasp of amazement. The merman turned his head briskly, his eye met hers. One
gloved hand brushed his brow; a broad streak of mud appeared there,
over which the blood meandered uncertainly. He looked up at the
maid in silence: in silence the maid looked down at him. He nodded,
with a pleasant smile.

"Good morning!" he said casually.

At this cheerful greeting, the astounded maid was near to tumbling
after, like Jill of the song.

"Er — good morning!" she gasped.

Silence. The merman reclined gently against the bank with a comfortable air of satisfaction. The color came flooding back to her
startled face.

"Oh, are you hurt?" she cried.

A puzzled frown struggled through the mud.

"Hurt?" he echoed. "Who, me? . . . Why, no — leastwise, I guess
not."

He wiggled his fingers, raised his arms, wagged his head doubtfully
and slowly, first sidewise and then up and down; shook himself guardedly, and finally raised tentative boot-tips to the surface. After this
painstaking inspection he settled contentedly back again.

"Oh, no, I'm all right," he reported. "Only I lost a big, black, fine,
young, nice horse somehow. You ain't seen nothing of him, have
you?"

"Then why don't you get out?" she demanded. "I believe you are
hurt."

"Get out? Why, yes, ma'am. Certainly. Why not?" But the girl
was already beginning to clamber down, grasping the shrubbery to
aid in the descent.

Now the bank was steep and sheer. So the merman rose, tactfully
clutching the grapevines behind him as a plausible excuse for turning
his back. It followed as a corollary of this generous act that he must

needs be lame, which he accordingly became. As this mishap became acute, his quick eyes roved down the cañon, where he saw what gave him pause; and he groaned sincerely under his breath. For the black horse had taken to the parked uplands, the dragging rope had tangled in a snaggy tree-root, and he was tracing weary circles in bootless effort to be free.

Tactful still, the dripping merman hobbled to the nearest shade wherefrom the luckless black horse should be invisible, eclipsed by the intervening ridge, and there sank down in a state of exhaustion, his back to a friendly tree-trunk.

CHAPTER II

First Aid

Oh woman! in our hours of ease
Uncertain, coy and hard to please;
But seen too oft, familiar with thy face
We first endure, then pity, then embrace!

A MOMENT LATER the girl was beside him, pity in her eyes.

"Let me see that cut on your head," she said. She dropped on her knee and parted the hair with a gentle touch.

"Why, you're real!" breathed the injured near-centaur, beaming with wonder and gratification.

She sat down limply and gave way to wild laughter.

"So are you!" she retorted. "Why, that is exactly what I was thinking! I thought maybe I was asleep and having an extraordinary dream. That wound on your head is not serious, if that's all." She brushed back a wisp of hair that blew across her eyes.

"I hurt this head just the other day," observed the bedraggled victim, as one who has an assortment of heads from which to choose. He pulled off his soaked gloves and regarded them ruefully. " 'Them that go down to deep waters!' That was a regular triumph of matter over mind, wasn't it?"

"It's a wonder you're alive! My! How frightened I was! Aren't you hurt — truly? Ribs or anything?"

The patient's elbows made a convulsive movement to guard the threatened ribs.

"Oh, no, ma'am. I ain't hurt a bit — indeed I ain't," he said truthfully; but his eyes had the languid droop of one who says the thing that is not. "Don't you worry none about me — not one bit. Sorry I frightened you. That black horse now — " He stopped to consider fully the case of the black horse. "Well, you see, ma'am, that black horse, he ain't exactly right plumb gentle." His eyelids drooped again.

The girl considered. She believed him — both that he was not badly hurt and that the black horse was not exactly gentle. And her suspicions were aroused. His slow drawl was getting slower; his cowboyese broader — a mode of speech quite inconsistent with that first sprightly remark about the little eohippus. What manner of cowboy was this, from whose tongue a learned scientific term tripped spontaneously in so stressful a moment — who quoted scraps of the litany unaware? Also, her own eyes were none of the slowest. She had noted that the limping did not begin until he was clear of the pool. Still, that might happen if one were excited; but this one had been singularly calm, "more than usual ca'm," she mentally quoted. . . . Of course, if he really were badly hurt — which she didn't believe one bit — a little bruised and jarred, maybe — the only thing for her to do would be to go back to camp and get help. . . . That meant the renewal of Lake's hateful attentions and — for the other girls, the sharing of her find. . . . She stole another look at her find and thrilled with all the pride of the discoverer. . . . No doubt he was shaken and bruised, after all. He must be suffering. What a splendid rider he was!

"What made you so absurd? Why didn't you get out of the water, then, if you are not hurt?" she snapped suddenly.

The drooped lids raised; brown eyes looked steadily into brown eyes.

"I didn't want to wake up," he said.

The candor of this explanation threw her, for the moment, into a vivid and becoming confusion. The dusky roses leaped to her cheeks; the long, dark lashes quivered and fell. Then she rose to the occasion.

"And how about the little eohippus?" she demanded. "That doesn't seem to go well with some of your other talk."

"Oh!" He regarded her with pained but unflinching innocence. "The Latin, you mean? Why ma'am, that's most all the Latin I know — that and some more big words in that song. I learned that song off of Frank John, just like a poll-parrot.".

"Sing it! And eohippus isn't Latin. It's Greek."

"Why, ma'am, I can't, just now — I'm so muddy; but I'll tell it to you. Maybe I'll sing it to you some other time." A sidelong glance accompanied this little suggestion. The girl's face was blank and non-committal; so he resumed: "It goes like this:

> Said the little Eohippus,
> "I'm going to be a horse,
> And on my midde finger-nails
> To run my earthly course" —

No; that wasn't the first. It begins:

> There was once a little animal
> No bigger than a fox,
> And on five toes he scampered —

"Of course you know, ma'am — Frank John he told me about it — that horses were little like that, 'way back. And this one he set his silly head that he was going to be a really-truly horse, like the song says. And folks told him he couldn't — couldn't possibly be done, nohow. And sure enough he did. It's a foolish song, really. I only sing parts of it when I feel like that — like it couldn't be done and I was going to do it, you know. The boys call it my song. Look here, ma'am!" He fished in his vest pocket and produced tobacco and papers, matches — last of all, a tiny turquoise horse, an inch long. "I had a jeweler-man put five toes on his feet once to make him be a little eohippus. Going to make a watch-charm of him sometime. He's a lucky little eohippus, I think. Peso gave him to me when — never mind when. Peso's a Mescalero Indian, you know, chief of police at the agency." He gingerly dropped the little horse into her eager palm.

It was a singularly grotesque and angular little beast, high-stepping, high-headed, with a level stare, at once complacent and haughty. Despite the first unprepossessing rigidity of outline, there was somehow a sprightly air, something endearing, in the stiff, purposed stride, the alert, inquiring ears, the stern and watchful eye. Each tiny hoof was faintly graven to semblance of five tinier toes; there, the work showed fresh.

"The cunning little monster!" Prison grime was on him; she groomed and polished at his dingy sides until the wonderful color shone out triumphant. "What is it that makes him such a dear? Oh, I know. It's something — well, childlike, you know. Think of the grown-up child that toiled with pride and joy at the making of him — dear me, how many lifetimes since! — and fondly put him by as a complete horse." She held him up in the sun: the ingrate met her caress with the same obdurate and indomitable glare. She laughed her rapturous delight: "There! How much better you look! Oh, you darling! Aren't you absurd? Straight-backed, stiff-legged, thick-necked, square-headed — and that ridiculously baleful eye! It's too high up and too far forward, you know — and your ears are too big — and you have such a malignant look! Never mind; now that you're all nice and clean, I'm going to reward you." Her lips just brushed him — the lucky little eohippus.

The owner of the lucky little horse was not able to repress one
swift, dismal glance at his own vast dishevelment, nor, as his shrinking
hands, entirely of their own volition, crept stealthily to hiding, the
slightest upward rolling of a hopeful eye toward the leaping waters
of the spring; but, if one might judge from her sedate and matter-of-
fact tones, that eloquent glance was wasted on the girl.

"You ought to take better care of him, you know," she said as she
restored the little monster to his owner. Then she laughed. "Hasn't
he a fierce and warlike appearance, though?"

"Sure. That's resolution. Look at those legs!" said the owner
fondly. "He spurns the ground. He's going somewheres. He's going
to be a horse! And them ears — one cocked forward and the other
back, strictly on the *cuidado!* He'll make it. He'll certainly do to
take along! Yes, ma'am, I'll take right good care of him." He regarded the homely beast with awe; he swathed him in cigarette papers
with tenderest care. "I'll leave him at home after this. He might get
hurt. I might sometime want to give him to — somebody."

The girl sprang up.

"Now I must get some water and wash that head," she announced
briskly.

"Oh, no — I can't let you do that. I can walk. I ain't hurt a bit, I
keep telling you." In proof of which he walked to the pool with a
palpably clever assumption of steadiness. The girl fluttered solicitous
at his elbow. Then she ran ahead, climbed up to the spring and extended a firm, cool hand, which he took shamelessly, and so came to
the fairy waterfall.

Here he made himself presentable as to face and hands. It is just
possible there was a certain expectancy in his eye as he neared the
close of these labors; but if there were it passed unnoted. The girl
bathed the injured head with her handkerchief, and brushed back his
hair with a dainty caressing motion that thrilled him until the color
rose beneath the tan. There was a glint of gray in the wavy black
hair, she noted.

She stepped back to regard her handiwork. "Now you look better!" she said approvingly. Then, slightly flurried, not without a memory of a previous and not dissimilar remark of hers, she was off up
the hill: whence, despite his shocked protest, she brought back the
lost gun and hat.

Her eyes were sparkling when she returned, her face glowing. Ignoring his reproachful gaze, she wrung out her handkerchief, led the
patient firmly down the hill and to his saddle, made him trim off a
saddle-string, and bound the handkerchief to the wound. She fitted
the sombrero gently.

"There! Don't this head feel better now?" she queried gayly, with fine disregard for grammar. "And now what? Won't you come back to camp with me? Mr. Lake will be glad to put you up or to let you have a horse. Do you live far away? I do hope you are not one of those Rosebud men. Mr. La——" She bit her speech off midword.

"No men there except this Mr. Lake?" asked the cowboy idly.

"Oh, yes; there's Mr. Herbert — he's gone riding with Lettie — and Mr. White; but it was Mr. Lake who got up the camping party. Mother and Aunt Lot, and a crowd of us girls — La Luz girls, you know. Mother and I are visiting Mr. Lake's sister. He's going to give us a masquerade ball when we get back, next week."

The cowboy looked down his nose for consultation, and his nose gave a meditative little tweak.

"What Lake is it? There's some several Lakes around here. Is it Lake of Agua Chiquite — wears his hair décolleté; talks like he had a washboard in his throat; tailor-made face; walks like a duck on stilts; general sort of pouter-pigeon effect?"

At this envenomed description, Miss Ellinor Hoffman promptly choked.

"I don't know anything about your Agua Chiquite. I never heard of the place before. He is a banker in Arcadia. He keeps a general store there. You must know him, surely." So far her voice was rather stern and purposely resentful, as became Mr. Lake's guest; but there were complications, rankling memories of Mr. Lake — of unwelcome attentions persistently forced upon her. She spoiled the rebuke by adding tartly, "But I think he is the man you mean!" and felt her wrongs avenged.

The cowboy's face cleared.

"Well, I don't use Arcadia much, you see. I mostly range down Rainbow River. Arcadia folks — why, they're mostly newcomers, health-seekers and people just living on their incomes — not working folks much, except the railroaders and lumbermen. Now about getting home. You see, ma'am, some of the boys are riding down that way" — he jerked his thumb to indicate the last flight of the imperfectly gentle horse — "and they're right apt to see my runaway eohippus and sure to see the rope-drag; so they'll likely amble along the back track to see how much who's hurt. So I guess I'd better stay here. They may be along most any time. Thank you kindly, just the same. Of course, if they don't come at all — Is your camp far?"

"Not — not very," said Ellinor. The mere fact was that Miss Ellinor had set out ostensibly by a sketching expedition with another girl, had turned aside to explore, and exploring had fetched a circuit that had left her much closer to her starting-place than to her goal. He misinterpreted the slight hesitation.

"Well, ma'am, thank you again; but I mustn't be keeping you longer. I really ought to see you safe back to your camp; but — you'll understand — under the circumstances — you'll excuse me?"

He did not want to implicate Mr. Lake, so he took a limping step forward to justify his rudeness.

"And you hardly able to walk? Ridiculous! What I ought to do is to go back to camp and get someone — get Mr. White to help you." Thus, at once accepting his unspoken explanation, and offering her own apology in turn, she threw aside the air of guarded hostility that had marked the last minutes and threw herself anew into this joyous adventure. "When — or if — your friends find you, won't it hurt you to ride?" she asked, and smiled deliberate encouragement.

"I can be as modest as anybody when there's anything to be modest about; but in this case I guess I'll now declare that I can ride anything that a saddle will stay on. . . . I reckon," he added reflectively, "the boys'll have right smart to say about me being throwed."

"But you weren't thrown! You rode magnificently!" Her eyes flashed admiration.

"Yes'm. That's what I hoped you'd say," said the admired one complacently. "Go on, ma'am. Say it again."

"It was splendid! The saddle turned — that's all!"

He slowly surveyed the scene of his late exploit.

"Ye-es, that was some riding — for a while," he admitted. "But you see, that saddle now, scarred up that way — why, they'll think the eohippus wasted me and then dragged the saddle off under a tree. Leastways, they'll say they think so, frequent. Best not to let on and to make no excuses. It'll be easier that way. We're great on guying here. That's most all the fun we have. We sure got this joshing game down fine. Just wondering what all the boys'd say — that was why I didn't get out of the water at first, before — before I thought I was asleep, you know."

"So you'll actually tell a lie to keep from being thought a liar? I'm disappointed in you."

"Why, ma'am, I won't say anything. They'll do the talking."

"It'll be deceitful, just the same," she began, and checked herself suddenly. A small twinge struck her at the thought of poor Maud, really sketching on Thumb Butte, and now disconsolately wondering what had become of lunch and fellow-artist; but she quelled this pang with a sage thought of the greatest good to the greatest number, and clapped her hands in delight. "Oh, what a silly I am, to be sure! I've got a lunch basket up there, but I forgot all about it in the excitement.

I'm sure there's plenty for two. Shall I bring it down to you or can you climb up if I help you? There's water in the canteen — and it's beautiful up there."

"I can make it, I guess," said the invited guest — the consummate and unblushing hypocrite. Make it he did, with her strong hand to aid; and the glen rang to the laughter of them. While behind them, all unnoted, Johnny Dines reined up on the hillside; took one sweeping glance at that joyous progress, the scarred hillside, the saddle and the dejected eohippus in the background; grinned comprehension, and discreetly withdrew.

CHAPTER III

Maxwelton Braes

> Oh the song — the song in the blood!
> Magic walks the forest; there's bewitchment on the air —
> Spring is at the flood!
>
> *— The Gypsy Heart*

> Well, sir, this here feller, he lit a cigarrette an' throwed away the match, an' it fell in a powder kaig; an' do you know, more'n half that powder burned up before they could put it out! Yes, sir!
>
> *— Wildcat Thompson*

Ellinor opened her basket and spread its tempting wares with pretty hostly care — or is there such a word as hostessly?

"There! All ready, Mr. —— I declare, this is too absurd! We don't even know each other's names!" Her conscious eye fell upon the ampleness of the feast — amazing since it purported to have been put up for one alone; and her face lit up with mischievous delight. She curtsied. "If you please, I'm the Ultimate Consumer!"

He rose, bowing gravely.

"I am the Personal Devil. Glad to meet you."

"Oh! I've heard of you!" remarked the Ultimate Consumer sweetly. She sat down and extended her hand across the spotless linen. "Mr. Lake says — "

The Personal Devil flushed. It was not because of the proffered hand, which he took unhesitatingly and held rather firmly. The blush was unmistakably caused by anger.

"There is no connection whatever," he stated, grimly enough, "between the truth and Mr. Lake's organs of speech."

"Oh!" cried the Ultimate Consumer triumphantly. "So you're Mr. Beebe?"

"Bransford — Jeff Bransford," corrected the Personal Devil crustily. He wilfully relapsed to his former slipshod speech. "Beebe, he's gone to the Pecos work, him and Ballinger. Mr. John Wesley Also-Ran Pringle's gone to Old Mexico to bring back another bunch of black, long-horned Chihuahuas. You now behold before you the last re- maining Rose of Rosebud. But, why Beebe?"

"Why does Mr. Lake hate all of you so, Mr. Bransford?"

"Because we are infamous scoundrels. Why Beebe?"

"I can't eat with one hand, Mr. Bransford," she said demurely. He looked at the prisoned hand with a start and released it grudgingly. "Help yourself," said his hostess cheerfully. "There's sandwiches, and roast beef and olives, for a mild beginning."

"Why Beebe?" he said doggedly.

"Help yourself to the salad and then please pass it over this way. Thank you."

"Why Beebe?"

"Oh, very well, then! Because of the little eohippus, you know — and other things you said."

"I see!" said the aggrieved Bransford. "Because I'm not from Ohio, like Beebe, I'm not supposed — "

"Oh, if you're going to be fussy! I'm from California myself, Mr. Bransford. Out in the country at that. Don't let's quarrel, please. We were having such a lovely time. And I'll tell you a secret. It's un- grateful of me, and I ought not to; but I don't care — I don't like Mr. Lake much since we came on this trip. And I don't believe — " She paused, pinkly conscious of the unconventional statement involved in this sudden unbelief.

" — what Lake says about us?" A much-mollified Bransford finished the sentence for her.

She nodded. Then, to change the subject:

"You do speak cowboy talk one minute — and all booky, polite and proper the next, you know. Why?"

"Bad associations," said Bransford ambiguously. "Also for 'tis my nature to, as little dogs they do delight to bark and bite. That beef sure tastes like more."

. . . . . .

"And now you may smoke while I pack up," announced the girl when dessert was over, at long last. "And please, there is something I want to ask you about. Will you tell me truly?"

"Um — you sing?"

"Yes — a little."

"If you will sing for me afterward?"

"Certainly. With pleasure."

"All right, then. What's the story about?"

Ellinor gave him her eyes. "Did you rob the post office at Escondido — Really?"

Now it might well be embarrassing to be asked if you had committed a felony; but there was that behind the words of this naïve query — in look, in tone, in mental attitude — an unflinching and implicit faith that, since he had seen fit to do this thing, it must needs have been the right and wise thing to do, which stirred the felon's pulses to a pleasant flutter and caused a certain tough and powerful muscle to thump foolishly at his ribs. The delicious intimacy, the baseless faith, was sweet to him.

"Sure, I did!" he answered lightly. "Lake is one talkative little man, isn't he? But, shucks! What can you expect? 'The beast will do after his kind.' "

"And you'll tell me about it?"

"After I smoke. Got to study up some plausible excuses, you know."

She studied him as she packed. It was a good face — lined, strong, expressive, vivid; gay, resolute, confident, alert — reckless, perhaps. There were lines of it disused, fallen to abeyance. What was well with the man had prospered; what was ill with him had faded and dimmed. He was not a young man — thirty-seven, thirty-eight — (she was twenty-four) — but there was an unquenchable boyishness about him, despite the few frosty hairs at his temples. He bore his hard years jauntily; youth danced in his eyes. The explorer nodded to herself, well pleased. He was interesting — different.

The tale suffered from Bransford's telling, as any tale will suffer when marred by the inevitable, barbarous modesty of its hero. It was a long story, cozily confidential; and there were interruptions. The sun was low ere it was done.

"Now the song," said Jeff, "and then — " He did not complete the sentence; his face clouded.

"What shall I sing?"

"How can I tell? What you will. What can I know about good songs — or anything else?" responded Bransford in sudden moodiness and dejection — for, after the song, the end of everything! He flinched at the premonition of irrevocable loss.

The girl made no answer. This is what she sang. No; you shall not be told of her voice. Perhaps there is a voice that you remember, that echoes to you through the dusty years. How would you like to describe that?

Oh, Sandy has monie and Sandy has land,
And Sandy has housen, sae fine and sae grand —
But I'd rather hae Jamie, wi' nocht in his hand,
Than Sandy, wi' all of his housen and land.

My father looks sulky; my mither looks soor;
They gloom upon Jamie because he is poor.
I lo'e them baith deary, as a docther should do;
But I lo'e them not half sae weel, dear Jamie, as you!

I sit at my cribbie, I spin at my wheel;
I think o' the laddie that lo'es me sae weel.
Oh, he had but saxpence, he brak it in twa.
And he gied me the half o't ere he gaed awa'!

He said: "Lo'e me lang, lassie, though I gang awa'!"
He said: "Lo'e me lang, lassie, though I gang awa'!"
Bland simmer is cooming; cauld winter's awa',
And I'll wed wi' Jamie in spite o' them a'!

Jeff's back was to a tree, his hat over his eyes. He pushed it up.
"Thank you," he said; and then, quite directly: "Are you rich?"
"Not — very," said Ellinor, a little breathless at the blunt query.
"I'm going to be rich," said Jeff steadily.
" 'I'm going to be a horse,' quoth the little eohippus." The girl
retorted saucily, though secretly alarmed at the import of this exam-
ination.
"Ex-actly. So that's settled. What is your name?"
"Hoffman."
"Where do you live, Hoffman?"
"Ellinor," supplemented the girl.
"Ellinor, then. Where do you live, Ellinor?"
"In New York — just now. Not in town. Upstate. On a farm. You
see, grandfather's growing old — and he wanted father to come back."
"New York's not far," said Jeff.
A sudden panic seized the girl. What next? In swift, instinctive
self-defense she rose and tripped to the tree where lay her neglected
sketch-book, bent over — and started back with a little cry of alarm.
With a spring and a rush, Jeff was at her side, caught her up and
glared watchfully at bush and shrub and tufted grass.
"Mr. Bransford! Put me down!"
"What was it? A rattlesnake?"
"A snake? What an idea! I just noticed how late it was. I must go."
Crestfallen, sheepishly, Mr. Bransford put her down, thrust his
hands into his pockets, tilted his chin and whistled an aggravating
little trill from the Rye twostep.

"Mr. Bransford!" said Ellinor haughtily.

Mr. Bransford's face expressed patient attention.

"Are you lame?"

Mr. Bransford's eye estimated the distance covered during the recent snake episode, and then gave to Miss Hoffman a look of profound respect. His shoulders humped up slightly; his head bowed to the stroke: he stood upon one foot and traced the Rainbow brand in the dust with the other.

"I told you all along I wasn't hurt," he said aggrieved. "Didn't I, now?"

"Are you lame?" she repeated severely, ignoring his truthful saying.

" 'Not — very.' " The quotation marks were clearly audible.

"Are you lame at all?"

"No, ma'am — not what you might call really lame. Uh — no, ma'am."

"And you deceived me like that!" Indignation checked her. "Oh, I am so disappointed in you! That was a fine, manly thing for you to do!"

"It was such a lovely time," observed the culprit doggedly. "And such a chance might never happen again. And it isn't my fault I wasn't hurt, you know. I'm sure I wish I was."

She gave him an icy glare.

"Now see what you've done! Your men haven't come and you won't stay with Mr. Lake. How are you going to get home? Oh, I forgot — you can walk, as you should have done at first."

The guilty wretch wilted yet further. He shuffled his feet; he writhed; he positively squirmed. He ventured a timid upward glance. It seemed to give him courage. Prompted, doubtless, by the same feeling which drives one to dive headlong into dreaded cold water, he said, in a burst of candor:

"Well, you see, ma'am, that little horse now — he really ain't got far. He got tangled up over there a ways — "

The girl wheeled and shot a swift, startled glance at the little eohippus on the hillside, who had long since given over his futile struggles and was now nibbling grass with becoming resignation. She turned back to Bransford. Slowly, scathingly, she looked him over from head to foot and slowly back again. Her expression ran the gamut — wonder, anger, scorn, withering contempt.

"I think I hate you!" she flamed at him.

Amazement triumphed over the other emotions then — a real amazement: the detected imposter had resumed his former debonair bearing and met her scornful eye with a slow and provoking smile.

"Oh, no, you don't," he said reassuringly. "On the contrary, you don't hate me at all!"

"I'm going home, anyhow," she retorted bitterly. "You may draw your own conclusions."

Still, she did not go, which possibly had a confusing effect upon his inferences.

"Just one minute, ma'am, if you please. How did you know so pat where the little black horse was? *I* didn't tell you."

Little waves of scarlet followed each other to her burning face.

"I'm not going to stay another moment. You're detestable! And it's nearly sundown."

"Oh, you needn't hurry. It's not far."

She followed his gesture. To her intense mortification she saw the blue smoke of her home campfire flaunting up from a gully not half a mile away. It was her turn to droop now. She drooped.

There was a painful silence. Then, in a far-off, hard, judicial tone:

"How long, ma'am, if I may ask, have you known that the little black horse was tangled up?"

Miss Ellinor's eyes shifted wildly. She broke a twig from a mahogany bush and examined the swelling buds with minutest care.

"Well?" said her ruthless inquisitor sternly.

"Since — since I went for your hat," she confessed in a half whisper.

"To deceive me so!" Pain, grief, surprise, reproach, were in his words. "Have you anything to say?" he added sadly.

A slender shoe peeped out beneath her denim skirt and tapped on a buried boulder. Ellinor regarded the toetip with interest and curiosity. Then, half-audibly:

"We were having such a good time. . . . And it might never happen again!"

He captured both her hands. She drew back a little — ever so little; she trembled slightly, but her eyes met his frankly and bravely.

"No, no! . . . Not now. . . . Go, now, Mr. Bransford. Go at once. We will have a pleasant day to remember."

"Until the next pleasant day," said resolute Bransford, openly exultant. "But see here, now — I can't go to Lake's camp or to Lake's ball" — here Miss Ellinor pouted distinctly — "or anything that is Lake's. After your masked ball, then what?"

"New York; but it's only so far — on the map." She held her hands apart very slightly to indicate the distance. "On a little map, that is."

"I'll drop in Saturday," said Jeff.

"Do! I want to hear you sing the rest about the little eohippus."

"If you'll sing about Sandy!" suggested Jeff.

"Why not? Good-bye now — I must go."

"And you won't sing about Sandy to anyone else?"

The girl considered doubtfully.

"Why — I don't know — I've known you for a very little while, if you please." She gathered up her belongings. "But we're friends?"

"*No! No!*" said Jeff vehemently. "You won't sing it to anyone else — Ellinor?"

She drew a line in the dust.

"If you won't cross that line," she said, "I'll tell you."

Mr. Bransford grasped a sapling with a firm clutch and shook it to try its strength.

"A bird in the bush is the noblest work of God," he announced. "I'll take a chance."

Her eyes were shining.

"You've promised!" she said. She paused: when she spoke again her voice was low and a trifle unsteady. "I won't sing about Sandy to — anyone else — Jeff!"

Then she fled.

Like Lot's wife, she looked back from the hillside. Jeff clung desperately to the sapling with one hand; from the other a handkerchief — hers — fluttered a good-bye message. She threw him a farewell, with an ambiguous gesture.

.   .   .   .

It was late when Jeff reached Rosebud Camp. He unsaddled Nigger Baby, the little and not entirely gentle black horse, rather unobtrusively; but Johnny Dines sauntered out during the process, announcing supper.

"Huh!" sniffed Jeff. "S'pose I thought you'd wait until I come to get it?"

Nothing more alarming than tallies was broached during supper, however. Afterward, Johnny tilted his chair back and, through cigarette smoke, contemplated the ceiling with innocent eyes.

"Nigger Babe looks drawed," he suggested.

"Uh-huh. Had one of them poor spells of his."

Puff, puff.

"Your saddle's skinned up a heap."

"Run under a tree."

Johnny's look of innocence grew more pronounced.

"How'd you get your clothes so wet?"

"Rain," said Jeff.

Puff, puff.

"You look right muddy too."

"Dust in the air," said Jeff.

"Ah! — yes." Silence during the rolling of another cigarette. Then: "How'd you get that cut on your head?"

Jeff's hand went to his head and felt the bump there. He regarded his fingers in some perplexity.

"That? Oh, that's where I bit myself!" He stalked off to bed in gloomy dignity.

Half an hour later Johnny called softly:

"Jeff!"

Jeff grunted sulkily.

"Camping party down near Mayhill. Lot o' girls. I saw one of 'em. Young person with eyes and hair."

Jeff grunted again. There was a long silence.

"Nice bear!" There was no answer.

"*Good* old bear!" said Johnny tearfully. No answer. "Mister Bear, if I give you a nice, good, juicy bite — "

"*U-ugg-rrh!*" said Jeff.

"Then," said Johnny decidedly, "I'll sleep in the yard."

CHAPTER IV

The Road to Rome

Behold, one journeyed in the night.
He sang amid the wind and rain;
My wet sands gave his feet delight —
When will that traveler come again?
— *The Heart of the Road*
ANNA HEMPSTEAD BRANCH

A HYPOTENUSE, as has been well said, is the longest side of a right-angled triangle. There is no need for details. That we are all familiar with the use of this handy little article is shown by the existence of shortcuts at every available opportunity, and by keep-off-o'-the-grass signs in parks.

Now, had Jeff Bransford desired to go to Arcadia — to that masquerade, for instance — his direct route from Jackson's Ranch would have been cater-cornered across the desert, as has been amply demonstrated by Pythagoras and others.

That Jeff did not want to go to Arcadia — to the masked ball, for instance — is made apparent by the fact that the afternoon preceding

said ball saw him jogging southward toward Baird's, along the lonely
base of that inveterate triangle whereof Jackson's, Baird's and Arcadia
are the respective corners, leaving the fifty-five-mile hypotenuse far to
his left. It was also obvious from the tenor of his occasional self-
communings.

"I don't want to make a bally fool of myself — do I, old Grasshopper? Anyhow, you'll be too tired when we get to 'Gene's."

Grasshopper made no response, other than a plucky tossing of his
bit and a quickening cadence in his rhythmical stride, by way of pardonable bravado.

"I never forced myself in where my company wasn't wanted yet,
and I ain't going to begin now," asserted Jeff stoutly; adding, as a
fervent afterthought: "Damn Lake!"

His way lay along the plain, paralleling the long westward range,
just far enough out to dodge the jutting foothills; through bare white
levels where Grasshopper's hoofs left but a faint trace on the hard-
glazed earth. At intervals, tempting cross-roads branched away to
mountain springs. The cottonwood at Independent Springs came into
view round the granite shoulder of Strawberry, six miles to the right
of him. He roused himself from prolonged pondering of the marvelous silhouette, where San Andres unflung in broken masses against the
sky, to remark in a hushed whisper:

"I wonder if she'd be glad to see me?"

Several miles later he quoted musingly:

> For Ellinor — her Christian name was Ellinor —
> Had twenty-seven different kinds of hell in her!

After all, there are problems which Pythagoras never solved.

The longest road must have an end. Ritch's Ranch was passed far
to the right, lying low in the long shadow of Kaylor; then the mouth
of Hembrillo Cañon; far ahead, a shifting flicker of Baird's windmill
topped the brush. It grew taller; the upper tower took shape. He
dipped into the low, mirage-haunted basin, where the age-old Texas
Trail crosses the narrow western corner of the White Sands. When
he emerged the windmill was tall and silver-shining; the low iron roofs
of the house gloomed sullen in the sun.

Dust rose from the corral. Now Jeff's ostensible errand to the West
Side had been the search for strays; three days before he had prudently been three days' ride farther to the north. The reluctance with
which he had turned back southward was justified by the fact that
this critical afternoon found him within striking distance of Arcadia
— striking distance, that is, should he care for a bit of hard riding.

This was exactly what Jeff had fought against all along. So, when he saw the dust, he loped up.

It was as he had feared. A band of horses was in the waterpen, among them a red-roan head he knew — Copperhead, of Pringle's mount; confirmed runaway. Jeff shut the gate. For the first time that day, he permitted himself a discreet glance eastward to Arcadia.

"Three days," he said bitterly, while Grasshopper thrust his eager muzzle into the watertrough — "three days I have braced back my feet and slid, like a yearlin' at a brandin' bee — and look at me now! Oh, Copperhead, you darned old fool, see what you done now!"

In this morose mood he went to the house. There was no one at home. A note was tacked on the door.

Gone to Plomo. Back in two or three days. Beef hangs under platform on windmill tower. When you get it, oil the mill. Books and deck of cards in box under bed. Don't leave fire in stove when you go.   GENE BAIRD
N.B. — Feed the cat.

Jeff built a fire in the stove and unsaddled the weary Grasshopper. He found some corn, which he put into a woven-grass *morral* and hung on Grasshopper's nose. He went to the waterpen, roped out Copperhead and shut him in a side corral. Then he let the bunch go. They strained through the gate in a mad run, despite shrill and frantic remonstrance from Copperhead.

"Jeff," said Jeff soberly, "are you going to be a damned fool all your life? That girl doesn't care anything about you. She hasn't thought of you since. You stay right here and read the pretty books. That's the place for you."

This advice was sound and wise beyond cavil. So Jeff took it valiantly. After supper he hobbled Grasshopper and took off the nosebag. Then he went to the back room in pursuit of literature.

.   .   .   .

Have I leave for a slight digression, to commit a long-delayed act of justice — to correct a grievous wrong? Thank you.

We hear much of Mr. Andrew Carnegie and His Libraries, the Hall of Fame, the Little Red Schoolhouse, the Five-Foot Shelf, and the World's Best Books. A singular thing is that the most effective bit of philanthropy along these lines has gone unrecorded of a thankless world. This shall no longer be.

Know, then, that once upon a time a certain soulless corporation, rather in the tobacco trade, placed in each package of tobacco a coupon, each coupon redeemable by one paper-bound book. Whether they were moved by remorse to this action or by sordid hidden purposes of their own, or, again, by pure, disinterested and farseeing love of their kind, is not yet known; but the results remain. There were three hundred and three volumes on that list, mostly — but not altogether — fiction. And each one was a classic. Classics are cheap. They are not copyrighted. Could I but know the anonymous benefactor who enrolled that glorious company, how gladly would I drop a leaf on his bier or a cherry in his bitters!

Thus it was that, in one brief decade, the cowboys, with others, became comparatively literate. Cowboys all smoked. Doubtless that was a chief cause contributory to making them the wrecks they were. It destroyed their physique; it corroded and ate away their will power — leaving them seldom able to work over nineteen hours a day, except in emergencies; prone to abandon duty in the face of difficulty or danger, when human effort, raised to the nth power, could do no more — all things considered, the most efficient men of their hands on record.

Cowboys all smoked: and the most deepseated instinct of the human race is to get something for nothing. They got those books. In due course of time they read those books. Some were slow to take to it; but when you stay at lonely ranches, when you are left afoot until the waterholes dry up, so you may catch a horse in the waterpen — why, you must do something. The books were read. Then, having acquired the habit, they bought more books. Since the three hundred and three were all real books, and since the cowboys had been previously uncorrupted of predigested or sterilized fiction, or by "gift," "uplift" and "helpful" books, their composite taste had become surprisingly good, and they bought with discriminating care. Nay, more. A bookcase follows books; a bookcase demands a house; a house needs a keeper; a housekeeper needs everything. Hence alfalfa — houseplants — slotless tables — bankbooks. The chain which began with yellow coupons ends with Christmas trees. In some proudest niche in the Hall of Fame a grateful nation will yet honor that hitherto unrecognized educator, Front de Boeuf.[1]

Jeff pawed over the tattered yellow-backed volumes in profane discontent. He had read them all. Another box was under the bed, behind the first. Opening it, he saw a tangled mass of clothing, tumbled in the bachelor manner; with the rest, a much-used football outfit — canvas jacket, sweater, padded trousers, woolen stockings,

[1] "Bull Durham."

rubber noseguard, shinguards, ribbed shoes — all complete; for 'Gene Baird was fullback of the El Paso eleven.

Jeff segregated the gridiron wardrobe with hasty hands. His eye brightened; he spoke in an awed and almost reverent voice.

"I ain't mostly superstitious, but this looks like a leading. First, I'm here; second, Copperhead's here; third, no one else is here; and, for the final miracle, here's a costume made to my hand. Thirty-five miles. Ten o'clock, if I hurry. H'm! 'When first I put this uniform on' — how did that go? I'm forgetting all my songs. Getting old, I guess."

Rejecting the heavy shoes, as unmeet for waxed floors, and the shinguards, he rolled the rest of the uniform in his slicker and tied it behind his saddle. Then he rubbed his chin.

"Huh! That's a true saying, too. I am getting old. Youth turns to youth. Buck up, Jeff, you old fool! Have some pride about you and just a little old horse-sense."

Yet he unhobbled Grasshopper, who might then be trusted to find his way to Rainbow in about three days. He went to the corral and tossed a rope on snorting Copperhead. "No; I won't go!" he said, as he slipped on the bridle. "Just to uncock old Copperhead, I'll make a little horseride to Hospital Springs and look through the stock." He threw on the saddle with some difficulty — Copperhead was fat and frisky. "She don't want to see you, Jeff — an old has-been like you! No, no; I'd better not go. I won't! There, if I didn't leave that football stuff on the saddle! I'll take it off. It might get lost. Whoa, Copperhead!"

Copperhead, however, declined to whoa on any terms. His eyes bulged out; he reared, he pawed, he snorted, he bucked, he squealed, he did anything but whoa. Exasperated, Jeff caught the bridle by the cheek piece and swung into the saddle. After a few preliminaries in the pitching line, Jeff started bravely for Hospital Springs.

It was destined that this act of renunciation should be thwarted. Copperhead stopped and dug his feet in the ground as if about to take root. Jeff dug the spurs home. With an agonized bawl, Copperhead made a creditable ascension, shook himself and swapped ends before he hit the ground again. "*Wooh!*" he said. His nose was headed now for Arcadia; he followed his nose, his roan flanks fanned vigorously with a doubled rope.

"Headstrong, stubborn, unmanageable brute! Oh, well, have it your own way then, you old fool! You'll be sorry!" Copperhead leaped out to the loosened rein. "This is just plain kidnapping!" said Jeff.

Kidnapped and kidnapper were far out on the plain as night came on. Arcadia road stretched dimly to the east; the far lights of La Luz flashed through the leftward dusk; straight before them was a glint and sparkle in the sky, faint, diffused, wavering; beyond, a warm and mellow glow broke the blackness of the mountain wall, where the lights of low-hidden Arcadia beat up against Rainbow Rim.

Jeff was past his first vexation; he sang as he rode:

> There was ink on her thumb when I kissed her hand
> And she whispered: "If you should die
> I'd write you an epitaph, gloomy and grand!"
> "Time enough for that!" says I.

"Keep a-movin here, Copperhead! Time fugits right along. You will play hooky, will you? 'I'm going to be a horse!'"

CHAPTER V

The Maskers

> For Ellinor (her Chrstian name was Ellinor)
> Had twenty-seven dfferent kinds of hell in her.
> — RICHARD HOVEY

IT LACKED LITTLE of the eleventh hour when the football player reached the ballroom — last comer to the revels. A bandage round his head and a rubber noseguard, which also hid his mouth, served for a mask, eked out by crisscrossed strips of courtplaster. One arm was in a sling — for stage purposes only.

As he limped through the door, Diogenes hurried to meet him, held up his lantern, peered hopefully into the battered face and shook his disappointed head. "Stung again!" muttered Diogenes.

Jeff lisped in numbers which fully verified the cynic's misgiving. "7 — 11 — 4 — 11 — 44!" he announced jerkily. This was strictly in character and also excused him from entangling talk, leaving him free to search the whirl of dancers.

A bulky Rough Rider volunteered his help. He fixed a gleaming eyeglass on his nose and politely offered Jeff a Big Stick by way of a crutch. "Hit the line hard!" he barked. He bit the words off with a prize-bulldog effect. He had fine teeth.

Jeff waved him off. "16 — 2 — 1!" he proclaimed controversially. He felt his spirits sinking, with a growing doubt of his ability to identify the Only One, and was impatient of interruption. He kept his slow and watchful way down the floor.

Topsy broke away from her partner and stopped Jeff's crippled progress. Her short hair, braided to a dozen tight and tiny pigtails, bristled away in all directions.

"Laws, young marsta', you suhtenly does look puny!" she said. Then she clutched at her knee. "*Aie!*" she tittered, as a loose red stocking dropped flappingly to her ankle. Pray do not be shocked. The effect was startling; but a black stocking, decorously tight and smooth, was beneath the red one. Jeff's mathematics were not equal to the strain of adequate comment. Topsy dived to the rescue. "Got a string?" she giggled, as she hitched the fallen stocking back to place. "I cain't fix this good nohow!"

Jeff jerked his thumb over his shoulder. "Man over there with an eyeglass cord — maybe you can get that. What makes you act so?" He looked cold disapproval; nevertheless, he looked.

Topsy hung her head, still clutching at the stocking-top. "Dunno. I spec's it's 'cause Ise so wicked!" Finger in mouth, she looked after Jeff as he hobbled away.

A slender witch bounced from a chair and barred his way with a broom. Her eyes were brimming sorcery; her lips looked saucy challenge; she leaned close for a whispered word in his ear: "How would you like to tackle me?"

Poor Jeff! "10, 2 — 10, 2!" he promised huskily. Yet he ducked beneath the broom.

"But," said the little witch plaintively, "you're going away!" She dropped her broom and wept.

"8, 2 — 8, 2 — 8, 2!" said Jeff, almost in tears himself, and again fell back upon English. "Mere figures or mere words can't tell you how much I hate to; but I've got to follow the ball. I'm looking for a fellow."

"If he — if he doesn't love you," sobbed the stricken witch, "then you'll come back to me — won't you? I love a liar!"

"To the very stake!" vowed Jeff. Such heroic, if conditional, constancy was not to go unrewarded. A couple detached themselves from the dancers, threaded their way to a corner of the long hall and stood there in deep converse. Jeff quickened pulse and pace — for one was a Red Devil and the other wore the soft gray costume of a Friend. She was tall, this Quakeress, and the hobnobbing devil was of Jeff's own height. Jeff began to hope for a goal.

Briskly limping, he came to this engrossed couple and laid a friendly hand on the devil's shoulder.

"Brother," he said cordially, "will you please go to — home?"

The devil recoiled an astonished step.

"What? What!! Show me your license!"

"Twenty-three! — Please — there's a good devil — 23! I'm the right guard for this lady, I hope. Oh, please to go home!"

The devil took this request in very bad part.

"Go back fifteen yards for offside play and take a drop kick at yourself!" he suggested sourly.

A burly policeman, plainly conscious of fitting his uniform, paused for warning.

"No scrappin' now! Don't start nothin' or I'll run in the t'ree av yees!" he said, and sauntered on, twirling a graceful nightstick.

"Thee is a local man, judging from thy letters," said the Quaker lady, to relieve the somewhat strained situation. "What do they stand for? E.P.? Oh, yes — El Paso, of course!"

"I saw you first!" said the Red Devil. "And with your disposition you would naturally find me more suitable. Make your choice of gridirons! Send him back to the side lines! Disqualify him for interference!"

"Don't be hurried into a decision," said Jeff. "Eternity is a good while. Before it's over I'm going to be a — well, something more than a footballer. Golf, maybe — or tiddledywinks."

The Quakeress glanced attentively from one to the other.

"Doubtless he will do his best to forward Thy Majesty's interests," she interposed. "Why not give him a chance?"

The devil shrugged his shoulders. "I always prefer to give this branch of work my personal attention," he said stiffly.

"A specialty of thine?" mocked the girl.

The devil bowed sulkily.

"My heart is in it. Of course, if you prefer the bungling of a novice, there is no more to be said."

"Thy Majesty's manners have never been questioned," murmured the Quakeress, bowing dismissal. "So kind of you!"

The devil bowed deeply and turned, pausing to hurl a gloomy prophecy over his shoulder. "See you later!" he said, and stalked away with an ill grace.

Pigskin hero and girl Friend, left alone, eyed each other with mutual apprehension. The girl Friend was first to recover speech. Her red lips were prim below her vizor, her eyes downcast to hide their dancing lights. Timidly she spread out fanwise the dove color of her sober costume.

"How does thee like my gray gown?"

"Not at all," said Jeff brutally. "You're no friend of mine, I hope."

A most un-Quakerlike dimple trembled to her chin, relieving the firm austerity of straight lips. Also, Jeff caught a glimpse of her eyes through the vizor. They were crinkling — and they were brown. She ventured another tentative remark, and there was in it an undertone lingering, softly confidential.

"Is thee lame?"

"Not — very," said Jeff, and saw a faint color start to the unmasked moiety of the Quaker cheek. "Still, if I may have the next dance, I shall be glad if you will sit it out with me." Painfully he raised the beslinged arm in explanation. *Sobre las Olas* throbbed out its wistful call; they set their thoughts to its haunting measure.

"By all means!" She took his undamaged arm. "Let us find chairs."

Now there were chairs to the left of them, chairs to the right of them, chairs vacant everywhere; but the gallant Six Hundred themselves were not more heedless or undismayed than these two. Still, all the world did not wonder. On the contrary, not even the anxious devil saw them after they passed behind a knot of would-be dancers who were striving to disentangle themselves. For, seeing traffic thus blocked, the policeman rushed to unsnarl the tangle. Magnificently he flourished his stick. He adjured them roughly: "Move on yous! Move on!" Whereat, with one impulse, the tangle moved on the copper, swept over him, engulfed him, hustled him to the door and threw him out.

So screened, the chair-hunters vanished in far less than a psychological moment: for Jeff, in obedience to a faint or fancied pressure on his arm, dived through portières into a small room set apart for such as had the heart to prefer cards or chess. The room was deserted now and there was a broad window open to the night. Thus, thrice favored of Providence, they found themselves in the garden, chairless but cheerful.

A garden with one Eve is the perfect combination in a world awry. Muffled, the music and the sounds of the ballroom came faint and far to them; star-made shadows danced at their feet. The girl paused, expectant; but it was the unexpected that happened. The nimble tongue which had done such faithful service for Mr. Bransford now failed him quite: left him struggling, dumb, inarticulate, helpless — tongue and hand alike forgetful of their cunning.

Be sure the maid had adroitly heard much of Mr. Bransford, his deeds and misdeeds, during the tedious interval since their first meeting. Report had dwelt lovingly upon Mr. Bransford's eloquence at need. This awkward silence was a tribute of sincerity above question.

With difficulty Ellinor mastered a wild desire to ask where the

cat had gone. "Oh, come ye in peace here or come ye in war?"
Such injudicious quotation trembled on the tip of her tongue, but
she suppressed it — barely in time. She felt herself growing nervous
with the fear lest she should be hurried into some all too luminous
speech. And still Jeff stood there, lost, speechless, helpless, unready,
a clumsy oaf, an object of pity. Pity at last, or a kindred feeling,
drove her to the rescue. And, just as she had feared, she said, in
her generous haste, far too much.

"I thought you were not coming?"

The inflection made a question of this statement. Also, by implication, it answered so many questions yet unworded that Jeff was able
to use his tongue again; but it was not the trusty tongue of yore —
witness this wooden speech:

"You mean you thought I said I wasn't coming — don't you? You
knew I would come."

"Indeed? How should I know what you would do? I've only seen
you once. Aren't you forgetting that?"

"Why else did you make up as a Friend then?"

"Oh! Oh, dear, these men! There's conceit for you! I chose my
costume solely to trap Mr. Bransford's eye? Is that it? Doubtless
all my thoughts have centered on Mr. Bransford since I first saw
him!"

"You know I didn't mean that, Miss Ellinor. I — "

"Miss Hoffman, if you please!"

"Miss Hoffman. Don't be mean to me. I've only got an hour — "

"An hour! Do you imagine for one second — Why, I mustn't
stay here. This is really a farewell dance given in my honor. We
go back East day after tomorrow. I must go in."

"Only one little hour. And I have come a long ways for my hour.
They take their masks off at midnight — don't they? And of course
I can't stay after that. I want only just to ask you — "

"Why did you come then? Isn't it rather unusual to go uninvited
to a ball?"

"Why, I reckon you nearly know why I came, Miss Hoffman;
but if you want me to say precisely, ma'am — "

"I don't!"

"We'll keep that for a surprise, then. Another thing: I wanted to
find out just where you live in New York. I forgot to ask you. And
I couldn't very well go round asking folks after you're gone — could
I? Of course I didn't have any invitation — from Mr. Lake; but I
thought, if he didn't know it, he wouldn't mind me just stepping in
to get your address."

"Well, of all the assurance!" said Miss Ellinor. "Do you intend to start up a correspondence with me without even the formality of asking my consent?"

"Why, Miss Ellinor, ma'am, I thought — "

"Miss Hoffman, sir! Yes — and there's another thing. You said you had no invitation — from Mr. Lake. Does that mean, by any chance, that I invited you?"

"You didn't say a word about my coming," said Jeff. He was a flustered man, this poor Bransford, but he managed to put a slight stress upon the word "say."

Miss Ellinor — Miss Hoffman — caught this faint emphasis instantly.

"Oh, I didn't say anything? I just looked an invitation, I suppose?" she stormed. "Melting eyes — and that sort of thing? Tears in them, maybe? Poor girl! Poor little child! It would be cruel to let her go home without seeing me again. I will give her a little more happiness, poor thing, and write to her a while. Maybe it would be wiser, though, just to make a quarrel and break loose at once. She'll get over it in a little while after she gets back to New York. Well! Upon my word!"

As she advanced these horrible suppositions, Miss Hoffman had marked out a short beat of garden path — five steps and a turn; five steps back and whirl again — with, on the whole, a caged-tigress effect. With a double-quick at each turn to keep his place at her elbow, Jeff, utterly aghast at the damnable perversity of everything on earth, vainly endeavored to make co-ordinate and stumbling remonstrance. As she stopped for breath, Jeff heard his own voice at last, propounding to the world at large a stunned query as to whether the abode of lost spirits could afford aught to excel the present situation. The remark struck him: he paused to wonder what other things he had been saying.

Miss Ellinor walked her beat, vindictive. Her chin was at an angle of complacency. She turned up the perky corners of an imaginary mustache with an air, an exasperating little finger, separated from the others, pointing upward in hateful self-satisfaction. Her mouth wore a gratified masculine smirk, visible even in the starlight; her gait was a leisured and lordly strut; her hand waved airy pity. Jeff shrank back in horror.

"M-Miss Hoffman, I n-never d-dreamed — "

Miss Hoffman turned upon him swiftly.

"Never have I heard anything like it — never! You bring me out here willy-nilly, and by way of entertainment you virtually accuse me of throwing myself at your head."

"I never!" said Jeff indignantly. "I didn't — "

Miss Hoffman faced him crouchingly and shook an indictment from her fingers.

"First, you imply that I enticed you to come; second, expecting you, I dressed to catch your eye; third, I was watching eagerly for you — "

"Come — I say now!" The baited and exasperated victim walked headlong into the trap. "The first thing you did was to ask me if I was lame? Wasn't that question meant to find out who I was? When I answered, 'Not — very,' didn't you know at once that it was me?"

"There! That proves exactly what I was just saying," raged the delighted trapper. "You don't even deny it! You say in so many words that I have been courting you! I had to say something — didn't I? You wouldn't! You were limping, so I asked you if you were lame. What else could I have said? Did you want me to stand there like a stuffed Egyptian mummy? That's the thanks a girl gets for trying to help a great, awkward, blundering butter-fingers! Oh, if you could just see yourself! The irresistible conqueror! Not altogether unprincipled though! You *are* capable of compunction. I'll give you credit for that. Alarmed at your easy success, you try to spare me. It is noble of you — noble! You drag me out here, force a quarrel upon me — "

"Oh, by Jove now! Really!" Stung by the poignant injustice of crowding events, Jeff took the bit in his teeth and rushed to destruction. "Really, you must see yourself that I couldn't drag you out here! I have never been in that hall before. I didn't know the lay of the ground. I didn't even know that little side room was there. I thought you pressed my arm a little — " So the brainless colt, in the quicksands, flounders deeper with each effort to extricate himself.

If Miss Hoffman had been angry before she was furious now.

"So *that's* the way of it? Better and better! I dragged *you* out! Really, Mr. Bransford, I feel that I should take you back to your chaperone at once. You might be compromised, you know!"

Goaded to desperation, he acted on this hint at once. He turned, with stiff and stilted speech:

"I will take you back to the window, Miss Hoffman. Then there is nothing for me to do but go. I am sorry to have caused you even a moment's annoyance. Tomorrow you will see how you have twisted — I mean, how completely you have misinterpreted everything I have said. Perhaps some day you may forgive me. Here is the window. Good night — good-bye!"

Miss Hoffman lingered, however.

"Of course, if you apologize — "

"I do, Miss Hoffman. I beg your pardon most sincerely for any-thing I have ever said or done that could hurt you in any way."

"If you are sure you are sorry — if you take it all back and will never do such a thing again — perhaps I may forgive you."

"I won't — I am — I will!" said the abject and groveling wretch. Which was incoherent but pleasing. "I didn't mean anything the way you took it; but I'm sorry for everything."

"Then I didn't beguile you to come? Or mask as a Friend in the hope that you would identify me?"

"No, no!"

Miss Ellinor pressed her advantage cruelly. "Nor take stock of each new masker to see if he possibly wasn't the expected Mr. Bransford? Nor drag you into the garden? Nor squeeze your arm?" Her hands went to her face, her lissome body shook. "Oh, Mr. Bransford!" she sobbed between her fingers. "How could you — how *could* you say that?"

The clock chimed. A pealing voice beat out into the night: "Masks off!" A hundred voices swelled the cry; it was drowned in waves of laughter. It rose again tumultuously: *"Masks off! Masks off!"* Nearer came hateful voices too, that cried: *"Ellinor! Ellinor! Where are you?"*

"I must go!" said Jeff. "They'll be looking for you. No; you didn't do any of those things. You couldn't do any of those things. Good-bye!"

"Ellinor! Ellinor Hoffman!! Where are you?"

Miss Hoffman whipped off her mask. From the open window a shaft of light fell on her face. It was flushed, sparkling, radiant. "Masks off!" she said. "Stupid! . . . Oh, you great goose! Of course I did!" She stepped back into the shadow.

No one, as the copybook says justly, may be always wise. Con-versely, the most unwise of us blunders sometimes upon the right thing to do. With a glimmer of returning intelligence, Mr. Brans-ford laid his noseguard on the window-sill.

"Sir!" said Ellinor then. "How dare you?" Then she turned the other cheek. "Good-bye!" she whispered, and fled away to the ball-room.

Mr. Bransford, in the shadows, scratched his head dubiously.

"Her Christian name was Ellinor," he muttered. "Ellinor! H'm — Ellinor! Very appropriate name. . . . Very! . . . And I don't know yet where she lives!"

He wandered disconsolately away to the garden wall, forgetting the discarded noseguard.

CHAPTER VI

The Isle of Arcady

Then the moon shone out so broad and good
  That the barn-fowl crowed:
And the brown owl called to his mate in the wood
  That a dead man lay in the road!
— WILL WALLACE HARNEY

ARCADIA'S ASSETS were the railroad, two large modern sawmills, the climate and printer's ink. The railroad found it a patch of bare ground, six miles from water; put in successively a whistling-post, a signboard, a depot, townsite papers and a water-main from the Alamo; and, when the townsite papers were confirmed, established machine shops and made the new town the division headquarters and base for northward building.

The railroad then set up the sawmills, primarily to get out ties and timbers for its own lanky growth, and built a spur to bring the forest down from Rainbow to the mills. The word "down" is used advisedly. Arcadia nestled on the plain under the very eavespouts of Rainbow Range. The branch, following with slavish fidelity the lines of a twisted corkscrew, took twenty-seven miles, mostly tunnel and trestlework, to clamber to the logging camps, with a minimum grade that was purely prohibitive and a maximum that I dare not state; but there was a rise of six thousand feet in those twenty-seven miles. You can figure the average for yourself. And if the engine should run off the track at the end of her climb, she would light on the very roundhouse where she took breakfast, and spoil the shingles.

Yes, that was some railroad. There was a summer hotel — Cloud-land — on the summit, largely occupied by slackwire performers. Others walked up or rode a horse. They used stem-winding engines, with eight vertical cylinders on the right side and a shaft like a steamboat, with beveled cogwheel transmission on the axles. And they haven't had a wreck on that branch to date. No matter how late a train is, when an engine sees the tail-lights of her caboose ahead of her she stops and sends out flagmen.

The railroad, under the pseudonym of the Arcadia Development Company, also laid out streets and laid in a network of pipe-lines, and staked out lots until the sawmill protested for lack of tie-lumber. It put down miles of cement walks, fringed them with cottonwood saplings, telephone poles and electric lights. It built a hotel and a few streets of party-colored cottages — directoire, with lingerie tile roofs, organdy façades and peplum, intersecting panels and outside chimneys at the gable ends. It decreed a park, with nooks, lanes, mazes, lake, swans, ballground, grandstand, bandstand and the band appertaining thereunto — all of which apparently came into being over night. Then it employed a competent staff of word-artists and capitalized the climate.

The result was astonishing. The cottonwoods grew apace and a swift town grew with them — swift in every sense of the word. It took good money to buy good lots in Arcadia. People with money must be fed, served and amused by people wanting money. In three years the trees cast a pleasant shade and the company cast a balance, with gratifying results. They discounted the unearned increment for a generation to come.

It was a beneficent scheme, selling ozone and novelty, sunshine and delight. The buyers got far more than the worth of their money, the company got their money — and everyone was happy. Health and good spirits are a bargain at any price. There were sandstorms and hot days; but sand promotes digestion and digestion promotes cheerfulness. Heat merely enhanced the luxury of shaded hammocks. As an adventurer thawed out, he sent for seven others worse than himself. Arcadia became the metropolis of the county and, by special election, the county-seat. Courthouse, college and jail followed in quick succession.

For the company, Arcadia life was one grand, sweet song, with thus far, but a single discord. As has been said, Arcadia was laid out on the plain. There was higher ground on three sides — Rainbow Mountain to the east, the deltas of La Luz Creek and the Alamo to the north and south. New Mexico was dry, as a rule. After the second exception, when enthusiastic citizens went about on stilts to forward a project for changing the town's name to Venice, the company acknowledged its error handsomely. When dry land prevailed once more above the face of the waters, it built a mighty moat by way of the *amende honorable* — a moat with its one embankment on the inner side of the five-mile horseshoe about the town. This, with its attendant bridges, gave to Arcadia an aspect singularly medieval. It also furnished a convenient line of social demarcation. Chauffeurs, college professors, lawyers, gamblers, county officers, together with a few tradesmen and railroad officials, abode within "the Isle of Arcady," on more or less even terms with the Arcadians proper; millmen, railroaders, lumberjacks, and the underworld generally, dwelt without the pale.

The company rubbed its lamp again — and behold! an armory, a hospital and a library! It contributed liberally to churches and campaign funds; it exercised a general supervision over morals and manners. For example, in the deed to every lot sold was an ironclad, fire-tested, automatic and highly constitutional forfeiture clause, to the effect that sale or storage on the premises of any malt, vinous or spirituous liquors should immediately cause the title to revert to the company. The company's own vicarious saloon, on Lot Number One, was a sumptuous and magnificent affair. It was known as The Mint.

All this while we have been trying to reach the night watchman.

In the early youth of Arcadia there came to her borders a warlock Finn, of ruddy countenance and solid build. He had a Finnish name, and they called him Lars Porsena.

Lars P. had been a seafaring man. While spending a year's wage in San Francisco, he had wandered into Arcadia by accident. There, being unable to find the sea, he became a lumberjack — with a custom, when in spirits, of beating the watchman of that date into an omelet.

The indulgence of this penchant gave occasion for much adverse criticism. Fine and imprisonment failed to deter him from this playful habit. One watchman tried to dissuade Lars from his foible with a club, and his successor even went so far as to shoot him — to shoot Lars P., of course, not his predecessor — the successor's predecessor, not Lars Porsena's — if he ever had one, which he hadn't. (What we need is more pronouns.) He — the successor of the predecessor — resigned when Lars became convalescent; but Lars was no whit dismayed by this contretemps — in his first light-hearted moment he resumed his old amusement with unabated gayety.

Thus was one of our greatest railroad systems subjected to embarrassment and annoyance by the idiosyncracies of an ignorant but cheerful sailorman. The railroad resolved to submit no longer to such caprice. A middleweight of renown was imported, who — when he was able to be about again — bitterly reproached the president and demanded a bonus on the ground that he had knocked Lars down several times before he — Lars — got angry; and also because of a disquisition in the Finnish tongue which Lars Porsena had emitted during the procedure — which address, the prizefighter stated, had unnerved him and so led to his undoing. It was obviously, he said, of a nature inconceivably insulting; the memory of it rankled yet, though he had heard only the beginning and did not get the — But let that pass.

The thing became a scandal. Watchman succeeded watchman on the company payroll and the hospital list, until someone hit upon a happy and ingenious way to avoid this indignity. Lars Porsena was appointed watchman.

This statesmanlike policy bore gratifying results. Lars Porsena straightway abandoned his absurd and indefensible custom, and no imitator arose. Also, Arcadia within the moat — the island — which was the limit of his jurisdiction, became the most orderly spot in New Mexico.

. . . .

In the first gray of dawn, Uncle Sam, whistling down Main Street on his way home from the masquerade, found Lars Porsena lying on his face in a pool of blood.

The belated reveler knelt beside him. The watchman was shot, but still breathed. "Ho! Murder! Help! Murder!" shouted Uncle Sam. The alarm rolled crashing along the quiet street. Heads were thrust from windows; startled voices took up the outcry; other home-goers ran from every corner; hastily arrayed householders poured themselves from street doors.

Lars Porsena was in disastrous plight. He breathed, but that was about all. He was shot through the body. A trail of blood led back a few doors to Lake's Bank. A window was cut out; the blood began at the sill.

Messengers ran to telephone the doctor, the sheriff, Lake. The knot of men grew to a crowd. A rumor spread that there had been an unusual amount of currency in the bank overnight — a rumor presently confirmed by Basset, the bareheaded and white-faced cashier. It was near payday; in addition to the customary amount to cash checks for railroaders and mill hands — itself no mean sum — and the money for regular business, there had been provision for contemplated loans to promoters of new local industries.

The doctor came running, made a hasty examination, took emergency measures to stanch the freshly started blood, and swore wholeheartedly at the ambulance and the crowding Arcadians. He administered a stimulant. Lars Porsena fluttered his eyes weakly.

"Stand back, you idiots! Bash these fools' faces in for 'em, someone!" said the medical man. He bent over the watchman. "Who did it, Lars?"

Lars made a vain effort to speak. The doctor gave him another sip of restorative and took a pull himself.

"Try again, old man. You're badly hurt and you may not get another chance. Did you know him?"

Lars gathered all his strength to a broken speech:

"No. . . . Bank. . . . Found window. . . . Midnight . . . nearly. . . .
Shot me. . . . Didn't see him." He fell back on Uncle Sam's starry
vest.

"Ambulance coming," said Uncle Sam. "Will he live, doc?"
Doc shook his head doubtfully.

"Poor chance. Lost too much blood. If he had been found in time
he might have pulled through. Wonderful vitality. Ought to be
dead now, by the books. Still, there's a chance."

"I never thought," said Uncle Sam to Cyrano de Bergerac, as the
ambulance bore away its unconscious burden, "that I would ever be
so sorry at anything that could happen to Lars Porsena — after the
way he made me stop singing on my own birthday. He was one
grand old fighting machine!"

CHAPTER VII

States-General

> And they hae killed Sir Charlie Hay
> And laid the wyte on Geordie.
>
> — *Old Ballad*

THAT THE MASTER'S EYE is worth two servants had ever been Lake's
favorite maxim. He had not yet gone to bed when the message
reached him, where he kept his masterly eye on the proper closing
up of the ballroom. He came through the crowd now, shouldering
his way roughly, still in his police costume — helmet, tunic and belt.
In his wake came the sheriff, who had just arrived, scorching to the
scene on his trusty wheel.

On the bank steps, Lake turned to face the crowd. His strong
canine jaw was set to stubborn fighting lines; the helmet did not
wholly hide the black frown or the swollen veins at his temple.

"Come in, Thompson, and help the sheriff size the thing up — and
you, Alec" — he stabbed the air at his choice with a strong blunt
finger — "and Turnbull — you, Clarke — and you. . . . Bassett, you
keep the door. Admit no one!"

Lake was the local great man. Never had he appeared to such advantage to his admirers; never had his ascendancy seemed so unquestioned and so justified. As he stood beside the sheriff in the growing
light, the man was the incarnation of power — the power of wealth,
position, prestige, success. In this moment of yet unplumbed disaster, taken by surprise, summoned from a night of crowded pleas-

ure, he held his mastery, chose his men and measures with unhesitant decision — planned, ordered, kept to that blunt direct speech of his that wasted no word. A buzz went up from the unadmitted as the door swung shut behind him.

Lake had chosen well. Arcadia in epitome was within those pillaged walls. Thompson was president of the rival bank. Alec was division superintendent. Turnbull was the mill-master. Clarke was editor of the *Arcadian Day*. Clarke had been early to the storm-center; yet, of all the investigators, Clarke alone was not more or less disheveled. He was faultlessly appareled — even to the long Prince Albert and black string tie — in which, indeed, report said, he slept.

So much for capital, industry and the fourth estate. The last of the probers, whom Lake had drafted merely by the slighting personal pronoun "you," was nevertheless identifiable in private life by the name of Billy White — being, indeed, none other than our old friend the devil. His indigenous mustache still retained a Mephistophelian twist; he was becomingly arrayed in slippers, pajamas and a pink bathrobe, girdled at the waist with a most unhermitlike cord, having gone early and surly to bed. In this improvised committee he fitly represented Society: while the sheriff represented society at large and, ex officio, that incautious portion under duress. Yet one element was unrepresented; for Lake made a mistake which other great men have made — of failing to reckon with the masterless men, who dwell without the wall.

Lake led the way.

"Will the watchman die, Alec, d'you think?" whispered Billy, as they filed through the grilled door to the counting room.

"Don't know. Hope not. Game old rooster. Good watchman, too," said Turnbull, the mill-superintendent.

Lake turned on the lights. The wall-safe was blown open; fragments of the door were scattered among the overturned chairs.

In an open recess in the vault there was a dull yellow mass; the explosion had spilled the front rows of coin to a golden heap. Behind, some golden rouleaus were intact: others tottered precariously, as you have perhaps seen beautiful tall stacks of colored counters do. Gold pieces were strewn along the floor.

"Thank God, they didn't get all the gold anyhow!" said Lake, with a sigh of relief. "Then, of course, they didn't touch the silver; but there was a lot of greenbacks — over twenty-five thousand, I think. Basset will know. And I don't know how much gold is gone. Look round and see if they left anything incriminating, sheriff, anything that we can trace them by."

"He heard poor old Lars coming," said the sheriff. "Then, after he shot him, he hadn't the nerve to come back for the gold. This strikes me as being a bungler's job. Must have used an awful lot of dynamite to tear that door up like that! Funny no one heard the explosion. Can't be much of your gold gone, Lake. That compartment is pretty nearly as full as it will hold."

"Or heard him shoot our watchman," suggested Thompson. "Still, I don't know. There's blasting going on in the hills all the time and almost every one was at the masquerade or else asleep. How many times did they shoot old Lars — does anybody know? Is there any idea what time it was done?"

"He was shot once — right here," said Alec, indicating the spot on the flowered silk that had been part of his mandarin's dress. "Gun was held so close it burnt his shirt. Awful hole. Don't believe the old chap'll make it. He crawled along toward the telephone station till he dropped. Say! Central must have heard that shot! It's only two blocks away. She ought to be able to tell what time it was."

"Lars said it was just before midnight," said Clarke.

"Oh! — did he speak?" asked Lake. "How many robbers were there? Did he know any of them?"

"He didn't see anybody — shot just as he reached the window. Hope some one hangs for this!" said Clarke. "Lake, I wish you'd have this money picked up — I'm not used to walking on gold — or else have me watched."

Lake shook his head, angry at the untimely pleasantry. It was a pleasantry in effect only, put forward to hide uneditorial agitation and distress for Lars Porsena. Lake's undershot jaw thrust forward; he fingered the blot of whisker at his ear. It was a time for action, not for talk. He began his campaign.

"Look here, sheriff! You ought to wire up and down the line to keep a lookout. Hold all suspicious characters. Then get a posse to ride for some sign round the town. If we only had something to go on — some clue! Later we'll look through this town with a finetooth comb. Most likely they — or he, if there was only one — won't risk staying here. First of all, I've got to telegraph to El Paso for money to stave off a run on the bank. You'll help me, Thompson? Of course my burglar insurance will make good my loss — or most of it; but that'll take time. We mustn't risk a run. People lose their heads so. I'll give you a statement for the *Day*, Clarke, as soon as I find out where Mr. Thompson stands."

"I will back you up, sir. With the bulk of depositors' money loaned out, no bank, however solvent, can withstand a continued run without backing. I shall be glad to tide you over if only for my own protection. A panic is contagious —"

"Thanks," said Lake shortly, interrupting this stately financial discourse. "Then we shall do nicely. . . . Let's see — tomorrow's payday. You fellows" — he turned briskly to the two superintendents — "can't you hold up your payday, say, until Saturday? Stand your men off. The company stands good for their money. They can wait a while.

"No need to do that," said Alec. "I'll have the railroad checks drawn on St. Louis. The storekeepers'll cash 'em. If necessary I'll wire for authority to let Turnbull pay off the millhands with railroad checks. It's just taking money from one pocket to put it in the other, anyhow."

"Then that's all right! Now for the robbers!" The banker's face betrayed impatience. "My first duty was to protect my clients; but now we'll waste no more time. You gentlemen make a close search for any possible scrap of evidence while the sheriff and I write our telegrams. I must wire the burglar insurance company, too." He plunged a pen into an inkwell and fell to work.

Acting upon this hint, the sheriff took a desk. "Wish Phillips was here — my deputy," he sighed. "I've sent for him. He's got a better head than I have for noticing clues and things." This was eminently correct as well as modest. The sheriff was a Simon-pure Arcadian, the company's nominee; his deputy was a concession to the disgruntled Hinterland, where the unobservant rarely reach maturity.

"Oh, Alec!" said Lake over his shoulder, "you sit down, too, and wire all your conductors about their passengers last night. Yes, and the freight crews, too. We'll rush those through first. And can't you scare up another operator?" His pen scratched steadily over the paper. "More apt to be some of our local outlaws, though. In that case it will be easier to find their trail. They'll probably be on horseback."

"You were an — old-timer yourself, were you not?" asked Billy amiably. "If the robbers are frontiersmen they may be easier to get track of, as you suggest; but won't they be harder to get?" Billy spoke languidly. The others were searching assiduously for "clues" in the most approved manner, but Billy sprawled easily in a chair.

"We'll get 'em if we can find out who they were," snapped Lake, setting his strong jaw. He did not particularly like Billy — especially since their late trip to Rainbow. "There never was a man yet so good but there was one just a little better."

"By a good man, in this connection, you mean a bad man, I presume?" said Billy in a meditative drawl. "Were you a good man before you became a banker?"

"Look here! What's this?" The interruption came from Clarke. He pounced down between two fragments of the safe door and brought up an object which he held to the light.

At the startled tones, Lake spun round in his swivel-chair. He held out his hand.

"Really, I don't think I ever saw anything like this thing before," he said. "Any of you know what it is?"

"It's a noseguard," said Billy. Billy was a college man and had worn a nosepiece himself. He frowned unconsciously, remembering his successful rival of the masquerade.

"A noseguard? What for?"

"You wear it to protect your nose and teeth when playing football," explained Billy. "Keeps you from swearing, too. You hold this piece between your teeth; the other part goes over your nose, up between your eyes and fastens with this band around your forehead."

"Why! Why!" gasped Clarke, "there was a man at the masquerade togged out as a football player!"

"I saw him," said Alec. "And he wore one of these things. I saw him talking to Topsy."

"One of my guests?" demanded Lake scoffingly. "Oh, nonsense! Some young fellow has been in here yesterday, talking to the clerks, and dropped it. Who went as a football player, White? You know all these college boys. Know anything about this one?"

"Not a thing." There Billy lied — a prompt and loyal gentleman — reasoning that Buttinski, as he mentally styled the interloper who had misappropriated the Quaker lady, would have cared nothing at that time for a paltry thirty thousand. Thus was he guilty of a practice against which we are all vainly warned — of judging others by ourselves. Billy remembered very distinctly that Miss Ellinor had not reappeared until the midnight unmasking, and he therefore acquitted her companion of this particular crime, entirely without prejudice to Buttinski's felonious instincts in general. For the watchman had been shot before midnight. Billy made a tentative mental decision that this famous noseguard had been brought to the bank later and left there purposely; and resolved to keep his eye open.

"Oh, well, it's no great difference anyhow," said Lake. "Whoever it was dropped it here yesterday, I guess, and got another one for the masquerade."

"Hold on there!" said Clarke, holding the spotlight tenaciously.

"That don't go! This thing was on top of one of those pieces of the safe!"

For the first time Lake was startled from his iron composure.

"Are you sure?" he demanded, jumping up.

"Sure! It was right here against the sloping side of this piece — so."

"That puts a different light on the case, gentlemen," said Lake. "Luck is with us; and — "

"And, while I think of it," said Clarke, making the most of his unexpected opportunity, "I made notes of all the costumes and their wearers after the masks were off — for the paper, you know — and I saw no football player there. I remember that distinctly."

"I only saw him the one time," confirmed Alec, "and I stayed almost to the break-up. Whoever it was, he left early."

"But what possible motive could the robber have for going to the dance at all?" queried Lake in perplexity.

"Maybe he made his appearance there in a football suit purposely, so as to leave us someone to hunt for, and then committed the robbery and went back in another costume," suggested Clarke, pleased and not a little surprised at his own ingenuity. "In that case, he would have left this rubber thing here of design."

"H'm!" Lake was plainly struck with this theory. "And that's not such a bad idea, either! We'll look into this football matter after breakfast. You'll go to the hotel with me, gentlemen? Our womankind are all asleep after the ball. The sheriff will send someone to guard the bank. Meantime I'll call the cashier in and find out exactly how much money we're short. Send Basset in, will you, Billy? You stay at the door and keep that mob out."

CHAPTER VIII

Arcades Ambo

What means this, my lord?
Marry, this is miching mallecho; it means mischief.
— *Hamlet*

We are here to do what service we may, for honor and not for hire.
— Robert Louis Stevenson

WITH BILLY went the sheriff and Alec, the latter with a sheaf of telegrams.

"Now . . . how did Buttinski's noseguard get into this bank? That's what I'd like to know," said Billy to the doorknob, when the other committeemen had gone their ways. "I didn't bring it. I don't believe Buttinski did. . . . And Policeman Lake certainly saw us quarreling. He noticed the football player, right enough — and he pretends he didn't. Why — why — why does Policeman Lake pretend he didn't see that football player? Echo answers — why? . . . Denmark's all putrefied!"

The low sun cleared the housetops. The level rays fell along the window-sill; and Billy, staring fascinated at the single blotch of dried blood on the inner sill, saw something glitter and sparkle there beside it. He went closer. It was a dust of finely powdered glass. Billy whistled.

A light foot ran up the steps. There was a rap at the door.

"No entrance except on business. No business transacted here!" quoted Billy, startled from a deep study. A head appeared at the window. "Oh, it's you, Jimmy? That's different. Come in!"

It was Jimmy Phillips, the chief deputy. Billy knew him and liked him. He unbarred the door.

"Well, anything turned up yet?" demanded Jimmy. "I stopped in to see Lars. Him and me was old side partners."

"How's he making it, Jimmy?"

"Oh, doc said he had one chance in ten thousand; so he's all right, I guess," responded that brisk optimist. "They got any theory about the robber?"

"They have that. A perfectly sound theory, too — only it isn't true," said Billy in a low and guarded tone. "They'll tell you. I haven't got time. See here — if I give you the straight tip will you work it up and keep your head closed until you see which way the cat jumps? Can you keep it to yourself?"

"Mum as a sack of clams!" said Jimmy.

"Look at this a minute!" Billy pointed to the tiny particles of glass on the inner sill. "Got that? Then I'll dust it off. This is a case for your gummiest shoes. Now look at this!" He indicated the opening where the patch of glass had been cut from the big pane. Jimmy rubbed his finger very cautiously along the raw edge of the glass.

"Cut out from the inside — then carried out there? A frame-up?"

"Exactly. But I don't want anybody else to size it up for a frame-up — not now."

"But," said Jimmy good-naturedly, "I'd 'a' seen all that myself after a little if you hadn't 'a' showed me."

"Yes," said Billy dryly; "and then told somebody! That's why I brushed the glass-dust off. I've got inside information — some that

I'm going to share with you and some that I am not going to tell even you!"

"Trot it out!"

Straightway the banker reported this possible clue to the sheriff.

"Lake had the key of this front door in the policeman's uniform that he wore to the dance. Isn't that queer? If I were you I'd very quietly find out whether he went home to get that key after he got word that the bank was robbed. He was still in the ballroom when he got the message."

"You think it's a put-up job? Why?"

"There is something not just right about the man Lake. His mind is too ballbearing altogether. He herds those chumps in there round like so many sheep. He used 'em to make discoveries with and then showed 'em how to force 'em on him. Oh, they made a heap of progress! They've got evidence enough up in there to hang John the Baptist, with Lake all the time setting back in the breeching like a balky horse. It's Lake's bank, and the bank's got burglar insurance. Got that? If he gets the money and the insurance, too — see? And I happen to know he has been bucking the market. I dropped a roll with him myself. Then there's r-r-revenge! — as they say on the stage — and something else beside. Has Lake any bitter enemies?"

"Oodles of 'em!"

"But one worse than the others — one he hates most?"

Jimmy thought for a while. Then he nodded.

"Jeff Bransford, I reckon."

"Is he in town?"

"Not that I know of."

"Well, I never heard of your Mr. Bransford; but he's in town all right, all right! You'll see! Lake's got a case cooked up that'll hang some one higher than Haman; and I'll bet the first six years of my life against a Doctor Cook lecture ticket that the first letter of some one's name is Jeff Bransford."

"Maybe Jeff can prove he was somewhere else?" suggested Jimmy.

Billy evaded the issue.

"What sort of a man is this Bransford? Any good? Besides being an enemy of Lake's, I mean?"

"Mr. Bransford is one whom we all delight to humor," announced the deputy, after some reflection.

"Friend of yours?"

Jimmy reflected again.

"We-ll — yes!" he said. "He limps a little in cold weather, and I got a little small ditch plowed in my skull — but our horses was both young and wild, and the boys rode in between us before there was any harm done. I pulled him out of the Pecos since that, too, and poured some several barrels of water out o' him. Yes, we're good friends, I reckon."

"He'll shoot back on proper occasion, then? A good sport? Stand the gaff?"

"On proper occasion," rejoined Jimmy, "the other man will shoot back — if he's lucky. Yes, sir, Jeff's certainly one dead game sport at any turn in the road."

"Considering the source and spirit of your information, you sadden me," said Billy. "The better man he is, the better chance to hang. Has he got any close friends here?"

"He seldom ever comes here," said Jimmy. "All his friends is on Rainbow, specially South Rainbow; but his particular side partners is all away just now; leastways, all but one."

"Can't you write to that one?"

The deputy grinned hugely.

"And tell him to come break Jeff out o' jail?" said he. "That don't seem hardly right, considerin'. You write to him — Johnny Dines, Morningside. You might wire up to Cloudland and have it forwarded from there. I'll pay."

Billy made a note of it.

"They'll be out here in a jiffy now," he said. "Now, Jimmy, you listen to all they tell you; follow it up; make no comments; don't see anything and don't miss anything. Let Lake think he's having it all his own way and he'll make some kind of a break that will give him away. We haven't got a thing against him yet except the right guess. And you be careful to catch your friend without a fight. When you get him I want you to give him a message from me; but don't mention my name. Tell him to keep a stiff upper lip — that the devil takes care of his own. Say the devil told you himself — in person. I don't want to show my hand. I'm on the other side — see? That way I can be in Lake's counsels — force myself in, if necessary, after this morning."

"You think that if you give Lake rope enough — "

"Exactly. Here they come — I hear their chairs."

"Blonde or brunette?" said Jimmy casually.

"Eh? What's that?"

"The something else that you wouldn't tell me about," Jimmy explained. "Is she blonde or brunette?"

"Oh, go to hell!" said Billy.

CHAPTER IX

Taken

Lord Huntley then he did speak out —
O, fair mot fa' his body! —
"I here will fight doublet alane
Or ony thing ails Geordie!

"Whom has he robbed? What has he stole?
Or has he killed ony?
Or what's the crime that he has done
His foes they are so mony?"

—*Old Ballad*

HUE AND CRY, hubbub and mystery, swept the Isle of Arcady that morning, but the most painstaking search and query proved fruitless. It developed beyond doubt that the football man had not been seen since his one brief appearance on the ballroom floor. Search was transferred to the mainland where, as it neared noon, Lake's perseverance and thoroughness were rewarded. In Chihuahua suburb, beyond the north wall, Lake noted a sweat-marked, red-roan horse in the yard of Rosalio Marquez, better known, by reason of his profession, as Monte.

Straightway the banker reported this possible clue to the sheriff and to Billy, who was as tireless and determined in the chase as Lake himself. The other masqueraders had mostly abandoned the chase. He found them on the bridge of the La Luz sallyport.

"It may be worth looking into," Lake advised the sheriff. "Better send someone to reconnoiter — someone not known to be connected with your office. You go, Billy. If you find anything suspicious the sheriff can 'phone to the hospital if he needs me. I'm going over to see how the old watchman is — ought to have gone before. If he gets well I must do something handsome for him."

Billy fell in with this request. He had a well-founded confidence in Lake's luck and attached much more significance to the trifling matter of the red-roan horse than did the original discoverer — especially since the discoverer had bethought himself to go to the hospital on an errand of mercy. Billy now confidently expected early developments. And he preferred personally to conduct the arrest, so that he might interfere, if necessary, to prevent any wasting of good cartridges. He did not expect much trouble, however, providing the affair was conducted tactfully; reasoning that a dead game sport with a clean conscience and a light heart would not seriously object to a small arrest. Poor Billy's own heart was none of the lightest as he went on this loyal service to his presumably favored rival.

Bicycle-back, he accompanied the sheriff beyond the outworks to the Mexican quarter. Near the place indicated by the banker Billy left his wheel and strolled casually round the block. He saw the red-roan steed and noted the Double Rainbow branded on his thigh.

Monte was leaning in the adobe doorway, rolling a cigarette. Billy knew him, in a business way.

"Hello, Monte! Good horse you've got there."

"Yais — tha's nice hor-rse," said Monte.

"Want to sell him?"

"Thees ees not my hor-rse," explained Monte. "He ees of a frien'."

"I like his looks," said Billy. "Is your friend here? Or, if he's downtown, what's his name? I'd like to buy that horse."

"He ees weetheen, but he ees not apparent. He ees *dormiendo* — ah — yais —esleepin'. He was las' night to the *baile mascarada.*"

Billy nodded. "Yes; I was there myself." He decided to take a risk: assuming that his calculations were correct, *x* must equal Bransford. So he said carelessly: "Let's see, Bransford went as a sailor, didn't he? *Un marinero?*"

"Oh, no; he was atir-re' lak one — *qué cosa?* — what you call thees theeng? — *un balon para jugar con los pies?* Ah! si, si! — one feetball! Myself I come soon back. I have no beesness. The bes' people ees all for the dance," said Monte, with hand turned up and shrugging shoulder. "So, *media noche* — twelve of the clock, I am here back. I fin' here the hor-rse of my frien', and one *carta* — letter — that I am not to lock the door; *porque* he may come to esleep. So I am mek to r-repose myself. Later I am ar-rouse when my frien' am to r-retir-re heemself. Ah, *qué hombre!* I am yet to esmile to see heem in thees so r-redeeculous *vestidos!* He ees ver' gay. Ah! *qué* Jeff! Een all ways thees ees a man ver' *sufficiente*, cour-rageous, es-strong, formidable! Yet he ees keep the *disposición*, the hear-rt, of a seemple leetle chil' — *un muchacho!*"

"I'll come again," said Billy, and passed on. He had found out what he had come for. The absence of concealment dispelled any lingering doubt of Jeff Buttinski. Yet he could establish no alibi by Monte.

Perhaps Billy White may require here a little explanation. All things considered, Billy thought Jeff would be better off in jail, with a friend in the opposite camp working for his interest, than getting himself foolishly killed by a hasty posse. If we are cynical, we may say that, being young, Billy was not averse to the rôle of *deus ex machina*; perhaps a thought of friendly gratitude was not lacking. Then, too, adventure for àdventure's sake is motive enough — in youth. Or, as a final self-revelation, we may hint that if Jeff was a rival, so too was Lake — and one more eligible. Let us not be cynical, however, or cowardly. Let us say at once shamelessly what we very well know — that youth is the season for clean honor and high emprise; that boy's love is best and truest of all; that poor, honest Billy, in his own dogged and fantastic way, but sought to give true service where he — loved. There, we have said it; and we are shamed. How old are you, sir? Forty? Fifty? Most actions are the result of mixed motives, you say? Well, that is a notable concession — at your age. Let it go at that. Billy, then, acted from mixed motives.

When Billy brought back his motives — and the sheriff — Monte still held his negligent attitude in the doorway. He waved a graceful salute.

"I want to see Bransford," said the sheriff.

"He ees esleepin'," said Monte.

"Well, I want to see him anyway!" The sheriff laid a brusk hand on the gatelatch.

Monte waved his cigarette airily, flicked the ash from the end with a slender finger, and once more demonstrated that the hand is quicker than the eye. The portentously steady gun in the hand was the first intimation to the eye that the hand had moved at all. It was a very large gun as to caliber, the sheriff noted. As it was pointed directly at his nose he was favorably situated to observe — looking along the barrel — that the hammer stood at full cock.

"Per-rhaps you have some papers for heem?" suggested Monte, with gentle and delicate deference. He still leaned against the door-jamb. "But eef not eet ees bes' that you do not enter thees my leetle house to distur-rb my gues'. That would be to commeet a r-rudeness — no?"

The sheriff was a sufficiently brave man, if not precisely a brilliant one. Yet he showed now intelligence of the highest order. He dropped the latch.

"You, Billy, stop your laughing! Do you know, Mr. Monte, I think you are quite right?" he observed with a smiling politeness equal to Monte's own. "That would be rude, certainly. My mistake. An Englishman's house is his castle — that sort of thing? If you will excuse me now we will go and get the papers, as you so kindly pointed out."

They went away, the sheriff, Billy and motives — Billy still laughing immoderately.

Monte went inside and stirred up his guest with a prodding boot-toe.

"Meester Jeff," he demanded, "what you been a-doin' now?"

Jeff sat up, rumpled his hair, and rubbed his eyes.

"Sleepin'," he said.

"An' before? *Porqué*, the sheriff he has been. To mek an arres' of you, I t'eenk."

"Me?" said Jeff, rubbing his chin thoughtfully. "I haven't done anything that I can remember now!"

"Sure? No small leetle cr-rime? Not las' night? Me, I jus' got up. I have not hear'."

Jeff considered this suggestion carefully. "No. I am sure. Not for years. Some mistake, I guess. Or maybe he just wanted to see me about something else. Why didn't he come in?"

"I mek r-reques' of heem that he do not," said Monte.

"I see," Jeff laughed. "Come on; we'll go see him. You don't want to get into trouble."

They crossed the bridge and met the sheriff just within the fortifications, returning in a crowded automobile. Jeff held up his hand. The machine stopped and the posse deployed — except Billy, who acted as chauffeur.

"You wanted to see me, sheriff — at the hotel?"

"Why, yes, if you don't mind," said the sheriff.

"Good dinner? I ain't had breakfast yet!"

"First-class," said the sheriff cordially. "Won't your friend come too?"

"Ah, señor, you eshame me that I am not so hospitabble, ees eet not?" purred Monte, as he followed Jeff into the tonneau.

The sheriff reddened and Billy choked.

"Nothing of the sort," said the sheriff hastily, lapsing into literalness. "You were quite within your rights. For that matter, I know you were at your own bank, dealing, when the crime was committed. I am holding you for the present as a possible accessory; and, if not, then as a material witness. By the way, Monte, would you mind if I sent some men to look through your place? There is a matter of some thirty thousand dollars missing. Lake asked us to look for it. I have papers for it if you care to see them."

"Oh, no, señor!" said Monte. He handed over a key. "*La casa es suyo!*"

"Thank you," said the sheriff, with unmoved gravity. "Anything of yours you want 'em to bring, Bransford?"

"Why, no," said Jeff cheerfully. "I've got nothing there but my saddle, my gun and an old football suit that belongs to 'Gene Baird, over on the West Side; but if you want me to stay long, I wish you'd look after my horse."

"I too have lef' there my gun that I keep to protec' my leetle house," observed Monte. "Tell someone to keep eet for me. I am much attach' to that gun."

"Why, yes, I have seen that gun, I think," said the sheriff. "They'll look out for it. All right, Billy!"

The car turned back.

"Oh — you were speaking about Monte being an accessory. I didn't get in till 'way late last night, and I've been asleep all day," said Jeff apologetically. "Might I ask before or after exactly what fact Monte was an accessory?"

"Bank robbery, for one thing."

"Ah! . . . That would be Lake's bank? Anything else?"

The sheriff was not a patient man and he had borne much; also he liked Lars Porsena. Perfection, even in trifles, is rare and wins affection. He turned on Jeff with an angry growl.

"Murder!"

"Lake?" murmured Jeff hopefully.

The sheriff continued, ignoring and, indeed, only half sensing the purport of Jeff's comment:

"At least, the wound may not be mortal."

"That's too bad," said Jeff. He was, if possible, more cheerful than ever.

The sheriff glared at him. Billy, from the front seat, threw a word of explanation over his shoulder. "It's not Lake. The watchman."

"Oh, old Lars Porsena? That's different. Not a bad sort, Lars. Maybe he'll get well. Hope so. . . . And I shot him? Dear me! When did it happen?"

"You'll find out soon enough!" said the sheriff grimly. "Your preliminary's right away."

"Hell, I haven't had breakfast yet!" Jeff protested. "Feed us first or we won't be tried at all."

.   .   .   .

Within the jail, while the sheriff spoke with his warder, it occurred to Billy that, since Jimmy Phillips was not to be seen, he might as well carry his own friendly message. So he said guardedly:

"Buck up, old man! Keep a stiff upper lip and be careful what you say. This is only your preliminary trial, remember. Lots of things may happen before court sets. The devil looks after his own, you know."

Jeff had a good ear for voices, however, and Billy's mustache still kept more than a hint of Mephistopheles. Jeff slowly surveyed Billy's natty attire, with a lingering and insulting interest for such evidences of prosperity as silken hosiery and a rather fervid scarfpin. At last his eye met Billy's, and Billy was blushing.

"Does he?" drawled Jeff languidly. "Ah! . . . You own the car, then?"

Poor Billy!

Notwithstanding the ingratitude of this rebuff, Billy sought out Jimmy Phillips and recounted to him the circumstances of the arrest.

"Oh, naughty, naughty!" said the deputy, caressing his nose. "Lake's been a cowman on Rainbow. He knew the brand on that horse; he knew Jeff was chummy with Monte. He knew in all reason that Jeff was in there, and most likely he knew it all the time. So he sneaks off to see Lars — after shooting him from ambush, damn him! — and sends you to take Jeff. Looks like he might be willing for you and Jeff to damage either, which or both of yourselves, as the case may be."

"It looks so," said Billy.

"Must be a fine girl!" murmured Jimmy absently. "Well, what are you going to do? It looks pretty plain."

"It looks plain to us — but we haven't got a single tangible thing against Lake yet. We'd be laughed out of court if we brought an accusation against him. We'll have to wait and keep our eyes open."

"You're sure Lake did it? There was no rubber nosepiece at Monte's house. All the rest of the football outfit — but not that. That looks bad for Jeff."

"On the contrary, that is the strongest link against Lake. I dare say Buttinski — Mr. Bransford — is eminently capable of bank robbery at odd moments; but I know approximately where that noseguard was at sharp midnight — after the watchman was shot!" Here Billy swore mentally, having a very definite guess as to how Jeff might have lost the noseguard. "Lake, Clarke, Turnbull, Thompson, Alec or myself — one of the six of us — brought that noseguard to the bank after the robbery, and only one of the six had a motive — and a key."

"Only one of you had a key," corrected Jimmy cruelly. "But can't Jeff prove where he was, maybe?"

"He won't."

"I'd sure like to see her," said Jimmy.

CHAPTER X

The Alibi

And all love's clanging trumpets shocked and blew.

The executioner's argument was, that you couldn't cut off a head unless there was a body to cut it off from; that he had never had to do such a thing before, and he wasn't going to begin at *his* time of life. — *Alice in Wonderland.*

THE JUSTICE OF THE PEACE, when the country court was not in session, held hearings in the courtroom proper, which occupied the entire second story of the county courthouse. The room was crowded. It was a new courthouse; there are people impatient to try even a new hearse; and this bade fair to be Arcadia's first *cause célèbre.*

Jeff sat in the prisoner's stall, a target for boring eyes. He was conscious of an undesirable situation; exactly how tight a place it was he had no means of knowing until he should have heard the evidence. The room was plainly hostile; black looks were cast upon him. Deputy Phillips, as he entered arm in arm with the sometime devil, gave the prisoner an intent but non-committal look, which Jeff rightly interpreted as assurance of a friend in ambush; he felt unaccountably sure of the devil's fraternal aid; Monte, lolling within the rail of the witness-box, smiled across at him. Still, he would have felt better for another friendly face or two, he thought — say, John Wesley Pringle's.

Jeff looked from the open window. Cottonwoods, well watered, give swiftest growth of any trees and are therefore the dominant feature of new communities in dry lands. The courthouse yard was crowded with them: Jeff, from the window, could see nothing but their green plumes; and his thoughts ran naturally upon gardens — or, to be more accurate, upon a garden.

Would she lose faith in him? Had she heard yet? Would he be able to clear himself? No mere acquittal would do. Because of Ellinor, there must be no question, no verdict of Not Proven. She would go East tomorrow. Perhaps she would not hear of his arrest at all. He hoped not. The bank robbery, the murder — yes she would hear of them, perhaps; but why need she hear his name? Hers was a world so different! He fell into a muse at this.

Deputy Phillips passed and stood close to him, looking down from the window. His back was to Jeff; but, under cover of the confused hum of many voices, he spoke low from the corner of his mouth:

"Play your hand close to your bosom, old-timer! Wait for the draw and watch the dealer!" He strolled over to the other side of the judicial bench whence he came.

This vulgar speech betrayed Jimmy as one given to evil courses; but to Jeff that muttered warning was welcome as thunder of Blucher's squadrons to British squares at Waterloo.

Down the aisle came a procession consciously important — the prosecuting attorney; the bank's lawyer, who was to assist, "for the people"; and Lake himself. As they passed the gate Jeff smiled his sweetest.

"Hello, Wally!" Lake's name was Stephen Walter.

Wally made no verbal response; but his undershot jaw did the steeltrap act and there was a triumphant glitter in his eye. He turned his broad back pointedly — and Jeff smiled again.

The justice took his seat on the raised dais intervening between Jeff and the sheriff's desk. Court was opened. The usual tedious preliminaries followed. Jeff waived a jury trial, refused a lawyer and announced that he would call no witnesses at present.

In an impressive stillness the prosecutor rose for his opening statement. Condensed, it recounted the history of the crime, so far as known; fixed the time by the watchman's statement — to be confirmed, he said, by another witness, the telephone girl on duty at that hour, who had heard the explosion and the ensuing gunshot; touched upon that watchman's faithful service and his present desperate condition. He told of the late finding of the injured man, the meeting in the bank, the sum taken by the robber, and the discovery in the bank of the rubber nosepiece, which he submitted as Exhibit A. He cited the witnesses by whom he would prove each statement, and laid special stress upon the fact that the witness Clarke would testify that the nosepiece had been found upon the shattered fragments of the safe door — conclusive proof that it had been dropped after the crime. And he then held forth at some length upon the hand of providence, as manifested in the unconscious self-betrayal which had frustrated and brought to naught the prisoner's fiendish designs. On the whole, he spoke well of Providence.

Now Jeff had not once thought of the discarded noseguard since he first found it in his way; he began to see how tightly the net was drawn round him. "There was a serpent in the garden," he reflected. A word from Miss Hoffman would set him free. If she gave that word at once, it would be unpleasant for her; but if she gave it later, as a last resort, it would be more than unpleasant. And in that same hurried moment, Jeff knew that he would not call upon her for that word. All his crowded life, he had kept the happy knack of falling on his feet: the stars, that fought in their courses against Sisera, had ever fought for reckless Bransford. He decided, with lovable folly, to trust to chance, to his wits and to his friends.

"And now, Your Honor, we come to the unbreakable chain of evidence which fatally links the prisoner at the bar to this crime. We will prove that the prisoner was not invited to the masquerade ball given last night by Mr. Lake. We will prove — "

There was a stir in the courtroom; the prosecutor paused, disconcerted. Eyes were turned to the double door at the back of the courtroom. In the entryway at the head of the stairs huddled a group of shrinking girls. Before them, one foot upon the threshold, stood Ellinor Hoffman. She shook off a detaining hand and stepped into the room, head erect, proud, pale. Across the sea of curious faces her eyes met the prisoner's. Of all the courtroom, Billy and Deputy Phillips alone turned then to watch Jeff's face. They saw an almost imperceptible shake of his head, a finger on lip, a reassuring gesture — saw, too, the quick pulsebeat at his throat.

The color flooded back to Ellinor's face. Men nearest the door were swift to bring chairs. The prosecutor resumed his interrupted speech — his voice was deep, hard, vibrant.

"Your Honor, the counts against this man are fairly damning! We will prove that he was shaved in a barber shop in Arcadia at ten o'clock last night; that he then rode a roan horse; that the horse was then sweating profusely; that this horse was afterward found at the house of — but we will take that up later. We will prove by many witnesses that among the masqueraders was a man wearing a football suit, wearing a nosepiece similar — entirely similar — to the one found in the bank, which now lies before you. We will prove that this football player was not seen in the ballroom after the hour of eleven P.M. We will prove that when he was next seen, without the ballroom, it was not until sufficient time had elapsed for him to have committed this awful crime."

Ellinor half rose from her seat; again Jeff flashed a warning at her.

"We will prove this, Your Honor, by a most unwilling witness — Rosalio Marquez" — Monte smiled across at Jeff — "a friend of the prisoner, who, in his behalf, has not scrupled to defy the majesty of the law! We can prove by this witness, this reluctant witness, that when he returned to his home, shortly after midnight, he found there the prisoner's horse, which had not been there when Mr. Marquez left the house some four hours previously: and that, at some time subsequent to twelve o'clock, the witness Marquez was wakened by the entrance of the prisoner at the bar, clad in a football suit, but wearing no nosepiece with it! And we have the evidence of the sheriff's posse that they found in the home of the witness, Rosalio Marquez, the football suit — which we offer as Exhibit B. Nay, more! The prisoner did not deny, and indeed admitted, that this uniform was his; but — mark this! — the searching party found no nosepiece there!

"It is true, Your Honor, that the stolen money was not found upon the prisoner; it is true that the prisoner made no use of the opportunity to escape offered him by his lawless and disreputable friend, Rosalio Marquez — a common gambler! Doubtless, Your Honor, his cunning had devised some diabolical plan upon which he relied to absolve himself from suspicion; and now, trembling, he has for the first time learned of the fatal flaw in his concocted defense, which he had so fondly deemed invincible!"

All eyes, including the orator's, here turned upon the prisoner — to find him, so far from trembling, quite otherwise engaged. The prisoner's elbow was upon the rail, his chin in his hand; he regarded Mr. Lake attentively, with cheerful amusement and a quizzical smile which in some way subtly carried an expression of mockery and malicious triumph. To this fixed and disconcerting regard Mr. Lake opposed an iron front, but the effort required was apparent to all.

There was an uneasy rustling through the court. The prisoner's bearing was convincing, natural; this was no mere brazen assuming. The banker's forced composure was not natural! He should have been an angry banker. Of the two men, Lake was the less at ease. The prisoner's face turned at last toward the door. Blank unrecognition was in his eyes as they swept past Ellinor, but he shook his head once more, very slightly.

There was a sense of mystery in the air — a buzz and burr of whispers; a rustle of moving feet. The audience noticeably relaxed its implacable attitude toward the accused, eyed him with a different interest, seemed to feel for the first time that, after all, he was accused merely, and that his defense had not yet been heard. The prosecutor felt this subtle change; it lamed his periods.

"It is true, Your Honor, that no eye save God's saw this guilty man do this deed; but the web of circumstantial evidence is so closely drawn, so far-reaching, so unanswerable, so damning, that no defense can avail him except the improbable, the impossible establishment of an alibi so complete, so convincing, as to satisfy even his bitterest

enemy! We will ask you, Your Honor, when you have seen how fully
the evidence bears out our every contention, to commit the prisoner,
without bail, to answer the charge of robbery and attempted murder!"

Then, by the door, Jeff saw the girl start up. She swept down the
aisle, radiant, brave, unfearing, resolute, all half-gods gone; she shone
at him — proud, glowing, triumphant!

A hush fell upon the thrilled room. Jeff was on his feet, his hand
held out to stay her; his eyes spoke to hers. She stopped as at a command. Scarcely slower, Billy was at her side. "Wait! Wait!" he whispered. "See what he has to say. There will be always time for that."
Jeff's eyes held hers; she sank into an offered chair.

Cheated, disappointed, the court took breath again. Their dramatic
moment had been nothing but their own nerves; their own excited
imaginings had attached a pulse-fluttering significance to the flushed
cheeks of a prying girl, seeking a better place to see and hear, to
gratify her morbid curiosity.

Jeff turned to the bench.

"Your Honor, I have a perfectly good line of defense; and I trust
no friend of mine will undertake to change it. I will keep you but a
minute," he said colloquially. "I will not waste your time combating
the ingenious theory which the prosecution has built up, or in cross-
examination of their witnesses, who, I feel sure" — here he bowed to
the cloud of witnesses — "will testify only to the truth. I quite agree
with my learned friend" — another graceful bow — "that the case he
has so ably presented is so strong that it can successfully be rebutted
only by an alibi so clear and so incontestable, as my learned friend
has so aptly phrased it, as to convince if not satisfy . . . my bitterest
enemy!" The bow, the subtle, icy intonation, edged the words. The
courtroom thrilled again at the unspoken thought: *An enemy hath
done this thing!* If, in the stillness, the prisoner had quoted the words
aloud in fierce denunciation, the effect could not have been different
or more startling. "And that, Your Honor, is precisely what I propose to do!"

His honor was puzzled. He was a good judge of men; and the prisoner's face was not a bad face.

"But," he objected, "you have refused to call any witnesses for the
defense. Your unsupported word will count for nothing. You cannot prove an alibi alone."

"Can't I?" said Jeff. "Watch me!"

With a single motion he was through the open window. Bending
branches of the nearest cottonwood broke his fall — the other trees
hid his flight.

Behind him rose uproar, tumult and hullabaloo, a mass of struggling men at cross purposes. Gun in hand, the sheriff, stumbling over someone's foot — Monte's — ran to the window; but the faithful deputy was before him, blocking the way, firing with loving care — at one particular treetrunk. He was a good shot, Jimmy. He afterward showed with pride where each ball had struck in a scant six-inch space. Vainly the sheriff tried to force his way through. There was but one stairway, and it was jammed. Before the foremost pursuer had reached the open Jeff had borrowed one of the saddled horses hitched at the rack and was away to the hills.

As Billy struggled through the press, searching for Ellinor, he found himself at Jimmy's elbow.

"A dead game sport — any turn in the road!" agreed Billy.

The deputy nodded curtly; but his answer was inconsequent: "Rather in the brunette line — that bit of tangible evidence!"

CHAPTER XI

The Nettle, Danger

Bushel 'o' wheat, bushel o' rye —
All 'at ain't ready, holler "I"!

— Hide and Seek

DOUBLE MOUNTAIN lies lost in the desert, dwarfed by the greatness all about. Its form is that of a crater split from north to south into irregular halves. Through that narrow cleft ran a straight road, once the well-traveled thoroughfare from Rainbow to El Paso. For there was precious water within those upheaved walls; it was but three miles from portal to portal; the slight climb to the divide had not been grudged. Time was when campfires were nightly merry to light the narrow cliffs of Double Mountain; when songs were gay to echo from them; when this had been the only watering place to break the long span across the desert. The railroad had changed all this, and the silent leagues of that old road lay untrodden in the sun.

Not untrodden on this the day after Jeff had established his alibi. A traveler followed that lonely road to Double Mountain; and behind, halfway to Rainbow Range, was a streak of dust; which gained on him. The traveler's sorrel horse was weary, for it was the very horse Jeff Bransford had borrowed from the hitching-rail of the courthouse square; the traveler was that able negotiator himself; and the pur-

suing dust, to the best of Jeff's knowledge and belief, meant him no
good tidings.

"Now, I got safe away from the foothills before day," soliloquized
Jeff. "Some gentleman has overtaken me with a spyglass, I reckon.
Civilization's getting this country plumb ruined! And their horses are
fresh. Peg along, Alibi! Maybe I can pick up a stray horse at Double
Mountain. If I can't there's no sort of use trying to get away on you!
I'll play hide-and-go-seek-'em. That'll let you out, anyway, so cheer
up! You done fine, old man! If I ever get out of this I'll buy you
and make it all right with you. Pension you off if you think you'll
like it. Get along now!"

Twenty miles to Jeff's right the railroad paralleled the wagonroad
in an unbroken tangent of ninety miles' stretch. A southbound passenger train crawled along the west like a resolute centipede plodding to
a date: behind the fugitive, abreast, now far ahead, creeping along the
shining straightaway. Forty miles the hour was her schedule; yet
against this vast horizon she could hardly be said to change place until,
sighting beyond her puny length, a new angle of the far western wall
completed the trinomial line.

Escondido was hidden in a dip of plain — whence the name, Hidden,
when done into Saxon speech. The train was lost to sight when she
stopped there, but Jeff saw the tiny steam plume of her whistling rise
in the clear and taintless air; long after, the faint sound of it hummed
drowsily by, like passing, far-blown horns of faerie in a dream. And,
at no great interval thereafter, a low-lying dust appeared suddenly on
the hither rim of Escondido's sunken valley.

Jeff knew the land as you know your hallway. That line of dust
marked the trail from Escondido Valley to the farther gate of Double
Mountain. Even if he should be lucky enough to get a change of
mounts at the spring in Double Mountain Basin he would be inter-
cepted. Escape by flight was impossible. To fight his way out was
impossible. He had no gun; and, even if he had a gun, he could not see
his way to fight, under the circumstances. The men who hunted him
down were only doing the right thing as they saw it. Had Jeff been
guilty, it would have been a different affair. Being innocent, he could
make no fight for it. He was cornered.

> Said the little Eohippus:
> "I'm going to be a horse!"

So chanted Jeff, perceiving the hopelessness of his plight.

The best gift to man — or, if not the best, then at least the rarest —
is the power to meet the emergency: to do your best and a little better

than your best when nothing less will serve: to be a pinch hitter. It is to be thought that certain stages of affection, and more particularly the presence of its object, affect unfavorably the workings of pure intellect. Certain it is that capable Bransford, who had cut so sorry a figure in Eden garden, now, in these distressing but Eveless circumstances, rose to the occasion. Collected, resourceful, he grasped every possible angle of the situation and, with the rope virtually about his neck, cheerfully planned the impossible — the essence of his elastic plan being to climb that very rope, hand over hand, to safety.

"Going round the mountain is no good on a give-out horse. They'll follow my tracks," said Jeff to Jeff. Men who are much alone so shape their thoughts by voicing them, just as you practice conversation rather to make your own thought clear to yourself than to enlighten your victim — beg pardon — your neighbor. Just a slip of the tongue. *Vecino* is Spanish for neighbor, you know. Not so much to enlighten your neighbor as to find out for yourself precisely what it is you think. "Hiding in the Basin is no good. Can't get out. Would I were a bird! Only one way. Got to go straight up — disappear — vanish in the air. 'Up a chimney, up —' Naw, that's backward! 'Up a chimney, down or down a chimney, down; but not up a chimney, up, nor down a chimney, up!' So that's settled! Now let me see, says the little man. Mighty few Arcadians know me well enough not to be fooled — mebbe so. Lake? Lake won't come. He'll be busy. There's Jimmy; but Jimmy's got a shocking bad memory for faces sometimes, just now, my face. I think, maybe, I could manage Jimmy. The sheriff? That would be real awkward, I reckon. I'll just play the sheriff isn't in the bunch and build my little bluff according to that pleasing fancy; for if he comes along it is all off with little Jeff!

"Now lemme see! If Gwin's working that little old mine of his — why, he'll lie himself black in the face just for the principle of it. Mighty interestin' talker, Gwin is. And if no one's there, I'll be there. Not Jeff Bransford; he got away. I'll be Long — Tobe Long — working for Gwin. Tobe Long. I apprenticed my son to a miner, and the first thing he took was a new name!"

Far away on the side of Double Mountain he could even now see the white triangle of the tent at Gwin's mine — the Ophir — and the gray dump spilling down the hillside. There was no smoke to be seen. Jeff made up his mind there was no one at the mine — which was what he devoutly hoped — and further developed his gleeful hypothesis.

"Let's see now, Tobe. Got to study this all out. They most always leave all their kegs full of water when they go away, so they won't have to pack 'em up the first thing when they come back. If they did, I'm all right. If they didn't, I'm in a hell of a fix! They'll leave 'em full, though. Of course they did — else the kegs would all dry up and fall down." He glanced over his shoulder. "Them fellows are ten or twelve miles back, I reckon. They'll slow up so soon as they see I'm headed off. I'll have time to fix things up — if only there's water in the kegs at the mine! He patted Alibi's head: "Now, old man, do your damnedest! It's pretty tough on you, but your part will soon be over."

Alibi had made a poor night of it, what with doubling and twisting in the foothills, the bitter water of a gyp spring, and the scanty grass of a cedar thicket; but he did his plucky best. On the legal other hand, as Jeff had prophesied, the dustmakers behind had slackened their gait when they perceived, by the dust of Escondido trail, that their allies must cut the quarry off. So Alibi held his own with the pursuit.

He came to the rising ground leading to the sheer base of Double Mountain; then to the narrow Gap where the mountain had fallen asunder in some age-old cataclysm. To the left, the dump of Ophir Mine hung on the hillside above the pass; and on the broad trail zigzagging up to it were burrow-tracks, but no fresh tracks of men. The flaps of the white tent on the dump were tightly closed. There was no one at the mine. Jeff passed within the walls, through frowning gates of porphyry and gneiss, and urged Alibi up the canon. It was half a mile to the spring. On the way he found three shaggy burros grazing beside the road. He drove them into the small pen by the spring and tossed his rope on the largest one. Then he un-saddled Alibi, tied him to the fence by the bridle rein, and searched his pockets for an old letter. This found, he penciled a note and tied it to the saddle. It was brief:

En Route, Four P.M.

Please water my horse when he cools off.

Your little friend,
JEFF BRANSFORD

P.S. Excuse haste.

He made a plain trail of high-heeled boot-tracks to the spring, where he drank deep; thence beyond, through the sandy soil, to the nearest rocky ridge. Then, careful that every step fell on a bare rock, he came circuitously back to the corral, climbed the fence, made his way to the tied burro, improvised a bridle of cunning half-hitches, slipped from the fence to the burro's back — a burro, by the way, is a donkey — named the burro anew as Balaam, and went back down the cañon at the best pace of which the belabored and astonished Balaam was capable. As Jeff had hoped, the two other burros — or the other two burros, to be precise — followed sociably, braying remonstrance.

Without the mouth of the canon Jeff rode up the steep trail to the mine, also to the great disgust of his mount; but he must not walk — it would leave boot-tracks. For the same reason, after freeing Balaam, his first action was to pull off the telltale boots and replace them with the smallest pair of hobnailed miner's shoes in the tent. With these he carefully obliterated the few boot-tracks at the tent door.

The water-kegs were full: Jeff swore his joyful gratitude and turned his eye to the plain. The pursuing dust was still far away — seven miles, he estimated, or possibly eight. The three burros nibbled on the bushes below the dump; plainly intending to stay round camp with an eye for possible tips. Jeff gave his whole-hearted attention to the *mise-en-scène.*

Never did stage manager toil so hard, so faithfully, so effectively as this one — or with so great a need. He took stock of the available stage properties, beginning with a careful inventory of the grub-chest. To betray ignorance of its possibilities or deficiencies would be fatal. Following a narrow trail round a little shoulder of hill, he found the powder magazine. Taking three sticks of dynamite, with fuse and caps, he searched the tent for the candle-box, lit a candle and went into the tunnel with a brisk trot. "If this was a case of fight now, I'd have some pretty fair weapons here for close quarters," said Jeff; "but the way I'm fixed I can't. No fighting goes — unless Lake comes."

In the tunnel his luck held good. He found a number of good-sized chunks of rock stacked along the wall near the breast — evidently reserved for the ore pile at a more convenient season. Beneath three of the largest of these rocks he carefully adjusted the three sticks of giant powder, properly capped and fused, lit the fuses and retreated to the safety of the dump. Three muffled detonations followed at short intervals. Having thus announced the presence of mining operations, he built a fire on the kitchen side of the dump to further advertise a mind conscious of its own rectitude. The pleasant shadow of the hills was cool about him; the flame rose clear and bright in the windless air, to be seen from far away.

He looked at the location papers in the monument by the ore stack; simultaneously, by way of economizing time, emptying a can of salmon. This was partly for the added verisimilitude of the empty

tin, partly because he was ravenously hungry. You may guess how
he emptied the tin.

The mine had changed owners since Jeff's knowledge of it. It was
no longer Gwin's sole property. The notice bore the signature of J.
Gwin, C. W. Sanders and Walter Fleck. Jeff grinned and his eye
brightened. He knew Fleck only slightly; but Fleck's reputation
among the cowmen was good — that is to say, as you would say it,
very bad.

Pappy Sanders, postmaster and storekeeper of Escondido, was an
old and sorely tried friend of Jeff's. If Pappy had grub-staked the
outfit — A far-away plan began to shape vaguely in his fertile brain.
He took the little turquoise horse from his pocket and laid it in the
till of the violated trunk. Were you told about the violated trunk?
Never mind — he had done any amount of other things of which you
have not been told; for it was his task, in the brief time allotted to
him, to master all the innumerable details needful for an intelligent
reading of his part. He must make no blunders.

He toiled like two men, each swifter and more savagely efficient
than himself; he upset the prim, old he-maidenish order of that carefully packed, spick-and-span camp; he rumpled the beds; strewed
old clothes, books, candles, specimens, pipes and cigarette papers with
lavish hand; made untidy, sprawling heaps of tin plates; knives, forks
and spoons; spilled candle-grease and tobacco on the scoured table;
and generally gave things a cozy and habitable appearance.

He gave a hundred deft touches here and there. He spread an open
book face downward on the table. (It was *Alice in Wonderland*, and
he opened it at the Mock-Turtle.) Meanwhile an unoccupied eye
snatched titles from a shelf of books against possible question; he
penned a short note to himself — Mr. Tobe Long — in Gwin's handwriting, folded the note to creases, twisted it to a spill, lit it, burned
a corner of it, pinched it out and threw it under the table; and, while
doing these and other things, he somehow managed to shed every
article of Jeff Bransford's clothing and to put on the work-stained
garments of a miner.

The perspiration on his face was no stage make-up, but good, honest sweat. He rubbed stone-dust and sand on his sweaty arms and
into his sweaty hair; he rubbed most of it from his hair and into the
two-days' stubble on his face, simultaneously fishing razor and mug
from the trunk, leaving them in evidence on the table. He worked
stone-dust into his ears, behind his ears; he grimed it on forehead and
neck; he even dropped a little into his shoes, which all this while
had been performing independent miracles to make the camp look

comfortable. He threw on a dingy cap, thrust in the cap a miner's candlestick, with a lighted candle, that it might properly drip upon him while he arranged further details — and so faced the world as Tobe Long, a stooped and overworked man!

Mr. Tobe Long, working with feverish haste, dug a small cave half-way down the steep side of the dump farthest from the road and buried therein a tightly rolled bundle containing every article appertaining to the defunct Bransford, with the single exception of the little eohippus; a pocketknife, which a miner must have to cut powder and fuse, having been found in the trunk — what time also the little turquoise horse was transferred to Mr. Long's pocket to bring him luck in his new career — a poor thing compared with the cowman's keen blade, but better for Mr. Long's purposes, as smelling strongly of dynamite. Then Mr. Long — Tobe — hid the grave by sliding and shoveling broken rock down the dump upon it.

Next he threw into a wheelbarrow drills, spoon, tamping stick, gads, drill-hammer, rock-hammer, canteen, shovel and pick — taking care, even in his haste, to select a properly matched set of drills — and trundled the barrow up the drift at a pace which would give a Miners' Union the rabies. At the breast, he unshipped his cargo in right miner's fashion, the drills in a graduated stepladder row along the wall; loaded the barrow with broken ore, a bit of charred fuse showing at the top, and wheeled it out at the same unprofessional gait, leaving it on the dump just above the spot where his late sepulchral rites had freshened the appearance of the sunbeaten dump.

He next performed his ablutions in an amateurish and perfunctory fashion, scrupulously observing a well-defined waterline.

"There!" said Mr. Long. "I near made a break that time!" He went back to the barrow and trundled it assiduously to the tunnel's mouth and back several times, carefully never in quite the same place — finally leaving it not above the sepulchered spoil, but near the ore stack, as befitted its valuable contents. "I got to think of everything. One wrong break'll fix me good!" said Mr. Long. He felt his neck delicately, as if he detected some foreign presence there. "In the tunnel, now, there's only the one place where the wheel can go; so it don't matter so much in there."

The fire having now burned down to proper coals, Mr. Long set about supper; with the corner of his eye on the lookout for the pursuers of the late Bransford. He set the coffee-pot by the fire — they were now in the edge of the tarbrush; there were only two of them. He put on a pot of potatoes in their jackets — he could see them plainly, diminutive black horsemen twinkling through the brush; he sliced bacon into a frying-pan and put it aside to await his cue; he disposed of other cooking ware in lifelike attitudes near the fire — they were in the shadow of Double Mountain; their horses were jaded; they rode slowly. He dropped the sour-dough jar and placed the broken pieces where they would be inconspicuously visible. Having thus a perfectly obvious excuse for not having sour-dough bread, which requires thirty-six hours of running start for preliminary rising, Jeff — Mr. Tobe Long — mixed up a just-as-good baking-powder substitute — they rode like young men; they rode like young men not to the saddle born, and Tobe permitted himself a chuckle: "By hooky, I've got an even chance for my little bluff!"

He shook his head reprovingly at himself for this last admission. With every minute he looked more like Tobe Long than ever — if only there had been any Tobe Long to look like. His mind ran upon nuggets, pockets, placers, faults, true fissure veins, the cyanide process, concentrates, chlorides, sulphides, assays, leases and bonds; his face took on the strained wistfulness which marks the confirmed prospector: he *was* Tobe Long!

The bell rang.

CHAPTER XII

The Siege of Double Mountain

Timeo Danaos et dona ferentes.
— *The Dictionary*

"Ho-o-e-ee! Hello-o!"

As the curtain rose to the flying echoes Long stepped to the edge of the dump, frying-pan in hand, and sent back an answering shout in the startled high note of a lonely man taken unawares.

"Hello-o!" He brandished his hospitable pan. Then he put it down, cupped hands to mouth and trumpeted a hearty welcome: "Chuck! Come up! Supper's ready!"

"Can't! See any one go by about two hours ago?"

"Hey? Louder!"

"See a man on a sorrel horse?"

"No-o! I been in the tunnel. Come up!"

"Can't. We're after an outlaw!"

"What?"

"After a murderer!"

"Wait a minute! I'll be down. Too hard to yell so far."

Mr. Long started precipitately down the zigzag; but the riders had got all the information of interest that Mr. Long could furnish and they were eager to be in at the death.

"Can't wait! He's inside the mountain, somewheres. Some of the boys are waiting for him at the other end." They rode on.

Mr. Long posed for a statue of Disappointment, hung on the steep trail rather as if he might conclude to coil himself into a ball and roll down the hill to overtake them.

"Stop as you come back!" he bellowed. "Want to hear about it."

Did Jeff — Mr. Long — did Mr. Long now attempt to escape? Not so. Gifted with prevision beyond most, Mr. Long's mind misgave him that these young men would be baffled in their pleasing expectations. They would be back before sundown, very cross; and a miner's brogan leaves a track not to be missed.

That Mr. Long was unfeignedly fatigued from the varied efforts of the day need not be mentioned, for that alone would not have stayed his flight; but the nearest water, save Escondido, was thirty-five miles; and at Escondido he would be watched for — not to say that, when he was missed, some of the searching party would straightway go to Escondido to frustrate him. Present escape was not to be thought of.

Instead, Mr. Long made a hearty meal from the simple viands that had been in course of preparation when he was surprised, eked out by canned corn fried in bacon grease to a crisp, golden brown. Then, after a cigarette, he betook himself to sharpening tools with laudable industry. The tools were already sharp, but that did not stop Mr. Long. He built a fire in the forge, set up a stepladder of matched drills in the blackened water of the tempering tub; he thrust a gad and one short drill into the fire. When the gad was at a good cherry heat he thrust it hissing into the tub to bring the water to a convincing temperature; and when reheated he did it again. From time to time he held the one drill to the anvil and shaped it, drawing it alternately to a chisel bit or a bull bit. Mr. Long could sharpen a drill with any, having been, in very truth, a miner of sorts — he could toy thus with one drill without giving it any very careful attention, and his thoughts were now busy on how best to be Mr. Long.

Accordingly from time to time he added an artistic touch to Mr. Long — grime under his fingernails, a smudge of smut on an eyebrow. His hands displeased him. After some experimenting to get the proper heat of it he grasped the partially cooled gad with the drill-pincers and held it very lightly to a favored few of those portions of the hand known to chiromaniacs as the mounts of Jupiter, Saturn and other extinct immortals.

Satisfactory blisters-while-you-wait were thus obtained. These were pricked with a pin; some were torn to tatters, with dust and coal rubbed in to give them a venerable appearance. The pain was no light matter; but Mr. Long had a real affection for Mr. Brans-ford's neck, and it is trifles like these that make perfection.

The next expedient was even more heroic. Mr. Long assiduously put stone-dust in one eye, leaving it tearful, bloodshot and violently inflamed; and the other one was sympathetically red. "Bit o' steel in my eye," explained Mr. Long. Unselfish devotion such as this is all too rare.

All this while, at proper intervals, Mr. Long sharpened and resharp-ened that one long-suffering drill. He tripped into the tunnel and smote a mighty blow upon the country rock with a pick — therefore qualifying that pick for repointing — and laid it on the forge as next on the list.

What further outrage he meditated is not known, for he now heard a horse coming up the trail. He was beating out a merry tattoo when a white-hatted head rose through a trapdoor — rose above the level of the dump, rather.

Hammer in hand, Long straightened up joyfully as best he could, but could not straighten up the telltale droop of his shoulders. It was not altogether assumed, either, this hump. Jeff — Mr. Long — had not done so much work of this sort for years and there was a very real pain between his shoulderblades. Still, but for the exigencies of art, he might have borne his neck less turtlewise than he did.

"Hello! Get him? Where's your pardner?"

"Watching the gap." The young man, rather breathless from the climb, answered the last question first as he led his horse on the dump. "No, we didn't get him; but he can't get away. Hiding somewhere in the Basin afoot. Found his horse. Pretty well done up." The insolence of the outlaw's letter smote him afresh; he reddened. "No tracks going out of the Basin. Two of our friends guarding the other end. They say he can't get out over the cliffs anywhere. That so?" The speech came jerkily; he was still short of breath from his scramble.

"Not without a flying machine," said Long. "No way out that I know of, except where the wagonroad goes. What's he done?"

"Robbery! Murder! We'll see that he don't get out by the wagonroad," asserted the youth confidently. "Watch the gaps and starve him out!"

"Oh, speaking of starving," said Tobe, "go into the tent and I'll bring you some supper while you tell me about it. Baked up another batch of bread on the chance you'd come back."

"Why, thank you very much, Mr. — "

"Long — Tobe Long."

"Mr. Long. My name is Gurdon Steele. Glad to meet you. Why, if you will be so kind — that is what I came up to see you about. If you can let us have what we need of course we will pay you for it."

"Of course you won't!" It had not needed the offer to place Mr. Gurdon Steele quite accurately. He was a handsome lad, fresh-complexioned, dressed in the Western manner as practised on the Boardwalk. "You're welcome to what I got, sure; but I ain't got much variety. Gwin, the old liar, said he was coming out the twentieth — and sure enough he didn't; so the grub's running low. Table in the tent — come on!"

"Oh, no, I couldn't, you know! Rex — that's my partner — is quite as hungry as I am, you see; but if you could give me something — anything you have — to take down there? I really couldn't, you know!" The admirable doctrine of *noblesse oblige* in its delicate application by this politeness, was easier for its practitioner than to put it into words suited to the comprehension of his hearer; he concluded lamely: "I'll take it down there and we will eat it together."

"See here," said Tobe, "I'm as hungry to hear about your outlaw as you are to eat. I'll just throw my bedding and a lot of chuck on your saddle. We'll carry the coffee-pot and frying-pan in our hands — and the sugar-can and things like that. You can tank up and give me the news in small chunks at the same time. Afterward two of us can sleep while one stands guard."

This was done. It was growing dark when they reached the bottom of the hill. The third guardsman had built a fire.

"Rex, this is Mr. Long, who has been kind enough to grubstake us and share our watch with us."

Mr. Steele, you have observed, had accepted Mr. Long without question; but his first impression of Mr. Long had been gained under circumstances highly favorable to the designs of the latter gentleman. Mr. Steele had come upon him unexpectedly, finding him as it were *in medias res*, with all his skillfully arranged scenery to aid the illusion. The case was now otherwise — the thousand-tongued vouching of his background lacked to him; Mr. Long had naught save his own unthinkable audacity to belie his face withal. From the first instant Mr. Rex Griffith was the prey of suspicions — acute, bigoted, churlish, deep, dark, distrustful, damnable, and so on down to zealous. He had a sharp eye; he wore no puttees; and Mr. Long had a vaguely uncomfortable memory, holding over from some previous incarnation, of having seen that long, shrewd face in a courtroom.

The host, on hospitable rites intent, likewise all ears and eager questionings, was all unconscious of hostile surveillance. Nothing could be more carefree, more at ease than his bearing; his pleasant anticipatory excitement was the natural outlook for a lonely and newsless man. As the hart panteth for the water, so he thirsted for the story; but his impatient, hasty questions, following false scents, delayed the telling of the Arcadian tale. So innocent was he, so open and aboveboard, that Griffith, watching, alert, felt thoroughly ashamed of himself. Yet he watched, doubting still, though his reason rebelled at the monstrous imaginings of his heart. That the outlaw, unarmed and unasked, should venture — Pshaw! Such effrontery was inconceivable. He allowed Steele to tell the story, himself contributing only an occasional crafty question designed to enable his host to betray himself.

"Bransford?" interrupted Mr. Long. "Not Jeff Bransford — up South Rainbow way?"

"That's the man," said Steele.

"I don't believe it," said Long flatly. He was sipping coffee with his guests; he put his cup down. "I know him, a little. He don't —"

"Oh, there's no doubt of it!" interrupted Steele in his turn. He detailed the circumstances with skilful care. "Besides, why did he run away? Gee! You ought to have seen that escape! It was splendid!"

"Well, now, who'd 'a' thought that?" demanded Long, still only half convinced. "He didn't strike me like that kind of a man. Well, you never can tell! How come you fellows to be chasin' him?"

"You see," said Steele, "everyone was sure he had gone up to Rainbow. The sheriff and posse is up there now, looking for him; but we four — Stone and Harlow, the chaps at the other end, were with us, you know — we were up in the foothills on a deerhunt. We were out early — sun-up is the best time for deer, they tell me — and we had a spyglass. Well, we just happened to see a man ride out from between two hills, quite a way off. Stone noticed right away that he was riding a sorrel horse. It was a sorrel horse that Bransford stole, you know. We didn't suspect, though, who it was till a bit later. Then Rex tried to pick him up again and saw that he was going out of his way to avoid the ridges — keeping cover, you know. Then we caught on and took after him pell-mell. He had a big start; but he was riding slowly so as not to make a dust — that is, till he saw our dust. Then he lit out."

"You're not deputies, then?" said Long.

"Oh, no, not at all!" said Steele, secretly flattered. "So Harlow and Stone galloped off to town. The program was that they'd wire down to Escondido to have horses ready for them, come down on Number Six and head him off. They were not to tell anyone in Arcadia. There's five thousand dollars' reward out for him — but it isn't that exactly. It was a cowardly, beastly murder, don't you know; and we thought it would be rather a big thing if we could take him alone."

"You got him penned all right," said Tobe. "He can't get out, so far as I know, unless he runs over us or the men at the other end. By George, we must get away from this fire, too!" He set the example, dragging the bedding with him to the shelter of a big rock. "He could pick us off too slick here in the light. How're you going to get him? There's a heap of country in that Basin, all rough and broken, full o' boulders — mighty good cover."

"Starve him out!" said Griffith. This was base deceit. Deep in his heart he believed that the quarry sat beside him, well fed and contented. Yet the unthinkable insolence of it — if this were indeed Bransford — dulled his belief.

Long laughed as he spread down the bed. "He'll shoot a deer. Maybe, if he had it all planned out, he may have grub cached in there somewhere. There's watertanks in the rocks. Say, what are your pardners at the other side going to do for grub?"

"Oh, they brought out cheese and crackers and stuff," said Gurd.

"I'll tell you what, boys, you've bit off more than you can chaw," said Jeff — Tobe, that is. "He can't get out without a fight — but, then, you can't go in there to hunt for him without weakening your guard; and he'd be under shelter and have all the best of it. He'd shoot you so dead you'd never know what happened. I don't want none of it! I'd as lief put on boxing gloves and crawl into a hole after a bear! Look here, now, this is your show; but I'm a heap older'n you boys. Want to know what I think?"

"Certainly," said Rex.

"Goin' to talk turkey to me?" An avaricious light came into Long's eyes.

"Of course; you're in on the reward," said Rex diffidently and rather stiffly. "We are not in this for the money."

"I can use the money — whatever share you want to give me," said

Long dryly; "but if you take my advice my share won't be but a
little. I think you ought to keep under shelter at the mouth of this
cañon — one of you — and let the other one go to Escondido and send
for help, quick, and a lot of it."

"What's the matter with you going?" asked Griffith disingenuously.
He wanted Long to show his hand. It would never do to abandon the
siege of Double Mountain to arrest this *soi disant* Long on mere suspicion. On the other hand, Mr. Rex Griffith had no idea of letting
Long escape his clutches until his identity was established, one way
or the other, beyond all question.

That was why Long declined the offer. His honest gaze shifted.
"I ain't much of a rider," he said evasively. Young Griffith read correctly the thought which the excuse concealed. Evidently Long considered himself an elder soldier, if not a better, than either of his two
young guests, but wished to spare their feelings by not letting them
find it out. Griffith found this plain solution inconsistent with his
homicidal theory: a murderer, fleeing for his life, would have jumped
at the chance.

There are two sides to every question. Let us, this once, prove
both sides. Wholly oblivious to Griffith's lynx-eyed watchfulness and
his leading questions, Mr. Long yet recognized the futility of an attempt to ride away on Mr. Griffith's horse with Mr. Griffith's ben-
ison. There we have the other point of view.

"We'll have to send for grub anyway," pursued the sagacious Mr.
Long. "I've only got a little left; and that old liar, Gwin, won't be
out for four days — if he comes then. And — er — look here now — if
I was you boys I'd let the sheriff and his posse smoke your badger
out. They get paid to tend to that — and it looks to me like someone
was going to get hurt. You've done enough."

All this advice was so palpably sound that the doubter was, for the
second, staggered — for a second only. This was the man he had seen
in the prisoner's dock. He was morally sure of it. For all the difference of appearance, this was the man. · Yet those blasts — the far-seen
fire — the hearty welcome — this delivery of himself into their hands?
. . . Griffith scarcely knew what he did think. He blamed himself for
his unworthy suspicions; he blamed Gurdy more for having no suspicions at all.

"Anything else?" he said. "That sounds good."

Tobe studied for some time.

"Well," he said at last, "there may be some way he can get out. I
don't think he can — but he might find a way. He knows he's trapped;
but likely he has no idea yet how many of us there are. So we know

he'll try, and he won't be just climbing for fun. He'll take a chance."
Steele broke in:

"He didn't leave any rope on his saddle."

Tobe nodded.

"So he means to try it. Now here's five of us here. It seems to me
that someone ought to ride round the mountain the first thing in the
morning, and every day afterward — only here's hoping there won't
be many of 'em — to look for tracks. There isn't one chance in a hundred he can climb out; but if he goes out of here afoot we've got him
sure. The man on guard wants to keep in shelter. It's light tonight —
there's no chance for him to slip out without being seen. You say the
old watchman ain't dead yet, Mr. Griffith?"

"No. The latest bulletin was that he was almost holding his own."

"Hope he gets well," said Long. "Good old geezer! Now, cap, I've
worked hard and you've ridden hard. Better set your guards and let
the other two take a little snooze."

Griffith was not proof against the insidious flattery of this unhesitant
preference. He flushed with embarrassment and pleasure.

"Well, if I'm to be captain, Gurd will take the first guard — till
eleven. Then you come on till two, Mr. Long. I'll stand from then
on till daylight."

In five minutes Mr. Long was enjoying the calm and restful sleep of
fatigued innocence; but his poor captain was doomed to have a bad
night of it, with two Bransfords on his hands — one in the Basin and
one in the bed beside him. His head was dizzy with the vicious circle.
Like the gentlewoman of the nursery rhyme, he was tempted to cry:
"Lawk 'a' mercy on me, this is none of I!"

If he haled his bedmate to justice and the real Bransford got away
— that would be a nice predicament for an ambitious young man! He
was sensitive to ridicule, and he saw here such an opportunity to earn
it as knocks but once at any man's door.

If, on the other hand, while he held Bransford cooped tightly in
the Basin, this thrice-accursed Long should escape him and there
should be no Bransford in the Basin — What nonsense! What utter
twaddle! Bransford was in the Basin. He had found his horse and
saddle, his tracks; no tracks had come out of the Basin. Immediately
on the discovery of the outlaw's horse, Gurd had ridden back posthaste and held the pass while he, the captain, had gone to the mouth
of the southern cañon and posted his friends. He had watched for
tracks of a footman every step of the way, going and coming; there
had been no tracks. Bransford was in the Basin. He watched the face
of the sleeping man. But, by Heaven, this was Bransford!

Was ever a poor captain in such a predicament? A moment before he had fully and definitely decided once for all that this man was not Bransford; could not be Bransford; that it was not possible! His reason unwaveringly told him one thing, his eyesight the other! . . . Yet Bransford, or an unfortunate twin of his, lay now beside him — and, for further mockery, slept peacefully, serene, untroubled. . . . He looked upon the elusive Mr. Long with a species of horror! The face was drawn and lined. Yet, but forty-eight hours of tension would have left Bransford's face not otherwise. He had noticed Bransford's hands in the courtroom — noticed their well-kept whiteness, due, as he had decided, to the perennial cowboy glove. This man's hands as he had seen by the campfire, were blistered and calloused! Callouses were not made in a day. He took another look at Long. Oh, thunder!

He crept from bed. He whispered a word to sentry Steele; not to outline the distressing state of his own mind, but merely to request Steele not to shoot him, as he was going up to the mine.

He climbed up the trail, chewing the unpalatable thought that Gurdon had seen nothing amiss — yet Gurd had been at the trial! The captain began to wish he had never gone on that deerhunt.

He went into the tent, struck a match, lit a candle and examined everything closely. There was no gun in the camp and no cartridges. He found the spill of twisted paper under the table, smothered his qualms and read it. He noted the open book for future examination in English. And now Tobe's labors had their late reward, for Rex missed nothing. Every effort brought fresh disappointment and every disappointment spurred him to fresh effort. He went into the tunnel; he scrutinized everything, even to the drills in the tub. The food supply tallied with Long's account. No details escaped him and every detail confirmed the growing belief that he, Captain Griffith, was a doddering imbecile.

He returned to the outpost, convinced at last. Nevertheless, merely to quiet the ravings of his insubordinate instincts, now in open revolt, he restaked the horses nearer to camp and cautiously carried both saddles to the head of the bed. Concession merely encouraged the rebels to further and successful outrages — the government was overthrown.

He drew sentry Steele aside and imparted his doubts. That faithful follower heaped scorn, mockery, laughter and abuse upon his shrinking superior: recounted all the points, from the first blasts of dynamite to the present moment, which favored the charitable belief above mentioned as newly entertained by Captain Griffith concerning himself. This belief of Captain Griffith-was amply indorsed by his subordinate in terms of point and versatility.

"Of course they look alike. I noticed that the minute I saw him — the same amount of legs and arms, features all in the fore part of his head, hair on top, one body — wonderful! Why, you pitiful ass, that Bransford person was a mighty keen-looking man in any company. This fellow's a yokel — an old, rusty, cap-and-ball, single-shot muzzle-loader. The Bransford was an automatic, steel-frame, high velocity — "

"The better head he has the more apt he is to do the unexpected — "

"Aw, shut up! You've got incipient paresis! Stuff your ears in your mouth and go to sleep!"

The captain sought his couch convinced, but holding his first opinion, savagely minded to arrest Mr. Long rather than let him have a gun to stand guard with. He was spared the decision. Mr. Long declined Gurdon's proffered gun, saying that he would be right there and he was a poor shot anyway.

Gurdon slept; Long took his place — and Captain Rex, from the bed, watched the watcher. Never was there a more faithful sentinel than Mr. Long. Without relaxing his vigilance even to smoke, he strained every faculty lest the wily Bransford should creep out through the shadows. The captain saw him, a stooped figure, sitting motionless by his rock, always alert, peering this way and that, turning his head to listen. Once Tobe saw something. He crept noiselessly to the bed and shook his chief. Griffith came, with his gun. Something was stirring in the bushes. After a while it moved out of the shadows. It was a prowling coyote. The captain went back to bed once more convinced of Long's fidelity, but resolved to keep a relentless eye on him just the same. And all unawares, as he revolved the day's events in his mind, the captain dropped off to troubled sleep.

Mr. Long woke him at three. There had been a temptation to ride away, but the saddles were at the head of the bed, the ground was stony; he would be heard. He might have made an attempt to get both guns from under the pillow, but detection meant ruin for him, since to shoot these boys or to hurt them was out of the question. Escape by violence would have been easy and assured. Jeff preferred to trust his wits. He was enjoying himself very much.

When the captain got his relentless eyes open and realized what had chanced he saw the further doubt was unworthy. Half an hour later the unworthy captain stole noiselessly to Long's bedside and saw, to his utter rage and distraction, that Mr. Bransford was there again. It was almost too much to bear. He felt that he should always hate Long, even after Bransford was safely hanged. Bransford's head had slipped from Long's pillow. Hating himself, Griffith subtly withdrew the miner's folder overalls and went through the pockets.

He found there a knife smelling of dynamite, matches, a turquoise carved to what was plainly meant to be the form of a bad-tempered horse, and two small specimens of ore!

Altogether, the captain passed a wild and whirling night.

CHAPTER XIII

The Siege of Double Mountain (*Continued*)

> If the bowl had been stronger
> My tale had been longer.
> — *Mother Goose*

W HEN THE SUN peeped over Rainbow Range, Captain Griffith bent over Tobe Long's bed. His eyes were aching, burned and sunken; the lids twitched; his face was haggard and drawn — but he had arrived at an unalterable decision. This thing could not and should not go on. His brain reeled now — another such night would entitle him to state protection.

He shook Mr. Long roughly.

"See here! I believe you're Bransford himself!"

Thus taken off his guard, Long threw back the bedding, rose to one elbow, still half asleep, and reached for his shoes, laughing and yawning alternately. Then, as he woke up a little more, he saw a better way to dress, dropped the shoes and unfurled his pillow — which, by day, he wore as overalls. Fumbling behind him, where the pillow had lain, he found a much-soiled handkerchief and tenderly dabbed at his swollen eye.

"Bit of steel in my eye from a drill-head," he explained. "Jiminy, but it's sore!"

Plainly he took the accusation as a pleasantry calling for no answer.

"I mean it! I'm going to keep you under guard!" said Captain Griffith bitingly.

Poor, sleepy Tobe, halfway into his overalls, stared up at Mr. Griffith; his mouth dropped open — he was quite at a loss for words. The captain glared back at him. Tobe kicked the overalls off and cuddled back into bed.

"Bully!" he said. "Then I won't have to get breakfast!"

Gurdon Steele sat up in bed, a happy man. His eye gave Mr. Long a discreetly confidential look, as of one who restrains himself, out of instinctive politeness, from a sympathetic and meaningful tap of one's forehead. A new thought struck Mr. Long. He reached over behind

Steele for the rifle at the bed's edge and thrust it into the latter's hands.

"Here, Boy Scout! Watch me!" he whispered. "Don't let me escape while I sleep a few lines! I'm Bransford!"

Gurdy rubbed his eyes and giggled.

"Don't you mind Rex. That's the worst of this pipe habit. You never can tell how they'll break out next."

"Yes, laugh, you blind bat!" said Rex bitterly. "I've got him all the same, and I'm going to keep him while you go to Escondido!" His rifle was tucked under his arm; he patted the barrel significantly.

It slowly dawned upon Mr. Long that Captain Griffith was not joking, after all, and an angry man was he. He sat up in bed.

"Oh, piffle! Oh fudge! Oh pickled moonshine! If I'm Bransford what the deuce am I doing here? Why, you was both asleep! I could 'a' shot your silly heads off and you'd 'a' never woke up. You make me tired!"

"Don't mind him, Long. He'll feel better when he takes a nap," said Gurd joyfully. "He has poor spells like this and he misses his nurse. We always make allowances for him."

Mr. Long's indignation at last overcame his politeness, and in his wrath he attacked friend and foe indiscriminately.

"Do you mean to tell me that you two puling infants are out hunting down a man you never saw? Don't the men at the other side know him either? By jinks, you hike out o' this after breakfast and send for some grown-up men. I want part of that reward — and I'm going to have it! Look here!" He turned blackly to Gurdon. "Are you sure that Bransford, or anyone else, came in here at all yesterday, or did you dream it? Or was it all a damfool kid joke? Listen here! I worked like a dog yesterday. If you had me stand guard three hours, tired as I was, for nothing, there's going to be more to it. What kind of a sack-and-snipe trick is this, anyway? You just come one at a time and I'll lick the stuffin' out o' both o' you! I ain't feelin' like any schoolboy pranks just now."

"No, no; that part's all straight. Bransford's in there, all right," protested Gurdon. "If you hadn't been working in the tunnel you'd have seen him when he went by. Here's the note he left. And his horse and saddle are up at the spring. We left the horse there because he was lame and about all in. Bransford can't get away on him. Rex is just excited — that's all the matter with him. Hankering for glory! I told him last night not to make a driveling idiot of himself. Here, read this insolent note, will you?"

Long glowered at the note and flung it aside. "Anybody could 'a' wrote that! How am I to know this thing ain't some more of your

funny streaks? You take these horses to water and bring back Bransford's horse and saddle, and then I'll know what to believe. Be damn
sure you bring them, too, or we'll go to producing glory right here
— great gobs and chunks of it! You Griffith! put down that gun or
I'll knock your fool head off! I'm takin' charge of this outfit now,
and don't you forget it! And I don't want no maniac wanderin' round
me with a gun. You go to gatherin' up wood as fast as ever God'll
let you!"

"Say, I was mistaken," said the deposed leader, thoroughly convinced once more. "You do look like Bransford, you know." He laid
down his rifle obediently.

"Look like your grandmother's left hind foot!" sneered the outraged miner. "My eyes is brown and so's Bransford's. Outside o'
that — "

"No, but you do, a little," said his ally, Steele. "I noticed it myself,
last night. Not much — but still there's a resemblance. Poor Cap
Griffith just let his nerves and imagination run away with him — that's
all."

Long sniffed. "Funny I never heard of it before," he said. He was
somewhat mollified, nevertheless; and, while cooking breakfast, he received very graciously a stammered and half-hearted apology from
young Mr. Griffith, now reduced to the ranks. "Oh, that's all right,
kid. But say — you be careful and don't shoot your pardner when he
comes back."

Gurdon brought back the sorrel horse and the saddle, thereby allaying Mr. Long's wrathful mistrust that the whole affair was a practical
joke.

"I told you butter wouldn't suit the works!" said Rex triumphantly,
and watched the working of his test with a jealous eye.

Long knew his Alice. " 'But it was the best butter,' " he said. He
surveyed the sorrel horse; his eye brightened. "We'll whack up that
blood-money yet," he announced confidently. "Now I'm going to
walk over to the south side and get one of those fellows to ride sign
round the mountain. You boys can sleep, turn and turn about, till I
get back. Then I want Steele to go to Escondido and wire up to
Arcadia that we've got our bear by the tail and want help to turn
him loose, and tell Pappy Sanders to send me out some grub or I'll
skin him. Pappy's putting up for the mine, you know. I'll stay here
and keep an eye on Griffith." He gave that luckless warrior a jeering
look, as one who has forgiven but not forgotten.

"Why don't you ride one of our horses?" said Gurdon.

"Want to keep 'em fresh. Then if Bransford gets out over the cliffs you can run him down like a mad dog," said Tobe. "Besides, if I ride a fresh horse in here he'll maybe shoot me to get the horse; and if he could catch you lads away from shelter maybe so he'd make a dash for it, a-shootin'. See here! If I was dodgin' in here like him — know what I'd do? I'd just shoot a few lines on general principles to draw you away from the gates. Then if you went in to see about it I'd either kill you if I had to, or slip out if you give me the chance. You just stay right here, whatever happens. Keep under shelter and keep your horses right by you. We got him bottled up and we won't draw the cork till the sheriff comes. I'll tell 'em to do the same way at the other end. I won't take any gun with me and I'll stick to the big main road. That way Bransford won't feel no call to shoot me. Likely he's 'way up in the cliffs, anyhow."

"Ride the sorrel horse then, why don't you? He isn't lame enough to hurt much, but he's lame enough that Bransford won't want him." Thus Mr. Griffith, again dissimulating. Every detail of Mr. Long's plan forestalled suspicion. That these measures were precisely calculated to disarm suspicion now occurred to Griffith's stubborn mind. For he had a stubborn mind; the morning's coffee had cleared it of cobwebs, and it clung more tenaciously than ever to the untenable and thrice-exploded theory that Long and Bransford were one and inseparable, now and forever.

He meditated an ungenerous scheme for vindication and, to that end, wished Mr. Long to ride the sorrel horse. For Mr. Long, if he were indeed the murderer — as, of course, he was — would indubitably, upon some plausible pretext, attempt to pass the guards at the farther end of the trip, where was no clear-eyed Griffith on guard. What more plausible than a modification of the plan already rehearsed — for Long to tell the wardens that Griffith had sent him to telegraph to the sheriff? Let him once pass those warders on any pretext! That would be final betrayal, for all his shrewdness. There was no possibility that Long and Bransford could complete their escape on that lame sorrel. He would not be allowed to get much of a start — just enough to betray himself. Then he, Griffith, would bring them back in triumph.

It was a good scheme: all things considered, it reflected great credit upon Mr. Griffith's imagination. As in Poe's game of "odd or even," where you must outguess your opponent and follow his thought, Mr. Rex Griffith had guessed correctly in every respect. Such, indeed, had been Mr. Long's plan. Only Rex did not guess quite often enough. Mr. Long had guessed just one layer deeper — namely, that

Mr. Griffith would follow his thought correctly and also follow him. Therefore Mr. Long switched again. It was a bully game — better than poker. Mr. Long enjoyed it very much.

Just as Rex expected, Tobe allowed himself to be overpersuaded and rode the sorrel horse. He renamed the sorrel horse Goldie, on the spot, saddled him awkwardly, mounted in like manner, and rode into the shadowy depths of Double Mountain.

Once he was out of sight Mr. Griffith followed, despite the angry protest of Mr. Steele — alleging falsely that he was going to try for a deer.

Tobe rode slowly up the crooked and brush-lined cañon. Behind him, cautiously hidden, came Griffith, the hawk-eyed avenger — waiting at each bend until Mr. Long had passed the next one, for closer observation of how Mr. Long bore himself in solitude.

Mr. Long bore himself most disappointingly. He rode slowly and awkwardly, scanning with anxious care the hillsides before him. Not once did he look back lest he should detect Mr. Griffith. Near the summit the Goldie horse shield and jumped. It was only one little jump, whereunto Goldie had been privately instigated by Mr. Long's thumb — "thumbing" a horse, as done by one conversant with equine anatomy, produces surprising results! — but it caught Mr. Long unawares and tumbled him ignominiously in the dust.

Mr. Long sat in the sand and rubbed his shoulder: Goldie turned and looked down at him in unqualified astonishment. Mr. Long then cursed Mr. Bransford's sorrel horse; he cursed Mr. Bransford for bringing the sorrel horse; he cursed himself for riding the sorrel horse; he cursed Mr. Griffith, with one last, longest, heart-felt, crackling, hair-raising, comprehensive and masterly curse, for having persuaded him to ride the sorrel horse. Then he tied the sorrel horse to a bush and hobbled on afoot, saying it all over backward.

Poor Griffith experienced the most intense mortification — except one — of his life. This was conclusive. Bransford was reputed the best rider in Rainbow. This was Long. He was convinced, positively, finally and irrevocably. He did not even follow Mr. Long to the other side of Double Mountain, but turned back to camp, keeping a sharp eye out for traces of the real Bransford; to no effect. It was only by chance — a real chance — that, clambering on the gatepost cliffs to examine a curious whorl of gneiss, he happened to see Mr. Long as he returned. Mr. Long came afoot, leading the sorrel horse. Just before he came within sight of camp he led the horse up beside a boulder, climbed clumsily into the saddle, clutched the saddle horn, and so rode into camp. The act was so natural a one that Griffith, already convinced, was convinced again — the more so because Long preserved a discreet silence as to the misadventure with the sorrel horse.

Mr. Long reported profanely that the men on the other side had also been disposed to arrest him, and had been dissuaded with difficulty.

"So I guess I must look some like Bransford, though I would never 'a' guessed it. Reckon nobody knows what they really look like. Chances are a feller wouldn't know himself if he met him in the road. That squares you, kid. No hard feelings?"

"Not a bit. I certainly thought you were Bransford, at first," said Griffith.

"Well, the black-eyed one — Stone — he's coming round on the west side now, cutting sign. You be all ready to start for Escondido as soon as he gets here, Gurd. Say, you don't want to wait for the sheriff if he's up on Rainbow. You wire a lot of your friends to come on the train at nine o'clock tonight. Sheriff can come when he gets back. There ain't but a few horses at Escondido. You get Pappy Sanders to send your gang out in a wagon — such as can't find horses."

"Better take in both of ours, Gurd," said Griffith. He knew Long was all right, as has been said, but he was also newly persuaded of his own fallability. He had been mistaken about Long being Bransford; therefore he might be mistaken about Long being Long. In this spirit of humility he made the suggestion recorded above, and was grieved that Long endorsed it.

"And I want you to do two errands for me, kid. You give this to Pappy Sanders — the storekeeper, you know" — here he produced the little eohippus from his pocket — "and tell him to send it to a jeweler for me and get a hole bored in it so it'll balance. Want to use it for a watch-charm when I get a watch. And if we pull off this Bransford affair I'll have me a watch. Now don't you lose that! It's turquoise — worth a heap o' money. Besides, he's a lucky little horse."

"I'll put him in my pocketbook," said Gurdon.

"Better give him to Pappy first off, else you're liable to forget about him, he's so small. Then you tell Pappy to send me out some grub. I won't make out no bill. He's grubstakin' the mine; he'll know what to send. You just tell him I'm about out of patience. Tell him I want about everything there is, and want it quick; and a jar for sourdough — I broke mine. And get some newspapers." He hesitated perceptibly. "See here, boys, I hate to mention this; but old Pappy, him and this Jeff Bransford is purty good friends. I reckon Pappy won't much like it to furnish grub for you while you're puttin' the kibosh on Jeff.

You better get some of your own. You see how it is, don't you? 'Tain't like it was my chuck."

Stone came while they saddled. He spoke apart with Griffith as to Mr. Long, and a certain favor he bore to the escaped bank-robber; but Griffith, admitting his own self-deception in that line, outlined the history of the past unhappy night. Stone, who had suffered only a slight misgiving, was fully satisfied.

As Steele started for the railroad Mr. Stone set out to complete the circuit of Double Mountain, in the which he found no runaway tracks. And Griffith and Long, sleeping alternately — especially Griffith — kept faithful ward over the gloomy gate of Double Mountain.

CHAPTER XIV

Flight

Keep away from that wheelbarrow — what the hell do you know about machinery? — ELBERT HUBBARD.[1]

JUST AFTER DARK a horseman with a led horse came jogging round the mountain on the trail from Escondido. On the led horse was a pack bound rather slouchily, not to a packsaddle, but to an old riding saddle. The horses were unwilling to enter the circle of firelight, so the rider drew rein just beyond — a slender and boyish rider, with a flopping wide-brimmed hat too large for him.

"Oh, look who's here!" said Tobe, as one who greets an unexpected friend.

"Hello, Tobe! Here's your food, grub, chuck and provisions! Get your outlaw yet? Them other fellows will be out along toward midnight." He went on without waiting for an answer: "Put me on your payroll. Pappy said I was to go to work — and if you was going to quit work to hunt down his friend you'd better quit for good. Lead on to your little old mine. I don't know where it is, even."

"I'll go up and unpack, Rex," said Tobe; "but, of course, I'm not going to lose my part of that five thousand. Pappy's foolish. He's gettin' old. I'll be back after a while and bring down the papers."

Chatting of the trapped outlaw, the Ophir men climbed the zigzag

[1] It is not intimated that Mr. Hubbard wrote this — merely that he printed it. — AUTHOR.

to the mine. To Griffith, their voices dwindled to an indistinct murmur; a light glowed through the tent on the dump.

The stranger pressed into Jeff's hand something small and hard — the little eohippus. "Here's your little old token. Pappy caught on at once and sent me along to represent. Let's get this pack off and get out of here. Do we have to go down the same trail again?"

"Oh, no," said Jeff. "There's a wood-trail leads round the mountain to the east. Who're you? I don't know you."

"Charley Gibson. Pappy knows me. He sent the little stone horse to vouch for me. I'm O.K. Time enough to explain when we've made a clean getaway."

"You're damn right there," Jeff said. "That boy down yonder is nobody's fool. I'll light a candle in the tent and he'll think I'm reading the newspapers. That'll hold him a while."

"I'll be going on down the trail," said Gibson. "This way, isn't it?"

"Yes, that's the one. All right. Go slow and don't make any more noise than you can help."

Jeff would have liked his own proper clothing and effects, but there was no time for resuscitation. Lighting the candle, he acquired *Alice in Wonderland* and thrust it into the bosom of his shirt. It had been years since last he read that admirable work; his way now led either to hiding or to jail — and, with Alice to share his fate, he felt equal to either fortune. He left the candle burning: the tent shone with a mellow glow.

"If he didn't hear our horses coming down we're a little bit of all right," said Jeff, as he rejoined his rescuer on the level. "Even if he does, he may think we've gone to hobble 'em — only he'd think we ought to water 'em first. Now for the way of the transgressor, to Old Mexico. This little desert'll be one busy place tomorrow!"

They circled Double Mountain, making a wide detour to avoid rough going, and riding at a hard gallop until, behind and to their right, a red spark of fire came into view from behind a hitherto intervening shoulder, marking where Stone and Harlow held the southward pass.

Jeff drew rein and bore off obliquely toward the road at an easy trot.

"They're there yet. So that's all right!" he said. "They've just put on fresh wood. I saw it flame up just then." He was in high feather. He began to laugh, or, more accurately, he resumed his laughter, for he had been too mirthful for much speech. "That poor devil Griffith will wait and fidget and stew! He'll think I'm in the tent, reading the newspapers, reading about the Arcadian bank robbery, likely. He'll wait a while, then he'll yell at me. Then he'll think we've gone to hobble the horses. He won't want to leave the gap unguarded. He won't know what to think. Finally he'll go up to the mine and see that pack piled off any which way, and no saddles. Then he'll know, but he won't know what to do. He'll think we're for Old Mexico, but he won't know it for sure. And it's too dark to track us. Oh, my stars, but I bet he'll be mad!"

.   .   .   .

Which shows that we all make mistakes. Mr. Griffith, though young, was of firm character, as has been lightly intimated. He waited a reasonable time to allow for paper-reading, then he waited a little longer and shouted; but when there was no answer he knew at once precisely what had happened; he had not been a fool at all, whatever Steele and Bransford had assured him, and he was a bigger fool to have allowed himself to be persuaded that he had been. It is true that he didn't know what was best to do, but he knew exactly what he was going to do — and did it promptly. Seriously annoyed, he spurred through Double Mountain, gathered up Stone and Harlow, and followed the southward road. Bransford had been on the way to Old Mexico — he was on that road still; Griffith put everything on the one bold cast. While the others saddled he threw fresh fuel on the fire, with a rankling memory of the candle in the deserted tent and Hannibal at Saint Jo. For the first time Griffith had the better of the long battle of wits. That armful of fuel slowed Jeff from gallop to trot, turned assured victory into a doubtful contest; when the fugitives regained the El Paso road Griffith's vindictive little band was not five miles behind them.

The night was lightly clouded — not so dark but that the pursuers noticed — or thought they noticed — the fresh tracks in the road when they came to them. They stopped, struck matches and confirmed their hopes: two shod horses going south at a smart gait; the dirt was torn up too much for travelers on their lawful occasions. From that moment Griffith urged the chase unmercifully; the fleeing couple, in fancied security, lost ground with every mile.

.   .   .   .   .   .

"How on earth did you manage it? Didn't they know you?" demanded Gibson as the pace slackened.

"It wasn't me! It was Tobe Long! 'You may not have lived much under the sea, and perhaps you were never even introduced to a lobster,'" quoted Jeff. Rocking in the saddle, he gave a mirthful résumé of his little evanishment. "And, oh, just think of that candle burning away in that quiet, empty tent! If I could have seen Griffith's face!" he gloated. "Oh me! Oh my! . . . And he was so sure! . . . Say, Gibson, how do you come in this galley?" As a lone prospector his speech had been fittingly coarse; now, with every mile, he shook off the debasing influence of Mr. Long. "Kettle-washing makes black hands. Aren't you afraid you'll get into trouble?"

"Nobody knows I'm kettle-washing, except Pappy Sanders and you," said Gibson. "I was careful not to let your friend see me at the fire."

"I'll do you a good turn sometime," said Jeff. He rode on in silence for a while and presently was lost in his own thoughts, leaning over with his hands folded on his horse's neck. In a low and thoughtful voice he half repeated, half chanted to himself:

> Illilleo Legardi, in the garden there alone,
> There came to me no murmur of the fountain's undertone
> So mystically, magically mellow as your own!

Another silence. Then Jeff roused himself, with a start.

"I'll tell you what, Gibson, you'd better cut loose from me. So far as I can see, you are only a kid. You don't want to get mixed up in a murder scrape. This would go pretty hard with you if they can prove it on you. Of course, I'm awfully obliged to you and all that; but you'd better quit me while the quitting's good."

"Oh, no; I'll see you through," said Gibson lightly. "Besides, I know you had nothing to do with the murder."

"Oh, the hell you do!" said Jeff. "That's kind of you, I'm sure. See here, who'd sold you your chips, anyway? How'd you get in this game?"

"I got in this game, as you put it, because I jolly well wanted to," replied Charley, with becoming spirit. "That ought to be reason enough for anything in this country. Nothing against it in the rules — and I don't use the rules, anyhow. If you must have it all spelled out for you — I knew, or at least I'd heard, that your friends were away from Rainbow; so I judged you wouldn't go up there. Then I knew those four amateur Sherlocks — they're in my set in Arcadia. When two of the deerhunters, after starting at two A.M., came back to Arcadia the same morning they left, looking all wise and important, and slipped off on the train to Escondido, saying nothing to anyone — and when the other two didn't come home at all — I began to think; went down to the depot, found they had gone to Escondido, and I came on the next train. I found out Pappy was your friend; and when

he got your little hurry-up call I volunteered my services, seeing
Pappy was too old and not footloose anyhow — with a wife and property. That's the how of it."

"Oh, yes, that's all right; but what makes you think I'm innocent?"

"I know Mr. White, you see. And Mr. White seems to think that
at about the time the bank was robbed you were — in a garden!"
Charley's voice was edged with faint mockery.

"Huh!" said Jeff, startled. "Who in hell is Mr. White?"

"Mr. White — in hell — is the devil!" said Charley.

At this unexpected disclosure Jeff lashed his horse to a gallop — his
spurs, you remember, being certain feet under the Ophir dump — and
strove to bring his thoughts to bear upon this new situation. He
slowed down and Charley drew up beside him.

"You seem to have stayed quite a while — in a garden," suggested
Charley.

"That tongue of yours is going to get you into trouble yet," said
Jeff. "You'll never live to be grayheaded."

Charley was not to be daunted.

"Say, Jeff, she's pretty easy to get acquainted with, what? And
those eyes of hers — a little on the see-you-later style, aren't they?"

Jeff turned in his saddle.

"Now you look here, Mr. Charley Gibson! I'm under obligations to
you, and so on — but I've heard all of that kind of talk that's good —
sabe?"

"Oh, I know her," persisted Charley. "Know her by heart — know
her like a book. She made a fool of me, too. She drives 'em single,
double, tandem, random and four abreast!"

"You little beast!" Jeff launched his horse at the traducer, but Gibson spurred aside.

"Stop now, Jeffy! Easy does it! I've got a gun!"

"Shut your damn head then! Gun or no gun, don't you take that
girl's name in your mouth again, or — Hark! What's that?"

It was a clatter far behind — a ringing of swift hoofs on hard
ground.

"By George, they're coming! Griffith will be a man yet!" said Jeff
approvingly. "Come on, kid; we've got to burn the breeze! I suppose
that talk of yours is only your damn fool idea of fun, but I don't like
it. Cut it out, now, and ride like a drunk Indian!" He laughed loud
and long. "Think o' that candle, will you? — burning away with a
clear, bright, steady flame, and nobody within ten miles of it!"

They raced side by side; but Gibson, heedless of their perilous situation, or perhaps taking advantage of it, took a malicious delight in

goading Jeff to madness; and he refused either to be silent or to talk about candles, notwithstanding Jeff's preference for that topic.

"I'm not joking! I'm telling you for your own good." Here the tormentor prudently fell back half a length and raised his voice so as to be heard above the flying feet. "Hasn't she gone back to New York, I'd like to know, and left you to get out of it the best way you can? She could 'a' stayed if she'd wanted to. Don't tell me! Haven't I seen how she bosses her mother around. No, sir! She's willing to let you hang to save herself a little slander — or, more likely, a little talk!"

Jeff whirled his horse to his haunches, but once more Gibson was too quick for him. Gibson's horse was naturally the nimbler of the two, even without the advantage of spurs.

"That's a lie! She was going to tell — she was bound to tell; I made her keep silent. After I jumped out she couldn't well say anything. That's why I jumped. Was I going to make her a target for such vile tongues as yours — for me? Oh! You ought to be shot out of a red-hot cannon, through a barbed-wire fence, into hell! You lie, you coward, you know you lie! I'll cram it down your throat if you'll get off and throw that gun down!"

"Yah! It's likely I'll put the gun down!" scoffed Gibson. "Ride on, you fool! Do you want to hang? Ride on and keep ahead! Remember, I've got the gun!"

"Hanging's not so bad," snarled Jeff. "I'd rather be hung decently than be such a thing as you! Oh, if I just had a gun!"

The sound of pursuit was clearer now; and, of course, the pursuers could hear the pursued as well and fought for every inch.

Jeff rode on, furious at his helplessness. For several miles his tormentor raced behind in silence, fearing, if he persisted longer in his evil course, that Jeff would actually stop and give himself up. They gained now on their pursuers, who had pressed their horses overhard to make up the five-mile handicap.

As they came to a patch of sandy ground they eased the pace somewhat. Charley drew a little closer to Jeff.

"Now don't get mad. I had no idea you thought so much of the girl — "

"Shut up, will you?"

" — or I wouldn't have deviled you so. I'll quit. How was I to know you'd stop to fight for her with the very rope round your neck? It's a pity she'll never know about it. . . . You can't have seen her more than two or three times — and Heaven only knows where that was! On that camping trip, I reckon. What kind of a girl is she, anyhow, to hold clandestine interviews with a stranger? . . . She'll write to you by and by — a little scented note, with a little stilted, meaningless word of thanks. No, she won't. It'll be gushy: 'Oh, my hero! How can I ever repay you?' She won't let you out of her clutches — anybody, so long as it's a man! Here! None o' that! . . . Go on, now, if you want to live!"

"*Who the hell wants to live?*"

A noose flew back from the darkness. Jeff's horse darted aside and Gibson was jerked sprawling to the sand at a rope's end — hat flew one way, gun another. Jeff ran to the six-shooter.

"Who's got the gun now?" he jeered, as he loosened the rope. "I only wish we had two of 'em!"

"You harebrained idiot!" Charley grabbed up his hat and spit sand from his mouth. "Get your horse and ride, you unthinkable donkey!"

"Pleasure first, business afterward!" Jeff unbuckled Gibson's gun-belt and transferred it to his own waist, jerking Gibson to his feet in the violent process. "Now, you little blackguard, you either take back all that or you'll get the lickin' o' your life! You're too small; but all the same — "

"Oh, I'll take it back, you big bully — all I said and a lot more I only thought!" said Charley spitefully. He was almost crying with rage as he limped to his horse. "She's an angel on earth! Sure she is! Ride, you maniac — ride! Oh, you ought to be hung! I hope you do hang — you miserable ruffian!"

The following hoofs no longer rang sharply; they took on a muffled beat — they were in the sand's edge not a mile behind.

"Ride ahead, you! I've got the gun, remember!" observed Jeff significantly; "but if you slur that girl again I'll not shoot you — I'll naturally wear you out with this belt."

CHAPTER XV

Good-Bye

They have ridden the low moon out of the sky; their hoofs drum up the dawn. — *Two Strong Men*, KIPLING

"I'M NOT SPEAKING of her and I'm not going to," protested Gibson, in a changed tone. "I'll promise! My horse is failing, Jeff. I rode hard and fast from Escondido. Your horse carried nothing much but a saddle — that pack was mostly bluff, you know. And those fellows' horses have come twenty miles less than either of ours."

No answer.

"I don't believe we're going to make it, Jeff!" There was a forlorn little quaver in Charley's voice.

Jeff grunted. "Uh! Maybe not. Griffith'll be real pleased."

Gibson rode closer. "Can't we turn off the road and hide?"

"Till daylight," said Jeff. "Then they'll get us. No way out of this desert except across the edges somewhere. You go if you want to. They won't bother to hunt for you, maybe, if they get me."

"No. It's my fault. . . . I'll see it out. . . . I'm sorry Jeff — but it was so funny!" Here, rather to Jeff's surprise, Charley's dejection gave place to laughter.

They rode up a sandy slope where mesquites grew black along the road. Blown sand had lodged to hummocks in their thick and matted growth; the road was a sunken way.

"How far is it from here, Jeff?"

"Ten miles — maybe only eight — to the river. We're in Texas now — have been for an hour."

"Think we can make it?"

"*Quien sabe?*"

Gibson drew rein. "You go on. Your horse isn't so tired."

"Oh, I guess not!" said Jeff. "Come on."

The sound of pursuit came clear through the quiet night. There was silence for a little.

"What'll you do, Jeff? Fight?"

"I can't!" said Jeff. "Hurt those boys? I couldn't fight the way it is — hardly, even if 'twas the sheriff. I'll just hang, I reckon."

They reached the top of the little slope and turned down the other side.

"I don't altogether like this hanging idea," said Gibson. "I got you into this, Jeff; so I'll just get you out again — like the man in our town who was so wondrous wise. Going to use bramble bushes, too." Volatile Gibson, in the stress of danger, had forgotten his wrath. He was light-hearted and happy, frivolously gay. "Give me your rope and your gun, Jeff. Quick now! No, I won't mention your girl — not once! Hurry!"

"What are you going to do?" asked Jeff, thoroughly mystified.

"Ever read the 'Fool's Errand'?" Charley chuckled. "No? Well, I have. Jump off and tie the end of your rope to that mesquite root. Quick!"

He sprang down, snatched one end of the coil from Jeff's hand and stretched it taut across the road, a foot from the ground. "Now your gun! Quick!"

He snatched the gun, tied an end of his own saddle-rope to the stretched one, near the middle, plunged through the mesquite, over a hummock, paying out his rope as he went; wedged the gun firmly in the springing crotch of a mesquite tree, cocked it and tied the loose end of the trailing rope to the trigger. He ran back and sprang on his horse.

"Now ride! It's our last chance!"

"Kid, you're a wonder!" said Jeff. "You'll do to take along! They'll lope up when they turn down that slope, hit that rope and pile in a heap!"

"And my rope will fire the gun off!" shrilled joyous Charley. "They'll think it's us — an ambuscade — "

"They'll take to the sandhills," Jeff broke in. "They'll shoot into the bushes — they'll think it's us firing back, half the time. . . . They'll scatter out and surround that lonesome, harmless motte and watch it till daylight. You bet they won't go projecting round it any till daylight, either!" He looked up at the sky. "There's the morning star. See it? 'They have ridden the low moon out of the sky' — only there isn't any moon — 'their hoofs drum up the dawn.' Then they'll find our tracks — and if I only could see the captain's face! 'Oh, my threshings, and the corn of my floor!' . . . And by then we'll be in Mexico and asleep. . . . When Griffith finds that gun — oh, he'll never show his head in Arcadia again! . . . Say, Charley, I hope none of 'em get hurt when they strike your skip-rope."

"Huh! It's sandy! A heap you cared about me getting hurt when you dragged me from my horse!" said Gibson, rather snappishly. "You did hurt me, too. You nearly broke my neck and you cut my arms. And I got full of mesquite thorns when I set that gun. You don't care! I'm only the man that came to save your neck. That's the thanks I get! But the men that are trying to hang you — that's different! You'd better go back. They might get hurt. You'll be sorry sometime for the way you've treated me. There — it's too late now!"

A shot rang behind them. There was a brief silence. Then came a sharp fusillade, followed by scattering shots, dwindling to longer intervals.

Jeff clung to his saddle horn.

"I guess they ain't hurt much," he laughed. "Wish I could see 'em when they find out! Slow down, kid. We've got lots of time now."

"We haven't," protested Charley. "Keep moving. It's hard on the horses, but they'll have a lifetime to rest in. They've telegraphed all over the country. You want to cross the river before daylight. It would be too bad for you to be caught now! Is there any ford, do you know?"

"Not this time of year. River's up."

"Cross in a boat then?"

"Guess we'd better. That horse of yours is pretty well used up. Don't believe he could swim it."

"Oh, I'm not going over. I'll get up to El Paso. I've got friends there."

"You'll get caught."

"No, I won't. I'm not going across, I tell you, and that's all there is to it! I guess I'll have something to say about things. I'm going to see you safely over, and that's the last you'll ever see of Charley Gibson."

"Oh, well!" Jeff reflected a little. "If you're sure you won't come along, I'd rather swim. My horse is strong yet. You see, it takes time to find a boat, and a boat means a house and dogs; and I'll need my horse on the other side. How'll you get to El Paso? Griffith'll likely come down here about an hour by sun, 'cross lots, a-cryin'."

"I'll manage that," said Gibson curtly enough. "You tend to your own affair."

"Oh, all right!" Jeff rode ahead. He whistled; then he chanted his war song:

> Said the little Eohippus:
>   "I'm going to be a horse!
> And on my middle fingernails
>   To run my earthly course!"
> The Coryphodon was horrified;
>   The Dinoceras was shocked;
> And they chased young Eohippus,
>   But he skipped away and mocked.
>
> Said they: "You always were as small
>   And mean as now we see,
> And that's conclusive evidence
>   That you're always going to be.
> What! Be a great, tall, hadsome beast,
>   With hoofs to gallop on?
> Why! You'll have to change your nature!"
>   Said the Loxolophodon.

"Jeff!"

"Well!" Jeff turned his head. Charley was drooping visibly.

"Stop that foolish song!"

Jeff rode on in silence. This was a variable person, Gibson. They were dropping down from the mesa into the valley of the Rio Grande.

"Jeff!"

Jeff fell back beside Charley. "Tired, pardner?"

"Jeff, I'm terribly tired! I'm not used to riding so far; and I'm sleepy — so sleepy!"

"All right, pardner; we'll go slower. We'll walk. Most there now. There's the railroad."

"Keep on trotting. I can stand it. We must get to the river before daylight. Is it far?" Charley's voice was weary. The broad sombrero drooped sympathetically.

"Two miles to the river. El Paso's seven or eight miles up the line. Brace up, old man! You've done fine and dandy! It's just because the excitement is all over. Why should you go any farther, anyhow? There's Ysleta up the track a bit. Follow the road up there and flag the first train. That'll be best."

"No, no. I'll go all the way. I'll make out." Charley straightened himself with an effort.

They crossed the Espee tracks and came to a lane between cultivated fields.

"Jeff! I'd like to say something. It won't be breaking my promise really. . . . I didn't mean what I said about — you know. I was only teasing. She's a good enough girl, I guess — as girls go."

Jeff nodded. "I did not need to be told that."

"And you left her in a cruel position when you jumped out of the window. She *can't* tell now, so long as there's any other way. What a foolish thing to do! If you'd just said at first that you were in the garden — Oh, why didn't you? But after the chances you took rather than to tell — why, Jeff, it would be terrible for her now."

"I know that, too," said Jeff. "I suppose I was a fool; but I didn't want her to get mixed up with it, and at the same time I cared less about hanging than any time I can remember. You see, I didn't know till the last minute that the garden was going to cut any figure. And do you suppose I'd have that courthouseful of fools buzzing and whispering at her? Not much! Maybe it was foolish — but I'm glad I did it."

"I'm glad of it, too. If you had to be a fool," said Charley, "I'm glad you were that kind of a fool. Are you still mad at me?"

Since Charley had recanted, and more especially since he had taken considerate thought for the girl's compulsory silence, Jeff's anger had evaporated.

"That's all right, pardner. . . . Only you oughtn't never to talk that way about a girl — even for a joke. That's no good kind of a joke. Men, now, that's different. See here, I'll give you an order to a fellow in El Paso — Hibler — to pay for your horses and your gun. Here's your belt, too."

Charley shook his head impatiently. "I don't want any money. Settle with Pappy for the horses. I won't take this one back. Keep the belt. You may want it to beat me with sometime. What are you going to do, Jeff? Aren't you ever coming back?"

"Sure I'll come back — if only to see Griffith again. I'll write to John Wesley Pringle — he's my mainest side pardner — and sick him on to find out who robbed that bank — to prove it, rather. I just about almost nearly know who it was. Old Wes'll straighten things out a-flying. I'll be back in no time. I got to come back, Charley!"

The river was in sight. The stars were fading; there was a flush in the east, a smell of dawn in the air.

"Jeff, I wish you'd do something for me."

"Sure, Charley. What is it?"

"I wish you'd give me that little turquoise horse to remember you by."

Jeff was silent for a little. He had framed out another plan for the little eohippus — namely, to give him to Miss Ellinor. He sighed; but he owed a good deal to Charley.

"All right, Charley. Take good care of him — he's a lucky little horse. I think a heap of him. Here we are!"

The trees were distinct in the growing light. Jeff rode into the river; the muddy water swirled about his horse's knees. He halted for parting; Gibson rode in beside him. Jeff took the precious Alice book from his bosom, put it in the crown of his miner's cap and jammed the cap tightly on his head.

"Better change your mind, Charley. Come along. We'll rout somebody out and order a dish of stewed eggs.

> "There is another shore, you know, upon the other side.
> The farther off from England the nearer 'tis to France;
> Then turn not pale, beloved snail, but come and join the dance.
> Will you — wont you — "

" 'No, I won't! I told you once!' " snapped the beloved snail.

"Here's the little eohippus horse then." As Charley took it Jeff wrung his hand. "By George, I've got to change my notion of Arcadia people. If there's many like you and Griffith, Arcadia's going to crowd the map! . . . Well — so long!"

"It looks awful wide, Jeff!"

"Oh, I'll be all right — swim it myself if the horse plays out — and if I don't have no cramps, as I might, of course, after this ride. Well — here goes nothin'! Take care of the little horse. I hope he brings you good luck!"

"Well — so long, then!"

Bransford rode into the muddy waters. They came to the horse's breast, his neck; he plunged in, sank, rose, and was borne away down the swift current, breasting the flood stoutly — and so went quartering across to the farther bank. It took a long time. It was quite light when the horse found footing on a sandbar half a mile below, rested, and splashed whitely through the shallows to the bank. Gibson swung his sombrero. Jeff waved his hand, rode to the fringing bushes, and was gone.

CHAPTER XVI

The Land of Afternoon

Dreaming once more love's old sad dream divine.

Los Banos de Santa Eulalia del Norte, otherwise known as Mud Springs, is a Mexican hamlet with one street of about the same length. Los Baños and Co. lies in a loop of the Rio Grande, half of a long day from El Paso, in mere miles; otherwise a contemporary of Damascus and Arpad.

Thither, mindful of the hot springs which supply the preliminaries of the name, Mr. Bransford made his way: mindful too, of sturdy old Don Francisco, a friend twice bound by ancient service given and returned.

He climbed the slow long ridges to the high *mesa:* for the river bent here in a long ox-bow, where a bold promontory shouldered far out to bar the way: weary miles were to be saved by crossing the neck of this ox-bow, and the tough horse tired and lagged.

The slow sun rose as he reached the Rim. It showed the wide expanse of desert behind him, flooded with trembling light; eastward, beyond the river, the buttressed and fantastic peaks of Fray Cristobal; their jutting shadows streaming into the gulf beyond, athwart the silvery ribbon of gleaming water, twining in mazy loops across the valley floor: it showed the black Rim at his feet, a frowning level wall of lava cliff, where the plain broke abruptly into the chasm beneath; the iron desolation of the steep sides, boulder-strewn, savage and forbidding:

"A land of old up-heaven from the abyss."

Long since, there had been a flourishing Mexican town in the valley. A wagon road had painfully climbed a long ridge to the Rim, twisting, doubling, turning, clinging hazardously to the hillside, its outer edge a wall built up with stone, till it came to the shoulder under the tremendous barrier. From there it turned northward, paralleling the Rim in mile-long curve above a deep gorge; turning, in a last desperate climb, to a solitary gateway in the black wall, torn out by flood-waters through slow centuries. Smallpox had smitten the people; the treacherous river had devastated the fertile valley, and, subsiding, left the rich fields a waste of sand. The town was long deserted; the disused road was gullied and torn by flood, the soil washed away, leaving a heaped and crumbled track of tangled stone. But it was the only practicable way as far as the sandhills, and Jeff led his horse down the ruined path, with many a turning back and scrambling detour.

The shadows of the eastern hills drew back before him as he reached the sand-dunes. When he rode through the silent streets of what had been Alamocita, the sun peered over Fray Cristobal, gilding the crumbling walls, where love and laughter had made music, where youth and hope and happiness had been. . . . Silent now and deserted, given over to lizard and bat and owl, the smiling gardens choked with sand and grass, springing with *mesquite* and *tornillo;* a few fruit trees, gnarled and tangled, drooping for days departed, when young mothers sang low lullaby beneath their branches. . . . Passed away and forgotten — hopes and fears, tears and smiles, birth and death, joy and sorrow, hatred and sin and shame, falsehood and truth and courage and love. The sun shone cheerfully on these gray ruins — as it had shone on a thousand such, and will shine.

Jeff turned down the river, past the broken *acequias,* to where a massive spur of basaltic rock had turned the fury of the floods and spared a few fields. In this sheltered cove dwelt Don Francisco Escobar in true pastoral and patriarchal manner; his stalwart sons and daughters, with their sons and daughters in turn, in clustering *adobes* around him: for neighbors, the allied family of Gonzales y Ortega.

A cheerful settlement, this of Los Baños, nestling at the foot of the friendly rampart, sheltered alike from flood and wind. South and west the close black Rim walled the horizon, the fantasy of Fray Cristobal closed in the narrow east: but northward, beyond the low sand-hills and the blue heat-haze, the high peaks of Organ, Guadalupe and Rainbow swam across the sleepy air, far and soft and dim.

In their fields the *gente* of Gonzales y Ortega and of Escobar raised ample crops of alfalfa, wheat, corn, *frijoles* and *chili,* with orchard, vineyard and garden. Their cows, sheep and goats grazed the foot-hills between river and Rim, watched by the young men or boys, penned nightly in the great corrals in the old Spanish fashion; as if the Moor still swooped and forayed. Their horses roamed the hills at will, only a few being kept in the alfalfa pasture. They ground their own grain, tanned their cow-hides at home. Mattress and pillow were wool of their raising, their blankets and cloth their own weave. There were granaries, a wine-press, a forge, a cumbrous stone mill, a great *adobe* oven like a monstrous beehive.

Once a year their oxen drew the great high-sided wagons up the sandy road to El Paso, and returned with the year's marketing — salt, axes, iron and steel, powder and lead, bolts of white domestic or *manta* for sheets and shirtings, matches, tea, coffee, tobacco and sugar. Perhaps, if the saints had been kind, there were a few ribbons, trinkets or brightly colored prints of Joseph and Virgin and Child, St. John the Beloved, The Annunciation, The Children and Christ; perhaps an American rifle or a plow. But, for the most part, they held not with innovations; plowed, sowed and reaped as their fathers did, threshing with oxen or goats.

The women sewed by hand, cooked on fireplaces; or, better still, in the open air under the trees, with few and simple utensils. The family ate from whitest and cleanest of sheepskins spread on the floor. But, the walls were snowy with whitewash, the earthen floors smooth and clean, the coarse linen fresh and white. The scant furniture of the rooms — a pine bed, a chair or two, a mirror, a brass candlestick (with home-made candles), a cheap print on the wall, a great chest for clothes, blankets and simple treasures, the bright fire in the cozy fireplace — all combined to give an indescribable air of cheerfulness, of homely comfort and of rest. This quiet corner, where people still lived as simply as when Abraham went up from Ur of the Chaldees, in the spring-time of the world, held, for seeing eyes, an incommunicable charm.

When Jeff came at last to Casa Escobar, the cattle were already on the hills, the pigs and chickens far afield. Don Francisco, white-haired, erect, welcomed him eagerly, indeed, but with stately courtesy.

"Is it thou indeed, my son? Now, my old eyes are gladdened this day. Enter, then, *amigo mio*, thrice-welcome — the house is thine in very truth. Nay, the young men shall care for thy horse."

He raised his voice. Three tall sons, Abran, Zenobio, Donociano, came at the summons, gave Bransford grave greeting, and stood to await their father's commands. Fathers of families themselves, they presumed not to sit unbidden, to join in the conversation, or to loiter.

Breakfast was served presently, in high state, on the table reserved for honored guests. Savory venison, chile, fish, eggs, *tortillas, tole, enchiladas,* cream and steaming coffee — such was the fare. Don Francisco sat gravely by to bear him company, while a silently hovering damsel anticipated every need.

Thence, when his host could urge no more upon him, to the deep shading cottonwoods. Wine was brought and the "makings" of cigarettes — corn-husks, handcut; a great jar of tobacco; and a brazier of mesquite embers. At a little distance women washed, wove or sewed; the young men made buckskin, fashioned quirts, whips, ropes, bridle-reins, tie-straps, hobbles, pack-sacks, and *chaparejos* of raw-hide; made cinches of horse-hair; wrought ox-yokes, plow-beams and other things needful for their simple husbandry.

Meanwhile, Don Francisco entertained his guest with grave and leisurely recital of the year's annals. Mateo, son of Sebastian, had slain a great bear in the Pass of All the Winds; Alicia, daughter of their eldest, was wed with young Roman de la O, of Cañada Nogales, to the much healing of feud and ancient hatred; Diego, son of Eusebio, was proving a bold and fearless rider of wild horses, with reason, as behooved his father's son; he had carried away the *gallo* at the *Fiesta de San Juan*, with the fleet dun colt "creased" from the wild bunch at Quemado; the herds had grown, the crops prospered, all sorrow passed them by, through the intercession of the blessed saints.

The year's trophies were brought. He fingered with simple pride the great pelt of the silver-tip. Antlers there were and lion-skins, gleaming prisms of quartz, flint arrowheads and agates brought in by the shepherds, the costly Navajo blanket won by the fleet-limbed dun at Cañada races.

Hither came presently another visitor — Florentino, breaker of wild horses, despite his fifty years; wizened and withered and small, merry and cheerful, singer of forgotten folk-songs; chanting, even as he came, the song of Macario Romero — Macario, riding joyous and light-hearted, spite of warning, omen and sign, love-lured to doom and death.

> "Concedame una licencia
> Voy á ir á ver á me Chata."

> Dice Macario Romero,
>   Parando en los estribos:
> "Madre, pues, esto voy á ver,
>   Si todos son mis amigos!"

And so, listening, weary and outworn, Jeff fell asleep.

.   .   .   .

Observe now, how Nature insists upon averages. Mr. Jeff Bransford was, as has been seen, an energetic man; but outraged nerves will have their revenge. After making proper amends to his damaged eye, Jeff's remnant of energy kept up long enough to dispatch young Tomás Escobar y Mendoza to El Paso with a message to Hibler: which message enjoined Hibler at once to carry tidings to John Wesley Pringle, somewhere in Chihuahua, asking him kindly to set right what Arcadian times were out of joint, as he, Jeff, felt the climate of Old Mexico more favorable for his throat trouble than that of New Mexico; with a postscript asking Hibler for money by bearer. And young Tomás was instructed to buy, at Juárez, a complete outfit of clothing for Jeff, including a gun.

This done, the reaction set in — aided, perhaps, by the enervating lassitude of the hot baths and the sleepy atmosphere of that forgotten village. Jeff spent the better part of a week asleep, or half awake at best. He had pleasant dreams, too. One — perhaps the best dream of all — was that on their wedding trip they should follow again the devious line of his flight from Arcadia. That would need a prairie schooner — no, a prairie steamboat — a prairie yacht! He would tell her all the hideous details — show her the mine, the camp of the besiegers, the ambuscade on the road. And if he could have Ellinor meet Griffith and Gibson for a crowning touch!

After the strenuous violence of hand-strokes, here was a drowsy and peaceful time. The wine of that land was good, the shade pleasant, the Alician philosophy more delightful than of yore; he had all the accessories, but one, of an earthly paradise.

Man is ungrateful. Jeff was a man; neglectful of present bounties, his dreaming thoughts were all of the absent accessory and of a time when that absence should be no more, nor paradise be empty.

Life, like the Gryphon's classical master, had taught him Laughter and Grief. He turned now the forgotten pages of the book of his years. Enough black pages were there; as you will know well, having yourself searched old records before now, with tears. He cast up that long account — the wasted lendings, the outlawed debts, the dishonored promises, the talents of his stewardship, unprofitable and brought to naught; set down — how gladly! — the items on the credit side. So men have set the good upon one side and the evil on the other since Crusoe's day, and before; against the time when the Great Accountant, Whose values are not ours, shall strike a final balance.

Take that book at your elbow — yes, either one; it doesn't matter. Now turn to where the hero first discovers his frightful condition — long after it has become neighborhood property. . . . He bent his head in humility. He was not worthy of her! . . . Something like that? Those may not be the precise words; but he groaned. He always groans. By-the-way, how this man-saying must amuse womankind!

Yes, and they actually say it too — real, live, flesh-and-blood men. Who was it said life was a poor imitation of literature? Happily, either these people are insincere or they reconsider the matter — else what should we do for families?

It is to be said that Jeff Bransford lacked this becoming delicacy. If he groaned he swore also; if he decided that Miss Ellinor Hoffman deserved a better man than he was, he also highly resolved that she should not have him.

"For, after all, you know," said Jeff to Alice:

> I'm sure he's nothing extra — a quiet man and plain,
> And modest — though there isn't much of which he could be vain.
> And had I mind to chant his praise, this were the kindest line —
> Somehow, she loves him dearly — this little love of mine!

CHAPTER XVII

Twentieth Century

> And there that hulking Prejudice
> Sat all across the road.
>
> .   .   .   .
>
> I took my hat, I took my coat,
> My load I settled fair,
> I approached that awful incubus
> With an absent-minded air —
> And I walked directly through him
> As if he wasn't there!
>
> — *An Obstacle*
> CHARLOTTE PERKINS STETSON

JOHNNY DINES rode with a pleasant jingle down the shady street of Los Baños de Santa Eulalia del Norte. His saddle was new, carven, wrought with silver; his bridle shone as the sun, his spurs as bright stars; he shed music from his feet. Jeff saw him turn to Casa Escobar: apple blossoms made a fragrant lane for him. He paused at Jeff's tree.

"*Alto Alli!*" said Johnny. The words, as sharp command, can be managed in two brisk syllables. The sound is then: "*Altwai!*" It is a crisp and startling sound, and the sense of it in our idiom is: "Hands up!"

Jeff had been taking a late breakfast *al fresco;* he made glad room on his bench.

"Light, stranger, and look at your saddle! Pretty slick saddle, too.

Guess your playmates must 'a' went home talking to themselves last night."

"They're going to kill a maverick for you at Arcadia and give a barbecue," said Johnny. The cult of *nil admirari* reaches its highest pitch of prosperity in the cow-countries, and Johnny knew that it was for him to broach tidings unasked.

"Oh, that reminds me — how's old Lars Porsena?" said Jeff, now free to question.

"Him? He's all right," said Johnny casually. "Goin' to marry one or more of the nurses. They're holdin' elimination contests now."

"Say, Johnny, when you go back, I wish you'd tell him I didn't do it. Cross my heart and hope to die if I did."

"Oh, he knows it wasn't you!" said Johnny.

Jeff shook his head doubtfully.

"Evidence was pretty strong — pretty strong! Who was it then?"

"Why, Lake himself — the old hog!"

"If Lake keeps on like this he's going to have people down on him," said Jeff. "Who did the holmesing — John Wesley?"

"Oh, John Wesley! John Wesley!" said Dines scornfully. "You think the sun rises and sets in old John Wesley Pringle. Naw; he didn't get back till it was all over. I cannot tell a lie. I did it with my little hatchet!"

"Must have had it sharpened up!" said Jeff. "Tell it to me!"

"Why, there isn't much to tell," said Dines, suddenly modest. "Come to think of it, I had right considerable help. There was a young college chap — he first put it into my head that it wasn't you."

"That would be the devil?" said Jeff, ignoring the insult.

"Just so. Name's White — and so's he: Billy White, S.M. and G.P."

"I don't just remember them degrees," said Jeff.

"Aw, keep still and you'll hear more. They stand for Some Man and Good People. Well, as I was a-saying, Billy he seemed to think it wasn't you. He stuck to it that Buttinski — that's what he calls you — was in a garden just when the bank was robbed."

Johnny contemplated the apple tree over his head. It was a wandering and sober glance, but a muscle twitched in his cheek, and he made no further explanation about the garden.

"And then I remembered about Nigger Babe throwin' you off, and I began to think maybe you didn't crack the safe after all. And there was some other things — little things — that made Billy and Jimmy Phillips — he was takin' cards in the game too — made 'em think maybe it was Lake; but it wasn't no proof — not to say proof. And there's where I come in."

"Well?" said Jeff, as Johnny paused.

"Simple enough, once you knowed how," said Johnny modestly. "I'd been reading lots of them detective books — Sherlock Holmes and all them fellows. I got Billy to have his folks toll Lake's sister away for the night, so she wouldn't be scared. Then me and Billy and Jimmy Phillips and Monte, we broke in and blowed up Lake's private safe. No trouble at all. Since the bank-robbin' every one had been tellin' round just how it ought to be done — crackin' safes. Funny how a fellow picks up little scraps of useful knowledge like that — things you'd think he'd remember might come in handy most any time — and then forgets all about 'em. I wrote it down this time. Won't forget it again."

"Well?" said Jeff again.

"Oh, yes. And there was the nice money — all the notes and all of the gold he could tote."

Jeff's eye wandered to the new saddle.

"I kept some of the yellow stuff as a souvenir — half a quart, or maybe a pint," said Johnny. "I don't want no reward for doin' a good deed. . . . And that's all."

"Lake is a long, ugly word," said Jeff thoughtfully.

"Well, what do you say?" prompted Johnny.

"Oh, thank you, thank you!" said Jeff. "You showed marvelous penetration — marvelous! But say, Johnny, if the money hadn't been there wouldn't that have been awkward?"

"Oh, Billy was pretty sure Lake was the man. And we figured he hadn't bothered to move it — you being the goat that way. What made you be a goat, Jeff? That whole performance was the most idiotic break I ever knew a grown-up man to get off. I knew you were not strictly accountable, but why didn't you say, 'Judge, your Honor, sir, at the time the bank was being robbed I was in a garden with a young lady, talking about the hereafter, and here and the here-tofore?' "

"On the contrary, what made your Billy think it was Lake?"

Johnny told him, in detail.

"Pretty good article of plain thinking, wasn't it?" he concluded. "Yet he mightn't have got started on the right track at all if he hadn't had the straight tip about your bein' in a garden." Johnny's eye reverted to the apple tree. "Lake found your noseguard, you know, where you left it. I reckon maybe he saw you leave it there — Say, Jeff! Lake's grandfather must have been a white man. Anyhow, he's got one decent drop of blood in him, from somewhere. For when we arrested him, he didn't say a word about the garden. That was rather a good stunt, I think. Bully for Lake, just once!"

"Right you are! And Mr. J. Dines, I've been thinking —" Jeff began.

Johnny glanced at him anxiously.

" — and I've about come to the conclusion that we're some narrow contracted and bigoted on Rainbow. We don't know it all. We ain't the only pebble. From what I've seen of these Arcadia men they seem to be pretty good stuff — and like as not it's just the same way all along the beach. There's your Mr. White, and Griffith, and Gibson — did I tell you about Gibson?"

Johnny flashed a brilliant smile. His smiles always looked larger than they really were, because Johnny was a very small man.

"I saw Griffith and he gave me his version — several times. He's real upset, Griffith. . . . Last time he told me, he leaned up against my neck and wept because there was only ten commandments!"

"Didn't see Gibson, did you? You know him?"

"Nope. Pappy picked him up — or he picked Pappy up, rather. Hasn't been seen since. I guess Gibby, old boy, has gone to the wild bunch. He wouldn't suspect you of bein' innocent, and he dreamed he dwelt in marble walls, makin' shoes for the state. So he gets cold feet and he just naturally evaporates — good-night!"

"Yes — he said he was going to hike out, or something to that effect," responded Jeff absently — the fact being that he was not thinking of Gibson, at all, but was pondering deeply upon Miss Ellinor Hoffman. Had she gone to New York according to the original plan? It did not seem probable. Her face stood out before him — bright, vivid, sparkling, as he had seen her last, in the court-room of Arcadia. Good heavens! Was that only a week ago? Seven days? It seemed like seven years! — No — she had not gone — at least, certainly not until she was sure that he, Jeff, had made good his escape. Then, perhaps, she might have gone. Perhaps her mother had made her go. Oh, well! — New York wasn't far, as he had told her that first wonderful day on Rainbow Rim. What a marvelous day that was!

Jeff was suddenly struck with the thought that he had never seen Ellinor's mother. Great Scott! She had a father, too! How annoying! He meditated upon this unpleasant theme for a space. Then, as if groping in a dark room, he had suddenly turned on the light, his thought changed to — *What a girl! Ah, what a wonderful girl! Where is she?*

Looking up, Jeff became once more aware of Johnny Dines, leg curled around the horn of the new saddle, elbow on knee, cheek on hand, contemplating his poor friend with benevolent pity. And then Jeff knew that he could make no queries of Johnny Dines.

Johnny spake soothingly.

"You are in North America. This is the Twentieth Century. Your name is Bransford. That round bright object is the sun. This direction is East. This way is called 'up.' This is a stream of water that you see. It is called the Rio River Grand Big. We are advertised by our loving friends. I cannot sing the old songs. There's a reason. Two of a kind flock together. Never trump your pardner's ace. It's a wise child that dreads the fire. Wake up! Come out of it! Change cars!"

"I ought to kill you," said Jeff. "Now giggle, you idiot, and make everybody hate you! — Wait till I say *Adiós* to my old compadre and the rest of the Escobar *gente* and I'll side you to El Paso."

"Not I. Little Johnny, he'll make San Elizario ferry by noon and Helm's by dark. Thought maybe so you'd be going 'long."

"Why, no," said Jeff uneasily. "I guess maybe I'll go up to El Paso and june around a spell."

"Oh, well — just as you say! Such bein' the case, I'll be jogging."

"Better wait till after dinner — I'll square it with Don Francisco if . . . anything's missing."

"No — that makes too long a jaunt for this afternoon. Me for San Elizario. So long!"

But beyond the first *acequia* he turned and rode back.

"Funny thing, Jeff! Remember me telling you about a girl I saw on Mayhill, the day Nigger Babe throwed you off? Now, what was that girl's name? — I've forgotten again. Oh yes! — Hoffman — Miss Ellinor Hoffman. Well — she's at Arcadia still. The mother lady was all for going back to New York — but, no, sir! Girl says she's twenty-one, likes Arcadia, and she's going to stay a spell. Leastwise, so I hear."

"I *will* kill you!" said Jeff. "Here, wait till I saddle my nag and say good-bye."

.   .   .   .

Beyond San Elizario, as they climbed the Pass of All the Winds, the two friends halted to breathe their horses.

"Jeff," said Johnny, rather soberly, "you can kick me after I say my little piece — I'll think poorly of you if you don't — but ain't you making maybe a mistake? That girl, now — nice girl, and all that — but that girl's got money, Jeff."

"I hate a fool worse than a knave, any day in the week," said Jeff: "and the man that would let money keep him from the only girl — why, Johnny, he's so much more of a fool than the other fellow is a scoundrel — "

"I get you!" said **Johnny.** "You mean that a submarine boat is better built for roping steers than a mogul engine is skilful at painting steeples, and you wonder if you can't get a fresh horse somewhere and go on through to Arcadia tonight?"

"Something like that," admitted Jeff. "Besides," he added lightly, "while I'd like that girl just as well if I didn't have a cent — why, as it happens, I'm pretty well fixed, myself. I've got money to throw at the little dicky-birds — all kinds of money. Got a fifty-one per cent interest in a copper mine over in Harqua Hala that's been payin' me all the way from ten to five thousand clear per each and every year for the last seven years, besides what I pay a lad for lookout to keep anybody but himself from stealing any of it. He's been buyin' real estate for me in Los Angeles lately."

Johnny's jaw dropped in unaffected amazement.

"All this while? Before you and Leo hit Rainbow?"

"Sure!" said Jeff.

"And you workin' for forty a month and stealin' your own beef? — then saving up and buying your little old brand along with Beebe and Leo and old Wes', joggin' along, workin' like a yaller dog with fleas?"

"Why not? Wasn't I having a heap of fun? Where can I see any better time than I had here, or find better friends? Money's no good by itself. I haven't drawn a dollar from Arizona since I left. It was fun to make the mine go round at first; but when it got so it'd work I looked for something else more amusing."

"I should think you'd want to travel, anyhow."

"Travel?" echoed Jeff. "Travel? Why, you damn fool, I'm here now!"

"Will you stay here, if you marry her, Jeff?"

"So you've no objection to make, if I've got a few dollars? That squares everything all right, does it? Not a yeep of protest from you now? See here, you everlasting fool! I'm just the same man I was fifteen minutes ago when you thought I didn't have any money. If I'm fit for her now, I was then. If I wasn't good enough then, I'm not good enough now."

"But I wasn't thinking of her — I was thinking of — how it would look."

"Look? Who cares how it looks? Just a silly prejudice! 'They say — what say they — let them say!' Johnny, maybe I was just stringin' you. If I was lying about the money — how about it then? Changed your mind again?"

"You wasn't lyin', was you?"

"Shan't tell you! It doesn't really make any difference, anyhow."

CHAPTER XVIII

At the Rainbow's End

Helen's lips are drifting dust;
Ilion is consumed with rust;
All the galleons of Greece
Drink the ocean's dreamless peace;
Lost was Solomon's purple show
Restless centuries ago;
Stately empires wax and wane —
Babylon, Barbary and Spain —
Only one thing, undefaced,
Lasts, though all the worlds lie waste
And the heavens are overturned,
Dear, how long ago we learned!
— FREDERICK LAWRENCE KNOWLES

STARLIT AND MOONLIGHT leagues, the slow, fresh dawn; in the cool of the morning, Bransford came to the crest of the ground-swell known as Frenchman's Ridge, and saw low-lying Arcadia dim against the north, a toy town huddling close to the shelter of Rainbow Range; he splashed through the shallow waters of Alamo, failing to a trickle before it sank in the desert sands; and so came at last to the moat of Arcadia. With what joyous and eager-choking heart-beat you may well guess: not the needlessness of those swift pulses or of that joy. For Ellinor was not there. With Mrs. Hoffman, she had gone to visit the Sutherlands at Rainbow's End. And Jeff could not go on. Arcadia rose to greet him in impromptu Roman holiday.

Poor Bransford has never known clearly what chanced on that awful day. There is a jumbled, whirling memory of endless kaleidoscopic troops of joyful Arcadians: Billy White, Monte, Jimmy, Clarke, the grim-smiling sheriff, the judge. It was dimly borne upon him by one or both of the two last, that there were yet certain formalities to be observed in the matter of his escape from custody of the Law and of the horse he had borrowed from the courthouse square. Indeed, it seemed to Jeff, in a hazy afterthought, that perhaps the sheriff had arrested him again. If so, it had slipped Jeff's mind, swallowed up in a gruesome horror of congratulations, handshakings, back-slappings, badinage and questions; heaped on a hero heartsick, dazed and dumb. Pleading weariness, he tore himself away at last, almost by violence, and flung himself down in a darkened bedroom of the Arcadian Atalanta.

One thing was clear. Headlight was there, Aforesaid Smith, Madison: but his nearest friends, Pringle, Beebe and Ballinger, though they had hastened back to Arcadia to fight Jeff's battles, were ostentatiously absent from his hollow and hateful triumph: Johnny Dines had pointedly refused to share his night ride from Helm's: and Jeff knew why, sadly enough. The gods take pay for the goods they give: and now that goodly fellowship was broken. The thought clung fast: it haunted his tossing and troubled slumbers, where Ellinor came through a sunset glow, swift-footed to meet him: where his friends rode slow and silent into the glimmering dusk, smaller and smaller, black against the sky.

·   ·   ·   ·   ·   ·   ·

The Sutherland place made an outer corner of Rainbow's End, bowered about by a double row of close and interlaced cottonwoods on two sides, by vigorous orchards on the other two.

The house had once been a one-storied adobe, heroically proportioned, thick-walled, cool against summer, warm in what went by the name of winter. The old-time princely hospitality was unchanged, but Sutherland had bought lots in Arcadia of early days; and now, the old gray walls of the house were smooth with creamy stucco wrought of gypsum from the White Sands; the windows were widened and there was a superimposed story, overhanging, wide and low. The gables were double-windowed, shingled and stained nut-brown, the gently sloping roof shingled, dormered and soft green: the overflow projecting to broad verandas on either side, very like an umbrella: a bungalow with two birthdays — 1866: 1896.

Miss Ellinor Hoffman had deserted veranda, rocking-chair and hammock. With a sewing basket beside her, she sat on a pine bench under a cottonwood of 1867, ostensibly basting together a kimono tinted like a dripping seashell, and faced with peach-blossom.

The work went slowly. Her seat was at the desert corner of the homestead which was itself the desert outpost of a desert town: and her blood stirred to these splendid horizons. The mysterious desert scoffed and questioned, drew her with promise of strange joys and strange griefs. The iron-hard mountains beckoned and challenged from afar, wove her their spells of wavering lights and shadows; the misty warp and woof of them shifting to swift fantastic hues of trembling rose and blue and violet, half veiling, half revealing, steeps unguessed and dreamed-of sheltered valleys — and all the myriad-voice of moaning waste and world-rimming hill cried "Come!"

Faint, fitful undertone of drowsy chords, far pealing of elfin bells;

that was pulsing of busy *acequias*, tinkling of mimic waterfalls. The clean breath of the desert crooned by — bearing a grateful fragrance of apple-blossoms near; it rippled the deepest green of alfalfa to undulating sheen of purple and flashing gold.

The broad fields were dwarfed to play-garden prettiness by the vastness of overwhelming desert, to right, to left, before; whose nearer blotches of black and gray and brown faded, far off, to a nameless shimmer, its silent leagues dwindling to immeasurable blur, merging indistinguishable in the burning sunset.

"East by up," overguarding the oasis, the colossal bulk of Rainbow walled out the world with grim-tiered cliffs, cleft only by the deep-gashed gates of Rainbow Pass, where the swift river broke through to the rich fields of Rainbow's End, bringing fulfilment of the fabled pot of gold — or, unused, to shrink and fail and die in the thirsty sand.

Below, the whilom channel wandered forlorn — Rainbow no longer, but Lost River — to a disconsolate delta, waterless save as infrequent floods found turbulent way to the Sink, when wild horse and antelope revisited their old haunts for the tender green luxury of these brief, belated springs.

Incidentally, Miss Hoffman's outpost commanded a good view of Arcadia road, winding white through the black tar-brush. Had she looked, she might have seen a slow horseman, tiny on the bare plain below the tar-brush, larger as he climbed the gentle slope along that white-winding road.

But she bent industrious to her work, smiling to herself, half-singing, half-humming a foolish and lilty little tune:

> A tisket a tasket — a green and yellow basket;
> I wrote a letter to my love and on the road I lost it —
> I crissed it, I crossed it — I locked it in a casket;
> I missed it, I lost it —

And here Miss Hoffman did an unaccountable thing. Wise Penelope unraveled by night the work she wove by day. Like her in this, Miss Ellinor Hoffman now placidly snipped and ripped the basting threads, unraveled them patiently, and set to work afresh.

> Now, there's no such thing as a Ginko tree;
> There never was — though there ought to be.
> And 'tis also true, though most absurd,
> There's no such thing as a Wallabye bird!

Miss Hoffman was all in white, with a white middy blouse trimmed in scarlet, a scarlet ribbon in her dark hair: a fine-linked gold chain showed at her neck. A very pretty picture she made, cool and fresh

against the deep shade and the green — but of course she did not know
it. She held the shaping kimono at arm's length, admiring the delicate
color, and fell to work again.

> Oh, the jolly miller, he lives by himself!
> As the wheel rolls around he gathers in his pelf,
> A hand in the hopper and another in the bag —
> As the wheel rolls around he calls out, "*Grab!*"

So intent and preoccupied was she, that she did not hear the approaching horse.

"Good evening!"

"Oh!" Miss Hoffman jumped, dropping the long-suffering kimono.
A horseman, with bared head, had reined up in the shaded road alongside. "How silly of me not to hear you coming! If you're looking for
Mr. Sutherland, he's not here — Mr. David Sutherland that is. But
Mr. Henry Sutherland is here — or was awhile ago — maybe half an
hour since. He was trying to get up a set of tennis. Perhaps they're
playing — over there on the other side of the house. And yet, if they
were there, we'd hear them laughing — don't you think?"

Mr. Bransford — for it was Mr. Bransford, and he was all dressed
in clothes — waited with extreme patience for the conclusion of these
feverish and hurried remarks.

"But I'm not looking for Sutherland. I'm looking for you!"

"Oh!" said Ellinor again. Then, after a long and deliberate survey,
the light of recognition dawned slowly in her eyes. "Oh, I *do* know
you, don't I? To be sure I do! You're Mr.—— the gentleman I met on
Rainbow Mountain, near Mayhill — Mr. — ah yes — Bransford!"

"Why, so I am!" said Jeff, leaning on the saddle-horn. One half
of Mr. Bransford wondered if he had not been making a fool of himself and taking a great deal for granted: the other half, though considerably alarmed, was not at all deceived.

Miss Ellinor did not actually put her finger in the corner of her
mouth — she merely looked as if she had. "Ah! — Won't you . . . get
down?" she said helplessly. "What a beautiful horse!"

"Why, yes — thank you — I believe I will."

He left the beautiful horse to stand with dangling reins, and came
over to the bench, silent and rather grim.

"Won't you sit down?" said Ellinor politely. "Fine day, isn't it?"

"It's a wonderful day — a marvelous day — a stupendous day!" said
this exasperated young man. "No, I guess it's not worth while to sit
down. I just wanted to find out where you lived. I asked you once
before, you know, and you didn't tell me."

"Didn't I? Oh, do sit down! You look so grumpy — tired, I mean."
Rather grudgingly, she swept the sewing basket from the bench to the
grass.

Jeff's eyes followed the action. He saw — if you call it seeing — the
snipped threads on the grass, the yet unpicked bastings, white against
the peach-pink facing; but he was a mere man, hardly circumstanced,
and these eloquent tidings were wasted upon his clumsy intellect: as
had been the surprising good fortune of finding Miss Ellinor exactly
where she was.

Nerving himself with memory of the Quaker Lady at the masquerade — if, indeed, that had ever really happened — Jeff took the offered
seat.

The young lady matched two edges together, smoothed them, eyed
the result critically, and plied a nimble needle. Then she turned clear
and guileless eyes on her glooming seatmate.

"You look older, somehow, than I thought you were, now that I
remember," she observed, biting the thread. "You've been away
haven't you?"

"Thought you were going away, yourself, so wild and fierce?" said
Jeff, evading. *Been away, indeed.*

Ellinor threaded her needle.

"Mamma *was* talking of going for a while," she said tranquilly.
"But I'm rather glad we didn't. We're having a splendid time here —
and Mr. White's going to take us to the White Sands next week. He'll
be down tomorrow — at least I think so. He's fine! He took us to
Mescalero early in the spring. And the young people here at Rainbow's End are simply delightful. You must meet some of them. Listen!
There they are now — I hear them. They *are* playing tennis. Come
on up and I'll introduce you. I can finish this thing any time." She
tossed the poor kimono into the basket.

"No," said this unhappy young man, rising. "I believe I'll go on
back. Good-bye, Miss Ell — Miss Hoffman. I wish you much happiness!"

"Why — surely you're not going now? There are some nice girls
here — they have heard so much of you, but they say they've never
met you. Don't you want — "

Jeff groaned, fumbling blindly at the bridle. "No, I wish I'd never
seen a girl!"

"Why-y! That's not very polite, is it? — Are — are you — mad to
me?" said Ellinor in a meek little voice.

"Mad? No," said Jeff bitterly. "I'm just coming to my senses. I've
been dreaming. Now I've woke up!"

"Angry, I mean, of course. I just say it that way — 'are you mad to me' — sometimes — to be — to be — nice, Mr. Bransford!"

"You needn't bother! Good-bye!"

"But I'll see you again — "

"*Never!*"

" — when you're not so — cross?"

Jeff reached for his stirrup.

"Oh, well! If you're going to be huffy! Never it is, then, by all means! No — wait! I must give you back your present."

"I have never given you a present. Some other man, doubtless. You should keep a list!" said Jeff, with bitter and cutting scorn.

The girl turned half away from him and hid her face with trembling hands; her shoulders shook with emotion.

"Look the other way, sir! Turn your head! You shall have your present back and then if you're so anxious to go — Go!"

"Miss Hoffman, I never gave you a present in my life," Jeff protested.

"You did!" sobbed Ellinor. She turned upon him, stamping her foot. "You said, when you gave it to me, that you hoped it would bring me good luck. And you've forgotten! *You'd* better keep a list! Turn your head away, I tell you!"

Confused, mazed, bewildered, Jeff obeyed her.

She sprang to her feet. She was laughing, blushing, glowing. In her hand was the little gold chain.

"Now, you may look. Hold out your hand, sir!"

Jeff's mind was whirling; he held out his hand. She laid a little gold locket in his palm. It was warm, that little locket.

"I have never seen this locket before in my life!" gasped Jeff.

"Open it!"

He opened it. The little eohippus glared up at him.

"Ellinor — *Charley Gibson!*"

"Tobe! Jeff! — *Jamie!*"

The little eohippus stared unwinking from the grass.

THE BEGINNING

The Trusty Knaves

THE TRUSTY KNAVES

CHAPTER I

A SMALL AND SCATTERED HERD grazed over the False Divide between
Plomo and Horsethief, and turned down into Gridiron; something
around six hundred head of cattle. They were thin and weak,
gaunted for water. A little bunch of saddle ponies, with a few extra
work horses, grazed apart, well to one side of the wagon road for
the sake of better grass, and a few hundred yards ahead of the cattle;
with a similar interval, a small band of white Angoras flanked them,
with a small boy for viceroy. The herders were five: George
Carmody, square-faced and grizzled — Old George, although he was
barely more than forty — three children, Judge, Jim and Jenny, step-
laddered from Judge's eighteen down to Jenny's twelve; and Charlie
Bird. Charlie had been wagon boss when the B 4 brand was great.
Dogged and faithful, he followed its fallen fortunes. Drought was
upon the land, the price of cattle had fallen from thirty dollars to
twelve, still falling. The B 4 was struggling westward for rumored
grass of Arizona.

Jenny was the horse wrangler; small Jimmy, on the small Ginger
pony, drove the goats. A mile ahead, four horses drew the canvas-
covered chuck wagon, and Lee Carmody sat in the shade of the tilt
to drive. It may be said here that the five dusty herders were cheerful herders as well, and that Lee Carmody's face was as comely and
pleasant as it was when Old George was Young George, and she was
Young George's young wife. It was one of our folkways to take
good and bad as they come, with little boasting and with no complaint.

High in the north, close above them, a sharp black ridge made a

fin on the crest of False Divide. At the scarp of this ridge a horse
and his rider stood motionless, outlined against the sky, looking down
upon the weary herd. The rider leaned forward, both hands on the
saddle horn. A scanty wind beat back the broad brim of a hat already
tip-tilted to heaven and clinging precariously to his head. The
stronger cattle in the lead began to string out, moving faster. Seeing
this, the horse herd moved on to check them. The observer lifted his
reins, and his horse picked his downward way gingerly through the
broken lava of the ridge. Man and horse turned into the dust behind
the plodding drag. George Carmody angled across to meet them.

The newcomer was tall, noticeably slender, something under middle
age. His face was long, thin, quiet, freckled so darkly that each
freckle stood out, embossed against that tanned and leathern face.
Thick, unruly hair, blown back against that tiptilt hat, was darkest
red, all but black. His nose was long and straight and thin, with a
hooked tip. A brindled mustache was ragged above an uncurving
thin-lipped mouth; wide-set pale blue eyes were watchful, but
friendly. He raised an open palm in salute.

"Howdy, stranger! Guess them lead cattle smell water, don't they?
I see 'em stringin' out."

"Yes." The tall man fell in beside Carmody. "Windmill in the
draw, beyond that next little rise. Two mile or so."

"Your place?"

The tall man shook his head. "Patterson's place. Ladder Line Camp.
Got most a dozen wells and still reaching out. Controls pretty much
all this end of our peaceful valley, Erie does. Gives the Railroad
brand — like this." He traced the Railroad brand with a finger on his
horse's neck. "Only we call it the Ladder, mostly. Me, I'm way west
and south, beyond the railroad. Over on the Gavilan." His eyes
rose to a far-off jumble of splintered hills; he pointed with a blunt
chin, Indian fashion; pursing his lips, again in Indian fashion. "Name
of Farr."

"Yes. I saw your brand."

Farr nodded, raising his bridle hand for brief inspection. Long
cuffs of heavy leather protected his forearms nearly all the way from
wrist to elbow, so making those arms useful to shield a face as it
crashed through brush. On each cuff and on the saddle a
brand was carved. His horse's thigh wore the same brand.

"That's me — Elmer Farr. Only nobody hardly ever calls me Elmer.
They call me Jack. Or Slim. I saw your brand, too. B 4. You're
Carmody. Heard you was coming. Knew your cousin Pat, down in
Llano."

"Pat's dead, Mr. Farr. Or did you know that?"

"Yes," said Farr. . . . "Them dogies of yours are tol'able thin, Mr. Carmody."

"They are so. And feeble. But nothing to what they was. Had their bellies full for a week now. Feed is right good this side of the river. Dry but good. They're gaining. Why, there's good pickin' right here; and only two miles from water, you say. Is it as good beyond that windmill?"

"Better. Three miles the other side grass is high as ever it was. We ain't stocked up here yet, hardly a-tall. Why, us ranchers haven't had any trouble with each other yet; and I reckon we're the sorriest bunch that ever forked a horse."

Carmody squinted at the sun. "Three miles and two — that will make it dark when we get to the bed ground. Well, Mr. Farr, I'm goin' to ooze along ahead and see about getting water — fill the barrel and all that. My wife, she's the cook. Want to side me? . . . That's good. I'll tell the boys."

They made a wide detour to pass the herd. "Plenty of water, I hope? And is there anybody at home, maybe?" said Carmody.

"Lots of water, and Bert is shoeing horses. I was there for dinner. But it might be a pious idea to get Bert to hitch a mule to the horse power. This wind isn't any too brisk and I don't know how deep the water is in the tank. Mr. Carmody, you must have had a hard time on the Flats, over east."

"I'll tell a man. That just about put the kibosh on 'em. But the river was worse, because they was already weak and jaded then from crossing the desert. Not a spear of grass for fifteen miles either side of the Rio Grande. So I just nicely had to buy a stack of hay and scatter it for 'em. Stayed there two nights. Man, it took every cent I had in the world, and five unbranded calves besides. Only I would 'a' lost the calves anyway. Their mammies wasn't giving no milk. Fellow said he'd teach 'em to drink milk out of a pail, so I traded 'em for more hay."

They passed the herd and the horse herd; they overtook the wagon, passed it, and came to the ranch. The windmill turned slowly. The bars were up at the gates of the water pen. Albert Garst was shoeing a thankless horse. Farr called and Garst came to the gate, sweating and dusty, bareheaded and curly-haired. His hat lay on the sand near the thankless horse and he wore two horseshoe nails in the corner of his mouth, held there by clamping teeth.

"Gennenlum to see you, Albert. . . . Mr. Carmody, this is Bert Garst. Bert, this is Mr. Carmody."

Bert flushed, scowled, mumbled. This was not Bert's way; he was by habit a genial rascal. Farr pricked up his ears.

"Mr. Garst, have you got water enough pumped for my little bunch of stuff?" Carmody fished up an old pipe as he spoke. "About six hundred head, besides the *remuda* and a passel of goats."

Albert Garst flushed to deep crimson. Sweat trickled down his nose. "Why, yes, sir, plenty of water, I guess. But now — dog-gone it, I hate this, mister — Erie said, from now on I was to charge every herd five cents a head for water."

"Aw, hell!" said Farr, and laughed. It was an ugly and sneering laugh. Garst rolled wrathful eyes his way.

"That is something new. And it's awkward, sir," said Carmody gravely. "For money is just what I haven't got. Down on the river I loaded up the chuck wagon, and it took my last dollar."

"Well, that's my orders," said Garst, "and I got no leeway. It's a new one on me, too, and I don't get any particular pleasure out of it. If I stretch the price, can't you turn over a couple of yearlings, or something?"

Carmody's face hardened. "You look like a cowman and you ought to know better than that. No other brand goes on B 4 cattle. No man on any range has any right to any cowbrute branded B 4. I sell no cow stuff, except to ship back to the States. I'll have to pay you with a pony, I reckon — and God knows I've none to spare. If I had anything fat enough for beef, now — "

A sharp, barking laugh, checked abruptly. That was Farr. Albert Garst whirled upon him.

"Can't you keep your long nose out of this?" he snarled.

"Why, Albert, can't a body laugh?" said Farr soothingly. "I was just thinking of all the fat stuff about here — yours and everybody's." His eyes widened a trifle and regarded the red-faced Garst with close attention. Not a stare, or a threatening look — steady and thoughtful contemplation. He put both hands on the saddle horn and leaned forward. "This is all foolishness, Bert, and you know it. We'll water these thirsty cattle now, and see about maybe paying some way when we get around to it. Let down the bars, Carmody."

"You just think so!" Albert made one quick step, his hand shot out and reached behind the gatepost. A double-barreled shotgun leaped to his shoulder, the hammer clicked, the muzzle jerked in to rake Farr at the waistband. "Now, you long, lean, red-muzzled son of Satan, if you move one finger towards your gun I'll blow you in two!"

Farr's contemplative eyes held unchanged, motionless. "Albert," said Farr, in a soft drawl which ended in a rising note, "what kind of shot have you got in them cartridges?"

"Buckshot, you old hyena! Buckshot at ten feet!"

"Then," said Farr gently, "we'll have to settle it some other way. I'll tell you what, my boy. I'll give you my note. Pay it tomorrow in Target."

"Note, me eye! You'll give me a check."

"Sure enough! I just can't get used to that new bank of ours. Always forgetting it. . . . All right, Albert; you win. Let the hammer down. I won't shoot." Moving those attentive eyes at last, he glanced down at his unbuttoned vest and fished out a new check book and a new pencil. He made ready to write, using his saddle horn for table.

"I want you both to understand that I have no gun on me," said Carmody; his voice was hard. "It is not my habit to let another man do my fighting for me, or pay for me."

"Eh? Oh, that's all right," said Farr. "Sure, I knew you had no gun. And you can pay me back when you get good and ready."

"Well, sir, I'm obliged to you, sir — I am so. I'll remember this."

"Oh, that's all right. You can do somebody a turn sometime. . . . Nice fat cattle you got, Albert. . . . Pay to the order of Erie Patterson, thirty dollars."

"Make that thirty-five," said Albert. "Forty or fifty head of horses and a bunch of goats."

Farr raised his head and his disconcerting eyes were again unwinking and motionless. "Thirty dollars. Your damned old gun might miss fire." He signed his name and tore out the check.

Albert leaned his shotgun against the fence and took down the bars. The B 4 wagon came around a curve in the twisting draw, the saddle horses close behind.

"Have your wagon drive around the tank, Mr. Carmody," said Albert. "You'll find a faucet and a hose there to fill your barrel with."

The horse herd passed through the gate and made for the troughs. Farr had ridden aside to get out of the dust. He came back now and leaned on the saddle horn again. "Albert," he said, and his drawl was slower than ever, "would you mind letting me see one of those cartridges?"

"Oh, my Lord! I thought you was gone. You'll keep on fooling around till somebody gets hurt."

"Why, Albert, I ain't in no fix to hurt nobody. The'retically, I'm done dead. You had me, if you was a mind to pull the trigger. So I'm in no mind to shoot you. Our gunning is all done, now and ever

after, so far as I'm concerned. I just wanted to know if that was sure-
enough buckshot in them cartridges."

"I told you so, didn't I? Are you calling me a liar?"

"Now, now," said Farr, "I just almost know you wouldn't lie — not
of a Wednesday. But I kinder like to see."

"I think," said Albert, "that you are absolutely the most aggravating, cantankerous old idiot in the whole round world."

He took the shotgun, hesitated perceptibly, broke it, slipped out one
of the cartridges and tossed it up to the horseman. "There, you old
fool! Are you satisfied now?"

Farr caught the cartridge, dug out wadding with his knife, and
dropped eight buckshot into his cupped palm. He nodded. "All right,
Albert. No grudge. No feud. But if you had deceived me and stuck
me up with a mess of bird shot, I shouldn't have liked it one mite. I
could take a mess of bird shot and then plug you, I judge." He paused
for rumination. "I'll tell you what, Albert. No gun grudge, but why
couldn't we arrange a little fist feud for a follow-up? Sometime when
we're not busy?"

"Any time you say, and no time like right this very now. Hop
down off that horse and I'll break you in two!"

Farr considered this proposition and shook his head regretfully. "I
aim to be right busy, next three or four days, finding out what Erie
Patterson means by charging for water. When did anybody ever hear
of such doings as that? Thirty dollars ain't no more to him than five
cents. This calls for my able mind. I can 'tend to you later. Any time
you see me comin', and me with no gun on me, you set out the lini-
ment and bandages handy. I'll bring some arniky along." He paused
for meditations which seemed to be pleasant, for his straight mouth
curved to a smile. "So you think you can break me in two, do you?"

"I know I can!"

"Mebbe so, mebbe so. I'll tell you what — I'll make you a little bet
on that. I like you, Albert, and I sort of hate to see you working for
this Railroad brand. So we'll fix it like this: If I lick you good and
plenty — lay you out cold — then you'll come over and work for me."

"And if I have to carry you to bed, what do I get out of it?"

"If you do that I'll be dead and you'll be leaving here in a hurry.
So you stand to win either way. . . . I'll bring the buckboard. We
won't either one of us feel like riding a horse."

CHAPTER II

It was a queer country. There were days when the circling mountains were near and clear, sharp and shining, where a thousand facets threw back the sun, every dimple and wrinkle showing plain, each gorge and cleft black and beckoning; when every wandering ridge and ground swell of the great plain was cameo-clear, and you were a brisk, upstanding man who rode, prancing and mettlesome, on affairs of weight and consequence; a sprightly person, interesting to yourself and to others.

But this was not one of those days. When Farr was an hour on the short cut from Line Camp to Target, the air fell hot and still, the far-off ranges made an unangled, wavering blur, blue beyond a trembling, sun-shot haze of dancing dust motes. The ridged and rolling plain was sea-flat now, smudged, undimensioned, vague and dim; and Elmer Farr saw himself a meaningless midge, creeping unnoticed beneath a brazen sky. This salutary frame of mind was dispelled when he topped a rise and saw below him the long loops of Corkscrew Draw, and a horse climbing to him on a zigzag trail — Johnny Pardee on his Strawberry horse. Farr drew rein and waited.

The trail was sharp and stiff. The last scramble climbed a staircase ledge of limestone. Strawberry puffed noisily, his nostrils dilating. Brown Jug held his head high, gazing beyond the canyon deeps with a lofty expression which implied that Strawberry was disgracefully fat, and also gave a distinct impression that Jug had both hands in his pockets, head up and chest out. Which was absurd, because Jug was Farr's horse and had no pockets. Strawberry snorted and laid his ears back. Johnny slid off.

"Slim, you got any water in that canteen?"

"Sure have."

"Gimme," said Johnny. As he drank, Farr climbed stiffly from his horse and sat on the ledge with his feet hanging over. To him, there, came Johnny with the canteen — a young and smaller man, with a sparkling face, unlined and smooth. That boyish face was deceptive. This was a man proved and trusted. At twenty-two, Johnny was foreman of the Packsaddle outfit, with men of twice his age, tough and seasoned — men of name and standing in the cow country — glad to be one of that hard and choosy bunch. He sat cross-legged beside Farr and rolled himself a smoke.

"Johnny," said Farr dreamily, "did you ever see any of this here driven snow?"

"All I know about snow is that I wish I had some to put in this canteen. Anything gnawing on you, old-timer? If you feel a sort of unusual sensation creeping around just above and back of your eyes, why, that might be an idea, you know. Driven snow, you said? Yes, yes; go on!"

"Once I was pure, like that," said Farr. "But it was a long while ago. I have done so much meanness myself, that my mind has soured on me. I'm not simple and trustful like I was. No, sir; I'm given to low suspicions, and I got one coming on right now."

"Tell it to me."

"Fork that fat plug of yours, then, and side me to Target. Tell you as we go."

"I was sort of wishful to drop in on Albert."

"Now, now; nothing to do till the round-up begins. You saunter along with me and Jug, and I'll tell you the sad story of my life."

"Poor Albert, he had no liking for that job — none whatever," said Farr in conclusion of the sad story. "He was all het up. I had me nearly two hours to study on it and I've made all the guesses there is. Me and Jug have just about got it ciphered out. Erie Patterson, he knew all about this Carmody a-coming, and him out of money. He done instructed Albert to get Carmody riled up, so he'd yank his old forty-come-odd and throw down on Albert and water his bossy cows by main force."

"Huh! Damn likely — and Albert to maybe get himself shot some?"

"Yes, sir. Just like that. That's why Albert didn't like it. That's how come that shotgun leaning against the gatepost — just in case. Loaded with buckshot. Buckshot in the middle of this plain, with nothing bigger'n a quail between here and the hills? This play is the only way to make any sense of that buckshot. Albert was willing to be stuck up, but he didn't yearn to be actually killed, if it really came to shooting. And when I put in — well, I've deviled Albert right smart, off and on, and he is just a little leery of me. He jumped up to see what he hung by."

"But why? Why pull off a risky stunt like that?"

"Why egg Carmody on to make a gun play? Simple. Then they jerk him to jail, law him to a frazzle, and buy his little bunch of cattle at half price."

"Why, Jack! How you do talk!"

"It's the only way that makes any sense. No one would take such a chance for just thirty dollars. They aim to annex those cattle. . . .

What's that? Who's they? Erie Patterson for one — and whoever we catch at it. It doesn't follow that Albert was in on that part. Probably wasn't. Albert is sort of fair to middlin'. Patterson just about told him to charge for watering that herd, but not to use no gun to collect with. Albert's pure and innocent face told me he was studyin' about why. And he didn't half like it."

"But Erie is out of cash," objected Johnny, "spreadin' himself all over the shop, and he's borrowed from our new, shiny bank up to his neck. You know that. You're one of the straw bosses in the bank and you passed on his notes. Erie's got no money to buy more cattle with."

"Just so. Therefore, there's someone else in on the deal. That's the point. Have you maybe noticed of late any queer goings-on in this happy valley of ours?"

"I have so. Leaving to one side the normal amount of clerical errors in the branding business. Granger takes up a homestead for himself on the Temporal. His house burns down. Another long lad settles at Carizo, and his house burns up. Freight cars looted on the Target side tracks. More freight cars robbed at the same place. Ore stolen from freight wagons in Target. Drunks rolled at Target. Reemarkable hands held at Jim's Gem against prosperous visitors from the East. Mines salted for prosperous visitors. And so on down the line."

"Johnny," said Farr, "I do believe they have been doing it on purpose."

"You mean a gang?"

"Just that. A nice new jail and it full all the time, but never a man for anything really low-down and ornery — drunk and disorderly; disturbing the peace; toting deadly weapons — the like of that. Jail till they rustle money for a big fine. Profiting thereby — town marshal, sheriff, Hissoner Francis Truesdale Humphries, J. P., and lawyers. Not one of 'em turning a hand at anything really useful; and catching not one of the skunks that have been doing the dirty work."

"So you think law and lawbreakers — "

"Partners. You said it. Then, thinks I, why not get about six or some reliable rascals together and look-see? So I thought of you right off — and here you're the first man I meet. A leading, I calls it."

"Well, where do you propose to start to untangle?"

"Done started. Erie Patterson, rairoader — takes his name from a railroad; calls his brand the Railroad. Ex-conductor on the T.C. Made his start dividing cash fares with the company. You know that?"

"Oh, si! Tossed the money up to the ceiling. What didn't come down went to the company. Go on."

"So Patterson quits the T.C. and goes in for cattle. You and me and most, we call his brand the Ladder, but Erie himself, he always calls it the Railroad brand. Some several old railroaders working for him. Dave Salt for one. Railroad bull — don't know a cow from a caboose. Killer, I guess. Well! Next point. Young fella me lad, can you go down to them locked cars on the siding and pick out one loaded with wagons? Or windmills? Or saddles? Or general merchandise? No, says you. Well, someone picked out just what they wanted. Never a car broken into at Target yet but it was loaded with something mighty handy to use around here. No pianos or farming implements ever bothered yet. Well?"

"Inside information?"

"Nothing else. And then? As to the Carmody case? The next step?"

"Humph! Cattle ranches, railroaders, law, somebody with money enough to buy that herd — "

"What's the matter with Kames? He's a lawyer."

"And was once a lawyer for the T.C. in a small way; till they fired him. Why? Not for lack of brains. He's a slick one — Kames. But I must stick to the Carmody case. . . . Says dear old Elmer to me, sezzee: What's the next move?" Johnny reflected, and spoke slowly, handling words as a man handles his feet when he walks a rope: "The man is broke. And I want to get him in bad and buy him in at forced sale. Oh, *si!* . . . And I tried to force him into a ranikiboo play at Line Camp. Well? So I could set John Law on him? Oh, *si!* And Carmody can't go through Gridiron Flat without watering at Target. And the T.C. Railroad pipes the Target water from the hills. Why, the next play is to have the agent charge him for watering at the stock pens."

"Correct. Let's ride!"

"But, Slim, the T.C. will never stand for that. Their play is to boost the cattle business."

"What does the T.C. know about what goes on here? If the earth opened and swallowed Target, San Francisco wouldn't know it till steer-shipping time. That yellow-bellied station agent could do it on his own. Let's you and me sort of permeate around and begin to Stop, Look and Listen. And," said Slim Jack Elmer Farr, "we want to gather in some re-enforcements. This will be a nifty job and us two are not enough."

"So far," said Johnny Pardee, "this has been mighty small potatoes for a gang, if there is a gang. Picayunish, petty larceny. Piking."

"Maybe they're just getting started," Farr suggested. "Feeling their way. Trying out candidates. But they stole enough from the railroad already to outfit a man-sized general-merchandise store, and if they aim to grab a whole brand of cattle this crack, that ain't exactly hen-roost stuff. That ain't all, either. Them nesters that got burned out by act of God, they were single men. The drunks, they was grown up. And nobody ever grieved themselves into the grave on account of pilfering from a railroad, or any kind of company or corporation, or the good old Government. But this Carmody guy, he's got a woman and three kids. That's different. 'Tain't just like rolling a drunk or robbing a train, or an express company, or — Why, Johnny! Johnny Pardee!" Farr reined in his horse. His eyes narrowed, his lips slightly parted, wrinkles ridged his dusty brow, he held his head side-wise, as if he listened to something far-off and faint.

"Slim Jack," said Johnny Pardee, "come out of it! 'I would not chide thee, Marguerite, nor mar one joy of thine so sweet' — but you've not been hitting it up again, have you? Excuse me for mention-ing it, but you do, you know, when the sign is just right. Why, you old fool, you're plumb agitated. What's eating you now?"

"Johnny," said the old fool, drawling, "I've been pretty lenient in my judgments about robbing trains and banks, and so on. Boys will be boys, and all that sort of thing. Banks back in Missouri and Illinois, you know. But this little bank here — why, that bank is yours and mine and everybody's! If anything was to happen to that bank, I'd be real peevish. I would so. I seem to see the whole subject in a new light, sort of. Miners, storekeepers, cowmen, everybody roundabout, all the way from Argentine to the border, they got a little money tucked away in there. Not such a gosh-awful lot, all told, but so long as it was scattered about, it would 'a' needed a lot of exertion to have made way with that money. Now we got it all bunched up for 'em, handy as a pocket in a shirt."

"Roll over. You're having a nightmare. Mr. Cleveland done wrote and cautioned us to humor you all we could. But this is too much."

"Listen, infant! Who was the prime mover in getting up this bank? I ask you. Ellis Kames, lawyer. Now what does Ellis Kames do? His open-and-aboveboard business? Livin' on the unlucky."

Johnny interrupted: "Also, sharing the spoil with the strong arm of the law. Who is the strong arm? Jim Yewell, town marshal; Steve Davis, sheriff; and the justice of the peace. Did any one of the four of them ever earn one round hard dollar by actual producing? The answer is: Not since they hit Gridiron. They are just like ticks in a cow's ear. Lilies of the field. The question now is: If I was sheriff, and if I then robbed a bank, and if I was then equipped with warrant and handcuffs, and went out looking for myself — would I ever catch myself?"

"Who's loony now?" said Slim Jack Elmer Farr.

The two friends reached Target soon after sunset, but it was ten o'clock when Farr tapped at the door of the telegraph office. Paul Nichols, the night operator, had barely time to close the door when the sounder stammered and choked.

Paul waved his hand. "Newspapers. Help yourself," he said as he slid into a chair and snatched up a pencil.

The sounder stuttered and spluttered and then settled to a snare-drum rataplan of train orders, while the flying pencil took them down. After which, young Paul pushed back his chair and turned a cheerful face on his guest. "Well, old Rain-in-the-Face, what's on your chest?"

"I hardly know how to set about this," said Farr. "Are you scary, or dishonest, or part human? Do I bully you, bribe you, or just take a chance that you're decent?"

Paul laughed. "Far be it from me to set up any fixed rules. You just try whichever way you think will get the best results. I gather," said Paul, "that you want me to do something. Probably something that I shouldn't hadn't oughtn't."

"No such thing. If you come projecting out to my ranch and asked me what hosses would work, I'd tell you. Whereas and aforesaid, to wit, namely, ss., I don't know as much about railroads as you do about horses. You tell me. Prick up your ears and listen to my tale of woe." So saying, he gave the bare outlines of the sale of water to the B 4 herd, but said no word of shotgun or suspicions. "New stuff, that is. I've seen water sold before, but that was where a man went off in the big middle of a desert and dug him a well for that purpose. In that case, he earned his money. But here, with plenty wells, shallow water — one stockman charging another — it's a low-down outrage. Dirty work at the crossroads. Now look! Erie Patterson and Mr. Wade Barton, station agent and your esteemed chief, are thick as thieves in a mill. What I look for is for Patterson to set Barton up to charge our wandering cowman for watering here in Target shipping pens. What I aim to do is to stop that short, never to go again. My idea is to wire one big howl and one promise true that if the T.C. pulls that stuff, I will henceforth and forever, amen, with all my friends, if any, drive my steers over and ship 'em on the Sante Fé. Signed, Elmer Farr. How about it? Where do I wire to who to tell him why?"

"My dear old fossil," said Paul, "your unworthy surmise proves you to be yourself no better than an evil-hearted rogue. Speaking as your lifelong friend of the last three days, I would advise you," said Paul, "to tuck in your shirt and otherwise readjust your attire."

"My fair child," said Farr, "it is just because of that evil heart you speak of that I know exactly what another low-lifed scoundrel will do under a given set of circumstances. This being thus, we will now proceed. Tell it to me!"

"A railroad doesn't care any more about freight than you do about your left eye," said the operator. "The man you want is the general freight agent. You know what will happen if you send that wire, I suppose?"

"Barton will be kicked out, heels over head."

"Not by a jugful. Someone will listen in and tip Barton off. He will then make no mention of any charge for water. If anybody is wishing trouble on your Texas outfit, they'll try something else. You'll be out the price of one night message, and the T.C. will mark opposite your name 'Buttinsky, Trouble-Maker.' "

"Right as rain," said the cowman. "You write me off the name and address of the big head devil in the main office. I'll fix up my telegram and make it stiff. If Mr. Agent doesn't make any charge for watering that herd, you are hereby authorized to kick me good and hard at high noon on the Plaza. But if he tries to spring his holdup on Brother Carmody, I give him my telegram to send."

"He'll back down," said Paul.

"Sure he will. And right afterward, when I get around to it, he'll lose his job for grafting."

Paul leaned back in his chair, rolled his eyes to the ceiling, made a church with his finger tips, and coughed delicately. "You mentioned a bribe, I believe?" he suggested.

Farr rose and made for the door.

"You speak too late, brother. I've got what I want and I have no more use for you." He slammed the door behind him and went whistling down the hall.

CHAPTER III

GRIDIRON FLAT was high and hot. It lay exactly where the backbone of the continent should have been. Events had happened here, leaving mountains scattered and tossed like jackstraws of a baby god. They made a broken circle about Gridiron; a boundary, but not a wall. The shining ranges lay crisscross, cater-cornered, end on, every way except wallwise — tower, saw tooth, ax edge, spearhead, cone, pyramid. In the north, dominant, giving the flat a name, stood the prodigious bulk of San Lorenzo. From granite reaches of those far-off hills, water was piped to Target — pure water, which would not cake in boiler tubes. Following the compass points were Staircase, Plomo, Horsethief, Moncayo, Breen's, Gavilan, Argentine, with a pass for every comma. The Trans-Continental was a young and hasty railroad then, and a branch line to the silver town of Argentine climbed through Silver Gap, between San Lorenzo and Argentine Peak. Anyone who now cares for a little railroad of his own might today do well to apply to the T.C. for the Argentine Spur. The T.C. will pay for the deed and give you a bonus.

Gridiron was not really flat. It looked that way, but when you crossed it, you found it to be a deep saucer. Pusher engines from Target led a dog's life helping trains up Heartbreak Hill on the west, and eastward to Misery on the False Divide. Nor was that all. Target, the metropolis, perched midway of the plain in the center of an S-shaped boss. The T.C., young and hasty, as aforesaid, had built a straightaway from Misery to Heartbreak, and thereby crossed that S ridge three times. Pres Lewis, freighting ore down from Staircase, spoke of this fact to his wheelers, as the freight train bobbed up and down before them, and smiled indulgently, as if the T.C. were a favorite child of his.

Despite the high mountains roundabout, this low and crooked ridge was reputed to be the true watershed. Legend told that the run-off of the rainy season found its way northward to the Californian Gulf, westward to the Mexican Gulf. It seemed improbable. There was no visible outlet; whichever way you looked was uphill. Moreover, the seas mentioned did not lie in the directions mentioned, and it never rained, anyhow. Target shrugged at that drainage system as an innocent myth, like Santa Claus, or that stork story. Who cared, anyhow?

Gridiron was grassy, bare, bushy, treeless, cedared, flinty, sandy, dusty, hard, stony, gravelly, gray, white, brown and red — everything except muddy and green. And from every pass not served by the T.C., wagon roads came to Target like spokes to a hub. Imports — postage stamps, playing cards and schoolma'ams. Exports — beef, wool and silver. They ship no silver from Target now.

That was what Pres Lewis was freighting — silver concentrates, sacked for shipment to the smelter. That mile of thin red sand had been heavy going, and as the wagons rolled out to hard road again, the steaming horses stopped unbidden, to rest and puff before they tackled the last grade into Target. Such was the custom. Pres swung down from the saddle for the better resting of Punch, the wheeler. Punch eyed him comfortably. Beyond question, Punch was wondering if they would load out in the morning, or lay over two nights in Target, as sometimes happened.

Lindauer Place was the heart of Target, the oldest building, and the best. It fronted the Plaza, one massive block from street to street; one story high, but such a story! To begin with, the stone foundations rose three feet above ground. For the floor was level with the porch and the porch was wagon high. Lindauer had a solid mind, and these solid walls were to serve his children's children. Three-foot adobe, they rose fifteen feet to the ceiling. Then the flat roof; then the high parapet, sure defense against arrow and bullet, which had once been a very fort in war, but was now only a habit. Three and fifteen and one and four, making twenty-three feet high for one story of service.

Later advices report that a new device has replaced the wagon, and that it has been needful to raise the street level before Lindauer Place so that long porch may be running-board high. The plans we make! It was the successors of Herman Lindauer who filled in that street with concrete. Lindauer's sons are in California now, planning wisely for their sons.

Lindauer's General Store sprawled along the east end of the block. There were no catalogues. You asked for what you wanted and it was handed over the counter. Holland House, the best and only hotel of Target, fronted west and north on the other corner. Sandwiched between was Jim's Gem, saloon and house of chance, long and narrow, lamplit by night and by day. A door opening from the hotel lobby to the bar, a door direct from Lindauer's, explained why this dark and narrow site was desirable.

Two features are yet untold of the Lindauer Block. In the great open spaces of the Lindauer Store, newly partitioned in brick, a small corner fronted the Plaza in plate glass, overlooked East Street through high new windows, magnificent with new iron grilles, ornate and twisted; and in front a new sign was blue and gold and glorious:

THE FIRST BANK OF TARGET

The other feature was that the wagon-high platform of thick planks was roofed over to make a shaded porch before hotel, saloon and store — a porch fourteen feet wide and a block long, a porch with iron hitching rings for horse or team, with benches, tables and chairs for the uses of men; a porch which was to be danced on in a later year; a porch which was lobby, assembly room and senate hall for Target and for Gridiron. And John Cecil Calvert sat tiptilt on that porch, forty years ago.

John Cecil Calvert was one-and-twenty, fresh from Ann Arbor. This was his second day in Target. His eyes drank in the splendor of a sun-drenched world, his mind revolved the curious and interesting information he had obtained, by dint of eager questioning, during the crowded hours of those two days. The latest information, from a grizzled prospector with a pack horse, was hardly ten minutes old. It dealt with gold on the Gila.

May the story speak apart with the reader, softly, but with no ungenerous motive? Softly, that this dreaming boy may not hear it? If, in that vanished year, you had spoken, in any company, the name of Ashtabula, that heavy word had checked all laughter and all song. There are few save those for whom grief made that name immortal who now remember that, in almost the last night of our Centennial Year, a transcontinental train went through a bridge at Ashtabula, and carried a hundred souls to death by water and fire. John Cecil's parents died together there. That is why, for more than a dozen years, the orphan's ways had been guided by trustees, to Europe and to Ann Arbor. And that was why John Cecil was now in Target. A month gone, Commencement and majority arrived together in the same dazzling week. And so, just a little weary of guidance, John Cecil, his own master, set forth upon his wander-year — which had not ended yet.

Another man — a grave and quiet man, tall, dark and broad-shouldered — shared the porch with John Cecil. His hair was really red, but it looked like black hair; he wore a black hat and rather gave the impression of a man in black, but in reality he had faded blue shirt, and faded blue overalls, pulled down over his boots; an inconspicuous man. He sat hunched over on a wooden bench and carved upon it a strange device — a fox-and-goose board, he told John Cecil, in answer to a direct question. To other direct questions he answered briefly, that he did not know, being himself a stranger in Target. So John Cecil abandoned him as unprofitable, and reverted to the information so recently imparted by the more voluble prospector. He mused on the sufferings, the resourcefulness and loyalty, and the final disaster of the old Spaniards who had hidden that treasure beset by savages; and how strangely that faded map, traced by the one survivor, had come down through two centuries. It was a good story.

Many heads had gone to the making of it, and the years had lent it polish. But, of course, John Cecil did not know that.

A team of horses came through narrow West Street to the Plaza; behind them, not a wagon but a second team, their stretchers taut to a heavy chain; a third team, a fourth. John Cecil rose up to see, ran down the steps to see. Span by span, a twenty-horse team crossed the railroad track and filed into the Plaza, drawing an enormous, high-sided wagon. Trailed behind by a short stub of tongue was a second wagon, smaller indeed, but double-sized for all that. The driver rode the near wheel horse. A single line, with one end buckled to the saddle horn, passed forward through turret rings on the hames of each near horse — excepting only the swing team — and led at last to the bit of the near leader. A slender jockey stick crossed from the leader's bit to his mate's; the other horses pulled free and unguided, except for individual lines to each member of the swing team, just in front of the wheelers. A wide strap led from the saddle horn back to a ring at the top of the vurving brake lever, ten feet long and as thick as a man's wrist. John Cecil watched with all his eyes. A water cask was slung by iron bands to the side of the trail wagon; there was a chuck box in the rear. The driver gave two gentle jerks on the long line, the leaders sidestepped to the right, obliqued and polkaed; the other teams followed, sidewise and forward at once, keeping 'ware and wide of the chain; curving majestically, the two wagons drew to a halt, close against the platform of Lindauer's store. The horses let the chain fall slack and stood at ease; the driver swung off and Lindauer bustled bareheaded to meet him. Little tufts of hair stood up to frame a bald patch on that frosted head. They shook hands warmly.

"Well, Hermie! Long time no see um!"

"Long time no see!" Lindauer echoed. "Not since that Apache scrap. Why, Pres, that's been three years! But where's Scotty? Sick? Drunk, maybe? I knew something was wrong. He was due here yesterday."

"Broke his leg."

"Dear, dear! Kicked?"

"Wagon tongue. Climbing Staircase Hill; chain stiff as a crowbar, wheel hit a rock, tongue whipped around, snapped back — bingo! So I came down as emergency driver."

"Tch! Tch! Bad hurt, is he?"

"Pretty bad. Big bone broke and the bruise hurts him worse than the bone. Eighteen tons of ore back of that tongue and twelve tons of horses in front — that strikes a pretty stiff blow."

"That makes three times I've known it to happen that way," said Lindauer soberly. "Three times to my own knowledge. In rough

country they aim to keep their feet high, or else ride sideways. But
they forget. Poor Scotty! He'll have a siege of it. Of course, his
pay goes on, and his expenses. Scotty knows that. . . . How about it,
Pres? You want to stick till Scotty's up and around again?"

"Shucks, no. Just came down to oblige. I'm no freighter. I'm a
blacksmith, me. Freighting don't appeal to me at all. Too much like
work. I hope you have your man all ready to load this ore on the
car. I don't hanker for it."

"No car," said Lindauer. "Rotten service. Should have been here
yesterday. Drive over in the feed corral, Pres. Unhitch and feed.
By that time I'll have a man to take over — Jake Blun or somebody."

"Why not make camp and hobble 'em, if you have to wait for your
car? Plenty grass, and feed costs money."

"Plenty grass, but harness costs money," said the merchant. "Target
has gone bad since you were here. They'd steal harness, ore, chains
and wagons, unless there was someone on the job night and day. Not
like old times. It's disgusting. Let me know when you're ready, and
I'll send you back in the stage."

Pres shook his head. "Not going back — not straight off. I'm tired
of blacksmithing, seems like. I got me three copper claims and a
shack at Jim River, and I aim to mosey up there and do assessment
work. Bimeby, after I investigate a little."

"Jim River? Never heard of it."

Pres Lewis twisted a silky brown beard. "Over on the Gavilan, in
the roughs. Jim River is just about as long as your freight team, and
a foot wide." He examined his hobnailed shoes and looked up sheepishly. "You see, I was born on the James River," he explained, "in
Virginia. Some time since."

"I see," said Herman. His old eyes rolled slowly from end to end
of Lindauer Place — very much as if he were casting about for another
name to give it.

Continuing that slow circle, the freight wagon made a complete
turn and recrossed the railroad tracks. Forty sharp ears pricked up
and canted alertly toward the great gates of Gray's Feed Corral, and
eighty eager feet reached out briskly to that haven of lucky horses.

In the corral, Pres Lewis was just dropping the first traces, when
a pleasant young voice spoke beside him.

"I beg your pardon," said the pleasant young voice, "but would
you let me help you unharness, and then let me ask you some questions? About the freighting and the horses. I know how to manage
two horses, but how about twenty? There are so many things I
want to know," said the young voice, rather breathlessly. "How

you train them, and how much you can haul, and how far you come, and what the ore is worth. I don't know anything about this country, you see; and there is so much to learn. I'll be awfully obliged if you'll tell me about things. My name is John Cecil Calvert." He pronounced it Kolvert.

The driver's lifted eyes, large and slow and smoky-brown, saw a pleasant young face, an eager young face. He pulled a small memorandum book from a hip pocket of his blue overalls, thumbed the pages forward and back, and scanned one page closely. "My name is — Lewis," he said haltingly. He held the book nearer his eyes and peered again: "Pres Lewis," he added. "Pres Lewis, the experienced man, who, out of the goodness of his heart, dispenses vast quantities of information gratis, like free lunch and salvation. . . . Well, unhitch a span at a time and let 'em go. We'll unharness in the stalls. Now, just what was it you wanted to know?"

"First of all, I suppose that's the reason for these big open squares, isn't it? So these long freight outfits can have room to turn around? I saw these great squares — plazas, is it? — in Santa Fé and Socorro. But I didn't happen to see any twenty-horse teams there."

Pres Lewis stopped work and stared at his questioner. To tell the truth, the experienced man was somewhat taken aback. "Frank John," said he, "I'll be honest with you. Leastways, as honest as I can be, after all these years. I've been watching freight teams turn around in these plazas ever since you was a baby, and never once thought why the plaza was made big. I thought they was just a habit. And here you've guessed how come, first off. One reason, anyway. There would be other reasons. And if you should ask me, Frank John — "

"My name is John Cecil Calvert," the young man spoke coldly.

Pres waved the protest aside. "Yes, yes; I heard you. And if you can use your eyes and your brains to such good effect, you can find out nearly anything you want to know, with a little patience, without asking questions. Perhaps I ought to tell you, Frank John, that asking questions is not fashionable in these parts."

"Why?" said Frank John.

CHAPTER IV

Twenty horses were unharnessed, watered, fed with good grama hay and Kansas corn; and Frank John had learned much. Twenty names; from Prince and Charlie, the swing team, to Tom and Jerry, the leaders; with Frank John's own explanation — the correct one — as to why the mate of any Charlie horse is always Prince. How the swing team, on short curves, hopped the chain and pulled the end of the tongue at almost a right angle to the pull of the chain, and why. How the trail wagon was dropped, for deep sand and high, hard hills; how it was coupled on again; and how hard it was to do that little stunt with no swamper to help; how sad a thing it was to be a swamper. Armed with currycomb and brush, they were smoothing over sweat-salted shoulders, and the older man was imparting other lore of the road, when a hurly-burly of shouts and laughter arose from an inner corral. At the same time, Lon Gray, owner of the feed corral, crossed behind the stalls.

Pres called to him, "Hi, Lon; what's going on in the other pen?"

"Johnny Pardee topping off a bronc'," Gray answered indifferently.

"Frank John, you seen any horses broke yet?" said Pres. . . . "No? Come on, then. We'll finish the currying later."

Well-dressed onlookers sat on the gate, so the newcomers climbed over. A laughing crowd shouted encouragement to a mouse-colored horse that pitched a frantic circle, making the stirrups pop with every pitch. Most of them knew Pres Lewis and roared greetings to him — Erie Patterson with three of his men, Dave Salt, Newt Somers and Bartolome Pino; Tolson, the assayer; Nash, the grocer; Hugh Monro, of the bridge gang; Breen, McKee and Goddard, miners from Argentine; Jim Yewell, the town marshal, and Steve Davis, the sheriff. There were some whom Lewis did not know — two who seemed to be "drummers," and a well-dressed, round man with a plump, pink face and a gray goatee. These three sat on the gate, and Pres noted a fourth stranger inside, a broad-shouldered man who leaned against the gatepost and whittled on a yucca stalk, with his head bent to watch his handiwork, so that a black hat brim flopped over his eyes; a man in two shades of faded blue, a man with red hair that pretended to be black.

"Oh, lookit Johnny Pardee, with new chaps and shiny conchos on 'em!" said Pres. "Ain't he just too sweet? All he lacks is a snakeskin hatband and a coupla guns. Nice nag you got there, Johnny. Your horse?"

"Naw, I'm just breaking him. He belongs to Mr. Hawkins, there." He jerked his chin at the whittler.

That person raised his head and glanced out from under his flopping hat brim.

"That statement isn't exactly right," he corrected mildly. "The little *grullo* still belongs to Mr. Patterson. If he gentles down and quits bucking for keeps, I buy him. But if his heart is real bad, he's no mount for old Bill Hawkins, and Mr. Patterson keeps him and sells me a kind one. . . . That right, Mr. Patterson?"

"That's the deal," said Patterson. "Personally, I hope the *grullo* don't gentle to suit you. I like his looks, and I priced him too cheap to you."

The mouse-colored horse desisted from his exercises, snorted loudly, ran on the rope experimentally, whirled at the rope's end, and faced his captor, head up, but slightly a-tremble. Johnny walked toward him slowly, patiently, coiling the rope as he went. With low and soothing speech he put out his hand toward a black nose; after two slight flurries, was able to pat that nose, to rub the dark head gently. "His name is Smoky, I think," said Johnny softly, and without turning his head. His left hand, holding the coiled rope, slipped up and closed firmly around the cheek piece of the bridle, his right hand moved slowly to the saddle horn, his foot was in the stirrup. Johnny eased into the saddle smoothly, loosened his hold on the cheek piece, held the hackamore reins taut, and patted the quivering neck. "Come, boy! "C-chk!" Smoky made two cautious sidewise steps, three —

"Whoopee!" Dave Salt shouted, and sent his big gray sombrero sailing through the air into the bronco's face. The bronco fairly screamed with fright as he went up into the air, and fence-railed, bawling, across the coral, zigzag bucking. Johnny rode easily, surely, as if he were part of the horse. Three jumps, four, five — At the next plunge, saddle and man left the horse's back together; the hind cinch held for a second, the horse twisted and plunged, saddle and Johnny rolled in the dust together.

Smoky leaped high in air, twisted zigzag again and came down almost on top of his fallen rider. He bucked again, stiff-legged, bawling, straight up and straight down; he bunched all his feet together and lit fairly on Johnny's thigh. His feet slipped from the thick leggins. Men ran toward him, shouting. The horse was high in air again, head between his feet. Johnny tried to crawl and roll from under. Again those bunched feet slid from the protecting leggins. The horse dropped and lay still. Johnny rolled clear, half dragged by grasping hands.

"You hurt, Johnny?" gasped Munro, who was the nearest.

"Don't think so. Scared. Them leggins saved my bacon, that time."

"Who fired that shot?" Those thunder tones were the town marshal's. Frank John remembered then, vaguely, that he had heard a shot somewhere. Oh! Was that why the mouse-colored horse lay so still? "Who fired that gun, I say? I've warned you fellows not to pack your guns in town."

"Oh, to hell with your guns, and you too!" said Hugh Munro. He glared upon authority with a hard eye. Here the plump old gentleman climbed down on the other side of the gate and departed. The "drummers" followed him. "Here's a boy barely missed a most unpleasant death, and you can't wait to see if his leg's broke or what, before you go to blowing off your empty head about guns. Tough on that poor devil of a horse — but suppose he'd come down on Johnny's belly?"

"I tell you this gun-toting has got to stop. The law — "

"Shut up, you windbag! . . . How about it, Johnny? Leg broke?"

"Guess not. Help me up." Johnny stood up and experimented shakily. "Nothing broke. Just scared. Not so bad bruised, either. Them good old chaps, they're next thing to armor." He hobbled painfully to his saddle.

Pres Lewis spoke up then, in a mild and honeyed voice. "That gun, now, Mr. Marshal — that was me. I couldn't see Johnny killed, trifling as he is. Humph! Jim Yewell, marshal, 'with a star on his breast and a sir to his name.' I wasn't knowin' to your new dignities, fair sir and Mr. Marshal — not till after I done shot and some kind friend showed me your star. You was just lookout for a faro game when I knew you."

"But you can't carry guns in this town," said the sheriff heavily. "That's final. We're going to enforce the law."

"Now, now, sheriff; go easy. I've just nicely got in. Not five minutes since I unharnessed. I know your new law. I've got a right to carry a gun on the road for protection, and I haven't been in a house yet. Just got unharnessed."

"You give me that gun!" thundered Marshall Yewell.

Lewis took a square of plug tobacco from his pocket, scrutinized it, selected a corner and gnawed a segment from it. "You keep your voice down, brother," he said, restoring the mutilated plug to its pocket. "If you bellow at me any more I'm liable to prophesy against you. You just turn your mind back and see what happened when people crowded me into foretelling. When you got any communications for me, I want 'em sweet and low, like the wind of the western sea. You remember that. And that gun — well, whilst you and Mr. Munro was conversing together, I passed that gun through the gate to old Lon and told him to keep it for me in the office. So that's all right. I don't want to hear any more about that gun."

Frank John's eyes were bulging. His new and kindly friend was an unblushing liar. Lewis was in his shirt sleeves, he had worn no gun; starting quicker, he had been in front of Frank John as the shot was fired, when both were plunging in to help the luckless Pardee. Moreover, that man Lon Gray had been at the gate in time to hear the second lie, which concerned him; hearing it, he had nodded his gray head and turned back to the office. Partners in iniquity! Doubtless this man Gray would have a pistol ready to match the lie, with an empty shell to represent the one which had ended life for the luckless horse. . . . But, after all, who had fired that shot?

"All right, Lewis," said Erie Patterson smoothly. "Nobody's going to make any trouble about that gun, of course. It's a good thing for young Pardee you hadn't put it up yet."

"Only, if you can shoot like that," said the sheriff, "you may look to be called on a posse, 'most any time. That horse was hit plumb between the eyes. I got a wire last night that Bill Doolin was seen this side of Roswell, coming this way. He's wanted, five thousand dollars' worth. So maybe I'll have use for you and your gun."

"Bill Doolin?" echoed Lewis blankly.

"Why, man; surely you've heard of Bill Doolin — train robber, bank robber? The Indian Territory was always the wild spot on any map. Forty-eight deputy United States marshals killed there in four years. One marshal a month. Tough men in the territory, and Doolin is the toughest and the shrewdest. But here lately they've been making the Nations too hot to hold him."

"I been in the high country, blacksmithing and mining," said Lewis apologetically. "I never heard about the Centennial till day before yesterday."

"There is one point which has not yet been touched upon," said Patterson. "Just who pays for my horse?" He glanced at Pres Lewis as he spoke.

"I'm sorry for your loss, Mr. Patterson, and I'm a good deal sorrier for. that *grullo* horse. His splendid days are over. And it wasn't his fault at all. He was trying to understand, that bronc' was; hoping it would turn out all right. Then somebody sailed a hat at him. I'd like to pay for that horse; I would so. But I promised not to do that. Never. Promised faithfully. Why not let him pay that made the trouble? . . . Who's bareheaded?"

Dave Salt was bareheaded — Erie Patterson's straw boss, reputed to be a tough citizen. He looked the part. "I didn't mean any harm," he said. "Just wanted to see a little fun. Where is my hat, anyway?"

It was Hawkins, the big man with the black hat, who answered this question. He sat quietly on the dead horse, still whittling. He pointed with his knife to a spot midway between himself and Johnny Pardee, who sat upon his saddle blankets, feeling cautiously on his injured leg.

Dave Salt broke into a wild roaring, half howl and half bellow. "My new hat! Cut in four pieces! I'll have blood for this!"

The big man looked up with smiling, kindly eyes. "I hope you don't suspect me, just because I was setting here handy with my knife open."

Johnny Pardee rose and limped painfully to his saddle. "Look at this, Salt! You're not the only one hurt. Someone has been mighty free with a knife before ever you threw your hat. See this off latigo of mine? Someone cut it where it doubles over the ring — cut it almost through, so it was bound to bust in three or four jumps. See it?"

"You little runt; you did this?" snarled Salt. He leaned in act to step.

But the man Hawkins moved noiselessly and spoke now into Dave Salt's ear. "On the other hand, neighbor," he said softly, "your hat seems to have been worked on by a very sharp knife. Now, my knife is very sharp. See it?" He held the knife out for inspection. For that purpose he reached over Dave's shoulder, holding the knife about one inch from Dave's jugular vein. Simultaneously, his left hand reached under Dave's coat and abstracted a .45-caliber revolver from a holster stuck under the waistband of Dave's natty doeskin; he tossed it back to a snappy double play — Breen to McKee to Munro. Munro shoved it under his coat. "Under the circumstances," sighed Bill Hawkins regretfully, "sooner than have you jump onto a cripple half your size, perhaps I had better take the blame for your hat. Any objections?"

"I cut up the hat meself," snapped Breen. "Out of respect for the horse — poor baste! By way of mourning, like!"

"Here!" cried a loud voice by the gate. "I want this squabbling stopped, right now. Hear me!" Slim Jack Farr sat his horse without, and looked over the gate. "Sheriff there? And the marshal? You're both wanted, right off."

"What is it? A shooting scrape?" said the sheriff, making for the gate.

"Next thing to it. There's an old geezer over to the stockyards with a bunch of cattle to water. And he's trying to force the station agent, Mr. Wade Barton — you know him, Erie — he's trying to make the agent take pay for that water — five cents a head. Barton refused to take any money, and he's afraid Carmody — that's this old codger with the cows — is going to use violence to force this money on him. You'd better come over and protect him."

Peaceful assayer, peaceful grocer, had oozed unnoticed, long since. The lawlike faction, officers and the four Ladder men, departed together, crestfallen, defied, muttering and malcontent. The miners went next, loftily, nose in air, followed by the painful progress of young Pardee, aided by Breen's shoulder on the left and Munro's on the right; the latter openly carrying Dave Salt's gun as spoil of war. Pres Lewis and his pupil were left alone.

Pres looked down at the dead horse. He bent to stroke the dark head, once only, but not ungently. "Poor fellow!" said Pres. "That was hard luck! All over now! Come on, Frank John, you'll be wanting to go to the water pen for a squint at that herd and the chuck wagon, and so on. I'll finish up the currying."

Young Frank John gave his head a shaking then, and stretched himself. "I feel like one who treads alone, Mr. Lewis, some banquet hall deserted," said Frank John. "Before I go, you might tell me, as between one gentleman and a blacksmith — who shot that horse?"

CHAPTER V

"What was all that goose grease Elmer was giving us?" asked Pres. He sat at supper with Johnny Pardee in the big dining room of the Holland House. The room was crowded with hungry and noisy people; these two were at a small table near a window.

"What was who giving us?"

"Old Elmer — Elmer Farr."

"Jack Farr? You're always calling people out of their names. Disrespectful. That Michigan kid spoke real bitter about it."

"Who — Frank John? You been getting acquainted with Frank John?"

"He has my family history ever since Columbus crossed the Delaware," said Johnny. "When I quit him, he was getting statistics about the B 4 outfit. Persistent cuss!"

"So am I," said Pres. "Information is what I'm after. Passing lightly over the point that old Elmer's name is really Elmer Farr and not Jack Farr."

"I declare, I'd forgotten that," said Johnny. "Jack, we call him, and Slim. Say, Mr. Lewis, who do you suppose cut my cinch? That was sure one dirty trick, if ever I knew one. I think it was Dave Salt himself. One of the Ladder men, anyhow. They was all there while I was getting a hackamore on that unlucky horse and teaching him to lead a little. Them Ladders is due for a showdown. They've been crowding all us little fellows nine ways from the jack. I've had an elegant sufficiency myself."

"Be that as it may, beloved, will you, Johnny Pardee, now tell me, Pres Lewis, just exactly what Slim Jack Elmer Farr meant by that windy about somebody paying for water for them dogies? Take your time, me laddie buck. Only bear in mind what I just said. Perhaps I would do better to explain that the reason that I ask you is because I want to know."

"In that case," said Johnny, "I'll tell you; although you may possibly have noticed that us cowmen don't consult much with miners and railroaders and storekeepers and freighters and sheep herders and blacksmiths — that sort of people. Of course, we think they ought to be allowed to vote, and pay taxes, and so on; or maybe we buy 'em a drink when we feel good-natured and mellow, but we don't really consider them overmuch in our calculations."

"You give me no news. Many's the laugh we have at your airs and graces. But if some people — people with a fairly good opinion of themselves, too — if they knew half what I know about them — "

Johnny held up his hand. "Oh, in that case, I'll tell you. It was like this." His voice sank to an undertone. It was a long telling.

"Uh-huh! So you and Elmer think the Ladder outfit aim to bedevil — "

"Jack Farr thinks, and I just back his play to the limit. If this Carmody man gives any excuse for these buzzards to sic the law on him, he's right in the middle of a bad fix. His cattle can just nicely keep their feet; and they've got to lay over a spell, come hell or high water. Me and Farr and our bunch, we aim to help Carmody herd 'em — to make sure he doesn't have trouble shoved on him — while we're studying how about it, and what next. He ain't got no money, either. This Bill Hawkins, that I was breaking the pony for, he bought one of Carmody's top horses this evening. I reckon that's every cent the old chap has to his name."

"How come his horses ain't poor, too?" said Lewis.

"Shucks! Carmody himself, he's right chunky. But the crew is just three kids out of the cradle, and Charlie Bird, the right bower. He's a little dried-up old herring, no bigger'n a pint of cider. That cavvyard is in right good shape. Thin, but peart."

"Well," said Pres judicially, "if you will insist on bringing your troubles to me, I suppose I'll have to take charge." Here Johnny sniffed. Pres regarded him austerely for a moment, and then continued: "Why don't you take this herd out to your ranch? Or why don't some of your crowd do it — whichever one has the best lay?"

"That's what it comes to — there or thereabouts. Those cattle are in no shape to tackle what's waitin' for 'em west of Heartbreak Hill. And let me tell you, mister, right then is where and when sorrow begins. The Gridiron has been all crosswise this long time — the Ladders and the Rockingchair on one side, and us little fellows on the other. The Chair outfit isn't so bad, but Patterson has been siding in with Troy Ware on every little friction and dispute, and muched him along till Troy thinks Erie is just as fine as silk. And Troy's riders are hard hombres. Trouble brewing. This Carmody play will just about bring it to a boil. They claim we run more cattle already than we got water for. And we don't stack up very well. Ladders and Chairs, they make just even twenty; lacking some three, or maybe four, that'll quit 'em when they begin dealin' from the bottom. And a lot of money. And the sheriff. And the town marshal. And the tinhorn vote, maybe. Aid and comfort and God knows what else, from some of the railroaders. Us fellows — let me see; Farr, Dal Cline, Aurelio Sais and me — that's four — and Cat Knapp and that Englishman, Carbray, and Larry Denny, that works for Carbray — seven of us, all told. The Packsaddle men are all on a big pasear down in Mexico and won't be back till round-up time."

"Vent slips!" said Lewis. "And the three punchers that you expect to quit when the dirty work starts — three good men — that's eleven, and this upstanding Munro and me, that makes sixteen. What can be fairer than that? Not to mention Carmody himself, and his little old hired man."

"That listens fine," said Johnny. "But you know what happened to the ten little niggers standing in a line?"

"Something happened — I don't just recollect what," said Lewis, frowning with the effort to remember. "And then there were but nine."

Johnny nodded. "And so on. That's the idea. We don't want to start anything. They'll start it. At night, or from a dry gulch. And then we'll lose on the first clash. Our best men, likely."

"Oh, I'll be cautious," said Pres.

Johnny ignored this levity and proceeded with a gloomy face: "I don't like it, just because I've naturally got good sense. What is more to the point, Jack Farr don't like it, either; nor Aurelio Sais — and both of 'em have been through one or two of these things already. Oh, why can't people have some sense?"

"I have," said Pres grandly. "It shall never be said that you sought help and leadership from me in vain. You know Jim River?"

"Jim River? Aw, what kind of guff are you springing now?"

"No guff. This is good medicine. Jim River's mine. Over in the Gavilan, beyond Farr's layout. Mighty few have been there. Jim River is maybe fifty yards long, an inch deep, and one mouse jump across. Rough, but good grass, good browse, plenty water, plenty mountain lions and bear. Them dogies will do fine there, if the old man will rustle himself two or three hound dogs and chase the varmints out."

"Out onto us?" suggested Johnny.

Pres considered this. "There may be something to that," he admitted. "All right. Then you get some hounds and chase 'em elsewhere. Kill 'em when you tree 'em. Good practice for the great day a-coming. The big point is, this wise and wary scheme will postpone that great day till you're better fixed. Jim River is over the divide. Not one of these cattle need ever range in Gridiron, and so your two cattle companies won't have any grievance."

"Terms?" said Johnny.

"Let's see. This is August. Here's the lay: The B 4 brand can run at Jim River until after steer selling, next spring, for no dollars and no cents. After that, if the old man wants to stick around, we can dicker. If he elects to go on, it won't cost him nary a cent. To be sure, if he sees fit to build a wagon road, I'll never tear it down. In the meantime, he'll have to pack in his provender. Oh, yes. Deer and quail and rabbits. Right good shack too. Two-room rock house. Dirt roof."

"This is right clever of you, Mr. Lewis."

"Isn't it?" said Mr. Lewis enthusiastically. "Isn't that just like me? You don't half know how fine it is, either. I was planning on something quite different. I've always tried to lead an honest life, and now I'm little better than a cowman. But maybe Carmody'll move on. It's pretty rough in there, and lonesome. I sorter intended to do a little counterfeiting there this winter. Oh, well! At any rate, this will give your crowd time to practice shooting, against the hour of need."

"I knew I was forgetting something," said Johnny, pushing back his plate. "Who was it shot that horse?"

"I didn't see. But when questions was asked and nobody spoke up, I judged that whoever it was had his reasons. Nobody had anything on me, so I up and claims the glory."

"Oh, I knew it wasn't you. I saw your work with a six-shooter once. Didn't know that, did you? I was about ten or twelve years old and quiet for my age. Over at Ojo Caliente, before they moved the Apaches from there and started all this hell we been having. . . . Now, this horse, he was shot smack through the brain pan, and him bucking. That let you out, and every other man I ever knew, barring two or three."

"I see!" said Pres Lewis. "You think it was the pink, fat man on the gate? With the goatee and the linen duster?" His eyes roved the dining hall as he spoke, and rested for a little on Mr. Hawkins, who sat alone in the rear at a corner table, with his back to the wall. Johnny's glance followed his; Mr. Hawkins was eating busily, but he looked up at this juncture. Pres waved a slight salute, which Hawkins acknowledged with a nod. Pres turned to face Johnny then. Their eyes met.

"This horse that 'Enry 'Awkins bought — was he a good one?"

"His name is Bill, not Henry," corrected Johnny. "That horse? A tough one, anyway, and gentle. He got one of these smoke-colored horses, and I never saw one yet but was a stayer."

"Gunwise?"

"Benefactor, chieftian, Great White Father, I didn't hear the trade made. But I'll make a little wager with you. I'll bet you twenty good dollars, current with the merchant, to one of your own make, that the new Hawkins horse is gunwise."

"Trust 'Enry for that! No, Mr. Pardee, I couldn't make that bet. Thank you just the same. And I need the money too. 'Enry looks to me like a good man," said Pres. "Yes, sir, if I needed a good man right bad, I'd take a chance on 'Enry. By the way, who was that quartered out Salt friend's hat?"

"I didn't see," said Johnny.

"I don't feel hungry at all," said Pres. "Can you make out to ride a right gentle horse without hurting your leg too much? 'Cause if you can, let's you and me ride over to the bed ground and carry the good news. Spring Jim River on your friend — or was it your friend's friend? And hadn't you or Farr or somebody better tell Patterson that if the herd can lay over three days, real peaceful and quiet, Carmody will move them on, then? It may save trouble. If Carmody tells 'em, they'll frame up a fight on him, sure."

"Farr is hitting up the booze. I wish he wouldn't," said Johnny. "He's ugly. Dangerous to enemies, friends, strangers and himself. Leave him be. And they don't like me much. I'll get Aurelio to tell 'em tomorrow. They're superstitious about Aurelio. If he advises 'em to lay off, they'll consider it. But why three days? Wouldn't it be shrewd and knowing to get that herd away right sudden and soon? . . . Ps-st! Hold everything! Here comes the sheriff."

Steve Davis came ponderously between the tables, with Patterson and Troy Ware in his wake. Ware was general manager of the Rockingchair outfit, the biggest cattle company in those parts. North Gridiron was half of the Rockingchair range. The other half lay north beyond the mountains, on the Feliz and the Gato.

The two cattlemen were smiling, but the sheriff's heavy face was worried. He was holding a yellow telegram in his hand.

"Gentlemen, I may need you on my posse sure enough. I wish **you** wouldn't leave town. I just had another wire. Bill Doolin was seen near Palomas Hot Springs, yesterday was a week ago. Positively identified."

"Doolin is bothered with rheumatism, it seems," said Troy Ware, "and it is thought that he would have stayed near the springs if unmolested. But they went there to look for him — and now where is he?"

"Read this wire, Mr. Lewis," said the sheriff. "Now, it's like this: I'm keeping good men on the lookout in every settlement, and if he comes into my bailiwick, we're going to stop everything and get him."

"I'm crippled," said Johnny. "Leave me out."

"I have married me a yoke of oxen and a vineyard — " Pres began.

"That's enough, Mr. Lewis. You will consider yourself a member of my posse. I need men like you. Your pay starts in the morning. Stay here in town until further developments. . . . As for you, Johnny, I'll have to send the doctor to look at that leg."

"Doctor, my foot! You come to my room and see for yourself. I'm black and blue from my knee to my hip, and you make it worse. You saw that horse jump on me. I'm going home in a buckboard, that's where I'm going."

"Steve, I guess there's no doubt but what the boy is hurt," said Erie Patterson, smiling. "There's plenty without him."

"All right, then. But you're done made a deputy, Mr. Lewis. Hold yourself in readiness for duty." Following the cattlemen, he made for the saloon door.

" 'So shines a good deed in a naughty world,' " said Pres. "See what I get for being a crack shot. Come on, Johnny; I got a horse tied out there for you. Say, this will be a joke on the sheriff if he sticks me up to shoot it out with Bill Doolin on the strength of one accidental shot."

"It'll be a joke on somebody," said Johnny, as they went out into the falling dusk.

"About that unanswered question," said Pres, as they rode along slowly down the deserted street. " 'Why three days?' says you. Because I think your friend Carmody ought to ride out to take a look at Jim River before he takes his cattle in there. When I say it's rough, what I mean is that it's sure-enough rough. Say, you've been through Soledad Canyon, east of Las Cruces? I know you have; heard you tell about visiting Jeff Isaacks there. Well, Jim River is like that, and more so. Why, Johnny, right behind my house there's a pinky granite needle half a mile up — straight up — one side sharp like another, slick as glass. That thing must have shoved up all at once, right through the crust, like you'd stick a knife through a tambourine. That was long ago," said Pres. "There were no gods then, and circles had no centers."

CHAPTER VI

IT was past eight when the news bearers returned. Their business had been of the briefest. "Jim River listens good," said Carmody. "I owe you a day in harvest. Maybe you'll never collect it yourself, but the worst that can happen will be that I'll do a turn for somebody else. Thankee." Upon which, Lewis had declared for that delayed investigation.

That broad balcony of Lindauer Place was lighted by hanging lamps, square in glass and ironwork; and there a goodly portion of Target took their ease. The two friends went into the hotel lobby, finding there Troy Ware, Max Hollocher, who was the bank cashier, and Chris Holl, chatting together from the comfort of the deepest armchairs. Through the open door from the saloon floated strange sounds, as of one who bellowed a lullaby:

> Oh, the Prodigal Son was a son of a gun!
> He was! He was!
> He shuffled the cards and he played for mon!
> He did! He did!

"Hark!" said Johnny. "Don't I hear something? Is it — can it be — "

"It is," said Chris Holl. "Jack Farr, just as drunk as he can be. Of course, when I say 'drunk,' I don't mean really drunk. I never saw Elmer unconscious."

"I could do with a drink myself," said Pres. "But I don't want to get tangled up with no drunks. Let's slip through into the back and make signs to the bar creature. Won't you boys join us?"

The boys excused themselves with thanks. Farr was noisy at the bar, with townsmen and several of the Ladders assisting. Their passing was unnoticed. In the rear they noted, together with hilarious tables of pitch, seven-up, solo, a quiet four-handed poker game. The players were Blondy Black, Eastman Hall and Sam Clark — three youths who would in time be tin-horn gamblers — and for the fourth none other than young Frank John, who was enjoying himself very much. They were all boys. Young Sam Clark — Lithpin Tham — was even younger than Frank John. The newcomers took a near-by table, and, for a starter, investigated the beer. The big poker games were in private rooms at the back, where, through the open transom, Erie Patterson and the sheriff were audible.

For Johnny and Pres, investigation of spiced rum followed, with a preliminary round of seven-up to see who should pay for it. After which the investigators passed into Lindauer's store, where business was brisk.

"They're trimming the lad," said Johnny. "They're letting him win on purpose now. Blondy called him once and our visiting friend showed down kings and fours. Blondy threw in his hand and Frank John raked the pot. But I saw Blondy's cards, and he had aces up."

"Sure, I saw that," said Pres. "We'll horn in. Listen!" Johnny listened; and thereafter Pres sought out Lindauer and, when his turn came, spoke aside with him:

"Hermie, I'm out of money. Can I borrow some of your shiny new bank?"

"Certainly, my friend. First thing in the morning."

"No, no," said Pres. "I want it tonight. About two hundred, maybe. Till my ship comes in."

"Against the rules, Pres. Office hours, nine to four. We got to keep our own rules, ain't it? Same with the notes. If you own real estate — not squatter's right, but patented land, or town lots — then we lend on your name. But if you own no land yourself, you must have a landowner's indorsement."

"That's a hell of a note," said Pres, embarrassed. "I don't own no land, and well you know it. Why, Hermie, it's your bank, isn't it? You're the president. You know I'll pay you back, don't you?"

"Sure, sure," said the banker. "But we are not lending our own money. It is the stockholders' money, the depositors' money, and we must hold to the safeguards agreed upon. All this is well understood in older countries, but here you are like children yet."

"Oh, well, lend it to me yourself."

"But I can't do that," said Lindauer. "The stockholders and officers are bound not to lend money themselves, or to go on any man's note."

"Why, Hermie!" The would-be borrower's face was both crestfallen and pained.

"Now, Pres! Now, Pres!" protested Hermie. "Don't you see, it's got to be that way? Just as we may not borrow for ourselves from our own bank. No, you get Cline, or Sais, or some other friend to go on your note, and that will be O.K."

"Oh, well. . . . I suppose I can get a bill of goods on tick, anyway?"

"Anything in the store, old friend," said Lindauer, much relieved. "You must not take it amiss — what I said. It is the custom. You are not used to banking yet, ain't it?"

Lewis took out a stub of a pencil, rolled his eyes for better consideration, and presently handed his old friend a brief list:

2 packs star-backed playing cards
20 five-dollar bills
10 ten-dollar bills
Charge to acct. of

P. B. LEWIS

Lindauer viewed these items with starting eyes. "All ridght! All ridght!" he cried, and threw up both hands. "Robber, I'll fill your bill myself! Come back to the safe. Such a man!"

Pres divided his purchases fairly with Pardee. After a whispered consultation they trooped back into the Gem and halted beside the poker table.

"Any room for two good players? Who's the banker? What's the come-in?" demanded Johnny.

"Free for all. Ten dollars come-in. All jackpots," said Eastman Hall civilly, but without enthusiasm.

The newcomers drew up chairs between Frank John and Lithpin Tham. With a flourish, Johnny spread out a neat bunch of greenbacks. "I'm playing this much behind my stack," he announced.

"Same here," said Lewis.

"You know, this is just a friendly little game," remonstrated Blondy. "You don't want to go to bulling it."

"Oh, no, nothing like that," said Pres. "Just want to be able to tap the winners, so long as I can. I expect to do my playing mostly with Pardee, anyhow. Got it in for him."

It was even so. The newcomers made no splurge, played a few pots, made no raises, and stayed about even with the board; not without pointed comment. Several rounds passed with the mill run of hands. Then, Pres Lewis dealing, Frank John and his original playmates passed in turn. Johnny opened for three dollars. Pres raised him seven. Frank John, Blondy, Hall and Lithpin Tham passed in turn. Johnny shoved in seven dollars, considered, and raised back for ten.

"I'll see that," said Pres. "Cards, if any?"

"Three right off the top," said Johnny.

"And three to me," said Pres. "Your bet, my son."

"Ten," said Johnny.

"And ten more."

"And ten better," said Johnny.

"Call you." Pres pushed his money in without hesitation. "That's all I got in front of me, barrin' a few white chips. What you got?"

"Queens."

The older man's face fell perceptibly. "How many?" he questioned gloomily.

"Two."

"That's good," said Pres heavily.

Johnny showed them to him — two queens and three trash cards. Lewis tossed in his hand. "Gimme another stack, banker," said he, and laid another roll of bills on the table.

Four stunned gamblers gazed on one another with a wild surmise. "That is magnificent," murmured Frank John, "but it is not poker."

Blondy Black leaned over the table. "The house rules — we forgot to tell you — the house rules are that the left bower beats big casino and you can't trump your partner's ace with pinochle unless high and low will put you out."

Lewis plucked up spirit. "That's all right; I'm just baiting Johnny along. I'll get him presently and go south with him."

Cautious playing followed. The first comers were distrustful, having no desire to get tangled in another orgy of wild betting. Only a few hands elapsed until, with Lewis dealing, the pot was passed up to Pardee again. He opened, and Pres Lewis raised him ten. The four other men passed out. Johnny started to throw his hand in the deck, reconsidered, studied, picked up a ten-dollar bill, all but dropped it in the pot, drew it back, folded it, creased it, refolded it to a lamplighter, and finally took up another bill of the same dimensions and pushed both in the pot.

"See that and raise you ten," said Pres.

"Ten right back at you."

" 'Another for Hector,' " said Pres. "Your ten and my ten, which is all the tens in stock at the present writing. Only this time I shove in my few but useful white checks."

"I call that," said Johnny.

Pres picked up the cards. "How many?"

"Help yourself."

Pres laid the pack down. "All right. What have you got?"

"Not at all. What have you got? I called you."

"Oh, just a flush."

"Same here," said Johnny. "Only this is a straight flush."

"Mine is a straight flush too," Lewis confessed. "How high is yours?"

"Just a little one. Ace high."

"Mine is ace high too," said Pres, absently. He raised guileless eyes to meet Johnny's. "I suppose you know that, in case of ties, spades outrank the other suits. It doesn't often happen, but them's the rules. Spades, hearts, diamonds, clubs."

"I never heard of such a rule in my life," said Johnny, "and I doubt if anybody else ever did. But that suits me. Here's mine." He laid down the ace, king, queen, jack and ten of spades.

"That's odd," said Pres. To the shocked gaze of the noncombatants he spread out a black fan of spades — ace, king, queen, jack and ten.

"Well, well! It's a tie!" said Johnny without emotion. "We'll have to divide the pot." Lewis shoved his hand into the discard and Johnny's five cards went in with them; they fell to dividing the pot.

"Fellows, I got to go," said Eastman Hall in a cracked and horrified voice. "Cash in. I am not feeling well. I am not feeling well at all."

"Thith ith thure going to be a lethon to me," said Lithpin Tham.

"But I don't understand," said Frank John, bewildered. Lewis and Pardee had departed to return, as unsatisfactory, the money advanced by Lindauer. Lithpin Tham and Hall were seeking forgetfulness at the bar. "They weren't trying to get our money. To all intents and purposes, they only played those two hands with each other. What was the idea?"

"Well, I'll tell you," said Blondy Black. "We was leading you on, see? Baiting you. We wasn't cheating you, because there was no necessity of it. Suppose when you started in tonight you lost your first ten-dollar stack, and then another stack, and then another — why, you might have got discouraged and quit, like as not. But you lost ten dollars and bought another stack and won, and had twenty dollars in front of you, and lost that, and bought another stack, and won back to thirty dollars, and so on, till you had bought forty or fifty dollars' worth, and had it about all in front of you. That was to make you think it was no difference how much you lost, because you could always win it back. Your mistake. When you get to hurrying the game and grabbing at the cards and trying to play in every pot — then you're stuck! And it don't make any difference then how much you lose, you keep on buying. That is why I am seriously considering being a professional tinhorn. It seems silly to work."

"But what has all that got to do with this clowning? Two ace-high spade flushes — what did they gain by that?"

"Dear — oh, dear!" said Blondy. "That was to break up the game in a nice pleasant way, without hurting anybody's feelings — so you wouldn't lose your shirt. Hey! Listen up in front! That Mr. Farr, he is making tall talk. We'd better get out of here, you and me both. This is no place for innocent young boys!"

CHAPTER VII

Target ish no good town," said Jack Farr. He stood sidewise to the bar, leaning heavily on his left elbow, so that he faced Newt Somers, Bart Pino and Dave Salt, a little farther up the bar. Farr was in his shirt sleeves, as indeed were the others, and it was evident that none of them carried guns. It was also evident, in connection with Farr's truculent face, that his befuddled mind had spotted his more calcitrant body in the position he would have chosen had he worn a gun on his right hip, with a reasonable expectancy that he might want to use it. In the long and slender fingers of his right hand, not too steadily, he held a half-filled whisky glass "Target ish no good town," he repeated. "A large housh ish unaccount'bly mishing, a shide track and a puffeckly good train of cars dishappeared overnight; a gentleman puts a mess of bread in the oven to bake, shlips away to get a small drink, and when he comesh back his stove is gone. Yesh!"

The words were painfully spaced and slow. He drank his liquor and sent the glass sliding along the bar. Then he glanced around. Ellis Kames, the lawyer, came through from the hotel, looked at Farr, sized up the situation, shrugged his shoulders and passed on through the front door without stopping for a good-night drink. Hawkins slouched inattentive in a chair against the wall. Beyond him, near the door, Marshal Yewell sat on a small table littered with newspapers. Farr turned his eyes upon the marshal and took up his tirade again:

"We got a sheriff and a tall marshal and a comfort'ble jail. What happensh? Ish that jail full of crooks? No-o-o! Somebody runsh hish horse down the street, or shings about 'lonely now sheems everything' — Here, I'll shing it!" His eyes grew round; his voice was tearful and husky:

> Shoon beyond the harbor bar
> Shall my bark be shailing far —

The song was interrupted. The sheriff and Patterson came from the poker room, passed beyond the singer to the bar and ordered drinks. Farr glowered at the interruption. Lewis and Pardee came in from the store, the latter painfully dragging a stiffened leg. They leaned against the wall beside the door leading from the store. Frank John joined them at this observation post.

Farr lifted up his voice to address the universe in general. "I wash telling you," he said. "Sho they puts 'em in jail for shinging On the Banksh of the Old Tennesshee, or for toting gunsh. Man orter tote a gun — "

"We sometimes put drunks in jail, too," said the marshal. As he spoke, the Gem's Jim came from the poker room where he had been banking; Jim, the proprietor, tallow-faced, wearing the black coat and white vest of the professional gambler. He stood at the end of the bar and eyed the tipsy Farr reflectively, lifting a questioning eyebrow at the marshal. The slouching Hawkins sat up straighter in his chair.

Farr fixed his disconcerting eyes upon the marshal's face. It was not a threatening glance; merely observant and thoughtful, as of one who charges his memory with something for future reference.

"Drunksh, yesh, but no thieves or housh burners. Never the one that picked the drunk mansh pocket when he's down with hish head under him."

"I see where you are going to sleep tonight," said the marshal.

"Can you shee no further?" jeered Farr. "You've got a star on your vest and a gun on your hip, and I ain't got neither one. But, man, have you no mishgivingsh? Closh your eyes now, and try if you cannot shee where you and me might meet yet in a loneshome plashe, and a chill wind blowing?"

"Do you threaten me?"

"No, no! Daydreamin', thash all. Me threaten? Me? Tell you what; boy could stick live coal in corncob and run me clear out of town. And me besh man in town too. Heap the besh! For," said Jack Farr simply, and lapsing by degrees into a barbaric chant, " 'I am a jolly baker and I bake bread brown!' No, shir, Misher Marshal, shir; you're dead right 'bout drunksh. Damn nuishance. Shoutin' an' shingin' . . .

> Sho early in the morning came a knocking at my door.
> Tirra, la, tirra la, lay!

" 'Sthurbin' peace. Thash bad! Gotter stop! But your Steve Sheriff's all wrong about gunsh. Man orter pack gun! Man gotter pack gun! Needsh gunsh where they burn down houshs and cut cinches." He flicked a pale eye toward the three Ladder men.

"Anyone that says I cut that cinch is a damned liar!" howled Salt.

Smack! Farr's open hand slapped full on the thrusting face, punctuation to the word; pivot and arm and wrist adding speed to the blow. Salt went spinning to the floor.

Pino and Somers plunged over him and grappled Farr together. Dazed, paralyzed, Frank John saw the marshal running, gun in hand; Patterson and the sheriff beyond him, charging down; Jim, the saloonkeeper, heaving up a chair to strike. Lewis leaped forward, Johnny Pardee behind, Frank John one second later. That made him too late. In that blink of time, before he could even overtake the crippled

Pardee, it was all over. Lewis caught up the saloonkeeper and hurled him crashing. Farr broke loose from Pino and struck Somers in the face. A streak that was Bill Hawkins left his chair. He hurled his muscular body through the air in a perfect football tackle, caught Farr around the knees and brought him down, dragging Somers with him. Hawkins made a convulsive scramble and fell on Farr's chest and his one free arm. Simultaneously, Lewis sat on Farr's legs. Hawkins smiled up at the marshal and lifted a hand, palm out.

"I got him for you," he said. "Want me to help you lead him to jail?"

Quick work. Salt had not yet had time to get to his feet. The sheriff and Patterson, with only twenty feet to travel, were still too late.

"Get up, you!" said the marshal. "Will you come peaceable or do we put the handcuffs on you?"

"Lemme think it over," said Farr dispassionately. He sat up, inspected the wreck that had been his shirt, and reached for his hat. At last he came to a decision. "Oh, peash'ble, I guess. Help me up, shomebody."

"Take his other arm, Hawkins," said the marshal. "Sheriff, can't you and Erie go down to the judge's house before he turns in? I want to consult with him and you. I'll be down as soon as I get Farr tucked into bed."

"Well, that's over," said Johnny. "Pres, I'll get a bottle and we'll go up to my room, where it's quiet. Come on, Frank John. But we'll have some coffee and pie first, steak and eggs and a few little fixin's. I haven't had a thing to eat since supper. Pres pays."

Johnny pulled off his boots, not without a groaning, and stretched himself on the bed. As a medicinal measure, Johnny was using for his injury the popular New Mexican panacea of letting nature take her course. The two guests selected the best and only chairs.

"Well," said Frank John, explosively indignant, "are you going to let your friend go to jail? Can't you bail him out?"

"Best place for him," said Johnny heartlessly. "He'll be sobered up by morning. He certainly is one plumb pest when he's full. Sad about Jack. Sober, he could clean out that whole bunch. But when he's sober there's no fight. It's too blamed bad."

"And as if three to one wasn't odds enough against him," cried the boy bitterly, "that big lubber of a Hawkins had to make a fourth — to curry favor with the officers, I suppose."

Lewis and Pardee exchanged glances. There was laughter in their eyes. But when Frank John looked his way, the Lewis eyes were filmed and dreamy.

"The brave boy seized the brawny Indian and hurled him over the beetling precipice into the seething waves below," Pres murmured joyfully, groping in the dead past. Then he turned his head, blinked, and came back reluctantly to the present. " 'Enry was just in time to keep the marshal from shooting Farr," he explained. "If 'Enry jumps the marshal, Tinhorn Jim beats Farr's brains out with that chair — so far as 'Enry knows. So 'Enry 'Awkins, he has just one finger snap of time to decide and do. He downed Farr. Good man, 'Enry. I warm my hands at him."

"What? You mean Hawkins was on Farr's side?"

"Just that. Otherwise, old Elmer was due to stop a bullet."

"You don't think the marshal meant murder?" demanded Frank John, horrified.

"Then why the gun? He didn't need no gun to make the arrest," said Johnny. "Sheriff didn't pull his gun — notice that, Pres? We'll have to remember that, come settling day. And the Rockingchair boys are not so bad either — not when you stack 'em up beside the Ladders. Coming back to the murder, Frank John; the sheriff didn't mean murder, but the marshal did. Jim Yewell had the inclination and the opportunity. Jack Farr talked like a fool, was bound to start a row, did start a row. He was a stumbling block to Yewell and his gang. And what Farr said was true, every word. Target is no place at all, just because there's an organized gang of crooks here, running wild. What I don't see is why the good men don't get together and clean up Gridiron so it will be fit to live in."

"Really good men, they never do much of anything — not when it's risky," said Pres. "Always fussing about the rules, stopping for Sunday and advice of counsel. Then, they foster a brutal prejudice against guessing, good men do. Worst of all, they wonder does it pay. That's fatal — that last. What you want is a few trusty knaves. Let's count. Elmer, the sot, the trouble hunter. No question about Elmer. Johnny, the cowman. That's two. Passing on with averted heads, hastily but kindly, I'm the next."

Frank John laughed.

"Do you doubt my rascality, then? When you've seen with your own eyes?" demanded Pres indignantly. "You see me drink and gamble and cheat in a poker game. You saw me make the fifth to jump on one poor drunken donkey in a barroom row — "

"Rats! You just caught hold of Farr's legs to square yourself for standing the saloonkeeper on his head," said Frank John, shrewdly enough. "If the sheriff had seen fit to call you to account, you would have claimed you thought Jim Gem was siding with Farr."

"It did answer a lot of questions, me hopping his hump that way," said Pres dryly. "And it certainly didn't hurt Farr any. That idea may have occurred to me. And so, Frank John, according to your own say, I'm a liar, too — or would have been if the sheriff had seen fit. As a matter of fact, however, mighty few sheriffs ever do see fit," said Pres dreamily. "They never did see fit. It's a habit with them. Now we'll tally up — gambler, cheat, liar and bully. Oh, I qualify, all right. That's three. And 'Enry 'Awkins makes Number Four."

"Come! I say! Five minutes ago Hawkins was a good man, and who so loud to praise him as you?"

"I may have used the words," Pres admitted. "But it is barely possible that 'good man' doesn't mean here just what it does in Maryland and Michigan."

"A good man means generous, loyal and brave," said Frank John hotly. "Here or in hell!"

Lewis went on placidly, ignoring the interruption: "Mistrusted 'Enry from the start. Too quiet. Fine, big, broad-shouldered man, inconspicuous, melted into the landscape like a quail. Hiring a bronc' broke, and him bow-legged as a pair of tongs. Walks on the right-hand side, no matter who he's walkin' with. Shooting that poor devil of a horse — "

"Oh, was that who it was?"

" — to save Johnny's worthless hide, and doing it without any gun that anybody saw. And that makes another lie I told. Four knaves. You are the fifth, Frank John. Take off your coat and pitch in, but keep your shirt on."

"Me? What have I done?" Frank John blushed with not-unbecoming confusion. It was plain he took the charge of knavery as an unmerited accolade. "And what use could I be to your league of rogues?"

Unspoken, a half-forgotten line flashed through his mind. Where had he read that, or heard it? Oxford, Carlisle, The Highlands, Normandy, Avignon? "*We are the lost. Queen Honor —*" How did it go? . . . "*Queen Honor is the deathless —*" Who had said that? How could he have forgotten? . . . "*A battered rascal guard still closes round her.*" . . . His blood tingled hot and proud; it flushed his boyish face with pleasure.

"As for your first asking, son — well, for one thing, you keep mighty bad company," said Pres. "And for the other point, you don't seem to realize that you'd be simply invaluable to us. You could go around asking questions when, if we'd do the like, we would never see sundown. Besides, we could explain things to you — "

"Oh, I know! You could explain, so you'd know what you meant yourself. You don't know that most of the time. You act by instinct, mostly, like the other wild animals. And by the time you spelled it out so I could get a glimmer, the rest would have it down like a plain, straight road so that the wayfaring man may not err therein. Thank you most to pieces, but I'm going home."

"Don't think of such a silly thing. That would be rank wasteful. Quite aside from the civic service you can up and go and do in this blessed emergency, you want to consider your education. You don't appreciate your opportunities, Frank John. You have a fine inquiring mind; and you want to remember that in a thousand years, or some such, historians will publicly offer their right eye to know what you can see now, at first-hand; just as they puzzle and stew and guess about Harold the Saxon, nowadays. Ain't people funny? Heavens to Betsy, how they'd raise the roof, them sharps, if they could lay hands on a few anecdotes by Little John, in his own handwrite, about Robin Hood and the proud Sheriff of Nottingham! But if they'd found those same letters while Little John was alive, they would have lit the kitchen fire with 'em. Ain't that queer? Well, you take warning by that, and keep your eyes open. Here you are, living in the ancient days and the springtime of the world, with a priceless chance to get the low-down on how we scramble through with a certain cheerfulness and something not far removed from decency, and make merry with small cause. You stick around, Frank John, and watch our ways and means. . . . Besides, we need you."

"No, I thank you. I'm not taking any. I'd only be a clog on you. I don't fit in here. I don't see closely enough, I don't think quickly enough, and I don't move quickly enough. Target is no place at all for me. I'm going back home. As John Cecil Calvert, among his own people, I can pass muster. Not here."

So, in humility and all good faith, John Cecil Calvert spoke his mind. It was his last recorded utterance — as John Cecil Calvert. Today, when New Mexicans would boast, they point to Frank John, pillar and landmark, name giver. It was he who gave to the Blue Bedroom that beloved name; incidentally, for many old-timers, Frank John was their only approach to the treasures of the English tongue.

Frank John did not go back home. For, as he rose to go, a discreet tapping came at the door. Frank John opened it. Hawkins stood framed there, upstanding, alert and tall, his face alight, his eyes dancing, finger on lip. He stepped in and closed the door softly.

CHAPTER VIII

IT WAS ONLY FOUR BLOCKS to the jail, two east and two south. It was a leisurely saunter. The prisoner draped one affectionate arm on the marshal's shoulder, held fast the Hawkins coat sleeve with the other hand, and chatted brightly of night and stars and the fishes of the deep; bidding them a cheery good-night as Knowles, the jailer, ushered him to a cell.

"Mr. Hawkins, will you stop in at Judge Humphries' place with me?" said the marshal as they turned back. He spoke in undertones.

"What for? I was thinking some of bed."

"Got a proposition to make to you. . . . What's the matter? What are you stoppin' for?" The marshal turned his head for the last words. Hawkins had halted in his tracks.

"You got no square business to spring on me in the middle of the night," said Hawkins bluntly. "Look here, Yewell; this looks like some shenanigan."

"Sh-h-h! Not so loud. Shenanigan? Why, yes, it is, in a way. But it is only a necessary stratagem of the law. We want your help — the sheriff and Erie and me," said Yewell. "We was considerin' you for the job this afternoon, mainly because you and Dave Salt tangled up. On account of that, nobody would think of you pulling a job for our crowd. Seein' the way you arose and shone durin' the recent ruckus with Farr, we could hardly do better. You're not squeamish, I judge."

Mr. Hawkins nibbled at the edges of this remark, wide-eyed and alert. Under his wide hat, his face was undecipherable in the star-light, but his voice was harsh:

"Why at the judge's? Why not at the hotel? Listen, fellow; I don't go into anything blind. Give it a name."

"Here on the street? Think I'm crazy? That's why we go to the judge's, and why we go in the dark. It's a night job, and tonight is the night."

"You give it a name," said Hawkins stubbornly. "I can always say no and go home to bed, if I don't like it. I dance for no man's piping, unless I call the tune."

"Conscience ache ye?" sneered Yewell. "Well, all I got to say is, you don't look it."

"Give it a name," said Hawkins. "This is the third and last time. Tell it to me!"

"There's houses along here. Want everybody to hear us? Vacant lot down the street a ways. Tell you there." He strode on through the starlight. Hawkins followed him a step behind.

Thrifty cottonwoods lined the street before the vacant lot. In the dark shadows the marshal stopped and spoke in an angry whisper:

"It's the Carmody outfit. They're camped out of town a ways and they shoved their little old horse herd over the ridge, a mile or so farther on, where the grass is better. We want you to run off that horse herd. Not steal 'em, just chase 'em off to the mountains any which way, and as much farther as you see fit. Then you can leave them and double back by some different route. Tell you why, up to the house, but that's all we want you to do. Month's pay for one night's work. Half a night — 'twill be midnight by the time you get your horse and get started."

"Shucks, is that all? I thought, by the way you was taking on, you wanted me to hide a train of cars in a well, or burn somebody in bed. But why tonight? Why not tomorrow night, so I could scatter 'em and get back before day and no one the wiser? The way you've got it framed out, I'll be suspected."

"And you act like a cowman, too," said Yewell, irritated. "Don't you see, their cattle are dog-tired, so they couldn't get 'em farther out this evening, waterin' as late as they did? Tomorrow they'll water at noon and shove the herd 'way out to good grass, and the horse herd will be right beside the bed ground. It's tonight or never. Come on, let's go talk it up."

"But why go up to the house?" asked Hawkins. "Why don't I go on from here? I don't care to have everybody know my business. Why take all Target in on the deal?"

"You're the most cautious man I ever saw! Why, there's nobody there but the sheriff and Erie and the judge; and we're all in it. Four heads are better than one, and we don't want to overlook any bets. This has to come off as slick as grease. Give you instructions after we consider every angle. Got to get your money, too. And I want you to be sure the law is back of you, so you won't get scary and spoil it all," said the marshal with an ill-concealed sneer. "Most suspicious fool I ever did see. Come on, we're wasting time."

The judge's house was set back from the street. Francis Truesdale Humphries had not favored adobe. He was from New Hampshire, and his house was of wood, weather-boarded, painted white, with green facings. In memory of other skies, the house perched upon stilts, boarded up to the hollow semblance of a basement. The large front room served as office; behind was a bedroom, with a kitchen beyond, which was also the dining room. The judge was unmarried. Hawkins remembered the place from daylight, because it was so unlike its neighbors. The back yard was surrounded by a high board fence. There, in earlier days, Humphries had raised chickens, to the great joy of Target. The far-flung New England conscience — or perhaps a habit — drove him to keep it whitewashed still. In the rear of this yard, flush with the alley, stood the abandoned chicken house, now falling to decay; flanked by a shed which was meant to stable one horse, before the judge had learned the good old New Mexico method of keeping horses; which is to turn your horse loose on the flat. Then, when you wanted to go somewhere, you could walk or wait till your horse came in for water.

The judge's curtains were drawn, but lines of light streamed out at the edge to show the tiny lawn. The graveled walk was neatly bordered by beer bottles set on end, necks down; a clipped lilac centered the lawn, and morning-glories latticed the covered porch.

The marshal tapped and entered. The sheriff looked like a tired man — which he was — a heavy man, sullen and slow and slightly bewildered, a man on whom the years were telling. He had thrown hat, coat and gun on a settle by the door, and was now sprawled on a sofa near the unlit fireplace, his boots toppled together for mutual support where he had kicked them off. He sat up grudgingly as Patterson and Judge Humphries rose to greet the newcomer. Erie Patterson was cordial and frank in his welcome. The judge was fluttered.

"Well, here's your Hawkins," announced the marshal. "Judge, you are the very spit and image of respectability, safety, and all that. You take this geezer in hand and reason with him. Most uneasy critter I ever did see. I've known a lady to leave her happy home for less persuasion. Sit up, Hawkins. You're among friends."

"I done heard about that lady," said Hawkins, smiling. "Heard it on night guard." He crooned softly, with no unpleasant voice:

> Oh, would you leave your home and would you leave your baby,
> And would you leave your own true love for to go with Black Jack Davy?

"The answer is, I will." So saying, he sank on the settle and looked up inquiringly at Judge Humphries.

"My dear fellow," said the judge, "it's quite simple. We want to know more about the Carmody outfit. But if the sheriff or anybody else goes prowling around them, they'll be suspicious and we'll learn nothing. The more so as there has been some unfortunate friction between them and Erie's men, as I hear. There is where you come in. No risk at all, since you act at the behest of the law. You are to run their horses off and scatter them. They will come to us with their complaints; the sheriff and Mr. Yewell will raise a posse, find the horses, and so become friendly and intimate with them at their own asking."

"The fact is," said Erie Patterson, watching Hawkins and glimpsing

incredulity behind his attentive eye — "and this is the strictest confidence, mind you — the fact is, we suspect Carmody of some knowledge — if indeed it goes no further than that — of this man Bill
Doolin."

"The outlaw? Is that the way the land lies?" cried Hawkins
eagerly. He eyed his informant shrewdly. So doing, he heard, slight
but distinct, the faint protest of a chair in the next room, the shuffle
of a cautious foot. Greed showed in his eyes as he went on, "There'll
be a reward for his capture or safe burial, I'm hearing?"

"There is, indeed," said Erie, smiling. "It is that reward which stirs
us up. Naturally, no suspicion must fall on us about this horse herd.
We are all going back up to be in evidence in the saloon just as soon
as you start."

"I'm not," said the sheriff shortly. "I'm going to bed, right here
and soon."

"Well, the rest of us are going," said Erie. "My reputation is none
so good but what an alibi is welcome. The rest of our boys are there
now, lapping it up. There's where you come in, Mr. Hawkins. This
Carmody man will snoop around and inquire about our crowd the
first thing."

"I'm the very man you want!" said Hawkins, flushing with enthusiasm. "I hung back a bit at first. It looked fishy to me, and that's a
fact. But I'm with you now. All I hope is that it isn't a false alarm.
I'd like to finger some small slice of that reward money."

"Carmody and Doolin are old friends; we're dead sure of that
much," said the marshal, and Hawkins turned trustful eyes upon him.
"Our thought, and hope, is that Doolin keeps in touch with him.
Hides out in the hills, but comes in by night for supplies and information. You notice all tracks, will you?"

Hawkins' face fell and lengthened; the eager light fled from his
eyes. "What if this devil, Doolin, was to catch me in my little enterprise during the course of his night prowling? Where would my
month's pay be then? 'No risk at all!' says you. I'd call it one hell
of a risk. Too much for that money. I might have known it. Easy
money is the hardest, always."

"Pshaw! There's no danger. Doolin would have no business at the
horse herd. Why should he? He might be at the wagon, but it is
the wagon you must shun. You know where they're camped?"
Hawkins nodded. "Give him his money, Erie. Pay him double. This
has got to be done tonight, remember."

Erie slid three double eagles into a waiting hand. But Hawkins
looked at the golden tokens without satisfaction. "Say, I'm a top
hand," he said. "I don't work for no thirty a month. But I'll tell you

what I'll do. I've got a good rifle over in the feed corral, with my saddle. But on such a chancy business as this, in the dark, a six-shooter beats any rifle. Give me a good six-shooter and I'm your man."

"In the devil's name, take that six-shooter layin' there by you and get out of here!" said the sheriff. "It'll be morning before you get started, and I got a jail full of guns. You take the horses to the foot-hills of San Lorenzo before daylight, and I don't care if you never come back!"

"Oh, I'll be back," said Hawkins. "I'm interested in Bill Doolin and that reward money. Nuff talk. 'Night, everybody!" He took up gun belt and gun, and buckled the belt on as he went down the walk. He crossed the street diagonally, walking briskly. At the street corner, close at hand, he turned north toward the feed corral, where his horse was. But he did not go there. He went north one block, east one block, turned south one block, stopping at the corner, peering cautiously to make sure that the judge's street was deserted; crossed the judge's street, turned down the judge's alley, slinking in the shadows, noiseless. He was delayed somewhat at the door of the judge's one-horse stable, which was hooked inside; lifted the hook with a poking gun barrel, fastened it behind him, crept like a ghost through the judge's garden, crawled without sound in a shadowed detour, and wormed himself under the kitchen, into the false basement beneath the judge's house. Slowly, with infinite caution, he came snakewise under the front room. There were holes in the floor and thrusting shafts of light and the sound of many voices.

"All right, boys!" said the marshal. He had been watching Hawkins from below a lifted corner of curtain; he rose now and dusted his knees.

The bedroom door opened and three men tramped out, blinking in the sudden change from darkness to light — Dave Salt; Nash, the grocer; Ellis Kames, the lawyer.

"Where's that bottle?" demanded Salt savagely. "Thought you was going to keep up that yap all night. Where's your glasses, judge?"

"In that wall cupboard. Help yourself; you're up on your hind legs."

"I thought I would have to sneeze in spite of everthing. I'm next with that bottle, Dave." Thus Nash for Cash, Groceries.

"It hands me a laugh to think of that poor boob, and what a surprise he's going to get," said Ellis Kames, darkly handsome, fault-

lessly attired, as attire went in that day — a Prince Albert coat, a black
string tie, a glossy black hat.

"He was a shy fish," said Yewell. "Shy, but greedy. Only for that
reward he might have backed out. Then where would your fine plan
have been, Ellis?"

"Then I would have hatched another plan. I concocted this one,
you will do me the justice to observe, in some haste, owing to your
joint desire to involve Carmody and get the B 4 cattle at forced sale.
I rather plume myself on that plan, for an impromptu. 'An excellent
plot, very good friends.' "

The allusion was lost. "Too many if's and and's," growled the
sheriff. "Something will slip up on you. The old army game is the
surest and safest."

"In many ways I quite agree with you, Steve," said Ellis Kames
tranquilly. . . . "If you are quite done with that bottle, Nash? . . .
Thanks." He poured a stiff drink, tossed it off, passed the bottle, and
wiped his mustache delicately with a bordered kerchief. "The bank
money is ours, certainly, any time we choose to take it. Personally,
I believe we might get more by waiting longer — although I may be
in error. This is not a rich country, and there is not much loose
money that is not already on deposit here. But this scheme works
both ways. We get the cash and Carmody gets in bad. Other things
being equal, I would cast my vote for this lay, just to see that white-
livered boob of a Hawkins buried as Bill Doolin. That hands me a
laugh!"

"Simplest way is the best way," said the sheriff stubbornly. "This
has to run like a time-table. And you know how often trains are
late."

"Let's go over it, then, to make sure it works like a time-table.
Everybody set your watches together before we leave. Bank opens
at nine. Somers is in the bar, setting 'em up, to make sure everybody's in off the street. Salt has a smoky horse, in the side street — a
horse which looks very much like the Hawkins horse. He's dressed
just like Hawkins, with a floppy black hat like Hawkins wears.
Salt, as everyone knows, bought him a new pearl-gray hat last night,
on account of an accident to his old one. There we are — nine o'clock,
street empty. Salt's watching. Now comes my part. I go into the
bank, make a deposit, come out when the bank's empty and go in
the saloon, where I am drinking deep when the robbery occurs. That
gives Salt the tip. He put on his little old mask, slips in and holds up
the flaxy cashier, puts the money in a meal sack and hops his horse.
He rides down that street to the alley, sees the sheriff a block down

the street, walking his way, bringing friend Farr up from jail to stand trial. So the bold bandit whirls into the alley across from the bank. Farr sees that, and can swear to it. . . . Get that, Salt?"

Salt scowled. "What's the idea? You taking all that pains to be sure the sheriff will be coming down the street at just that exact minute. Kames, are you insinuating that I might doublecross my friends and light out with all of it?"

"My dear Dave! What an idea! You pain me, you do indeed. That was to have Farr — no friend of ours — able to swear the robber went down the alley. That you couldn't ride down the street and over the hills to Mexico, because Steve would shoot your eye out and earn high praise as an efficient peace officer, in case your evil spirit prompted you not to turn down that alley, as per schedule — that is just a coincidence."

"To hell with all of you," snarled Salt. "Let someone else pull your chestnuts from the fire. I won't."

"There, there," said Erie. "You shan't do it if you don't want to. But I think you might, Davy. You're the only one of us as big as Hawkins, and Hawkins, he's just about Bill Doolin's size, from all accounts, and we might get that reward, being this is a hot country and all. Bank robber tracked up and killed resisting — had to bury him — Doolin seen and positively identified near by, only a week ago; suspicious actions of the man Carmody, supposed to have been Doolin's confederate — why, it's a fair cinch! And the real Doolin won't be seen again — not if he hears of it. That will be his chance, and he'll be smart enough to take it. He's married, and he'd quit — so I hear — if the officers would let up on him — as they would, if they thought he was dead. That five thousand would help, Dave, if you felt like going through with it. Never mind Kames; he always has to have his little joke." Erie's voice was honeyed, almost cooing. "You think it over, and do whatever you think best. But I think you might go on with it, Dave, so long as none of the rest of us can fill the bill. Look at what I have in my hand, Dave. Don't you think you might go on with it?"

What Patterson had in his hand was cocked, and the muzzle was so adjusted as to cover a point just above Dave's belt buckle. Dave thought he might go on with his part, and said so, while sweat rolled into his eyes.

"Another little joke of mine, friend Dave," remarked Kames, "is that Jim Yewell will be at the back door of the saloon at just that exact minute — as you so aptly phrased it — just to make sure that your evil spirit doesn't turn you up the wrong alley. As a further coincidence, Newt Somers will stand at the end of the bar, next to the

front door, and that door opened. I am a poor shot myself," said
the lawyer apologetically, "but Newt is considered well above the
average, I believe. And since Bart Pino will be sitting on the judge's
porch at that exact minute, cleaning the judge's rifle for him —
really, it would seem that the robber must infallibly be shot, unless
indeed he turned up the alley back of the Nash for Cash grocery
store. Cheer up, Dave. Your part is nearly over. You only have to
carry that money a hundred and fifty feet, be the same more or less.
Then a quick dash, and you're in the clear. . . . Your turn, Erie.
Speak your piece."

"At nine sharp, Nash and I are in his office at the rear of the store —
just the two of us. Nash has a brown leather valise, neither new nor
old, unnoticeable. The valise is open. I have a double-barreled shotgun. The shotgun is loaded. Buckshot, I believe. There is a back
door in the office, leading to the alley. The door is open. I stand by
the back door with the shotgun. As Dave races by, he throws the
sackful of money — if I remember rightly — through the open door.
That's right, isn't it, Dave?"

Dave confirmed this.

"We all want to be letter-perfect in our parts," observed Patterson
pleasantly, "so that everything will go off smoothly. To resume:
Dave throws the sack into us at the open door; we dump the money
into the satchel; Nash locks the satchel, giving me the key to the
satchel; we pop the satchel in the safe, we turn the combination, we
dispose of the meal sack — ordinary meal sack; fifty like it in Nash's
lumber room. Questioned, however, it appears that the back door was
shut and not open. Mr. Nash and I did not see the robber pass, but
we heard a horse running. We opened the door and looked, just in
time to see a man and a horse turn out of the alley into the street —
the street just beyond the judge's house. That's all we know."

"You confirm this, Mr. Nash?"

"That's how it was," said Nash. "Horse was running as hard as he
could go. Couldn't see its color for the dust. . . . And the money is
safe in the safe."

"Safe in the safe!" Kames repeated. "Safe, because friend Nash has
too much property to leave. Not to mention the enormous line
carried in his store — and paid for, gentlemen, as I made it my business
to ascertain — paid for, except for a few recent invoices. Aside from
that, Nash owns real estate and a substantial block of stock in the
Railroad cattle ranches. We may be quite sure that Mr. Nash will
never contemplate other than a fair and equitable division of the
spoil. So much for that. The money is safe; and now we must see
to it that Dave Salt is safe. He has borne the burden and heat of the

day; he has taken more risk than any other — oh, far more risk! He is to have a double share for his pains, and he is to have an unbreakable alibi. He throws the money into Nash's office, as related. Then, and not till then, Dave goes on full tilt up the alley, unmolested, as fast as his horse can run, till he comes to the door of the Humphries stable. That door is open. He rides in and jumps off; he closes the door and hooks it from within. Bart Pino is in the stable, and Bart Pino's new saddle, creaking new, with silver conchas, gaudy Navajo blanket and a bridle to match, is in the stable.

"Bart strips off the shabby old saddle and bridle — the judge's, long disused, unnoticeable — and replaces it with his own beautiful rig. With a gentle horse the change can be made in one minute by a man in haste. This is a gentle horse, and Bart has reasons for haste. Let us now go back to Dave. Jumping off, Dave runs to the front of the back yard, where his own horse stands, ready saddled with Dave's own saddle, well known to everyone. Judge Humphries awaits him there with Dave's new hat — the one he is wearing now. He takes from Dave the old, black, floppy hat — Dave has already dropped his mask in the alley. The high board fence hides all these hurried transactions. Bart joins Dave there; they lead their horses through the gate to the front of the judge's house; the judge has gone in with the floppy black hat. The alarm is given. Dave and Bart proceed down the street, the judge accompanying them afoot, chatting together. To be sure, Bartolome Pino is riding a smoke-colored horse. That is nothing. There are many such horses. The bandit was an American and his saddle was old. This smoky horse is appareled like the sun and ridden by a Mexican with irreproachable companions, who will vouch for him if questioned. No man will think twice of the smoky horse. . . . Go on, judge; tell us what you know about this case."

"Well, after breakfast I was cleaning my rifle, and when I went to put it together it wouldn't fit. So Dave and Pino was riding by and I asked them to help me. What time? Oh, half-past eight, or some such matter — I didn't notice. They was there 'bout half an hour on my front porch, Bart tinkering with my rifle and Dave fixing him a hackamore. Their horses? They tied 'em back of the house, seems like. Yes, they went back for 'em when we heard the hue and cry, because I was quite a ways up the street before they overtook me. Did I see anybody that might have been the robber? Come to think of it, I did see somebody, two or three blocks down, crossing the street and riding pretty fast. Didn't notice him particular. Why should I? Except that he seemed to be in a hurry. Riding north, he was. Come to think of it, I believe he had a black hat, this fellow.

I couldn't be absolutely sure of that, but I seem to remember it that way. This was a big man, you say? I swan I don't know whether this fellow I saw was big or not. He was kinder humped over, I noticed."

"That's the lay," said Kames. "See any flaws in it, anybody? The ayes have it. The rest is simple and governed by circumstances. We'll make up a posse and scour the country. More accurately, the authorities will do this. I'm not up to hard riding myself, as you all know. Carmody will miss his horses by sunup or before. He'll think they're just drifted, and hunt for them. It is not at all likely that he'll make a report before nine. Possibly not at all. If he comes, or sends word, the sheriff details a bunch to go with him and follow up the tracks. They'll find the horse herd, and they'll be sure to find the track where Hawkins rode off alone, because someone will be along who knows there'll be such a track."

"I'll be one," said Yewell, interrupting. "Me and Erie go with the horse-trailing bunch; taking along a few outsiders for the looks of it. We'll find that track and insist on following it up. If just us two goes alone, so much the better."

"That's the idea. You overtake Hawkins, on a smoky horse, wearing a floppy hat. Maybe you meet him coming back. In either case he resists arrest and you have to kill him. You've got the bank robber, but not the money. Accomplice likely; although he may have hidden it. An accomplice? Who? Who is this Carmody, this stranger? Isn't it queer that his horse herd should be run off just then, and at no other time? If Carmody, or his man Bird, or both, are out ostensibly looking for their horses, doesn't that look as though they were in collusion with the robber, hiding the money for him? And if, by any lucky chance, Carmody comes up with a report of his missing horses before the bank robbery, then it's as plain as the nose on your face. He wanted to draw as many as possible on the sheriff's posse, looking for horse thieves, to give the bank robbers a break. Anybody can see that, when the horses are found, and not one missing. However, we can hardly expect that much luck. Carmody will hunt his own horses, probably. But if we don't hear from his camp before the posse starts, we'll ride out by his camp to make inquiries. Then we'll send a bunch to hunt the stolen horses. And the dead robber — is it possible that this is Doolin himself? It is possible. Same general description, anyhow. Sheriff hasn't got back yet. When he comes he can wire and see. But we'll have to bury this long lad right now. He ain't keeping any too good. They can always dig him up for identification. . . . Boys, this is good! It works like a watch. Any questions?

No? . . . Oh, yes, one thing more. . . . Steve, didn't you remember
hearing, a long time ago, that Bill Doolin and this Carmody was close
friends?"

"I don't remember anything of the kind!" roared the sheriff. He
arose and pounded violently on the table. His big red face fairly
swelled with rage. "And no other man is going to remember it. It's
a dirty rotten deal all the way around, without that. Carmody's
going to have his chance without any perjury from me. Why don't
you leave Carmody out of it? He's got a family. I don't give a damn
about Hawkins. Don't like him; never did — surly, black-muzzled
swine. But if you try to hang it onto Carmody I hope you make a
botch of the whole job. Know what I think? I think I'm going to
stake Carmody enough to get him and his herd out of here. Kames,
you leave Carmody out of this or I'll shoot you in the belly! Hear
me?"

"Come on, boys; let's go uptown," said Nash for Cash. "You'll need
slickers tomorrow. Some folks have rheumatism when a rain is coming on, but it works on the sheriff's conscience. I've seen him this
way before. He always gets over it. . . . Coming, judge?"

"No, I'll stay here with Steve."

"Good night, then."

Mr. Hawkins began to wriggle out while the feet of the departing
conspirators allowed him to make a comparatively speedy escape by
covering any small noises he might make. He effected his retreat in
short order as far as the alley, but was quite unable to hook the stable
door behind him. He contented himself with propping it shut with a
stone, confident that the habits of small boys would account for this
small circumstance, should it be noticed. Two blocks away he paused
to take stock. He was woefully begrimed and becobwebbed. He
wiped his face with a handkerchief; he brushed his clothes with his
hat, and then brushed the hat with the handkerchief. Then he
scratched his nose and took counsel with himself in a guarded
whisper:

"That sheriff? Kind of pitiful, isn't it, Bill? . . . H'm! That's odd
too. If that clever marshal hadn't told me that Bill Doolin and this
Carmody was old friends, I'd have turned him down, and that would
have been the end of it. But that statement interested me — and so it
was only the beginning! Lying," said Bill Hawkins sagely, "is a bad
habit. . . . That Nash, too. I don't take to Nash, somehow. Rheumatism is no subject for joking."

He looked up at the sky. The clock said twelve and past. He made

his way swiftly to Holland House, listened in the hall, heard there a
low humming of voices, and tapped on Pardee's door.

CHAPTER IX

When Hawkins joined the conferees in Johnny Pardee's room
Frank John could hardly recognize him; this supple light-foot had so
little in common with the clumsy oaf of yesterday, humped and
slouching. And then he remembered that twice before, in decisive
action, this same Hawkins had been swifter than his eyes could follow.
Frank John pondered this.

The scrutiny was mutual. The newcomer eyed Frank John doubtfully and with some perplexity. One Hawkins eyebrow shot up; the
other, after some deliberation, followed slowly; and he bent an inquiring gaze on the other occupants of the now-crowded little room.

"The boy with the taffy-colored hair is all right, 'Enry," said Pres
Lewis, answering the unspoken query. "He'll do to take along. A
little lacking in experience, it may be, but something whispers in my
ear that he has some on the way. What with one thing and you shining like a Japanese lantern on a Christmas tree, fairly oozin' information at every pore, I seem to hear afar ancestral voices prophesying
war." He transferred himself to the bed and waved his hand at the
vacated chair. "Sit down and relieve your mind, 'Enry. Frank John
will stand hitched. Didn't you notice him bulging to battle a while
ago, a little late, but headed the right way? When so softly you came
tapping, just now, we was in the very act of offering him the keys
of the city on a lordly dish."

'Enry's doubtful face cleared with this assurance. "This is no kid's
play, but I'll take your word for him. And a chair is the last thing
I need just now. Listen, Lewis, will you do my askings first and wait
till later to find out why? If I stop to explain it, it will be too late."

"Adventures first; explanations take such a dreadful time," murmured Lewis, nursing his hands between his knees. "Next room on
one side is mine; Frank John's on the other. Nobody in them. Shoot!"

"Yes, and my empty room across the hall. For all that, I'm closing
the window, if we smother," said Hawkins. "Eavesdropping has happened, to my certain knowledge." He lowered his voice to the key
of caution. "Here's the lay: You come with me and wait at the far
corner of the plaza. I'll get my horse from Gray's corral. Then you
ride your prettiest out to Carmody's wagon and carry a message for

me. I'll wait here for you, and when you get back, us four will go into executive session and I'll tell you all about why."

"What's the message?"

"I'll tell you the odds and ends as we go, but the main items must be written, or they wouldn't believe in them, and you a stranger. The fact is, when I bulldogged our drunk a while ago, I plumb won the young affections of both money and brains, and they propositioned me to do dirt for 'em, cash in advance, right off. With hints of more to follow. First chore was to run off the B 4 horse herd." Here Johnny made comment, but 'Enry held up his hand. "No questions. Tell you later. Going on one o'clock right now. I'm delegatin' the job to Carmody's man, Charlie Bird. He must be off and gone as quick as he can. It's my job and I'm supposed to be well on the way."

"Carmody must have a heap of confidence in you," said Johnny.

"Never saw the man in my life till I bought a horse of him yesterday evenin'. But Charlie, he'll do what I tell him, and the old man will do what Charlie tells him. So that's all right." Hawkins turned to Frank John: "You got paper and pencil? Well and good; write what I tell you."

So Frank John sat by a little table and wrote from dictation, as follows:

Friend Charlie: You and Carmody do just like I say, without wasting a minute. Don't fail. Don't make any move different to what I tell you. Important. I am banking on you. One, put your saddle on this horse of mine. Two, send me another horse by bearer, as good as this one, or as good as you got. Three, you take this horse and push your horse herd out to the San Lorenzo Mountain, right off, just as fast as you can. That's the big mountain, due north. I am supposed to do this, paid for it. And you got no time to waste. Four, tell Carmody not to make no report in the morning. When somebody comes he is to say the horses drifted and you went after them about sunrise, that you'll get 'em. Act like he wasn't a mite uneasy — which he needn't be. Five, about ten in the morning, or a little later, you catch you another horse and drift your horse herd back, but leave my horse behind to be found and wondered at. Better push him on a couple of miles beyond your herd, and then you hustle right back and move your herd before he can get with them. If you meet anyone, make your story match the one Carmody is to tell. You didn't see my horse or anyone like me. But for everything else you see, tell it straight and careless. Your horses drifted; you didn't think they'd do the like of that; you'll hobble them tonight.

The bearer, Mr. Lewis, is all right. He cannot tell you the why of this, because I have not had time to tell him yet.

Charlie, I seen you yesterday at the stock pens, but I dodged you. So long.

"That's all. Here; I'll sign it," said Hawkins. He took the pencil and traced an extravagantly wide capital S, an inch high, crossing it with two long, perpendicular lines; the whole making a firm and exceedingly plump dollar mark.

"That was the brand me and Charlie Bird planned to have together when we were boys," said Hawkins, musing. "Some folks are born with two strikes on them. . . . That's nonsense. That's doin' the baby act. It's not luck; it's the man. Every time. I had as good a chance as Charlie Bird did, every bit."

"Charlie Bird?" said Frank John. His eyes were round with astonishment. "That little dried-up manikin? He told me he had neither kith nor kin left alive. Poor, alone, hardly a shirt to his back, working for day wages and in all human probability not drawing even that; following a ruined and falling house. I don't see what Charlie Bird has that any man can envy."

Hawkins folded the note and handed it to Pres Lewis. He lifted up his eyes and regarded Frank John attentively. "Don't you?" he said, at last. "Well, Mr. Lewis, we'll go get my horse."

"Friend with the countersign," said Hawkins, ten minutes later, as he swung down from the smoky horse and handed the rein to Lewis. "When you ride up to that camp, you ride a-whistlin' real loud and pleasant. That Charlie Bird, he's half Cherokee and half white, and them's two bad breeds. Don't know about Carmody, but from his tell yesterday, his patience is pretty well given out. You whistle. One or the other of 'em will be with the herd, and the other a-snoozin', so you'll have to step lively. It's all to the good that they don't know why, so they won't have nothin' to hide. But you hurry on back. I got a heap to tell you. Leave the new horse and my saddle with Gray till you call or send an order. But you bring my old rifle up to your friend's room."

The program fell behind the schedule. It was later than two o'clock when the stolen horse herd, with the owner's right hand in charge, took the road for San Lorenzo. Haste though he might, it was half-past when Pres rejoined the conference room; finding there two young men of highly divergent pasts who were now wholly at one, each merely a mass of quivering curiosity; and Mr. 'Enry 'Awkins tranquilly asleep in his chair.

" 'The time has come . . .' " said Pres rather loudly, " 'to talk of many things — ' Hi! Don't shake him, Johnny. You donkey, you ought to know better than that. . . . 'Enry! Executive session! Up and tell us why."

So 'Enry up and told them.

"But, Mr. Hawkins," broke in Frank John, when the story came to where 'Enry had wormed his way under the house as reporter, "you must have had a very strong hunch that the marshal was lying, to cause you to take such an extraordinary step as that."

"I knew he was lying," said Hawkins dryly. "No guesswork about it. And it wasn't a step. I tell you I crawled on my belly like a snake, expectin' to bite a rattler any minute, over dead men's bones, and shiny what-are-yous, and ha'nts whisperin' 'Boo' to me, and a cold skel'ton hand ketchin' me by the ankles. You gentlemen may not believe me, but I was glad to get out in the starlight again."

The session was long. Hawkins' memory was excellent and he told the story with gusto and with excellent mimicry — plausible marshal, timid judge, complacent Kames, arrogant Patterson, baited Salt and the berserk sheriff. As he told of the system of checks and balances devised for the better guidance of Dave Salt, Hawkins paused for meditation. A look of wonderment spread over his dark face.

"That's odd too," he said. "What an outlaw needs in his pardners is just what an honest man wants in his, no more and no less. J'ever think of that? They both want a man they can depend on, come hell or high water. Cowards, traitors, jellyfish — God hates 'em and the devil won't have 'em. This Dave Salt and his likes ain't worth a damn a dozen!"

The story was ended at last, and once more Frank John spoke out of turn, having much yet to learn : "Splendid! And now you can send the whole bunch to the pen."

"Who? Me?" said 'Enry 'Awkins, touching his own chest with an astonished forefinger. "Me, a stranger; my word against Law and Order in person? Me, in a witness box, ownin' up to shameless eaves-droppin'? I guess not. We don't tell nothin' to nobody."

"You set an ambuscade then? Take them in the act?" cried Frank John eagerly; and, in the painful silence that ensued, became aware that he had sinned greatly. It was a bad moment for the boy. Dating from that small point, Frank John began a chastened and unquestioning career.

"And catch Dave Salt, with his own pals shooting him up like a cullender? Damn likely. That's what the dirty dogs planned. If anybody happened to catch on to Dave and go to foggin' him, his own crowd would shoot him down themselves and be in the clear. 'Works like a watch,' says that lousy lawyer, braggin' and boastin', swelled up like a frog in a churn. Well, just because Mr. Kames thought he was smart enough to make his layout foolproof, hog-tight, bull-strong and horse-high, we'll let him pull his play. Then we'll pull ours, like I'm going to tell you; and we make high, low, Jick, Jack, Jill, Jenny and the game card."

"Give us your powders," said Pres.

They crowded around the little table. Slowly, painstakingly, with keenest foresight, Hawkins gave them their powders. Discussion followed — substitutions, elaboration, strengthening. Dawn sparkled in the east when Hawkins went tiptoe through the hall, bearing his boots and a blanket from his bed. He slipped softly up a half-forgotten stairway in the trunk room at the rear, opened a rusted door, and so came to the long-deserted roof of Lindauer Place — a roof that had once been Fort Lindauer, and famed.

Behind him Johnny Pardee drew a long face. "And me with a game leg," he groaned. "Ain't that luck for you?" Then he brightened perceptibly. "Say, Pres! Gayly the Troubadour, he's just about taken over your job as First Assistant Providence, hasn't he?"

"Who? 'Enry? My son, 'Enry is a great medicine man. He has covered every possible chance, I think. And now to bed, the bilin' of us. It's half-past four this very now. I'm leaving word with the desk to wake us at eight. This will be one long, hard day for all and sundry."

But Pres was mistaken. 'Enry had left at least one chance uncovered. To be Assistant Providence is not a desirable job.

'Enry woke shortly after sunrise, strove with all diligence to sleep again — and failed, much to his disgust. He sought to peer through the loopholes where once long rifles had beaten off Apache bands. He found two of every three given up to birds' nests, old or new; so quickly fades the glory of this world. Crouched and cautious, he made his rounds, peering out to the four corners of the world. Smoke curled from a hundred chimneys, dogs ran upon pressing errands, jaunty horsemen went to and fro, wagons were astir, a baby crowded from a window to see a man bareheaded below, who swung a lusty ax at the woodpile. He watched a breakfasting through near-by windows, a kiss snatched at a door. He saw, beyond the plaza, the night operator bringing in the switch lights, section hands trudging to meet the hour of seven, a grumbling engine at the water tank. He saw the B 4 herd, grazing fanwise from the bed ground. And upon every side, in town and out of it, in the sandy streets, on the low sandy slopes, by barrow pit or roadside, stray beer bottles sparkled in the low sun.

The Holland House gong called loud in air, but ham and eggs with hot coffee were not for 'Enry — doomed by a hard fate to be twenty miles away with an ill-gotten cavvyard of horses. After tedious eternities, private Pres came discreetly to the roof, shortly after eight, with smuggled sandwiches. He took back 'Enry's blankets, lest an ovezealous chambermaid should remark upon their absence. The next eternity was shorter; and at long last, barely three minutes before nine by 'Enry's watch, Herman Lindauer came puffing up the steep stairs, with protesting brows in an astonished face. On his heels came Johnny Pardee.

"Sh-h! Keep your head down and your voice down," said 'Enry.

"What is this?" said Lindauer, whose English was excellent except in stress and agitation. "Pres Lewis says I must come with Johnny, that it is all right, that I must not disobey you the slightest. And what Pres Lewis says I do, every time, you betcha! But what goes on?"

"Look at the roof of that house across the alley from Nash's place," said Johnny. "Aurelio Sais is there with a double-barreled shotgun loaded with buckshot. That house belongs to some of Aurelio's *gente*. He is to stick his head up for you to see, just as the clock strikes nine; so you'll know he's in on the play. Aurelio, he's one of the best."

"Keep your head down, Mr. Lindauer — look through that little loophole," urged Hawkins. . . . "No, this one here. It slopes the right way for you to see Aurelio. Don't look over the wall, whatever happens. If we're seen everything is ruined."

Aurelio Sais popped up a flame-red head for brief inspection. "I see him," said Lindauer. 'Enry's hand made a brisk arc above the wall, an arc invisible from the street. Aurelio vanished. "You I don't know," said Lindauer, "but Pres and Aurelio, with my life I trust them. . . . Why, who is that?"

A swift clatter of unseen feet below; a horse came partly into his field of vision, gathering speed, a smoke-colored horse, a rider in faded blue, a large man with a flop-brimmed black hat. A half horse and a half man; more he could not see, because of his angled loophole, until they whirled into the alley. The rider hurled a meal sack through the open door and thundered up the alley.

"Watch now!" said Johnny. "He'll ride in the open door of Humphries old stable. See him? I'm not looking through no porthole, so you may know we savvy what's going on. We're wise to the whole thing." A shout came from the street in front, another answered. There was a swift tumult, the sound of running feet. "Look down now. You'll see the sheriff looking up the alley in ten or twelve seconds — coming from the right, just too late to see which way the robber went. See him?"

"That robber was made up to look like me, you know," said 'Enry. "That's why you're here — so I can help you get your money back — me and Aurelio. Aurelio's not to show up."

"The sheriff, I see him, pointing up the alley — waving, shouting," wheezed Lindauer. "Robber? A conspiracy, what? The bank?"

"Yes — and the sheriff is in on it — Yewell — Patterson — others. Hold on to yourself. You don't lose a cent, and a new day comes to Target — " A roar of indistinguishable voices, thunder of frenzied feet, a howling mob about the sheriff, frantic, gesticulating.

"But, Johnny — if you knew beforehand? Why, then?"

"Your money is now in Nash's safe, and in no more danger than when it was in your own. Less. Nash is in the gang, and he is to keep the money till the dust blows over. You get every cent back an hour from now, or as soon as the posse gets started. When that money comes out of that safe you'll be the man that takes it out. Then we get them piecemeal, separated. There's the man to thank — Hawkins. He brought the whole rotten mess to light. Everything provided for. Good men to watch Nash's front door — Munro and Tolson. Aurelio guards the back."

"What's that they're calling?" said Lindauer, trembling. His face went red and white.

"They're yellin' 'Bill Doolin,'" answered Johnny contemptuously. "They planned to blame it on him. It wasn't Doolin robbed your bank. It was your friends and neighbors. Yes, and your own directors, some of them. Well, go down and keep a stiff upper lip. All you have to do is not to tell any living soul one word of what we told you. Look as if you was scared! Try to make it natural. That's it — that's good. You got a right to look scared. Just help to get the posse started, quick as you can. Hurry, now; you're overdue."

A dervish whirl of hubbub, confusion and madness in the street below, till the sheriff leaped into a wagon and his bull voice bellowed above the tumult:

"Keep still, everybody! Shut up, I say! Stop it, you fools! . . . Gray, we want every horse and saddle in your corral, no matter who they belong to. . . . Yewell, you line up all the riding men and have them dig up rifles — them that has 'em. . . . Patterson, you see that they're mounted — those that haven't horses of their own. . . . Lindauer, see that everybody has arms and ammunition and canteens. . . . Holl, put up everything in the shop for lunches. . . . Lewis, you run down to the other restaurants, and commandeer all they got cooked, and tell 'em to keep on cooking till we leave. . . . Hollocher, go to Troy Ware's house and tell him to bring all his men that's in town. . . . Kames, you're no good on a horse. You and the judge take charge here while we're gone. I'll want you to send some wires for me — tell you presently. And you two read all telegrams that come for me, and send messengers after us if necessary. . . . Now, judge, what was that you was trying to tell us? You saw him? Where?"

"I saw somebody who might or might not have been the robber," said the judge modestly. "Going north like hell in a hand basket. Dave and Bart was both with me, but I don't know whether they saw him or not. I thought nothing of it at the time, of course. Not till we heard the yelling down here."

"That's him, I guess," said the sheriff. "Where's Aurelio Sais and Munro? Find 'em, somebody. Tolson too. We want every fighting man in town." He turned to Farr, his forgotten prisoner, who sat tranquilly on the curb and smoked a peaceful pipe, swinging a foot in careless happiness. "Farr, that lets you in. Lets you out, rather." He chuckled at his own joke.

Farr removed his pipe and twisted his head back to look. "I guess not," he said indignantly. "Drunk and disorderly. Ten and ten. I pay no fine; so you can make it twenty. Who'll make it forty? Do I hear forty? It is going to be main hot today. . . . Glad I'm not out on the blisterin' flat."

"Drop it, you old fool. You're on my posse."

"I demand my rights as an American citizen," said Farr stubbornly. "I was drunk as a lord, and quarrelsome. By all good rights I ought to be in jail all the rest of this month, anyway. Fine business this is. Put you in jail for carrying a gun; yank you out of jail illegally, and force you to pack a gun about none of your business, and get shot all to hell! I guess not!"

"Stop this clowning, you crazy fool. You're losing priceless time for me. You have to serve on a posse when summoned."

"And if I don't you can punish me, eh?" said Farr severely. "Send me to jail? All right, here I am. Do you expect me to take myself down and lock myself up?"

Farr made this play from his own inexhaustible stock of deviltry. He was as yet quite uninformed as to the league of knaves and their private purposes. A leaguer now interfered. This did not suit their book at all. They wanted Slim Jack Elmer on that posse.

"Oh, Jack, shut up!" said Johnny Pardee. "A joke's a joke. Quit it! You're delayin' the posse, just as the sheriff says. Of course you're goin'. That was Bill Doolin that robbed this bank, and you don't want him to get away with a play like that. We'll be a laughingstock."

More he might have said, but here, at last, he caught the prisoner's eye. Farr got that urgent message, literally, 'in the bat of an eye,' as the saying goes.

"Doolin, eh?" said Farr, with wakening interest. "That's different. I supposed all the time it was Albert Garst. I'd sure hate to shoot Albert."

"Double-damned fool!" growled the sheriff. "All the same, I'd not be sorry to have old Elmer Farr at my back, if I was to meet up with Bill Doolin."

"You've insulted me, Steve Davis," said Farr. "Your posse will split up and I'm not going with you. I'm going to be at Jim Yewell's back!" His face brightened with that thought. He rose to go, and sidled toward Yewell with a spreading and golden smile.

Yewell looked most unhappy at this suggestion. But Pres Lewis laughed loud and long, and slapped the marshal on the back. "He's pulling your leg, Jim! He needs one drink to settle his tummy, and then he'll feel a heap better. You take me and Erie and Farr with you and we'll do our damnedest to get Doolin; just us four."

"Doolin, hell!" said the sheriff. "Where's that man Hawkins? I believe it was Hawkins? I saw him. He looked like Hawkins; he wore a black hat, and his horse looked just like the Hawkins horse."

"That's so. Where is Hawkins?" said Lewis, and his face fell at the unwelcome thought. "I haven't seen him either, come to think of it. Now what do you think about that? Oh, blast the luck!"

"Lon Gray says Hawkins got his horse and beat it between twelve and one," said the saloon keeper.

"Shucks!" said the marshal. "I bet that's who done it. And here I was banking on a split in that reward money for Doolin! Never mind; our bank will pay handsome for Hawkins, and we'll get him or bust a tug."

"They will, if we get the money when we get Hawkins," declared Erie Patterson soberly. "But if he's managed to get rid of it some way, gentlemen, our bank is busted flat! Leastwise, all except what me and other unlucky guys has borrowed of 'em. I bet they wish now they had loaned us more. I wanted them to do that, too — but they turned me down. Say, Lewis — Where's Lewis gone to, all of a sudden?"

Lewis had gone to Gray's corral, all of a sudden. A horrible and unforeseen thought had arisen before him. These people noticed brands. They would see the new B 4 horse he had brought up in the dead watches of the night. Questioned, Lon Gray would tell of that late coming; attention called, some would remember the Hawkins saddle — and then the fat would be in the fire for a fact! Fortunately Lon Gray was an old friend, and it is an untouchable and priceless privilege of integrity that it may do the questionable, unquestioned and unhindered. Sweating profusely, Lewis contrived to speak apart with Lon Gray. That B 4 horse and saddle must be hidden away when the unmounted came for the commandeered horses. Right as rain, said Lon Gray, and would Pres go peddle his papers, and stew no more about that horse?

Messengers rode headlong to warn the Packsaddle, Cline, Carberry, Cat Knapp and the south. Telegrams went forth to rouse up east and west against the bandit; a wire went to Argentine to organize and move east behind the mountains to join Troy Ware's men on the Gato. The posse was organized with surprising swiftness, ready and waiting before Troy Ware and his retainers had arrived from Ware's town house to join them. Even then, three good men were not to be found — Aurelio Sais, Munro, Tolson. The sheriff would wait no longer, and departed, cursing those three by name. The posse rode north together, a goodly cavalcade, planning inquiry as to any glimpse of the fugitive at the Carmody herd before they separated to comb the country.

As prearranged, Lindauer came to the stairway, shortly after the posse had fairly started, and summoned the watcher to come down. But Hawkins called to the banker to come up on the roof instead, and waited there, despite Lindauer's fuming impatience, until he saw the posse gather around the B 4 wagon, linger there for a space, and then ride on — to separate beyond into three parties, spreading fanwise, north, northeast and nearly east. He noted with keen satisfaction that the smallest body rode northeast toward Staircase — five men, his sharp eyes assured him. Common sense had told them that the Ladder men would go east to search the Ladder range; that the largest body of men would go to comb the enormous bulk of San Lorenzo; that Troy Ware's men would go that way into their own country, passing beyond in due time to their northern range on the Feliz; that the sheriff would head them, the sooner to get in touch with the contingent which would be starting from Argentine. It was logical to suppose that the Staircase party would be headed by the marshal; that Pres, as a Staircase man familiar with the country, would be a second; that Farr, in accordance with his expressed determination, his recent wordy altercation with the sheriff, and the known bad feeling between himself and the Ladders, would make a third. It was 'Enry's hope that the marshal's distrust and fear of Farr, together with the influence of Lewis, would determine that Erie Patterson would be the fourth. This was probable; Lewis was a known man, his word listened to. Such a decision was the more likely, since the Ladders would pick up their foreman for leader — Curly Parker, a tried fighting man — and since Erie was next friend and crony to the marshal. As to the fifth, that was sure to be none other than Frank John, the disciple. Hawkins was a little surprised that one or two others had not been detailed with this party, but ascribed it to good management by Pres Lewis.

He came downstairs, highly elated. But he made a further delay in the dining room — chaperoned and vouched for by the banker — to absorb one steaming cup of coffee; which same he had sadly missed. They were joined there by Johnny Pardee, excused from active service for cause. Lindauer strictly enjoined the dining room to absolute silence as to Hawkins — whereat the dining room, in one collective bound, leaped nimbly to the not-unnatural conclusion that Hawkins was a secret-service man in the banker's employ — a luckless detective, since this robbing had been pulled off while he had been on other affairs. Guarding against another robbery of freight cars, the dining room rather thought, and so expressed itself, sagely enough, to kitchen and office. However, the hotel kept honorable silence as toward outsiders.

The streets were deserted, the remaining buzzers now buzzing in the saloon. So Lindauer, Hawkins and Johnny passed unnoticed into the street on their way to recover the stolen money and bear it back to its own proper home.

CHAPTER X

Mr. Ellis Kames sauntered across the Plaza from the freight depot, and idly flipped with a slender cane at pebbles in the path. Two small Mexican urchins played at marbles in that smoothly beaten path. They rose on their knees to yield the right of way. But Mr. Kames waved his hand airily and stepped aside, leaning on his cane to watch the game with smiling indulgence. From time to time he glanced about him, beaming upon the world with vague benevolence. A puff of smoke feathered and grew over the False Divide. Mr. Kames smiled. That was the Westbound Limited, toiling over Misery. That train was a short half hour away, was due to leave Target at ten-thirty-five. He took out a small penknife with a handle of glistening pearl, delicately cut the tip from the most crooked of all corkscrew cheroots, lit it, puffed with a cheerful satisfaction that was pleasant to see, glanced again at that low smoke in the east, flourished his cane in amiable salute to the marble players, and took up his loitering way.

The cane went gently tip-tap up the steps to the prosperous establishment of Nash for Cash. Mr. Kames turned in here. One customer stood at the counter. Kames waited idly until her small wants were filled; scanning the well-stocked shelves so absently that he didn't remark the customer's departure.

"Yes, Mr. Kames?" said the clerk at last.

"Ah, Walter," said Kames, recalling his vagrant thoughts with an effort. "Oh, yes! Mr. Nash is in the private office, I presume?" The cane lifted.

"Yes, sir. Shall I announce you, sir?"

"Oh, no, it is an appointment. Er — Walter, please do not let anyone disturb us."

"I will see to it, sir."

Kames glanced around the empty store, smiling faintly. "I see that your fellow clerk — Churchill, is it? — was a member of the posse."

"Yes, sir. Mr. Nash said he could spare one of us. And so," said Walter, blushing, "we tossed up a coin, and Churchill won."

"Ah, youth, youth!" said Kames, smiling, with half a sigh. "A sad blow to the community, this robbery." He passed on languidly and opened the office door.

Nash jumped in his chair and rose with a flushed face. Kames smiled again, and seated himself, half standing, on the corner of Nash's low desk. "My dear fellow," said Kames pleasantly, "you must learn to control your nerves. You are quite on edge."

"You startled me."

"Tut, tut, Charles! You invite suspicion. Sit down — sit down. Take it easy. My dear man, pattern yourself upon me. You have no cause for alarm. You were never safer in your life. Our little stroke of business went off smoothly, and not one of us will ever know the touch of suspicion. But you are sadly upset. I feared this. That was why I dropped in — to quiet you, if needed, and get you back to normal. Brace yourself, Charles. You do not take enough exercise, I fear. You should walk abroad in the cool of the day. Better still, you should have a saddle horse. I would strongly advise you to ride."

"Perhaps I will."

"Begin this very afternoon," urged Kames warmly. "That's good advice. But perhaps it will be difficult to get a saddle horse today. Because of our late misfortune, the riding men and the fighting men are all gone." He opened his watch, glanced at it, and slid from the desk to his feet as he returned the watch to his pocket. With the same movement a revolver shone in his hand, making a double click as he thrust the muzzle against Nash's ear. "That is the reason, my dear Charles, that you must open your safe," said Kames kindly. "The fighting men have all gone north, and I am going south."

His dear Charles will never be so white in his coffin as he was in that evil dream. "Ellis! For God's sake!"

"Not at all," said Ellis. "For my sake entirely. I had always contemplated this, as a possibility. When Lindauer's cashier told him that our haul was even larger than our highest hopes, I knew the time had come for a bold stroke. I trust, for your own sake — "

"Ellis! You wouldn't kill me?"

"If you think not, raise your voice," said Kames savagely. "If you think not, hesitate. Make one second's delay. Move, Nash! Your life hangs on a hair!"

Nash went to the safe, stumbling, all but falling. He groped at the combination, he swung the great door open.

"Pass that valise out," said Kames. Nash obeyed. Kames shoved it back with his foot. "Put your right hand behind you. I'll not have you shooting at me as I leave. Quick, man! Death is at your shoulder!"

Nash thrust his arm back; a handcuff snapped on his wrist. "Now your left hand behind you. Clear around!"

But as the left hand came back, Kames snapped the empty cuff on the shank of the long handle of the safe door. Instantly, a second handcuff gripped Nash's left wrist. Kames jerked the loose end back and shackled it, as he had done with the first, on the handle of the safe. He thrust the revolver into a scabbard under his long coat, so that it hung at his left side, butt forward, just in front of the hip socket. He stepped back and picked up the brown valise.

"You can always explain, Charles — in case you should choose to give the alarm. Good-bye!"

Nash fell to his knees as he realized his awful situation. "They'll kill me," he whispered with bloodless lips.

"It will be your part to be gone," said Kames. "I advised riding, you remember." He threw open the back door and stepped out into the alley.

Shooting his eyes to right and left, he made for the street. The first two steps were hasty, almost a run. The man was not iron. But with the third step he began to slow down, meaning the next step to fall into the casual, unhurried walk of a mind at peace. He heard a slight noise above him and glanced up.

Aurelio Sais looked over the parapet of the house across the alley, holding a double-barreled shotgun upon him. The muzzle was not ten feet from his head. "Keep your eyes like that," said Aurelio without heat or hurry. "If you look down — if your hands move ever so slightly — that will be all. You are holding the little bag in your right hand. Hold it — oh, so still! That is not wise for a man in such busi-

ness. You should always keep the gun hand free. I saw the whole
play through the window, Mr. Kames. I am surprised at you. To rob
is not well, but to break the faith — oh, that is shameless! Think, I beg
you, how that unlucky Nash now hears you and sees you — and with
how much joy." His steady eye looked down the barrels without
moving, but his voice rose to a great shout:

"Ho-o-o! Hawkins! Munro! Johnny Pardee! *A mi!*"

On their way to the Nash store, Lindauer, Hawkins and Pardee
were midstreet as that wild cry rang out. Hawkins went then to war.
It is not too much to say that he removed himself from that place.
When Lindauer and the lame Pardee reached the entrance to the alley,
Hawkins had already searched Kames for weapons. The brown valise
was at his feet, with the Kames revolver beside it; his rifle covered the
double traitor. Aurelio laughed down from his wall.

"Johnny," said Hawkins, a little breathlessly, "will you take this
rifle? I am close to pulling the trigger, and that is what I do not want
to do." He kicked the brown bag viciously. The unshaken man was
shaken now, color came and went in his dark face. "If this play had
gone wrong — and me thinking I was so smart! Never again do I peer
into the future. Things happen that you don't expect — like this."

"'Enry," said Johnny Pardee, "I am beginning to think that Ellis
Kames is not reliable. That's what fooled you. Kames ain't dependable."

"I will come down now," said Aurelio. "I observed through the window. He was most unhappy, that Nash, for he must account for that
money to his friends, it seems. That *pobrecito!* And now he hears
us and is curious as to his future. But if Nash is terrified, this man is
crushed and broken. Look, all this time he has not said one word."

It was true. The cunning man was voiceless now, his crooked
tongue had failed him; his face was the face of a fiend. A train whistle
came to his ears; the westbound was coming into Target. Kames
trembled at the sound. Aurelio joined them as they listened.

"Think!" said Hawkins in a great voice. "If this clever Kames
had gone quietly out the front way, stopping at the counter to have
his valise wrapped and tied, he might have walked over to the train
and made a clean getaway." He drew out his knife, he slashed the
bag across; he spread the gash apart and looked in. "That's the money,
all right. I was beginning to be afraid Nash had switched the bag on
Kames. I'm losing faith in everybody. . . . Take it, Lindauer; I'll not
draw a long breath till it's back in the safe. I was near losing it for
you. I had the brilliant idea to throw a gun down on the cashier and
make him put it back in the safe. That's all off now. I want it to go

back, and do it quick. Aurelio, are any of your folks in there?"

"Not one. My *tío*, he is old. And I sent him away, not knowing what might happen here."

"That's good. Johnny, do you think you can take this shotgun and hold Mr. Kames in Aurelio's house till Aurelio and I come for him?"

"I can try," said Johnny. "At least I'll make a reasonable effort to hold him. But if he gets away after I give him both barrels, I can't help it. He'll just have to go. I can't run."

"This play simplifies matters," said Hawkins. "We will have a little more to do. Then Aurelio and I will take Mr. Kames off your hands. We won't let word get out, and if we possibly can, we'll get him out of town without attracting any attention."

"Why not?" said Aurelio. "There are few left to see. The railroad men have their own troubles. And if anyone notes us, what is there to see? Three friends, riding out together. No more than that. We can make it a point with Mr. Kames that he shall go quietly. Besides, what can he say? What can he ever say? Take him in, Johnny."

"Oh, Mr. Hollocher," said Lindauer, to his distracted cashier, when the three friends had arrived safely in the bank, "here is that money that was taken a while ago." He shoved the violated valise through the wicket.

The cashier plunged trembling hands into the bills and lifted them. "But — but — " he gurgled, with bulging eyes fixed upon Hawkins.

Lindauer laid an affectionate hand upon the suspect's shoulder. "It was not Mr. Hawkins," he said, laughing. "The robber was dressed like him, purposely, so that Hawkins should have the blame. Max, that this bank is not ruined, we owe it to many brave friends, but most of all to this good friend here. And this town, Max, from now on it will be a fit place to live in. And we shall owe it to Mr. Hawkins."

"Shucks!" said Mr. Hawkins, embarrassed. "Mr. Max, you want to check up that money. It may not be all there. For all we know, Dave Salt got a chance to shovel a handful of it down in his pants. I wouldn't put it past him." He turned to Lindauer. "You spoke of thanking me. If you mean it, let me work this thing out my own way. You could send a few to the pen — Salt and Nash and Kames for sure. For the others, you'd only have my word. Even so, what I know covers only a small part of the gang. Your town is rotten with crooks, all working together. I don't want to send any man to the pen. And I particularly want to manage so that no one gets killed this trip. But if you'll not let it be known for twenty-four hours that you got your money back — if you won't say a word about Kames — in fact, if you won't say nothing to nobody about anything — you leave it to me and I'll throw such a scare into this burg that the last and least will think the devil is clawing at his elbow. You'll not need to clean up. Them that stays in Target will sure have a clean conscience."

"It is a go," said Lindauer. . . . "You hear, Max? . . . You hear, Aurelio?"

"That ain't all, either," said Hawkins. "They won't get together again, somewhere else, and do it all over. Somebody tipped the mitt and they'll suspect everybody. If two of these men ever meet in California, one will head for Australia and the other for the North Pole. But I'll have to be boss till sundown today. Is it a go?"

"Surely. But you will not find the bank ungrateful."

"That's good. You can give me a box of ca'tridges, then, and collect from the bank. . . . Come on, Mr. Lindauer; you and me and Aurelio have got a couple of short visits to make. Then me and Aurelio'll buy us a small snack of dinner — after which the two of us will take Mr. Kames and proceed to bring the fear of God to Gridiron. We'll want a horse for Kames. Here, let's take Aurelio visiting with us."

"I declare," said Lindauer, in the street, "it seems like Sunday, don't it?"

"It does so. Nobody seen us since I come alive, not even when Aurelio was yelling bloody murder. They're all talking it up, in the saloon."

They visited the Nash store first. The office door was shut, and customers went about the store. Walter, the clerk, was busy and cheerful. It was evident that Nash had not seen fit to give the alarm. In his private mind, Mr. Hawkins felt confident that Nash was now on his travels; a guess that lacked something to fit the fact. Nash had seen Kames taken, had heard every word spoken in the alley. He knew that his own guilt was established beyond question, and his only hope was for mercy; and he now awaited the next turn of the wheel with what patience he could muster, not uncomforted by recent events in the alley.

It was Hawkins who opened the office door. His jaw dropped when he saw that Nash was shackled to his own safe. He pointed, voiceless; color swept his face as he turned to Lindauer and Aurelio.

"I told him this morning not to do that!" said Hawkins, and bit his lip with vexation. "Here I preached up as far as fourthly to you fellows, over in the bank, just to give Nash time to make his get-away — and behold you, he hasn't budged."

Nash turned imploring eyes on the banker. "You'll help me get loose, Hermie?" he faltered. "For the sake of old times?"

But Lindauer, whose contempt had wasted no word on Kames, flamed now to anger. His friendship with Nash was a thing long past, but he felt betrayed. He spread out his hands.

"How are we to know you wanted loose? It is your place and you might run it to suit yourself. If you choose to make such arrangements, why should I interfere? If you want loose you should attend to it. Nobody will stop you. I'll sell your clerk a file for cash. I bid you good day."

"But, Hermie, we are making one big mistake," said Aurelio when they reached the street once more.

"Yes. We should send these thugs to the pen for life," said Hermie, wiping his wrist across his brow.

"Not that. If all was known that I know," said Aurelio, "one who would now be serving time would be Aurelio Sais. I know just how Mr. Hawkins feels. Also, his way will be best for us. Only the leaders were concerned in robbing your bank. If we send them up, the main army would still be with us. The other way, fear will be at their backs. Fear of the unknown. The Gridiron gang is a smashed egg, and all the king's horses and all the king's men can never get it together again. But that was not what I meant. Hawkins is supposed to have been Bill Doolin, and to have robbed your bank — and it is only good luck that somebody has not taken a shot at him already. Don't you think it would be pleasant if you would go over to the Jim Gem saloon and make oration? You don't have to explain. Tell them that it was impossible for Hawkins to have robbed your bank, because he was closeted with you at the time of the robbery."

"Sure! We have been taking chances." He started to go, but the Mexican caught at his sleeve. "Another thing, amigo. You're overlooking one bet." Aurelio's speech was cold and precise as a usual thing, smacking of the schools. But now, in his anxiety not to give offense to his friend, he became almost colloquial. "You want to clean up Target, Hermie? Well, there is one thing you can do that will be a big help. Make your store larger — or your hotel. The Holland House hasn't near enough bedrooms. Why don't you make your saloon into bedrooms?"

"But — but it is not my saloon. I just rent it to Jim," said Lindauer, flushing. "The guests want their liquor, and my customers in the store. I like a little drink myself."

"I like a little drink, too. That's not the question. Jim's Gem makes the headquarters of crime under your roof. Kick him out. He can find other places. You know very well that when you want to hire a man to shoot someone in the back, you never mention the matter to a man that's working. You go straight to the saloon. Don't you?"

"Always. I remember now," admitted Lindauer fretfully. He flapped his hands wingwise. "All righd, all righd — don't sing no hymns! Have it your own way. I make me a fine big hotel and lose money by it." He turned back to Lindauer Place, grumbling and muttering, still winging his way.

Judge Humphries was slipping a pan of sour-dough biscuit into the oven when Aurelio knocked. He came to the door wiping his hands, a smile of welcome spreading to greet Aurelio; a smile which became fixed and frozen as he saw who stood beyond.

Hawkins sniffed. "Lord 'a' mercy, is that wool I smell burning? Judge, have you went and burned up that old black hat? Why, you old skeesicks, I wanted that hat for Exhibit A. . . . Never mind, I'll use this one of mine. The grateful bank will just nicely have to buy me a new one, 'cause I need this for a special purpose, and my money is low, and I'm taking the road right sho'tly. . . . Judge, I'm taking that old saddle and bridle, out behind. Kames wants it. Be around and get it after a bit. Good-bye, Judge! C'mon, 'Relio. Don't you see the judge wants to think it over?"

A modest sign upon the wall near the judge's front door caught his eye. It was this notice to the world:

FRANCIS TRUESDALE HUMPHRIES

Justice of the Peace

Notary Public

Land Laws

Location Notices

Blanks of All Kinds

Hawkins paused and considered this sign long and earnestly. "You got a pencil, Aurelio?" he said at last. "Well, wish you'd write a little note on this sign for me."

"Ready," said Aurelio, and wrote there as dictated:

Gone to Europe. May not be back till sundown.

CHAPTER XI

WHEN THE TIME came for the posse to split and fan, there was argument, even as foreseen by Hawkins on the housetop. Marshal Yewell did not want Farr, and said as much with point and vigor; while Farr would hear of no other decision. Also, Erie Patterson inclined strongly to go with his own men. It required all the firmness and persuasion that Lewis could bring to bear to make the arrangement according to his wish. Once over the hill to Staircase, he pointed out, the marshal could pick up more men. As to old Elmer, he was only exercising a perverse and misbegotten sense of humor. Elmer would be a good man in a pinch. He asked Erie to recall that cowboys had never functioned for two masters, and never would. They would work for the foreman or they would work for the owner, but the world never went well when both were on the job.

"You side us, Erie, and let Curly rod your peelers," said the jovial Lewis. "You can help to keep an eye on old Elmer, so the marshal's nerves can sorter quiet down."

Moreover, as to the aid of Frank John, the marshal showed a singular lack of enthusiasm; shrugging his wide shoulders and wrinkling his aristocratic Roman nose. Thus in disfavor, Farr and Frank John tagged along in the blistering heat, far behind to escape the dust; and to my first, my second imparted much information about my third, fourth and fifth; in fact, about Gridiron as a whole, with a spirited résumé of all that Farr had missed during his brief imprisonment.

They rode swiftly. That is to say — in order that there shall be no misunderstanding in this matter — the trot they used for distance was a long, steady, reaching trot. They stood up in their stirrups, leaning forward, steady on the bit. This forced-draft gait was good for six miles an hour; which means many miles from sun to sun, as may be verified with pencil and paper if you are of a mathematical turn. Or, it may be verified by riding. In the latter case you will observe that the long, hard trot will take you, in the time mentioned, just twice as far as the same horse can carry you at the gay gallop — with the further advantage that you would still have a live horse the next morning. It was expressly provided in the Treaty of Guadalupe-Hidalgo that no posse should gallop except when the fugitive was actually visible, and then only when the prisoner was not only in sight, but also out of gunshot. It is believed that moving pictures have changed all this. But they have never told the horses.

Eighteen miles brought them to one o'clock and the foothills. Erie spoke of the good lunch at his saddle horn, and the marshal spoke of Gib Newell's ranch at Clingstone, just over the divide and eight miles farther on — not trotting miles but climbing miles. Once more Lewis overruled them:

"Up that second little side canyon on the left-hand side, just beyond the second bend, is a place we ought to look," said he. "The old Red Sleeve mine. Natural hide-out, little spring, lookout and back stairs — everything. Place where a man could hide a year and never be found. Many's the time I've thought about it, studyin' what I'd do if I had spunk enough. Why not go make a look-see there? If we

don't find no trace of our bold bandit, we can eat our lunch and then
toddle along up to Clingstone."

"Red Sleeve?" echoed Erie. "Why, I thought that was the old
Mangas Mine."

"Same thing. Red Sleeve is Mangas Colorado in English. Low-
grade copper. No good. Bless my soul and body! Near twenty years
since I was up there, workin' for Bige Witherspoon. Man, that's a
long time ago! Grant was President, the Frenchies was fighting Bis-
marck, and I had a girl in Santa Rita, 'n' one night, as I was comin'
home, I stumbled over a star. This was a fine country then."

Avoiding discussion, he waved his hand to hurry up the laggards,
and turned from the road. His mind thus made up, the marshal soon
took the lead, quite unsuspicious of the fact that his ways were gently
guided. The rear guard closed up briskly and rejoined the others at
the first bend of the canyon.

There was a short box, then another sharp bend. The canyon
opened to a natural amphitheater, gracious and wide, parked with
spicy cedar and spicy juniper. Beyond was a low, rolling divide,
wavy and meandering, topped on the very crest by a spiny dike;
like nothing so much as the woodcuts of the Chinese wall in the back
of the geography book. And in that dike there was a gap, and in that
gap there was a house, sagging and weather-gray; and near that house
there sprawled an old mining dump, melting into the hill, reclaimed
now by grass and wild poppies and firefly bush; and on that dump
there was a windlass; exactly like a riddle.

The answer was soon found. There was no track of horse or man;
the ghastly house was a skull, with eyeless sockets where windows had
been, and an open door between; bleached and gray, the windlass
posts stood out against the sky line, spectral and startling. Unurged,
curious, the marshal led the way, sidelong against the slope. Patterson was next. Because, no man has lived who could resist the impulse
to look down a well or a shaft. It is compulsory.

Lewis and Farr pulled their rifles from the scabbards. Frank John
wished that he hadn't come and was glad he did. The leaders left their
horses at the edge of the dump and went directly to the shaft, without
once looking back. Long planks covered it, with boulders to hold
them down. They rolled away the smallest boulder, levered the plank
aside and knelt to peer down the shaft. Lewis made a long arm and
jerked Yewell's gun from the scabbard at his hip. Farr would have
done as much for Patterson. But Erie Patterson heard, or saw, or
sensed — himself could not tell you how. With an inch to spare, with
half a fraction of some small part of a second, his body dived forward
from that crouching position on hands and knees, lunged like a sword

thrust, twisting in the air as he plunged. He fell on his back across the planking, his clutching hand all but touching his gun, but with the gun partly under him as he had fallen. He held his hand there, unmoving, and looked up with steady, unfearing eyes.

"I'll never rot in the pen!" said Erie Patterson. "You'll get me, of course. But when one foot moves this way I go for my gun."

Farr's rifle covered him, Farr's foot was almost touching his, but the clear eyes did not waver, and there was no shadow in them. The man was beautiful. Lewis still held his rifle thwartwise in his left hand; his right hand held the marshal's revolver trained upon Patterson's ribs, all but touching them. The marshal made no observation. The marshal was sickly green and frozen where he knelt. Frank John was trying to breathe.

"You fool, I've got a bead on your gizzard!" cried Farr.

"And I've got my eye on your belt buckle," said Patterson, with an even voice. "It's a bad draw, but the longer you talk the better my chances. I hit my crazy bone when I did a flop. Nasty jar, but it's better now. And I've arched my hip enough to let my gun loose. Come on, I'm ready. I've lived free, and I'll die that way!"

"I get your point, Erie," said Pres approvingly. "But you're all wrong. Just hold your horses, will you? Nobody wants to put you in the pen."

"No, nor I won't hang, either," said Erie. There was no bravado in his defiance. "You can never bury me cheaper, and I'll take company with me. You may hang Erie Patterson's dead body, but you'll never hang me."

"Why, Erie!" said Farr. "Such an idea never entered my head."

"Liar!"

"I'm not moving till we get the news into your thick skull," said Farr patiently. "Don't you move, either. If I was to kill you, you might never get over it."

"Farr's telling you true," said Pres Lewis. "This isn't the law. This is a private enterprise — one of them Italian vendettas, like Troy Ware's got on his new house."

"I don't believe any such a thing. What have I ever done to you?"

"You don't understand, son. This here little feud has got nothing to do with the past. It's all in the future. You ain't never goin' to forgive me. I feel it in my bones. No, sir, in all the years to come, you're always goin' to feel a grudge against old Pres. And you can have long years to get even, if you'll just be reasonable and unbuckle that belt with your left hand, and then get up, right hand first, leaving your gun lay. Then we can talk it over. You're just so heady, we can't talk good while you've got that gun handy. If you had the brains God gives a grasshopper, you'd know that we never meant to kill you. If we did, why are you living along all over the shop?"

Patterson considered this at some length. "Oh, I believe that much of it," he conceded. "You don't want to kill me, but you want my gun. You don't get it. That gun stands between me and the pen."

"No such thing," said Farr. "I swan, Erie, I'm getting out of patience with you. You deserve the pen, of course. Who don't? But it was set down beforehand that nobody was to go to the pen this trip. And nobody to get killed, if it could be managed convenient."

"What are you driving at then, you speckle-faced maniac?"

"I don't rightly know all the ins and outs of it myself, me being in jail," said the maniac, pleasantly enough, but with a wary eye upon his opponent's gizzard. "It seems the Almighty sent His pussonal representative to look over this neck of the woods, near as I can make out. Sort of inspector like — and he has an idee you're the lost Charlie Ross. I think he is the Angel Gabriel, maybe, from all I hear. What he says goes, anyhow, just like he was the doctor. And from what Frank John tells me, back there in the dust, Gabe is a heap more tender-hearted than ever I gave him credit for. 'Gosh, I don't want nobody sent to no pen,' says Gabe. 'They might not be satisfied there. I know I wouldn't be.'"

"It wasn't Gabriel," said Pres. "It was Abijah K. Witherspoon. And what Farr says is true. The last words Bige said to me: 'Woodman, whatever you do,' he says, 'you spare that tree, if it's anyways possible.' And he ain't going to be any too well pleased, either, me setting your mind at ease, like this. His idea was that you'd be speculating and worrying about your past life, and how much of it had leaked out — and here I do believe you're planning along for the future right now. It's discouraging, that's what it is," said Lewis. "But Bige would have done the same, if he'd been here. He didn't know you had so much internal economy. How could he? Well, you never can tell till you try. But I'm real pleased with you, Erie. I am so. Now you be reasonable. Nobody's asking you to give up your gun. You just get up and go away and leave your gun where it is."

"Indeed, Mr. Patterson, I heard them agree that no one was to be imprisoned, or even arrested," said Frank John, speaking for the first time. "Word of honor," he added earnestly. "Why should a boy, a perfect stranger, lie to you, perjure himself about it?"

Patterson turned this idea over in his mind. "Huh! Something in that too. All right, then. My back itches, anyhow." He raised his right hand high, unbuckled his belt, and got up, holding to the windlass post; he rubbed his right elbow, gingerly. "That elbow's still tingling," he said. "That was hard luck, me doing that. Put me plumb out of business."

"There, Frank John; I told you we needed you," said Pres. "Nothing like a good old Maryland name to make a little party respectable. Erie didn't half believe us — but just a word from you, and everything was lovely. Now, Frank John, you pick up these extra guns and tote 'em over by the horses. If anybody starts to come that way, you flip a pebble at 'em. . . . Yewell, get up and stand over there by Erie, so Elmer can keep an eye on both of you." He began moving the boulders from the rotting planks. "Come to think of it, I camped here a spell, only last year, deer hunting. The windlass is over in the old house. We'll bring the windlass over and take our saddle ropes — "

"Like hell!" said Erie, and plunged over the steep dump. But Frank John started with him, two steps and a long jump, and landed on Patterson's shoulders while both were in the air. They rolled together in rolling stones and dust, they struggled to their knees at the foot of the dump, bruised, bleeding, breathless from the fall. Lewis was just behind; the two together grappled with this dauntless enemy and brought him down, struggling manfully, wordless. Farr herded the marshal to the horses, before his rifle, took down a saddle rope; he brought marshal and rope to the writhing huddle below; they bound Patterson hand and foot, helpless, but still defiant.

"Liar!" said Erie. His eyes were blazing.

"I shall expect a written apology for that before the week is out," replied Lewis, with great dignity. "Just as soon as you are safe on the bounding billow, you drop me a post card. But it's just as well. If you think, for a day or two, that you're going to the pen, that will be next best to actually going there. We are going to send down grub and water to you — with you, rather. Make you all nice and comfy. You can be thinking it over. You'll have lots of time. There's a short tunnel, running north from the bottom of the shaft. That's the place I was telling you about — where a man could hide. Shaft is a hundred feet deep, even. Ten assessment works. Three saddle ropes will just nicely make it. Come on, marshal. We'll let you down first. You stay here, Erie."

"You go to hell!" said Erie.

Taking Yewell with them, they brought the windlass from the deserted house, rigged it on the posts and turned it till the three saddle ropes were tied together and neatly wound to the end, leaving only a loop for the marshal's foot. Lewis brought from his saddle bags a folded newspaper and a candle. "I've thought of everything, Yewell," he said cheerfully. He lit the newspaper and dropped it down the shaft. "That's to test it out for foul air," he explained. "It burns all right, so that part is over. I'd hate to have you poisoned. And the candle, that's because rattlesnakes fall in sometimes, or skunks. That'll give you light to kill 'em by, if so be you find any. You take your canteens and lunch, this trip. Then we'll send Erie down to you and you can untie him." In spite of frantic prayers and entreaties, they forced Yewell to put foot and hand to the rope, and lowered away. Canteens and lunch were draped over his shoulders.

"I hope that rope don't break on you, Jim," said Farr kindly, as the marshal's head disappeared in the shaft. "Purty good rope, though. I guess it will hold you."

The calculation was exact. When the rope went slack only a yard remained on the windlass. "All right below?" said Lewis. "Take your foot out. Now you look for snakes while we get Erie."

The three of them carried Erie, who enlivened the short journey by his opinions, some of which were novel and unexpected. All were new to Frank John.

They tied the windlass rope to Erie's bonds securely. "Matches? Tobacco?" said Pres, patting Erie's pockets. "We can spare you another sack. . . . No? All right then. We got to send you down tied, Erie. If we didn't I do believe you'd let go, just out of spite. You suhtenly are the beatin'est man!"

Erie expressed his thanks for this compliment in suitable terms. They lowered away then. But when a few feet of rope had been paid out Pres stopped the windlass. "I declare, Erie, I forgot to ask you for the key to that valise!" he said. . . . "Elmer, we'll have to pull this bundle up again."

"Oh, we can cut the valise open," said Elmer. "I don't want to work this windlass all day. I want to eat. I'm all hot and flustered. . . . Frank John, you can be bringing the lunch and canteens over here."

The bundle made no reply, probably because its thoughts were running on keys and valises. They lowered it to the bottom and Yewell untied it from the windlass rope. They did not wind the windlass up this time, but pulled the rope up hand over hand, untied it and coiled it neatly to three blameless saddle ropes again.

Lewis sat with his legs hanging in the shaft, held a canteen between his legs, pulled the cork and gazed mildly at hill and sky. " 'It is a far, far better thing I do now than I have ever done before,' " he murmured mistily.

"Huh?" said Elmer. But Frank John, something overwrought and strained of spirit, strangled in his water drinking. He had not yet learned the management of a canteen.

They ate their lunch to the last crumb, dropping its wrappings into the shaft. Then Pres sighed comfortably, took out a plug of tobacco, turned it critically, this way and that, worried off a propitious corner, and gazed down at the spark of light that was the candle.

"Erie," he called down, "are you there?"

Erie indicated that he was there. Pres listened admiringly, and waited for a strategic moment.

"What do you want us to do with your horses?" Pres inquired, as Erie paused for breath. "And your guns?"

Erie told him what he might do with the horses and the guns. A drowsy silence followed. Elmer lit his pipe. Then Pres spoke to the shaft again:

"It's sure blazing hot up here, fellows. Reg'lar old scorcher. Thunder-heads peeping up above the hills. I betcha we're going to have a rain. If it does, you boys had better go in the tunnel, so's to keep dry."

The shaft made no answer.

"Erie, are you still down there? Anything we can send you out from town? Deck of cards, or a bottle? Mail? Newspapers?"

Erie replied, in effect, that he wanted for nothing; and blew out the candle.

"Oh, all right, if that's the way you feel about it. But we'll send you some more grub and water anyway — tomorrow, or maybe next day. Erie, you don't know any good songs, do you? Mrs. Lofty? Beautiful Mabel Clare?" He cleared his throat and sang huskily, with trembling tenderness:

> In the gloaming, oh, my darling,
> Think not bitter-lee of me!

"Hey? What's that?" Looking down, Lewis could no longer see those moving shadows in the dusk below. The other members of the posse had retired to the privacy of their tunnel. It was plain that they lacked artistic feeling.

Lewis rose up and squinted at the sun. "Oh, well, if you don't want to be friendly we'll go on in to Target."

CHAPTER XII

Hawkins and Aurelia Sais made an early dinner, well before midday, through courtesy of the management. They strolled to the feed corral. The new horse, sent to substitute for the vanished Smoky, was a stockingfoot sorrel, and Hawkins greeted him at once as Mittens, though without previous acquaintance.

"He looks like that kind of a horse," said 'Enry, none too well pleased. " 'Two white feet, buy him; three white feet, try him,' " he quoted. "This varmint has got four white feet. Oh, well! Mr. Gray, Pres Lewis left this horse here, and I haven't any more papers than a road lizard. What with the wild excitement and all, Lewis plumb forgot."

"Sais says you're to take him. That's good."

"And we want another for the day," said Aurelio. "No saddle. Mr. Hawkins has another saddle."

"A slow horse, named Terrapin," amended Hawkins. "We want a slow horse, most particular. . . . Aurelio, would you mind callin' me 'Enry? Mr. Hawkins seems so stiff and formal, and I'm tired of Hawkins, anyway. Bill is such a common name — awful common. But 'Enry sounds friendly. You call me 'Enry, and I'll call you 'Eadlight."

Aurelio laughed, pushing back his high-crowned and tomato-colored Mexican hat to show a mop of flaming hair. "Make it Goldie," he suggested. "That's my name in English. And my gray horse is Plata. Silver and gold."

They led Terrapin into the alley behind the Humphries' horse box, to saddle him with the sorry rig they found there. They found no saddle blanket, so they went into the house to take one from the judge's bed. The judge was not within. A scorchy smell filled the kitchen. Goldie opened the oven. The biscuits were burned. They passed into the front room. The door was open. A watchful and bright-eyed tortoise-shell cat curled on the cushion of the rocking-chair, and purred under Goldie's hand. A book lay open on the table, face down to hold the place; Aurelio spread out his hands. *"Se fué!"* he said solemnly. " 'Enry, the judge is gone."

"Just as well," said 'Enry. "He was a purty old man and he couldn't stand the razzle-dazzle we're dealing. Goldie, Old Man Lindauer says you're due to be sheriff, soon as they can get his resignation to Davis. I guess that includes the custody of the cat. That cat's going to be right lonesome. Bring him along. His name is Grayback."

They saddled Terrapin, and behind the saddle they tied a black hat, a small and slashed valise and a meal sack; they walked down the alley, leading the horses. Goldie carried the cat, making small reassuring noises in golden Spanish; he knocked at his *tío's* door.

"We come for Kames," he stated simply, as Johnny Pardee opened to him.

"Moses in the bulrushes!" said Johnny. "I thought you was never coming. What in time have you been doing?"

"You run on and peddle your papers, Johnny. Grub pile ready, and what you don't know won't hurt you. Mr. Kames and Goldie and me are going to take a little ride," said 'Enry. "It may be the last ride we will ever take together," he added, not without emotion.

Kames shrieked: "Johnny, he means to murder me! Don't let them take me; come with them if they take me. They don't intend to take me to jail. Come with me, for God's sake."

"I got to go to dinner," said Johnny. "Get Nash to go with you."

"Nash's place is closed," said 'Enry. "I saw that poor little clerk's face through the window. Scared stiff, he was. 'D-bye, buster!"

"Good-bye? Why, 'Enry, you'll be back?"

"After what's going to happen to Kames? Not likely. Folks are mighty supicious of these accidents, like this. Take keer of yourself, kid. Watch your cinches!"

Aurelio took Kames by the arm and towed him out into the alley. "You remember Ouray, Kames? His name is Terrapin now. And you know Ouray is not what you might call a fast horse. All right, then. We'll allow you to keep with us till we get out of town. Then you ride ahead, out of earshot. You poison the air. When you come to a fork in the road, you look back. I'll motion to you which way to go. Then you can use your own judgment. It would be better for you to take the way I show you. If you meet anyone coming, give 'em the road — and ride wide. Not a word out of you, good or bad, to anyone. You are practically extinct."

"Aurelio, what are you going to do with me? Oh, have pity! What are you going to do?" A thin scream, like an animal's, burst from Kames' quivering lips. In his abject terror the coward buckled and fell, and clasped his hands together, groveling in the sand, where Goldie surveyed him with loathing and disgust.

"Get up, you white-livered hound!" he said. "Get on that horse. Don't open your filthy mouth again. What will we do? Not what you are afraid of; and nothing that you'll ever guess. Ride!" As the lawyer mounted, his eyes fell, for the first time, on the evidence behind the saddle, and he lacked but little of a stroke.

"That meal sack isn't really the same one," said 'Enry. "I meant to get the one Dave had, but when I saw how you had fixed up Nash, I was so flabbergasted I forgot. You might have knocked me down with a crowbar. You mustn't mind what Sais says. That's just his way. He's so blamed upright. You've got a right to be scared."

They crossed the railroad beyond the stockyards, and circled back to Staircase road, leaving the Carmody herd on the left. No need to make inquiries, said 'Enry; if Pres Lewis had failed to make up his party as planned, he, 'Enry, would have had word of it. Far to the left, a dust cloud on the plain, coming down from San Lorenzo; a dust that was, by all the doctrines of chance and probability, Charlie Bird returning with the recovered herd. 'Enry wondered if Charlie Bird had found the thief; and if so, was it a case of kill or capture? Kames rode on before, twenty yards, thirty; a drooped and dejected wreck of a man, he who had been so jaunty and so arrogant, so scornful of the humble and the poor.

High above them and far away, black spots wove dimly through the dark bushes along the winding road. A glitter of light on metal, figures that shaped and grew, became men and horses, became three men and five horses, became a slender man, a blocky man, a short man. Aurelio drew rein where a soapweed clump made shade, for the sun was hot and hot. He waved the dismal Kames from the road, waved him to circle back, keeping his distance; stopped him at last where he could be well watched. Goldie sat under a soapweed then, and held his rifle across his knees.

"Bless my soul, if it isn't the gifted 'Enry and little Goldilocks!" said Pres. "But who is that out yonder? Isn't that neighbor Kames?"

"Light down, light down. That is what was Kames. But how about you? Whatever has happened to our wandering boy today?"

"Frank John," said Elmer, "has been to war. Don't he look it?"

He looked it. The man all tattered and torn had never a shirt so split and fluttering. His hands looked like a cat fight, his face was raked across where he had used it for a sled runner on the loose rock of the Mangas dump, an ear lopped askew for lack of needed repairs, one eye was puffed and swollen, beautifully black; and no swash-buckler of all time had ever borne himself so proudly, not even the storied hero who could strut while sitting down.

"He did that planting Patterson, as per agreement," said Lewis, paternally proud. "I must tell you about Patterson. Not now, though. Kames first. What has Kames been and gone and done now?"

"You'd never guess. Get down, all of you, and I'll tell you about Kames."

"Oh and ah," said Elmer politely, in a small, mouse voice. He stifled a yawn with three slender fingers. "If that is all — if you're quite sure that is all — why, you got no more use for me, and I'll go on about my business. You fellows can all go back to Mangas mine together, or you can all go back to town together, or you can stay right here and swap stories. I don't care. I'm going to cut across to the Ladder Line Camp and see if I can't persuade Albert Garst to work for me. You boys just prattle away." He swung into the saddle, but paused for a moment. "It's going to be right queer, though, when the sheriff gets back. Nobody owning Erie's cattle or Nash's store. Property squandering around loose, right and left. Marshal gone, judge gone. And nobody saying a word. I declare, that's goin' to be real shivery and scaresome."

'Enry wore a shamefaced look. "I think maybe the sheriff won't come back," he said, much embarrassed. "I think possibly that jailer or somebody might slip out and put a bug in the sheriff's ear. In fact, I know he will. Weak-minded of me, I know. But I keep thinking about him standing up for the Carmody woman and the Carmody kids. Dave Salt, he's just a tool and a cat's-paw. But that dumb, pot-bellied old sheriff is some part of a man, even yet."

"I know," said Pres soberly. "Elmer and me and the youngster, we hog-tied a real man today, and let him down that shaft like a calf in a crate. . . . What makes 'em go bad, 'Enry? Why can't they be straight?"

'Enry made a wry face and shook his head. "Well, there's no use of everybody looking at me for information," said Elmer with decision. "Because I'm done and gone. This conversation is getting entirely too personal to suit me." He flicked his quirt and set out on his promised visit.

"Frank John is tired," said Pres. "Goldie, you go back to town with him, and me and 'Enry will escort the wearisome Kames out to the mine and drop him in. We want one of your saddle ropes, though. Kames hasn't got any on his saddle."

Clouds hurried across the sky when they came to the dump of that old mine, and the sun was nearing the hills. They ordered the outcast to dismount. Kames thought his hour had come; knew it when he saw his relentless guards take from his saddle all the hateful baggage at which he had shuddered through those dreadful hours. Why should they do that, except they meant killing? They would leave that damning evidence with his body.

Pres Lewis leaned on the windlass and shouted down the shaft: "Hoo-o! You down there yet? . . . This is Lewis. You remember me — Pres Lewis? Sending some stuff down. Get back in your tunnel; I'm going to drop it." The meal sack fluttered down the shaft. He heard a smothered oath from below. After an interval, to allow for reflection, he dropped down that rolled black hat and the brown bag.

"That will give them something to study about," said Hawkins. Kames' heart leaped. It was not death, then. They rigged the rope to the windlass, and Kames put his foot in the loop willingly enough. To live — only to live!

"You explain to them, Mr. Kames," said Pres kindly. They lowered

him to the bottom and rode away; they left the rope there, hanging
in the shaft.

"How long do you think it'll take them to climb that rope?" said
'Enry as they turned the first bend.

"No time at all. I betcha Erie is halfway up now — unless he
wanted to hear the explanations first. I would sure admire to hear
what kind of a tale Kames puts up. I don't think it will be so good.
He doesn't seem quite up to the mark today — Kames. What will
they think? What will they say? What will they do?"

"Hoof it to the nearest Ladder well, get horses and scatter. And
to the day of their death, not one will ever know why he wasn't
killed or jugged."

"Well, how about it, 'Enry? Do we go to town or ease over to
Clingstone for the night? It's about eight miles to Clingstone, and
getting late."

They were on the main road now, and the smoke of Target's
engines lay far below them. 'Enry stretched out his hand.

"Lewis, there's the only place in the world that thinks well of me."
His mouth twisted to a crooked smile. "So I'm moving on before
they change their minds. You go on to Clingstone. I'll mosey over to
that line camp Farr was heading for, if I can find it, and pull out soon
in the morning. So this is *adiós*. Take keer of yo'self."

"I guess not," said Pres. "You might run up against some of the
Ladder boys, and you want someone to tell 'em it was all a mistake.
I'll side you."

'Enry grinned. "I'd just about forgot they was looking for me," he
admitted. "Had a lot on my mind today, and not overmuch sleep last
night. Besides, I might not find the camp at night. Been there, but it
was from the other side, and daytime. Well, thank you kindly, Mr.
Pres. This is right clever of you. Is it far?"

"All of that. There's a short cut through the hills, for them that
knows it. Let me lead that horse a spell, 'Enry. If he keeps on holding back I'll ride him myself and lead mine. You roll you a smoke
and look pleasant. Night is right on us. Soon be time for taps." He
threw up his head and sang, and echoes brought the slow words back
to him:

> Go to sleep. Day is gone. Night is on!

"Gosh, I'm tired," said 'Enry. "These jugglers, that keep three
balls in the air, and a plate and a glass of water, a butcher knife and a
canary bird — do you suppose they ever get dizzy, so they can't stop?
I feel like that."

"I get you. Especially about the bird. Erie Patterson isn't yellow, but he certainly is a bird! I guess I won't forget Erie — not ever. What a waste!"

"I seen things today I ain't goin' to forget for quite a spell, either. Queerest of all was that empty house and them burned biscuits, tea-kettle singing away on the stove, and the cat a-waiting. That's a nice cat. You tell Goldie I said for him to be good to that cat. And then Lindauer, when he agreed to ditch the Gem. Sawin' the air with his little fat arms, and the sun beatin' down on his shiny bald head. "All righd, all righd — don't sing no hymns!" he says, fanning his head. Funny to think that'll be the last I'll ever see him."

The way grew wide here, crossing a walled valley, and the two rode side by side. Clouds drifted low over Gridiron; close above them the rose glow of sunset fell over the broken battlements of Horse-Thief Hill.

"Now I've done it again!" announced 'Enry. "Come away without paying my bill at the hotel, and left my things there. You tell Old Man Lindauer to pay the bill and charge it to the bank; and you can keep the things, if you want 'em, or burn them. Just some duds. . . . But there was one thing — a little tintype. Oh, well!"

Pres said, "Drop me a post card when you get time, and give me some friend's address. I'll send the picture to your friend and you can get it later. It will not be traced."

'Enry rode on in silence for a space. Then he lifted quiet eyes. "Did you know all the time who I was?" he asked.

"Not till last night. Not till you said the marshal was lying to you."

'Enry ridged his forehead in puzzlement. Then he shrugged. "I'm tired, I guess. How was it?"

"Young Frank John put his finger on the place when he said you must have some extraordinary motive to make you act the silly way you did. You said it was because you knew the marshal was lying to you, and that there was no guesswork about it. But what the marshal said might have been perfectly true, for all you had any chance to know — all except just one thing. He told you that Bill Doolin and Carmody were old friends. And you had already told us that you had never seen Carmody before — when you sent me out with the letter. And you sent the letter to Charlie Bird; not to Carmody. That's all."

'Enry nodded. "I didn't want to see Charlie. I liked Charlie when we was boys." There was a long pause. "And Charlie liked me — then." He rode on in silence. Lewis took the lead as the swift twilight dimmed. They climbed athwart a high hillside and a smother of mist was all about; the black void of night rushed upon them. Shod feet struck fire from the flinty hill. They rounded a shoulder to a steep descent, and came to an open ridge below the fog.

"This is the home stretch," said Lewis. "One long straight ridge to the Line Camp, couple or three miles yet." He checked his horse and waited until the other drew alongside. "'Enry," said Lewis earnestly, "why not stay here and play out the string? You've got good friends here. Make your play."

"No go. It is soon or late with me. This is my bed, like I made it."

"Target thinks well of you, 'Enry."

"Even that much I did not come by honestly," said the other bitterly. "Lewis, I come to look that bank over myself. Only that I got a down on that gang — You see how it is. Can I build on such a foundation as that?"

"Well, you wouldn't be deceiving me, anyhow," urged Pres. "Why not try Jim River? I can make Jim River a sanctuary. You and me, 'Enry, we'd make quite a pair."

"I'd only drag you down with me. No go. Don't waste your time on me," said 'Enry. "I'll quit you here, I think. I know my way now and I guess I'll move on till morning. Couldn't sleep and I don't feel like talking, down at the camp."

The black and enormous night was about them as they parted on that bleak and shrill hillside. "There is only one thing you can do for me," said 'Enry steadily. "Target is the one place on earth that will remember me kindly. Let it be Hawkins they remember. Let them wonder what ever did become of Hawkins, and speak kindly of him by campfires. Good-bye."

"I'm no great shakes myself," said Lewis, and his voice was warm in the night. "Such as I am, I wish you well. And I give you Merve Woody's toast:

> Here's at ye, and here's to'ard ye;
> If we'd never seed ye, we'd a-never knowed ye!

"So long, friend. Take keer of yourself!"

There were no lights in the line-camp house, no sound of horses from the sheds. Pres opened the door and struck a match. He saw an overturned table and broken dishes all about. A lamp lay by the door, and shattered glass beyond. He picked up the lamp and shook it. There was some oil left in it yet, so he lit it with a second match. When the flame burned clear, he raised the lamp high and looked about. The room was littered with broken chairs and crockery, boxes, tinware, trampled towels and torn clothes. The table was splintered, the stove was upset and ashes lay along the floor amid the crushed and battered pipe and ruined stoveware. There was no bedding in the broken bunk. Pres shook his head sadly.

"Old Elmer," he said, "has no tact."

The Desire
of the Moth

THE DESIRE OF THE MOTH

CHAPTER I

Little Next Door — her years are few —
Loves me, more than her elders do;
Says, my wrinkles become me so;
Marvels much at the tales I know.
Says, we shall marry when she is grown —

THE LITTLE HAPPY SONG stopped short. John Wesley Pringle, at the mesa's last headland, drew rein to readjust his geography. This was new country to him.

Close behind, Organ Mountain flung up a fantasy of spires, needle-sharp and bare and golden. The long straight range — saw-toothed limestone save for this twenty-mile sheer upheaval of the Organ — stretched away to north and south against the unclouded sky, till distance turned the barren gray to blue-black, to blue, to misty haze; till the sharp, square-angled masses rounded to hillocks — to a blur — a wavy line — nothing.

More than a hundred miles to the northwest, two midget mountains wavered in the sky. John Wesley nodded at their unforgotten shapes and pieced this vast landscape to the patchwork map in his head. Those toy hills were San Mateo and Magdalena. Pringle had passed that way on a bygone year, headed east. He was going west, now.

"I'm too prosperous here," he had explained to Beebe and Ballinger, his partners on Rainbow. "I'm tedious to myself. Guess I'll take a *pasear* back to Prescott. Railroads? Who, me? Why, son, I like to travel when I go anywheres. Just starting and arriving don't delight me any. Besides, I don't know that strip along the border. I'll ride."

It was a tidy step to Prescott — say, as far as from Philadelphia to Savannah, or from Richmond to Augusta; but John Wesley had made many such rides in the Odyssey of his wander years. Some of them had been made in haste. But there was no haste now. Sam Bass, his corn-fed sorrel, was hardly less sleek and sturdy than at the start,

though a third of the way was behind him. Pringle rode by easy
stages, and where he found himself pleased, there he tarried for a
space.

With another friendly nod to the northward hills that marked a
day of his past, Pringle turned his eyes to the westlands, outspread
and vast before him. To his right the desert stretched away, a mighty
plain dotted with low hills, rimmed with a curving, jagged range. Beyond that range was a nothingness, a hiatus that marked the sunken
valley of the Rio Grande; beyond that, a headlong infinity of unknown ranges, tier on tier, yellow or brown or blue; broken, tumbled,
huddled, scattered, with gulfs between to tell of unseen plains and
hidden happy valleys — altogether giving an impression of rushing
toward him, resistless, like the waves of a stormy sea.

At his feet the plain broke away sharply,·in a series of steplike sandy
benches, to where the Rio Grande bore quartering across the desert,
turning to the Mexican sea; the Mesilla Valley here, a slender ribbon
of mossy green, broidered with loops of flashing river — a ribbon six
miles by forty, orchard, woodland, and green field, greener for the
desolate gray desert beyond and the yellow hills of sand edging the
valley floor. Below him Las Uvas, chief town of the valley, lay bask-
ing in the sun, tiny square and street bordered with greenery: its
domino houses white-walled in the sun, with larger splashes of red
from the courthouse or church or school.

Far on the westering desert, beyond the valley, Pringle saw a white
feather of smoke from a toiling train; beyond that a twisting gap in
the blue of the westmost range.

"That's our road." He lifted his bridle rein. "Amble along, Sam!"

To that amble he crooned to himself, pleasantly, half-dreamily —
as if he voiced indirectly some inner thought — quaint snatches of old
song:

> She came to the gate and she peeped in —
> Grass and the weeds up to her chin;
> Said, "A rake and a hoe and a fantail plow
> Would suit you better than a wife just now."

And again:

> Schooldays are over now,
>   Lost all our bliss;
> But love remembers yet
>   Quarrel and kiss.
> Still, as in days of yore —

Then, after a long silence, with a thoughtful earnestness that Rainbow would scarce have credited, he quoted a verse from what he was
wont to call Billy Beebe's Bible:

One Moment in Annihilation's waste,
One Moment of the Well of Life to taste —
The Stars are setting, and the Caravan
Starts for the Dawn of — Nothing. Oh, make haste!

After late dinner at the Gadsden Purchase, Pringle had tidings of
the Motion Picture Palace; and thither he bent his steps. He was late
and the palace was a very small palace indeed; it was with difficulty
that he spied in the semi-darkness an empty seat in a side section. A fat
lady and a fatter man, in the seats nearest the aisle, obligingly moved
over rather than risk any attempt to squeeze by.

Beyond them, as he took the end seat, Pringle was dimly aware
of a girl who looked at him rather attentively.

He turned his mind to the screen, where a natty and noble young
man, with a chin, bit off his words distinctly and smote his extended
palm with folded gloves to emphasize the remarks he was making to
a far less natty man with black mustaches. John Wesley rightly concluded that this second man, who gnashed his teeth so convincingly,
and at whom an incredibly beautiful young lady looked with haughty
disdain, was the villain, and foiled.

The blond and shaven hero, with a magnificent gesture, motioned
the villain to begone! That baffled person, after waiting long enough
to register despair, spread his fingers across his brow and be-went; the
hero turned, held out his arms; the scornful young beauty crept into
them. Click! On the screen appeared a scroll:

Keep Your Seats. Two Minutes to Change Reels.

The lights were turned on. Pringle looked at the crowd — girls,
grandmas, mothers with their families, many boys, and few men;
Americans, Mexicans, well-dressed folk and roughly dressed, all together. Many were leaving; among them Pringle's fat and obliging
neighbors rose with a pleasant: "Excuse me, please!"

A stream of newcomers trickled in through the door. As Pringle
sat down the lights were dimmed again. Simultaneously the girl he
had noticed beyond the fat couple moved over to the seat next to his
own. Pringle did not look at her; and a little later he felt a hand on
his sleeve.

"Tut, tut!" said Pringle in a tolerant undertone. "Why, chicken,
you're not trying to get gay with your old Uncle Dudley, are you?"

"John Wesley Pringle!" came the answer in a furious whisper, each
indignant word a missile. "How dare you! How dare you speak to me
like that?"

"What!" said Pringle, peering. "What! Stella Vorhis! I can hardly
believe it!"

"But it's oh-so-true!" said Stella, rising. "Let's go — we can't talk here."

"That was one awful break I made. I most sincerely and humbly beg your pardon," Pringle said on the sidewalk.

Stella laughed.

"That's all right — I understand — forget it! You hadn't looked at me. But I knew you when you first came in — only I wasn't sure till the lights were turned on. Of course it would be great fun to tease you — pretend to be shocked and dreadfully angry, and all that — but I haven't got time. And oh, John Wesley, I'm so delighted to see you again! Let's go over to the park. Not but what I was dreadfully angry, sure enough, until I had a second to think. Why don't you say you're glad to see me — after five years?"

"Stella! You know I am. Six years, please. But I thought you were still in Prescott?"

"We came here three years ago. Here's a bench. Now tell it to me!"

But Pringle stood beside and looked down at her without speech, with a smile unexpected from a face so lean, so brown, so year-bitten and iron-hard — a smile which happily changed that face and softened it.

The girl's eyes danced at him.

"I'm so glad you've come, John Wesley! Good old Wes!"

"So I am — both those little things. Six years!" he said slowly. "Dear me — dear both of us! That will make you twenty-five. You don't look a day over twenty-four! But you're still Stella Vorhis?"

She met his gaze gravely; then her lids drooped and a wave of red flushed her face.

"I am Stella Vorhis — yet."

"Meaning — for a little while yet?"

"Meaning, for a little while yet. That will come later, John Wesley. Oh, I'll tell you, but not just now. You tell about John Wesley, first — and remember, anything you say may be used against you. Where have you been? Were you dead? Why didn't you write? Has the world used you well? Sit down, Mr. John Wesley Also-Ran Pringle, and give an account of yourself!"

He sat beside her: she laid her hand across his gnarled brown fingers with an unconscious caress.

"It's good to see you, old-timer! Begin now — I, John Wesley Pringle, am come from going to and fro upon the earth and from walking up and down in it. But I didn't ask you where you were living. Perhaps you have a — home of your own now."

John Wesley firmly lifted her slim fingers from his hand and as firmly deposited them in her lap.

"Kindly keep your hands to yourself, young woman," he said with stately dignity. "Here is an exact account of all my time since I saw you: I have been hungry, thirsty, sleepy, tired. To remedy these evils, upon expert advice I have eaten, drunk, slept, and rested. I have worked and played, been dull and gay, busy and idle, foolish and unwise. That's all. Oh, yes — I'm living in Rainbow Mountain; cattle. Two pardners — nice boys but educated. Had another one; he's married now, poor dear — and just as happy as if he had some sense."

"You're not?"

"Not what — happy or married?"

"Married, silly!"

"And I'm not. Now it's your turn. Where do you live? Here in town?"

"Oh, no. Dad's got a farm twenty miles up the river and a ranch out on the flat. I just came down on the morning train to do a little shopping and go back on the four-forty-eight — and I'll have to be starting soon. You'll walk down to the station with me?"

"But the sad story of your life?" objected Pringle.

"Oh, I'll tell you that by installments. You're to make us a long, long visit, you know — just as long as you can stay. You're horseback, of course? Well, then, ride up tonight. Ask for Aden Station. We live just beyond there."

"But the Major was a very hostile major when I saw him last."

"Oh, father's got all over that. He hadn't heard your side of it then. He often speaks of you now and he'll be glad to see you."

"Tomorrow, then. My horse is tired — I'll stay here tonight."

"You'll find dad changed," said the girl. "This is the first time in his life he has ever been at ease about money matters. He's really quite well-to-do."

"That's good. I'm doing well in that line too. I forgot to tell you." There was no elation in his voice; he looked back with a pang to the bold and splendid years of their poverty. "Then the Major will quit wandering round like a lost cat, won't he?"

"I think he likes it here — only for the crazy-mad political feeling; and I think he's settled down for good."

"High time, I think, at his age."

"You needn't talk! Dad's only ten years older than you are." She leaned her cheek on her hand, she brushed back a little stray tendril of midnight hair from her dark eyes, and considered him thoughtfully.

"Why, John Wesley, I've known you nearly all my life and you don't look much older now than when I first saw you."

"That was in Virginia City. You were just six years old and your pony ran away with you. We were great old chums for a month or so. The next time I saw you was — "

"At Bakersfield — at mother's funeral," said the girl softly. "Then you came to Prescott, and you had lost your thumb in the meantime; and I was Little Next Door to you — "

"And Prescott and me, we agreed it was best for both of us that I should go away."

"Yes; and when you came back you were going to stay. Why didn't you stay, John Wesley?"

"I think," said Pringle reflectively, "that I have forgotten that."

"Do you know, John Wesley, I have never been back to any place we have left once? And of all the people I have ever known, you are the only one I have ever lost track of and found again. And you're always just same old John Wesley; always gay and cheerful; nearly always in trouble; always strong and resourceful — "

"How true!" said Pringle. "Yes, yes; go on!"

"Well, you are! And you're so — so reliable; like Faithful John in the fairy story. You're different from anyone else I know. You're a good boy; when you are grown up you shall have a yoke of oxen, over and above your wages."

"This is very gratifying indeed," observed Pringle. "But — a sweetly solemn thought comes to me. You were going to tell me about another boy — the onliest little boy?"

"He's not a boy," said Stella, flushing hotly. "He's a man — a man's man. You'll like him, John Wesley — he's just your kind. I'm not going to tell you. You'll see him at our house, with the others. And he'll be the very one you'd pick out for me yourself. Of course you'll want to tease me by pretending to guess someone else; but you'll know which one he is, without me telling you. He stands out apart from all other men in every way. Come on, John Wesley — it's time to go down to the station."

Pringle caught step with her.

"And how long — if a reliable old faithful John may ask — before you become Stella Some-One-Else?"

"At Christmas. And I am a very lucky girl, John. What an absurd convention it is that people are never supposed to congratulate the girl — as if no man was ever worth having! Silly, isn't it?"

"Very silly. But then, it's a silly world."

"A delightful world," said Stella, her eyes sparkling. "You don't know how happy I am. Or perhaps you do know. Tell me honestly, did you ever 1—like anyone, this way?"

"I refuse to answer, by advice of counsel," said John Wesley. "I'll say this much, though. X marks no spot where any Annie Laurie gave me her promise true."

When the train had gone John Wesley wandered disconsolately back to his hotel and rested his elbows on the bar. The white-aproned attendant hastened to serve him.

"What will it be, sir?"

"Give me a gin pitfall," said John Wesley.

CHAPTER II

Cold feet?"

"Horrible!" said Anastacio.

Matthew Lisner, sheriff of Dona Ana, bent a hard eye on his subordinate.

"It's got to be done," he urged. "To elect our ticket we must have all the respectable and responsible people of the valley. If we can provoke Foy into an outbreak—"

"Not we—you," corrected Anastacio. "Myself, I do not feel provoking."

"Are you going to lay down on me?"

"If you care to put it that way—yes. Kit Foy is just the man to leave alone."

"Now, listen!" said the sheriff impatiently. "Half the valley is owned by newcomers, men of substance, who, with the votes they influence or control, will decide the election. Foy is half a hero with them, because of these vague old stories. But let them be stirred up to violence now and you'll see! They won't see any romance in it— just an open outrage; they will flock to us to the last man. Ours is the party of law and order—"

"Law to order, some say."

The veins swelled in the sheriff's heavy face and thick neck; he regarded his deputy darkly.

"That comes well from you, Barela! Don't you see, with the law on our side all these men of substance will be with us unconditionally? I tell you, Christopher Foy is the brains of his party. Once he is discredited—"

"And I tell you that I am the brains of your party and I'll have

nothing to do with your fine plan. 'Tis an old stratagem to call oppression, law, and resistance to oppression, lawlessness. You tried just
that in ninety-six, didn't you? And I never could hear that our side
had any the best of it or that the good name of Dona Ana was in any
way bettered by our wars. Come, Mr. Lisner — the Kingdom of Lady
Ann has been quiet now for nearly eight years. Let us leave it so.
For myself, the last row brought me reputation and place, made me
chief deputy under two sheriffs — so I need have the less hesitation
in setting forth my passionate preference for peace."

"You have as much to gain as I have," growled the sheriff. "Besides your own cinch, you have one of your *gente* for deputy in
every precinct in the county."

"Exactly! And if we have wars again, who but the Barelas would
bear the brunt? No, no, Mr. Matt Lisner; while I may be a merely
ornamental chief deputy, it will never be denied that I am a very
careful chief to my *gente*. Be sure that I shall think more than once
or twice before I set a man of my men at a useless hazard to pleasure
you — or to re-elect you."

"You speak plainly."

"I intend to. I speak for three hundred — and we vote solid. Make
no mistake, Mr. Lisner. You need me in your business, but I can do
nicely without you."

"Perhaps you'd like to be sheriff yourself."

"I might like it — except that I am not as young and foolish as I
was," said Anastacio, smiling. "Now that I am so old, and so wise
and all, it is clear to see that neither myself nor any of the fighting
men of the mad old days — on either side — should be sheriff."

"You were not always so thoughtful of the best interests of the dear
pee-pul," sneered the sheriff.

"That I wasn't. I was as silly and hot-brained a fool as either side
could boast. But you, Sheriff, are neither silly nor hot-headed. In
cold blood you are planning that men shall die; that other men shall
rot in prison. Why? For hate and revenge? Not even that. Oh, a
little spice of revenge, perhaps; Foy and his friends made you something of a laughing stock. But your main motive is — money. And I
don't see why. You've got all the money any one man needs now."

"I notice you get your share."

"I hope so. But, even as a money-making proposition, your troubled-
voters policy is a mistake. All the mountain men want is to be let
alone, and you might be sheriff for life for all they care. But you
fan up every little bicker into a lawsuit — don't I know? Just for the
mileage — ten cents a mile each way in a country that's jam full of

miles from one edge to the other; ten cents a mile each way for each
and every arrest and subpoena. You drag them to court twice a year —
the farmer at seed time and harvest, the cowman from the spring and
fall round-ups. It hurts, it cripples them, they ride thirty miles to vote
against you; it costs you all the extra mileage money to offset their
votes. As a final folly, you purpose deliberately to stir up the old
factions. What was it Napoleon said? 'It is worse than a crime: it is
a blunder.' I'll tell you now, not a Barela nor an Ascarate shall stir
a foot in such a quarrel. If you want to bait Kit Foy, do it yourself
— or set your city police on him."

"I will."

A faint tinge of color came to the clear olive of Anastacio's cheek
as he rose.

"But don't promise my place to any of them, sheriff. I might hear
of it."

"Stranger," said Ben Creagan, "you can't play pool! I can't — and I
beat you four straight games. You better toddle your little trotters off
to bed." The words alone might have been mere playfulness; glance
and tone made plain the purposed offense.

The after-supper crowd in the hotel barroom had suddenly slipped
away, leaving Max Barkeep, three others, and John Wesley Pringle —
the last not unnoting of nudge and whisper attending the exodus.
Since that, Pringle had suffered, unprotesting, more gratuitous insults
than he had met in all the rest of his stormy years. His curiosity was
aroused; he played the stupid, unseeing, patient, and timid person he
was so eminently not. Plainly these people desired his absence; and
Pringle highly resolved to know why. He now blinked mildly.

"But I'm not sleepy a-tall," he objected.

He tried and missed an easy shot; he chalked his cue with assiduous
care.

"Here, you! Quit knockin' those balls round!" bawled Max, the
bartender. "What you think this is — a kindergarten?"

"Why, I paid for all the games I lost, didn't I?" asked Pringle, much
abashed.

He mopped his face. It was warm, though the windows and doors
were open.

"Well, nobody's going to play any more with you," snapped Max.
"You bore 'em."

He pyramided the balls and covered the table. With a sad and lingering backward look Pringle slouched abjectly through the wide-
arched doorway to the bar.

"Come on, fellers — have something."

"Naw!" snarled José Espalin. "I'm a-tryin' to theenk. Shut up, won't you?"

Pringle sighed patiently at the rebuff and stole a timid glance at the thinker. Espalin was a lean little dried-up manikin, with legs, arms, and mustaches disproportionately long for his dwarfish body. His black, wiry hair hung in ragged witchlocks; his black pin-point eyes were glittering, cold, and venomous. He looked, thought Pringle, very much like a spider.

"I'm steerin' you right, old man," said Creagan. "You'd better drag it for bed."

"I ain't sleepy, I tell you."

Espalin leaped up, snarling.

"Say! You lukeing for troubles, maybe? Bell, I theenk thees *hombre* got a gun. Shall we freesk him?"

As he flung the query over his shoulder his beady little eyes did not leave Pringle's.

Bell Applegate got leisurely to his feet — a tall man, well set up, with a smooth-shaved, florid face and red hair.

"If he has we'll jack him in the jug." He threw back the lapel of his coat, displaying a silver star.

"But I ain't got no gun," protested John Wesley meekly. "You-all can see for yourself."

"We will — don't worry! Don't you make one wrong move or I'll put out your light!"

"Be you the sheriff?"

"Police. Go to him, Ben!"

"No gun," reported Ben after a swift search of the shrinking captive.

"I done told you so, didn't I?"

"Mighty good thing for you, old rooster. Gun-toting is strictly barred in Las Uvas. You got to take your gun off fifteen minutes after you get in from the road and you can't put it on till fifteen minutes before you take the road again."

"Is that — er — police regulations or state law?"

"State law — and has been any time these twenty-five years. Say, you doddering old fool, what do you think this is — a night school?"

"I — I guess I'll go to bed," said Pringle miserably.

"I — I guess if you come back I'll throw you out," mimicked Ben with a guffaw.

Pringle made no answer. He shuffled into the hall and up the stairway to his bedroom. He unlocked the door noisily; he opened it; noisily; he took his sixshooter and belt from the wall quietly and closed the door, noisily again; he locked it — from the outside. Then he did a curious thing; he sat down very gently and removed his boots.

The four in the barroom listened, grinning. When they heard Pringle's door slam shut Bell Applegate nodded and Creagan went out on the street. Behind him, at a table near the pool-room door, the law planned ways and means in a slinking undertone.

"You keep in the background, Joe. Let us do the talking. Foy just naturally despises you — we might not get him to stay the fifteen minutes out. You stay back there. Remember now, don't shoot till Ben lets him get his arm loose. *Sabe?*"

"Maybe Meester Ben don't find heem."

"Oh, yes, he will. Ditch meeting tonight. Ought to be out about now. Setting the time to use the water and assessing *fatiga* work. Every last man with a water right will be there, sure, and Foy's got a dozen. Max, you are to be a witness, remember, and you mustn't be mixed up in it. Got your story straight?"

"Foy he comes in and makes a war-talk about Dick Marr," recited Max. "After we powwow awhile you see his gun. You tell him he's under arrest for carryin' concealed weapons. You and Ben grabbed his arm; he jerked loose and went after his gun. And then Joe shot him."

"That's it. We'll all stick to that. S-st! Here they come!"

There are men whose faces stand out in a crowd, men you turn to look after on the street. Such — quite apart from his sprightly past — was Christopher Foy, who now entered with Creagan. He was about thirty, above middle height, every mold and line of him slender and fine and strong. His face was resolute, vivacious, intelligent; his eyes were large and brown, pleasant and fearless. A wide black hat, pushed back now, showed a broad forehead white against crisp coal-black hair and the pleasant tan of neck and cheek. But it was not his dark, forceful face alone that lent him such distinction. Rather it was the perfect poise and balance of the man, the ease and unconscious grace of every swift and sure motion. He wore a working garb now — blue overalls and a blue rowdy. But he wore them with an air that made him well dressed.

Foy paused for a second; Applegate rose.

"Well, Chris!" he laughed. "There has been a time when you might not have fancied this particular bunch — hey? All over now, please the pigs. Come in and give it a name. Beer for mine."

"I'll smoke," said Foy.

"Me too," said Espalin.

He lit a cigar and returned to his chair. Ben Creagan passed behind the bar and handed over a six-shooter and a cartridge belt.

"Here, Chris — here's the gun I borrowed of you when I broke mine. Much obliged."

Foy twirled the cylinder to make sure the hammer was on an empty chamber and buckled the belt under his rowdy.

"My hardware is mostly plows and scrapers and irrigating hoes nowadays," he remarked. "Good thing too."

"All the same, Foy, I'd keep a gun with me if I were you. Dick Marr is drinking again — and when he soaks it up he gets discontented over old times, you know." Applegate lowered his voice, with a significant glance at Espalin. "He threatened your life today. I thought you ought to know it."

Foy considered his cigar.

"That's awkward," he replied briefly.

"Chris," said Ben, "this isn't the first time. Dick's heart is bad to you. I'm sorry. He was my friend and you were not. But you're not looking for any trouble now. Dick is. And I'm afraid he'll keep on till he gets it. Me and the sheriff we managed to get him off to bed, but he says he's going to shoot you on sight — and I believe he means it. You ought to have him bound over to keep the peace."

Foy smiled and shook his head.

"I can't do that — and it would only make him madder than ever. But I'll get out of his way and keep out of his way. I'll go up to the Jornado tonight and stay with the Bar Cross boys awhile. He won't come up there."

"You'll enjoy having people tellin' how you run away to keep from meeting Dick Marr?" said Applegate incredulously.

"Why shouldn't they say it? It will be exactly true," responded Foy quietly, "and you're authorized to say so. I'm learning some sense now; I'm getting to own quite a mess of property; I'm going to be married soon; and I don't want to fight anyone. Besides, quite apart from my own interests, other men will be drawn into it if I shoot it out with Marr. No knowing where it will stop. No, sir; I'll go punch cows till Marr quiets down. Maybe it's just the whisky talking. Dick isn't such a bad fellow when he's not fighting booze. Or maybe he'll go away. He hasn't much to keep him here."

"Say, I could get a job offered to him out in San Simon," said Applegate, brightening.

His eye rested on the clock over the long mirror. He stepped over to the show case, clipped the end from a cigar and obtained a light from a shapely bronze lady with a torch. When he came back he fell in on Foy's left; at Foy's right Creagan leaned his elbows on the bar.

"Well, I'm obliged to you, boys," said Foy. "This one's on me. Come on, Joe — have a hoot."

"Thanks, no," said Espalin. "I not dreenkin' none thees times. Eef I dreenk some I get full, and loose my job maybe."

"Vichy," said Foy. "Take something yourself, Max."

As Mr. Max poured the drinks an odd experience befell Mr. José Espalin. His tilted chair leaned against the casing of the billiard-room door. As Max filled the first glass Espalin became suddenly aware of something round and hard and cold pressed against his right temple. Mr. Espalin felt some curiosity, but he sat perfectly still. The object shifted a few inches; Mr. Espalin perceived from the tail of his eye the large, unfeeling muzzle of a six-shooter; beyond it, a glimpse of the forgotten elderly stranger, Mr. Pringle.

Only Mr. Pringle's fighting face appeared, and that but for a moment; he laid a finger to lip and crouched, hidden by the partition and by Espalin's body. Mr. Espalin gathered that Pringle desired no outcry and shunned observation; he sat motionless accordingly; he felt a hand at his belt, which removed his gun.

"Happy days!" said Foy, and raised his glass to his lips.

Creagan seized the uplifted wrist with both hands, Applegate pounced on the other arm. Pringle leaped through the doorway. But something happened swifter than Pringle's swift rush. Foy's knee shot up to Applegate's stomach. Applegate fell, sprawling. Foy hurled himself on Creagan and bore him crashing to the floor. Foy whirled over; he rose on one hand and knee, gun drawn, visibly annoyed; also considerably astonished at the unexpected advent of Mr. Pringle. Applegate lay groaning on the floor. Pringle kicked his gun from the holster and set foot upon it; one of his own guns covered the bartender and the other kept watch on Espalin, silent on his still-tilted chair.

"Who're you!" challenged Foy.

"Friend with the countersign. Don't shoot! Don't shoot me, anyhow."

Foy rose from hand and knee to knee and foot. This rescuer, so opportunely arrived from nowhere, seemed to be an ally. But to avoid mistakes, Foy's gun followed Pringle's motions, at the same time willing and able to blow out Creagan's brains if advisable. He also acquired Creagan's gun quite subconsciously.

"Let me introduce myself, gentlemen," said Pringle. "I'm Jack-in-a-Pinch, Little Friend of the Under Dog — see Who's This? page two-thirteen. My German friend, come out from behind that bar —

hands up — step lively! Spot yourself! My Mexican friend, join Mr. Max. Move, you poisonous little spider — jump! That's better! Gentlemen — be seated! Right there — smack, slapdab on the floor. Sit down and think. Say! I'm serious. Am I going to have to kill some few of you just because you don't know who I am? I'll count three! One! two! — That's it. Very good — hold that — register anticipation! I am a worldly man," said Pringle with emotion, "but this spectacle touches me — it does indeed!"

"I'll get square with you!" gurgled Applegate, as fiercely as his breathless condition would permit.

"George — may I call you George? I don't know your name. You may get square with me, George — but you'll never be square with anyone. You are a rhomboidinaltitudinous isosohedronal catawampus, George!"

George raved unprintably. He made a motion to rise, but reconsidered it as he noted the tension of Pringle's trigger finger.

"Don't be an old fuss-budget, George," said Pringle reprovingly. "Because I forgot to tell you — I've got my gun now — and yours. You won't need to arrest me, though, for I'm hitting the trail in fifteen minutes. But if I wasn't going — and if you had your gun — you couldn't arrest one side of me. You couldn't arrest one of my old boots! Listen, George! You heard this Chris-gentleman give his reasons for wanting peace? Yes? Well, it's oh-so-different here. I hate peace! I loathe, detest, abhor and abominate peace! My very soul with strong disgust is stirred — by peace! I'm growing younger every year, I don't own any property here, I'm not going to be married; I ain't feeling pretty well anyhow; and if you don't think I'll shoot, try to get up! Just look as if you thought you wanted to wish to try to make an effort to get up."

"How — who — " began Creagan; but Pringle cut him short.

"Ask me no more, sweet! You have no speaking part here. We'll do the talking. I just love to talk. I am the original tongue-tied man; I ebb and flow. Don't let me hear a word from any of you! Well, pardner?"

Foy, still kneeling in fascinated amaze, now rose. Creagan's nose was bleeding profusely.

"That was one awful wallop you handed our gimlet-eyed friend," said Pringle admiringly. "Neatest bit of work I ever saw. Sir, to you! My compliments!" He placed a chair near the front door and sat down. "I feel like a lion in a den of Daniels," he sighed.

"But how did you happen to be here so handy?" inquired Foy.

"Didn't happen — I did it on purpose," said John Wesley. "You

see, these four birds tipped their hand. All evening they been instruct-
ing me where I got off. They would-ed I had the wings of a dove,
so I might fly far, far away and be at rest. Now, I put it to you, do
I look like a dove?"

"Not at present," laughed Foy.

"Well, I didn't like it — nobody would. I see there was a hen on,
I knew the lay of the ground from looking after my horse. So I
clomped off to bed, got my good old Excalibur gun — full name
X. L. V. Caliber — slipped off my boots, tippytoed down the back
stairs like a Barred Rock cat, oozed in by the side door — and here I
be! I overheard their pleasant little plan to do you. I meant to do
the big rescue act, but you mobilize too quick for me. All the same,
maybe it's as well I chipped in, because — take a look at them cartridges in your gun, will you? Your own gun — the one they borrowed from you."

Foy twisted a bullet from a cartridge. There was no powder. The
four men on the floor looked unhappy under his thoughtful eye.

"Nice little plant — what? Do we kill 'em?" said Pringle cheerfully.
"I don't know the rules well enough to break them. What was the
big idea? Was they vexed at you, son?"

"It would seem so," said Foy, smiling. "We had a little war here
a spell back. I suspect they wanted to stir it up again for political
effect. Election this fall."

"And you were not in their party? I see!" said Pringle, nodding
intelligently. "Well, they sure had it fixed to make your side lose one
vote — fixed good and proper. The Ben-boy was to let your right
hand loose and the Joe-boy was to shoot you as you pulled your
gun. Why, if you had lived to make a statement your own story
woulda mighty near let them out."

"I believe that I am greatly obliged to you, sir."

"I believe you are," said Pringle. "And — but, also, I know the two
gentlemen you were drinking with should be very grateful to you.
They had just half a second more to live — and you beat me to it.
Too bad! Well, what next?"

Foy pondered a little.

"I guess I'll go up to the Bar Cross wagon, as I intended, till things
simmer down. The Las Uvas warriors seldom ever bother the Bar
Cross Range. My horse is hitched up the street. How'd you like to
go along with me, stranger? You and me would make a fair-sized
crowd."

"I'd like it fine and dandy," said Pringle. "But I got a little visit
to make tomorrow. Maybe I'll join you later. I like Las Uvas," stated

John Wesley, beaming. "Nice, lively little place! I think I'll settle down here after a bit. Some of the young fellows are shy on good manners. But I can teach 'em. I'd enjoy it. . . . Now, let's see: If you'll hold these lads a few minutes I'll get my boots and saddle up and bring my horse to the door; then I'll pay Max my hotel bill and talk to them while you get your horse; and we'll ride together till we get out in the open. How's that for a lay?"

That was a good lay, it seemed; and it was carried out — with one addition: After Foy brought his horse he rang Central and called up the sheriff.

"Hello! That you, Mr. Lisner? This is Kitty Foy," he said sweetly. "Sheriff, I hate to bother you, but old Nueces River, your chief of police, is out of town. And I thought you ought to know that the police force is all balled up. They're here at the Gadsden Purchase. Bell Applegate is sick — seems to be indigestion; Espalin is having a nervous spell; and Ben Creagan is bleeding from his happiest vein. You'd better come see to 'em. Good-bye!"

Pringle smiled benevolently from the door.

"There! I almost forgot to tell you boys. We disapprove of your actions oh-very-much! You know you were doing what was very, very wrong — like three little mice that were playing in the barn though the old mouse said: 'Little mice, beware! When the owl comes singing "Too-whoo" take care!' If you do it again we shall consider it deliberately unfriendly of you. . . . Well, I'll toddle my decrepit old bones out of this. Eleven o'clock! How time has flown, to be sure! Thank you for a pleasant evening. Good-bye, George. Good-bye, all! Be good little boys — go nighty-nighty!"

They raced to the corner, scurried down the first side street, turned again, and slowed to a gallop. Pringle was in high feather; he caroled blithesome as he rode:

> So those three little owls flew back up in the barn —
>   Inky, dinky, doodum, day!
> And they said, "Those little mice make us feel so nice and warm!"
>   Inky, dinky, doodum, day!
> Then they all began to sing, "Too-whit! Too-who!"
> I don't think much of this song, do you?
> But there's one thing about it — 'tis certainly true —
>   Inky, dinky, doodum, day!

They reached the open; the gallop became a trot.

"I go north here," said Foy at the cross-roads above the town. "Which way for you?"

"North too," said Pringle. "I don't know just where, but you can tell me. I go to a railroad station first — Aden. Then to the Vorhis place?"

"Vorhis? I'm going there myself," said Foy. "You didn't tell me your name yet."

"Pringle."

"What? Not John Wesley Pringle? Great Scott, man! I've heard Stella talk about you a thousand times. Say, I'm sure glad to meet you! My name's Foy — Christopher Foy."

"Why, yes," said Pringle. "I think I've heard Stella speak of you, too."

CHAPTER III

BEING A CHILD must have been great fun — once. Nowadays one would as lief be a Strasburg goose. When you and I went to school it was not quite so bad. True, neither of us could now extract a cube root with a stump puller, and it is sad to reflect how little call life has made for duodecimals. Sometimes it seems that all our struggle with moody verbs and insubordinate conjunctions was a wicked waste — poor little sleepy puzzleheads! But there were certain joyous facts which we remember yet. Lake Erie was very like a whale; Lake Ontario was a seal; and Italy was a boot.

The great Chihuahuan desert is a boot too; a larger boot than Italy. The leg of it is in Mexico, the toe is in Arizona, the heel in New Mexico; and the Jornado is in the boot-heel.

El Jornado del Muerto — the Journey of the Dead Man! From what dim old legend has the name come down? No one knows. The name has outlived the story.

Perhaps some grim, hard-riding Spaniard made his last ride here; weary at last of war, turned his dead face back to Spain and the pleasant valleys of his childhood. We have a glimpse of him, small in the mighty silence; his faithful few about him, with fearful backward glances; a gray sea of waving grama breaking at their feet; the great mountains looking down on them. Plymouth Rock is unnamed yet. — Then the mist shuts down.

The Santa Fé Trail reaches across the Jornado; tradition tells of vague, wild battles with Apache and Navajo; there are grave-cairns on lone dim ridges, whereon each passer casts a stone. Young mothers dreamed over the cradles of those who now sleep here, undreaming; here is the end of all dreams.

Doniphan passed this way; Kit Carson rode here; the Texans journeyed north along that old road in '62 — to return no more.

These were but passers-by. The history of the Jornado, of indwellers named and known, begins with six Americans, as follows: Sandoval, a Mexican; Toussaint, a Frenchman; Fest, a German; Martin, a German; Roullier, a Swiss; and Teagarden, a Welshman.

You might have thought the Jornado a vast and savage waste or a pleasant place and a various. That depended upon you. Materials for either opinion were plenty; lava flow, saccaton flats, rolling sand hills, sagebrush, mesquite and yucca, bunch grass and shallow lakes, bench and hill, ridge and groundswell and wandering draw; always the great mountains round about; the mountains and the warm sun over all.

A certain rich man desired to be President — to please his wife, perhaps. He was a favorite son sure of his home-state vote in any grand old national convention. He gave largely to charities and campaign funds, and his left hand would have been justly astonished to know what his right hand was about.

Those were bargain-counter days. Fumbling the wares, our candidate saw, among other things, that New Mexico had six conventional votes. He sent after them.

So the Bar Cross Cattle Company was founded; range, the Jornado. Our candidate provided the money and a manager, also ambidextrous with instructions to get those votes and incidentally to double the money, as a good and faithful manager should.

He got the six votes, but our candidate never became president. Poor fellow, his millions could not bring him happiness. He died, an embittered and disappointed man, in the obscurity of the United States Senate.

The Bar Cross brand was the sole fruit of that ambition. Other ranches had dwindled or vanished; favored by environment the Bar Cross, almost alone, withstood the devastating march of progress. It was still a mark of distinction to be a Bar Cross man. The good old customs — and certain bad old customs, too — still held on the Bar Cross range, fifty miles by one hundred, on the Jornado. Scattered here and there were smaller ranches: among them the V H — the Vorhis Ranch.

Stella Vorhis and John Wesley, far out on the plain, rode through the pleasant afternoon. The V H Ranch was in sight now, huddled low before them; beyond, a cluster of low hills rose from the plain, visible center of a world fresh, eager, and boundless.

The girl's eyes kindled with delight as they sought the far horizons, the misty parapets gleaming up through the golden air; she was one who found dear and beautiful this gray land, silent and ensunned. She flung up her hand exultingly.

"Isn't it wonderful, John Wesley? Do you know what it makes me think of? This:

> . . . Magic casements, opening on the foam
> Of perilous seas, in faery lands forlorn!

"Think, John! This country hasn't changed a bit since the day Columbus set out from Spain."

"How true! Fine old bird, Columbus—he saw America first. Great head he showed, too, getting himself named Christopher. Otherwise you might have said, 'the day Antony discovered Cleopatra'—or something like that. Wise old Chris!"

Stella's eyes narrowed reflectively.

"John Wesley, you've been reading! You never used to know anything about Mark Antony."

"I cribbed that remark from Billy Beebe and he swiped it from a magazine. I don't know much about Mark, even this very yet. Good old easy Mark!"

"That's the how of it. You've been absorbing knowledge from those pardners of yours. Your talk shows it. You're changed a lot— that way. Every other way you're the same old Wes!"

"Now, that sounds better!" said Pringle in his most complacent tones. "I want to talk about myself, always, Stella May Vorhis; we've come thirty miles and I've heard Christopher Foy, Foy, Foy, all the way! It's exasperating! It's sickening!"

But Stella was not to be flustered. She held her head proudly.

"It's you that have been talking about him. I told you you'd like him, John Wesley."

"Yes, you did—and I do. He's a self-starter. He's a peppermist. He's a regular guy. It wasn't only the way he smashed those thugs— taken by surprise and all—but that he had judgment enough not to shoot when there was no need for it; that's what gets me! And then he went and spoiled it all."

"How?"

"Hiking on up to the ranch with the Major, without even waking you up. Why, if it was me, do you s'pose I'd leave another man— no matter how old and safe he was—to tell such a story as that his own way and hog all the credit for himself? That Las Uvas push is a four-flush—he needn't stir a peg for them. No, sir! I'd have stayed right there till you got ready to come—and every time I'd narrate that tale about the scrap it would get scarier and scarier."

"I know, without telling, what my Chris does is the brave thing, the best thing," said the girl, with softly shining eyes. "And he never brags — any more than you do, Wes. You're always making fun of yourself. And I'm afraid you don't know how serious a menace this Las Uvas gang is. It isn't what Chris may do or may not do. All they want is a pretext. Why, John, there are men down there who are really quite truthful — as men go — till they get on the witness stand. But the minute they're under oath they begin to lie. Force of habit, I guess. The whole courthouse ring hates Chris and fears him — especially Matt Lisner, the sheriff. In the old trouble, whenever he was outwitted or outfought, Chris did it. Besides — " She paused; the color swept to her cheek.

"Besides — you. Yes, yes," grumbled Pringle. "Might have been expected. These women! Does the Foy-boy know?"

"He knows that Lisner wanted to marry me," said Stella. Neck and cheek were crimson now; but it was characteristic that her level eyes met Pringle's fearlessly. "But before that — he — he persecuted me, John. Chris must not know. He would kill him. But I wanted you to know in case anything happened to Chris. There is nothing they will stick at, these men. Lisner is the vilest; he hates Chris worst of all." She was in deep distress; there were tears in her eyes as she smiled at him. "And I wish — oh, John Wesley, you don't know how I wish you were staying here — dear old friend!"

"As a dear and highly valuable old friend," said Pringle sedately, "let me point out how shrewd and sensible a plan it would be for you and your Chris to go on a honeymoon at once — and never come back."

"I am beginning to think so. Up to last night I had only my fears to go on."

"But now you know. We managed to make a joke of last night — but what that push had in mind was plain murder. I would dearly like," said John Wesley, "to visit Las Uvas — some dark night — in a Zeppelin."

At the corral gate the Major met them, with a face so troubled that Stella cried out in alarm:

"Father! What is it? Chris?"

"Stella — be brave! Dick Marr was killed at midnight — and they're swearing it off on Chris."

"But John Wesley was with him."

"That's just it. Applegate and Creagan tell it that they saw Chris leaving town at eleven o'clock, that he said he was coming up here, and that he made a war-talk about Marr. But not a word about Pringle or the fight at the hotel. Joe Espalin doesn't appear — no claim that he saw Foy at all."

"That looks ugly," observed Pringle.

"Ugly! Your testimony is to be thrown out as a lie made of whole cloth. Espalin and the barkeeper don't appear. They're afraid the Mexican will get tangled up, and Max will swear he didn't see Chris at all. It's cut and dried. You are to be canceled. Marr was found this morning at the first cross-road above town. His watch was stopped at ten minutes to twelve — mashed, it seemed, where it hit on a stone when he fell. If they had told about the mix-up with you and Chris last night, I might have thought they really believed Chris killed Marr — or suspected it. As it stands, we know the whole thing is a black, rotten conspiracy."

"But where's Chris?" demanded Stella, trembling.

"We have none of us seen Chris — you want to remember that. You won't have to lie, Stella — you didn't see him. Pringle, I bank on you."

"Sure! I can lie and stick to it, though I'm sadly out of practice," said Pringle. "But hadn't we better fix up the same history to tell? And where's your man Hargis that stays here? Will he do?"

"Unsaddle and I'll tell you. We've only got a few minutes. I saw the dust of them coming down from the north as I drove in this bunch of saddle horses. Some of them went up by train to Upham, you know. Hargis has gone to the round-up, and I'm just as well pleased. I'm not sure he can be trusted. We are to know not the first word of what has happened. We haven't seen Chris and haven't heard of the murder. Come in — we'll start dinner and be taken by surprise. Pringle, throw your gun over on the bunk. Stella, get that look off your face. After you hear the news you can look any old way and it'll be natural enough. But you've got to be unconcerned and unsuspicious when they first come."

He started a fire. Stella set about preparing dinner.

"Who brought the news?" she asked.

"Joe Cowan — and a relay. Someone rode to Jeff Isaack's ranch as fast as ever a horse could go. Jeff came to Quartzite; Dodd passed the word on to Goldenburg's and Cowan came here. At every ranch they drove all the fresh saddle horses out of the way, so a posse couldn't get a remount without losing time. Kitty Foy has got good friends, and they don't believe he'd shoot any man in the back."

"And Foy's drifted with Cowan?"

"He hadn't a chance to get clear," said the Major. "We had no fresh horses here. They've sworn in a small army of deputies. Nearly a hundred men are out hunting for him by this time. One posse was to go up the San Andres on the east, leaving a man at every waterhole. The sheriff wired for a special train, took a carload of saddle horses and dropped a couple of men off at every station. At Upham the rest of them were to unload and string out across the Jornado, so as to cut Chris off from the Bar Cross round-up at Alaman. It's some of that bunch I saw coming, I guess. And the others were to scatter out and come up the middle of the plain. They'll drag the Jornado with a fine-toothed comb."

"How's he to get away, then?"

"Cowan took Kit's horse and led his own, which was about to give out. He turned back east, up a draw where he won't be seen unless somebody's right on top of him. Eight or ten miles out he'll turn Foy's horse loose; he'll carry the extra saddle on a ways and drop it in a washout. They'll find Foy's horse and think he's roped a fresh one. Then Cowan will start up a fresh bunch of mares and raise a big dust. He will ride straight to the first posse he sees, claiming he's run his horse down chasing the mares. That'll let him out — maybe."

"And Foy?"

"We rode my horse double to the edge of the hills, to where he could walk on a ledge and leave no tracks," said the Major. "Then I went on. I rounded up this bunch of saddle horses and brought them back. He went up on Little Thumb Butte. It's all bluffs and bowlders there. Up on the highest big cliff, at the very top, is a deep crack that winds up in a cave like a tunnel. You know the place, Stella?"

"Yes. But, dad, they'll hunt out the hills the first thing."

"They will not!" said the Major triumphantly. "They'll read our sign; they'll see where four shod horses came up the road. I'll claim one of them was a horse I was leading — that'll be that bald-faced roan out in the corral. We all want to stick to that."

"But he's bigger than any of our horses," objected Pringle. "They'll know better by the tracks."

"Exactly! So they'll find a fresh-shod track going east — a track matching the fourth track we left on the road. They'll reason we're trying to keep them from following that track. So they'll follow it up; they'll find Kit's give-out horse and then they'll know they're right."

"It seems to me," said Pringle reflectively, "that friend Cowan may have an interesting time if they get him."

The Major permitted himself a grin.

"He yanked the shoes off his horse before he left. Once he mixes his tracks up with a bunch of wild mares he'll be all right. They may think, but they can't prove anything. And Foy'll be all right — if only the posse follows the plain trail."

"It's too much to hope," said Stella. "They'll split up. Some of them will hunt out the hills anyway — tomorrow, if not today."

"That's my idea of it," said Pringle.

"They won't find the cave if they do," said Vorhis hopefully. "If he can get to the Bar Cross they'll see him through, once they hear his story. Not telling about that clean-up you and Kit made last night is a dead giveaway."

"Any chance of Foy slipping out afoot?"

"Too far. But he could stand a siege till we could get word to his friends if, by any chance, the posse should find his cave. He took my rifle. He can see them coming; he'll have every advantage against attack; and there's another way out of the cave, up on top of the hill. There's just one thing against him. There wasn't even a canteen here. He took some jerky and canned stuff — but only one measly beer bottle of water. When that's used up it's going to be a dull time for him. We can't get water to him very handy without leaving some sign. We mustn't get hostile with the posse. Take it easy — you especially, Pringle. Stella and me, they know where we stand. But you're a stranger. Maybe they'll let you go on. If you once get away — bring the Bar Cross boys and they'll take Foy out of here in broad day."

"Very pretty — but there's four men in Las Uvas that know me — and three of them are police. Maybe they'll stay in the city though — being police?"

"No, they won't," said the Major gloomily. "They'll be along — deputized, of course. Maybe they won't be in the first batch though. Your part is to be the disinterested traveler, wanting to be on your way."

"It won't work, Major. This is a put-up job. Even if Applegate and his strikers aren't along they've given my description. Somebody will know I was with Foy last night, and they'll know I'm lying."

The Major sighed. "That's so, too. I'm afraid you're in for trouble."

"I'm used to that," said Pringle lightly. "Once, in Arizona — "

"Don't throw it up to me, John," said the Major a trifle sheepishly. "I'll say this though: I wouldn't ask for a better man in a tight than you."

"Thanks so much!" murmured Pringle. "And that Sir Hubert Stanley thing."

"One more point, John: You don't know Foy. I do. Foy'll never give up. He's desperate — and he's not pleased. There's no question of surrender and standing trial; understand that. He'd be lynched, probably, if they ever got him in Las Uvas. A trial, even, would be just lynching under another name. They don't want to capture him anyway — they want a chance to kill him."

"I wouldn't want the job," said Pringle.

"Hush!" said Stella. "I hear them coming. Talk about something else — the war in Europe."

The Major picked up a paper.

"What do you think about the United States building a big navy, John?" he asked casually.

Stealthy footsteps rustled without.

"Fine!" said Pringle. "I'm strong for it. We want dreadnoughts, and lots of 'em — biggest we can build. But that ain't all. When we make the navy appropriations we ought to set by about fifty-some-odd million and build a big multiple-track railroad, so we can carry our navy inland in case of war. The ocean is no place for a battle-ship these days."

"Stop your kidding!"

"I'm not kidding," said John Wesley indignantly. "I never was twice as serious in my whole life. My plan is sound, statesmanlike — "

"Shut up, you idiot! I want to read."

"Oh, very well, then! I'll grind the coffee."

Men crept close to the open door on each side of the kitchen. Stella slipped a pan of biscuits in the oven; she laid the table briskly, with a merry clatter of tinware; her face was cheerful and unclouded. The Major leaned back in one chair, his feet on another; he was deep in the paper; he puffed his pipe. John Wesley Pringle twirled the coffee mill between his knees and sang a merry tune:

> There were three little mice, playing in the barn
>   Inky, dinky, doodum, day!
> Though they knew they were doing what was very, very wrong —
>   Inky, dinky, doodum, day!
> And the song of the owls, it sounded so nice
> That closer and closer crept the three little mice
> And the owls came and gobbled them —

A shadow fell across the floor.

"Hands up!" said the sheriff of Dona Ana. "We want Chris Foy!"

CHAPTER IV

NAVAJO, Pima and Hopi enjoy seven cardinal points — north, east, west, south, up, down, and right here. In these and any intermediate directions from the Vorhis Ranch the diligent *posse comitatus* made swift and jealous search through the slow hours of afternoon. It commandeered the V H saddle horses in the corral; it searched for sign in the soft earth of the wandering draws between the dozen low hills scattered round Big Thumb Butte and Little Thumb Butte; it rode circles round the ranch; the sign of Christopher Foy's shod horse was found and followed hotfoot by a detachment. Eight men had arrived in the first bunch, with the sheriff; others from every angle joined by twos and threes from hour to hour till the number rose to above a score. A hasty election provided a protesting cook and a horse wrangler; a V H beef was slaughtered.

The posse was rather equally divided between two classes — simpletons and fools. The first unquestionably believed Foy to be a base and cowardly murderer, out of law, whom it were most righteous to harry; else, as the storied juryman put it, "How came he there?" The other party were of those who hold that evil-doing may permanently prosper and endure.

In the big living room of the adobe ranch house much time had been wasted in cross-questions and foolish answers. Stella Vorhis had been banished to her own room and Sheriff Matt Lisner had privately told off a man to make sure she did not escape.

Lisner and Ben Creagan, crossest of the four examiners, had been prepared to meet by crushing denial an eager and indignant statement from Pringle, adducing the Gadsden House affair and his subsequent companying with Foy as proof positive of Foy's innocence. That no such accusation came from Pringle set these able but mystified deniers entirely at a loss, left the denial high and dry. Creagan mopped his brow furtively.

"Vorhis," said Sheriff Matt, red and angry from an hour's endeavor, "I think you're telling a pack of lies — every word of it. You know mighty well where Foy is."

The Major's gray goatee quivered.

"Guess I'll tell you lies if I want to," he retorted defiantly.

"But, Sheriff, he may be telling us the truth," urged Paul Breslin. "Foy may very well have ridden here alone before Vorhis got here.

I've known the Major a long time. He isn't the man to protect a red-handed murderer."

"Aw, bah! How do you know I won't? How do you know he's a murderer? You make me sick!" declared the Major hotly. Breslin was an honest, well-meaning farmer; the Major was furious to find such a man allied with Foy's foes — certain sign that other decent blockheads would do likewise. "Matt Lisner tells you Kit Foy is a murderer and you believe him implicitly: Matt Lisner tells you I'm a liar — but you stumble at that. Why? Because you think about me — that's why! Why don't you try that plan about Foy — thinking?"

"But Foy's run away," stammered Breslin, disconcerted.

"Run away, hell! He's not here, you mean. According to your precious story, Foy was leaving before Marr was killed — or before you say Marr was killed. Why don't you look for him with the Bar Cross round-up? There's where he started for, you say?"

"I wired up and had a trusty man go out there quietly at once. He's staying there still — quietly," said the sheriff. "Foy isn't there — and the Bar Cross hasn't heard of the killing yet. It won't do, Major. Foy's run away."

John Wesley Pringle, limp, slack, and rumpled in his chair, yawned, stretching his arms wide.

"This man Foy," he ventured amiably, "if he really run away, he done a wise little stunt for himself, I think. Because every little ever and anon, thin scraps of talk float in from your cookfire in the yard, — and there's a heap of it about ropes and lynching, for instance. If he hasn't run away yet, he'd better — and I'll tell him so if I see him. Stubby, red-faced, spindlin', thickset, jolly little man, ain't he? Heavy-complected, broad-shouldered, dark blond, very tall and slender, weighs about a hundred and ninety, with a pale skin and hollow-cheeked, plump, serious face?"

At this ill-timed and unthinkable levity Breslin stared in bewilderment; Lisner glared, gripping his fist convulsively; and Mr. Ben Creagan, an uneasy third inquisitor, breathed hard through his nose. Anastacio Barela, the fourth and last inquisitor, maintained unmoved the disinterested attitude he had held since the interrogation began. Feet crossed, he lounged in his chair, graceful, silent, smoking, listening, idly observant of wall and ceiling.

No answer being forthcoming to his query Pringle launched another:

"Speaking of faces, Creagan, old sport, what's happened to you and your nose? You look like someone had spread you on the minutes." He eyed Creagan with solicitous interest.

Mr. Creagan's battered face betrayed emotion. Pringle's shameless mendacity shocked him. But it was Creagan's sorry plight that he must affect never to have seen this insolent Pringle before. The sheriff's face mottled with wrath. Pringle reflected swiftly: The sheriff's rage hinted strongly that he was in Creagan's confidence and hence was no stranger to last night's mishap at the hotel; their silence proclaimed their treacherous intent.

On the other hand, these two, if not the others, knew very well that Pringle had left town with Foy and had probably stayed with him; that the Major must know all that Foy and Pringle knew. Evidently, Pringle decided, these two, at least, could expect no direct information from their persistent questionings; what they hoped for was unconscious betrayal by some slip of the tongue. As for young Breslin, Pringle had long since sized him up for what the Major knew him to be — a good-hearted, right-meaning simpleton. In the indifferent-seeming Anastacio, Pringle recognized an unknown quantity.

That, for a certainty, Christopher Foy had not killed Marr, was a positive bit of knowledge which Pringle shared only with the murderer himself and with that murderer's accomplices, if any. So much was plain, and Pringle felt a curiosity, perhaps pardonable, as to who the murderer really was.

Duty and inclination thus happily wedded, Pringle set himself to goad ferret-eyed Creagan and the heavy-jawed sheriff into unwise speech. And inattentive Anastacio had a shrewd surmise at Pringle's design. He knew nothing of the fight at the Gadsden House, but he sensed an unexplained tension — and he knew his chief.

"And this man, too — what about him?" said Breslin, regarding Pringle with a puzzled face. "Granted that the Major might have a motive for shielding Foy — he may even believe Foy to be innocent — why should this stranger put himself in danger for Foy?"

"Here, now — none of that!" said Pringle with some asperity. "I may be a stranger to you, but I'm an old friend of the Major's. I'm his guest, eating his grub and drinking his baccy; if he sees fit to tell any lies I back him up, of course. Haven't you got any principle at all? What do you think I am?"

"I know what you are," said the sheriff. "You're a damned liar!"

"An amateur only," said Pringle modestly. "I never take money for it." He put by a whisp of his frosted hair, the better to scrutinize, with insulting slowness, the sheriff's savage face. "Your ears are very large!" he murmured at last. "And red!"

The sheriff leaped up.

"You insolent cur-dog!" he roared.

" 'To stand and be still to the Birken'ead drill is a dam' tough bullet to chew,' " quoted Pringle evenly. "But he done it — old Pringle — John Wesley Pringle — liar and cur-dog too! We'll discuss the cur-dog later. Now, about the liar. You're mighty certain, seems to me. Why? How do you know I'm lying? For I am lying — I'll not deceive you. I'm lying; you know I'm lying; I know that you know I'm lying: and you apprehend clearly that I am aware that you are cognizant of the fact that I am fully assured that you know I am lying. Just like that! What a very peculiar set of happenstances. I am a nervous woman and this makes my head go round!"

"The worst day's work you ever did for yourself," said the angry sheriff, "was when you butted into this business."

"Yes, yes; go on. Was this today or yesterday — at the hotel?"

"Liar!" roared Lisner. "You never were at the Gadsden House."

"Who said I was?"

The words cracked like a whiplash. Simultaneously, Pringle's tilted chair came down to its four legs and Pringle sat poised, his weight on the balls of his feet, ready for a spring. The sheriff paused midway of a step; his mottled face grew ashen. A gurgle very like a smothered chuckle came from Anastacio. Creagan flung himself into the breach.

"Aw, Matt, let's have the girl in here. We can't get nothing from these stiff-necked idiots."

"Might as well," agreed Lisner in a tone that tried to be contemptuous but trembled. "We're wasting time here."

"Lisner," said the Major in his gentlest tone, "be well advised and leave my daughter be."

"And if I don't?" sneered Lisner. He had no real desire to question Stella, but welcomed the change of venue as a diversion from his late indiscretion. "If, in the performance of my duty, I put a few civil questions to Miss Vorhis — in the presence of her father, mind you — then what?"

"But you won't!" said the Major softly.

"Do you know, Sheriff, I think the Major has the right idea?" said Pringle. "We won't bother the young lady."

"Who's going to stop me?"

Anastacio, in his turn, brought his chair to the floor, at the same time unclasping his hands from behind his head.

"I'll do that little thing, Sheriff," he announced mildly. "Miss Vorhis has already told us that she has not seen Foy since yesterday noon. That is quite sufficient."

Silence.

"This makes me fidgety. Somebody say something, quick — anything!" begged Pringle. "All right, then; I will. Let's go back — we've dropped a stitch. That goes about me being a liar and a damned one, Sheriff; but I'm hurt to have you think I'm a cur-dog. You're the sheriff, doin' your duty, as you so aptly observed. And you've done took my gun away. But if bein' a cur-dog should happen to vex me — honest, Sheriff, I'm that sensitive that I'll tell you now — not hissing or gritting or gnashing my teeth — just telling you — the first time I meet you in a strictly private and unofficial way I'm goin' to remold you closer to my heart's desire!"

"You brazen hussy! You know you lied!"

"You're still harpin' on that, Sheriff? That doesn't make it any easier to be a cur-dog. How did you know I lied? You say so, mighty positive — but what are your reasons? Why don't you tell your associates? There is an honest man in this room. I am not sure there are not two — "

Anastacio's eyes again removed themselves from the ceiling.

"If you mean me — and somehow I am quite clear as to that — "

"I mean Mr. Breslin."

"Oh, him — of course!" said Anastacio in a shocked voice. "Breslin, by all means, for the one you were sure of. But the second man, the one you had hopes of — who should that be but me? I thank you. I am touched. I am myself indifferent honest, as Shakespere puts it."

"If you think I am going to stay here to be insulted — "

"You are!" taunted John Wesley Pringle. "You'll stay right here. What? Leave me here to tell what I have to say to an honest man and a half? Impossible! You'll not let me out of your sight."

"My amateur Ananias," interrupted Anastacio dispassionately, "you are, unintentionally, perhaps, doing me half of a grave injustice. In this particular instance — for this day and date only — I am as pure as a new-mown hay. To prevent all misapprehension let me say now that I never thought Foy killed Dick Marr."

"In heaven's name, why?" demanded Breslin.

"My honest but thick-skulled friend, let me put in my oar," implored the Major. "Let me show you that Matt Lisner never thought Foy was guilty. Foy said last night, before the killing, that he was coming up here, didn't he?"

"Hey, Major — hold up!" cried Pringle. But Vorhis was not to be stopped.

"Don't you see, you doddering imbecile? If Foy had really killed Dick Marr he might have gone to any other place in the world — but he wouldn't have come here."

"Aha! So Foy did come here, hey?" croaked the sheriff, triumphant in his turn. "Thanks, Major, for the information, though I was sure before, humanly speaking, that he came this way."

"Which is another way of saying that you don't think Foy did the killing — that you don't even suspect him of it," said Anastacio, as the Major subsided, crestfallen. "Matt Lisner, I know that you hate Foy. I know that you welcome this chance to get rid of him. Make no mistake, Breslin. I was not wanted here. I wasn't asked and none of my people were brought along. I tagged along, though — to wait. It's one of the best little things I do — waiting. And I came to protect Foy, not to capture him. I came to keep right at his side, in case he surrendered without a fight — for fear he might be killed . . . escaping . . . on the way back. It's a way that we have in Las Uvas!"

Lisner threw a look of hate at his deputy.

"You don't mean to tell me there's any danger of anything like that?" said Breslin, staggered and aghast.

"Every danger. That's an old gag — the *ley fuga*."

"You lie!" bawled Creagan. His six-shooter covered Anastacio.

"That'll keep. Put up your gun, Bennie," said Anastacio with great composure. "Supper's most ready. Besides, the Barelas won't like it if you shoot me this way. There's a lot of the Barelas, Ben. I'll tell you what I'll do, though — I'll slip the idea to my crowd, and any time you want to kill me on an even break, no Barela or Ascarate will take it up. Put it right in your little holster — put it up, I say! That's right. You see, Breslin? Don't let Foy out of your sight if he should be taken."

"But he'll never let himself be taken alive," said Vorhis. "Even if anyone wants to take him — alive. Pass the word to your friends, Breslin, unless you want them to take part in a deliberate, foreplanned murder."

"Damn you, what do you mean?" shouted the sheriff.

"By God, sir, I mean just what I say!"

"Why, girls!" said Pringle. "You shock me! This is most unladylike. This is scandalous talk. Be nice! Please — pretty please! See, here comes some more pussy-foot posse — three, six, eleven hungry men. Have they got Foy? No; they have not got Foy. Is he up? He is up. Look who's here too! Good old Applegate and Brother Espalin. I wonder now if they're goin' to give me the cut direct, like Creagan did? You notice, Mr. Breslin."

The horsemen rode into the corral.

"No; don't go, Sheriff," said Anastacio. "I'm anxious to see if those two will recognize Ananias the Amateur. They'll be here directly. You, either, Creagan. Else I'll shoot you both in the back, accidentally, cleaning my gun."

From without was the sound of spurred feet in haste; three men appeared at the open door.

"Why, if it ain't George! Good old George!" cried Pringle, rising with outstretched arms. "And my dear friend Espalin! What a charming reunion!"

Applegate's eyes threw a startled question at his chief and at Creagan; Espalin slipped swiftly back through the door.

"I don't know you, sir," said Applegate.

"George! You're never going to disown me. Joe's gone, too. Nobody loves me!"

The third man, a grizzled and bristly old warrior with a limp, broke in with a roar.

"What in hell's going on here?" he stormed.

"You are, for one thing, if you don't moderate your voice," said Anastacio. "Nueces, you bellow like the bulls of Bashan. Mr. Applegate, meet Mr. Pringle."

"What does he mean, then, by such monkeyshines?" demanded the other — old Nueces River, chief of police, ex-ranger, and, for this occasion, deputy sheriff. "I got no time for foolishness. And you can't run no whizzer on me, Barela. Don't you try it!"

"Oh, they're just joking, Nueces," said the Major. "Tell us how about it. Here, I'll light the lamp; it's getting dark. Find any sign of Foy?"

Nueces leveled a belligerent finger at the Major.

"You've been joking, too! I've heard about you. Lisner, I'm ashamed of you! Let Vorhis pull the wool over your eyes, while you sit here and jaw all afternoon, doing nothing!"

"Why, what did you find out?"

"A-plenty. Them stiffs you sent out found Foy's horse, to begin with."

"Sure it was Foy's horse?" queried Lisner eagerly.

"Sure! I know the horse — that big calico horse of his."

"Why didn't you follow him up?"

"Follow hell! Oh, some of the silly fools are milling round out there — going over to the San Andres tonight to take a big hunt manana. Not me. That horse was a blind. They pottered round tryin' to find some trace of Foy — blind fools! — till I met up with 'em. I'd done gathered in that mizzable red-headed Joe Cowan on a give-out horse, claimin' he'd been chousin' after broom-tails. He'd planted Foy's horse, I reckon. But it can't be proved, so I let him go. He'll have to walk in; that's one good thing."

"But Foy — where do you figure Foy's gone?"

"Maybe he simply was not," suggested Pringle, "like Enoch when he was translated into all European languages, including the Scandinavian."

"Pringle, if you say another word I'll have you gagged!" said the exasperated sheriff. "Don't you reckon, Nueces, that Cowan brought Foy a barefooted horse? He can't have gone on afoot or you'd have seen his tracks."

"Sheriff, you certainly are an easy mark!" returned Nueces, in great disgust. "Foy didn't go on afoot or horseback, because he was never there. I've told you twice: Cowan left that calico horse on purpose for us to find. Vorhis is Foy's friend. Can't you see, if Foy had tried to get away by hard riding he would have had a fresh horse, not the one he rode from Las Uvas, and you wouldn't have found a penful of fresh horses to chase him with? Not in a thousand years! That was to make it nice and easy for you to ride on — a six-year-old kid could see through it! It's a wonder you didn't all fall for it and chase away. No, sir! Foy either stopped down on the river and sent his horse on to fool us — or, more likely, he's up in the Buttes. Did you look there?"

"I sent the boys round to out sign. I didn't feel justified in hunting out the rough places till we had more men. Too much cover for him."

"And none for you, I s'pose? Mamma! but you're a fine sheriff! Look now: After we started back here we sighted a dust comin' 'way up north. We went over, and 'twas Hargis, the Major's buckaroo, throwin' in a bunch from the round-up. He didn't know nothin' and was not right sure of that — till I mentioned your reward. Soon as ever I mentioned twenty-five hundred, he loosened up right smart."

"Well? Did he know where Foy was?"

"No; but he knew of the place where I judge Foy is, this very yet. Gosh!" said Nueces River in deep disgust, "it beats hell what men will do for a little dirty money! Seems there's a cave near the top of the least of them two buttes — the roughest one — a cave with two mouths, one right on the big top. Nobody much knows where it is, only the V H outfit."

Pringle had edged across the room. He now plucked at Bell Applegate's sleeve.

"Say, is that right about that reward — twenty-five hundred?" he whispered. His eyes glistened.

"Forty-five," said Bell behind his hand. "The Masons, they put up a thousand, and Dick's old uncle — that would have let Dick starve or work — he tacked on a thousand more. Dead or alive!" He looked down at Pringle's face, at Pringle's working fingers, opening and shutting avariciously; he sneered. "Don't you wish you may get it? S-sh! Hear what the old man's saying."

During the whispered colloquy the old ranger had kept on:

"There's where he is, a twenty-to-one shot! He'll lay quiet, likely, thinkin' we'll miss him. Brush growin' over both the cave mouths, Hargis says, so you might pass right by if you didn't know where to look. These short nights he couldn't never get clear on foot. Thirty mile to the next water — we'd find his tracks and catch him. But he might make a break to get away, at that. Never can tell about a he-man like that. We can't take no chances. We'll pick a bit of supper and then we surround that hill, quiet as mice, and close up on him. He can't see us to shoot if we're fool enough to make any noise. Come daylight, we'll have him cornered, every man behind a bowlder. If he shows up he's our meat; if he don't we'll starve him out."

"And suppose he isn't there?" said Creagan. "What would we look like, watching an empty cave two or three days?"

"What do we look like now? Give you three guesses," retorted Nueces. "And how'd we look rushin' that empty cave if it didn't happen to be empty? Excuse me! I'd druther get three grand hee-haws and a tiger for bein' ridiculous than to have folks tiptoe by a-whisperin': 'How natural he looks!' I been a pretty tough old bird in my day — but goin' up a tunnel after Kitty Foy ain't my idea of foresight."

"Some man — some good man, too — will have to stay here and stand guard on the Major and this fresh guy, Pringle," said the sheriff thoughtfully. "He'll get his slice of the money, of course."

"You'll find a many glad to take that end of the job; for," said Nueces River, "it is in my wise old noddle some of us are going to be festerin' in Abraham's bosom before we earn that reward money. Leave Applegate — he's in bad shape for climbing anyway; bruise on his belly big as a washpan."

"Bronc' bucked me over on the saddle horn," explained Applegate. "Sure, I'll stay. And the Pringle person will be right here when you get back, too."

"Let the Major take some supper in to Miss Vorhis," suggested Breslin. "I'll keep an eye on him. He can eat with her and cheer her up a little. This is hard lines for a girl."

Lisner shrugged his shoulders.

"We have to keep her here till Foy's caught. She might bring a sight of trouble down on us."

"Say, what's the matter with me going out and eating a few?" asked Pringle.

"You stay here! You talk too much with your mouth," replied the sheriff. "I'll send in a snack for you and Bell. Come on, boys."

They filed out to the cook's fire in the walled courtyard.

"George, dear," said Pringle when the two were left alone, "is that right about the reward? 'Cause I sure want to get in on it."

"Damn likely. You knew where Foy was. You know where he is now. Why didn't you tell us, if you wanted in on the reward?"

"Why, George, I didn't know there was any reward. Besides, him and me split up as soon as we got clear of town."

"You're a damn liar!"

"That's what the sheriff said. Somebody must 'a' give me away," complained John Wesley. He rolled a cigarette and walked to the table. "All the same, you're making a mistake. You hadn't ought to roil me. Just for that, soon as they're all off on their man hunt, I'm goin' to study up some scheme to get away."

"I got a picture of you gettin' away!"

"George," said John Wesley, "you see that front door? Well, that's what we call in theatrical circles a practical door. Along toward morning I'm going out through that practical door. You'll see!"

He raised the lamp, held the cigarette over the chimney top and puffed till he got a light; so doing he smoked the chimney. To inspect the damage he raised the lamp higher. Swifter than thought he hurled it at his warder's head. The blazing lamp struck Applegate between the eyes. Pringle's fist flashed up and smote him grievously under the jaw; he fell crashing; the half-drawn gun clattered from his slackened fingers. Pringle caught it up and plunged into the dark through the practical door.

He ran down the adobe wall of the water pen; a bullet whizzed by; he turned the corner; he whisked over the wall, back into the water pen. Shouts, curses, the sound of rushing feet without the wall. Pringle crouched in the deep shadow of the wall, groped his way to the long row of watering troughs, and wormed himself under the upper trough, where the creaking windmill and the splashing of water from the supply pipe would drown out the sound of his labored breath.

Horsemen boiled from the yard gate with uproar and hullabaloo; Pringle heard their shouts; he saw the glare of soapweeds, fired to help their search.

The lights died away; the shouts grew fainter: they swelled again as the searchers straggled back, vociferous. Pringle caught scraps of talk as they watered their horses.

"Clean getaway!"

"One bad actor, that *hombre!*"

"Regular Go-Getter!"

"Batting average about thirteen hundred, I should figger."

"Life-size he-man! Where do you suppose — "

"Saw a lad make just such another break once in Van Zandt County — "

"Say! Who're you crowdin'?"

"Hi, fellers! Bill's giving some more history of the state of Van Zandt!"

"Applegate's pretty bad hurt."

" — in a gopher hole and near broke my fool neck."

"Where'd this old geezer come from, anyway? Never heard of him before!"

" 'Tain't fair, just when we was all crowdin' up for supper! He might have waited."

"This will be merry hell and repeat if he hooks up with Foy," said Creagan's voice, adding a vivid description of Pringle.

Old Nueces answered, raising his voice:

"He's afoot. We got to beat him to it. Let's ride!"

"That's right," said the sheriff. "But we'll grab something to eat first. Saddle up, Hargis, and lead us to your little old cave. Robbins, while we snatch a bite you bunch what canteens we've got and fill 'em up. Then you watch the old man and that girl, and let Breslin come with us. You can eat after we've gone."

"Don't let the girl heave a pillow at you, Robbins!" warned a voice.

"Better not stop to eat," urged Nueces.

"We can lope up and get to the foot of Thumb Butte before Pringle gets halfway — if he's going there at all. Most likely he's had a hand in the Marr killing and is just running away to save his own precious neck," said the sheriff. "We'll scatter out around the hill when we get to the roughs, and go up afoot till every man can see or hear his neighbor, so Pringle can't get through. Then we'll wait till daylight."

"That may suit you," retorted Nueces. "Me, I don't intend for any man that will buck a gun with a lamp to throw in with Kit Foy while I stuff my paunch. That sort is just the build to do a mile in nothing flat — and it's only three miles to the hill. I'm goin' now, and I'm goin' hellity-larrup! Come on, anybody with more brains than

belly — I'm off to light a line of soapweeds on that hill so this Mr.
Pringle-With-the-Punch don't walk himself by. If he wants up he'll
have to hoof it around the other side of the hill. We won't make any
light on the north side. That Bar Cross outfit is too damn inquisitive.
The night herders would see it; they'd smell trouble; and like as not
the whole bilin' of 'em would come pryin' down here by daylight.
Guess they haven't heard about Foy or they'd be here now. They're
strong for Foy. Come on, you waddies!"

Mr. Pringle-With-the-Punch, squeezed, cramped, and muddy
under the trough, heard this supperless plan with displeasure; his hope
had been otherwise. He heard the sound of hurried mounting; from
the thunder of galloping hoofs it would seem that a goodly number
of the posse had come up to the specifications laid down by the old
ranger.

The others clanked away, leaving their horses standing. The man
Robbins grumbled from saddle to saddle and gathered canteens. As
he filled them from the supply pipe directly above Mr. Pringle's head,
he set them on the ground within easy reach of Mr. Pringle's hand.
Acting on this hint Mr. Pringle's hand withdrew a canteen, quite unostentatiously. An unnecessary precaution, as it turned out; Mr. Robbins, having filled that batch, went to the horses farther down the
troughs to look for more canteens. So Pringle wriggled out with his
canteen, selected a horse, and rode quietly through the gate.

"Going already?" called Robbins as he passed.

Secure under cover of darkness, Pringle answered in the voice of
one who, riding, eats:

"Yes, indeedy; I ain't no hawg. Wasn't much hungry nohow!"

CHAPTER V

AT THE FOOT of Little Thumb Butte a lengthening semicircle of fire
flared through the night. John Wesley Pringle swung far out on the
plain to circle round it.

"This takes time," he muttered to himself, "but at least I know
where not to go. That old rip-snorter sure put a spoke in my wheel!
Looks like Foy might see them lights and drift out away from this.
But he won't, I guess — they said his hidey-hole was right on top, and
the shoulder of the hill will hide the fires from him. Probably asleep,
anyhow, thinkin' he's safe. I slep' three hours this morning at the
Major's; but Foy he didn't sleep any. Even if he did leave, they'd

track him up in the morning and get him — and he knows it. Somebody's goin' to be awfully annoyed when he misses this horse."

He could see the riders, dim-flitting as they passed between him
and the flames. Once he stopped to listen; he heard the remaining
half of the man-hunt leaving the ranch. They were riding hard. Thereafter Pringle had no mercy on his horse. Ride as he might, those who
followed had the inner circle; when he rounded the fires and struck
the hill his start was perilously slight. While the footing was soft he
urged the wearied horse up the slope; at the first rocky space he
abandoned the poor beast lest the floundering of shod hoofs should betray him. He took off saddle and bridle; he hung the canteen over his
shoulder and pressed on afoot.

A light breeze had overcast the stars with thin and fleecy clouds.
This made for Pringle's safety; it also made the going harder — and it
would have been hard going by daylight.

The slope became steeper; ledges of rock, little at first, became
larger and more frequent; he came to bluffs that barred his progress,
slow and painful at best; he was forced to search to left or right for
broken places where he could climb. Bits of rock, dislodged by his
feet, fell clattering despite his utmost care; he heard the like from
below, to the left, to the right. The short night wore swiftly on.

With equal fortune John Wesley should have maintained his lead.
But he found more than his share of no-thoroughfares. Before long
his ears told him that men were almost abreast of him on each side.
He was handicapped now, because he must shun any chance meeting.
His immediate neighbors, however, had no such fear; they edged
closer and closer together as they climbed. At last, stopped against
a perpendicular wall ten feet high, he heard them creeping toward him
from both sides, with a guarded "Coo-ee!" each to the other; John
Wesley slipped down the hill to the nearest bush. His neighbors came
together and held a whispered discourse. They viewed the barrier
with marked patience, it seemed; they sat down in friendly fashion
and smoked cigarette after cigarette; the hum of their hushed voices
reached Pringle, murmuring and indistinct. It might almost be
thought that they were willing for others to precede them in the place
of honor. A faint glow showed in the east; the moon had thoughts of
rising.

After an interminable half-hour the two worthies passed on to the
right. Pringle took to the left, more swiftly. Time for caution had
passed; moonlight might betray him. When he found a way up that
unlucky wall others of the search party farther to the left were well
beyond him.

Perhaps a quarter of a mile away, the last sheer cliff, the Thumb which gave the hill its name, frowned above him, a hundred feet from base to crest. Pringle bore obliquely up to the right. Speed was his best safety now; he pushed on boldly, cheered by the thought that if seen by any of the posse he would be taken for one of their own number. But Foy, seeing him, would make the same mistake! It was an uncomfortable reflection.

The pitch was less abrupt now, and there were no more ledges; instead, boulders were strewn along the rounded slope, with bush and stunted tree between. Through these Pringle breasted his way, seeking even more to protect himself from above than from below, forced at times to crawl through an open space exposed to possible fire from both sides; so came at last to the masses of splintered and broken rock at the foot of the cliff, where he sank breathless and panting.

The tethered constellations paled in the sky; the moon rose and lit the cliff with silver fire. The worst was yet to come. Foy would ask no questions of any prowler, that was sure; he would reason that a friend would call out boldly. And John Wesley had no idea where Foy and his cave might be. Yet he must be found.

With a hearty swig at the canteen Pringle crept off to the right. The moonlight beat full upon the cliff. He had little trouble in that ruin of broken stone to find cover from foes below; but at each turn he confidently looked forward to a bullet from his friend.

"Foy! Foy!" he called softly as he crawled. "It's Pringle! Don't shoot!"

After a space he came to an angle where the cliff turned abruptly west and dwindled sharply in height. He remembered what the Major had said — the upper entrance of the cave came out on the highest crest of the hill. He turned back to retrace his painful way. The smell of dawn was in the air; the east sparkled. No sound came from the ambush all around. The end was near.

He passed by his starting-point; he crept on by slide and bush and stone. The moon magic faded and paled, mingled with the swift gray of dawn. He held his perilous way. Cold sweat stood on his brow. If Foy or a foe of Foy were on the cliff now, how easy to topple down a stone upon him! The absolute stillness was painful. A thought came to him of Stella Vorhis — her laughing eyes, her misty hair, the little hand that had lingered upon his own. Such a little, little hand!

Before him a narrow slit opened in the wall — such a crevice as the Major had described.

"Foy! Oh, Foy!" he called. No answer came. He raised his voice a little louder. "Foy! Speak if you're there! It's Pringle!"

A gentle voice answered from the cleft:

"Let us hope, for your sake, that you are not mistaken about that. I should be dreadfully vexed if you were deceiving me. The voice is the voice of Pringle, but how about the face? I can only see your back."

"I would raise my head, so you could take a nice look by the well-known cold gray light of the justly celebrated dawn," rejoined Pringle, "if I wasn't reasonably sure that a rifle shot would promptly mar the classic outlines of my face. They're all around you, Foy. Hargis, he gave you away. Don't show a fingernail of yourself. Let me crawl up behind that big rock ahead and then you can identify me."

"It's you, all right," said Foy when Pringle reached the rock and straightened himself up.

"I told you so," said Pringle, peering into the shadows of the cleft. "I can't see you. And how am I going to get to you? There are twenty men with point-blank range. I'm muddy, scratched, bruised, tired and hungry, sleepy and cross — and there's thirty feet in the open between here and you, and it nearly broad daylight. If I try to cross that I'll run twenty-five hundred pounds to the ton, pure lead. Well, we can put up a pretty nifty fight, even so. You go back to the other outlet of your cave and I'll stay here. I'm kinder lonesome, too. . . . Toss me some cartridges first. I only got five. I left in a hurry. You got forty-fives?"

"Plenty. But you can't stay there. They'll pot you from the top of the bluff, first off. Besides, you got a canteen, I see. You back up to that mountain mahogany bush, slip under it, and worm down through the rocks till you come to a little scrub-oak tree and a big granite boulder. They'll give you shelter to cross the ridge into a deep ravine that leads here where I am. You'll be out of sight all the way up once you hit the ravine. I'd — I'd worm along pretty spry if I was you, going down as far as the scrub oak — say, about as swift as a rattlesnake strikes — and pray any little prayers you happen to remember. And say, Pringle, before you go . . . I'm rather obliged to you for coming up here; risking taking cold and all. If it'll cheer you up any I'll undertake that anyone getting you on the trip will think there's one gosh-awful echo here."

"S'long!" said Pringle.

He wriggled backward and disappeared. Ten minutes later he writhed under the bush at Foy's feet.

"Never saw me!" he said. "But I'll always sleep in coils after this — always supposing we got any after this coming to us."

"One more crawl," said Foy, leading the way. "We'll go up on top. Regular fort up there. If we've got to die we'll die in the sun."

He stooped at what seemed the end of the passage and crawled out of sight under the low branches of a stunted cedar. Pringle followed and found himself in the pitch dark.

"Grab hold of my coat tail. I know my way, feeling the wall. Watch your step or you'll bark your shins."

The cave floor was smooth underfoot, except for scattered rocks; it rose and dipped, but the general trend was sharply upward.

"You're quite an institution, Pringle. You've made good Stella's word of you — the best ever!" said Foy as they mounted. "But you can't do me any good, really. I'll enjoy your company, but I wish you hadn't come."

"That's all right. I always like to finish what I begin."

"Well," remarked Foy cheerfully, "I reckon we've reached the big finish, both of us. I don't see any way out. All they've got to do is to sit tight till we starve out for water. Wish you was out of it. It's going to be tough on Stella, losing her friend and — and me, both at once. How's she making out? Full of fight and hope to the last, I'll bet."

"They had me under herd; but she was wishing for the Bar Cross buddies to butt in, I believe. Reckon your sheriff-man guessed it. He had her under guard, too."

"Nice man, the sheriff! How'd you get away from your herder?"

"He don't just remember," said Pringle.

"Who was it?"

"Applegate. Dreadful absent-minded, Applegate is. Ouch! There went my other shin. Had any sleep?"

"Most all night. Something woke me up about two hours ago, and I kept on the lookout ever since."

"That was me, I guess. I had to step lively. They was crowding me."

"If the Bar Cross happened to get word," observed Foy thoughtfully, "we might stand some hack. But they won't. It's good-bye, vain world, for ours! Say, in case a miracle happens for you, just make a memo about the sheriff being a nuisance, will you?"

"I'll tie a string on my finger. Anything else?"

"You might stick around and cheer Stella up a little. I'll do as much for you sometime. I'm thinking she'll feel pretty bad at first. Here we are!"

A faint glimmer showed ahead. They crawled under low bushes·

and stumbled out, in what seemed at first a dazzle of light; into a small saucer-shaped plat of earth a few feet across, enclosed by an irregular oval made by great blocks of stone, man-high. Below, a succession of little cliffs fell away, stair fashion, to an exceeding high and narrow gap which separated Little Thumb Butte from its greater neighbor, Big Thumb Butte.

"Castle Craney Crow," smiled Foy with a proprietary wave of his hand. "Just right for our business, isn't it? Make yourself at home, while I take a peep around about." He bent to peer through bush and crack. "Nothing stirring," he announced. He leaned his rifle against a walling rock. "Let's have a look at that water."

He raised the canteen to his lips. Pringle struck swift and hard to the tilted chin. Foy dropped like a poled bullock; his head struck heavily against the sharp corner of a rock. Pringle pounced on the stricken man. He threw Foy's six-shooter aside; he pulled Foy's wrists behind him and tied them tightly with a handkerchief. Then he rolled his captive over.

Foy's eyes opened; they rolled back till only the whites were visible; his lips twitched. Pringle hastily bound his handkerchief to the gash the stone had made; he sprinkled the blood-streaked face with water; he spilled drops of water between the parted lips. Foy did not revive.

Pringle stuck his hat on the rifle muzzle and waved it over the parapet of rock.

"Hello!" he shouted. "Bring on your reward! I've got Foy! It's me — Pringle! Come get him; and be quick — he's bleeding mighty bad."

"Come out, you! Hands up and no monkey business!" answered a startled voice not fifty yards away.

"Who's that? That you, Nueces? Give me your word and I'll lug him out. No time to lose — he's hurt, and hurt bad."

"You play fair and we will. I give my word!" shouted Nueces.

"Here goes!" Pringle pitched the rifle over. A moment later he staggered out between the rocks, bearing Foy's heavy weight in his arms. The head hung helpless, blood-spattered; the body was limp and slack; the legs dragged sprawling; the dreaded hands were bound.

Pringle laid his burden on the grass.

"Here he is, you hyenas! His hands are tied — are you still afraid of him? Damn you! The man's bleeding to death!"

CHAPTER VI

You treacherous, dirty hound!" said Breslin.

"Of all the low-down skunks I ever seen, you sure are the skunkiest!" said Nueces. "The sheriff was right after all. Cur-dog fits you to a T." He finished washing out the cut on Foy's head as he spoke. "Now the bandages, Anastacio. We'll have the blood stopped in a jiffy. Funny he hasn't come to. It's been a long while. It ain't the head ails him. This isn't such a deep cut; it oughtn't to put him out. Just happened to strike a vein." He bound up the cut with the deftness of experience.

"I hit him under the jaw," observed Pringle. "That's what did the business for him. He'll be around directly."

Anastacio looked up at Pringle; measureless contempt was in his eyes.

"Judas Iscariot could have sublet his job to you at half price if you'd been in the neighborhood. You are the limit, plus! I hope to see you fry in a New English hell!"

"Oh, that's all right, too," said Pringle unabashed. "I might just as well have that forty-five hundred as anyone. It wouldn't amount to much split amongst all you fellows, but it's quite a bundle for one man. That'll keep the wolf from the well-known door for quite a while."

"You won't touch a cent of it!" declared the sheriff.

"Won't I, though? We'll see about that. I captured him alone, didn't I? Oh, I reckon I'll finger the money, alrighty!"

"Here, fellows; give him a bait of whisky," said Creagan.

Breslin, kneeling at Foy's side, took the extended flask. They administered the stimulant cautiously, a sip at a time. Foy's eyes flickered; his breath came freer.

"He's coming!" said Breslin. "Give him a sip of water now."

"He'll be O.K. in five minutes, far as settin' up goes," said old Nueces, well pleased; "but he ain't goin' to be any too peart for quite some time — not for gettin' down off o' this hill. See — he's battin' his eyes and working his hands around. He sure heard the birdies sing!"

"The rest of you boys had just as well go on down to the shack," directed the sheriff. "Creagan and Joe and me will take care of Foy till he's able to move or be moved, and bring him into camp. You just lead up our three horses and an extra one for Foy — up as far as you can fetch 'em. One of you can ride home behind someone. Call down to the bunch under the cliff that we've got 'em, and for them to hike out to the ranch and take a nap. You'd better turn old Vorhis loose — and that girl. They can't do any harm now."

"Bring my horse, too," said Anastacio. "I'm staying. I want to be sure the invalid gets . . . proper care."

"Me too," said Breslin.

"And I'm staying to kinder superintend," said Nueces dryly. "Sheriff," he added, as the main body of the posse fell off down the hill — "and you, too, Barela — I don't just know what's going on here, but I'm stayin' with you to a fare-you-well. You two seem to be bucking each other."

No one answered.

"Sulky, hey? Well, anyhow, call it off long enough to drive this Pringle thing away from here. He ain't fittin' for no man to herd with."

"I'm staying right with this man Foy till I get that reward," announced Pringle. "Those are my superintentions. Much I care what you think about me! There's other places besides this."

Breslin raised his eye from Foy's face and regarded Pringle without heat — a steady, contemplative look, as of one who studies some strange and interesting animal. Then he waved his hand down the pass, where certain of the departing posse, were bringing the saddle horses in obedience to the sheriff's instructions.

"They'll carry a nice report of you," observed Breslin quietly. "What do you suppose that little girl will think?"

A flicker of red came to Pringle's hard brown face. Even the scorn of Espalin and Creagan had left him unabashed, but now he winced visibly; and, for once, he had no reply to make.

Foy gasped, struggled to a sitting position, aided by his oddly assorted ministrants, gazed round in a dazed condition and lapsed back into unconsciousness.

"I'll take my dyin' oath it ain't the cut that ails him," said the ranger, tucking a coat under Foy's blood-stained head. "That must have been a horrible jolt on his jaw, Pringle. You're no kind of a man at all — no part of a man. You're a shameless, black-hearted traitor; but I got to hand it to you as a slugger. Two knock-outs in one day — and such men as them! I don't understand it."

"He 'most keel Applegate," said the Mexican.

"Aw, it's easy!" said Pringle eagerly. "There ain't one man in a thousand knows how to fight. It ain't cussin' and grittin' your teeth, and swellin' up your biceps and clenching your fists up tight that does the trick. You want to hit like there wasn't anybody there. I'll show you sometime."

He paused inquiringly, as if to book any acceptance of this kindly offer. No such engagements being made, Pringle continued:

"Supposin' you was throwin' a baseball and your hand struck a man accidentally; you'd hurt him every time — only you'd break your arm that way. That ain't the way to strike. I'll show you."

"That wasn't no olive branch I was holdin' out," stated Nueces River. "You'll show me nothin' — turncoat!"

"It helps a lot, too, when the man you hit is not expecting it," suggested Anastacio smoothly. "You might show me sometime — when I'm looking for it."

"Now what's biting you?" demanded Pringle testily. "What did you expect me to do — send 'em a note by registered mail?"

"I'm not speaking about Applegate. That was all right. I am speaking about your friend."

"Here; Kit's coming to life again," said Lisner.

Kitty Foy rolled over; they propped him up; he looked round rather wildly from one to the other. His face cleared. His eye fell upon Pringle, where it rested with a steady intentness. When he spoke, at last, he ignored the others entirely.

"And I thought you were my friend, Pringle. I trusted you!" he said with ominous quietness. "I'll make a note of it. I have a good memory, Pringle — and good friends. Give me some water, someone. I feel sick."

Espalin brought a canteen.

"Take your time, Chris," said Lisner. "Tell us when you feel able to go."

"I'll be all right after a little. Say, boys, it was the queerest feeling — coming to, I mean. I could almost hear your voices, first. Then I heard them a long ways off but I couldn't make any sense to the words. Here; let me lean my back up against this rock and sit quiet for a while. Then we'll go. I'm giddy yet."

"I've got it!" announced Nueces a moment later. "Barela, he's hankering to be sheriff — that's the trouble. He wanted to take Chris himself, to help things along. That would be quite a feather in any man's hat — done fair. And the sheriff, natural enough, he don't want nothing of the kind."

"That's it," said Anastacio, amusement in his eyes. "I knew you were a good gunman, Nueces, but I never suspected you of brains before."

"What's the matter with that guess?" said Nueces sulkily. "Kid, you're always ridin' me. Don't you try to use any spurs!"

"I'm in on that," said Pringle, rising brightly. "That's my happy chance to join in this lovin' conversation. Speaking about gunmen, I'm a beaut! See that hawk screechin' around up there? Well, watch!"

The hawk soared high above. Pringle barely raised Foy's rifle to his shoulder as he fired; the hawk tumbled headlong. Pringle jerked the lever, throwing another cartridge into the barrel, as if to fire again at the falling bird. Inconceivably swift, the cocked rifle whirled to cover the seated posse.

"Steady!" said Pringle. "I'm watchin' you, Nueces! Chris, when you're able to walk, go on down and pick you a horse from that bunch. Unsaddle the others and drive 'em along a ways as you go." Still speaking, he edged behind the cover of a high rock. "I'll address the meetin' till you get a good head start. . . . Steady in the boat!"

"Well, by Heck!" said Nueces.

"And I thought you had betrayed me!" cried Foy.

"Well, I hadn't. This was the only show to get off. . . . I hate to kill you, Nueces; but I will if you make a move."

"Hell! I ain't makin' no move! What do you think I am — a damn fool?" said Nueces. "If I moved any it was because I am about to crack under the justly celebrated strain. Say, young fellow, it strikes me that you change sides pretty often."

"Yes; I am the Acrobat of the Breakfast Table," said Pringle modestly. "Thanks for the young fellow. That listens good."

"Look out I don't have you performing on a tight rope yet!" growled the sheriff hoarsely. "There'll be more to this. You haven't got out of the country yet."

"That will be all from you, Sheriff. You, too, Creagan — and Espalin. Not a word or I'll shoot. And I don't care how soon you begin to talk. That goes!"

Espalin shriveled up; the sheriff and Creagan sat sullen and silent. Foy got to his feet rather unsteadily.

"Chris, you might slip around and gather up their guns," said Pringle. "Pick out one for yourself. I left yours where I threw it when I picked it out of your belt. I meant to knock you out, Chris — there wasn't any other way; but I didn't mean to plumb kill you. You hit your head on a rock when you fell. It wouldn't have done any good to have got the drop on you. You had made up your mind not to surrender. You would have shot anyhow; and, of course, I couldn't shoot. I'd just have got myself killed for nothing. No good to play I'd taken you prisoner. This crowd knew you wouldn't be taken — except by treachery. So I played traitor. As it was, when I knocked you out you didn't look much like no put-up job. You was bleeding like a stuck pig."

"Hold on, there, before you try to take my gun!" warned old Nueces River as Foy came to him for his gun, collecting. "You got the big drop on me, Pringle, and I wouldn't raise a hand to keep Chris from getting off anyhow — not now. But I used to be a ranger — and the rangers were sworn never to give up their guns."

"How about it, Pringle?" asked Foy, who had already relieved the sheriff and his satellites of their guns. "He'll do exactly as he says — both ways."

"I wasn't done talking yet," said Nueces, irritably. "But I'll let Chris take my gun, on one condition."

"What's that?" inquired Pringle.

"Why, if you ain't busy next Saturday I'd like to have you call around — about one o'clock, say — and kick me good and hard."

"Let him keep his gun. He called me a young fellow. And I don't want Breslin's, anyway. He's all right. Not to play any favorites, let Anastacio keep his. There are times," said Pringle, "when I have great hopes of Anastacio. I'm thinking some of taking him in hand to see if I can't make a man of him."

"Ananias the Amateur," said Anastacio, "I thank you for those kind words. And I'd like to see you Saturday about two — when you get through with Nueces. I'm next on the waiting list. This will be a lesson to me never to let my opinion of a man be changed by anything he may do."

"If you fellows feel that way," said Foy, "how about me? How do you suppose I feel? This man has risked his life fifty times for me — and what did I think of him?"

"If you ask me, Christopher," said Anastacio, "I think you were quite excusable. It was all very well to dissemble his love — but I should feel doubtful of any man that handed me such a wallop as that until the matter had been fully explained."

"What I want to know, Pringle, is, how the deuce you got up here so slick?" said Nueces.

"Oh, that's easy! I can run a mile in nothing flat."

"Oh — that's it? You hid in the water pen?"

"Under the troughs. Bright idea of yours, them fires! I knew just where not to go. After you left I hooked a horse. If you'd had sense enough to go with the sheriff and eat your supper like a human being I'd 'a' hooked two horses, and Chris and me would now be getting farther and farther. I don't want you ever to do that again. Suppose Chris had killed me when I tried to knock him out? Fine large name I would 'a' left for myself, wouldn't I?"

"If you had fought it out with us," said Breslin musingly, "you would have been killed — both of you; and you would have killed others. Mr. Pringle, you have done a fine thing. I apologize to you."

"Why, that all goes without saying, my boy. As for my part — why, I don't bother much about a blue tin heaven or a comic-supplement hell, but I'm right smart interested in right here and now. It's a right nice little old world, take it by and large, and I like to help out at whatever comes my way, if it takes fourteen innings. But, so long as you feel that way about it, maybe you'll believe me now, when I say that Christopher Foy was with me all last night and he didn't shoot Dick Marr."

"That's right," said Foy. "I don't know who killed Dick Marr; but I do know that Creagan, Joe Espalin, and Applegate intended to kill me last night. They gave me back my six-shooter, that Ben Creagan had borrowed — and it was loaded with blanks. Then they pitched onto me, and if it hadn't been for Pringle they'd have got me sure! We left town at eleven o'clock and rode straight to the Vorhis Ranch."

"I believe you," said Anastacio. "You skip along now, Chris. You're fit to ride."

"Why shouldn't I stay and see it out?"

"It won't do. For one thing, your thinker isn't working as per invoice," said Nueces River. "You're in no fix to do yourself justice. We'll look after your interests. You know some of the posse might be coming back, askin' fool questions. Pull your freight up to the Bar Cross till we send for you."

"Well — if you think Pringle isn't running any risks I'll go."

"We'll take care of Pringle. Guess we'll make him sheriff next fall, maybe — just to keep Anastacio in his place. Drift!"

"No sheriffin' for mine, thanks. Contracting is my line. Subcontracting!"

"So long, boys! You know what I'd like to say. You gave me a square deal, you three chaps," said Foy. "Get word to Stella as soon as ever you can. She thinks I'm a prisoner, you know. You know what I want to say there, Pringle — tell her for me. . . . Say! Why don't you all go in now? You boys all know that Stella's engaged to me, don't you? What's the good of keeping her in suspense? Go on to the ranch, right away."

"I told you your head wasn't working just right," jeered Nueces. "We want to give you a good start. They'll be after you again, and you're in no fix to do any hard riding. But one of us will go. Breslin, you go."

"Too late," observed Anastacio quietly. "There is Miss Vorhis now, with her father. They're climbing to the Gap. Go on, Foy."

"They've got a led horse," said Nueces as Stella and the Major came to the highest point of the Gap. "Who's that for? Chris? But they couldn't know about Chris. And how did they get here so quick? Don't seem like they've had hardly time."

Stella dismounted; she pressed on up the hill to meet her lover. The first sunshafts struck into the Gap, lit up the narrow walls with red glory.

Magic Casements! thought Pringle.

"Watch Foy get over the ground!" said Anastacio. "He'll break his neck before he gets down. I don't blame him. He's nearly down. Look the other way, boys!"

They looked the other way, and there were none to see that meeting. Unless, perhaps, the gods looked down from high Olympus — the poor immortals — and turned away, disconsolate, to the cheerless fields of asphodel.

"But they're not going away," said Breslin after a suitable interval. "They're waiting; and the Major's waving his hat at us."

"I'll go see what they want," said Anastacio.

In a few minutes he was back, rather breathless and extremely agitated in appearance.

"Well? Spill it!" said Neuces. "Get your breath first. What's the trouble?"

"Applegate's dead. Joe Espalin, I arrest you for the murder of Richard Marr! Applegate confessed!"

"He lied! He lied!" screamed Espalin. "I was with Ben till daylight, at the monte game; they all tell you. The sheriff he try to make me keel heem — he try to buy me to do eet — he keel Dick Marr heemself!"

"That's right!" spoke Creagan, suddenly white and haggard. His voice was a cringing whine; his eyes groveled. "Marr was at Lisner's house. We all went over there after the fight. Lisner waked Marr up — he'd been tryin' to egg Marr on to kill Foy all day, but Marr was too drunk. He was sobering up when we waked him. Lisner tried to rib him up to go after Foy and waylay him — told him he had been threatening Foy's life while he was drunk, and that Foy'd kill him if he didn't get Foy first. Dick said he wouldn't do it — he'd go along to help arrest Foy, but that's all he'd do. The sheriff and Joe went out together for a powwow. The sheriff came back alone, black as thunder — him and Dick rode off together — "

The sheriff sprang to his feet, his heavy face bloated and blotched with terror.

"He cursed me; he tried to pull his gun!" he wailed. His eyes protruded, glaring; one hand clutched at his throat, the other spread out before him as he tottered, stumbling. "Oh, my God!" he sobbed.

"That will do nicely," said Anastacio. "You're guilty as hell! I'll put your own handcuffs on you. Oddly enough, the law provides that when it is necessary to arrest the sheriff the duty falls to the coroner. It is very appropriate. You must pardon me, Mr. Lisner, if I seem unsympathetic. Dick Marr was your friend! And you have not been entirely fair with Foy, I fear. . . . Creagan, we'll hold you and Joe for complicity and for conspiracy in Foy's case. We'll arrest Applegate, too, when we get to camp. He'll be awfully vexed."

"What!" shrieked the sheriff, raising his manacled hands. "Liar! Murderer!"

"So Applegate's not dead? Well, I'm just as well pleased," said Pringle.

"Not even hurt badly. I was after the Man Lower Down. What the Major told me was that the Barelas were at the ranch — more than enough to hold Lisner's crowd down. They come at daylight. I was expecting that, and waiting. As I told you, that's the best thing I do — waiting."

"But how did you know?" demanded Breslin, puzzled.

"I didn't know, for sure. I had a hunch and I played it. So I killed poor Applegate — temporarily. It worked out just right and nothing to carry."

"One of the mainest matters with the widely known world," said Pringle wearily, "is that people won't play their hunches. They haven't spunk enough to believe what they know. Let me spell it out for you in words of two cylinders, Breslin: You saw that I knew Creagan and Applegate, while they positively refused to know me at any price; you heard the sheriff deny that I was at the Gadsden House before I'd claimed anything of the sort. Of course you didn't know anything about the fight at the Gadsden House, but that was enough to show you something wasn't right, just the same. You had all the material to build a nice plump hunch. It all went over your head. You put me in mind of the lightning bug:

> The lightning bug is brilliant,
> But it hasn't any mind;
> It wanders through creation
> With its headlight on behind.

"Come on — let's move. I'm fair dead for sleep."

"Just a minute!" said Anastacio. "I want to call your attention to the big dust off in the north. I've been watching it half an hour. That dust, if I'm not mistaken, is the Bar Cross coming; they've heard the news!"

"So, Mr. Lisner, you hadn't a chance to get by with it," said Pringle slowly and thoughtfully. "If I hadn't balked you, the Barelas stood ready; if the Barelas failed, yonder big dust was on the way; half your own posse would have turned on you for half a guess at the truth. It's a real nice little world — and it hates a lie. A good many people lay their fine-drawn plans, but they mostly don't come off! Men are but dust, they tell us. Magnificent dust! This nice little old world of ours, in the long run, is going right. You can't beat the Game! Once, yes — or twice — not in the long run. The Percentage is all against you. You can't beat the Game!"

"It's up to you, Sheriff," said Anastacio briskly. "I can turn you over to the Bar Cross outfit and they'll hang you now; or I can turn you over to the Barelas and you will be hung later. Dick Marr was your friend! Take your choice. You go on down, Pringle, while the sheriff is looking over the relative advantages of the two propositions. I think Miss Vorhis may have something to say to you."

She came to meet him; Foy and the Major waited by the horses.

"John!" she said. "Faithful John!" She sought his hands.

"There now, honey — don't take on so! Don't! It's all right! You know what the poet says:

> Cast your bread upon the waters
> And you may live to say:
> "Oh, how I wish I had the crust
> That once I threw away!"

Her throat was pulsing swiftly; her eyes were brimming with tears, bruised for lost sleep.

"Dearest and kindest friend! When I think what you have done for me — that you faced shame worse than death — guarded by unprovable honor — John! John!"

"Why, you musn't, honey — you mustn't do that! Why, Stella, you're crying — for me! You mustn't do that, Little Next Door!"

"If you had been killed, taking Chris — or after you gave him up — no one but me would have ever believed but that you meant it!"

"But you believed, Stella?"

"Oh, I knew! I knew!"

"Even when you first heard of it?"

"I never doubted you — not one instant! I knew what you meant to do. You knew I loved him. The led horse was for you. I thought Chris would be gone. Why, John Wesley, I have known you all my life! You couldn't do that! You couldn't! Oh, kiss me, kiss me — faithful John!"

But he bent and kissed her hands — lest, looking into his eyes, she should read in the book of his life one long, long chapter — that bore her name.

Hit the Line Hard

HIT THE LINE HARD

CHAPTER I

Neighbor Jones gazed meditatively from his room in the Saragossa House: an unwelcome guest buzzed empty boastings in his ear. He saw, between narrowed lids, the dazzle of bright tracks, the Saragossa Station, the bright green of irrigated fields beyond, merged to a vague and half-sensed background. The object of his attentive consideration was nearer at hand, by the west-most track — a long, squat warehouse, battered and dingy red. And from this shabby beginning, while the bore droned endlessly on, Neighbor Jones wove romance for his private delight.

The warehouse was decked all about by a wide, high platform. A low-pitched roof reached far out beyond the building to overhang this platform, so that the whole bore a singular resemblance to Noah's Ark of happy memory. A forlorn and forgotten ark: the warped shingles, the peeling, blistered paint, the frayed and splintered planks, were eloquent of past prosperity and of change, neglect and decay.

The gable end was crowded with huge lettering of whitish gray. When those gray letters were white the sign had read:

BROWN, ALMANDARES & COMPANY

GENERAL MERCHANDISE

BEST PRICES

FOR WOOL AND HIDES

Long ago the firm name had been painted out; but the old letters broke dim and ghostly through, persisted stubborn under the paint that would blot them, hid and haunted beyond the letters of a later name:

MARTIN BENNETT

Bennett had been the Company.

Neighbor Jones sprawled largely in his tilted chair, smoking with vast and enviable enjoyment. One hand was pocketed. The other, big, strong, blunt-fingered, tapped on the window sill a brave tattoo of ringing hoofs — no finicky, miminy tanbark trot, but steady and measured, a great horse breasting the wind and the rain. To this strong cadence Neighbor Jones trolled a merry stave from the amazing ballad of the Chisholm Trail:

> Foot in the saddle and a hand on the horn;
> Best old cowboy ever was born.
> Hi, yi-yi-yippy, yippy hi-yi-yi!
> Hi — yi-yi-yippy-yippy-yea! —

In the lines of the long taper from broad shoulders to booted feet; in the massive broad-browed head; the tawny hair; the square, ruddy-brown face; the narrowed sleepy eyes — in every mold and motion of the man, balanced and poised, there was something lionlike; something one might do well to remark.

But his one companion, the Kansas City Kid, remarked none of those things. The Kansas City Kid was otherwise engrossed — with his own cleverness.

"Oh, I'll show you, all right! There's one born every minute," said the K. C. Kid crisply. "How many hands? Five? Five is right. Second hand for Jones; first hand is the winner. Watch me close!"

He shuffled the cards with a brisk and careless swing, cutting them once, twice, thrice, with flourish and slap; shuffled again, with a smooth ripple pleasant to the ear, and shoved the deck across for a final cut.

"See anything wrong? No? Here we go! Watch!" He dealt five poker hands, face down. "Now then, look! You've got three tens and a pair of trays. First hand has jacks up, opens, stands a raise from you, draws one black jack." Illustrating, the Kid flipped the top card from the deck. It was the spade jack. "Then you bet your fool head off. He should worry. And that's the way they trimmed you — see?"

Neighbor Jones blinked a little and twisted his tawny-gold hair to a peak, retaining unshaded and unchanged his look of sleepy good nature.

"Smooth work!" he said approvingly.

"You're dead right, it's smooth work!" asserted the gratified artist. "Some class to that! Them guys that got yours couldn't do any such work — they was raw! I'm showing you what I got, so you can figure out the surprise party you and me can hand to 'em — see? Say, they pulled a lot of stunts the Old Ladies' Home is wise to back in my town — strippers, short cards, holdouts, cold decks — old stuff! Honest, they make me sick! I can steal the gold out of their teeth and they'll never miss it!"

Jones looked at the man with wonder and pity. The poor wretch was proud of his sorry accomplishment, displayed it with pleasure, thought himself envied for it. By this shameful skill he had come so far, in the pride and heyday of youth — to such dire shifts, such ebbs and shallows; to empty days, joyless, friendless, without hope of any better morrow. No dupe he had gulled but might grieve for him, cut off, clean aside from all purpose or meaning of life.

"Well?" said the Kid impatiently.

The contemplative gentleman roused himself.

"Someway I don't like this idea of being cheated pretty well." His voice was a mild and regretful drawl. "Never had much use for Beck; but I did think old Scanlon was a square old sport!"

"Square sport! Why, you poor simp, you never had a look in!" sneered the sharper. Then he wrinkled his brows in some perplexity. "What I don't see is why they didn't skin the Eastern chap too. They could 'a' had that gink's wad — that Drake; but they let him down easy. Oh well, we should worry! It will leave all the more for us."

"For us?" echoed Neighbor, puzzled.

"Sure, Mike! You get hold of a good piece of money and we'll do a brother act. You and me, we ain't never been chummy — they won't tumble. We'll sit in with 'em and string along with 'em till the big money gets out in the open — just holding enough cards to keep in the swim. When I give you the office, go get 'em! I'll slip big ones to Beck and the college Johnny — and the top hand to you, of course — and we'll split fifty-fifty."

Neighbor's mind groped back along the dusty years for a half-forgotten adage.

"If a dog bites you once," he said with halting speech, "shame on him; if you bite a dog — shame on you!"

"Huh? I don't get you."

"Besides," said Neighbor placidly, "you'll be going away now."

"Not me. Saragossa looks good to me."

"You'll be going away," repeated Neighbor patiently, "on the next train — any direction — and never coming back!"

"What?" The Kid jumped up, blazing wrath. "Why you cheap skate — you quitter! Are you goin' to throw me down? You come-on! You piker — "

"Boob?" suggested Neigbor kindly. "Mutt? Sucker?"

"You hick! You yellow hound — "

"Sit down," advised Neighbor quietly.

"You ought to lose your money! For ten cents — "

"Sit down," said Neighbor more quietly. The pocketed hand produced a dime and slid it across the table. "Go on with that ten-cent job you had on your mind, whatever it was," said Neighbor. "There's the money. Pick it up!"

Weight and inches, the two men evened up fairly well. Also, the ivory butt of a forty-four peeped from the Kid's waistband. But Neighbor's eye was convincing; here was a man who meant the thing he said. The younger man shifted his own eyes uneasily, checked, faltered and sat down.

"Pick up your dime!" said Neighbor. The Kid complied with a mumbling in his throat. "That's right," said Jones. "Now, don't you be too proud to take advice from a yellow hound. First, don't you bother your poor head about me losing my money. My money don't cost me anything," he explained — "I work for it. Next, about Beck — I'll sleep on this matter and look it over from all sides. No hurry. If I'm not just pleased with Beck for cheating me I'll adjust the matter with him — but I'll not cheat him. I never try to beat a man at his own game. Toddle along, now. I hear a train coming. By-by!"

"It's the freight. I'll go on the five-o'clock passenger — not before."

"Oh, yes you will!" said Jones confidently. "You've only accused Beck of cheating, but you've proved it on yourself. The boys won't like it. It is best to leave me thus, dear — best for you and best for me." His eyes wandered to the window and rested calculatingly on the Fowler cottonwood across the street. It was a historic tree; Joel Fowler had been hanged thereon by disapproving friends.

The Kid caught the glance and the unspoken allusion; sweat beaded his forehead.

"Aw, lemme wait for the passenger!" he protested. "I gotta go up to the Windsor to pay what I owe and get my suit case."

Neighbor arose.

"There, there! Don't you fret," he said, patting the other man's shoulder kindly. "Give me the money. I'll pay your bill and keep the suit case. You just run along."

"Good lord, man! Those clothes cost me — "

"Now, now! Never mind — that's all right — everything's all right!" said Neighbor soothingly. "We're just about of a size." He nudged the Kid's ribs with a confidential elbow. "Sly old dog! You had some of my money too, didn't you? Yes; and I'll keep that cunning little gun of yours as a souvenir." The last remark came after — not before — Neighbor's acquisition of the cunning little gun. "Come on, my boy, we'll mosey along over to the station. Here's our hats, on the bed."

He linked his arm with the victim's: he sang with a joyous and martial note:

> Hark! From the tombs a doleful sound;
> Maryland, my Maryland!
> My love lies buried underground;
> Maryland, my Maryland!

CHAPTER II

IT WAS NEARING TWO P.M. when Mr. Jones, after speeding the parting Kid, made his way uptown. Upstairs was the word in his thought. Saragossa is built that way. Let Saragossa Mountain, close and great and golden, stand for the house; the town will then be the front steps. The first step is Venice, in the lush green of the valley — railroad buildings, coal chute, ferryman, warehouses, two nth-class hotels, a few farmhouses, all on stilts, being a few feet above the Rio Grande at low water and a few feet under it at high water. Whence the name, Venice.

On the first rising ground to the westward is the business quarter, as close to the railroad as safety permits. A step up comes to a sheltered, sunny terrace and to the Old Town — the Mexican village dating back to before the great uprising of 1680. Another, a steep and high step, rose to the residence section, on a strip of yellow mesa; for Saragossa has water piped from the high hills, so please you, and is not confined to the lowlands, like most of her New Mexican sisters. Still above, on the fifth and last step, smelter and mining town clung to a yellow-brown slope reached by a spur of railroad looping in a long bow-knot from the valley below.

Above all, sheer and steep, circling about, sheltering, brooding, hung Saragossa Mountain, rose and gold in midday or morning sun; blue and rose-edged when the long shadows thrust eastward stealthily, steadily — crept like kittens at play, or like them fell off, down those old, old steps.

Something of all this Neighbor saw and put into thoughts — not into words. Saw, too, all beyond and all about, the vast and sun-drenched land of all colors and all shapes — valley and plain and mesa, shelf and slope and curve, and bend and broken ridge and hill; great ranges against the turquoise sky, near or far, or far beyond belief, saw-toothed or wall-straight or rounded — every one precisely unlike any other visible mountain or any other possible mountain. By this cause his step was sprightly and glad, his eye bright, his chin well up — a very sincere way of thanking God.

Now, as he swung along the street, he voiced these thoughts in a little hymn of praise. At least it sounded like a hymn of praise as he sang it to a healthy and manful tune; resonant, ringing, reverberant:

> Plunged in a gulf of dark despair
> Maryland, my Maryland!

On three sides of the shaded plaza business was housed in modern comfort. In sharp contrast, all along the north, sprawled an unbroken, staring huddle of haphazard buildings — frame, brick and adobe, tall and squat jumbled together, broad-fronted or pinched. At the river-ward corner, massive, ill-kept but dominant still, was a great structure of graystone once the luckless home of Brown and Almandares.

Squalid, faded and time-stained, like Falstaff's rabble of recruits, this long row stuck sinister to the eye. Any stranger, seeing what blight had fallen ominous and threatening all about him, seeing on door after door the same repeated name, might well guess the whole ugly story. For this long, forlorn row housed Bennett's General Stores. Bennett sold everything but tunnels.

Here was Neighbor's nearest errand. After a little delay he was shown into the great man's private office.

Bennett turned slowly in his revolving chair; a tall spare man, with a thin straggle of sandy hair and a sharp, narrow face, close-shaven; which might have been a pleasant face but for a pinched and cruel mouth, a mean, pinched nose, and a shifty eye.

Here arose a curious contradiction. The man had held the whip hand for years, his conscious manner was overbearing and arrogant, but his eyes betrayed him, and all the unconscious lines of his face were slinking and furtive. He now wore an austere frown.

"Mr. Jones, I hear you have been gambling."

"Oh, *si!*" said Mr. Jones; and he made those simple words convey enthusiasm, brightness and joy. "And — but also, what do you suppose I hear about you? Give you three guesses."

"What!" Bennett gasped incredulously; he crashed his fist down on the desk. "How about that mortgage?"

Jones beamed triumphant.

"You see? You don't like it yourself — meddlin', pryin' and loose talk."

"I'll fix you! This'll be the worst day's work you ever did — trying to get smart with me!"

"Percival Pulcifer, will you kindly retain your rompers?" said Neighbor with eminent cheerfulness. "Now hark and heed! You did not ask me to sit down. You are not a nice old man. I do not like you much. Don't you touch that bell! . . . I shall now sit down. Smoke? No? Well, I'll roll one."

Rolling one with tender care, Neighbor cocked a pleasant but rather impish eye on the seething financier and blithely prattled on:

"Allow me to say, Mr. Banker, that you are overlooking one point: You have a mortgage on my cattle, but you haven't got any mortgage on me. Got that — clear?"

The banker gurgled, black faced and choking.

"I'll ruin you! I'll smash you!"

"Percival Pulcifer Peterkin Pool!"

For some reason, not at first easily apparent, these harmless words, which Jones syllabled with great firmness, made the banker writhe. He was wonted to hate — but ridicule was new to him and it hurt.

"You might at least show some respect for my gray hairs," he interrupted indignantly.

"Oh, dye your gray hairs!" said Neighbor simply. "Damn your old gray hairs! Shoot, if you must, that old gray head! You're an old gray-headed scoundrel — that's what you are!"

"Of course," observed the gray-haired one, gathering himself together, "you will be ready with the money on the nail?"

"Now you're talking sense!" cried Neighbor warmly. "Now you're getting down to facts." He threw back his head and sang with great heartiness and zest:

> That day of wrath, that dreadful day;
> Maryland, my Maryland!
> When heaven and earth shall pass away;
> Maryland, my Maryland!

Clerks beyond the glass partition turned startled faces that way. In that gloomy, haunted counting room, used only to the tones of meekness or despair, the echoes rolled thunderous:

> When, shriveling like a parched scroll,
> The flaming heavens together roll —

"Will I have the money? *Quien sabe?* If I don't the brand is yours — party of the first part, his heirs, executors and assigns forever — nary a whimper from this corner. If I knew for certain I'd tell you, for you have a plain right to know that; but that first line of talk was just sickening drivel. If you held a mortgage on a man's stuff, would that give you any right to go snoopin' round and compel him to get in a poker game — hey? Would that look nice? Whaddy you mean then — how dast you, then — try to tell me not to play poker — meddling in my private affairs? How dare you? Shame-y! Shame-y! S-s-h!"

"Jones," said the other thickly, "I think the devil himself is in you today. You poor, headstrong fool! I sent for you to do you a kindness."

Jones rose anxiously.

"Shall I call a doctor?"

"Well, I did; but you make it hard for me."

"Yes, yes! And you not used to doing kind things either!" said Jones sympathetically. "Go on. We're all with you. Give it a name."

Bennett paced up and down, clasping his hands behind his back.

"You know I have a cattle ranch out Luna Way? Ever been there?"

"Not any. I stick to the east side. Saragossa is my furthest west; and, as you know, I've never been here before. But don't let me interrupt. You were working yourself up to a kindness."

Bennett flinched at his careless contempt, but he forced himself to go on.

"I was intending to offer you a job as my foreman."

Neighbor sat down with an air of relief.

"You don't need no doctor. It's yourself you're trying to be kind to. Go on with your talk. For a starter — what would I do with my own cattle?"

"Sell, get a friend to run them; let them out on shares. You wouldn't need to worry about the mortgage. It could stand over — you'll be getting good money. And," said the financier diffidently, spacing the words and dropping his voice to tones singularly flat and even, "If — everything — went — all — right, the — mortgage — might — be — canceled."

"Yes? How jolly! But what's the matter with the west-side cowmen? Can't you get some of the V T waddies? Should think you'd rather use home talent."

Bennett resumed his measured pacing. At the end of each beat he turned, always away from Neighbor's eyes, so that he marked out a distinct figure eight. Other men, unhappy debtors, had walked that narrow space, many of them; perhaps none so fiend-ridden as he who now tracked back and forth. The jeers of this uncringing debtor galled him to the quick, yet his purpose drove him on.

"We have been having a little trouble on the ranch. For many reasons I do not think it wise to get a local man." He coughed gently, and went on in the same low and listless manner of speech he had used in his hint about the mortgage. "Trouble was between my boys and the Quinliven outfit — the Double Dee — about one of my watering places. I have no legal title, but the spring is mine by all the customs of the country. There was some shooting, I believe. No one was hurt, fortunately, but there is hard feeling. I must put a stop to it. For his part in the deplorable affair I let my foreman go — Tom Garst. Know him?"

"Sure!"

"So I thought I would get you for the place."

"Me being a notorious peacemaker and cheekturner, suffering long, and kind, not easily provoked — yes, yes!"

"Quinliven himself would be willing to let the matter drop, I think; but young Roger Drake — why, you know young Drake — he was one of your poker party!"

"The college lad — yes."

"Nephew of Old Drake, Quinliven's partner, who died a month or two ago," continued Bennett, sedulously avoiding Neighbor's eye. "Young Drake is hot-headed; says he's going to hold that spring anyhow. He — will — require — careful — handling." Again that slow, significant spacing of the words.

As lifelessly Neighbor answered:

"And — if — I — handle — him — carefully; if — everything — turns — out — all — right, the —mortgage — will — be — canceled?"

"Yes," said Bennett. He busied himself at his desk.

In a startled silence Neighbor rose, fold after fold, interminable and slow. He fumbled for matches, pipe and tobacco; thoughtfully, thoroughly, he constructed a smoke. Then he raised his eyes. Many a hard Ulysses-year had passed over him, this old Neighbor; but his eyes were clear and unstained yet. They now observed Mr. Bennett attentively.

"Sorry," said Neighbor Jones. "I haven't got a thing fit to wear."

At the door he turned. "Now, I'll tell you what you do," he said kindly. He spread out his left hand and drew a diagram down the palm: "You go to hell and take the first turn to the left!"

CHAPTER III

Ducky Drake — Roger Olcott Drake, Second — dawdled over a four-o'clock breakfast. He was in bathrobe and slippers, his feet on a second chair; the morning paper was propped before him and the low western sun peeped through his windows.

The room phone rang. "Hel-lo-o! Gentleman to see Mr. Drake — shall we show him up?" . . . "Use your own judgment; the last time I tried to show a man up he worked my face over." Bring him up, the telephone meant. Mr. Drake desired particulars: "What is the gentleman's silly name?" . . . "Jones. Cowpunch; six or seven feet up; incredibly sober." . . . "Sure, Moike! Bring him along! Say, send some good smokes, will you? — and some swipes. What's that? What do I mean, swipes? Beer, you idiot — beer!"

A clear eye, bright and black; a clean fresh-colored skin; a frank and pleasant face — that was Ducky. He met his visitor at the door.

"Glad to see you, Mr. Neighbor — welcome to our well-known midst! Weather! Chair! How's every little thing? You look chirpy enough. Shan't I have breakfast sent up for you?"

"No, thank you; I got up at noon. You can give me a little help though."

"Put it on the table, George. That's all." George, known in private life as Gregorio, departed, and Ducky turned to his guest. "Whaddy you mean — help?" he demanded grinning sympathetically. "Did they put the kibosh on you good and proper after I quit last night?" He pushed the cigars over and began operations with a corkscrew.

"Oh, no — nothing like that. I want some advice."

"Advice? This is the right shop." Roger struck a Pecksniff pose, waved the corkscrew aloft, and declaimed grandly: "Put your eggs in one basket. Get on the wagon. Hitch your wagon to a star. Mind your step! When in doubt, play trumps. Be sure you're ahead and then go right home."

"Not advice exactly — information."

"Oh!" said Ducky. "A straight line is the shortest distance between two points; the woman who hesitations is lost; a Cobb in the club is worth two in the bush; lead-pencil signatures are good in law; a receiver is as bad as a promoter; hospitality is the thief of time; absinthe makes the heart grow fonder."

Neighbor shoved a bottle of beer into his host's hand.

"Drink, pretty creature, drink! Let me explain: What I want is to ask some questions — about words, and so on. You're a college Johnny, ain't you?"

"Booze Arts, Harvard," said Ducky. "Not graduated yet."

"Man staying here in the Windsor with you — was staying here, gone now — used a lot of words I don't quite savvy." Neighbor leaned forward, blinking earnestly. "What is the precise distinction between a mutt, a simp, a gink and a boob? And what did he mean by saying all the time, 'I should worry!'?"

Ducky placed the tips of his fingers accurately together, and held his head on one side, birdwise, pursing his lips precisely.

"The phrase I should worry is derived from the Hebrew verb to bibble, meaning to worry — I should bibble; you should bibble; he or she should bibble. Plural: we should bibble; ye should bibble; they should bibble.

"Mutt, simp, gink and boob are scientific terms employed rather indiscriminately by philosophers of an idealistic tendency. Broadly speaking, the words denote one whose speech, manner, education, habits or clothes differ in any respect from your own; categorically, a thinker whose opinions and ideals do not correspond in every particular with your own. Exactly equivalent terms are — in religion, heretic or infidel; in politics, demagogue, blatherskite!"

"Thank you," said Neighbor humbly. "Myself, I understood him to mean almost the same thing as a sucker; because this fellow — it was the K. C. Kid, that sat on your left — he spoke of you and me being mutts and simps, and all them things; and at the same time he said we'd been swindled, cheated or skinned in that little poker game."

Ducky made a passionate comment.

"That alley-goat could sure stack the cards. He showed me that," said Neighbor, and related the painful story of the K. C. Kid's flitting.

"We are the victims of the highly accomplished fact," said Roger. "We can't very well squeal; but can they do this to us with the well-known impunity?"

"No," said Neighbor; "they cannot. I'll make a note of it. We'll not squeal and we'll not cheat; but we'll give 'em their comeuppances someway. I do not, as a general thing, hold myself up for the admiration of the good and wise; but I must say that I've always got what I went after if I wanted it hard enough."

" 'Don't flinch; don't foul; hit the line hard!' " said Roger. The words snapped like a lash.

"Who said that? He did? Good for him once! And I want this, hard. When I get my auger in, I'll give it another twist for you, Mr. Ducky, in case you are not here. You haven't lost much anyhow.

That's funny too! Huh! Our tinhorn friend noticed that. Seems like they didn't want to rob you; and yet your wool was enough sight longer'n mine. I don't get the idea. I like to understand things as I go along."

"I won away quite a wad, all right; but you might say I wasn't a loser at all compared to what I was two or three nights ago. I was certain-lee in bad!" Ducky performed a hospitable rite. "Well, we'll have to give up poker at Beck's. Here's how!"

"That brings me up to the main point," said Neighbor casually. "What have you been and gone and done? Because a gentleman just offered me the highest market price for your scalp."

"What?"

"He wanted me to abate you — to abolish you — to beef you — to murder you! Don't be so dumb! So I thought I'd drop in and get your views."

"What's the joke?"

"It's no joke. This *hombre* sure wants you killed off. You'll save time by taking that for proved. And," said Neighbor wistfully, "I needed the money too."

"But who — who — "

"Not at all," said Jones. "Why — why? You tell me why, why first, and see how well it fits in with who, who. I know the answer all right, but I haven't heard the riddle yet."

"Oi, yoi, yoi!" Young Drake sat up with a sudden alertness and stared hard at his visitor. "It's Uncle Ducky's money — that's why — I'll bet a cooky!"

"Not with me, you won't," said Neighbor; "for if your Uncle Ducky left any worldly goods the gentleman that offers a bounty for you is the very man to covet those goods. Just how getting you killed would bring him in anything I don't almost see."

"That's just it!" cried Roger Drake. "He's got the money now — or somebody has; I haven't. I'm trying to find it."

"Son," said Neighbor judicially, "this sounds real thrillin'. Tell it to me."

Young Drake hesitated.

"No offense, Mr. Jones; but I have been strongly advised to say nothing."

Neighbor nodded eagerly.

"Yes, yes! Mystery; sorcery; silence; wisdom! 'But how do you know I'm honest?' says the lad in the story. 'Why,' says the other chap, 'didn't you just tell me so?' Well, I'm honest. Go on! Also curious. That's why I want to be told; but here is why you should want to tell me: If we were back in New York town you'd under-stand the ins and outs of things that I couldn't make a guess at, and that it would take you large, dreary centuries to tell me about. Ever think of that?"

"I gotcha!" said Roger joyously. "And this is your country, you mean; while I'm a mere stranger — "

"Correct! Move up one girl! I never saw a merer stranger than you, Mr. Ducky. You're so mere that none know you but to love you. Why, the boys you've met up with out on the range couldn't even be hired to kill you, and they had to offer me the chance. Durned if I believe I'm going to do it myself! G'wan now; let's hear the sad story of your life."

CHAPTER IV

WHEN I THINK of that poor little answer waiting all alone for its own dear riddle," said Ducky, much affected, "I can't refuse. But I'll only hit the high places. Uncle Roger is dead, and it isn't a pleasant stunt to rake up all his faults and catalogue 'em."

He reflected a little while.

"My uncle put me through college and named me as his sole heir, for the reason — I had it from his own lips — that he lost father's little property for him. Uncle Roger was the elder brother, head of the family, and all that.

"He had a mighty high idea of the Drakes, did Uncle Roger, and he never liked my mother. To the day of her death he was barely civil to her. That's what I couldn't forgive in him, for all his cold and formal kindness to me. Damn it! He ignored her and she was worth a hundred like Roger Drake.

"From all accounts, my Uncle Roger was a warm baby at college. He was the only original Ducky Drake; all others were base imitations. Come back to li'l ol' N' York — lawyer; man about town; clubs; Tottie Twinkletoes; birds and bottles at proper temperatures! New York took his roll away from him.

"Did he buckle down to business and, by frugal industry — and so on? He did not. He faded away into the dim blue and the tall green. Honest, Jonesy, this is rotten of me — knockin' like this! But if you're going to help me play Money, money, who's got Uncle Ducky's money? this is what you want to know. It was the keynote of his character that he wanted all the beastly junk money will buy, but wasn't willing to hop out and hustle for the money. He wanted it quick, easy and often."

"Mind if I take notes?"

"'Eavings, no! Well, six years afterwards he came back. A distant relative — great-aunt or something — had left him a sizable legacy. Business of killing calf. So he took his money and poor old dad's and set to work to found an estate. Mother didn't know about it. I happened along about that time and she took quite a fancy to me; didn't notice other things.

"It doesn't seem possible that anyone could consistently lose money in real estate in a thrifty, growing burg like New York, does it? Uncle Roger did. Then he ducked again.

"Some ten years later, back to New York — who comes here? Is it my long-lost uncle? It is. Talked vaguely of holdings in New Mexico. Had the mazuma, and spent it. He stayed all winter; then back to New Mex. That's been the program ever since — four to six months in New York, the rest out here. But he didn't talk about New Mexico and he didn't urge us to visit him there.

"To do him justice, he made good on one point. He came through with good hard coin for dad. He was really very fond of poor old dad, and he'd always been sore at himself about losing dad's wad. And, as I said, he put his ungrateful nephew through school.

"Two months ago we found him dead in his bed — heart disease. His will left all his property to me unconditionally. But where and what was his property? He hadn't told us; and naturally dad hadn't felt like asking him.

"Saragossa was his post office. Except a pass book for his New York bank we found no papers in his effects — not so much as a letter. We applied at the bank — Ahem! Huh? Mr. Drake had opened an account with them years ago; the balance was so much — about one winter's spending for Uncle Roger. We pressed 'em a little. Very irregular, said the bank; but, under the circumstances — ahem! It had been Mr. Drake's custom to make one large deposit each year, checking out the greater part of it before he put in more. What was a little unusual, he generally made these deposits personally and in cash; sometimes — ahem! — there had been drafts from Albuquerque or El Paso.

"So there we were! How much property? According to the pass book, Uncle Roger had been spending, on the average, about seven thousand a year, including his two extravagances — father and yours truly. Said property was evidently in the grand state of New Mex. But where, what and how much? Had Uncle Roger spent all his income or only part of it? All of it, we judged; for, with all respect to your so wonderful Southwest, my Uncle Roger thought life in any place more than half an hour away from Broadway was a frost. If he stayed there only four months in the year, it was because supplies didn't hold out."

"I knew of your uncle — never saw him," said Neighbor. "He lived very quietly. Stayed at the ranch mighty close; made no friends and no enemies. No mixer. Had no visitors from the outside. Hunted a little. No cowman. He didn't know anything about cattle, he wouldn't learn anything about cattle, and he didn't care anything about cattle. Left all to his partner. That's his rep, according to campfire talk. One thing's certain — your uncle didn't make any seven thousand per from the ranch, or any big part of it. The Double Dee outfit doesn't sell three hundred steers a year. Your uncle only got half of that and paid half the expenses. No, sir — that Double Dee brand helped some, but it was mostly a blind for something else."

"That's what I'm headed for," said Ducky. "Dad's an invalid; so I came out. At Albuquerque Mr. Drake had bought drafts at the banks. The hotels knew him but none of the business men had ever heard of him. El Paso, ditto. So he couldn't have been engaged in any business openly, aside from the ranch. I came to Saragossa. You know what I found here. Uncle Roger's whole bunch of cattle would have made about a year's pocket money for him. His partner offered me ten thousand for my half of the ranch and cattle. That's enough to keep the wolf from the well-known door, but hardly what was expected."

"Grab it! That's more than it's worth. I know. Jim-Ike, my new neighbor, worked that country last year."

"Quinliven — Uncle Ducky's pardner — showed me the tally book. According to that, my share would be about that much."

Jones bent his head to hide a significant smile.

"Take it! Well, what did he say about your uncle?"

"He didn't believe my uncle owned any property here. Didn't know what he might have back East. Close-mouthed codger, he was.

"My own idea all along had been that my uncle had a secret mine. I put this up to Quinliven. Secret mine? Rubbish! No one could work a secret mine in this country — where everything was known; where the smoke of the strange camp fire was something of vital interest, to be looked into at once; where every cowpuncher had the time, ability and inclination to follow up any strange track.

"Fat chance, when all the freight from a country as big as an Eastern state was handled through one depot! Everybody knew all ore shipped — where it came from and what it run. Rubbish! Placer mines? 'Mai dear-r sir-r, to wash placer dirt, you must have water; and where water is, in New Mexico, is a frequented and public place.' Nuggets? Pish! Bosh! Nowt!

"I questioned my uncle's banker and his lawyer. Great astonishment. Nothing knowing. Mr. Bennett showed me the joint account of Quinliven & Drake, with a very small balance. My uncle kept no private account; he knew of no other investment my uncle had made; no such sums as I mentioned passed through his hands. The lawyer is now trying to solve my problem for me."

"Who's the lawyer?"

"He's a Mexican — a Mr. Octaviano Baca — and, at first, it seemed a rum start that Uncle Roger should have a native for his attorney. But he's a live one, all right; a very shrewd, keen person, indeed. Educated, too — good company; witty; speaks English with fluency and precision — much better English than I do. But doubtless you are acquainted with him. He is, I am told, something of a political power, having great influence with the natives."

Neighbor chuckled. He knew what young Drake did not. Octaviano Baca was the Boss — King of Saragossa.

"Know him by sight; never met him. But we know all about everything here, even people we've never seen. In this country our campfire talks take the place of Bradstreet and Dun, or Who's Who. Great help. They ain't afraid to say what they think, them firelighters; and they ain't afraid to think what they say! We're all catalogued. . . . 'Jones, Neighbor. Good old wagon, but needs greasing. Use no hooks.' . . . That's me. I'm mighty proud of that biography too. So it is Baca and Bennett that are looking after your interests?"

"Baca alone now," corrected Ducky. "Bennett helped at first, making inquiries from his business connections, and so on. We thought if we could unearth some investment of my uncle's we might follow it up; but there was a silly gunplay on the range between Bennett's men and ours, and Bennett thought he had better withdraw from the investigation; because Quinliven took it up, you know — grouchy old sorehead! — talked pretty rough to Bennett, and took our account over to the other bank."

"What was the trouble about — mavericks?"

"I hardly know — pure cussedness, I guess. Nothing worth quarreling about. Tommy Garst and one of our boys had some words about some spring in the mountains. All foolishness — nobody had any real title to it and everybody's cattle watered there; so it made no difference who claimed it. But they got to shooting over it — silly fools! Both gone now."

"Nobody hurt?"

"Dah!" said Ducky scornfully. "Well, how about that answer?"

Neighbor looked at his own toes with painstaking speculative interest. To assist the process he cocked his head on one side and screwed his mouth up. At last he glanced over at Ducky.

"I know a lot if I could only think of it," he announced plaintively. With a thoughtful face and apparently without his own knowledge, he broke into song, with a gay, lilting voice:

> Here I am, a-comin' on the run —
> Best durn cowboy 'at ever pulled a gun!
> Hi-yi-yi-yippy; yippy-yi-yi-yi!
> Hi-yi-yi-yippy; yippy-yea!

Ducky sniffed.

"Why don't you learn a tune if you want to sing?"

Neighbor looked round with puckered eyes.

"Why, I ain't singin' — not exactly!" he answered dreamily. "I'm thinkin' — thinkin' about your troubles and how to make 'em all come out right in the next number. I've got a two-story mind, you see. One of 'em is diggin' away for you, hard, while the other one is singin', foot-loose, or talking to you. Me and the real serious-mind, we're studyin' right now; we don't hardly sense what I'm sayin' to you. And that's a real nice tune too. I don't like to have you make fun of that tune. That's a saddle song. That tune goes to a trotting horse. You try it."

"Why, so it does!" said Ducky after a brief experiment.

"Can you make your fingers go gallop-y? Well, do it, and I'll show you another. But don't talk to me. I'm thinking fine and close, like walkin' a rope; and you'll throw me off."

So Ducky made his fingers go gallop-y and Neighbor kept time to it:

> Percival Pulcifer Peterkin Pool,
> Cloaked and mittened and ready for school;
> Cloaked and muffled and gloved and spurred.
> Gee! Wasn't Peter a wise old bird?

"Any more?" demanded Ducky, highly diverted.

"Yes; here's a pacing tune. They say," added Neighbor absently, "They say, back in Maryland and Virginia, that old King James Fifth wrote this song — allowing for some expurgating and change o' names — Albuquerque for Edinburg — to give it local color. Hark!

> Oh, when I got to Albuquerque I taken down my sign —
> Trra-la-la, tirra-la-la, lay!
> Oh, when I got to Albuquerque I taken down my sign,
> For they're all educated there in the riding line —
> Ti-ri-laddy and a ti-ri-lay!

Here Neighbor brought his tilted chair back to level, removed his clasped hands from the back of his head, and shook off his dreamy expression.

"Well, I guess I'll have to give it up for this time," he sighed.

"Yah!" said Ducky, grinning. "A pish and three long tushes! You big stiff! I thought you were going to tell me money, money, who's got the money? and where Uncle Roger plucked it in the first place. Little Ducky, he sticks to his first guess — mines — and counterfeiting, for place."

"Where he got it? Where — My poor, poor boy!" said Neighbor. "My poor misguided lamb, I wasn't studying on who's got your uncle's money; I was figuring on a harder thing — and that's how you and me are going to get it. I know where your uncle's money is. I know it was really cash money, too, and not property. And I know how he got it!"

Ducky stared.

"Business of gasp!" he said. "Demonstrated! Produce!"

"Wait a minute!" said Neighbor, holding up a warning hand. "How do you bate your breath? If you know, do it!"

"She's bated. Break it to me!"

"I'll tell you first and give you the reasons afterward; it makes the reasons sound so much more reasonable, that way."

" 'You may fire when ready, Gridley!' "

"Hist!" said Neighbor, weird, shaky and spook-eyed. "Listen to the evil old man of Haunted Hill! Your uncle was the Man Higher Up! He made his money backing gambling hells! U-r-r-r-r-h! The men who have now got that money-money are Beck, Baca, Scanlon, Quin- liven and Bennett! And the men who are now going to get that money-money — open another bottle, Ducky — are Roger Olcott Drake, Second — Present! — and Neighbor Jones — Present! But how? How? How?"

CHAPTER V

Roger Drake caught his breath. "Sir, do you inhale it or do you use a needle? Can you prove any of that?"

"Prove it!" returned Neighbor indignantly. "I don't have to prove it — I know it. It's just gemimini-mentally got to be that way. There ain't no proofs — the kind to convince a jury of peers; but there's no other way to account for what's happened, and, if you're not a natural-born peer, I can show you."

"Among the many beauties that add luster to my character are an aptitude to be shown and a simple willingness to try anything — once. Go to it, old summit! Wise me up!"

"Ver-ree well! Let us examine the simple and jolly facts — well known, but not to you. Tavy Baca is abso-lute-ly the Big Noise in Saragossa County — accent on loot. Nominations and appointments f.o.b. for cash with order. Special terms for convictions and acquittals. Try our land-office decisions. Small graft of all kinds. Corpses to order in neat hardwood boxes. Very Roycrofty. See us before trying elsewhere.

"Laying all juries aside, he's a smart lawyer — Baca. He might be immensely wealthy, but every Mexican within a radius, when he's sick, lazy or in trouble, makes a beeline for Baca and comes away with a jingle in his pocket. It's like packin' water in a sieve.

"Gambling, as perhaps you know, is completely stamped out in New Mexico since she joined the glorious sisterhood. Baca would be getting a juicy rake-off from Beck's game. Or, since Baca was your uncle's lawyer, uncle made the necessary arrangements himself, likely."

"But how do you know my uncle was behind Beck?"

"I don't — that comes later. I am now giving you known facts only, and you can build for yourself wherever they'll fit.

"Bennett owns a heap of other people's property. He began life by ruining Brown and Almandares — take thy bill and write down fifty — deliberately smashed 'em so he could get the wreckage. As he began, he kept on — a wrecker. He has no heart, lungs, lights or liver. I knew Almandares; and the good Lord never made a better man than that old Mexican.

"Let me at once show you the impassable gulf between Bennett and a common cheat like Beck, or like Scanlon — blacklegs, card sharps, flimflammers. With the Beck kind, you lose only what they win. The Bennett kind gladly makes you lose ten dollars so he can get one. To end with, Beck and Scanlon showed a tenderness toward you not wholly explained by your many charms of face and form. It was magnificent, but it was not poker. And there's where I first got the hunch.

"Having stolen the big bundle, they, or either of them, felt a certain delicacy about cheating you for your small change; so what they won from you they won fair. But Banker Bennett, with his share to put up in moth balls, he's so scared you might find out and pry it away from him that he wants to hire you killed!"

Ducky Drake made an impassioned remark. It was a household word.

"What makes it a good deal worse," added Jones with exceeding bitterness, "is that he picked on me to let the contracts to."

"Well, but — "

"But, nothing! That is one word I can't bear. He offered to cancel the mortgage on my stuff if I'd expurgate you. That means nearly two thousand perfectly good bucks. Why? Would Bennett do that from civic pride? Nary! He's got a big bunch of your money — that's why. Is there any other possible reason?"

"Mere as I am," said Ducky, "I can see that. There is not. But how does all this involve the others? And what makes you hook up my uncle with the kitty industry?"

"When a man loves money and not work; when a man has run through three fortunes, two of 'em his own; when he turns up with a taxable income made in Saragossa County — how did he make it? How can he make it? Openly, in mines, sheep, cattle, storekeeping, liquor or law. But, except for one cattle ranch, misses' size, your uncle had no business relations — openly.

"What kind of business is done secretly? Business that is very profitable and not well thought of; counterfeiting — smuggling — gambling. This wasn't smuggling — too far from the border. Nor counterfeiting — else he might have printed off enough to let him live in New York. Also, it couldn't possibly be counterfeiting, because it was gambling.

"Now, Beck and Scanlon run the only dens in Saragossa and at Ridgepole. Because they are all involved, your uncle must have been hooked up with gambling; and because your uncle was hooked up with gambling, they're all involved."

Ducky looked dazed; with tolerable reason.

"Quinliven is involved bad and big and sure. He offered to take your cattle for the full number on the tally book. No cowman would do that. The calves on that tally are sold, lost, strayed, stolen, eaten, skinned, and gone with the wild bunch. Quinnie, he wanted to get little Ducky out of the country.

"That shooting scrape was all fake; so you wouldn't suspect him and Banker Bennett of standin' in. Real sincere people don't empty their guns and not hit anybody — it ain't respectable. But Bennett he intended to make that water hole the explanation of your bein' found dead and promiscuous. That's what he proposed to me."

"Oh, goils, pinch me!"

"Baca is involved by being your uncle's lawyer, and yet not knowing how your uncle extracted that nice little income from Saragossa County; and by being your lawyer and not finding out. And old

Beck and Scanlon are involved by their conscientious scruples in not wanting the last rag off your back."

Ducky remonstrated.

"Hi! You put that last in to make it easy — like the Englishman who always added 'and barks like a dog' to all his riddles, to make 'em harder. You're throwing the long arm of coincidence out of socket. It won't wash, my Angular-Saxon friend! You're a good old super-dreadnought and the best hand at a standing high guess I've ever seen — but we can't go to court waving any wild, wet tale like that."

"Court? Oh, Jemima! Who said court? Let Tavy Baca pick the jury and you couldn't convict one of that push on his own written confession. The right hunch is goin' to be the best evidence, where we settle this case — and that's out of court."

"Do you mean to use force?"

"Thank you, I shouldn't wish any pie. Why, Ducky dear, some of that outfit would lock horns with Julius K. Caesar if he looked ogle-eyed at 'em. Tavy Baca especially is a cold proposition — the worst west of a given point. Only one skunk in the firm. That's Bennett. No, sir; if you want to touch that tainted money — "

"I do. Let me leave no chance for misapprehension. I want to roll in it! I want to puddle my paddies in it!"

"Then you've got to guess quick and guess right and guess hard; you've got to mean what you think, and dig in your toes when you pray! To handle this contract you have got to have the hunch, the punch, the pep and the wallop!"

"But, even if you're right — "

"If you say that again I'll quit you!" declared Jones indignantly.

"Don't say dem crool woids to me!" begged Ducky. "You're horribly right — but where are you going to begin? It's like climbing a glass wall."

"Oh, no — not so bad as that! We have one highly important circumstance in our favor. They haven't divided the spoils yet. If they had they wouldn't be trying to get you out of the way. And when they do divide — about this time look out for squalls; for I judge that most of that cash was left on deposit with Bennett. The hell-house-keepers will have the rest — what they had for the house roll when they heard that Uncle Roger had cashed in, and what they've won or lost since.

"When you came on and it became plain that you didn't know anything about your uncle's business, there they were! Bennett couldn't keep it all — the gamblers would give the snap away unless they got their share. They couldn't get it all — Bennett would tell you first."

"Oh, my, my! Birds in their little nests should not fall out!"

Jones ignored the interruption.

"Baca and Quinliven horned in too — they each want a slice; but Bennett won't let it out of his hands till you go home. He's afraid you'll find instructions from your uncle or some sort of a statement."

"Uncle Roger knew, in a vague, general way, that men died; but he thought that was only other people — people in the papers," explained Roger. "And yet he must have kept a pass book, receipts — something to show for his deposits."

"Exactly! Beck and Baca, between them, have got the pass book, and hold it over Bennett's head for a club, likely. That's real funny. Bennett's the one that's taken all the risks, this load. Generally it's somebody else that takes the chances, while Bennett gets the profit."

"Well! You certainly are a wise old fowl!" said Roger with explosive emphasis.

"If your uncle had trusted him, I think, maybe, Quinliven might have come across — I judge he would. I reckon Quinnie, old boy, was just uncle's blind; but he guessed something and butted in to blackmail the blackmailers. To make it nice and pleasant all round, him and Baca will be wanting the gamesters to throw the house roll into the pool along with the rest, and then split it all up, even Stephen. I would right much admire to witness the executive session of that firm when they declare the final dividend!" said Neighbor with a chuckle. Then his brow clouded.

"But I can't. Because we're going to get it. To begin with, suppose you step round and take Quinnie up on his offer for your cattle. Stick out for cash. He hasn't got it, but he'll make the others dig it up from the sinking fund. Right then that company will begin to get a pain in the stumick-ache. They'll see you makin' ready to go 'way and they'll all begin playing for position. You hang to your cattle selling as though you didn't have another idea on earth."

Neighbor Jones rose to go.

"And while you start that I'm going round and throw the clutch of circumstance into the high gear."

CHAPTER VI

In the lobby of the Windsor Hotel, as Neighbor Jones came down the stairs, Mr. Octaviano Baca chatted with a little knot of guests. A well-set-up man, tall and strong, with a dark, intelligent face marred and pitted by smallpox but still pleasing, he carried his two score years with the ease of twenty. A gay man, a friendly man, his manner was suave and easy; his dress, place considered, rigorously correct — frock coat, top hat, stick, gloves and gun. The gun was covered, not concealed, by the coat; a chivalrous concession to the law, of which he was so much an ornament.

Baca was born to riches, and born to the leadership of the clans. He had brains in his own right; but it was his entire and often proved willingness to waive any advantage and to discuss any moot point with that gun which had won him admiration from the many and forgiveness from the few.

Mr. Jones sank into a quiet chair and read the newspapers. When Mr. Baca, after several false starts, left his friends and went out on the street, Mr. Jones rose and followed him. Mr. Baca turned in at Beck's place, Jones behind him.

Gambling was completely eliminated in Saragossa, but the saloon was in high favor legally; so Beck and Scanlon kept a saloon openly on the ground floor. The poker rooms and the crap, monte, roulette and faro layouts were upstairs. Their existence was a profound secret. No stranger could find the gambling den in Saragossa without asking somebody — anyone would do; unless, indeed, he heard, as he passed, the whir of the ivory ball or the clicking of chips.

Baca, with a nod and a smile for the bar, passed on to join a laughing crowd behind, where two native boys were enjoying a bout with the gloves. Neighbor leaned on the bar. The partners were ill matched. Beck was tall, portly and, except for a conscientious, professional smile, of a severe countenance, blond, florid and flaxen. Scanlon was a slender wisp of a blue-eyed Irishman, dried up, wizened and silent.

"Well, boys," said Neighbor jovially, "I got to go back to the hills and grow a new fleece. Till then, you've lost my game. Sorry."

Beck frowned.

"I hate to see a good fellow go bust. If boys like you had plenty of money I wouldn't never have to work. Well, hurry on back! And come straight here the first night, before you waste any on clothes and saddles and stuff." He lowered his voice for Neighbor's ears. "Say, if you're short, you know — hotel bills, and so on — come round." He jerked a confidential thumb at the house safe.

"Not so bad as that!" laughed Neighbor. "But you want to sharpen your shears up. They pulled a little this time." He passed on to the circle round the boxers.

It was late dusk when, after certain sociable beverages, Mr. Baca bethought himself of supper and started homeward. As he swung

along the sidewalk Mr. Jones was close behind. Mr. Baca took the
first turn to the left: Mr. Jones took the first turn to the left. Mr.
Baca cut across the Park: Mr. Jones also cut across the Park, now
almost at his quarry's heels. Mr. Baca wheeled.

"Did you wish to speak with me?"

Neighbor came forward, with an air of relief.

"Why — er — not exactly; but I'd just as lief as not. And it'll be
easier for me, now it's getting so dark. You see," he said confi-
dentially, "I'm shadowing you!"

"You're — what?"

"Shadowing you. You seemed to have plenty of money; and I
thought," said Neighbor hopefully, "that I might catch you doing
something wrong and blackmail you."

"Are you trying to break into jail?" demanded Baca sharply. "You
are either intoxicated or mentally deficient. In either case — "

"No, no," said Neighbor soothingly. "I'm not drunk. I really need
the money."

"Except that I doubt your sanity," said the outraged lawyer, "I'd
make you regret this bitterly. Do you know who I am?"

"Sure! You're Tavy Baca — Boss, Prosecuting Attorney and two-
gun man. And please don't talk that way about me," Neighbor
pleaded in an injured voice. "It makes me feel bad. You wouldn't like
it yourself. Don't you know me? I'm not insane. I'm Jones — Neighbor Jones. I've been bucking the poker game at Beck's. But there —
you don't know about the poker game, of course — you being Prosecuting Attorney and all."

"See here!" said Baca with a dull, ugly note, "if you're looking for
trouble you can get enough for a mess!"

"Not trouble — money!"

"I warn you now," Baca advised. "Do not follow me another step.
I'm going."

Jones burst into joyous laughter with so free and unfeigned a note
that Baca turned again.

"Come!" cried Jones. "I know what you think I'm going to say —
that before I started I left a sealed envelope with a friend and told
him if I didn't come back by X o'clock to break the seal and be guided
by the contents — that's what you thought I'd say. But you're wrong!"
Unhesitatingly he took the few steps separating him from that silent,
angry figure in the starlight. "Nobody knows what I'm up to but
you and me and God, and you're not right sure. So don't waste any
more breath on warnings. I'm warned — and you are!"

Without a word Baca turned at right angles to his homeward
course, and led the way swiftly up the dark and steep street to a dark

and silent quarter of the Mexican suburb. Toward the street, these old adobe homes presented a blank wall; windows, and all doors save one, fronting on the inclosed *patio*.

"It's like this," said Jones cheerfully, pressing along the narrow way a yard behind: "I had a nice little bunch of cows — nigh onto two hundred — out in the Monuments. And Bennett, he was projecting about like a roarin' lion out there; and he says: 'Jones, why don't you buy the Bar Nothing brand?' 'No money,' says I. . . . I say, Baca, don't go so fast! This ain't no Marathon! Lonesome, shivery place, isn't it?"

The silent figure walked still swifter.

"Oh, all right, then! 'I'll lend you the money,' says Bennett, 'an' take a mortgage on both brands.' 'There'll come a drought,' says I, 'and them cattle will lay down and die on me, a lot of 'em; and I'll find myself in a fix.' And he did, and they did, and I did."

No word from Baca. In the black shadow of the dark unlighted houses he passed swiftly and unhesitatingly. Jones continued:

"Since that I paid him all but eighteen hundred-odd; and now the mortgage comes due pretty sudden, and I stand to lose both brands. . . . Say, Baca, where're you takin' me to? Some gang of thugs? You can do that all right — but I'll get you first and I'll get you hard, and I'll get you sure! Don't make any mistake!"

Baca gave way to his feelings.

"Oh, bother!" he said, and stopped, irresolute.

"What do you mean anyway, actin' the way you do?" demanded Jones, mopping his forehead. "Wouldn't it sound silly, if I lay a-dyin', for you to threaten me with jail and shootin' and law? They'd sound real futile, wouldn't they? Well, I'm dying right now. I've been a long time at it; but there ain't no cure for what ails me but death. I refer, of course, to the malady of living."

"Damn your eyes!" cried the exasperated King of Saragossa; and he began rapidly to retrace his steps.

"And so," continued the dying man, keeping pace, "I don't never back up. When I start out to blackmail a man he might just as well be nice about it, 'cause I'm going to blackmail him."

Despite himself Baca had to laugh.

"What are you going to blackmail me for?"

"About two thousand," said Jones.

"But what have I done?"

"Good Lord, man!" said Jones blankly. "I don't know!"

"Come!" said Baca, and clapped his persecutor on the back. "I like a brave man, even if he is a damned fool! Come home to supper with me. I've got a little bachelor establishment beyond the Park, with an old Mexican *hombre* who can give you the best meal in town."

"You're on! And after supper, then we can fix up that mortgage, can't we? I want to specify that now, so I can eat your salt without prejudice."

"And now," said Baca, replenishing his guest's wine-glass, "about the blackmail. Of what particular misdeed do you accuse me?"

"When you asked me to supper," said Jones thoughtfully, "you virtually admitted there was something. You see that? But I don't like to intrude on your private affairs — to butt in, as we say in Harvard."

The host fixed keen eyes on him.

"As we say in Harvard? Yes," he purred. "Go on!"

"It is very distasteful to me. Instead of me naming your crime — or crimes — why could you not beg me to accept a suitable sum as a recognition of my good taste? Just as you please! It's up to you."

"As we say in Harvard!" suggested Baca lightly, lifting his brows with another piercing look.

"As we say in Harvard," agreed Jones. "Any sum, so long as it comes to exactly two thousand. Or, you might use your influence to get Bennett to cancel my mortgage — that would be the same thing. He offered to cancel it once this afternoon — on a condition."

"And that condition?"

"Was not acceptable. It betrayed too plainly the influence — the style, we might say — of the James brothers."

"William and Henry?"

"Jesse and Frank. Man, dear," said Neighbor with sudden, vehement bitterness, "you and me, we're no great shakes. You're goin' to rob young Drake and I'm going to take hush money for it; but this man Bennett is a stinking, rancid, gray-headed old synonym. He is so scared he won't be happy till he gets that boy killed. If I was as big a coward as that, durned if I'd steal at all!"

Baca struck the table sharply; splotches of angry red flamed in his cheeks.

"And I told him I wouldn't stand for it! Damn him! Look here, Jones, you ought to be boiled in oil for your stupefying insolence; but, just to punish him, I'll make Bennett pay your price. It will be like drawing teeth; give me time."

CHAPTER VII

THE RAIN DRENCHED in long shudders. Here and there a late lamp blurred dimly at a pane; high-posted street lamps, at unequal and ineffectual distances, glowed red through the slant lines of rain, reflected faintly from puddle and gutter at their feet. Alone, bent, boring into the storm, Martin Bennett shouldered his way to Baca's door under the rushing night.

A gush of yellow struck across the dark — the door opened at his first summons; he was waited for. The master of the house helped him from his raincoat and ushered him through crimson portières into a warm and lighted room. Three men sat before an open fire, where a table gleamed with glasses and bottles. There were two other doors, hung, like the first, with warm, bright colors, reflecting and tingeing the light from fire and lamp — a cheerful contrast to the raw, bleak night outside.

Here the good cheer ceased. The three faces, as they turned to scowl at the newcomer, were sullen, distrustful and lowering.

Despite the raincoat, Bennett was sodden to his knees; his hands and face and feet were soaked and streaming. No friendly voice arose to remark on his plight; an ominous silence had prevailed since the street door had opened to him. He bent shivering to the fire. With no word the host filled and brought to him a stiff glass of liquor. Bennett drained it eagerly and a little color crept back into his pinched features.

Owen Quinliven broke silence then, with a growl deep in his throat. "Thought you'd better come, eh?" His mustached lip bristled.

"The storm was so bad. I thought it might let up after a while," said Bennett miserably.

"Don't make that an excuse," said Beck with a cold sneer. "You might have slipped over to our place, a short block; or you could have had us meet you at your own office."

"Gentlemen! Gentlemen!" expostulated Baca, with a curling lip. "You do not understand. Mr. Bennett has his position to think of. Mr. Bennett is highly respectable. He could not let it be known that he had traffic with professional gamblers like Mr. Beck and the estimable Scanlon." He bowed ironically; the estimable Scanlon rolled a slow, wicked little eye, and Baca's cheek twitched as he went on: "I say nothing as you observe, of myself or of our worthy friend Quinliven, who, as I perceive, is in a very bad temper."

Quinliven glowered at the speaker like a baited bull. He was a huge, burly man with a shaggy, brindled head, a bull neck, a russet face knotted with hard red lumps, and small, fiery, amber-colored eyes under a thick tangle of bushy brows. The veins swelled in his neck as he answered.

"Well, he'll have some traffic with me, and do it quick! Here I've talked young Drake into selling out and going home; I'm giving him twenty-five hundred dollars too much, standin' the loss out of my share — and me not getting a full share at all! All I get is the cattle, while the rest of you pull down nearly twelve thousand apiece, net cash. That part is all right though. That's my own proposition. I don't begrudge the little extra money to the boy, and I want him to get away from here for his own sake as well as for mine. This crawling, slimy Bennett thing is bound to have that boy killed." He glared at the steaming banker by the fire. "I don't see how that man got by with it so long. He wouldn't last long on the range. And now, after I've made the trade, Bennett hems and haws, and hangs fire about giving up the money."

"You don't understand," protested the wretched banker. "You'll get your share; but it would inconvenience me dreadfully to take that amount of money immediately from a little private bank like mine. In ninety days, or even sixty, I can so adjust my affairs as to settle with all of you."

"My heart bleeds for you," said Beck sympathetically. "For I'm going to inconvenience you a heap more. You'll adjust your affairs in less than ninety hours, or even sixty. I've been fooled with long enough. That pass book calls for a little over forty-six thousand dollars. We expected to get half. Instead we've got to split it four ways. Young Drake is going and I want my split right now."

"What about me?" cried the banker in wild and desperate indignation. "What do I get? Barely a fourth! And you two have Drake's money already — heaven knows how much!"

"Heaven don't" said Beck.

"But do I get any of that?" shouted the outraged banker.

"You do not," returned Beck. "In the first place, the men are different. You stepped out of your class when you started to mingle with the likes of us. Why should you bother to rob a perfect stranger anyhow? And you with money corded up! I don't understand it."

"Bennett!" cried the ranchman, "if I stood in your shoes, before I'd allow any man to use me like we're using you, I'd go to Drake and give that money up. I'd say: 'Young fellow, I meant to rob you; but my conscience troubles me, and so do my feet.' You ain't got the gall, and you're too big a hog. I dare you to!"

"And in the next place," continued the complacent gambler, ignoring the interruption, "there's not one scrap of paper to connect our money with Old Drake. Part of it is ours anyhow, that we've made honestly — "

"At poker," corrected Scanlon.

"At poker, I should say. But we've got your receipts, Mr. Banker. That's what makes you squirm! And they're where you can't get 'em; so it won't do you any good to get any of us murdered, the way you tried to do that boy."

"He tried it again yesterday," interposed Baca softly.

Quinliven brought his heavy hand crashing down on the table.

"You damned coward! I told you to drop that!" His red mustache prickled fiercely; above his eyes the red tufts knotted to bunches. He glanced round at his fellows. "Look here; there's no damn sense in hurting that kid, the way things stand. If Drake gets killed over this I'm going to see that Bennett swings for it if I have to swing with him — the yellow cur!"

The banker shriveled under his look.

"Your sentiments do you vast credit," observed Baca suavely. "I concur most heartily. But, my good fellow, why bawl your remarks?" He accompanied the query with a pleasant smile.

Scanlon raised his head to watch. The ranchman's fingers worked and quivered; for a moment it seemed as though he would leap on his tormentor; but he settled back.

"I'm with you," said Scanlon.

Then, noting that Beck did not commit himself to this self-denying ordinance, he filled a glass with wine and, as he drank it, observed his partner narrowly from the tail of his eye.

"You may rest easy, Mr. Quinliven," observed Baca, straddling with his back to the fire and his hands to the blaze. "There will be no need for you to carry out your chivalrous intention. I assure you that while I live I am perfectly cap ble of selecting a jury that will hang Mr. Bennett without the disastrous concomitant you mention; and I shall take great pleasure in doing so should need arise. I should hate to see you hanged, Quinliven — I should indeed! You distress me! But I fear — " He left the sentence unfinished, shaking his head sorrowfully. "Mr. Bennett, I am sure, will bear himself to conform with our wishes. However, I find myself in full accord with Mr. Bennett in the matter of the moneys now in the hands of Messrs. Beck and Scanlon, and wrongfully withheld from our little pool."

"That will be a plenty," said Beck. "For fear of mistakes I will now declare myself. We admit that we have a bundle of the Drake money and we announce that we are going to keep it. How much, is nobody's business but our own. In consideration of that fact, however, the two of us lay claim to only one full share of the Drake deposit. That gives us twelve thousand; Bennett as much; the Honorable Prosecuting Attorney the same; the Double Dee brand to Quinliven. That's final!"

"I suppose you know, Mr. Beck," said Baca, cupping his chin, "your little joint can be closed any time I lift a finger?"

"Baca," said Scanlon, with level eyes, "you'll close nawthin'! We bought protection from you. We'll get what we bought. When you feel any doubts comin' on, don't talk to Beck about it. Talk to me! And," he added with venomous intensity, "one more word about any divvy on our poker roll and that pass book goes to Ducky Drake!" He tapped his breast. "I've got the pass book — not Beck."

"Well, well," said Baca indulgently, "have your own way. Far be it from me to question any gentleman's ultimatum, and so, perhaps, bring a discordant note into our charming evening. Let us pass on to the next subject. Is everybody happy? No! Mr. Bennett is not happy. Mr. Bennett is a very able man, as we all know — exemplar to the young — a rich man, merchant prince, and all that. And yet we can quite understand that he may be temporarily embarrassed for actual cash. I, for one, am willing to allow him a reasonable time. He cannot hide his real estate; so we shall be taking no risks. Doubtless we can stand off young Drake for the price of his cattle by giving him good security."

The silent Scanlon leaped up and snarled in unimaginable ferocity.

"If there's any more shilly-shally there'll be a Standing Room Only sign on the gates of hell and the devil sending out a hurry-up call for the police!" His voice swelled in breathless crescendo. "I'm sick of you — the whole pack and pilin'! I want to get so far away from here it'll take nine dollars to send me a postcard; so far east they'll give me change for a cent; so far north the sun don't go down till after dark." His eyes were ablaze with blistering scorn. "Gawd! Look at yourselves! Quinliven — the honorable, high-minded, grave-robbing pardner — "

"Here!" bellowed Quinliven savagely. "I came through with the cattle, straight as a die! That's as far as I was any pardner of Drake's. You don't know how that man treated me! It wasn't only me doing all the work — but his cold, sneering, overbearing — "

"Shut up, you polled Angus bull!" yelled Scanlon, with a howl of joyous truculence. "And Bennett — faugh! P-t-t-h!"

Scanlon spat in the fire, and wheeled on the other gambler. Beck's face was black with concentrated hate. The little man pointed a taunting finger.

"Look at Beck!" he jeered. "Guess what he knows I think of 'im! And I know him — he's me pardner! Fish mouth and mackerel eye — Yah! And all three of you knuckle down to Baca! Year after year you let yourselves be bullyragged, browbeaten, lorded over by a jury-packing, witness-bribing shyster — a grafter, a crook, a dirty Mexican — "

Without hesitation or change of countenance Baca walked across the open space toward him.

"Not one step more!" said Scanlon.

Baca stopped in his tracks.

"You nervy little runt," he said, half in admiration, "you mean it! Well, I mean this, too. If I'm a crook — and there is much in favor of that contention — it is because my personal inclination lies that way, and not in the least because of my Mexican blood. I am quite clear on that point. Leave out the part about the dirty Mexican and I don't take that other step. Otherwise, I step! Choose!"

"I withdraw the Mexican!" said Scanlon ungrudgingly. "Gawd! I believe you're the best of the rotten bunch!"

"Go on then: 'Grafter, crook' — " prompted Baca.

"Why — er — really!" stammered Scanlon. Then he brightened. " 'There has been so much said, and, on the whole so well said,' " he beamed, canting his head on one side with a flat, oily smile, " 'that I will not further detail you.' "

He seated himself, with a toothy, self-satisfied expression; but the allusion was lost on all except the delighted Baca.

In glum silence, Quinliven reached for a bottle and glared at the little Irishman, who smiled evilly back at him.

"There is one more point," observed Baca in his best courtroom manner, "on which I touch with a certain delicacy and as it were, with hesitation. I am reluctant to grieve further a spirit already distressed; but the fact is, gentlemen, our impulsive friend here" — he laid a gentle hand on Bennett's shoulder and Bennett squeaked — "undertook yesterday to employ this man Jones — Neighbor Jones — to murder our friend Drake. I take this most unkindly."

He teetered on his tiptoes; he twirled his eyeglasses; his hand made a pleasant jingle with key ring and coin; his face expressed a keen sense of well-being and social benevolence.

"As a matter of abstract principle, even before we had learned to love our young friend Drake, we decided that such a step was unnecessary and inexpedient; and so informed Mr. Bennett. But the idea of slaying Mr. Drake seems to have become an obsession with Mr. Bennett — or, as English Ben would put it, a fad. As English Ben would say, again, Mr. Bennett is a beastly blighter."

He adjusted the eyeglasses and beamed round on his cowed and sullen confederates, goaded, for his delight, to madness and desperation; and on the one uncowed co-devil, the mordant and cynical Scanlon.

"Our young Eastern friend has endeared himself to our hearts. I

do not exaggerate when I say that we feel quite an avuncular interest
in his fortunes. We are deeply hurt by Mr. Bennett's persistence; but
let us not be severe. In this case retribution has been, as we might
say, automatic, for the man Jones, by some means, has acquired an
inkling of the posture in which our affairs lie in the little matter of the
Drake estate; though I believe he suspects only Bennett and myself.
Bennett, I judge, has talked too much. And — such is the wickedness
and perfidy of the human mind — the man Jones makes a shameless
demand on us for two thousand dollars, money current with the
merchant, as the price of silence. Alas, that such things can be!"

His hands, now deep in his trousers pockets, expressed a lively
abhorrence for the perfidy of the man Jones.

"This iniquitous demand is no better than blackmail and might be
resisted in our courts of justice; but, inasmuch as Mr. Bennett's san-
guinary disposition has brought on us this fresh complication, would
it not be well to permit Mr. Bennett to pay this two thousand from
his private pocket? I pause for reply."

Bennett let out a screech between a howl and a shriek.

"This is infamous! You're robbing me! Oh, why did I ever have
dealings with such desperadoes?"

"Why, indeed?" said Baca tranquilly. "I think, if you will permit
me to criticize, that was a mistake in judgment on your part, Mr.
Bennett. You have not the temperament for it."

"He pays!" said Scanlon, gloating.

"He pays!" echoed the rancher.

"You're robbing me!" Bennett crumpled to a wailing heap.

"We're not, ye black scut!" snapped Scanlon, perking the unfortunate banker upright by the collar. "But we will! We're now holding
to the exact bargain we proposed and you agreed to; but if ever little
Mickey S. has need or desire av the red, red gold or the green, green
greenback, 'tis back here he will come to you. May Gawd have
mercy on your soul! Sit up, ye spineless jellyfish — sit up!"

Beck, sitting mute in a cold fury of hate, raised his eyes.

"This Neighbor Jones — I had a letter about him today. He's caught
on, someway, that we've been workin' him over in the shop; and he's
layin' for us, I guess. That big lump that called himself the Kansas
City Kid — 'twas him that wrote the letter. Jones accused him of
cheating and drove him out of town — took his gun, made him leave
his clothes, and hike. That's a dangerous man, Baca. Now I think of
it, young Drake quit us at the same time. Jones told him our game
was crooked, likely."

"Them two was together all this forenoon — I seen 'em," contributed Quinliven. "Is Jones maybe fixing to give you the double cross?"

Baca considered with contracted brow.

"Possibly; but not necessarily so," he said. "Drake agreed to sell last night. Perhaps he merely got wise to himself — to use his own phrase — and decided to sell out and go home while the going was good. Jones would be his natural associate, the two having been bucking the game together; but Jones expects to get clear of his debt by sticking to me. He could gain nothing by telling Drake. We are too powerful. He knows there is no way to make us disgorge — disgorge is the word, I think, in this connection. I find Jones most amusing, myself. If he wearies me — "

"Don't you figure Jones for any easy mark," warned Scanlon. "If he tries to hand us something — look out! He is a bad actor!"

"Leave him to me," said Baca with a tightening of the lips. "I'll take measures to improve his acting. Never mind Jones. We have now satisfactorily adjusted the preliminaries, have we not? It is established, I believe, that Mr. Scanlon and myself constitute a clear majority of this meeting. Any objection? In that case, let us now get down to the sad and sordid business before us. It is the sense of the meeting, as I take it, that Mr. Bennet shall bring to this room, by ten o'clock tomorrow — no; tomorrow is Sunday — by ten o'clock on Monday, the purchase money for the Double Dee cattle."

"Oh-h!" It was a mournful howl, a dog's hopeless plaint to the moon; emitted, however, by one of the gentlemen present.

"Objection overruled. You will, also, Mr. Bennett, provide twenty-four thousand dollars to satisfy the other equities, here held in the Drake estate."

Scanlon held up a finger.

"Cash, you moind! No checks or drafts, to be headed off. Coin or greenbacks! I will not be chipracked by this slippery ould man. He is the human greased pig."

By a prodigious effort Bennett pulled himself together; his face was very pale.

"To provide that much cash, without warning, is impossible. I should have nothing left to do the bank's business with; in fact, I have not half that amount of actual cash in the safe."

He stood up and grasped the back of a chair — his knuckles were white as he gripped; his voice grew firmer.

"I'll be open with you, gentlemen. I am too much extended; I am bitterly cramped for ready money. Give me time to turn round; don't force me to take this money out of the business now. Once let the ordinary loans be refused to a few customers; let the rumor of it go abroad; let my Eastern creditors once hear of it — and I must inevitably stand a heavy loss. They will demand immediate payment, and that I cannot make without sacrifice."

"What would your creditors think if they knew what we know?" answered Beck. "You'll make your sacrifice right now, within forty-eight hours, for your preferred creditors, here present."

"Baca! I appeal to you. Help me! I'll be honest. To pay out this sum will not ruin me, but it'll cripple me so that it may take me years to recover. At the very best I shall lose far more than the pitiful remnant of the Drake money you leave me. Give me time to turn round! Give me thirty days!"

"Thirty hours," said Beck; "Monday morning."

"I tell you it will cost me two dollars for every one I pay over to you now," the banker pleaded. "Let me give you certificates of deposit."

"That's what you gave Drake!" said Scanlon.

For the first time in the somber silence that followed they heard the loud clock on the mantel — tick, tock — tick, tock — tick, tock!

Baca spoke at last slowly and thoughtfully.

"Bennett, you have good standard securities in the El Paso National, pledged for a comparatively small amount, as I happen to know. You can sell them by wire and have the money here by the last train on Monday. That's what you'd better do. Personally I am not inclined — "

"Here is too much talk," said Scanlon. "Cash or smash!"

Bennett threw up his hand in a gesture of despair.

"I'll get it on Monday. Let me go home."

"There now! I knew you would do the right thing if we forced you to!" Baca went to the window. "It is not raining hard; so perhaps you had better go home, as you suggest Mr. Bennett. You seem fatigued. But the rest of you will stay with me for the night, I trust. I have good beds; here is wine and fire; and we can have a quiet rubber. No stakes, of course." He twisted his mouth and cocked an eyebrow at Beck.

"I'm gone!" announced Beck. He brushed by without a glance at the others, jerked his hat and slicker from the rack, and flung out into the night.

"Now who would suspect the urbane and lovable Beck of being so sensitive?" asked Baca, rocking on his feet. "We shall not have our whist game after all. You two will stay, however? Yes? That's good!" said the host. "Have a glass of wine before you go, Bennett. No? Let me help you on with your raincoat, then. You have your rubbers?" He held the door open. "Good night!"

CHAPTER VIII

BECK DID NOT TAKE his way to his own rooms despite the lateness of the hour. He followed the street at his left, the one that led to Bennett's home. A little later the door opened and Bennett took the same path at a slower gait.

A head projected itself cautiously above the adobe wall that fenced the Baca garden, looked forth swiftly, and vanished. After a few seconds the head appeared again, farther away, where a lilac overhung the wall. Screened by this background the head, with the body appertaining thereunto, heaved, scrambling over the wall, and followed, with infinite caution, the way of the two transgressors, keeping at a discreet distance behind the slower one.

It was quite dark, though a few pale stars glimmered through rushing clouds; the rain was a mere drizzle. Head and appurtenant body — the latter slickered and bulky — paused to listen. They heard plainly the plup of Bennett's feet before them, and sat resolutely down on the sloppy stone walk. There was a swift unlacing of shoes, a knotting of laces. Slinging the shoes about the neck between them, they took up the pursuit, swift and noiseless, slinking in the deeper shadows, darting across the open spaces, and ever creeping closer and closer — a blacker darkness against the dark.

When Bennett had passed through Baca's door, framed for an instant, black against a blowing square of light, Beck had been watching from far down the street. Assured that Bennett was coming, he then walked on swiftly for two or three blocks. Where a long row of cottonwoods made dark the way, he waited in the shadows. He heard the slow steps of his approaching victim, noted their feebleness, and waited impatiently until Bennett passed his tree.

The gambler pounced on him; he crushed his puffy hand over Bennett's mouth.

"It's me, Beck! If you make a sound, damn you, I'll kill you! Feel that gun at the back of your neck?" He took his hand away. "What's the matter with you? You old fool, can't you stand up? I won't hurt you — unless you try to talk. If you say just one word to me I'm going to kill you. I mean it!" His speech was low and guarded. "I've heard enough talk tonight to do me quite some time. That Scanlon and Baca — I'll show them how to ride me!"

He peered up and down the deserted street.

"Walk on, now! Here; take my arm, you poor old fool! Let's go down and inspect your bank!"

Bennett gave a heart-rending groan; his knees sagged, and he clung limply to his captor's arm.

"If it will make you feel any better," said Beck with a little note of comfort in his voice, "I'm going to rob my own safe next."

This assurance did not have the desired effect. With many exhortations, slowly, painfully, they negotiated the distance to the Bennett headquarters in the old Almandares Block.

With a strong hand on his collar and the muzzle of a forty-four pressed between his shoulder blades, the unfortunate banker unlocked the door, threaded the long, crowded aisles in the pitch dark, and came at last to his private office. At his captor's command he lighted a single gas jet near the safe; it made a wan and spectral light in the doleful place; in the corners of the great room the shadows crowded and trampled.

With his shriveled face contorted in dumb protest, with tears on his ash-pale cheeks, the wretched man groped at the combination. Strange thoughts must have passed through his mind as he knelt there, delaying desperately, hoping for the impossible.

Vainly, with a fiendish face, Beck urged and threatened; still the shaking fingers fumbled, without result. With a horrible snarl the gambler clasped Bennett's wrist, twisted it up and back to the shoulder blades, and pushed it violently forward. Stifling a shriek, the tortured wretch pitched over on his face and lay there groveling, gasping, his free hand clawing at the boards of the floor.

The gambler raised him up, releasing the pressure on the twisted arm; Bennett twirled the knobs, the tumblers clicked, the bolts snicked from their sockets; the great door swung open.

"Now the little doors and the drawers!" Beck directed. He was sweating freely. For a moment it had seemed that Bennett would defy him at the last. "Don't leave anything locked on me! Man, the sweat's just pouring from you. That looks like a lot of money, to me. There, I forgot one thing! I saw one of those little electric flashlights in your show window yesterday. I want it. Lead me to it."

After some delay in the dark the flashlight was found. By its aid the robber compelled his victim to search out and carry a neat traveling bag, certain coiled ropes, two silk handkerchiefs, and a round from a loose stool; and drove him back to the office.

Here, heedless of voiceless protest and despairing tears, he gagged the master of the counting house with the silk handkerchiefs and the chair round, and then, with scientific precision, proceeded to bind him hand and foot.

"There!" he said, after a final painstaking inspection. "That'll hold you a while! It's a pity you're a bachelor. If you had a family they might find you here tomorrow. As it is I'm afraid you'll have to wait till Monday morning. If you'll excuse me I'll turn out the gas now. Somebody might see it. I can do my packing by the searchlight."

He sized up the stacks of gold, thumbed the bills, made a rough calculation, rolled on the prisoner an eye dark with suspicion, and remarked with great fervor, that he would be damned — Oh! Oh! He packed the money neatly in the bag. Then he turned the flashlight on Bennett's livid face — a hopeless face, seared with greed and fear and all the unlovely passions.

"Bennett, you're the most contemptible liar God ever let live!" His voice rang deep with scorn. "All that talk about your bein' broke — and here's thirty-one thousand and some dollars — not counting the chicken feed, which I leave for you. Say, do you know what I think?" He held the flashlight closer to the quivering face. "I think you've reached the end of your rope. I think you're about ready for a smash-up. By jingo, that's it! You've been speculating deep or you never would have stolen Drake's deposit.

"It's my notion that you intended to take this little wad and skip for Old Mex — maybe selling them El Paso securities before we missed you. I beat you to it, old hand! You can settle with my lovely companions on Monday. I reckon they'll be pretty sore, too, after all that big talk they made — Scanlon especially. We have about twenty-six thousand in our safe and I'm taking that. Well, I gotta go. S'long!"

But he came back at once. Bennett could not see his face; but the man's voice, for the first time since the hold-up, carried a human note.

"I kind of hate it, too —you layin' here tied up this way all that time. It's going to be pretty tough. You'll have to overlook it, old man. There wasn't any other way. It was that or kill you. If it'll make you any easier in your mind you've got my dyin' oath that I'd 'a' killed you in a holy minute if you hadn't come through, or if you'd 'a' made one wrong move. Bein' tied up is a lot better than being dead." A new thought struck him. "I've got it!" he cried triumphantly. "Quick as I get to Juárez I'll wire somebody to let you go. That won't be so bad. I won't waste a minute. Buck up! I'm gone now."

Once in the open Beck trod with a jubilant step. It was darker now and raining steadily; the smell of dawn was in the air; he quickened his pace. No sign of life was on the street.

The gambler came to his place of business, took out his key ring, and entered noiselessly. He worked swiftly. A through freight went south before daylight, stopping at Saragossa for water; he would have time to make it nicely. Very quickly the money in the safe was stowed in his traveling bag. There was a little silver in stacks. Though the bag was quite heavy enough already — for much of the money had been gold pieces — Beck took the silver too.

Then a better thought came to him. He counted out nine silver dollars and put them back in the safe; he laid a blank check, face down, on the floor of the safe, with a dollar on each end like paper weights. And in the slender lance of light cast by the electric flash he penciled a brief note:

Dear Scanlon: I am leaving you nine dollars to send me a post-card.

He snapped out the flashlight, stuck it in his pocket, and tiptoed to the front door, laughing softly.

Man is the slave of habit. Outside Beck turned to lock the door — a most illogical thing to do. He placed the bag between his feet, fumbled for the keyhole and inserted the key. Then he stiffened. He felt the cold muzzle of a gun against his temple, and a gentle voice said:

"Let me carry your bag."

Frozen with horror, the gambler felt a hand remove his own gun and the flashlight.

"What's this?" demanded the voice. "Oh, I see — a searchlight! That'll be nice. Keep your hands right where they are!" The hand felt for further weapons. "All right!" said the voice. "Now open up and we'll go upstairs. You tote the baggage. Close the door gently, please. March!"

There was nothing else to do; so Beck marched.

"I may not do as good a job on you as you did with Bennett," said the voice apologetically; "but I'll fix you up some way. While you was tyin' Bennett up I raided the whole durn neighborhood for clothesline. This'll be one awful grouchy town on wash-day!"

Beck's scalp prickled with an agonizing memory of Bennett's ghastly face, as he had seen it last; the hair began to rise. He stopped on the stairs rebelliously.

"I wish you would yell once, or balk — or something," said the voice hopefully. "It'd save me a heap o' trouble — trussing you up. G'wan, now!"

The gambler g'waned.

CHAPTER IX

THE SKY was washed clean; the sound of church bells floated across the sunny meadows; the winds were still, save as a light and loitering air wandered by, poignant with a spicy tang, the sweet alloy of earth.

Listening to those peaceful bells, Mr. Drake and Mr. Jones lolled at ease in the modest hostelry favored by the latter gentleman, and looked out on a freshened and sparkling world. As the last echo died away Mr. Drake resumed the conversation:

"I gotta hand it to you, Mr. Weisenheimer. That's a great bean of yours! You've made your case. Uncle had money; it's gone; somebody's got it: x is eager to give too much for my brand; y offers an exorbitant price for my scalp; z is willing to pay you to keep quiet. How long will it take two men to dig two graves if the age of the first man is twice that of the second one? And who should have the custody of the child? Perfectly simple!"

"But you can't explain it any other way."

"Hang it! I don't want to explain it any other way. You're right — but you can't go ahead. Your wind-up is good; but can you put it over? How do you propose to go ahead about collecting? It reminds me of a little passage in Shakespeare that my chum sprung on the Frosh class in English. I remember it because Kitty, the prof, was so justly indignant:

> Deep and dangerous,
> As full of peril and adventurous spirit
> As to o'erwalk a current roaring loud
> On the unsteadfast footing of a spear;
> If he fall in — good night!

"It is widely believed," replied Neighbor, "that you cannot catch a weasel asleep; but I think it can be done, with patience. Don't be in such a hurry — be calm!"

"I want you to know I can be as calm as anybody when there's anything to be calm about," retorted Ducky with some acerbity. "It isn't so much the money — not but what I could use that to buy food with — but those fellows are not doing me right."

"There's our one best chance," said Neighbor, more seriously than was his wont. "They're doing wrong. Doing right is as easy as sticking a needle in the eye of a camel; but to do wrong takes a steady, dead lift. Every tendency and every fact pulls against it like the force of gravity at four P.M. I'm not particularly bitter against my own dear little sins, but I do believe that, in the long run, the way of the transgressor is really hard."

There came a tap at the door; Mr. Jones was wanted at the phone.

"Hello! This is Baca!" the telephone said; and could Mr. Jones step up to the house? It thought that matters might be arranged. "*Immediatamente!*" said Mr. Jones, and hung up.

"Now, Ducky," he counseled, as they walked uptown, "you notice close, and I'll show you some diplomacy. I'll make Baca commit himself so deep that it will amount to a full confession. You still don't quite believe what you think. When I am done with him you'll have no doubts. That's your great trouble, son — you don't think hard enough. You don't concentrate. You will not give to the matter in hand the full impact of your mind. You think straight enough but you haven't got the punch.

Baca lifted a sarcastic eyebrow at Ducky's presence and bent a questioning look on Neighbor Jones, but showed them into the curtained room of the previous night's conference. Refreshments were offered and declined.

"Well, Mr. Jones, if you are still of the same mind tomorrow morning at ten o'clock your mortgage will be released to you on the terms you mentioned."

Neighbor wore a shamefaced look. He twiddled with his hat.

"Maybe I didn't do just right about that, Mr. Baca. I only wanted to draw you." He looked up and smiled. "You see, we knew all the time that you fellows had Drake's money," he said chattily. "My proposition was to make you tip your hand — to convince Mr. Ducky that my reasoning was strictly O.K., if not logical."

Mr. Baca received this rather staggering communication point-blank but, aside from a heightened color, bore up under it with surprising spirit. Indeed, he seemed less disconcerted than Ducky Drake.

"Ah!" said the lawyer. "You don't lose much time in getting to the point, do you? Your candor is most commendable, and it shall be my endeavor to observe a little frankness with you. It is better so. Deceit and subterfuge are foreign to my disposition. Though not anticipating this particular turn of affairs, I have been forewarned against you, Mr. Jones, and have made my preparations accordingly. Felipe!"

One of the portières slid aside, revealing a slim brown young man with a heavy revolver, and a fat brown young man with a rifle. At the other door the curtains parted for a glimpse of an older Mexican with a benign and philosophical face and a long white beard. His armament consisted of one double-barreled shotgun. All these men wore appreciative grins, and all these weapons were accurately disposed to rake Mr. Jones amidships.

"My executive staff!" announced the lawyer urbanely.

Neighbor nodded to the staff. Fascinated Ducky did the same.

"So pleased!" he murmured.

Baca paused for a moment to enjoy his triumph. Then he waved his hand.

"That will do." The portières slid together.

"I'm not scared," explained Neighbor Jones earnestly. "That noise you hear is only my teeth chattering!"

"Oh, you punch!" Ducky drew a long breath. "If I had three wishes I'd want to be a puzzle picture — find Ducky Drake!" Then he giggled. " 'Gee! Sumpin' must 'a' happened to Ole!' " he suggested lightly.

"Did you ever hear of the old Texan's advice to his boy?" asked Baca. " 'My son, don't steal cattle; but if you do steal cattle, never give 'em up!' It is an admirable maxim and one which, in part, has been my guide."

"In part? Mr. Evers said in part: 'My dear Mister Umpire — my very dear sir — is it not possible that you erred in your decision?' " murmured Ducky with an air of reminiscent abstraction.

"Drake!" said the lawyer, "whatever else you may have to complain of at my hands, you owe me your life — once and twice."

"Am I to be both your prisoner and your judge?" asked Ducky. "What inference am I to draw?"

Baca snapped his fingers.

"My dear young friend, I do not care that for your inference! Be well guided. Leave Saragossa today and never come back. The money for your cattle will be forthcoming when you send a deed; get some lawyer or a bank to attend to the details of exchange."

"Oh! By the way, how about that mortgage of mine?" inquired Neighbor.

"Pray accept my apologies, Mr. Jones. I charged you with insolence: you are merely impudent. You grow wearisome. Your caliber is about twenty-two short, Jones!" said Baca, tapping a monitory finger with a pencil. "I am no man to get gay with. When you measured your brains against mine you flattered yourself considerably. I am not to be bluffed. I am not to be forced. Judge for yourself what chance you have of outwitting me. And, as for the courts — 'Fo' de land's sake, Br'er Fox, whatever you does — don't t'row me in de brieh bush!' "

Neighbor blinked mildly.

"Oh, well! When two men play at one game one of 'em has to

lose!" he said philosophically. "Never mind about the mortgage. I've got no family anyway; so where's the diff? You win!"

"I win!" repeated the other. "And now you will pay forfeit. Day before yesterday, Mr. Jones, you drove a young man out of town. You made him leave his suitcase — "

"Oh, pshaw! I forgot that suitcase. I must get it."

"You will not! And you took his gun. That was an arbitrary act, Mr. Jones; and now you are to receive fitting punishment for it. The northbound accommodation leaves here at eleven-forty. You will board that train, accompanied by Mr. Drake and escorted by myself. You will never come back."

"I hate to interrupt when you're going so good; but it'll be better for all hands if I declare myself now. You might propose something I shouldn't want to do," said Neighbor Jones. "I'm holding no grudge against you for outwitting me, and I'm willing you should crow a little; but don't rub it in. I'm not the kind to be evened with a tinhorn gambler. So I take that suitcase with me. I value it highly. It is a keepsake."

"Pardon me; but I really do not see where you are in any position to dictate terms."

"It is a remarkable fact," said Neighbor Jones with great composure, "that in spite of all the brag about the Southwest as a health resort, the death rate here is precisely the same as that of the crowded East Side of the city of New York — namely, one per capita. Such being the case, since I can die but once and must die that once — I should worry! — as we say in dear old Harvard. Therefore, though you may do all the dictating, I will make bold to mention the only terms that will be acceptable or accepted. I have no fancy for humble pie — my digestion ain't good."

"There is a certain force to your contention, certainly," conceded Baca, bending an attentive regard on his opponent. "You put it in a new light. Come, I must revise my former estimate of you, I see. And then?"

"Then, this!" — Neighbor checked off the counts with the thumb and fingers of his left hand — "I am perfectly willing to leave town and I never expect to come back — but I won't promise not to come back. Ducky can have his trunk packed and sent after him — leastly because he wouldn't have time to pack, and lastly because there was no question of a threat about his baggage. Me. I'll take my duds."

"Are you sure?"

"I'm sure. And I'll keep my gun. It's become a habit with me — that gun."

"We shall have to insist on the gun, I'm afraid."

"Baca," said Neighbor severely, "do you want me to nonplus you?"

"Why, no," said Baca after consideration; "I don't."

"Be a little ware, then. Don't bank too much on your militia. Any insurance company would rate you as a bad risk if they suspected you of any designs on my gun."

"Jones," said Baca, "you please me. Have it your own way. By all means march out with the honors of war, side arms and flags flying. Only you needn't march — I'll take you down in the car."

Jones rose and looked at the clock.

"Well, let's go, then. . . . One thing more: You send the money for the cattle on to Albuquerque tomorrow, and we will both pass our words that we'll never, after this day and hour, try to recover the Drake money from you or make any claim to it. Yes, we will, Ducky. Do as I say and save your cow money. You can't collect a cent from Bennett and Baca, and there's no use in trying. . . . All right — he'll promise if you will, Baca."

"It's a go!" said Baca.

"Shake, then!"

A big touring car purred at the door. At Baca's invitation Ducky drove, with Jones beside him; while the bearded philosopher sat with Baca in the tonneau. During the exchange of views in the house the excitement had kept Drake's spirits up, but he cooled down now, and showed some natural depression, realizing the extent and hopelessness of his loss. But Jones was in no way abashed.

"I see the smoke. You'll have to hurry, if you want that suitcase," said Baca as they drew up at Neighbor's hotel.

"Oh, no — got her all packed; it won't take but a minute. Come along, if you're afraid I'll give you the slip."

"I'm not," said Baca. "What good would it do you?"

"I guess that's right," grinned Jones. "I've done my worst now." He hurried in, thrust a bill into the hotelkeeper's hand and grabbed up the suitcase, now his own, which had once belonged to the Kansas City Kid. The car trundled them to the station just in time to buy tickets.

"Well, good-bye, Baca! Oh, say! Here's a V I borrowed from Beck. Wish you'd give it to him as you go back uptown, and tell him I'm much obliged. Give him my best. He sleeps up over the joint, you know."

"All right; I'll hand it to him. Hi! You're forgetting your suitcase."

"Oh, yes! Well, here she comes. So long!"

"Glad to have met you. So long!"

There were no other passengers. The little jerkwater train halted for a bare moment to let them on and then chugged stolidly on her way. They stood on the platform of the rear car; the greenwood closed in beside the right of way, so that the last Ducky saw of Saragossa was the receding triangle made by the station, the old Almandares Warehouse, and a black doll waving from a toy car. Ducky sighed.

"No hard feelings, kid?"

"Of course not," said Ducky stoutly. "You're not to blame. Besides, I don't believe we should ever have recovered that money. That crowd got it, all right — I know that anyway. I knew it before, but I didn't know that I knew it — wasn't sure; not sure enough, for instance, to sanction an attempt to take it by force."

"Yes," assented Neighbor musingly. "I thought of that. That's why I took you up to Baca's place with me. I sure wasn't expectin' an ambush, though. Pretty smart fellow, Baca!"

"Yes; and if we had tried force we might jolly well have been killed," said Drake brightening.

"Maybe it's all turned out for the best, Ducky. Well, let's go in."

"That's a heavy bag you have there," said Ducky, lifting it.

"Yes," said Neighbor carelessly. "A good share of it was gold."

"A good share — *huh?* Whadda you mean — gold?"

"Why, your uncle's estate. It's in there, under my clothes. Beck had it in a new bag, but I put it in mine when I counted it."

"*What!*"

"Don't say what — say sir! Beck, he stole it from his pals last night. They ain't found it out yet; but Tavy will be untyin' Beck about now."

"*What?*"

Ducky was on his knees, struggling with the snaps of the suit case.

"Don't spill any of it, Ducky. Yes; I gagged Beck and hogtied him up in his own poker room. Some job — believe me! I put four aces in his vest pocket."

Consider
the Lizard

CONSIDER THE LIZARD

JOHNNY BUILT THE BREAKFAST. Todd unharnessed and watered the team from twenty-gallon casks slung amidships on the deep-sea wagon — the roadrunner — of Oasis. Serving out hobbles and corn, he filled a canteen, saturating the cloth cover, and hung it to cool, unstoppered. Later, he spread a tarp under the wagon and suggins thereupon, fore and aft, for skipper and crew. They had driven twenty-five miles since moonrise: their high purpose was to make a little six-hour nooning, dinner about three P.M., and a home-stretch spurt to Oasis.

Hot biscuits, black coffee, bacon and reckless rabbit; then the shade of the wagon, coat and boots for heading. It will be pleasant to remember these things hereafter.

Seen from this point of view, the world has no limits. Between the wagon spokes it stretched away to a quivering heat-haze, where there was no more to see. In vain Todd assured himself that he had but to raise his head to see the far-off mountains. It did not help; he still felt like a very small Saint Simeon Stylites on a very large pillar drifting in empty space. Next, prompted by the blistering glare of the sun, came the reflection, new to Todd, that interstellar space must be perpetual sunlight. He said as much aloud.

"Huh? What's that?" said Johnny's drowsy voice.

Todd repeated his statement.

"Suppose it does — what you goin' to do about it, you little runt? Go to sleep!"

"Little? Come — I like that!" said Todd in tones exceedingly bitter,

the inference being he did not like that. "I'm five-feet-six, half an
inch taller than you, and I outweigh you twenty pounds."

"Fat," said the voice scornfully. "Piffly fat!"

Todd's eyes filled with tears. A lizard from nowhere appeared on
the felly. His tail curled aquiver; he cocked an impudent eye at
Todd, as who should say: "Huh! Fat little runt!" He winked; he
thrust out a swift black tongue; his throat pulsed stormily. Tears
gave way to a cherubic smile. Todd began a mental note of the
visitor's color-scheme. Presto! The lizard blinked, whisked, frisked —
and was gone. Todd vainly tried to eke out his notes by memories of
all the lizards he had ever seen. He had a vague impression of gray or
olive green, black bars. Oh, confound it!

"Johnny, what color is a lizard?"

"Idiot!"

"Yah! You can't tell! You don't know. That's the trouble with
you outdoor men. You don't use what few and elementary faculties
you have. A trained and intelligent observer like myself can tell you
more about your own country, after a week of it, than you have
found out for yourself in a lifetime. But a lizard's markings are so
strikingly beautiful, at once fantastic and orderly — man, dear man!
Haven't you any idea what an ordinary lizard looks like?"

"Sure! Beautiful fleshmarks, at once fantastic and orderly, sort of —
er — gray color and — and brown stripes, I reckon."

Todd groaned.

"Stripes? You great gipe! There's just one stripe — wavy dull-
brown stripe down his back. Then there's an elaborate double row
of tesselated designs on each side, alternating in shape and color —
first, a bright brown T, and then a red circle like a target, with a
green bull's-eye. And every other T is upside down. Stripes! Sweet
spirit hear my prayer!"

"What's a gipe?" said Johnny fearfully.

"You are. A gutteral gipe — a gruesome, gibbering, gutteral gipe!"

"Well, anyhow," said Johnny, after a crushed silence, "that's your
specialty — fauna and floradoras. Things you know nothing about,
your eyes ain't such a much. Cards, now. Ever notice what court
cards look alike?"

Todd winced at this unkind speech. He was a field naturalist of
some note and of an affectionate disposition, now field-naturally list-
ing the smaller Southwestern mammalia for the Smithsonian and
making yet other researches on the side. For the rest, in his own
habitat Todd had been triumphant and undisputed champion rummy
player: it grieved his proud spirit that New Mexicans, irrespective of
age, sex or color, languidly and gently beat him at it. The game of

Con Quien is native to the Southwest. It is easy to see how the name was corrupted to "Coon Can" in transplanting: but why it is pronounced "Rummy" is not known. It beats Cholmondeley.

"King o' diamonds has one eye, meat-ax, Vandyke, and reverse english on his curls," said Johnny Dines dreamily. "The other three are left-handed; they got swords and two eyes apiece, and they all part their beards in the middle. But the king of clubs, he had his trimmed lately on an election bet. King of hearts wears his Buffalo Bills curling to his neck on the left side and curling away from his neck on the right side; and his upper lip is shaved, and he's fixing to fetch somebody a wollop with his sticker. All the queens are packin' posies; and she of spades is twiddlin' hers, real flirty, and she's got a chair-leg for emergencies."

Todd raised to his elbow very cautiously. Johnny was stealthily fingering an old deck; his drawling persiflage was to gain time for research. Todd glared.

The able mariner continued his discourse:

"The Jack of hearts, he stole some tarts, and he's only got one eye and a battle-ax. The other three carry doodads and dingbats. Jack of spades, one eye and two entirely different suits of curls — gets 'em a-comin' and a-goin'. I'll fix yours that way this evenin' if you want. . . . Oh, well, just as you say! Spade cards all have their little coatees trimmed with spades, and the diamonds all wear diamonds; but the others — "

Todd pounced upon his perfidious companion and shook him violently.

"Cheater! Sneak! Jackass! *Je vous accuse! Canaille!* Cutthroat! Scab! Demagogue! Mugwump! No principle — no sportsmanship — not even common decency!"

He clasped his left hand to the back of Johnny's neck just below the ears; he rubbed Johnny's chin firmly with finger and thumb — this exercise is known as the "suasion." If you have bristles under your skin get some discreet friend to try it on you.

"Ouch! Help! Yelp! Leggo!"

Johnny made a furious attempt to bump his assailant's head against the reach, and so broke loose from the suasion.

"Cheat, will you?"

"Oh, what's the matter with you, you fat swab? What you howling about? Didn't you swell up like a hoptoad just now — coming the high and mighty over me, and you lookin' at a lizard all the time?"

"It's a black lie!" hissed Todd. "I'm incapable of such an action. I wasn't looking at any lizard at all. I just made that up!"

2

For sheer skillful engineering, New Mexican railroads know no rivals. Neglecting fractions, spurs and feeders, consider only the trunklines. Four of them were built from border to border without touching a town!

Ill-natured people speak of townsites and hogsties in this connection. They say — these malicious ones — that when many-millioned railroads came begging, as is the custom, for gifts of land and cash, those hardheaded and benighted Southwestern towns cordially declined, mentioning terms of barter and sale. Nor could any high-salaried press agent manufacture enthusiasm, charm he never so wisely. The New Mexican's mind was, and is sometimes to this day, a primitive affair. But, as it has never been misused as a storehouse for odds and ends of useless information, he uses this mind or thinker, such as it is, to do his thinking with; and resolutely prefers to do his thinking with his own mind rather than with any other mind soever — even a mind with all the latest new-fangled improvements.

So far from an offering of yards on a lordly dish, garnished with bonus and bonds, the railroads faced the astounding and insulting proposition that they should buy what they needed, just as you and I have to do.

Hence new townsites were hatched in an incubator, hand-raised, coddled and taught to gobble the unearned increment. New Mexico is a land of twin cities. Commonly one name serves for both towns, with a prefixed Old or New. When the old town was left too far afield there are two names — as in the case of Mesilla and Las Cruces.

Not one of these recalcitrant old cities got a station within her borders — and not one weakened. They had been wont to freight from Independence by ox team; their unit of distance was twenty-five miles, and a little jaunt to the station held no terrors for them. They were hardy old towns and they foraged for themselves a goodly share of the increment they had earned by a few centuries of hardship.

Also, in some instances, Old Town made annual visits of condolence in the matter of a few feet of Rio Grande water in New Town's first floor. In these pious pilgrimages Old Town sat on the bank, offering sympathy and advice. Results varied, but an enjoyable time was had.

Now you know why Oasis Station is one mile west of Oasis. It remains to be seen why the station agent's family firmly declined to live in the rooms above the depot — thoughtfully provided for their use and in fixing the agent's salary — but dwelt in Oasis proper: why even the section hands trudged a mile to work and back again.

After all, human nature is one of the most natural things possible.

Oasis irresistibly brings to mind — if you have that kind of mind —
Emerson's noble line of those lives which "advance the standard of
humanity some furlongs farther into chaos." Physically, that is —
pushing out garden, orchard and field, a league of brave defiance to
the besieging desert. It is a convincing desert — no semi-arid nonsense
about it. In reaction that same human nature has made Oasis a riotous
bravado of shade.

The town was founded that year in which Paris began to speak
patronizingly of the young man Bonaparte, who had shown some
military ability at Toulon. Each generation of Oasis made sorties
against the desert, with conquest of new fields: builded new streets,
and lovingly lined those streets with cottonwoods. They arch and
meet now, those old trees, home of a million mocking-birds to thrill
the dawn with unimaginable sweetness. Literally the town cannot be
seen from the outside. There are no towers and minarets and things.
The houses are adobe, one story high and a block long — recumbent
skyscrapers.

Strangers arriving by rail condemn this prodigality of shade trees
as wasting the slender resources of water and soil; but those who come
in from the desert find no fault with the arching cottonwoods.

Indeed, Oasis has all the drawbacks you mention and some you
would never guess; civically speaking, it is "link'd with one virtue and
a thousand crimes."

Yet — for that deep and cool and generous shade, and the brave
tinkling of her hundred acequias — men in the world's showplaces
think with a pang of that dim and far old town, and name her puny
river with a kindling eye, as Naaman spake of Abana and Pharpar,
rivers of Damascus.

Now you know why the night operator of Oasis curses the company from franchise to dividends, standing up or sitting down, walking or lying, sleeping or waking.

He is lonesome. His nearest neighbor is one mile away.

So much was needful. In addition it will do you no harm to know
that a near-by mountain range about the size of Palestine makes the
eastern horizon for Oasis — a range never lower than highest Leb-
anon, capped by a peak to peer Mont Blanc, overhanging Oasis; or that
the visible West, desert and mountains beyond, is pretty much the size
and shape of England. For these things are dominant, ever-present,
unescapable — they draw out the minds of men; they teach a sense of
proportion.

The westbound flyer is an aristocratic institution — excess fare; limited baggage; carrying only through passengers, through mail, through

express. Running south through New Mexico, it is not immediately apparent where the westbound flyer gets the title. That is not even the name of the train. It is only what the name of the train is called. The name of the train, officially, is The Goldplate Limited — but the train really is Number One. Towns where it does not stop mention it, with rancor, as Flossy.

Flossy is due at Oasis at eight-fifteen P.M. It stops there to drop passengers from St. Louis or beyond, to take passengers for Los Angeles or beyond, and for derailment or collision — not otherwise.

Flossy paused rather snippily this particular eight-fifteen. Miss Carroll qualified, coming all the way from Covington to visit her brother, the Indian agent at Mescalero. That gentleman is waiting with a Government ambulance. In a moment he will whisk her away and you will see them no more. Delightful people, no doubt — important to us only because for them the Limited stopped at Oasis.

Yeardsley, the express messenger, yelled to the night operator and dropped a heavy box from his door — a stout and padlocked chest not unlike those in which valuable express is carried, but smaller, new and unpainted.

"Here you are, Oasis! — P. Crandall, La Golendrina Mining Company — Rush! Here's your waybill."

"First time we ever got express off the flyer!" said the night man. "Ugh! Heap heavy!"

"Thought I might as well dump it off, so long as we stopped here — "

"All aboard!"

" — instead of takin' it on to Mecca to come back on the local."

The messenger shouted back the last words as the train moved off. Turning into his car he noticed a man and a heavy gun. The man wore a new cap, a mask made of a new handkerchief, and a voluminous new slicker, which reached the floor. The gun was cocked and pointed accurately at the messenger's left eye.

"That's right!" said the man behind the gun. He referred to Yeardsley's hands, which were stretched up in search of an imaginary trapeze. A second man appeared, arrayed precisely like the first. He carried a sack. The long oilskins made a perfect disguise, completely hiding the form. Evidently they had climbed in at the farther door during that brief chat with the operator. Number two passed swiftly through the door to the other half of the car, the baggage compartment.

"Goin' to rain, do you think?" said Yeardsley.

Number One smothered a laugh. Number Two returned escorting the baggage-wrangler. He secured Yeardsley's gun and took a long rope from the sack.

"Hands behind you!" said Number One.

The messenger's hands were bound quickly and securely.

"Now sit down," advised the spokesman.

"Say, there's no good doing this! Timelock on the safe, you know!" remonstrated the messenger as his feet were swiftly knotted to the chairlegs and a turn taken round his body.

"Yes; set for eight-thirty-seven — so you can check up contents with your relief between Mecca and El Paso. Don't worry — we'll tend to that. Goin' to back up in a minute. We'll jolly the passengers while we wait on your little old lock. A swell bunch like that ought to shell out a nice piece of money."

Meanwhile the baggageman was trussed up by Number Two's nimble fingers.

"Gag 'em?" queried that deft bandit, speaking for the first time.

"Shucks, no! What's the use? No one living along the track or in ten mile of it. Let 'em holler if they want to. It develops the lungs." He turned to the captives. "Now, old hands, we hate to do you this way. Take it easy. The boys have got your pardner in the mailcar hog-tied the same way, if that'll make you feel any better."

He pulled the bell cord and the train slowed down. Before it stopped two other robbers — capped, masked and slickered — swung in at the side door.

From the sack-of-all-trades the chief took a set of climbing-irons, a pair of pliers, and a pair of incredibly large shoes — all fire-new. Leaving these behind, he threw the sack over his shoulder. "We must leave you now — going to take up a little collection!" he explained. They filed into the vestibule.

The affair passed off pleasantly. The train stopped and instantly backed up. Passengers remarked the presence of fishermen three — Wynken, Blynken and Nod — come to fish for the herring fish that live in this beautiful sea. To be sure, there were four fishermen instead of three. What of it? The Three Guardsmen were four. A single fisherman so far inland would have been noteworthy; at four the passengers assumed the attitude of those who say *La sus!* — especially as regards the hands. Trainmen, when met, were held under herd.

Wynken held attention in the first car, Blynken in the second, while Nod and his sack-bearing chief passed into the third and last. The train was backing at full speed.

"The congregation will now stand up!" announced the spokesman — "except the ladies, who will be getting their offerings ready. Hands up, please!"

While his brother-in-arms kept the assembly amused, Nod induced the porter to carry the famous sack; and into it dropped pocketbooks, watches, rings, and such trinkets. He did not indulge in any brilliant badinage. His chief was the entertainer: Nod's was a practical, sordid mind, wholly intent on fish. They passed into the middle car, taking the conductor and the porter with them.

By this time they had backed past the station. But financial operations were transacted much faster now, for there were two willing workers instead of one. Four miles north of Oasis, negotiations were satisfactorily concluded: the train stopped on a northward slope. A procession trooped back from the engine; the engineer and fireman, followed by a fifth outlaw in the regulation uniform — cap, yellow slicker, mask and gun. At his instigation the fireman undid the couplings between the Pullman and the baggage coach ahead. A bandit opened the vestibule door and dropped off, tripping back to the engine with Number Five. The other three stepped over to the platform of the baggage car, first uncoupling the bell cord.

"Well, so long, old sports!" said the cheerful chieftain to the train crew, still under herd. "Put out a flag! We'll send the expressman and his pals back to you afoot in a few minutes — don't shoot 'em when they come."

He took the sack of valuables and tipped the porter; he pulled the bell cord and the first half of the flyer, under the new management, slid away into the night.

It stopped something like half a mile south. One robber took the pliers and climbing-irons and departed, obviously to cut the telegraph wires — stepping, all shod, as he was, into those mighty brogans. Another went to the mail car, cut loose the clerk and brought him back. The leader did the same kindly service to the baggageman and turned him over to his mate for guarding. Then he looked at the messenger's watch and laid it on the safe.

"Eight-thirty-five," he said, cutting the ropes. He picked up the watch and held it open in his hand. "At eight-thirty-seven I'll say, Go! Then you get to working the combination on that safe. If it's open at eight-thirty-eight you can hike along back to the Goldplate." He held the gun — cocked — in the other hand. "And if it isn't you won't! Go!"

The messenger twirled the knobs earnestly and opened the outer and inner doors. So at eight-thirty-eight he dropped out of the side door and the man on guard climbed in.

"Thanks! Be good to yourselves, gentlemen! Toddle along now!" said the leading man. "Got those wires cut? Hop on, then. All aboard!"

3

Mecca, the county seat, is fourteen miles south of Oasis, where the next little stream runs down from the mountains. Those miles are pure desert and no man lives between the two towns. Mecca cannot see the approach of southbound trains until they pass the cut through a low ridge, a mile north of town; just north of this ridge a thirty-mile spur leaves the main line to bring lumber from the mountains. Mecca is a railroad town — division point, machine shops and all that.

At eight-seventeen Oasis reported Number One by on time. At eight-twenty-five the train dispatcher sent orders through to a freight train at Malaga, forty miles north. At eight-thirty-five, or thereabout, the flyer's headlight should have flashed into sight; she was due at Mecca at eight-thirty-seven.

She did not come. The dispatcher called Oasis. There was no answer. For minutes he clicked out the imperative call: O S — O S — O S. He began to sweat, with visions of a wreck. He took down the receiver.

"Hello! Get me the Oasis depot — quick!"

He heard the sharp, decisive call for Oasis Central before he hung up. He called an assistant and set him to pounding the O S call. There was a bare chance that the operator was merely out of the depot. He looked at the clock and shuddered. On time fourteen miles away, the flyer was now fifteen minutes late! The telephone rang:

"Oasis says depot don't answer."

"Get me Lipton's saloon then. Tell her if any one's on the line to cut 'em off!" Sweat was rolling down his face. "Hello! Is this Lipton?"

"Lipton's not here and the barkeep don't speak English. This is Johnny Dines. Can I do anything for you?"

"Yes. This is the train dispatcher at Mecca. The flyer's not in yet. I can't get the Oasis depot. Please go down and see what's the matter with him. I'll have the wrecker out — What's that?"

"Wait a minute! . . . Hold your wrecker! Your flyer's been held up! She just left here a-goin' south, hell-for-leather, carryin' the black flag! Hold the wire! Your operator's here — run all the way up. He'll report to you as soon as he gets his breath."

The dispatcher got his own breath. Train robbery was bad, but not like a wreck. He looked at the time. It was nine o'clock.

A special was slung together with a jerk. It pranced at the heart-breaking delay while the destined passengers were found and gathered up by phone and message — the sheriff, and Ben Cafferty, the railroad's special officer; the division superintendent; the Wells Fargo agent; linemen for telegraph repairs; gangs of doctors and sectionmen for possible other repairs.

The special crept her way cautiously. On any mile of the single track they might smash into the piratical flyer, coming without lights or standing still without them — or a rail might be taken out to wreck inquiry and delay pursuit; but they did not meet her. They made Oasis about ten o'clock, finding there part of Number One's train crew, who had walked in, and the entire male population of Oasis.

Down from the north, while they questioned her trainmen, came the hysterical Pullmans of Flossy, pushed by a blasphemous freight train. Plainly, then, the black-flag half of the train had run down within a mile of Mecca and backed up on the High Line spur — perhaps had gone all the way to the lumber woods with her booty. And traffic was piling up from both ways!

The break in the telephone wire was found and mended a few poles away. A second special was ordered up the spur to capture the outlaw train; the sheriff called up men of Mecca to go with it as his representatives, and set himself to get the facts of the robbery from the victims.

The railroad straightened out its own tangles in its own way. North and south went linemen to mend the breaks, using the special and the peevish engine of the sidetracked freight. From the crowd the sheriff picked men for deputies to go with them — Bat Wilson, his ranch partner, and Petey Crandall, of the Golendrina. They reported all wires cut — through and local, railroad and commercial — at about the same distance on each side of town, and the same set of footprints at each break — the track of gigantic shoes; for the first impulse of the frontiersmen is to "read sign."

"And there's something dead wrong about this thing, Bill," declared Bat Wilson; "for we could see the marks of climbin'-irons on both them two poles — but a man to fit them shoes could 'a' bit the wires in two without ever stretchin' hisself! Them was sure the largest brogans ever made in captivity!"

Meanwhile the investigators — sheriff, superintendent and detective — had elicited two new facts, upon which passengers and crew were at one: None of the robbers had been either notably tall or very short; also, since their hands had been ungloved, it was certain that not one of them was a Mexican. Upon this latter discovery the Mexicans of

Oasis drew apart, somewhat ostentatiously, with expressions of pained and sniffy virtue.

"And now," said Sheriff Bill Hamilton to his coadjutors, "we'll go in and interview this night operator. Let's see — I want a lot of men to get out at daylight and ride sign on both sides of the track. Pete, you see to that. I'll have a bunch hike out from Mecca and Cadiz and ride the High Line. I guess the robbers went that route all right; but, so long as we're up here, we'll just take a look round. Bat, you come with me. You, too, Cornish — you come in and take notes and take notice. You're an educated man."

Then up spake Johnny Dines:

"I'll just declare myself in on this, sheriff, if you don't mind — me and my pardner. We'd like to hear Mr. Operator. We heard him once, briefly, and we'd like to hear it all."

Hamilton leveled his brows at this.

"Who do you represent, Johnny?"

Todd strutted out and patted his chest.

"We represent ourselves — and other innocent men here present, if any."

"I will ask you to notice," said Johnny grandly, "that all these Oassassins and Oassistants are under suspicion except my friend and myself, who are very short men of high character. Besides," he added sadly, "we didn't come in time — just got in tonight. That ain't all either. My pardner is a very intelligent man, he tells me."

The sheriff shrugged his shoulders, rather annoyed at the intrusion.

"Oh, very well! It isn't often there's any devilment afoot you're not mixed up in, Johnny — I suppose that you want to make the most of it."

The superintendent called in one of his young men to hold down the key, making eight in the party. They moved toward the depot door. The sheriff stopped and pointed:

"Whose rig is that? I'm going to take a look!"

It was a covered wagon, backed up to the freight platform at the farther end. Bat laughed.

"Good eye, Bill! It's yours. I brought down a couple of hind-quarters of beef to ship to Mecca — was aimin' to load up some freight, but it hadn't come; so I unhitched and went back to town. Take a good look and maybe you'll find the money!"

As they went into the office the sheriff spoke to the superintendent: "You examine him, Mr. Jones — he's your man."

Mr. Jones delayed his operations while the party were finding seats. There were only three chairs in the room. Todd and Bat Wilson sat on a chest; Johnny and the detective climbed on the ticket counter;

Bert Cornish opened the baggage room and dragged in a new flat-topped trunk. The superintendent eyed this performance askance. He privately disliked having so many present at the inquiry.

Cornish caught the glance and laughed frankly.

"It's my trunk, Mr. Jones. I just got in yesterday from a little *pasear* in Oklahoma. Have a seat with me, Mr. Sheriff?"

The superintendent began:

"Let me see — your name is Blinn, is it not — Fred Blinn? Well, Mr. Blinn, we wish to ask you some questions. How long have you worked here?"

"Two months."

"Has Number One ever stopped here before?"

"Not since I have been here."

"Mr. Blinn, did you know that Number One was to stop here to-night?"

"Certainly, sir. A message came for Mr. Carroll, at the Agency, saying his sister would arrive tonight."

"Did you tell anyone?"

Blinn flushed with obvious resentment. He was a young man, good-looking, well-dressed, with big blue eyes and reddish hair.

"I telephoned the message to Mr. Carroll, at Mescalero — if you call that telling. Anyone could have heard it who cared to rubber."

"Are you sure you spoke to no one else?"

Blinn reflected.

"Why, yes, sir — I spoke of it to Mr. Howe in a jocular way when he relieved me yesterday morning."

"And to no one else?"

"To no one else."

"Now, Mr. Blinn, you came on duty last night at six, I believe?"

"At six-thirty. Mr. Howe lights the switchlamps at night and I bring them back in the morning."

"Isn't that irregular? Are you not supposed to have the care of the lamps?"

"Perhaps. It is an arrangement between ourselves. We get the work done." The tone was sullen and defiant.

"May I ask the reason for the change?"

"You may. It is for our own convenience. Mr. Howe hangs out the lamps, and also fills and cleans them for me — work which must be done in daytime. In return, I do some of his office work for him at night."

"Let the matter rest for the present. Now, Mr. Blinn, after you came on tonight did you see any men around or in the depot?"

"No, sir — not until Mr. Carroll and his men came, about eight. Oh, yes, I did too — Mr. Wilson, over there, shipped some beef about seven or a little after."

"Could there have been any men in or about the freight cars on the sidetrack?"

"Certainly, sir. There might have been a hundred. It is no part of my duties to look for burglars under the bed."

"Easy — Blinn — easy!" said Ben Cafferty. "Keep your shirt on! You're taking the wrong tack."

"How'd you like it yourself?" rejoined Blinn hotly. "Don't you suppose if I'd seen masked men hanging about I should have mentioned it before? What's the sense of baiting me like this? It gets me rattled and it don't catch you any train robbers." He jumped up and snapped his fingers at Superintendent Jones. "Do you mean to insinuate that I've got an engine and two cars hid in my vest pocket? Because, if you do, I don't like it, job or no job — I'll tell you that right now!"

Cornish laughed.

"Mr. Sheriff, you called me in here. Am I supposed to keep my mouth shut or may I offer an observation?"

"Let's have it."

"Well, then — our redheaded friend is young and excitable; but the general bearing of his remarks strikes me as extremely judicious. Where we ought to be is up on the High Line, where the outlaws went. To hurry things up — if Mr. Jones will not be offended — I suggest that we allow Mr. Blinn to tell his story his own way, just so we'll get done quicker."

"All right!" said Jones grimly. "Young man, I am sorry if I hurt your feelings about that missing engine. Go ahead!"

"There's not much to tell. The young lady got off. The messenger threw off a box. I reported Number One to Mr. Davis, about eight-eighteen, having been delayed a little to take the check for the young lady's trunk."

"Did Carroll go to Mescalero or did he stop at the hotel?" asked Wilson.

Blinn glared at him rebelliously.

"How do I know? Suppose you find out! See here, Mr. Jones, I judge there'll be a big reward out for these outlaws. If you'll let me turn the office over to this new man you brought in I'll go look for 'em — if these gentlemen don't intend to."

"All in good time. We want to hear your story before we do anything else. Go on!"

The operator chafed at what he seemed to consider a useless harrying and delay.

"Well, I didn't hear the flyer backing up till she was right here. She didn't whistle. I ran out on the platform. She was going fast. I saw a man in the gangway keeping the engine men covered with a six-shooter. The fireman was throwing in coal and the firebox was open; so I could see plainly. The robber was masked and wrapped up in a long slicker. I ran back and tried to call up Mecca. I got no answer. I tried every wire I could use. I called for a long time — both Mr. Davis and the Mecca depot. Then I rang up Oasis on the telephone — and couldn't get them."

"What time was this?"

"I didn't notice at first. I was excited. When I gave it up and went to the telephone it was eight-thirty."

Ben Cafferty nodded.

"The dispatcher got orders for Number Twenty-Seven through to Malaga at eight-twenty-five. They must have left a man to cut the wires where they backed up. He would have had just about enough time. What next, Blinn?"

"Well, I called up Mecca again — maybe half a minute. Then I began calling to the north — Saragossa, Santa Rosa, Tucumcari. I thought we could get over the Central to the Santa Fe, and so down to El Paso and back up to Mecca. They didn't answer and I heard the train coming back again. I ran down to the north switch. I could see there wasn't any lighted cars behind; and, at first, I intended to wreck 'em. Then I weakened and let 'em go by. They were running close to a mile a minute. I thought the engineer and fireman were still aboard. If I had only known I could have put them in the ditch! Then I ran up town and gave the alarm — and that's all."

"Let's see that switchkey," said the sheriff curtly.

The baited operator almost flung the switchkey at the sheriff. "Think I'd swallowed it?" he sneered. But that taciturn officer showed the key to Cafferty, without retort, and when Cafferty nodded, he tossed it back.

"H'm! What about the express package that came in on the flyer? Did you bring it in?" asked Bat.

"You're sitting on it!" said Blinn wrathfully. "What did you think I'd do with it? Hang it on the semaphore?"

"Well, you didn't say," replied Bat weakly.

Todd moved and looked at the label attentively.

"Didn't say?" snapped Blinn. "When you brand a calf you turn it loose afterward, don't you? Shut up, you fellows! They're calling O S."

So, like the snowy-haired Lieutenant General Bangs, "they stopped to take the message down, and this is what they learned":

The missing half of the train had been found on the High Line spur, barely a quarter of a mile from the junction. The postal clerk was certain the mail had not been tampered with. The express safe was innocent of treasure — in it, piled in a neat and orderly array, five slickers, five masks, five caps; climbing-irons, pliers and a pair of enormous shoes. The whole was capped by a waybill, on which was penciled the insulting legend: Exhibit A.

"Oh, you Captain Kidd!" murmured Todd.

"They're on the way for us now — be here any minute," said Jones. "We'll go down at once. Mr. Blinn, you are exonerated from all blame or suspicion. So far as I can see you did everything any man could have done. If you wish to go along with us you may. Thompson, you will act as operator until further orders."

"You two mighty innocent people can come along if you want to," said Hamilton.

"Why, thankee, sheriff — I guess we'll go to bed," said Johnny. "Me and Todd, we been a-driving nights. We'll take a good sound sleep and tomorrow we'll wake up with our little heads all nice and clear. Then we'll stir round and find that money."

Once outside the door he took Todd firmly by the arm. "If you want to find out what color a lizard is," he said, "you've got to look close!"

4

East and west and south and north, the riders flashed in the morning sunlight, seeking for signs and finding none — save the derisive trail of a malicious giant, where the telegraph wires were cut. No fresh track of men afoot, on horseback or in wagons left the railroad along the scene of last night's adventure — except, of course, round the depot at Oasis, where the thoughtless — or thoughtful — had trampled everywhere. It was as if the wooden shoe had come down from the skies bearing homeward the fishermen three — Wynken and Blynken and Nod. And where, oh, where was all that money gone?

Wild reports were abroad concerning the amount of booty — beginning with any amount and going as far as you liked. The express company would give no figures of their loss, but they offered one thousand dollars apiece for the robbers. Rewards by railroad, county and state totaled as much more.

At Lipton's, the social center, Oasis talked it over. Entire familiarity with local conditions had been shown in this brilliant affair; it was plainly the work of local talent, and Oasis was uplifted accordingly.

Everyone knew everyone else; no one man was missing and unaccounted for — much less five, they had unsuspected ability in town. It was as Johnny Dines had said — every American in Oasis was under a cloud. They showed the effect of this cruel suspicion in their own peculiar way.

To this gathering came Johnny and Todd, fresh from a combined dinner and breakfast and smiling sleepily.

"Hello, you train-robbers!" was Johnny's greeting. "Anything new?"

"Mecca claims all the credit to herself," grumbled Lipton. "To hear them tell it, they beat their way up from there on a freight train, went back to the junction on the head end of Number One, and walked on home, packing the sack of boodle. Mecca was always a hateful town!"

"Dern likely too!" said the town doctor indignantly. "That stroke of business was planned and pulled off by men right in this room likely."

"At least one man went down on the engine — probably two," objected Johnny. "How'd they get back?"

The doctor smiled knowingly and turned the subject.

A seedy man bustled in the doorway and elbowed the bar importantly.

"You know that little bill you got chalked up against me, Tobe? I'll be round and settle it in a few days — soon as things simmer down a little."

Two shabby and mournful seven-up players sat in the corner. "That team of horses, Sim," said one in a confidential undertone, "that you was pricin' the other day and that I offered you so cheap — I don't want to sell 'em now. I've changed my mind."

"Well," said Sim in the same guarded but plainly audible tone, "I've about concluded to get me an automobile anyway."

"What I don't see," said Todd dreamily, "is where you fellows got all those new slickers!"

"Them? I had 'em shipped — " Lipton corrected himself hastily: "I mean, neither does the sheriff. He's inquiring about it in every store within a hundred miles — that and the rest of the stuff. It was all new — everything."

"Dines," said Todd loftily, "we do not want to associate with these — er — people. I think we had better saddle up and ride out in the — er — uncontaminated air."

"Quite right, me deah fella!" drawled Johnny. "A wuffianly lot they are, to be shu-ah!"

"Hold on a minute!" said Lipton. He fished two new bandannas from under the bar and shook them open. Each one had two eye-holes snipped out. "Take these. Every man in town has got one. When the sheriff and his bunch get back we're going to give 'em the Chautauqua salute!"

The innocents found an uncontaminated spot on a high knoll just out of town and lay in the shade of their horses.

"Now, Mr. Trained Observer, let's have an exhibition of that super-human sagacity of yours."

"You first, Johnny — you're better looking than I am. I've got my notebook. If you should happen to say anything sensible I'll jot it down."

"I am handsome!" admitted Johnny. "Such being the case, here goes! But I hardly know where to begin. This whole design is so beautiful — at once so fantastic and so orderly! . . . A few general reflections first. There was at least one railroad man on the job; at least one man who knew how to follow a trail, and so didn't propose to leave any — some old-timer; at least one Easterner — no one out here ever saw a cap; and at least one man who had mighty good reason to know that it isn't safe to monkey with Uncle Sam — else why was it they didn't touch a thing in the mail car? . . . Yet they hog-tied the postal clerk and put him off. Now what was that for? They didn't rob the mail. They could have left him in the car while they ran down to Mecca if that was all they did. . . . Consider the lizard! There was something they didn't want him to see — something besides cutting the wires and backing in over the High Line. Shucks, my head aches already!

"Now we'll get down to cases. We'll begin with that message for Carroll. They knew the Flossy train was to stop. Any operator along the line might have known that. But we'll just play, for the present, that our man Blinn stood in on the deal."

"Let X equal Fred Blinn — for the present," agreed Todd. "There was certainly someone on the job who knew exactly where the trains were, or they wouldn't have dared to back round so recklessly. We'll nominate Blinn for the goat. Anyway, he overplayed his part the first thing, in my opinion. Too fiery, he was — hotheaded, injured innocence, and all that. And for an excitable man he showed wonderful presence of mind in the emergency — thinking right offhand of wiring round by the Sante Fe, and throwing the train in the ditch!"

"If he's innocent — and he may be — he did it just as he tells it," said Dines. "If he is one of the bunch he told it to account for the elapsed time. It was nine o'clock when he came to Lipton's. That's

thirty minutes and more by his own account, since he saw 'em back
by. That was while the gang was doing something — making a getaway and hiding the stuff right here in Oasis, I guess. Ten to one they
stopped here. That the engine went down to the junction almost
proves that they went to Mecca. Therefore, as they're such a cunning bunch, they didn't. Yet at least one went to drive the engine.
Tut! Tut!" He scratched his head. "And the kings are all left-handed!
Now if they had all wanted to stay here they might have started the
engine up, and jumped off. But they didn't. They turned the switch
and backed up on the spur. They knew how to run an engine. But they
took a big chance of a smashup if Mecca had got nervous and started
a rescue train as soon as the flier didn't show up. There must have
been someone mighty anxious to get to Mecca — and, if our guess
about Blinn is correct, they had some reason for wanting to get there
by nine o'clock. Now who was it that had to be in Mecca by nine
o'clock, and why?"

"I can think of two persons, who — if they were in it — would have
a mighty good reason for wanting to be there by nine o'clock," said
Todd.

"Blest if I do!" said Johnny. "But that's the proper number — two
— engineer and fireman. Who was it? I don't keep up with you."

"You wouldn't. I'll tell you after a while. One thing at a time. The
train dispatcher says he used the wire at eight-twenty-five. Blinn says
it wouldn't work at some time before eight-thirty. The Limited
people said that when the train stopped the first time it backed up immediately; so if the wire was cut before eight-thirty, there must have
been still another man — and another pair of big shoes to make those
tracks. Do you think that likely?"

"No, I don't. That would mean one more man to split the money
with — and no need of it if Blinn was standing in with them as we
think. He could just play that he called up Mecca when the flier
backed by — he didn't actually have to call. They could cut the wires
south of town as they went down the last time."

"But we don't know that Blinn is guilty and we mustn't build entirely upon that. He may possibly be all right after all."

"Whoosh! Hooray! We've got him — by George! we've got him
dead to rights!" Johnny sat up, his big, black eyes snapping. "I
thought all the time that nobody could get up a lie that wouldn't
show through to field naturalists used to counting the spots on lizards.
Blinn said that he tried to call up Saragossa and the other towns to
the north at eight-thirty — remember? And we know positively, by
the evidence of the expressman and baggageman and the postal clerk,

that the north wire was being cut at eight-thirty-seven! Blinn lied seven whole minutes!"

Todd made a correction in his notes.

"X is Fred Blinn," he said. "What next?"

"You're next. Do you want me to do all the heavy work? Get to grindin' and find those other men! Who was it you knew about, so wild and fierce, that had good reason to be in Mecca by nine o'clock?"

"There are just two men alive who—provided they were in this thing and knew when Blinn was set to give an alarm—knew positively that they would be looked for in Mecca immediately afterward; and they were the very people to know best how inadvisable it is to trifle with the United States Mail. They were the sheriff and the railroad's special officer! And it is a ten-to-one shot that one of them—Cafferty—can drive an engine. But where's the money? And who were the other men?"

"The other men—why, they are the sheriff's posse! I am a man singularly free from vanity," said Johnny, "but I thought at the time 'twas a strange thing that Bill Hamilton should pick that bunch and leave me out—just as I thought it queer that he didn't notice what a break Blinn had made in not getting some capable person—like me—to size up the tracks before he gave the alarm and sent the whole blame town down there. You and me, we went down right off; but the sign was all mummuxed up before we got there—where they cut the telephone wire and where they hot-footed back to town."

"Maybe they didn't come back to town," suggested Todd. "Maybe they just stayed down there and oozed in with the crowd!"

"No, they didn't—they came uptown to set a good example marking out tracks. Bat Wilson and Petey Crandall are old-timers—they know what a telltale a footprint is if it's not queered. Whoever cut the telephone wire wouldn't wear those enormous shoes—'twould have been a giveaway on Blinn. And they had to come up to town to hide the money too. No! By Heck! I see it all now—perfectly clear from start to finish! Bat smuggled them down in his wagon to begin with—so they couldn't be seen by any accident and wouldn't leave any tracks. The slickers—"

Todd broke in:

"I see! The new slickers, new masks, new caps, new climbers, new pliers, new number fourteen shoes—Bert Cornish brought them the day before in his new trunk—after Blinn had wired him when Miss Carroll was coming. On the same train he had the chest sent—that new chest—by express, on the off chance that the messenger would drop it off when the train stopped here. Why, it works out like the

tabby end of a solitaire game! And the money — Of course! Come
along! It's all over but the shouting!"

"Shooting, maybe!" suggested Johnny grimly. "But I guess we can
surprise 'em. We will now send for Mr. Superintendent Jones. He's
all right. See how he rambled round with his questions! But them
others — they had the whole play rehearsed so fine they didn't waste a
word. There's that switchkey! If the sheriff hadn't borrowed it to
get in on the High Line with he would never have thought of asking
if Blinn had it. Too smart! Come along!"

They shunned the town and rode to the solitude of the depot, where
they had held deep converse with Agent Howe. An hour later, in
answer to their imperative summons, Superintendent Jones alighted
from a northbound freight, accompanied by a Man Some Higher Up
in express circles, who had hurried from El Paso to investigate.

"You claim you have a clue?" said Mr. Jones anxiously as they
came to the office.

"Why, you might call it a clue — certainly," said Todd. "We've
got the money anyhow!"

"What!"

"Yes — and we know the robbers; but we haven't got 'em yet.
They're out of town. Here's a list of their names — but don't open it
till we make good."

"Why, how on earth — "

"Exercise of pure reason," said Johnny. "We're very intelligent,
Todd and me, for all we're so handsome. At that, I don't mind admitting that we lost a little sleep on it. The money — well, we took a
little liberty, which we trust you'll excuse." He raised a saddle blanket,
which was spread over a chest — the chest! He kicked the lid open,
exposing currency in bundles; coin in stacks, sacks and packages; bill-
books, watches and jewelry.

"We knew it was either in this box or in a certain trunk we knew
of — but we felt a certain impatience to see it; so we didn't wait.
One of us tolled Mr. Howe away and the other just naturally unlocked it with an ax. It was very rude — but we had to do it. We
were getting palpitation of the heart."

"We busted the trunk too," said Todd. "No money in it or anything else that was in any way suspicious. Just a gentleman's wardrobe
and not much of that. That doesn't make any odds — we had a clear
case anyhow; but I'm sorry about breaking 'em open too," he added
wistfully. "I wanted to send for a bunch of keys, take out the money,
fill it up with junk, and let 'em take it home to divide. That would
have been jolly!"

"Well — this is the most extraordinary circumstance!" gasped the expressman. "Will you explain how it happens that you made these discoveries rather than the officers?"

"Johnny will," said Todd. "I furnish the brains for this establishment, but Johnny is the orator. Look at your list."

The superintendent unfolded the paper. This is what he saw:

CAFFERTY, Railroad Detective
HAMILTON, Sheriff
CRANDALL ⎫
WILSON ⎪
CORNISH ⎬ The Posse
BLINN ⎭

"You see," said Johnny, "it might have been some time before that bunch found the culprits."

"I can't believe it possible!" said Jones.

"I'll tell you what then — you believe half of it and maybe this gentleman can believe the other half."

"For Heaven's sake, man, tell us what happened here and how you found it out!"

Johnny shook his head sagely.

"I'll buy," said Jones. "Tell us what happened."

5

"To my notion," said Johnny, "Cornish must have planned the whole thing. If it was any other way he couldn't have been in it at all. He had to put something into the partnership — so he furnishes brains. Hamilton and Bat and Petey Crandall are old residenters — Bat is Hamilton's accomplice in the cow business. They've got plenty of brains, but they're the right-now kind of brains — not the day-after-tomorrow kind.

"Cornish's first idea was that if the sheriff and Detective Cafferty were in the play they might not arrest themselves. Or was that it? Was it the train-robbin' scheme that sent him corruptin' the officers, or knowing the officers that made him think of train-robbin'? Anyhow he got 'em. And Blinn — they had to have Blinn to make things come out even.

"They ciphered out every point. They knew the Flossy train dropped the diner at Saragossa after supper, to be picked up on the return trip. That left three coaches. They wanted to make out with just as few to divvy up with as they could have and be safe — so they

wouldn't be obliged to shoot anybody. You want to give 'em credit
for that. That made five men — one for the engine, one for manager
of each coach, and one to pass the plate. There's where the sheriff
takes in Bat and Petey, knowin' them to be reliable.

"I judge by this time the sheriff was kind of taking the lead. Anyhow him and Cafferty had seen too much of Uncle Sam's work from
the inside — they wouldn't hear to takin' a thing from the mail car.

"Everybody knew that Miss Carroll was coming pretty soon. So
Cornish he goes back to Oklahoma. Nobody notices that — he's always taking little trips. He buys all that new stuff and packs it in his
trunk.

"Then he rigs up this chest and sends it, or maybe leaves it — we
don't know where-all he's been — with some good responsible person
in Kansas City, to be sent by express on this particular train when
notified by telegraph. Anyway, the box came from Kansas City, as
per label. Cornish is mighty particular not to send it himself. He's
got a long head. You want to go easy on these lads, Mr. Jones — they
took a heap of pains to manage not to kill the express messenger. That
was the idea of sending that chest — so they could hop on quietly
while the messenger was dropping the chest out the door. Another
thing — all they set out to do was to keep clear themselves; they didn't
try to hang it on somebody else. That was decent of 'em. Mention
that to the court, will you? No; you needn't. I'll do it myself."

"I'll not forget it either," said Jones.

"All set then! Miss Carroll tells her brother when she'll be here —
night message of course; Blinn wires Cornish; Cornish wires his friend
to send the box, and then comes back from Oklahoma, a day ahead
of Miss Carroll, leaving his trunk in the depot.

"Last night, soon as Mr. Howe's gone, Bat Wilson brings the bunch
down here, all cozy and out of sight in his covered wagon. No
knowin' where he picked them up — different places, I reckon. Bat,
he takes his team to the pastures and slips back. The beef and the
freight was just a blind."

"The freight came today," said Howe.

"Yes," said Johnny admiringly. "They didn't miss many bets.
Just one thing they overlooked — there never was yet a man so good
but there was another one just a little better — except Ty Cobb.

"Well, they opened up little Bertie's trunk — in here — put on their
masquerade duds, and got over beyond the freight cars on the far
track before Lieutenant Carroll drove down with his little old ambulance.

"You know the rest — up to the time they coaxed the messenger to open the safe. While they were gone, Blinn opened up this box and dumped out what was in it — coal in little sacks packed tight — into the coalbin. They packed the swag in it, and they put back the sacks and enough coal to make it weigh about what it did before. There wasn't really any need of this. They could have put it in Cornish's trunk. I reckon that was Cornish's scheme, on the long chance that if anything went wrong Petey would be implicated and he wouldn't if nobody turned state's evidence. And I don't believe any of them fellows would do that — unless 'twas Cornish or Blinn.

"Yes, that was Bert Cornish. Just consider this: Blinn and Pete Crandall and Bat, they was all clamped down to this depot last night if things went wrong — Bat's wagon, the box for Pete's and Blinn's job. Hamilton and Ben Cafferty, they took their chance sloping with the train and maybe being seen when they walked the track from where they left it. They had to get home — for, of course, they was going to be called on right off to hunt down the perpetrators of this high-handed outrage. They had just nicely time to answer 'Present' to the roll call. But Bertie — He's certainly some slick crook! — he ain't takin' no chances. There ain't a thing on him right now but a moral certainty — that and him bein' on the sheriff's posse."

"That's the way it looks to me," said the expressman dryly, "unless the others implicate him — as, of course, they will."

"Do you think so?" said Todd anxiously. "Maybe we'd better slip a little loot in his trunk to save trouble?" This ingenious project was negatived.

"Well, but you've overlooked one thing!" said the expressman. "Didn't they have inside information as to what money was carried by express? It looks like it."

"Not at all," said Johnny. "Such information, to be of any value, would have to coincide with the date of Miss Carroll's arrival, which is entirely improbable. No, sir; they were sure of a pretty good thing from the passengers alone, and they just took a gambler's chance on the express. If they made a big haul from you, which I don't know — "

"He can only count up to nineteen!" explained Todd.

" — it just happened that way. That's all, I guess — only that they're all on the posse because they dassent trust each other! They aim to stick together till things quiet down, and then, in a day or two, take the box out to the mine and declare a dividend. You'd better put this stuff in the safe and watch the safe, I reckon. Don't you want to hire a good honest man to watch you?"

"You always want me to do all the work!" said Todd bitterly.

"But how are you going to capture your sheriff and his posse?" said Jones. "Won't it be dangerous?"

"Oh, them? Shucks! I don't know yet. I'll rig up some sort of deadfall, so we won't have to kill 'em. One good turn deserves another — and they sure was mighty thoughtful about the express messenger! Well, I guess we'll shack along uptown now. Hey! You silly ass! Where you going?"

The last words were addressed to Todd, who had walked out the front door, crossed the track, and was now heading out for the desert. Todd stopped and partly turned round.

"Me? I'm going to catch me a lizard. I want to see what they look like!"

6

Above the hitching rack flaunted a gay signboard, riotous in color, enormous in lettering:

LUIZ TRUJILLO: TIENDA BARATA

The sonorous syllables merely bespeak a cheap store — in the Spanish idiom, Store Cheap — preceded by the owner's name. Suspended from this eye-filling announcement was a smaller board of modest black and white, lettered with the pungent pleasantry:

Why Go Elsewhere to Be Cheated?

Luiz Trujillo knew his Oasis. This was effective psychology — color, magnificence, mass and processional pomp for the gay and volatile Latin — two sides of many-sided truth, in one ironic glimpse, for the sober Saxon. An unfortunate phrase, this last: please substitute "the graver Saxon."

Columbus stood the egg on end and John Milton invented Satan. Other people have done these things better since, but the credit remains with the first discoverers. So with Mr. Trujillo's literary venture, which stirred up emulation.

Mr. Lipton's establishment was a quadrangle. The hotel was on one side of the big gateway, the saloon on the other; the inclosed square was a feed corral, with stables in the rear; and over the gateway was a high arch, bearing the ambiguous legend:

ENTERTAINMENT WITHIN FOR
MAN AND BEAST

Johnny Dines sat at his balanced ease on the beam of the hitching rack. He was in his shirt sleeves; his hat was on the back of his head;

his heels clicked idly together; he twisted the ends of his drooping mustache; by and large, he presented the picture of a man without a care — presumably with a vacant mind; and he trolled a stave of astonishing import:

> Oh, the spring — the spring I sing!
> There's nothing like fried onions!
> Because the skies are almost overhead,
> Let us lean up against the seashore!

The sheriff and his party turned the corner from Cadiz Road — six dusty but jaunty horsemen. As they rode slowly down the long street, their coming suddenly became a triumphal progress. The windows blossomed with laughing girls; serious-eyed men strolled from every house. It was a beautiful, clear day; but all those serious-eyed men wore slickers or carried them rolled in a neat bundle; and every man, as the sheriff passed, fluttered a red and ostentatiously slitted kerchief.

"Got 'em in jail, Bill?"

"Never touched us!"

"Bet they bought you off!"

"Find any clues?" demanded one, wearing climbers slung conspicuously from his neck.

"Say, sheriff, what'll you give me to turn state's evidence?"

"Sheriff, these pesky fellers ain't using you right," said Lipton soothingly. "They oughta be ashamed! You come in and wash up. You must be all tired out. Supper'll be ready in a jiffy. Must be five o'clock or after."

He pulled out a watch, looked at it, shook it, held it to his ear. Then, from various pockets on his round and goodly person, he produced, one after another, five more watches, all of which he gravely consulted. In this process he dropped a pair of pliers from a side pocket and forthwith set a foot upon them, shod in the mightiest shoe Oasis could furnish. The posse grinned sheepishly.

No — they were not heartless, these people; the king's horses and the king's men could not have drawn them to this cruelly mistimed mockery had they known what waited.

The seven picked men who knew bore no hand in the foolery. There had been no discussion of this point; it was part of the fitness of things that they should not. Johnny Dines felt a twinge of pity — almost wished that the luckless wretches might sense their danger and turn and flee; but he had a better thought as well — of trainmen and messengers slaughtered without mercy — and he hardened his heart.

The sheriff paused before Trujillo's and fixed Johnny with a quizzical eye.

"Caught your men yet, Dines?"

"Not yet."

Todd came from the hotel, carrying a camera.

"Wait half a sec, sheriff, before you go in! I'm going to write this
thing up for the El Paso papers, and I'd like to get a photograph of
your crowd, guns and all, just as you came in from the manhunt.
Won't take but a minute! Oh, never mind the dust — it won't show.
We can't get a good picture in the shade. Just ride over in that sunny
place by Rosalio's, where we can have the adobe wall and the old
house for a background."

The posse complied, nothing loth. Todd planted his tripod and
proceeded to arrange his group.

"I want to take two exposures — in case one plate isn't good. Not
too close together now — don't let the horses crowd! And don't try
to line up — you're not soldiers! Sit naturally in the saddles. Blinn,
you're too stiff. Cornish, your hat's down over your eyes — push it
back a little! Hi! You other fellows — stand back! You're crowding
in the picture. I'll take some of you, all in good time, when you get
what's coming to you."

A crowd had followed, after the manner of humans. They stood
back obediently; Johnny Dines and five others, all in shirtsleeves, even
jumped over into the garden and ducked behind the crumbling wall
to make sure they were out of the way.

Todd dived under the camera cloth. He popped up his head again.

"That's pretty fair! When we're ready keep perfectly still till you
hear the machine click the second time. But don't look at the camera.
Hold your heads up like you would if you were out on the plains
looking at something a long way off. There! That's good! Hold
that!"

He made another dive and the camera clicked once — twice. Todd
came up smiling.

"Now one more — a profile this time. Just turn your heads a little
toward the garden wall."

The posse obeyed — and were annoyed to observe six shotguns
rested on the garden wall — each man looking down the barrels of an
individual shotgun to a steady eye beyond.

"Look pleasant, please!" said Johnny Dines.

The Perfect Day

=|||=

THE PERFECT DAY

MR. TUBS WHEELER sat on the shady porch before his store. He was short, sleek and substantial, shirt-sleeved because of the heat; he was in his own particular swivel chair, his feet were upon the porch rail, and he looked out tolerantly upon a world rather excessively be-sunned.

It was a large world, for the store perched on a wide ridge sep-arating and overlooking two great valleys. From the west, a mile of brown river made a dead set at this ridge, and met it head on, just facing the store. The ridge was too strong — as yet; thwarted and foaming the Rio Grande turned southward, at right angles, and pres-ently swerved yet further to the southwest, leaving behind it a per-pendicular bank thirty feet high and half a mile long. Hence the name, Box Toe Ridge.

To the north the American Bend — sometimes ironically called Happy Valley — spread out a green half-circle against a background of frowning hill and sandy slope that led to the desert; to the south, Mr. Wheeler's left hand as he sat, the Doña Ana Valley, wide and green between jutting broken mesas of black lava, stretched away be-yond the line of vision, dotted with orchard and hearth-smoke. It was a famed and fertile spot, cultivated for more than two centuries; the American Bend was a new enterprise, anticipating the big dam now being built by the Reclamation Service.

The fencing table lands were high, but beyond them saw-toothed peaks of far-off ranges notched the sky wherever the eye turned. Indeed there was a very desirable range in Mr. Wheeler's back yard;

a dozen miles square of warm-hued granite, knob and sharp cone and slender spire: The Doña Ana Hills. In many lands mountains so neat and ornamental would have been famous. In New Mexico they lost out, like the brave men before Agamemnon, lacking a press-agent.

It was some eighty yards from Mr. Wheeler's feet to the precipice at the end of Box Toe, and in those scanty yards a single-track railroad, the wagonroad and the big Doña Ana Mother-Ditch crowded, jostling, following the river's curve. Railroad, highway, ditch, river, was the sequence; the railroad barely missed Wheeler's home. The highway ran in a deep and narrow depression between track and high-banked ditch until it came to the store; there it crossed the track for more room. Directly opposite this crossing, Wheeler's private road bridged the ditch and turned north to the low-lying fields of his farm. A little further up the rails was a stubby side track, a covered platform and a crane for catching mail-sacks from passing trains. Wheeler was postmaster, and the flag-station was named for him. It looked just like a town, on the map.

Far down the narrow highroad a shod hoof rang on a stone. A string of horses swung jauntily into sight, each with a rawhide hobble around his neck. A shuffling pack horse brought up the rear. A tall horseman lolled easily in the saddle, one comfortable leg curled round the horn. Wheeler knew the horses.

"Humph! That fool, Spud Wallis!" he sniffed.

The fool, Spud Wallis, drew rein before the store. He was a tall, raw-boned, broad-shouldered man with a berry-brown face. He cocked a twinkling blue eye at Mr. Wheeler's feet in respectful silence. The loose horses promptly took to the hillside for browsing.

The feet withdrew with a bounce and Mr. Wheeler's face appeared.

"Oh-h!" said Spud. "Excuse me; didn't see you. Know where the Tumble-T wagon is? They was workin' the Pigeon Tank country last I heard, but maybe they've drifted north."

"Left this morning for Point o' Rocks," said Mr. Wheeler shortly.

Mr. Wallis rolled his eye at the sun. "I can terrapin along up there this evenin'." There was no answer. "After dinner," added Mr. Wallis, pointedly.

Mr. Tubs Wheeler leveled an accusing hand at the prospective guest. "Now, young man, you just natchelly mosey right along out of this!"

"Why, Mis-ter Wheeler!" said the young man in shocked reproach. "I am suhprized! An old-timer like you, and grudge a body a meal's victuals."

"Meal's victuals be blowed!" said Wheeler wrathfully. "It ain't the grub — you know it, confound you. I ain't going to have you making up to my girl."

"Oh-h! I see-ee! Gertie?" said Spud. His elbow was on the saddle horn; his chin went to his palm for a little meditation. Then he looked up, frank-eyed. "Say, that's a good idea. I might do a heap worse." He sparkled with enthusiasm. "I'll go see her right away now!"

"Ride, plague on you, ride! If you ever come fooling around here again — "

"But I'm not fooling. I'm right serious."

"I'll — I'll shoot you, and set the dog on you, and throw you in the 'cequia, and sue you for trespass!"

"Why, don't you reckon Gertie's going to get married sometime, same as other girls?" demanded Spud, hotly. "Think she never wants to see anybody but a cantankerous old frawg, like you?"

"You worthless, shiftless, poker-playin', cow-stealin', scape-gallows — "

"See here, old man — don't you ever talk about me to Miss Gertie like that — don't you dare to! Girls is awful queer. Like as not she'd up and set her heart on me, just to contrary you."

Mr. Tubs Wheeler towered tiptoe; he went glassy-eyed. He thumped his open palm with a pudgy fist and simultaneously came to his heels with a crash. Then he fought for self-control.

"Don't you worry — she won't never marry a measly thirty-dollar-a-month cowpuncher. She can take her pick of better than you. Look here, Spud — I ain't got anything against you, as a man, but I got to look out for my daughter. You see that. A fellow that wants a wife has got a right to get some stuff together first."

"Well," drawled Spud reflectively, "I never did put much energy in this money proposition. I been giving all my time to being alive — hard. But what's the matter with my little bunch of cows?"

"That's just it. You don't know nawthin' but cows — and cows is nix, *nada*. That day's over. The wise ones got from under like I did. Summerford, Joe Haskell, Herron — they got farms for themselves ready for the big ditch. Look at Joe Haskell, now. He done better runnin' cattle than ever you did. Right on the job every minute — not hellin' around like you. But he took a long look ahead. Now he's got as fine a piece of land as there is in the bend. And when there's no work for him on the farm, he goes teamin' on the dam. Never misses a chance to turn a dollar. There's a forehanded man."

"Yes, Joe stacks up pretty fair — but you want to remember that Joe's single yet," said Spud earnestly. "The married men always make the worst husbands."

"Married men — what's that?" said Wheeler, wrinkling his forehead to a puzzled frown. "Married men — Oh, the devil!"

"That's what I've always heard. Anyhow, Joe Haskell don't figure in this case. He likes someone else better than he does Gertie."

"Who?" demanded Mr. Tubs Wheeler, sharply.

"Why, just himself. So we'll leave him out of the question."

"We? *We!* Say, what do you think this is — a family council?"

Unheeding, Spud pushed back the index finger of his left hand to dispose of Joe Haskell, and took up the case of the middle finger. "And Herron?" he said consideringly. "H'm-m! Well, I don't want to knock, but really — " He thrust out a dubious under lip; he shrugged his shoulders.

"Well, what about Herron? And what about you, yourself? Don't you ever take a drink?"

Spud slid from the saddle. "I don't care if I do," he said.

"You banshee!" cried Wheeler. He made a conscientious effort at a scowl which ended in the disaster of a broad grin. "Come along with you."

When they returned to the porch, Spud Wallis sank into a chair and tugged diffidently at his mustache. "Say, Mr. Wheeler — you was speaking about foresight and so on — how about you taking forty acres of your claim up on this ridge? What was the idea? You can't farm here."

Wheeler permitted himself a superior smile. "That, my son, illustrates just what I was pointing out." Here he interrupted himself, pivoting his chair with a squeaking of springs. "Hi! There's another automobile. Third one this month."

Wallis looked. A hooded touring car stood in the deep road between track and ditch. Two men were on their hands and knees, peering under. A sound of clinking steel came through the heated air.

"Broke down, as usual. I shouldn't think that they'd come any higher up than Doña Ana with the hills and thorns and sand and all."

"A wagon will be coming along presently and want to get by," said Wheeler. "No knowin' how long they've been there, whilst we was confabing in the store. There — they're cranking her up now."

"I suppose when that good road gets through to the dam, the cars'll be thicker'n flies," said the young man disconsolately.

Wheeler chuckled. "And that brings us back to my forty acres of hill. Do you think they'll build that good road down there, where there's no room, and only a matter of years till the river gnaws the bank away? No, sir-ee! The Doña Ana Ditch'll go through the hill back of my house, and the good road will go over my hill — that's what. And they'll pay little old Tubs Wheeler a good big price for a right of way. Maybe the railroad'll have to move, too, sometime. And when Mr. Big Old He-Ditch comes here, Mr. Ditch'll take one good look, and make a big cut — or a tunnel, maybe — through my old ridge — and there's another right of way. Four — count 'em — four! You keep your eye on Tubby."

Spud gazed respectfully at the older man. "By Jo-ve, Mr. Wheeler, yuh suhtenly are a wondah!" he drawled. "And you want Gertie to have a man that'll cipher out plays like that? Well, suh, I don't blame you. What's the matter with that car? Stuck again?"

"Lost something, I guess — see 'em goin' back down the road all stooped over. Hey, they're calling to us. Must be something valuable. Let's go see."

Wallis made no answer. His hands were clasped at the back of his head and his eyes dreamily considered the country beyond the river.

"Come out of it!" said Wheeler, cheerfully, much mollified by the visitor's recent tribute to his discernment. "What's the matter with yuh?"

Spud returned to himself with a start. "Just a-studying," he said. "See how the river makes a big ox-bow loop opposite here? Looks like, instead of going to all that expense, the roads and ditches would throw in together and build a wing-dam, slant-wise, where the river heads this way and turn it right across the neck of land — maybe digging out some for a starter — and leave this place all safe and hunky, a mile out of danger and lots of room. It ought to be cheaper. Only one patch of land to buy, and that don't seem to be worth much — all grown up to tornillo and cottonwood saplings."

Wheeler's jaw fell. "Cracky, they could do that! Well!" he exclaimed. "That ground, now — it belongs to old Panlo Montoya's boy. Used to be a farm there twenty year ago. I'll just go over there and buy it tomorrow — then I'll be fixed, either way. Well, I'm sure obliged to you, Spud. I never thought of that," he admitted slowly. Privately Mr. Wheeler's opinion of Spud's business sense was poorer than ever.

"Oh, that's all right," said Spud generously. "Let's go see what's lost."

The strangers met them at the car. One was a middle-aged man of slight build and severe but prosperous appearance, with a panama hat, gold-rimmed eye-glasses, and close-clipped and grizzled mustache. He wore a duster and long black driving-gauntlets. The other was a much younger man. His stalwart six feet were arrayed in white flannel, his shirt sleeves were rolled up, his collar turned in. His face was smooth shaven; he had wide, honest brown eyes under heavy

brows; his mouth was small, red and well shaped. Curly chestnut hair
showed under his careless cap; his hands were soft, white, plump and
perfectly cared for.

"I beg your pardon, gentlemen," he said. "I have lost a very valuable diamond ring. Could we get you to help us look for it?"

"We will pay you well for your time," prompted the older man.

"Of course — certainly," said the young fellow, smiling pleasantly
and showing strong white teeth.

"Whether we find it or not," added the other.

"Oh, but I say, old chap, we must find it. I can't afford to lose that
ring, really."

"You stand to lose enough to buy you a box full of pretty rings
if we don't get to Grindstone tonight," said the little man.

"Sure we'll help you," said Wheeler. "Do you know where you
had it last?"

"Oh, yes," said the youth, leading the way. "It is somewhere between here and where we worked on the car. When we were
poking about at the works I took it off and laid it on the running-
board — on this side. The setting was loose and I was afraid I'd lose
the stone. Then I forgot about it. Deuced careless of me. See, here's
where we stopped. It's somewhere between here and the car. Oh,
we're sure to find it."

"I hope so, Robert," said his companion. "For we can't stay here
long. I'd rather buy you another ring."

"It isn't so much the value of it, Mr. Dwyer — though it cost a
pretty penny, I believe," said Robert. "But — it was poor old dad's."

"Oh!" said Dwyer, less brusquely. "In that case, we'll stay till the
last possible moment." Sifting the sand through his gloved fingers, he
looked up at Wheeler. "You see, we have to meet a party at Grindstone to sign up an important mining proposition. He comes on the
five-forty train and we have to be there. Phew! But it's hot!"

"It probably didn't fall off right at first," said Wheeler. "I'm going
to look a little further up."

"Yes, by that stony bit," assented Robert.

"It's going to be some job," said Wallis. "There's a heap of sand.
Look now — I got a mount of horses up here, aquandering all over
the country. I'll round 'em up and put 'em in the pen first, before
they stray off on me. I'll be right back. Any wagon that come along,
you want to make 'em drive on the other side of the road."

But he did not come right back. In fact, he did not come back at
all. "Reckon some of his horses quit him," said Wheeler, wiping his
dripping brow. "Just like his carelessness."

This guess, however, was not the right one. Half an hour after Spud's departure, Joe Haskell rode down from his farm. In the corral he found Spud's mount, and on the porch he found Spud himself in joyous conference with Miss Gertie Wheeler.

Joe glowered from the step.

"Well! You two seem to be enjoying yourselves," he said.

"Yes — don't we? It's right cool and pleasant here," said Spud. His eye wandered to the busy scene down the road; he leaned back luxuriously in Wheeler's swivel chair.

"What's up?" said Haskell, following Spud's gaze. "Lost something?"

Spud explained.

"Why aren't you out there helpin' 'em, then?" demanded Joe, acidly.

"Why, I ain't feelin' right well."

Joe did not look convinced. He sniffed; his black eyes snapped. "I'm going to hunt for that ring," he declared.

"Aw, stay here, Joe, and help us enjoy ourselves," drawled Spud. "It's broiling hot out there."

Joe scowled. "Thought you said you was going to start after supper tonight and go straight across to the round-up?"

"It came to me all of a sudden to make Pa Wheeler a little visit," said Spud.

"Spud Wallis," said Joe, earnestly, "you ought to be shot at sunrise on three successive mornings." He stalked gloomily down the sunken road to join the search party.

"Now, there goes a nice boy," said Spud, admiringly. "Plumb full of ginger. Good looker, too. And thrifty — my! Never see *him* laze around when there's a dollar in sight. Always up and doing. Why, he left camp this mornin' at break o' day, whilst I was poundin' my ear. 'A little more sleep, a little slumber, a little closing of the eyes to sleep' — that's my motto. Did you notice, Gertie, he didn't even say good morning to you? Someway, he didn't seem right pleased."

After much searching, Joe detached himself from his associates and marched back. Spud hailed him cheerfully.

"Find it, Joe?"

Joe shot him a triumphant look. "No, but you sure missed out, old-timer. They paid us ten dollars apiece for a starter — and there'll be a big reward to split. I'm going to lope down to Willit's and have a screen sent up to run the sand through."

He strode on to the corral.

"Spud Wallis," said Gertie, as soon as Joe was out of ear shot, "you're holding out something. I know you like a book. You're up to some devilment."

"Gertrude Lucretia," said Spud, "I'd scorn to deceive you. I am."

Joe whisked around the corner on a fat and fiery black.

"Joey, you'd better go down the tracks till you pass that auto," advised Spud sweetly. "That bronc's feeling his oats. He'll be scarey of that machine."

"You go right on with your visit, old boy," said Joe, pleasantly, "and I'll worry on with my horse, the best I can." He was a crack horseman, and perhaps not averse to proving it. He spurred over the track. Nearing the car the horse snorted, shied, plowed his forefeet in the sand, and stopped, all a-quiver. Joe's quirt slashed down; the black reared, whirled and bucked madly up the road.

"Ride him, cowboy! Sta-ay with him, you're doing well!" cried Spud. "Watch him sunfish!"

Joe plied whip and spur. The black swerved suddenly across the acequia bridge, then took off on the other side with a tremendous bound. Joe's hat flew off, he leaned over and wrapped his hand in the rein to turn the horse from the bluff; the rein snapped; pitching mightily, the black held straight on to the river. One plunge — two — at the third, horse and man, in a whirlwind of dust, went over the thirty-foot bank into the Rio Grande. The sound of a terrific splash rose to the silent porch.

Gertie gasped.

Spud bit his lip and smote his knee in vexation. "There!" he said. "I told him this morning not to do that!"

"Spud! He'll be killed!"

"Him? Lord, no! The water's deep under the bluff. We might go look." He picked up Joe's hat as they raced to the bank. "Wish *I* could ride like that," said Spud.

They were in mid-stream, swimming strongly. Joe clung to the horse's tail and acted as rudder. Spud sat happily on a boulder. He spoke to Joe's hat courteously but earnestly, and observed Joe's progress with grave and simple interest.

Joe looked back. The two on the ridge waved a friendly salute; Joe shook his fist.

"Beats all where that Joe Haskell is," grumbled Wheeler. "Maybe he went over the ridge. That's it — couldn't make his horse go by your car, I reckon."

Mr. Dwyer snapped his watch decisively. "Robert," he said, "we can't wait here any longer. Mr. Wheeler will doubtless find your ring. He can wire you at Grindstone when he does. If he doesn't — well, we can come back day after tomorrow, if you prefer. But we've got to be traveling."

"I suppose so," said Robert reluctantly. He considered a moment. "Mr. Wheeler, I shall depend on you and your friend to keep up the search. I have decided to double that reward — make it an even thousand. That is about all the ring is worth; but I wouldn't lose it for twice that. And if you don't find it — well, keep looking for it till we get back and I'll give you a hundred apiece anyway — keep wagons off and all that. If you find it, wire me. We had planned a deer hunt in the mountains, and I would hate to miss that."

"But you'll have an early dinner before you go?" urged Wheeler. "We can fly around and throw something together in a jiffy. Joe'll be back by that time."

Dwyer shook his head. "Thank you very much, but we'll just wash up and go on. We have an excellent lunch with us. The road, we hear, is very slow and sandy, and we want to be on time. Come, Robert."

The car drew up before the store. Spud leaned over the rail. "Find it?"

"No," said Wheeler. "They're going on. This way, gentlemen."

He ushered his guests in, with a black look for the young couple as he passed. He came back out at once.

"What's this? What's all this? Gertie, go in the house this minute and start dinner. Confound you, Spud, why didn't you come back?"

"I'm feeling poorly, Mr. Wheeler."

"Oh, go tell that to the submarines. You're a triflin' scoundrel, suh! Where's Joe?"

"Gone to Willit's, after a screen."

"How'd he go — over the ridge?"

"He went down the river."

"*What?*"

Spud explained and led his incredulous host out to the scene of Joe's exploit. Wheeler's bad humor disappeared in laughter.

"Well, that's a good one! We'll have to tell that to the strangers. You might as well stay to dinner, Spud."

"No," said Spud. "I'm feeling bad, I tell you. If you'll leave me put my horses in your pasture, I'll go up to Rincon on the passenger and see the doc."

"Yes — and make that an excuse to come back. Gertie, I thought I told you to go into the house."

"I ain't making any excuse to come back," said Spud, pained and grieved. "If you or Joe'll bring my string up to Point o' Rocks this evenin' I'll pay you what's right."

"Likely — and let someone else find that ring?"

"Well, then, I'll send one of the boys for 'em," said Spud wearily.

"Why, if you're really sick, boy, that's different. You come get 'em yourself. But don't make it a habit."

"Oh, that reminds me, Mr. Wheeler. If I make good as a business man — better than Joe, say — or as good as you — you'll have no further objection to me as a son-in-law, would you?"

"Now, Spud Wallis, don't you pester me — takin' advantage just because I'm a little mite sorry for you. Anyway, Joe'll show you up, any time you tackle him — and so will I."

"That's a bargain then. If I can outdo you and Joe —"

"Drat you, yes — and welcome. Shut up. Let's go tell the gentlemen about Joe and his horse."

They told the gentlemen as they were cranking the car. The gentlemen were greatly amused.

"He'll get well paid for it, at least," said Robert. "A thousand if you find the ring — a hundred apiece anyhow — that's the bargain. Here's my card. Wire me at the hotel at Grindstone. Good-bye."

They climbed into the car and whirled gaily away.

" 'Robert J. Whalen, Stationer, Designer and Engraver, 3741 Federal St., Chicago,' " Wheeler read aloud. "Nice chap. I'll just copy this off in my book before I lose the card."

"Seems like there was something else I wanted to tell you," mused Spud, "but I can't lay a finger on it. Store don't do much business, does it? Nobody here all morning."

"Only nights and Saturdays. Everybody busy — but you," retorted Wheeler. "There I forgot you was feeling so poorly. Now I'll go take another whirl at that ring. Here comes Joe."

Spud lifted Mr. Whalen's card from the counter, inspected it for a moment, and then tucked it away in his tally book.

Mr. Wheeler puffed into his enclosed courtyard, with an exultant whoop.

"You, Spud! We found it!" he shrilled jubilantly. "Spud, you good-for-nothing rascal, come out o' that kitchen!"

Spud appeared at the corral gate in all the dignity of conscious innocence.

"I haven't been near your old kitchen," he said. "I've unsaddled and unpacked and turned my sticks in your pasture. Got the ring, eh? That's good. Who found it—you or Joe?"

"Neither one. Feller came along the track—not a tramp exactly, but trampin'. He asked us what we'd lost, and I up and told him before I thought. He come on down and it wasn't fifteen minutes before he up and found it."

"Shucks! That's too bad. I was in hopes you or Joe'd get it."

Wheeler's eyelid fluttered on his cheek. "We ain't complaining any, Joe and me. We let him think it was ours and we dug up two hundred dollars for him and sent him hiking up the road."

"You're the schemers," said Spud, admiringly. "Well, I'm not grudging you your luck—you deserve it."

"Sure we do. Say, Spud, that ring's a daisy. Want to see it? Got it in my safe."

"No, my train'll be here directly—haven't got time. But where's Joe?"

"He's gone on home. Huffy—at you. But you'd better have been out there. You had the same chance Joe did, and missed it—as usual. Eight hundred and twenty dollars—purty good morning's work, I think. And you'd just as well have been in on it."

"Only eight hundred, isn't it?"

"They paid us twenty in advance, Spud," said Wheeler triumphantly, laying a fatherly hand on the young man's arm; "you see now why I don't make you welcome here. Whilst you was philanderin' around, Joe was on the job."

"But I'm not huffy," objected Spud, placidly, "and Joe is."

"There'll be other days for Joe. Most train time, Spud—so long! I'm going to tell Gertie the good news."

"Oh, I heard about it all right, papa," said Gertie, tripping demurely through the corral gate. "Congratulations! I'll expect a new dress."

Wheeler gave the pair a withering look. "Spud Wallis!" he said in a voice husky with emotion, "go flag that train! And I'm going right with you. There'll be no little tender partings, please."

"We thought of that," said Gertie, blushing and laughing. "Good-bye, Spud—again!"

"Good-bye, Gertie—again!"

"I'll kick the cat—I'll stop the clock—I'll bite the dog!" raved Wheeler. Then he grinned feebly. "I guess that's a horse on me, Spud. Make the most of it."

"There's the train," said Spud. "Come on."

They went down the steps. Spud waved his hat back and forth

across the track. The engine whistled twice in acknowledgment.

"Oh, I just thought what it was I wanted to tell you. No use for you to try to buy that place of Montoya's boy," said Spud as the train slowed up. The baggage car crept by; Spud swung on the smoker step. "Someone bought it a month ago."

"All aboard!"

The train gathered headway. Wheeler ran alongside, red-faced, and shouted up to Spud.

"Who bought it?"

Spud looked down at him benevolently.

"I did," he said.

The wagon road ran beside the track across the Bend. Spud kept close watch and was gratified, where the desert road left the river, to observe a touring car toiling up the sandy slope that led to the desert.

At Rincon, Spud did not see the doctor. Instead, while the train waited for dinner, he hunted up Charlie Simpson, his particular crony. When the train started again, both were passengers. Simpson carried a long repeating rifle tucked under his arm; it seemed unusually long because Simpson was a very small man.

At Rincon the railroad leaves the river, climbs painfully up Lookout Hill, and strikes across the desert. Spud got off at Hess, the second siding; Simpson waved joyous farewell from the car window.

The Tumble T wagon was in plain sight on the mesa beyond Lookout Draw, a great dust rose from the cutting-ground beyond. Spud set out for a two-mile walk to the wagon.

Where the first curve of the road hid them from Wheeler's, Messrs. Dwyer and Whalen drove the car under an overhanging cottonwood and halted. They opened the tool-box and laid the tools on the running board in businesslike fashion; but they did no repair-work, no overhauling. Instead, they spread robes out in the shade and composed themselves for a peaceful sleep.

Long afterward a man on foot came up the railroad track through the quivering heat. He was roughly clad and bore a little bundle on a stick. He stopped opposite the car and surveyed the sleepers with a look of infinite disgust. He wiped his dripping face with a red bandanna and then did a surprising thing. He clambered down the embankment and thrust a coarsely shod plebeian foot into Mr. Whalen's immaculate ribs.

"Wake up, bo," he said gruffly, "and pay for your night's lodgin'!"

Whalen sat up and rubbed his eyes.

"Ugh — aah — oah!" he said. "Well, Bill, did the hicks come through?"

"Two hundred — hundred and eighty net," said Bill crossly. "I tried to rub 'em for more, but the young 'un made such a squeal I took what I could get. Come now, let's get out of this."

"That's not so worse," said Dwyer. "That makes about twenty-one hundred in the old kick. Fairish clean up for a jay country like this, starting from a shoestring."

"A piker's game," said Whalen, throwing his robe in the car. "I'm sick of it. How many more rings have we got left?"

Bill gave him a venomous glance. "Yes, you tried out your big-league stuff on the coast — got us run out of Los Angeles, without gasolene money. This racket ain't swift enough for you, but it's getting us home, and then some. I think you guys is havin' it pretty soft, if anybody should ask me."

"Aw, what you beefin' about, you crab?" demanded Dwyer. "Didn't we poke around in that blistering sand an hour and a half? Where've you got any holler coming?"

"Hell, look at me!" said Bill, coarsely. He ran his fingers through the stubble on his face. "Don't you think I got any pride? I'm done, right now. Dig up a new one — you fellows are so smart."

Dwyer removed the number plate, Ill. 41372, and substituted Ky. 13306. "It's just as well," he said. "We've worked that gag for all the traffic will bear. Some of the yaps'll be letting out a long howl. 'Twon't be safe to work it again till we get up in Oklahoma."

"What you got them tools out for — the old wreck on the bum again?" growled Bill.

"Stalling, in case someone came by," explained Whalen.

"Well, get a wiggle," admonished Bill. He climbed into the tonneau, which was crowded with three suitcases and a goodly hamper. "You fellows drive awhile. I'm going to try some beer and a little sleep. Take the first right-hand road. It's fifteen miles shorter than following along the railroad, they say, and no worse."

They were a long hour climbing the sandy slope to the level of the desert. On the river, they enjoyed a substantial luncheon from the hamper. Then Bill opened his suitcase, shaved carefully, and attired himself in joyous apparel, giving him quite a collegiate air. His spirits and his vocabulary rose accordingly.

"Blooie!" he said, throwing the discarded garments into a mesquite bush. "Home, Jeems! Unless you chaps would like to get hep to a rippin' good show — eh, what? On second thoughts, Jeems, you may drive us down to Broadway. Take the High Bridge."

The going was much firmer; they bowled along at a fair pace. The road lay straight as a ruler across the great gray desert. It was a vast and limitless land, that far-seen plain. Some might have found it impressive, even beautiful; the silence, the loneliness, the dreaming levels, the interminable reaches of wide flung mountain, tiered and tangled, misty with distance or radiant with glancing lights on cliff and scar. But this distinguished party remained unimpressed. They saw it as some men see life — the small discomforts, sand and rock and thorn — unheeding the larger vision.

Little bunches of cattle, larger bands of horses, fled affrighted at this novel visitor to the desert. Far to the left, the roofs of Lookout peered over the skyline; later, they could see the low houses and the shining tracks. A freight train crawled up the hill, a string of match boxes for size, with a little black feather of smoke curling from a cigarette-sized smoke stack. A pusher engine detached itself and slid softly back down the hill. Ten miles ahead the Hess section-house stood up against the sky line.

It was past mid-afternoon when they drew near to Hess. They passed the day herd, a thousand head strung out for the Point of Rocks tank in the little low hills ahead. At the round-up wagon, half a mile to the right, the cook's fire blazed brightly; beyond it, a few riders held a bunch of cattle near the trampled round-up ground, the day's cut, waiting to throw in with the slow day herd. The horse-herd grazed beside the road, guarded by a youthful wrangler, hunched over and seemingly asleep in the saddle. A hundred yards further on the car came to the rim of Lookout Draw and turned down the steep and sandy slope.

Halfway down, Bill threw the brakes and stopped the car with a jerk. "Wake up, you fellows! Look there, will you?"

Down the slope from the Point of Rocks, across the draw, came a wild rider in a whirl of dust. Beyond and a little behind him another horseman raced at top speed. He was shooting at the first man; he was forcing him obliquely along toward the car. Scattered far behind, spread in a straggling fan across the draw, a dozen cowboys rode furiously after. A yell came from behind; the horse wrangler, frantically urging his horse with a doubled rope, tore down to the car; a tow-headed boy, wide-awake now, and pop-eyed with excitement screamed:

"Got a gun? Got a gun?"

"No — what's the matter?"

The answer came in gasps. "Train robber! Bill Panky! Ten thousand dollars reward! Great Cæsar's ghost, if I only had a rifle!" The wrangler whirled back toward the chuck wagons. "Go to the station — telegraph!" he shouted back over his shoulder.

"Go to the station, hey?" jeered Whalen. "In front of that scrap? I guess not! Can you turn around in this sand, Bill? *Lord! Look! Look!*"

The first pursuer gained on the fugitive; evidently he had the fresher horse. He was not firing now; he was reloading his revolver as he passed from sight behind a little ridge. Quick as thought the outlaw swerved to meet him. The pursuer flashed into the open, still loading his gun; the outlaw closed in, shooting. He fired once — twice — three times; the luckless cowboy clutched at the saddle horn, fell over along the horse's neck, hung for a second and rolled over in the deep sand.

Yells of wild rage, a popping of guns filled the air. Unheeding, the assassin rode close to the body and deliberately fired again — once — twice. Bullets puffed the sand about him, but he swooped down from his saddle, came up with the gun of his fallen foe, turned and thundered across to the car.

The occupants sat paralyzed with fear. In a hundred seconds the sane and orderly world had crumbled to a horrible nightmare. The horseman was upon them, he leaped off, he scrambled toward the car, gun in hand.

"Hit her up!" he commanded, jumping in. "Give her all you got!" The car leaped forward. "Climb over in front, you little fellow!"

The car lurched and bounded across the gullied draw. Bullets whined overhead, or spluttered in the dust before; the nearest cowboys were not more than two hundred yards away.

The outlaw prodded Bill with a gun muzzle. "You'll have us in the ditch! Sit up, you, or I'll blow you to Kingdom Come."

For Bill was trying to duck. Mr. Dwyer was scrunched on the floor in front, clinging desperately to Bill's leg. Mr. Whalen, in the tonneau, was trying to squeeze himself between two suit-cases, and poor Bill was manifesting a tendency to sit on his own shoulder blades.

Thus admonished, Bill sat up. On the smooth road beyond the draw, the car gathered speed and shot ahead with a roar; the shots and shouts grew fainter.

Behind them a strange thing took place. As the fleeing car topped the first raise, the avengers desisted, with one accord, and jogged soberly back in little groups of two's and three's.

Even more remarkable, perhaps, was the conduct of the murdered man. He brushed himself, rubbed the sand from his hair, took up his sombrero, mounted his horse, captured the loose horse left by his late assassin and led him to camp. The horse wrangler rode out to meet him.

"Spud Wallis, you red hellion," said the horse-wrangler, "them fellows'll be at the North Pole by sundown."

In the kidnapped car, conversation languished. The three owners thought of several things to say, but courteously repressed them.

"Pull her up, son," advised the new passenger. "We've made our get-away. Just let her trundle along. I want to do some heavy thinkin', and it distracts my attention when you loop the loops. There, that's better."

He was a powerful bulk of a man, great of body and bone; he filled the eye. In his left hand he held his enormous high-peaked Mexican sombrero of thick red felt, heavily braided with silver; the other hand, carelessly holding the six shooter, rested easily on his thigh. A massive head sat on a bullneck. His features were heavy but not ill-shaped; his mouth was tensed to a grim straight line; his mustache was black and long; his eyes were black and hard, his brows heavy and black, the thick tangle of hair jet-black; his great red-brown face was streaked with sweat and dust.

He turned his attention to his seat-mate, Mr. Robert Whalen. "What's the matter, brother? Got a chill?"

Mr. Whalen picked up spirit.

"Great Christopher K. Columbus!" he answered with some irritation. "I'm scared!"

Chauffeur Bill flung a remark over his shoulder. "Well, you needn't put on any high-and-mighty airs about it — so am I."

The robber laughed. He looked at Mr. Whalen, he looked at the pair in front; his eyes filmed with calculation. Then the hard lines of his face relaxed, and he sighed.

"I really ought to shake you fellows down for your change," he said apologetically, "but I haven't the heart to do it, the way the play come. It wouldn't seem right, somehow. You done me a good turn, and I'm grateful. Too bad, but that's the way I feel. You just carry me along till I get a horse and we'll call it square. But if you got any guns you'd better dump 'em overboard. Guns make me nervous."

"Shrimp's got one," said Bill. "Toss it out, Shrimp, as the gentleman tells you."

It appeared that Mr. Dwyer was Shrimp; he produced a dainty affair in silver and pearl.

The outlaw gave a cry of delight.

"Oh, what a cunning little thing!" he cooed. "Don't throw it away,

Mr. Shrimp. Isn't it sweet? I'll sew it on my hat. No — I'll use it for a scarf pin." He thrust his own gun in the holster and put the new one in his pocket. "Now we'll go 'long, all nice and cosy," he said.

The Point of Rocks lay far behind; the railroad was close to the left. In the north, Lear — section house, water-tank and telegraph shack — grew large against the sky. They crossed the railroad track and plowed through a stretch of sand.

"We follow the railroad as far as Lear," ordered Panky. "The telegraph operator keeps a saddle horse. Maybe he'll loan it to me."

Just out of Lear, they dipped down in a draw; Bill slowed to cross a deep and narrow wash. He eased the front wheels into the gully.

"Hands up! Stop her!"

Ten feet away a rifle barrel poked from behind a washed-out bank. It was pointed at Bill, but in a half second it swung to cover the tonneau.

"If it ain't Bill Panky! Don't move a hand!"

To steady himself in crossing the gully, Mr. Panky's hands had gripped at seat and stanchion. He now rigidly held that strained position. Mr. Panky did not so much as shift his eyes — such was his desire to please — but kept them focused between chauffeur Bill's shoulder-blades. The car stopped astride the ditch.

A man stepped cautiously from the wash-out — a little man with a long 30-40 repeater. He looked very much indeed like Mr. Charlie Simpson. The resemblance was not merely a freakish coincidence; this was Mr. Simpson's self. He held the muzzle of the long rifle within a foot of Mr. Panky's ribs.

"Put your hands on the back of the front seat!" he ordered. "Shut your eyes!"

Mr. Panky did this. The little man held the rifle in one hand and reached forward gingerly for Mr. Panky's six-shooter. Getting it, with a little audible sob of relief, he cocked it, backed off a step, and laid the rifle behind him.

"Get out!" he said. "Keep them hands up! Turn around. Back out!"

Panky meekly submitted while the little man frisked him for weapons.

"What — in — hell — is — this?" said the little man, in a rising crescendo of astonishment, when he came to the little pearl-handled gun. "Turn around, Bill, let's have a look at you!"

"Why, it's old Hank!" said Mr. Panky, apparently much gratified.

"Yes — it's old Hank." The little man sat down on the bank. He had a wizened, freckled face and a stubby red mustache, which now bristled to a snarl. "Old Hank — him you bullied and run over, and cheated out of his share on that Lordsbury money. Well, well! What a joyful surprise! I see this ortermobile a-coming, and I thinks I'll just pick up a little piece of money — and here I got the drop on old Bill Panky, and ten thousand perfectly good dollars reward for him, alive or dead. I hope this will always be a lesson to us."

Mr. Panky laughed uneasily. "You wouldn't do old Bill dirt like that, old fellow."

"Yes, I would," said Hank, positively.

"Not your old pardner. You ain't that kind, Hank — not you."

"Yes I am. You don't know me."

"I got a big bunch of money hid out, Hank — I'll whack up even with you — honest I will."

"No, you won't. You want a chance to put me to bed with a shovel — that's what you want. Lord love yer, Bill, I knows you like a book. Here's where I get even with you, for keeps. I'm gettin' old, Bill — it's time I was leading a better life. And that ten thousand will sorter ease my declinin' years."

"Maybe I was too rough on you," admitted Mr. Panky. "But I'll make it up to you. You keep the guns, Hank — take what dough this bunch has, if you want it — we'll get some horses and hit the brush for my hide-out."

"You'll hit the back track for Doña Ana," retorted Hank, ferociously. "Back out that car, you feller, and turn her round." He reached back for the rifle.

"You can't do that, Simp — Simpleton," said Panky. "They'll send you to the pen for that Lordsbury job."

"They'll let me off light, me givin' myself up and bringin' you in," asserted Hank confidently. "They want you, Bill. You'll swing for that conductor you got. They'll give me two or three years at most — maybe a full pardon. And you'll be hung till you's dead — dead — dead!"

"I'll give you all the money I got cached, Hank."

"You'll give me a shot in the back. To hell with your money!"

Panky wilted. He was trembling like a leaf. He cringed. "Take me to Grindstone, then, Hank," he pleaded abjectly. "The Tumble T outfit will lynch me if you take me back that way. I — killed a man down there this afternoon, Hank."

"You did? Is that right, you fellows?" Hank asked.

"He did," said Whalen. "Cold-blooded murder. Shot him twice after he was down. We saw it. Then he made us bring him up here. Don't you be afraid of us. We're with you — we take you in the machine wherever you want to go."

Hank surveyed the prisoner with ferocious joy. "That settles you. You can enjoy yourself guessing as we go back — but my guess is that the Tumble T boys don't lynch you — they'd rather see you hang in Doña Ana jail. But I don't care what they do. I get the reward just the same — alive or dead. And what's more, if you open your ugly head for just one more word, I'll kill you right now and here. I mean it." His fingers twitched along the rifle barrel.

By the car, the three partners had been holding a whispered and hasty conference. Now Dwyer came forward. He was very pale and his face had fallen in since the swift tragedy of an hour ago, but the light of greed was in his blinking eyes.

"Wait — wait a minute," he faltered. "We want to make you a proposition. We happen to have with us a considerable sum in ready cash. We wouldn't have told you this, but you couldn't very well rob us on your way to tell the court you wanted to reform. But why should you go to the penitentiary? Why wouldn't you have us pay you a good cash percentage right here, and let us have that reward, while you go free?"

"They might send you up for a long term, you know. You never can tell," urged Whalen. "Why, you might get sick and die there. This'll certainly be a lot better way for you."

"How much?" Hank did not move his little glowing eyes from his captive. "I never did care much for the penitentiary, nohow."

In turn Chauffeur Bill became the spokesman.

"Fifteen hundred dollars."

"That listens pretty good. Come again. You hadn't ought to try to hold out on an old man that way," said Hank sorrowfully. "I got the guns. Try once more."

"We can scrape up a little more, between us," admitted Dwyer reluctantly. "But it will leave us bare. We need some expense money."

"You give it here," returned Hank implacably. "Expense money be blowed! You can have the town of Doña Ana if you want it, or the whole Tumble T outfit, when you turn up with Panky. Give me two thousand, even, and it's a go. If you got any more you can keep it. But you got to go back the way you came. I'm goin' north — and I need room. The boys won't lynch him — not with you bringin' him in that way. If they'd caught him themselves they might of, likely. They'll take him to Doña Ana for you. That's my last word. Take it or leave it."

The money changed hands. Under Hank's gun, Panky was trussed up with suit-case straps, his hands behind his back, and was assisted into the car. Then his ankles were strapped together. Whalen took the steering wheel, with Dwyer beside him and the two Bills in the tonneau. The car turned back toward the Point of Rocks; behind it, Hank climbed to the railroad track and howled a truculent farewell.

No longer restrained by Hank's rifle, Mr. Panky chatted freely, mainly about Hank. His companions, being in high spirits, met these lively sallies with laughter and applause, and a pleasant time was had. After a few miles, however, Mr. Panky lapsed to sulky silence; rousing himself occasionally to communicate an afterthought.

A cool breeze tossed the wayside mesquites; their shadows danced long and black across the road; a far mountain notched black and sharp across the red sun; the car came again to Lookout Draw. It chugged up the sandy slope, it turned across the plain to the chuck-wagon.

Close at hand the bawling day-herd had reached the bed ground; gay riders circled in the dim dust, "bedding them down," singing, turning back wayward splashes of cattle to an ever-contracting circle.

A horseman trotted out to meet the car, waving his arm. "Gee whiz! Ain't you got no sense?" he cried in an angry voice. "Get away with that devil-wagon. You'll stampede these cattle. Go 'way round, if you want to get to camp."

Whalen made a wide detour, driving slowly over the grass hummocks; dusk had fallen when he reached the wagon.

By the bright fire stood a battery of steaming Dutch ovens and pots and a vast kettle of coffee, sending out a savory incense; in the firelight, a broad semi-circle of cowboys sat cross-legged, laughing and talking, or busy with plate and knife and fork.

"Supper all ready, strangers! Come and get it!"

The hail came from Cole, the foreman, as the car stopped.

"We've got your train-robber!" called Whalen triumphantly. "Here's your Bill Panky."

The semi-circle went suddenly hushed and still.

Cole rose and came forward. "Bully!" he said, heartily. "Good for you! There's a big reward offered for him — ten thousand, I think. You're in luck. Where'd you get him?"

It was a casual tone, considering the recent bloody affair of the afternoon, but Whalen, in his excitement failed to note this.

"Another man captured him," explained Whalen, modestly, "and turned him over to us to bring in." He tugged at the strap on the captive's legs. "I'll tell you about it later."

He took the prisoner's elbow, Bill assisting from behind, and helped him to the ground. Dwyer followed.

"Gosh, my feet are asleep," remarked the prisoner, to a vast silence. He shambled a step into the firelight. "Undo my arms, somebody."

Cole unbuckled the strap; the outlaw hobbled straight to a tin plate and cup. Cole spoke in a pained and shocked voice.

"Why, this isn't Bill Panky. This is old Jim Hendricks, and he isn't worth twenty dollars a dozen to anyone."

"But he killed a man here!"

Cole shook his head. "We were just playing moving-picture cowboys."

Whalen's heart stood still. Dwyer felt a cold faintness creeping over him and leaned heavily against the mud guard. "But our m-money!" gurgled Dwyer. "All we had — gave it to the man that caught him!"

A drawling voice rose from behind the fire. "What sort of a looking man? Little sawed-off runt, red eyes and brindled mustache?"

"That's him!"

"Oh, it's all right then!" said the voice. "I told him to do that." Spud Wallis, the speaker, rose and loitered over. "I'll take care of the money. You just make a little list of the rings you've lost lately, Mr. Whalen — your poor old dad's rings — and there won't be a bit of trouble. Jot down the names and amounts, you know, near as you remember, and I'll fix it all up for you as far as the money holds out."

Bill stepped into the car and grasped the steering-wheel firmly.

"Home, Jeems!" he said.

Beyond
the Desert

BEYOND THE DESERT

CHAPTER I

Beyond the Desert

MacGregor was in haste. He pressed forward in a close, fine rain. A huge and graceless hulk of a man, he rode craftily, a brisk jog, a brisk walk; where the trail was steep, he slipped from the saddle and led the way to the next smooth bit.

Hard by the head of the pass, where the peaks of San Quentin — monstrous, exaggerated, fantastic — frowned through fog and mist, he paused on a jutting shoulder in a brief lull between showers. The night drew near. The fog lifted for a space as a gust of wind whipped between the hills: far behind and below there was a glimpse of toiling horsemen, a black wavering line where the trail clung to the hillside.

MacGregor lifted the heavy brows that pent his piggy little red eyes. His face was a large red face, heavy, square, coarse-featured, stubbly. It now expressed no emotion. Unhurriedly, he took up a long thirty-forty from the sling below the stirrup leather, raised the sights high, and dropped two bullets in the trail before the advancing party. They shrank back to a huddling clump. The mist shut down.

Under shelter of his long slicker, he wiped the rifle carefully and returned it to the scabbard. "Persons of no experience," he grumbled. "They ride with small caution for a country of boulders and such-like cover. If the half o' them had stayed behind at yonder well and the best few followed, each with a led horse, they might well ha' caught me oop ere I could win across yonder weary plain. No judgment at all!"

The critic clicked his teeth disparagingly as he remounted.

"'Tis plain I have naught to fear from these gentry for all the heavy weight this red horse of mine must carry. For they will think twice and again at each bend and rockfall. Aweel — I hae seen worse days. Thanks to this good rain, I needna fear the desert either for mysel' or the beastie. Hunger and great weariness, pain and jostling death, these I can make shift to bear — but against naked thirst no man can strive for long — But beyont the desert? Ay, there's the kittle bit. There's a telephone line awa' to the north, and if the good folk of Datil be at all of enterprising mind, 'tis like I shall hear tidings."

Dawn found him beyond the desert, breasting the long slow ridges beneath the wooded mountain of the Datils. The storm was passed away. Behind, the far peaks of San Quentin fluttered on the horizon, dream-pale; and then, in one swift moment, flamed at a touch of sudden sun, radiant and rejoicing, sharp against a clean-washed sky. The desert brimmed with a golden flood of light, a flood which rolled eastward across the level, to check and break and foam against the dense, cool shadow of the Datil Range. So dense and so black was that shadow that the rambling building of the C L A ranch scarce bulked blacker: hardly to be seen, save for a thin wisp of wood smoke that feathered in the windless air.

"Ay," said the horseman. "Now the pot boils. And indeed I am wondering if my name is in that pot. For here comes one at a hard gallop — wrangling horses, belike. And now he sees me and swerves this way. Truly, I am very desirous that this man may be Mundy himself. I would ever like best to deal with principals — and Mundy is reputed a man of parts. Be it Clay Mundy or another, yon bit wire has gien him word and warning to mark who comes this way. I must e'en call science to my own employ. Hullo, Central! . . . Hullo! Give me Spunk, please. . . . Hullo, Spunk. MacGregor, speaking. Spunk, I am now come to a verra strait place, and I would be extremely blithe to hae your company. For to deal plainly wi' you, my neck is set on the venture, no less . . . I am obligit to you. Ye hae aye been dependable. See if you canna bring Common-sense wi' you. Hullo, Central! Gimme Brains . . . What's that? No answer? Try again, Central! Central, gin ye please. The affair is verra urgent."

The oncoming rider slowed down: MacGregor turned to meet him, his two hands resting on the saddle horn.

"'Tis Mundy's self, thanks be," he muttered. "Now, do you twa walk cannily, Spunk and Common-sense. Here is the narrow bit. Aha, Brains! Are ye there at the last of it? That's weel! I shall need you!"

He rode on at a walk. The riders drew abreast.

"Hands up, you!" Mundy's gun was drawn and leveled with incredible swiftness.

MacGregor's hands did not move from the saddle horn: he leaned on them easily. "And that is no just what ye might call a ceevil greeting, Mr. Mundy. Ye give me but a queer idea of your hospitality. Man, ye think puirly! Do ye see this rifle under my knee? Thirty-forty, smokeless — and had I meant ye ill, it was but stepping behind a bit bush to tumble you from the saddle or e'er ye clapped eyes on me."

"You have my name, I see," said Mundy. "And there is certainly some truth in your last saying. You might have taken a pot shot at me from ambush, easy enough. Guess you didn't know we were expecting you. Unless all signs fail, you are fresh from the loot of Luna. Now I've had about enough nonsense from you. Stick up those hands or I'll blow you into eternity."

"And that is a foolish obsairve," said MacGregor, composedly. " 'Into eternity!' says he! Man, I wonder at ye! We're in eternity just noo — every minute of it — as much as we e'er shall be. For the ambush, you do me great wrong. I was well knowing to yon mischief-making telephone — but I took my chance of finding you a man of sense. For my hands, they are very well where they are. You have me covered — what more would you wish? I have conscientious scruples aboot this hands-up business. It is undeegnified in the highest degree. Man, theenk ye I have nae self-luve at all! Hands up might be all verra weel for a slim young spark like you, wi' looks and grace to bear it off with. But me, wi' my years and the hulking carcass of me, in such a bairnly play — man, I should look just reedeeculous! The thing cannae be done."

"Very well. I am coming to get your gun. Keep your hands on the saddle horn. I have you covered, and if you crook a finger, I'll crook mine."

"'Tis early yet in the day, Mr. Mundy." MacGregor held the same attitude and the same unmoved composure. "Dinna be hasty in closing in upon me. I was thinking to propose a compromise."

"A compromise? And me with finger on trigger — me that could hit you blindfolded?"

"Nae doot of it at all. I am well acquaint wi' you by repute. Ye have the name of a man of speerit and of one skilly wi' his gun and unco' swift to the back o' that. Myself, I am slow on the draw. 'Tis lamentable, but I must needs admit it. I am no what ye might ca' preceesly neemble of body or of mind — but, man! if I'm slow, I'm extraordinary eefeecient! If you crook that finger you are speaking of, I am thinking the two of us may miss the breakfast cooking yonder. For myself, I am free to say I had far liefer crook elbows wi' you over a thick beefsteak."

"Fool! I can shoot you three times before you get to your gun."

"Nae doot, nae doot," said MacGregor pacifically. "It has been done — yet here am I, little the waur o't. Come, Mr. Mundy, I must deal plainly wi' you. Long ago, that place where your ranch is was pointit oot to me by yon square-capped peak behind for landmark — and I came here the noo rather than to any ither spot round aboot this wide circle of the plains of San Quentin, preceesly because ye are bespoken a man of parts and experience — and thereby the better able to judge weel and deal wisely with another man as good as yoursel'."

"Sure of that?"

"Positeeve. Now, understand me weel. I am laying no traps to tempt your eye to rove — so dinna look, but e'en take my word for it. But gin ye were free to look ye wad see, as I did just ere you came, some ten-twelve black specks coming this way ahindt me on the plain, a long hour back, or near two — and ye may draw your ain conclusions thereby. To speak the plain truth, I doot they mean me nae guid at a'."

"I should conclude that this was your unlucky day. Mr. Whatever-your-name-is. Quite aside from these gentlemen behind, or from myself — and you may possibly be underrating me — the whole country east of here is warned by telephone. Heavy, heavy hangs over your head!"

"I am a little struck wi' that circumstance myself," said MacGregor simply. "Ye see the seetuation wi' great clearness, Mr. Mundy. But I have seen worse days and have good hopes to come fairly off from this one yet. For if you can eenstruct me in what way I should be any worse off to be shot by you just now, than to be hanged in a tow from a pleasant juniper a little later, after tedious delays and parley-wows, I shall be the more obleegit. For then I can plainly see my way to give myself up to you. If you cannae do this, then I shall expect ye, as a reasoning man yourself, to note that ye can have naught to gain by changing shots wi' one who has naught to lose, and to conseeder the proposeetion I mak to you — as I should surely do and the cases were changed."

"You put it very attractively and I see your point," said Mundy. A slow smile lit up his face. He put his gun back in the scabbard. "Well, let's have it."

"And a verra guid choice, too. If it be not askin' too much, let us e'en be riding toward your ranch gate while ye hear my offer, for when the sun reaches here we should be seen — and yonder weary bodies gain on us while we stand here daffing."

They made a strange contrast: Mundy, smooth, slender and graceful, black of hair and eye, poised, lithe and tense, a man to turn and look after: MacGregor, stiff, unwieldy, awkward, gross, unkempt, battered, year-bitten.

"For the first of it, ye should know that not one of these gentry behind have seen my face, the which I kep' streectly covered durin' my brief stay in Luna. Second, though no great matter, ye may care to know that the bit stroke I pulled off in Luna was even less than justice. For within a year and a day a good friend of mine was there begowked and cozened by that same partnership — yes and that wi' treachery and broken trust to the back of it — of mair then I regained for him by plain and open force at noonday. So much for that — though I do not hold you squeamish. Third, for your own self, it is far known that you and the Wyandotte Company and Steel-foot Morgan are not agreeing verra weel — "

"You never heard that I've taken any the worst of it, did you?"

"No, but that they keep you weel occupied. Also, that hired warriors from the Tonto are to join wi' Webb of the Wyandotte. So hear me now. I need nae ask of ye if ye have ony but discreet persons aboot ye?"

Mundy laughed. "Boys are floating in the Malibu hills with a pack outfit. No one at the ranch today but Hurley, the water-mason. He's all right."

"Verra weel. Do you send him away betimes on that beastie atween your knees, and I will be water-mason to you — the mair that I can run your steam-pump as well as the best, though there will be small need of pumps till these rains be over. The story will be that the outlaw-body passed by night, unseen, liftin' your night-horse as he flitted, and leavin' this sorrel of mine. Your man Hurley can join your outfit and lose himself. That will be my gain, for I shall be blameless Maxwell, your water-mason — and who so eager to run down the runagate robber as he? And when they see how it is, that their man has got clean away, these men from Luna will know that the jig is definitely up and they will be all for the eating and sleeping."

"Very pretty, and it can be done — since they do not know you," agreed Mundy. "They will not be expecting their outlaw to call them in to breakfast, certainly. But I do not see where I am to gain anything."

"You are to hear, then," said the outlaw. "I will praise the bridge that carries me over, but I will do more too: I will mend that bridge. I will fight your battles with you against all comers. Not murder, you mind, but plain warfare against men fit for war."

"A fighting man, and slow on the draw?"

"I am that same, both the one and the other. Slow, I cannot deny it — slow, in compare with the best. But man, I'm experienced, I'm judgmatical, and I'm fine on the latter end. I'm a good person to have at your right hand or your left. Some way, I dinna prosper verra weel as chief man — but as the next best, there is none better rides leather."

"You come well recommended."

"By myself, you are meaning? And just that you may know the worth of that recommend, I am telling ye that my name is no exactly Maxwell. You have had word of me, your ownself, in El Paso, where indeed I saw your face, though you saw not mine. And I would have ye to observe, Mr. Mundy, that I keepit my name streectly to myself for such time as ye might have taken the sound of it as a threat, and give it to you now only when it comes mair as a promise. So now I offer you the naked choice, peace or war — and the last word is with you. A hundred miles and twenty, at the least of it, I have now made in sax-and-thirty hours — and blow high, blow low, I ride no step beyond yonder gate."

"I am decidedly inclined toward peace," said Clay Mundy, smiling again, "if only to hear you talk. For you talk convincingly. My own risk in the matter — which you have been kind enough not to mention — also moves me that way. And, after all, your late exploit at Luna is nothing to me. But as to your value in my little range war — you forgot to mention the name, you know."

"The name is MacGregor."

"Not Sandy MacGregor? Of Black Mountain?"

"That same. Plain shooting done neatly."

"You're on," said Clay Mundy.

So MacGregor became Maxwell, and Mundy's. The search party came, and swore, and slept; for they were weary. None mistrusted Maxwell, that kindly and capable cook, who sympathized so feelingly with them concerning the upness of the jig. In the seven-up tournament organized after that big sleep, Maxwell won the admiration of all and the money of most: and they went home mingling praises of their new friend with execrations of the escaped outlaw.

CHAPTER II

Pictured Rock

"And the herdsmen of Gerar did strive with Isaac's herdsmen, saying, The water is ours."

That was at the well Esek. The patriarchs were always quarreling with their neighbors or with each other over wells, pasturage and other things — mavericks, maybe. Abraham, Laban, Lot, Isaac, Jacob — they led a stirring life, following the best grass. You ought to read about them, sometime.

It is entirely probable that Terah went forth from Ur of the Chaldees either because the grass was short or because he had no friends on the grand jury.

Cattlemen have not changed much since then. They still swing a big loop: it is as risky as ever to let the stock out on shares: and we still have cattle wars wherever there is free range, because of the spirit so justly expressed by Farmer Jones: "He said he wasn't no land-hog — all he wants is just what joins his'n."

Human nature is the same on the plains of Mamre or of San Quentin: so there is no new thing to tell about the Mundy-Morgan war. Wrong and folly and stubbornness; small matter now whose first the blame; this might have been a page of history.

Strong warriors, able leaders, Ben "Steel-foot" Morgan, Webb of the Wyandotte outfit, and Clay Mundy; sharp and bitter hate was in their hearts, and the feud was more savage than the usual run of cattle wars: carried on (of course upon a higher plane than any "civilized" warfare. For there were restrictions, there were limits. To rise up from a man's table and war upon that man while the taste of his bread was still sweet in your mouth — such dealing would have been unspeakable infamy in the San Quentin country.

Again, you might be unfriendly with a man and yet meet on neutral ground or when each was on his lawful occasions, without trouble. It was not the custom to war without fresh offense, openly given. You must not smile and shoot. You must not shoot an unarmed man, and you must not shoot an unwarned man. Here is a nice distinction, but a clear one: you might not ambush your enemy; but when you fled and your enemy followed, you might then waylay and surprise without question to your honor, for they were presumed to be on their guard and sufficiently warned. The rattlesnake's code, to warn before he strikes, no better: a queer, lop-sided, topsy-turvy, jumbled and senseless code — but a code for all that. And it is worthy of note that no better standard has ever been kept with such faith as this barbarous code of the fighting man.

Round-up season passed with no fresh outbreak of hostilities. After the steer-shipping, Mr. Maxwell had been given a mount, a rope and a branding iron, and so turned loose to learn the range. This was equivalent to letters of Marque and Reprisal.

Mr. Maxwell was camped at Whitewater, alone. So far, he had passed a pleasant day. He had killed a fat buck at daybreak, when he wrangled horses. Later, he had ridden leisurely in nooks and corners, branding two of his employer's calves, overlooked by the roundup, two of the Y calves, and one long-eared yearling — a pleasing total of five for the C L A tally-book. So far his services had been confined to

such peaceful activities as these: the war had languished since the rains
set in. It was late October now, and the rains were still falling. The
desert was glorified with the magic of belated spring.

All day it had been cloudy. While Mr. Maxwell was branding his
maverick it began to sprinkle; when he turned it loose the sprinkle
had become rain, the clouds were banked dark and sullen against the
mountains. He wriggled into his slicker and started for camp, but the
rain turned to a blinding storm and he was glad to turn his back to its
fury and ride his straightest for the next shelter.

Pictured Rock is an overhanging cliff of limestone, sheltered from
three winds. Gray walls and creamy roof are close, covered with the
weird picture writing of Apache and Navajo, a record of the wars and
journeys of generations.

As he turned the bend in the canon, Maxwell saw a great light glowing under Pictured Rock, now veiled by the driving sheets of rain,
now beating out in gusts across the murky dark, reflected and magni-
fied by the cliff behind. Another, storm driven like himself, was before him. He paused at the hill-foot and shouted:

"Hullo, the house! Will your dog bite?"

"Hi!" It was a startled voice: a slender figure in a yellow slicker
appeared beside the fire. "Dog's dead, poor fellow — starved to death!
Come on up!"

The C L A man rode up the short zigzag of the trail to the fire-lit
level. He took but one glance and swept off his hat, for the face he
saw beneath the turned-up sombrero was the bright and sparkling face
of a girl.

"You will be Miss Bennie May Morgan? I saw you in Magdalena
at the steer-shipping."

"Quite right. And you are Mr. Sandy Maxwell, the new warrior
for Clay Mundy."

"Faces like ours are not easily forgot," said Maxwell.

Miss Bennie laughed. Her eyes crinkled when she laughed. "I will
give you a safe-conduct. Get down — unless you are afraid of hurting
your reputation, that is." She sat upon her saddle blankets where they
were spread before the fire, and leaned back against the saddle.

The C L A man climbed heavily down and strode to the fire, where
he stood dripping and silent. The grinding of boulders in the flooded
canon rose loud and louder, swelled to a steady ominous roar by the
multitudinous echoes of the hills.

"Well! How about that lunch?" demanded Miss Bennie sharply.
"It's past noon."

"Sorry, Miss Morgan, but I have not so much as a crumb. And that
is a bad thing, for you are far from home, and who knows when this

weary storm will be by? But doubtless they will be abroad to seek
for you."

Miss Bennie laid aside her hat and shook her curly head decidedly.
"Not for me. Dad thinks I'm visiting Effie at the X L and Effie thinks
I'm home by this time. But this storm won't last. The sun will be out
by three. You'll see! And now, if you please, since you can't feed me,
hadn't you better entertain me? Sit down, do!"

"It is like that I should prove entertaining for a young maid, too!"
said Maxwell, carrying a flat stone to the fire to serve for a seat.

"Oh, you never can tell! Suppose, for a starter, you tell me what
you are thinking so busily."

"I am thinking," said Maxwell, slowly, "that you are a bonnie lass
and a merry one. And I was thinking one more thing, too. The X L is
awa' to the southeast and the Morgan home ranch as far to the southwest. Now what may Miss Bennie Morgan need of so much northing,
ten long miles aside from the straight way, and her friend Effie thinking she was safe home and all? And then I thought to myself, the folk
at San Quentin are very quiet now. It is to be thought that the season
of great plenty has put them in better spunk with the world. And
it is an ill thing that a way cannae be found to make an end of this
brawling for good and all. And, thinks I, the bonny Earl of Murray
himself was not more goodly to the eye than Clay Mundy — and it is
a great peety for all concerned that Clay Mundy is not storm-bound
this day at Picture Rock, rather than I!"

"Well!" Miss Bennie gasped and laughed frankly, blushed red, neck
and cheek. "Oh, you men! And while you were making this up — "

"It is what I thought," said Maxwell stoutly. "Only I was nae
thinking words, d'ye see? I was just thinking thoughts. And it is no
verra easy to put thoughts into words."

"Well, then — while you were thinking all those preposterous
thoughts, I was seeing a wonderful picture, very much like this storm,
and this cave, and this fire, and us. If I were a painter, this is what I
would try to paint: a hill-side like this — so you might feel what you
could not see, the black night and the wild storm. The black night,
and a red fire glowing in a cave-mouth, and a wind-bent tree close
beside: and by the fire a man straining into the night at some unseen
danger; a cave-man, clad in skins, with long matted hair, broad-shouldered, long-armed, ferocious, brutal — but unafraid. He is half-
crouching, his knees bent to spring: he is peering under his hand: the
other hand clutches a knotted club: a dog strains beside his foot, snarling against the night, teeth bared, glaring, stiff legs braced back, neck
bristling: behind them, half-hidden, shrinking in the shadow — a
woman and a child. And the name of that picture would be 'Home!' "

Maxwell's heavy face lit up, his dull and little eye gleamed with an answering spark, his sluggish blood thrilled at the spirit and beauty of her: his voice rang with a heat of frank admiration. "And that is a brave thought you have conjured up, too, and I will be warrant you would be unco' fine woman to a cave-man — though I'm judgin' you would be having a bit club of your own." He paused, fixed her with a meditative eye, and spoke again in a lighter tone. "I recognize myself, and the dog is dead, puir fellow — starved to death, you said. But I would have you observe that the thoughts of the two of us differed but verra little when all is said — forbye it ran in my mind that a much younger person was to be cave-man to you. And you gave me safe-conduct, too! Are you to be man-sworn, then, and me trusting to you?"

"Now you are trying to torment me," said Miss Bennie, briskly. "I can't have that, you know. Better give it up. Roll a smoke. I know you want to. The storm is slackening already — we will be going soon."

"A pipe, since you are so kind," said Maxwell, fumbling for it.

"Do you admire your friend Clay Mundy so much?" said Miss Bennie next, elbows on knees, chin in hands.

Maxwell rolled a slow eye on her, and blew out a cloud of smoke. "My employer. I did not say friend, though if I like him no worse it may come to that yet. He has the devil's own beauty — which thing calls the louder to me, misshapen as you see me. He is a gallant horseman, fame cries him brave and proven. But I am not calling him friend yet till I know the heart of him. Fifty-and-five I am, and I can count on the fingers of my twa hands, the names of those I have been willing to call wholly friend — forbye one of those few was my enemy to my overthrow. So you will not be taking Clay Mundy to your cave upon my say-so till I am better acquaint wi' him. But dootless you know him verra well yourself."

Miss Bennie evaded this issue. She became suddenly gloomy. "It is plain that you are a stranger here, since you talk so glibly of any lasting peace in the San Quentin. A wicked, stiff-necked unreasoning pack, they are — dad and all! There has never been anything but wrong and hate here, outrage and revenge, and there never will be. It is enough to make one believe in the truth of original sin and total depravity!"

"No truth at all!" cried Maxwell warmly. "Oreeginal sin is just merely a fact — no truth at a'! Folks are aye graspin' at some puir halflin fact and settin' it up to be the truth. It takes at least three trees to make a row, and it needs at least three facts to make a truth. Mankind is blind, foolish and desperately wicked — yes, take it from me that am an old ruffian. But mankind is also eencurably good — wise and strong and splendid and kindly and brave — in your time of sorrow and danger you will find it so — and there's another glaring fact for you! With endless rain earth would drown, wi' endless sun it would be a cinder: look about you now, see what sun and rain and evil and good have wrought together, grass and flower and bud and fruit, the bonny world and the bonny race o' men! World and man, the machine Works! And there's the third fact for you, lassie, and the weightiest fact. We are a Going Concern: we pay a profit to our Owner! And for the truth behind these three facts, may not this be it: That if we are at once evil and good, it is the good God who made us that way, not in sloth, but because He wanted us to be that way? It is so I think. But it is a strange thing to me that I am most roundly abused for disrespect to the Maker whene'er I dare venture the mild guess that perhaps He knew what He was about!"

"A very fine sermon, reverend sir, though I did not get the text," said Miss Bennie, twinkling. "And now if you will give me your benediction, I will be on my way soon. The storm is breaking. It will clear as suddenly as it came on."

Maxwell shook out the saddle blankets and saddled her horse. "For the text it is this: 'And God saw everything that He had made and behold it was very good.' — And I am an old fool as well as an old ruffian," he grumbled, "for I have wearied you."

"Oh, no, you haven't. Your theology took my breath away, rather — that's all. It was so very unexpected."

"Of course, I will be seeing that you get safe home — "

"You mustn't. It would only make you a hard ride for nothing. No need of it at all. There is time for me to get home while the sun is still an hour high."

"It doesn't seem right," protested Maxwell.

"Really, I'd rather you wouldn't," said Miss Bennie earnestly. "I don't want to be rude, but I am still — " She gave him her eyes and blushed to her hair — " am still . . . north of where I should be, as you so shrewdly observed. And your camp lies farther yet to the north."

"Good-bye, then, Miss Morgan."

"Good-bye, Mr. MacGregor."

He stared after her as she rode clattering down the steep. "MacGregor!" he repeated. "MacGregor, says she! And never a soul of the San Quentin kens aught of the late MacGregor save Clay Mundy's own self! Here is news! Is she so unco' chief wi' him as that, then? And who told her whaur my camp was; she was glib to say that she

had time enow to go home or sundown — but she was careful she
didna say she was gaun there! Little lady, it is in my mind that you
are owre far north!"

She waved her hand gaily; her fresh young voice floated back to
him, lingering, soft and slow:

> He was a braw gallant,
>   And he rid at the ring;
> And the bonny Earl of Murray
>   Oh! He might have been a king.
>
> He was a braw gallant,
>   And he played at the glove;
> And the bonny Earl of Murray
>   Oh! He was the Queen's love!
>
> Oh! Lang may his lady
>   Luke owre the castle down,
> Ere she see the Earl of Murray
>   Come sounding thro' the town.

The girl passed from sight down the narrow canon. MacGregor-
Maxwell gave his head a shaking then, to clear his thoughts, and put
foot to stirrup. When he came to the beaten trail again, where the
horse's feet pattered rhythmically on the firm ground, MacGregor
half sang, half crooned, a plaintive and wandering air:

> Then I pray you do not trust the hawk again,
>   The cruel hawk that mocks thy love, like me.
> Oh, alone, betrayed and sad although I leave thee,
>   Yet the wandering traitor weeps, poor love, for thee —
>   Ay! Paloma azul!

"The de'il and his horns! Now why do I sing such an ill-omened
and unchancy song as that?" He shook his great shoulders, as if to shake
off a weight: he held his cupped hand to his mouth. "Hullo, Central!
Can you get Brains for me? . . . Try again, please . . . Now, Brains,
you are partly acquaint wi' this day's doings. But did you mark the
bonny blush of her at the name of Clay Mundy — and her so far from
the plain way, wi' no cause given? . . . Ye didna? . . . Brains, you're
but a cauld, feckless, dusty-dry thing, when all's said. Well then, I am
telling you of it. And what am I to do in such case as that? . . . A
little louder, please! . . . Oh! I am to see where Clay Mundy rides this
day, if it is any affair of mine — is that it? . . . Surely it is my business.
Any man is natural protector to any woman against any man except
himself. . . . And if he means her naething but good? . . . It is what
I will know. And then I will be best man — and to be best man at this
employ should be no empty form. For indeed I think the Morgans are
like to be little pleased.

"Aweel, Brains, I will e'en do your bidding, and I will seek proof where Clay Mundy fares this day — though I tell you plainly that I know very well now. And I scorn for a slow-speeritless, doddering sluggard — you and your proofs! You can but look through a hole in a stone wall, at the most of it. What are walls for but to leap over — can you tell me that? Show me once a braw lass and a high hard wall and a lad beyond, and I will show you a place where there shall be a fine climbing done — the more when the young folk are so bold and bonny as the twa of them yonder towards the sunset. . . . What's that? How do I know? . . . Brains, I wonder at ye, I fairly peety you — and that's the truth of it. Where else should he be?"

CHAPTER III

Good-Bye

"I thought it was you," said Miss Bennie May Morgan. "So I waited for you. Aren't you rather out of your own range, Mr. Maxwell? The Morgans'll get you if you don't watch out!"

With elaborate surprise, MacGregor took his bearings from the distant circling hills. "Why so I am! I was on my way to Datil," he explained. "I see now" — he jerked a thumb back over his shoulder — "that I should have ridden east-like this morning instead of west."

"It is shorter that way — and dryer," she agreed. "This road to Datil is very damp after you pass California."

"Shall I ride with you a bit on your way?" said MacGregor. "I can still get back to my camp before sundown. Mind you, I am not saying at all that I shall go to my camp by that hour, but only that there is time enough."

Then Miss Bennie Morgan knew where she stood. She flicked at her stirrup with a meditative quirt. "Why, I said something about like that to you last week at Pictured Rock, didn't I?"

"Very much like that."

"When you got lost today," said Miss Bennie thoughtfully, "I suppose you were composing a sermon?"

"Why, no, I wasnae. It was like this. Clay Mundy set off for Datil early this morning, you see, whilst I staid in camp, shoeing horses. He was riding his Jugador horse — fine I ken the crooked foot of him. And when later in the day I came upon the track of that twisted hoof, I found suddenly a great desire to go after him to Datil, where I have never yet been. And I said to myself, 'Plainly if you follow this track you will come to that place.' And so you see me here."

"And now that you're here, Mr. —— ?"

"Maxwell — not MacGregor," said MacGregor.

"Thank you; Maxwell. Not MacGregor. I must remember that." She turned clear, unflinching eyes upon him. "Well, let's have it!"

"Er — why — eh!" said MacGregor, and swallowed hard. "I don't quite understand you."

"Oh, yes you do!" said Miss Bennie cheerfully. "Don't squirm. What's on your mind?"

"It is now on my mind that it would be none such a bad scheme for me to turn tail bravely and run awa' from this place," said Mac-Gregor, truthfully; quite taken aback at this brisk and matter-of-fact directness.

In her innermost heart Miss Bennie knew certainly — without reason, as women know these things — that this grim old man-at-arms liked her very well, and came as a friend.

"Blackmail? Oh no — that is not in your line. And I do not take you for a tell-tale, either." She looked him over slowly and attentively; a cruel, contemplative glance. It brought a dull glow to MacGregor's leathern face, even before she spoke. "I see!" She dropped the reins and clapped her hands together. "You were planning to take Clay Mundy's place with me — is that it?"

MacGregor plucked up spirit at the taunt. "And that was an unkind speech of you, Miss Morgan."

Her eyes danced at him. "There is but one thing left, then. You have come to plead with me for your friend — your employer — to ask me to spare his youth and innocence — to demand of me, as the phrase goes, if my intentions are honorable. Is that it?"

"It is something verra like that, then, if I must brave your displeasure so far as to say it. And it is my poor opinion that so much was verra needful — though it was in my mind to give you but the bare hint that your secret was stumbled upon. For what one has chanced upon this day another may chance tomorrow. And there was something else besides, which I find ill to put to words to."

The girl dropped all pretense. "I think you meant kindly by me, Mr. MacGregor, and I thank you for it. And you must consider that our case is hard indeed. For where can we meet, if not secretly? Fifty miles each way, every ranch is lined up on one side or the other of this feud. One word to my father's ear will mean bloodshed and death — and then, whoever wins, Bennie Morgan must lose."

"Yet you must meet?" said MacGregor.

She met his eyes bravely. "Yet we must meet!" She said it proudly.

"You two should wed out of hand then, and put the round world between you and this place," said MacGregor.

Miss Bennie sighed. "That is what I tell Clay. It is the only way. Soon or late, if we live here, those two would clash, my father and my husband. If we go away, father may get over it in time. Clay does not want to go. He cannot bear to have it said that he had to run away from San Quentin. But I will never marry him till he is ready to go."

"He is a fool for his pains, and I will be the one who will tell him that same!" declared MacGregor, stoutly. "Him and his pride! He should be proud to run further and faster than ever man rode before on such an argument."

"No — you mustn't say one word to him about me — please! He would be furious — and he is a dangerous man!"

"I thank ye kindly for this unexpected care of my safety," said MacGregor humbly.

"Oh these men! Must you hear that you are so dangerous, too? There would be trouble, and you know it. Clay's as cross as a bear with a sore head, now — so I think he is coming to my way of thinking, and doesn't like to own up. Don't you say anything to him. I'll tell him — not that you have seen me, but that we might so easily be seen — and that our meetings must be few and far between. That will help to make up his mind, too, if he feels — " She checked herself, with a startled shyness in her sudden drooping lids: she was only a young girl, for all her frank and boyish courage. "I will warn him, then. And yet I think there is no man who would not think twice before he whispered evil of Ben Morgan's daughter and" — she held her head proud, she lifted her brave eyes — "and Clay Mundy's sweetheart!"

MacGregor checked his horse, his poor, dull face for once lit up and uplifted: whatever had been best of him in all his wasted and misspent life stirred at the call of her gallant girlhood.

"I think there will be no man so vile as to think an evil thing of you," he said. "Miss Morgan, I was a puir meddlin' fool to come here on such an errand — and yet I am glad that I came, too. And now I shall go back and trouble you nae mair. Yet there is one thing, too, before I turn back — and I think you will not laugh."

She faced him where he stood: so that he carried with him a memory of her dazzling youth against a dazzle of sun. "I shall not laugh."

"It is better than fifty years, they tell me, since last the San Quentin knew any such rains as these," said MacGregor slowly. "This place has the ill name of a desert. Yet all this day the air has been heavy with sweetness; all day long I have ridden stirrup-deep in strange bright flowers — and no man knows the name of them! Fifty years they have slept in the blistered brown earth, the seeds of these nameless flowers, waiting for this year of many rains. Lassie, there are only too many men, like me, of deserved and earned ill name, as of waste places where no good thing can flourish. And when you think of us, I would have you remember how this bright, belated spring-tide came to San Quentin. I would have you think there may be hidden seeds of good in us yet — if only the rains might come! And if ever you have any need of me — as is most unlike — I shall be leal friend to you, I shall stick at nothing in your service. It is so that I would have you think of old MacGregor. Good-bye!"

"I shall not forget," said Bennie. "But you said there was something else — something hard to put into words?"

MacGregor took off his hat. "I think there will be no need to say that — to you," he said.

Once more her eyes searched him and this time he did not flinch — so high he held her now in his thought. She read his answering look. "Yes — since this is the day for plain-speaking, let me say it for you. You mean . . . that it is not only whispering tongues I have to fear, or my father's anger — no, nor black death itself — but that I must fear myself most of all? But, Mr. MacGregor — there was need to say that indeed! And now you are my friend, for I have trusted you very greatly."

"Good-bye, then!" said MacGregor again. He bent over her hand. "Good-bye!"

CHAPTER IV

Skullspring

MacGregor worked out the Whitewater country and moved his camp to Bear Springs, on the southern frontier of the Mundy range. From here he rode the cedar brakes on the high flanks of the mountain, branding late calves. This work was most effectively done at early daybreak and at sundown, when the wild cattle ventured from the thickets into the open glades and valleys.

For a week, Milt Craig had ridden with him. But Milt had made his pack yesterday and moved on to the Cienaga, where MacGregor was to join him later, once he had picked up the few calves that still went unbranded in the Bear Spring country. So today MacGregor rode alone.

Ever drifting from one bunch of cattle to another and then on to another clump of red and white on the next hill-side, as the day wore on he found himself well across in the Wyandotte-Morgan country; prowling in the tangle of hills, south of the Magdalena road, which was the accepted dividing line.

As the sun rode on to afternoon, the prowler turned back, and made his way to Skullspring, with a thought of the trickle of water that dripped from the high cliffs there; and as he came down a ridge of backbone from the upper bench, he saw a little curl of smoke rising above the Skullspring bluff.

MacGregor remarked upon this fact to Neighbor his horse. "We are in a hostile country, Neighbor," said he. "For all we are so quiet and peaceful these days, it will be the part of prudence to have a look into this matter, least we go blundering in where we arenae much wanted." He tied Neighbor in a little hollow of the hill, and went down with infinite precaution to the edge of the cliff above Skullspring.

Three men were by the fire below — all strangers to MacGregor. That gentleman lay flat on the rock, peering through a bush, and looked them over. Clearly, they had only stopped at Skullspring for nooning. Two were cowboys: their saddled horses stood by. The younger of these two stowed a little grub-sack under the seat of a light buggy that stood by the fire. The third person, a tall man of about thirty, had the look of a town-man. He wore a black suit and a "hard-boiled" hat.

"I tell you," said the older cowboy, a sullen-faced young man. "I'll be good and glad a-plenty when this thing is over with. It's a shaky business."

"Don't get cold feet, Joe," advised the tall man. "You're getting big money, mighty big money, for a small risk."

"I notice there's none of these San Quentin *hombres* caring for any of it," grumbled Joe, sulkily.

"Aw, now, be reasonable," said the tall man. "He wouldn't risk letting any of the home people know. Too shaky. You get the chance just because you're a stranger. And because you're a stranger, you can get away without being noticed."

Plainly, here was mischief afoot. It seemed likely to MacGregor that Clay Mundy was to be the object of it.

The younger man of the party spoke up. "I'm not only goin' to get away, but I'm goin' to keep on gettin' away. I'm after that dough all right, all right — but lemme tell you, Mr. Hamerick, this country'll be too hot for me when it's over."

MacGregor barely breathed. It appeared that the tall man was Hamerick, for he answered. "I'm going away myself. But this is too good a chance for easy money, and we don't want to make a hash of it. Keep your nerve. Your part is easy. You take the first right-hand trail and drift south across that saddle-back pass yonder, so you'll get there before I do. You'll find the Bent ranch right under the pass. Nobody there. The Bents have all gone to Magdalena for supplies. Mrs. Bent is going to Socorro and Bent'll wait for her. You're to make yourselves at home, so there won't be anything suspicious — new men working there; sorry the Bents are gone, and all that." He kicked out the dying fire.

"And if anyone comes, then what?" Joe glowered at him with the question.

"Then you're strangers, passing by. It isn't at all likely that any-one'll come. The nearest ranch is twenty-five miles. But if anyone should come, it's all off, for today. We want to have the longest start we can get. And for Mundy, he has his own reasons. You'll ride out to good grass and make camp. If we see your fire, Mundy and me'll turn back. We'll pull it off tomorrow."

Mundy! MacGregor's heart leaped. Were the men to entice Mundy to the Bent ranch and murder him there, while he was off his guard, thinking himself among friends? MacGregor drew his gun, minded to fall upon the plotters without more ado: the vantage of ground more than made up for the odds of numbers. But he put back his gun. They were to separate. He would follow the man Hamerick and deal with him alone.

"I am to meet Mundy at that little sugar-loaf hill yonder, four or five miles out on the plain," said Hamerick. "I'll be late, too — jawing with you fellows this way. Then I'll go on down the wagon road to Bent's with him. The play is that I'm supposed to think the Bent folks are at home. You boys'll have plenty of time to get settled down."

"If we don't run into a wasp's nest," said Joe sulkily.

Hamerick scowled. "I'm the one that's taking the biggest risk, with this damned buggy — but I've got to have it, to play the part. I'll leave it, once I get safe back to my saddle."

"We three want to ride in three different directions," said Joe. "I wish it was over."

Hamerick gave him a sinister look. "You get no money till I get a-straddle of a horse again — I'll tell you that right now, my laddie-buck! This buggy's too easy to track up, if anything goes wrong.

You'd like it first-rate to ride off scot-free and leave me to hold the sack."

"I won't, eh!" Joe took a step forward, his ugly face blotched with crimson. "Damn you, I've took just about enough from you!"

Here the younger man interposed. "Oh, you both make me sick!" His voice was cutting and cold, venomous in its unforced evenness. "I guess I'll do a little telling now, myself. If you fellows get to fighting, I'll do my best to kill both of you. Got that?"

MacGregor almost hugged himself with delight. Oh, if they once get to shooting—if they only would! he thought. It would be a strange thing if between the four of us we should not do a good day's work of it!

"Now, now, Tait—"

"Don't Tait me!" said Tait, in the same deadly level. "This is a wise bunch for a ticklish job, ain't it? I know that no one but a dirty skunk would be found in such dirty work—but is that any reason why we should be fools, too? Hamerick's right, Joe. We'll string along with him till he gets to a saddle—and then may the devil take the hindmost! Maybe we'll find a saddle at the Bent ranch. If we do, all the better. The sooner I see the last of you two, the better pleased I'll be. For you Hamerick—you're engineerin' this thing, but when it comes down to brass tacks, I'm the best man, and don't you forget it. So if you've been plannin' any nice little plans to hold out part of the price on me and Joe, you can throw 'em over for excess baggage, right here. For I'm to put it up to the paymaster, right to your face —you won't have no chance to fool us. Now don't give up any more head to me! You'll stick to me against Joe till you're horseback again, with a fair chance for a getaway; Joe'll stick to me till we get a fair divvy on the money—and if either of you don't like it, you can double up on me whenever you feel lucky. I'm ready for you both any turn in the road."

The challenge went unmet. It was plain that Tait was to be master. MacGregor waited for no more. He rolled back from the bare rim with scarce more noise than a shadow would have made. He crawled to the nearest huddle of rocks and hid away. For a little, the muffled murmur of angry voices floated to him; then came the sound of wheels and a ringing of shod feet on rock; Tait and Joe toiled up the trail beyond the cliff-end, paced slowly by, black against the sky line, and dipped down into a dark hollow that twisted away towards Bent's Pass.

The tingling echoes died; and then MacGregor climbed back to Neighbor. The game was in his hands. Keeping to the ridge, he would gain a long mile on the wagon road, deep in the winding pass.

He was in high feather as he followed the plunging slope; he laughed as he rode; his eyes drank in the brightness of the day. This would be a rare jest to tell at campfires!

"Now I wonder who can be at the bottom of this bonny scheme?" he chuckled. "It doesnae sound much like the San Quentin folk, who, if reports be true, are accustomed to do their own murders. And, if the man Hamerick tells the whole story, what then? That will be for Mundy to say. Any rate, 'tis a fine thing for Clay Mundy that my dry throttle drove me to Skullspring just at that time."

When he came into the wagon road the buggy was just before him, close to the mouth of the pass. MacGregor struck into a gallop.

The stranger had been going at a brisk gait, but at sight of the horseman he slowed to a prim and mincing little trot.

"A fine day, sir," said MacGregor civilly, as he rode alongside.

"It certainly is," said the stranger. He was plainly ill at ease at this ill-timed meeting, but tried to carry it off. "How far is it to Old Fort Tularosa, can you tell me?"

MacGregor squinted across the plain. "A matter of forty miles, I should say. Goin' across?"

The stranger shook his head. "Not today. I think I will camp here for the night and have a look in the hills for a deer. You're not going to the Fort yourself, are you?"

MacGregor grinned cheerfully. Knowing what he did, he knew that this was Hamerick's device to try to shake off his unwelcome company. "Well, no; not today. The fact is, sir" — he bent over close and sunk his voice to a confidential whisper — "the fact is, if you're for camping here the night, I must even camp here, too."

"What!"

"Just that. And first of all, do you remark this little gun which I hold here in my hand? Then I will ask you to stop and to get out upon this side, holding to your lines verra carefully lest the beastie should run away, while I search you for any bit weapons of your ain. For you spoke very glibly of hunting a deer — and yet I do not see any rifle."

Hamerick groaned as he climbed out; he had not thought of that. "I haven't any rifle. My revolver is under the cushion — but of course you can search me, if you think I've got another. What the devil do you want anyway? If it's money you're after, you'll get most mighty little."

"All in good time, all in good time," said MacGregor cheerfully. He went through Hamerick for arms; finding none, he went through the buggy, finding the gun under the cushion. He inspected this carefully, tried it, and stuck it in his waistband.

"Will you kindly go aside some few steps, sir?" said MacGregor politely. "I am dry, and I would have a good swig of water from your canteen, but I didnae wish to set myself in that defenseless posture of holding a canteen to my throat whilst ye were still armed."

"You see I have no money, you have my gun, you have your drink — what more do you want of me?" spluttered Hamerick. "Let me go! I have an appointment — I'll be late now."

"With that deer, ye are meaning?" MacGregor sat cross-legged on the ground and whittled off a pipeful of tobacco with loving care. He puffed a while in great satisfaction, watching his fuming captive with twinkling eyes. "Do you know, sir," he said at last, between whiffs, "that is my puir opeenion, if you knew how you are like to keep that appointment of yours, you would be little made up with it?"

Hamerick stammered. He had no idea of what his captor was driving at, but he had his own reasons for great uneasiness. He pulled himself together with an effort. "I — I don't know what you mean. I see now that you are not a robber, as I first thought. You are mistaking me for some other man. You can't be doing yourself any possible good by keeping me here. I tell you I am waited for."

"Take my word for it, sir — if you knew my way of it, you would be less impatient for that tryst of yours."

"What — what the devil do you mean?"

"I will tell you then, Mr. Hamerick." At this unexpected sound of his own name, Hamerick started visibly. "If Clay Mundy is at all of my mind, this is what we shall do: We will set you on Clay Mundy's horse and put Clay Mundy's hat upon your head; and we two will get in your bit wagon and drive you before our guns — just at dusk, d'ye mind? — to the Bent ranch; and there, if I do not miss my guess, you will be shot to death by hands of your own hiring!"

Here MacGregor, gloating on that pleasant inward vision, was extremely disconcerted by the behavior of his prospective victim. So far from being appalled, Hamerick was black with rage; he stamped, he shook his fist, he struggled for speech in a choking fury.

"You fool! You poor spy! Idiot! Bungler! Why couldn't you tell me you were Mundy's man?"

"Steady, there! Are you meaning to face it out that you did not plan to murder Clay Mundy? Because we are going on now to see him."

Hamerick gathered up the reins eagerly. "Come on, then, damn you — before it's too late!" There was relief and triumph in his voice — and at the sound of it MacGregor sickened with a guess at the whole dreadful business; the bright day faded. "Me, kill Clay Mundy? Why,

you poor, pitiful bungler, Clay Mundy brought me here to play
preacher for him!"

MacGregor drew back. His face flamed; his eyes were terrible. He
jerked out Hamerick's gun and threw it at Hamerick's feet. There
was a dreadful break in his voice. "Protect yourself!" he said.

But Hamerick shrank back, white-lipped, cringing. "I won't! I
won't touch it!"

"Cur!"

"Oh, don't kill me, don't murder me!" Hamerick was wringing his
hands; he was almost screaming.

MacGregor turned shamed eyes away. He took up Hamerick's gun.
"Strip the harness from that horse then, take the bridle and ride! And
be quick, lest I think better of it. Go back the way you came, and
keep on going! For I shall tell your name and errand, and there is no
man of Morgan's men but will kill you at kirk or gallows-foot."

He watched in silence as Hamerick fled. Then he rode down the
pass, sick-hearted, brooding, grieving. He came to the mouth of the
pass: at the plain's edge he saw a horseman, near by, coming swiftly.
It was Clay Mundy.

CHAPTER V

No Dwelling More on Sea or Shore

MacGregor slowed up. The flush of burning wrath had died away;
his face was set to a heavy, impassive mask. He thrust Hamerick's gun
between his left knee and the stirrup-leather and gripped it there. He
rode on to meet Clay Mundy — and the nameless flowers of San Quentin were stirrup-high about him as he rode.

He drew rein so Mundy should come to his right side; and again,
as at their first meeting, he laid both hands on the saddle horn as he
halted.

Clay Mundy's face was dark with suspicion.

"Have you seen a fool in a buggy?" he demanded.

"I see a fool on a horse!" responded MacGregor calmly. "For
the person you seek, I have put such a word in his ear that he will
never stop this side of tidewater. What devil's work is this, Clay
Mundy?"

"You damned meddler! Are you coward as well as meddler, that
you dare not move your hands?"

"Put up your foolish gun, man — you cannae fricht me with it. The thing is done and shooting will never undo it. There will be no mock-marriage this day, nor ony day — and now shoot, if you will, and damned to you! Man! Have ye gone clean daft? Or did ye wish to proclaim it that ye were no match for the Morgans in war? And did ye think to live the week out? That had been a chance had you married her indeed, with bell and book — as whaur could ye find better mate? But after such black treachery as ye meant — Man, ye are not in your right mind, the devil is at your ear!"

"It is hard to kill a man who will not defend himself," said Mundy thickly. "I spared your life once because you amused me — "

"And because it was a verra judeecious thing, too — and you are well knowing to that same. Think ye I value my life owre high, or that I fear ye at all, that I come seeking you? Take shame to yourself, man! Have a better thought of it yet! Say you will marry the lassie before my eyes, and I will go with you on that errand; or turn you back and I will go with her back to the house of the Morgans — and for her sake, I will keep your shame to mysel'. Or, if it likes you better, you may even fall to the shooting."

"Fool!" said Mundy. "I can kill you before you can touch your gun."

"It is what I doubt," said MacGregor. "Please yourself. For me there is but the clean stab of death — but you must leave behind the name of a false traitor to be a hissing and a byword in the mouths of men."

"I will say this much, that I was wrong to call you coward," said Mundy, in a changed voice. "You are a bold and stubborn man, and I think there is a chance that you might get your gun — yes, and shoot straight, too. I will not marry the girl — but neither will I harm her. But I will not be driven further. I am not willing to skulk away while you tell her your way of the story. That would be too sorry a part. I will go on alone, and tell her, and send her home."

"You will say your man fled before the Morgans, or was taken by them, or some such lies, and lure her on to her ruin," said MacGregor. "I will not turn back."

"I will give you the minute to turn back," said Mundy.

"It is what I will never do!"

"Then you will die here," said Mundy.

"Think of me as one dead an hour gone," said MacGregor steadily. "My life is long since forfeit to every law of God or man. I am beyond the question. Think rather of yourself. You have the plain choice before you — a bonny wife to cherish, and bairns to your knee — life and love, peace and just dealing and quiet days — or at the other hand but dusty death and black shame to the back of that!"

As a snake strikes, Mundy's hand shot out: he jerked MacGregor's gun from the scabbard and threw it behind him. His face lit up with ferocious joy.

"You prating old windbag! How about it now? I'll be driven by no man on earth, much less by a wordy old bluffer like you."

"You used other speech but now. Ye are false in war as in love. But I carenae for hard words, so you deal justly with the lassie. Wed her with me to witness, or let her go free."

"Talk to the wind!" said Mundy.

"For the last time, Mundy, give it up! In the name of God!"

"Get off that horse and drag it! I give you your life — you're not worth my killing. Never be seen on the San Quentin again!"

"Mundy — "

"Get off, I say!" Mundy spurred close, his cocked gun swung shoulder high.

"Aweel," said MacGregor. He began to slide off slowly, his right hand on the saddle horn; his left hand went to the gun at his left knee; he thrust it up under Neighbor's neck and fired once, twice — again! Crash of flames, roaring of gun shots: he was on his back, Neighbor's feet were in his ribs; he fired once more, blindly, from under the trampling feet.

Breathless, crushed, he struggled to his knees, the blood pumping from two bullet-holes in his great body. A yard away, Clay Mundy lay on his face, crumpled and still, clutching a smoking gun.

"I didnae touch his face," said MacGregor. He threw both guns behind him; he turned Mundy over and opened his shirt. One wound was in his breast, close beside his heart; another was through the heart. MacGregor looked down upon him.

"The puir, mad, misguided lad!" he said between pain-wrung lips. "Surely he was gone horn-mad with hate and wrong and revenge."

He covered the dead man's face, and straightened the stiffening arms, and sat beside him: he looked at the low sun, the splendor of the western range; he held his hand to his own breast to stay the pulsing blood.

"And the puir lassie — she will hear this shameful tale of him! Had I looked forward and killed yonder knave Hamerick, she had blamed none but me. 'Twas ill done. . . . Ay, but she's young still. She will have a cave and a fire of her own yet."

There was silence a little space, and his hand slipped. Then he opened his dulling eyes:

"Hullo, Central! . . . Give me Body, please. . . . Hullo, Body! Hullo! That you, Body? . . . MacGregor's Soul, speaking. I am going away. Good luck to you — good-bye! . . . I don't know where."

Maid
Most Dear

MAID MOST DEAR

On the second day out, Eddie Early rode from the ferry up and up
across the yellow staircase mesas, over the high foothill range of Cuchillo Negro and down into Fairview for the night. On the third day
he turned to the northeast by the Yaples ranch to follow up through the
pines in a valley steep, narrow and winding, on a dim road which
crossed at every turn the onset of a little brawling river; through the
ghost towns which were once Robinson and Grafton. Beyond Grafton
he came to a deserted sawmill, where a mossy water-wheel turned forever, and his voice rang hollow on the great empty floor. Roundabout
were ruin and decay, thickets of tangled greenery where merry life
had been, staunch high stone of old fireplaces above fallen roofs and
rotted timbers and crumbled walls.

But here the rippling water still was gay to chuckle and sing, cool
and clear, brimming down the gray flume to plunge, splashing, into
the swaying and misty buckets of the old wheel, turning, turning
always, steadily, slowly, creaking, half in shadow and half in sun.
Above flume end and circling buckets, sunlit and spray drenched, a
rainbow fragment flashed and dazzled and danced, a miracle of confused and whirling senses, color, form and motion blended indistin-
guishably with the sound of falling water. Eddie blinked and shook
his head; he almost thought that mill-wheel was a dream.

He turned to the left here, up and up again, to the Continental
Divide, the Black Range. This pass, Fairview had told him, was nine
thousand feet above the sea; and from its crest Eddie looked down
upon a tossing limitless green sea, aspen and spruce and fir and pine,

wave after wave of twisting and knuckled ridges, troughs of inter-
twined and looping valleys; so twisting, vague and tangled, so endless
and vast, that those green waves seemed dizzily to ripple and flow, to
rise and fall; where island peaks thrust up above the welter, the wearied
eye clung gladly, grateful for something fixed and certain in this reeling and rushing chaos.

He turned down the Pacific Slope. A plunging league of greenwood, a league of broken glades; strange and unreal, as if he had
traveled in time as well as in space, he came into a dim and dreamy
world, a world of narrow farms, curved with the plunging valleys of
rail fences, ox teams, and log houses with clapboard roofs.

Women wore sunbonnets and the men, youngsters excepted, were
bearded. Those youngsters were few. Youth had passed on beyond
those high horizons to the rumored, fantastic far-off world. Here was
a country of old men and boys. They wore hickory shirts, they had
ropes of plaited rawhide, home-forged bits, and such saddles as were
made ten years before, twenty, thirty; even, once or twice, the old
time saddles with dinner plate horns, brass-studded, and a leather over-
skirt laced above all the saddle rig, with heavy wooden stirrups, five
inches wide. They used black powder rifles, clean and well-kept,
forty-four repeaters and the long forty-five-ninety; and he saw double-
barreled muzzle-loading shotguns in passing wagons.

Eddie found lodging for the night with a friendly farmer named
Akers. The house was in a great yard where hollyhocks grew, and
marigolds — a long log house with covered galleries between alternate
rooms. In these galleries hung scythes, guns, saddles; two-handled
cross-cut saws, bright double-bitted axes, augers of all sizes, a hundred things beside. Old-time ways held unchanged here; a well-sweep
by the kitchen door, bear skin rugs in the living room, water in cedar
buckets, a drinking gourd. Barefooted towheads whisked around corners or peered shyly through doors; grown daughters, smooth-haired
and buxom, helped their mother at a vast stick-and-clay fireplace, with
a great crane and a row of dutch ovens. A long table with a gay oil-
cloth cover, where Eddie ate supper with his host and the two oldest
boys; the women and children to eat later; fried chicken, corn bread,
corn on the cob, white butter, honey, apple pie and buttermilk; barley
hay and corn for the Cry Baby horse; dusk and moonlight, the crickets
calling in the dew, a corn-husk mattress to his bed, a Rising Sun
quilt, and deep dreams — of a splashing mill-wheel, turning, steady
and slow.

On the morrow in the cool freshness between dawn and day, the
Akers family stood before the log house to wave farewell to him. He

took a ridge trail according to directions, leaving the settlements. At nine Eddie was thankful for his slicker, a weight hitherto begrudged. A slow rain came with mist and fog; the sun was lost, the landmark hills were blotted out. Noon came and passed; and the traveler came to have grave doubts as to where his travels were tending. He found a hundred ridges and twenty trails, each ridge the same, each trail washed clean and trackless; little wandering rivers — so the dry country names them — three feet wide, ten, twenty; singing mirthful, and cheerfully running uphill, contrary to regulations and experience. It had been hours since Eddie's last guess at north or south, and now, in the dripping mist, he did not know up from down. Reason assured him, at each foot-high Niagara, that this water flow was downward; but his eyes refused to confirm these findings. So far as his eyes could influence him, every way was up.

"Cry Baby," said Eddie Early, " 'we are lost, the captain shouted, as he staggered up the stairs.' You and me, we thought we was old hands, down in the desert, with mountain ranges every which-a-way to show us what was what and a sky right overhead to tell us which way was up. Every damn way is up, here. We're in a hole under the cellar under the bottomless pit."

Cry Baby whimpered. He had always made little whinnying answers to his rider's remarks, from which endearing habit he had earned his name. But this was a real whimper, with feeling in it. Cry Baby knew very well that they were lost in this dim, rainy place, and he looked with apprehension at the horrible green stuff on the ground, so different from the gray grama of his beloved desert. "Oh, why did we ever leave our happy home?" said Cry Baby, plain as plain.

Wisps and streamers of fog clung in the pine tops. The vast horizons of the desert were shrunken to a wavering, mist-walled circle, moving with them through the thin forest, veiling all contours to sameness.

Eddie scouted to left, to right, prospecting new ridges and valleys, finding only the unbroken greenwood, the same dim aimless trails, no trace of use or habitation. With the first rains, evidently, the cattle had deserted the pine wood country for the high grassy plains, where now they could find precarious water at tank and *tinaja*. Eddie's watch said Twelve. It said One, and Cry Baby pricked sharp ears to the right and paused unbidden, midstep, one front foot absurdly checked a-curve in air.

"Hey, what do you think you are — a statue of Stop, Look and Listen?" said Eddie, chiding, but turning eyes where those brown ears pointed. Small sounds came from that quarter of the universe, uncer-

tain at first, then clearer, nearer, steadier; a shadowy bulk moved
vaguely through the mist, darkened and took shape; another horseman broke through from outer space into the dim circle of the
dwindled day. Cry Baby expressed his relief by a deep and vigorous
sigh. Unbidden once again, he stepped out briskly to meet the res-
cuers.

The new horse was a black horse, mud bespattered and something
weary, who bore himself aloof and haughtily incurious as to outsiders. The new man was dark, slender, young. A leather chin-strap
held a battered shapeless hat a-slant; in lieu of a slicker he wore bat-
winged chaps, old and scratched and torn, with a short and sadly worn
canvas jacket; the turned-up collar buttoned high at the neck, with
an effect weirdly Elizabethan. Above that collar rose a face like a
flame, bold, reckless and exultant, sparkling with eager life; a scratched
and mud-spotted face, with a quizzical mouth, shrewd black eyes and
a black foretop damply askew beneath the tilted and curving brim of
that work-worn hat. This was a hand. A gallant face, a strong face;
about twenty-five, thought Eddie, from the rueful vantage of ten
added years. Eddie noted with private amusement that this mud-
splashed face was smoothly shaven beneath the mud — freshly shaved,
here, back of beyond! — This fact might be useful. For it is not permitted to the cowman to be mastered by events, and Eddie felt himself placed on the defensive. Lost, a grown man — here was occasion
for ill-timed levity! His bronze face became guardedly expressionless.

"Which way you goin', stranger?" The black eyes were a-dance.

"With you," said Eddie, firmly.

"Not lost, I hope?"

"Oh, no. Just stealing cattle."

The black eyes swept slowly up and down the folds of Eddie's
voluminous slicker and the black brows arched in faint surprise.

"Not working at it today," Eddie explained. "Had an accident. . . .
Broke my bottle of bay rum. Too bad! So I quit everything and
pulled out for a fresh supply."

The stranger rubbed a finger delicately over a smooth cheek. Then
he twisted the silken wisp of mustache above a mirthful mouth. The
eyes crinkled.

"Come with me and you will find everything required by your
blond loveliness. You're sure in luck. I'm the only man in this place
that keeps it in stock. In fact, I'm the only man in the place."

"Nice place," said Eddie. "Roomy and everything."

"This place," said its inhabitant, "is called Salsipuedes. Do that into
English and it means — "

"Yeah, I know. It means 'Get out if you can.' Not what I called it, exactly. . . . No. But it's a good name. Fits fine. Anyway, I never crossed my own tracks, not once. Of course, I knew all along that the bark is thickest on the north side of a dog — but I didn't know which way was north."

The Salsipuedan laughed. He had accurately sized up the older and larger man. This man was a hand. An old hand, not further to be deviled. "No call to feel hacked, old-timer. In this fog, the oldest man in the world couldn't find his way without a bell. I'm letting my horse take me home — and I've been here four months. Every hill and hollow just like every other one."

"I noticed a certain similarity," said Eddie, "but I thought it was the same hill. Speaking of names, mine's Early."

"I'm Jackson. Tumble T hand, working odd corners for calves the wagon missed. Skid Jackson, more favorably known by my own fireside as Beefsteak John. Let's ride."

"In that case, call me Eddie. And yet — tarry a bit, as Uncle Jerry used to say. Your camp, now — is it on my way to Shard, Alma, Springerville and parts west? I'm looked for."

"So am I," said Skid. "They'll never find you. Best place in the world."

"Expected, I mean. Agreed to be in Holbrook on a set day. Good man depends on me to be there. So if your camp leads me in that general direction — ?" He pushed his hat back as he spoke. An amber crest rose inquiringly, bearing a broad forehead, strangely white between sun-bronze cheek and honey-colored hair.

"It doesn't. It lies to the south, and you want to head northwest. But there's a wagon road from my camp on, and in all this fog — Where did you start from this morning, anyhow?"

"The Jeff Akers place, on Cress Creek."

Skid whistled. "Man, you're right back where you started and way to the south. No wonder you didn't cross your own tracks. Two o'clock, nearly, and the fog getting thicker. You figure it out. Come onto camp, let your horse rest and fill up on corn and good barley hay. Start soon in the mornin' and you can make up a lot of it. Ranch every few miles, beyond Shard, so you can push on as far as you like and find a place to petrify when you're ready."

"Beefsteak, you said?"

"The finest. Mr. Early, did you ever notice how much better other people's beef tastes than your own?"

"Why no," said Eddie, hesitating. "No — I never noticed that." He paused, reflecting. "I never ate any of my own beef."

2

No clouds were in the clean-swept sky, none on the far-off mountains. For eight hours Eddie had ridden through the windless golden day; slowly, as befits a horseman. Leaving the Tumble T line-camp, he had dropped below the pines to oak, walnut, cedar and piñon, to rolling hills, turning up the deep winding cañon of Willow Creek, branch of the many-branched Gila. The cañon narrowed, between cliffs, widened to little valley farms, narrowed again to a box cañon curving between great red hills. The road climbed over a rocky promontory. Far in the west, he glimpsed the prodigious bulk of the Mogollon ,Mountains, beyond which lay his road through Alma, "the outlaw Capital," and on to Holbrook. He dropped down to join Willow Creek again, twisting through a maze of cedared hills. At a sudden bend, he came upon Shard unawares.

Shard was unprepossessing; Eddie's nose wrinkled in displeasure. Tatterdemalion cabins, with crazy fences, clung to the hill foot; a small dingy, weatherbeaten store neighbored a large dingy and weatherbeaten saloon. Faded letters on the two false fronts announced the one as

THE GILA MERCHANDISE COMPANY

and the saloon as

THE FIRST CHANCE

A huge mulberry tree threw a black shade over the plank platform before the saloon and a wide circle of the road, and there a dozen horses stood with dropped reins, patiently waiting the leisure of their lords. Loud talk jostled through the open door. Eddie went in.

Card players at a rear table glanced up. Booted and spurred, gun-belted, boisterous, a noisy line elbowed the bar, turning, some of them, as Eddie came in. Their faces were sodden, puffy, stupid. Eddie stood at the bar end, waiting. The men raised their glasses; the biggest bawled out a drunken toast:

"Here's to us, and to hell with the rest!"

Eddie beckoned. "A small whisky, please."

The barkeeper was bald-headed, with a cast in one eye, and a furtive, sneering face. "Any place here where they serve meals?" asked Eddie, as he took change for a dollar bill.

The bull-necked toast-giver hammered on the bar, and broke into a maudlin roar.

"A little service here, Ben!"

Eddie took a step aside till he stood with the end of the bar before him. "Mr. Ben is engaged at present," he said. His voice was cheerful, but his quiet eye held steadily on the one that wanted service; who glared truculently, opened his mouth to roar again, but thought better of it.

"Speak up, Mr. Ben. We don't want to keep the gentlemen waiting."

"There's a sort of a hotel around the bend a ways," mumbled the bartender.

A pleasant voice rose from the card table. "They only serve dinner between twelve and one. Home folks, home cooking. Doubt if you can get a meal there this time of day. Neighboring now, likely. Still, you might try."

"Thanks," said Eddie. But his eye did not wander. "I won't bother them. Get me some truck from the store. That will do me." He took three sidewise steps to the door, and disappeared.

"Seems like the hungry guy had it on you, McCabe," said his next neighbor, laughing discordantly. "What's the matter? Buffaloed?"

"Just that. You're a damned fool, Slagle — but I'm not. Both my hands was on the bar and his wasn't. And he had a mean gray eye. I seen it. Not good enough. Come on. Drinks is on me."

"Well, if you want to let him get off with that line of stuff, it's your lookout," said Slagle. "I wouldn't if it was me — that's all."

"Anyway, I butted in on him," said the big man.

"Yes, and you butted right out again," Slagle shrugged his shoulders. "If you're satisfied, I am. But you're some easy pleased."

Eddie bought a feed of corn from a graybeard in the store. With his knife he shaped a gunny sack to an improvised nosebag. He led Cry Baby to an open shed behind the store, unsaddled, tied him and hung the nose bag on a whinnying nose. Then he bought crackers, cheese and a tin of sardines. He opened the sardines at the counter; as an afterthought, he handed belt and gun to the graybeard. "Keep this for me till I'm ready to start," he said. Carrying these purchases, he went back into the saloon. A vacant table, littered with old newspapers, stood near a tall and rusty stove, which doubled as a waste basket in warm weather. Eddie drew up a chair, sat sidewise by this table and called for a bottle of beer. "And a glass, please," he added. "All right for me to eat here, if I spread an old newspaper on the table?"

"Sure," said the barkeep, "Help yourself. I'll open the beer and pour you out a glassful so it won't slop. Tray here, somewheres. I'll bring that."

Eddie took a deep pull at his beer. "Cold," he murmured with satisfaction. He sliced cheese and built a little pile of sandwiches; he

speared a sardine with his jackknife, and began on his first sandwich.
The noisy crew at the bar huddled together, with a busy gabble of
undertones. The huddle broke and one man stepped out into the
open space before Eddie, ten feet away. He planted his feet well
apart for steadiness. "Hey, you! Come have a drink," he said. It
was the man called Slagle. His face was mottled, sweating, drink-
inflamed.

Eddie glanced up, and jerked a thumb toward his beer glass. "No,
thanks. This beer will be all I can manage." He spoke with a mouthful of cracker crumbs.

Slagle jerked his gun. "Damn your impydent soul, you'll drink or
die! I'll show you!"

"Uncle Jerry always said I'd be killed in a barroom," said Eddie,
sadly. He bit into another sandwich.

"Aw, Slagle, cut it out. He ain't got no gun." This was the burly
loud-mouthed man who had asked for service; he twisted his shaggy
beard. Eddie turned gray eyes his way.

"Right, old Buffalo! Left my gun at the store, seein' you boys was
pretty well lit up. Thought that would leave me out of it." He
drained his glass of beer and picked up a sardine between finger and
thumb.

"Come on Slagle. Put your gun up," said the big man. "He ain't
hurtin' you."

"Shet your fool head, McCabe. I'm doing this! When I tell a man
to drink, he drinks."

Eddie shook his head regretfully. "Can't do it — not after I declared
myself. Bad example for the children. Can't back down."

"Then I'll kill you like a dog."

"Do that," said Eddie.

An angry voice rose from the card table, "Slagle, you drunken
fool —"

Slagle snarled, without turning his head. "Your guns is all behind
the bar. Try to get 'em!" The barrel of his cocked .45 dropped until
it pointed directly at Eddie's waistband.

"Now, you!" He broke into a murderous frenzy of obscenity.

A cracked and horrified falsetto shrilled from the card table. "You
fool, thath Eddie Early from Thalamanca, and if you thoot him that
way, and him with no gun, them fellowth will come up here and kill
every thon-of-a-gun in your outfit! If you wath thober —"

"Why, it's Lithpin Tham!" cried Eddie. "Sam, what are you doing
way up here?"

"I'm counting five!" said Slagle. "One! . . . Two!" From the corner of his eye, Eddie saw two men rise from the card table, saw a chair whirl up. "Three!"

"Look out, Slagle!" screamed the bartender. A chair crashed into Slagle's neck, his gun jerked, roaring; a second chair whirled through the air; he ducked.

Eddie Early pounced on the fallen gun and whirled. "Hell, you needn't put your hands up," he observed, speaking to Slagle's companions. "Shootin' you boys would be just murder, full as you are. Just hold steady."

The card players rushed behind the bar and grabbed their guns; Eddie rubbed his knuckles ruefully, and turned to contemplate his fallen foe. His fist had caught Slagle on the jaw; but as Slagle had crouched with his head turned, right fist had crashed into right jaw — a thing which may never have chanced before. The results were disastrous. Slagle fell over a chair, struck on head and neck. His body followed, rolling on, feet up with the impetus of that diving fall to poise precariously on its own shoulders, and toppled over, his legs straddled the disused stove, and brought it down; he lay with his head under him, the stove on him, and a cloud of soot from fallen stovepipe blackly glorious over all. The victor regarded him with some perplexity.

"I never saw him do that before," said Eddie.

Two cowboys dragged the fallen from the wreck. One knelt and listened. "No, he's breathing — sort of," he said. "Hell, that's too bad."

"You fellows had better get your waggish friend away from here," said Eddie. "Advise him a lot. If he doesn't mend his ways, somebody's going to sever his jocular vein."

Stumbling, muttering, the festal party carried Slagle out to the mulberry. The big man paused at the door to say: "No grudge. He had it a coming."

Eddie turned to Lithpin Tham. "Sam, you threw that chair. I saw you. Didn't think you had it in you."

"I'm thurprithed mythelf," said Sam, sheepishly. "Mithter Early, that ith the firth dethent thing I've done thinth I robbed a lawyer. But you never wath tho damned thuperior ath the reth of your crowd, and I thort of hated to thee you thot. . . . Mithter Early, this ith Bud Wilthon, that threw the other chair."

"Much obliged, Bud," said Eddie.

"Pleased to meet you," said Wilson. "And these three poor dumbbells are Shorty, Sooner and Dutch. No matter which is which. They're all poor fish. We're the whole C A P outfit."

"Dumb," agreed one of them. "Bud's the boss — so you can see how triflin' we are."

"I thuppoth," said Sam ruefully, "I might ath well be movin' on?" He looked up at Eddie with a vague wistfulness in his eye.

Wilson clapped him on the shoulder. "Shucks, Sam — we was all onto you, long ago. You didn't win any of our money, did you? Why, you dealt me four cold jacks, a while ago, and I didn't even stay."

"Oh!" said Sam. "I thought I'd thlipt."

"And we held out four cards on you," said Wilson. "One little spade, heart, diamond and club — passing 'em around, under the table, as needed. So that's all right. You stick around, Tham. I'll tell you what — you come out and wrangle horses for us a spell. I sort of like the way you handle a chair. Real prompt and earnest."

"Mithter Wilthon, you've done hired a wrangler," said Sam.

"Now for the unfinished business," said Eddie.

Dutch stared at him. "Great Scott, what you goin' to do now — start a morgue? I'd say you did a complete job already."

"Not at all," said Eddie. "Introduce me to the bartender."

"Ben Hill — you come here!" said Dutch.

Ben Hill shambled out from behind the bar, wiping his hands and smirking nervously. "This is it," said Dutch.

Eddie regarded Ben Hill in silence; Mr. Hill's oily smile faded. Eddie thrust out a long arm and a pointing finger, and paused. . . . Ben Hill cringed. " 'Look out, Slagle!' says you! . . . Me unarmed — you with plenty guns under the bar, and a sawed-off shotgun, too, or I miss my guess — Slagle working himself up to murder me . . . 'Look out, Slagle!' " He clutched Ben Hill's collar and jerked him down to his knees. "Roll out a whisky barrel, boys. Spreadeagle him, and I'll put the belt to him. Gimme a belt, somebody."

"Maybe we oughtn't to do that," said Wilson, dubiously. "We have to live here, you know."

"That's why you want to teach him to protect his customers. Live here myself, maybe," said Eddie. "I like Shard. Liveliest little town south of the Smith and Wesson line. Want to make the home town better and brighter. Stretch him out."

"You tempt me," said Bud. "We really ought to get a permit from the Forest Ranger, but here goes. Grab him, boys."

They stretched the luckless wretch across a barrel. He yelled, screamed, threatened death and fire. Eddie punched the cartridges from a heavy belt and grasped it firmly by the buckle end. "One for all and all for each! About three licks apiece? Want in, Tham?"

"Not me," said Lithpin Tham. "He detherveth it, of courth. But what if I got my dethervinths? Count me out. I'm gone. And you'd better take that thawed-off thot gun when you go. Get me?"

"I get you," said Eddie. "Fifteen, it is, then. You keep count, Mr. Hill, and if I don't stop when I get to fifteen, you mention it."

"Slagle and his friends are gone," said Bud. "Guess he wasn't hurt much."

"Just between us girls," said Sooner McCoy, "what are you going to do with that shotgun? You'll look right quaint ridin' down the street with that thing across the horn of your saddle."

"Yes, but think how quaint I'd look being carried along with the Dead March and no mourners," said Eddie. "Even if folks laugh at me, it'll be quite some comfort to know that I'm still able to hear 'em. That will help me to put up with it. Well, I got to get my gun from the store and saddle up."

Bud walked along with him. "It's high time we was pulling out for the ranch, ourselves. Won't you side with us, Mr. Early? 'Bout thirty miles out."

"Thanks just the same. By good rights, I ought to be going, but my idea of true politeness demands that I stick around a spell. Barkeep or this man Slagle may not be just satisfied. Guess I'll lay over twenty-four hours — say till after dinner tomorrow. They can't expect me to hang up here all fall to wait their convenience."

"Ben is just trash. But you might keep an eye on him," said Bud. "I really can't say about Slagle. All that bunch are K P men. Queer outfit. Been here two-three years. Tough, but they ain't friendly. Don't mix. Never ask anyone to the ranch, and if you drop in they're just barely civil. Little bunch of cattle, just off the Forest Reserve. They're not stealing cattle. Don't half work their own, and twice the men they need. Half of them ain't hands at all and the best are none too good. They hell around the little towns, but they don't ever all leave the ranch at once. Never less than two of 'em right there at the home ranch. Kirby and Payne, they're the owners. They're citified, but they're tough too. Only not our kind of tough. Not our sort of people, none of 'em, except Tom Copeland. Don't belong here. Something off-colored about the whole kit and bilin' of 'em. I don't see as you've got any call to wait to see how Slagle likes it — not if you don't feel that way. He asked for it."

"Oh, I'll wait a reasonable length of time to see if he wants some more. But it's a damn nuisance. My lunch got spilled, too," grumbled Eddie, saddling Cry Baby. "One swell place to get hung up, Shard.

What kind of a name is that for a town, anyway? Shard! How come?"

"Indian Pottery. Shard Springs, it was. Fritz Aude settled there and gave it the name. But, man — this isn't Shard, here. This is Hell's Bend. Just the off-scourings and riffraff. Hop that horse and I'll show you the cleanest, greenest little burg between hither and yon."

They doubled a sharp hill-corner; Bud reined in and threw out a hand. "There! Cowboy, you don't know your luck!"

The creek made half a mile of sweeping curve, the road followed the creek, and thrifty trees made the road shady; beyond the trees was a crescent of pleasant homes, some twenty in all, set well back from the road, pleasant with orchard, garden and yard.

Bud held his head high, his eyes sparkled. "Don't that look like home? Hear them bees — and the turtle doves cooing! Don't that look some different from Hell's Bend?"

"Oh yes, if you insist. Maybe, a little. This so-called hotel now — can you steer me to it?"

"We go back the other way," said Bud. "You come to a store, a barber shop and a blacksmith shop. Third house beyond. Finest grub you ever flopped a lip over. And say, Early — you seem the right sort. Listen, hard. You buy you a shave and a new shirt."

3

Bees hummed in the yard, the turf was thick, and elms made gracious archways. Apples reddened in the little orchard, grapes hung from a sheltered trellis; moss roses, marigolds, coxcomb, hollyhocks and yellow dahlias were thick beside the path. The house was adobe, long and low; a double house with a broad gallery between, roofed, open at the ends, gratefully cool and airy. There were spacious arm-chairs of wickerwork, a rocking chair, brightly blue, another of cherry; a corded and covered water jar, a Mexican *olla*, hung cooling from the *vigas*, swinging in the light breeze. A gay Navajo blanket covered a low table where magazines and papers were stacked. This was evidently the lobby. No one was visible and there was no bell. On either side of the gallery were open doorways with screen doors. Eddie knocked at the nearest door. No one came: he knocked again, more vigorously. A door opened behind him.

"Oh, are you the traveling public?" cried a clear and youthful voice.

Eddie turned and swept off his hat. A girl came across the passage-way; a girl of twenty, dark, slender, bright-eyed and flower-fresh.

"Right," said Eddie. "And you, I suppose, are the hotel?"

"Just now I am. My aunt and uncle are chumming around some-wheres. You've left your horse at the gate, I see. Come on, and I'll show you where to put him. If you're staying all night, that is."

"Oh, yes," said Eddie. "Longer, maybe. This is certainly one beautiful little place, Shard is. I expect you think it's the finest ever."

The girl walked beside him, unembarrassed and frank. "I am scarcely a judge," she said, smiling. "You see, Mr. Public, I've lived here all my life. Except for a few trips to Silver City and El Paso, I've never been out of these hills." Her head lifted, her eyes lingered on the long horizons, lovingly. "If it is any better outside, I'm willing to be cheated."

Eddie looked again at this back-of-beyond girl. Her face, which might have been sad, was joyous instead; her eyes, which might have been wistful, were mirthful and confident. "I was born here," she said. "Just over the Continental Divide, at an old sawmill above Grafton. And —"

"You were!" said Eddie. "Why, Miss Hotel, I was at that very sawmill Sunday. And let me tell you, that old wheel is turning yet, singing in the sun. I stopped there a long time, and wondered who ever used to live there. And here it was you, all the time."

"My parents died there, and then my aunt brought me here to Shard. There you have my whole history. How about yours?"

"I've been delayed," said Eddie. "But here I am."

"Miss Eva — soon after supper, what say if I hurl your saddle on your Wisenose horse, and we go for a little saunter in the hills?" asked Eddie. "I hear rumors of a moon."

The supper in question was not the one which followed immediately after the exchange of autobiographies outlined above. It was several suppers later. Two or three suppers later; Eddie was not quite sure as to the number. That was the time. The place was a cheerful living room, with an old piano which wore the unmistakable look of use — much different from the air of pianos which are only to be looked at, thank you. There were long shelves of old, old books — Dickens, Scott, Charles Reade, Cooper, William Black. *The Three Guardsmen, Lorna Doone, David Balfour, Steadman's Anthology, Alice* and *The Autocrat,* and *Huck, John Halifax, The Story of An African Farm, Innocents Abroad, Don Quixote,* Whittier, Longfellow, Tennyson, Byron, Poe, Burns, Shakespeare — that sort of thing. Lincoln's face looked from the wall, a steel engraving; a flag hung there, an old sword; Venice, glowing through a thin drifting mist, crowding feluccas at the wharves, their gay sails furled to the tilted yards; a fezzed and tasseled Arab, with a villainous grin, squatted in the sand and proffered a Dead Sea Apple to a skeptical camel; by the window a jaunty canary, eager, egotistical, and brave, poured forth a high and soaring melody of uncaged song. That was the place. As for the

girl, she was the same dark girl whom Eddie had met as Miss Hotel —
better known in private life as Eva Scales.

"That will be fine, Eddie."

"Well!" said an indignant voice. Skid Jackson stood in the doorway. An accusing finger covered the culprits alternately.

"The curse is come upon me," remarked Miss Eva Scales. She
folded her hands and took on the saintly aspect of a martyr.

"What's Aunt Gerda thinking about, and that mizzable Pete Jensen, lettin' you roam around with this Early creature, and him with a
crest like a cockatoo?"

Miss Eva's eyes roved to that amber crest and she made a little
twisting movement with her fingers.

"Why, it's Skid!" said Eddie, beaming. "Didn't know you, Skid,
you was all spruced up so."

Skid stalked tragically into the room. Ignoring Eddie's welcome,
he turned his finger on Eva. "Aren't you my own woman — mine to
me, as Frank John says?"

"I didn't say so," said the martyr.

"You never said you wasn't, and I said you was. That makes it practically unanimous. I'm surprised. No — not surprised. Grieved.
Pained. Affected."

He turned on Eddie. "You, Early — did I recommend this hotel to
you?" he demanded, glooming. "Not much. I took a lot of pains to
send you on to the O Bar O. Didn't you know, right off, that I
wouldn't want you hanging around here?"

"I suspected it, sort of," said Eddie, meekly. "This fatal gift of
beauty — "

"I'll fix that. And how about that hotfoot hustle of yours — off
where duty called you? You might have been in Holbrook, right
now."

"How time does glide away," said Eddie.

"And that good man waiting for you, too — strainin' his riggin',
watching the slow days drag by, and no Eddie Early."

"Life," said Eddie, "is full of trouble."

"You don't know how right you are," said Skid. He took a rocking chair and rolled a cigarette. "You're not riding out, searchin' for
no moon, fellow. Far from it. Soon after supper — and I'm most
starved now — you and me, we're going to take a turn behind the old
red barn, or words to that effect."

"I'm too heavy for you," said Eddie regretfully.

"I'm not so big, but I'm nimble," said Skid, eagerly. "Spry as a cat.
You'll be surprised."

"Not practical. I got forty pounds on you, Skid. And," said Eddie, "if you have writ your annals true, like Miss Eva was reading to me about, 'tis there that I'm reasonably spry myself, for a big man. And it isn't fair. You lick me, and I'm a big awkward lummox. I best you and I'm a big, overgrown bully. Never do at all. Have to think of something else. I'll tell you what! I'll take on that big forest ranger. He takes dinner here regular as noon comes. Silly old fool, Lamar is — thirty if he's a day! And you tackle Bud Wilson. He's just about your size."

"I named it to Bud, week or so ago," said Skid gloomily.

"Oh, did you?" said Eva. She dimpled. "What did Bud say to that?"

"He said for me to go to hell!"

"Don't you do it!" cried Eva. "The idea!"

"Then if you down Bud," continued Eddie, ignoring the interruption, "and if Lamar downs me — "

"I think you're a lunatic, you know," said Skid.

"I've got it!" announced Eddie. "We'll let Miss Eva have a say in this. You just give us a friendly hint, girl. Which one of us might just as well be on his way out to the far-off world? But why, and where to, and what earthly difference would it make to the unlucky devil?"

"Is this a proposal?" said Eva.

"It might be twisted to some such meaning by a designing mind, if you want to hold us to a careless word," said Eddie loftily. "But we would prefer you to consider it — ah — more in the light of a certain natural curiosity."

"I will give the matter careful consideration," said Eva, "and I'll let you know my views — oh, well — say, two years from now."

"Fine and dandy," said Eddie.

> "Take, O take those lips away,
> That so sweetly were forsworn,
> And those eyes, the break of day,
> Lights that do mislead the morn;
> But my kisses bring again, bring again
> Seals of love, but sealed in vain, sealed in vain."

A shaded lamp made a small golden cone by the old piano. Her voice was a natural contralto, rich and deep, flexible, poignant. An untrained voice, it is true, but also an unspoiled voice. Those were simple songs that Eva knew, a marriage of words and music, magic and beauty; songs that meant something. She was Mariana now, feeling all she sung. Her tunes were simple, too; homemade, oftener than not.

Skid Jackson had not even the excuse of leaves to turn. He stood beyond that glowing circle of light, leaning on the piano, and his eyes were all for her.

Old Pete Jensen sat by the fireplace, where a cedar fire snapped and crackled, not for warmth but for delight; his lined face changed to time with every song. White-haired and serene, Aunt Gerda rocked with her knitting at the light's edge. As for Eddie Early, he was in the window seat. The moon rode high, and beyond the green mountains white clouds rose and billowed — the fringes of the banners of the gods. He sat silent, incredulous; the enchanted night without, and within the sorcery of song. Unawares, he had stepped from the blazing noon of life into this unguessed kingdom of beauty and wonder and delight.

"Frank John's song," Skid ventured hopefully. "Can't you give us that? 'Pale hands I loved beside the —' something or other, Palomar? Couldn't be Palomar. Something long ago."

"Samovar?" Eva twinkled as she made this small suggestion.

"Eva! Aren't you ashamed?" said Aunt Gerda. "It was the Shalimar, I think; and the Shalimar was a river, maybe, somewhere. . . . Don't mind her, Skid."

"Oh, let the little lady have her sport," said Skid, unabashed. "I had it coming. San Antone to Bakersfield — that's my limit. Shalimar, eh? Sounds like the good old Bible. And what's a samovar? Oh, I know. Tea urn. Yes, yes! That's right, girl; kick him when he's down. 'Pale hands I loved beside the Samovar.' Frank John will like that — nix! He's nuts on that ditty. How about it, Eva? Do we hear it?"

The girl flaunted her slim brown fingers at him. "Don't you know any song about freckles, Skid? Doesn't anybody love freckles?"

"I do," said Pete Jensen stoutly. Don't you sing it for him. Give us Sir Patrick Spens. There's a good lass."

So she sang of the King's daughter of Noroway; of "Now we have harried all Bamboroughshire"; and of the bonny Earl of Murray, who was the Queenis luve. Then her voice rippled softly from Scotland to a ballad of Old England: "I loved a forester, gay, bold and free." Heartbreak was in it, and the breath of the greenwood; a mother crooning to her child:

> "And I will dream thee Alan Percy's son,
>   And dream poor Alan guards thy sleep with me
>   Lull-a-by! Lull-a-by!"

Aunt Gerda put up her knitting briskly. "Lullaby time it is," she said. "This singing is now done."

"Just one more, Auntie," begged Skid. "McCartney's song. Please! Then we go dreaming."

"Never heard that one," said Eddie. "McCartney? Who's he?"

"He wrote it — an Australian. He seems," said Skid, "to have been a lucky guy. Listen, Eddie."

Her fingers drifted caressingly to a prelude where night winds whispered and long waves broke on a white beach; a prelude which changed, rang clear and high, dawn after dark, joyous; the lark on the thorn and Pippa on her holiday:

> "Once I loved a lady,
> And put her in a song — "

The accompaniment danced on, gay and youthful, defiant of loss and change and death:

> "First we loved with laughter,
> Then we loved with tears;
> And that's the way a life goes by
> The dreaming years."

The interlude was longer now, the strong beat of chords, steady, relentless, like the inexorable march of the years. It faltered, and failed, and died away to silence; her hands lay idle on the keys.

Eddie's heart leaped with longing and the world centered on one small dark face in that golden circle. The brown hands stirred slowly, reluctantly, and strayed along the keys to a small, low melody, brave and faint and elfin; she took up the words again, an echo, wandering, hushed and far:

> "She and I are ghosts now,
> Haunting an old song;
> I belong to nowhere.
> Where do you belong?"

So he remembered her in years to come, and in his dreams he heard that song again.

4

Rosenthal's store was flanked on either side by long hitch racks. Between rack and store certain mimic craters, each centered by an iron peg, showed where Shard pitched horse shoes when the shade was right. Open horse sheds stood in the rear, with a walled feed corral of fabulous acreage between store and blacksmith shop. The store was built on a high stone foundation, making a vast basement store room, half-underground. On the downhill side a level doorway led to great sliding doors. Rosenthal's freight wagons rolled into the basement to unload, passing on, when empty, through a second set of

doors to scramble up a steep pitch on the high side. Rosenthal did
not believe in waste motion. Moreover, when a wagon came late
and weary, it was left there under lock and key, safe from weather,
to be unloaded in the morning. There was also a platform further
back, where goods might go directly to the store proper, when
desired.

The front porch perched on stilts at a level with the store itself;
that is to say the edge of the porch was as high as the box of a
lumber wagon, without sideboards. High, wide and substantial, that
covered porch; known to affectionate derision as the town hall.
Three-inch plank made the floor, broad steps, the full width of the
porch itself, rose to it at either end; and the columns which upheld
the roof were peeled logs, time-checked and weather-gray, carved by
industrious knives to brand-book and social register. Long benches
stood beneath the windows; mid porch, at casual hit-or-miss intervals,
were three tables. Negligent tables, confident, entirely at home, with
satellite wooden chairs; roomy, round-backed chairs with time-
polished arm-rests. Surviving chess-men threatened and warded on
the first table. Checkers and dominoes made little sprawling piles on
Two and Three. This was mail day and Rosenthal was postmaster;
Shard tripped and minced, stalked, hobbled, hurried and crept, up
the steps and through the doors; gulped its mail greedily, chattered
and bantered and bought, and made large eyes or glanced sidewise by
accident, under drooped lids, from the ambush of a shoulder. Twice
a week, Wednesdays and Saturdays, the stage came in from Silver
City, passed on to Summit and Clear Creek. You and I have a beg-
gerly dozen of holidays for each year, but Shard had all these and a
hundred great days besides.

Skid and Eddie, who did not patronize the mail, had the great porch
to themselves. Scornful of chair or bench, they faced each other on
the platform's edge, each with his back against a trusty tree. Eyes
half closed, his legs drawn up, Eddie leaned luxuriously against his
particular porch column, the corner one, and nursed his ankles. His
hat hung from one knee, and he smoked a droop-shouldered pipe.
Skid lopped sidewise against his post. He sat tailor fashion and
braided a cigarette, hat aslant, his foretop dangling askew over one
eye.

"This is all very well for you, J. Pierpont, but I'm supposed to turn
a day's work for the Tumble T, every now and then. 'Tain't right!"
said Skid.

One of Eddie's shoulders quivered to an almost imperceptible shrug
and a corner of his mouth drew down. One eye propped open for

a slow stare. It opened wider. "Brush your bangs back, sister," advised Eddie. "You look positively callus . . . Debauched, if you know what I mean. . . . Depraved. . . . Wanton."

"My jig hawse eating his fool head off, too," Skid complained. "You oughta move on, fellow. You'll lose that job."

"Jobs are a nuisance. Just like you say. They want you to work . . . Gosh, what's that?"

A blond giant came slowly through the door, paused, nodded, moved slowly to the other end of the porch and sat on the bench there, slowly, cautiously. He unfolded a slender newspaper and conned it earnestly, his lips moving with the words. His big blue eyes were slow and dreamy, a yellow ox-horn mustache drooped dejectedly, his big bony face was patient and melancholy, his massive hands were startling. Eddie's eyes opened wide now, incredulous.

"That's Windy Bill Nelson. Our deputy. Look him over, Sobersides. Sheriffs come and sheriffs go, but Bill goes on forever. One new-hatched sheriff come up and told Windy there was complaints about him being too high-handed, week ends. Asked him to resign. . . . Windy looked at him a spell, bit him off a chew of plug and says 'No.' Sheriff made a pass at him — and Windy threw him in the cooler over Sunday for disturbin' the peace. Held his job, too. Firm, Bill is. . . . After you, likely. Hear you stole Ben Hill's shotgun and beat up Slagle."

"Yeah," said Eddie. "I really ought to buy Slagle a hat or something. Only for him, I wouldn't be here now. Just getting myself a bite when — *Hey!*"

Without perceptible start, Windy Bill was halfway across the porch, his gun flaming. Eddie rolled from the porch in a four-foot drop. This account is not chronologically exact, for these events were simultaneous. To be sure, the first bullet had whistled close above Eddie's head, but Eddie was already twisting out and down. Skid dived headlong, lighting on fingers and toes. They crouched beak to beak, glaring. The gun roared again.

Eddie found voice. "What you grinnin' about, you damn heather-cat?"

"Thought I heard something drop," Skid explained.

"Take that nose away or I'll bite it," said Eddie. His groping hand closed on a smooth round cobblestone, the size of a pink sugar bowl; he rose up behind the sheltering corner post, glimpsed his assailant, and heaved mightily. As the cobble arched across, Eddie saw that the deputy had returned his gun to the holster, and now stood pensive and peaceful, his eyes intently following something across the street

and down the street. Not so intent but that he saw the flying cobblestone; he inclined his head gently, and the stone crashed through the
window. An impressive silence came from the store.

"Whaddy you mean, you ox-eyed walrus?" shouted Eddie and
took the steps at a gallop. Windy Bill gazed benevolently and thrust
out a long arm, pointing obliquely across the road. Impressed by this
large tranquillity, Eddie paused in his charge to look. He saw a long
low dust beyond the trees, a something before the dust, a bulk that
shaped to a running horse and a man crouched along that horse's
neck. Windy Bill beckoned and led the way diagonally across the
porch. He paused, searching; laid his finger on a freshly splintered
bullet hole, which had struck the bench at a sharp angle. Keeping
that finger there, Windy Bill pointed with the other hand.

"Saw a rifle poke around that far willow, takin' slow aim. You
take a sight!"

Eddie knelt and sighted. The line ran directly before the post
where he had been sitting. "Oh — that way? You wanted me to
move?" Windy Bill nodded. "Then why in hell didn't you say so,
you Siberian wart-hound?"

"You moved, didn't you? If I'd told you, you'd just ha' said
'Why?' " said Windy Bill. He spoke grudgingly. "And I maybe discouraged him from a second shot. Missed him. Too far for a six-
shooter."

Rosenthal's shiny bald head appeared cautiously at the door casing.
He saw three men in friendly converse, his brows lifted. "Was there
somethings?" he asked with a rising note.

"Snake," said Windy.

Rosy's eyebrow arched higher yet; his lips pursed. He thumbed
his chin thoughtfully, and peered up at the shattered glass. "Somebody breaks my windows," he observed.

"I broke your window," said Eddie. "Snake. I threw too high. I
pay for what I break."

"I run along now," said Rosenthal, politely.

Windy punched empty shells from his gun and reloaded, glancing
at Eddie. "You're Early? . . . Thought so. . . . K P came to town
yesterday. Whigamaleerie outfit, the K P is. Don't just figure them
out. . . . Seems like you might maybe go visiting a spell. I would."

"I been telling him that," said Skid.

"You and Bud Wilson friends?" Eddie nodded, fascinated by the
way the deputy slow-spaced his words, and made each word count.
"Then you go stay with Bud a coupla nights." Windy drew a chunk
of plug tobacco from his pocket, and gnawed at a corner. "Ben Hill,

he was saying something about a shotgun. . . . Sawed-off shotgun." He returned the plug to his pocket, and ruminated. "Well, you keep that shotgun. Ben Hill ain't fit to manage such."

A horseman drew abreast; a far-stepping blue roan horse, a tall rider with a dark still face. The roan's ears twitched, the rider turned eyes to the porch — and waved a hand in heart-high salute. The conferees waved back.

"Who's that?" asked Eddie. "Haven't seen him before."

"Tom Copeland . . . K P boss," said Windy. The words were half a sigh, and Skid looked up quickly. The deputy's eyes were narrowed, musing, saddened. "Only for the men he works for, and the men that work for him," said Windy Bill Nelson, "I'd kind of like to like that man."

"Windy, you're either drunk or in your second childhood. You haven't talked that much, all told, these last seven years. But you're right about Copeland," said Skid. To his own surprise he found himself speaking from a heavy heart. "Copeland might have been a real man. He had the makings. Spoiled like a good horse is, sometimes." He shook his head impatiently. "Eddie, old man! You don't know how I hate to see you go!" His voice was gushing, cooing, tender.

"I know it," said Eddie. "But you're going to hate it a heap worse to see me come back."

A tow-head of ten sidled from beside the store, and mounted halfway up the steps. His wide gold-brown eyes, sorting strangely with that flaxen hair, looked up adoringly at Eddie Early, hero-in-chief for two days now, because of a bronco riding in the Jones corral. "I saw him," stated the tow-head shyly.

Eddie's hand went to his pocket. When it came out, a silver coin clung in the shaped palm. "Know what that is?" asked Eddie.

The tow-head nodded vigorously. "It's a dollar."

"Well, then," said Eddie, "what did you see?"

The gold eyes sought the steps, considering, their silken lashes drooping; a toe scratched thoughtfully at a brown ankle. Then the eyes lifted trustingly.

"A snake," said tow-head.

"Right!" The dollar changed owners. "We men have to stick together," said Eddie.

"Did I hear you say you was going out to Bud's or something?" said Windy.

"No, you didn't. But you do now. Good weather for visiting," said Eddie. "You cheer up, Skid. Don't look so blue. I'll be back."

"Yes," said Skid. "That's what I'm blue about."

5

After the other men caught their mounts, Copeland roped out his private horse — a stocking-legged sorrel. Wilcox twisted his mouth at this, and spoke low for Slagle's private ear, sneeringly.

"The big boss don't ride with us today, it seems." He did not look as if his name was Wilcox. He looked more like a Lippi or a Cuneo.

"You boys ride Horse Mesa and brand up what calves you find," said Copeland. "Slagle and Wilcox and me, we won't be with you today."

Five men rode away. "What's up now?" asked Wilcox suspiciously.

"Making medicine with the chief. Come on."

They clanked into the house. Kirby heard them come through the hallway and threw open his door. His plump fingers were pink against the casing. "Anything wrong?" His small eyes glittered.

"Not a thing, Little Chin," said Copeland.

"Come in then. What's on the mind today?"

Copeland drew back and let his companions precede him. They threw their hats on a table and sat beside it, but Copeland stood by the door. His saturnine face wore a trace of mockery. His gun holster hung low and well forwards. Kirby noted this, and his plump face grew a shade less pink.

"I'm quitting," said Copeland. "I brought Slagle and Wilcox so they could square you with the boys. They're here to witness that you hand over my share."

"Quit? My good God, you can't do that! You'll spoil the best machine ever put together. Don't be a damned fool! In five years we'll have Jesse James lookin' like a piker!"

"I give you five months to go smash," said Copeland coldly. "It may be five weeks. Slagle tried to murder this man Early yesterday — from ambush."

"Well?"

"I warned him not to. . . . Just start when you're ready, Slagle, if you feel that way, and I'll practically spoil your entire forenoon. . . . I'm done, Kirby. I know Early by rep. He stands well with the best men in the desert country. Murdered that way, with no chance — well, it's like that lisping jasper told Slagle when he tried it before. They'll just naturally take the K P apart — if local talent doesn't do it first. They're ripe. Too much whisky and mouth and your special brand of gun-play."

"We figure that we're pretty smooth gunmen ourselves," said Wilcox. "Too smooth for these hicks."

"You three think you're good. I know you're not. You kill, but
you can't take it. You lack the essentials. Here I am, one to three —
and what are you going to do about it? I'd hate to have any one of
you catch me asleep, from now on. But now, you see," said Copeland
softly, "I'm awake. If you don't believe I am, hop to it. But if you're
wise, you'll slip me and look pleasant. If the bunch was real bright,
they'd give Slagle his piece too, while the subject was up, and kick
him to hell out of this. With him gone, you might last quite a while
yet, if you only knew how to act halfway human."

"You're turning your back on the best chance you ever had,"
wailed Kirby. "Other gangs hung close to one stamping ground and
got sold out by friends — or skirts. We come way out here, buy up
this place and stock it, and live quietly a year to establish ourselves.
Then when Payne tips us off, a bunch of us slip out and hop the cars
— some from Silver City, and some from Magdalena — pull a job in
California, Oklahoma or Nebraska — and slip back, no one the wiser.
Nobody comes and nobody cares. We don't touch the mail, we don't
work near home, or twice in the same state. Best of all, we have no
friends to sell us out, and there is no splurge afterwards, no chorus
girls. We bring the loot here, burn the give-away stuff, and deposit
it to the credit of the K P Company, in Silver City, El Paso, Magdalena, Albuquerque — a little at a time, never too much; draw out
some now and then and deposit it in other banks, a thousand miles
away. Never any suspicion; slow and steady. It took real brains to
work that all out. We'll have a million to the good in no time. Men
hand picked, no two from the same town, and you picked especial
to deal with these rubes around here and put up a front like a cattle
ranch. And here you want to spoil it!"

"Yes — I know all that. About sixty thousand in there from local
banks and as much more salted away back in Illinois. I'm not spoiling
it. Your thugs spoil it, because they won't take the trouble to fit in
with the scenery. I'm done, and I don't want to hear any more talk.
Produce. You've got nearly forty thousand right here in the safe
from this last lay. If you had any sense you'd give me and McCabe
the ranch and cattle for our part. I'd risk it with McCabe. The rest
of you had a damn sight better take this cash and what you have in
all these banks and split up before you get yourselves hung. That's
good advice. These hicks are going to get you, and get you good!
— Cattle ranch, me eye! I try to tell these slickers of yours just the
A B C of running cattle. They won't listen. The cows are wise to
'em, the horses are wise to 'em and the hicks are wise to 'em. They
know there's something phoney. And this Windy Bill Nelson is just

the guy to hang it on you. I'm telling you! I'm going. I'm gone.
But honest, I wish the bunch would break up and call it a day. You
haven't got a chance. You don't know how to treat folks. No?
Well, I've told you. Bear that in mind later.

"Talk's done. Shell out. I'm not going to be picayunish with you.
Count me out one hundred and fifty of them hundred-dollar bills.
That is well under what's coming to me, and you know it. That is
why I pitched on that figure. Round numbers. Hand it over!"

"And if we don't?" sneered Slagle.

"Then I'll take it all!" Copeland's gun leaped to his hand. "Slagle!
Your left hand! Unbuckle that belt. Back over to the wall. Wilcox!
Left hand! Careful! That's better. Back over to the wall." He
picked up the dropped guns cautiously, one eye on Kirby. "Now
Kirby! Open that safe!"

Kirby opened the safe and counted out the desired sum.

"Walk ahead to the corral, you three," said Copeland. At the
corral, Copeland tossed the captured guns into the tank; he swung into
the saddle. "Let's go, Sox!"

Sox raced down the cañon at full speed till a bend hid them from
possible rifle fire. Beyond this bend Copeland slowed down but held
a brisk gait until he could quit the narrow cañon for a short-cut trail
across open hills. From there he held to a gentle fox trot.

6

"Wisenose hasn't plumb forgot old Jig yet, has he?" observed Skid.

"Wisenose isn't that kind of a horse," said Eva.

"Well, I didn't know. Pirouettin' over the pinnacles with that
Early pony, that way, me and Jig might have slipped his mind, real
easy. Mighty interesting beast, that Early horse."

"Skid, I do wish you'd act sensible."

"Me?" Skid tapped his chest inquiringly. "Lady, I ain't been just
right in my head since that day. Here was me, hurrying on my way
from Minneapolis to St. Paul, and I just dropped in to get me a bite —
and here I am yet! Shard is certainly the delayingest place, and all
on account of your Aunt Gerda being such a good cook."

They rode briskly up the big road in the early morning. They
were en route to visit Kitty Leffingwell, nine miles out. Black Jig
and black Wisenose had made this little journey together more than
once; they stepped out cheerfully.

"These mounts of ours know where we're going. Well-matched
pair," said Skid. "We'll get us a buggy."

"You didn't pay close attention to what I told you," said Eva severely. "I said that I wanted two years to make up my mind. I said it very loud and clear."

"When you was taking the matter under serious consideration? Why, I took that to mean, natural enough, that you was just lettin' Eddie down easy. Good heavens, girl, you don't want to miss no chance like me! Two years, and me with my trusting disposition — you don't know what might happen."

"Yes, I know," said the girl, and caroled blithely,

> And for any Annie Laurie,
> I'd lay me doon and dee!

"Woman," said Skid, "there spoke your jealous heart! No use to argue about it. You're bespoke." He paused, reflecting. "I never did accumulate money much — me bein' right busy. But from now on, you just watch my smoke! We'll go out and see that world Eddie was mentioning. . . . Poor old Eddie!"

Shard boasted one telephone. A wire ran to Silver City and to the Forest Service. The bell rang now. Rosenthal answered it.

"Hello! That you, Rosy? . . . This is Lamar. Bill Nelson around? . . . Right there? Call him to the phone, will you?"

"Deputy wanted," said Rosenthal. Windy took up the receiver. "Hello! This is Nelson!"

"Lamar, at the Forest Service. Hell to pay. Big fire over west, towards Catlin Hill. Send out every able-bodied man in Shard and get word to the ranches."

"I'll be right out."

"No you won't. You got another job. Man murdered. Tom Copeland. McCabe come in just now to have me phone for him. They found the body in Squawberry, above the Cienega, he says — about six miles south from here. Someone's going back to the K P for a wagon. Rest of 'em off following the murderer — tracking him. Ambushed, McCabe says. He wants you to come right out. And for Mike's sake go easy on your posse. This fire's going to be hard to handle. Make them loafers from the Bend come out."

"You don't want 'em. I send you good men, right off. S'long!"

He hung up the receiver. "Fire," said he calmly, "And murder." He outlined the situation in fewest words. "Wait, I pick me a posse. Then the rest of you get going. Send the boys to tell the farmers, but don't you let no boys go to the fire. . . . I want you, Hi Benton, And the blacksmith. Where's Skid Jackson?"

"Rode off soon this mornin' — him and his girl," said Benton.

Windy scowled. "Then I take Myers. Get movin'!"

Ten minutes later, Shard was straggling up the telephone line. Long since, Windy was climbing the stony trail above Hell's Bend; the trail that led to the west country, a dozen miles shorter than the wagon road through Horseshoe Cañon.

The posse rode fast. Eight miles out, trail and road met — twenty by the wagon road. A little further up, the cañon forked three ways, and the wagon roads forked with it. The southern prong led to the C A P; the central road followed up the main cañon of the Squawberry to the K P, and the right-hand road led due north, curving steeply to the camp of the Forest Rangers. They pushed up Squawberry. Just below the Cienega — the swamp where the creek had its beginnings — they saw two riders, north of the Cienega, climbing the steep hill. Windy shouted and waved them down. They came breakneck and the posse loped to meet them. It was Bud Wilson and Sooner McCoy.

"Where you think you're going, Bud?" said Windy.

"Goin' to the fire. Saw a big smoke over there a piece. Going to help."

"No, you ain't. Come along. Need you. Tell you as we ride. Plenty gone to the fire."

In the road again, Windy explained to his new allies. "Thought you was K P men. Copeland got killed: they're after the murderer. So they claim. Six-eight K P men — and I ain't right easy in my mind about them. No knowing. You're on the posse. Where's the balance of your outfit?"

"Lost 'em in the brush. Early stayed at the shack; going back to Shard this afternoon."

"Wish they was here," said Windy. "Trouble comin'. My bones ache me."

McCabe sat beside the dead man. His eyes and face were dull with misery. Copeland's face was covered, his limbs straightened decently.

Hats came off as the riders dismounted. "What's the story, Mac?" said Nelson, gently.

"Wilcox and Slagle found us about nine o'clock — "

"Found who? Start at the beginning, McCabe. Steady does it."

"Five of us left early to work Horse Mesa: about sun up. Tom and Slagle and Wilcox stayed at the ranch for something. Kirby never rides with us. Tom started to town. Some later, Blackie Wilcox and Slagle, they started for the Cienega to pull bog. Cows getting stuck there some. They found Tom here, and found where he'd been ambushed." He jerked his chin toward the bush covered ridge, south of the road. "Hundred yards or more, they said. Plugged him plumb center. Never had a chanct. They found where the murderer had come down and looked him over and then went back, on the top of the hill, where he left his horse. Then he rode back the way he came."

"Which way was that?" asked Benton.

"Down the ridge. Then they hunted us up and brought us down here. Cramer staid with the body, while I rode over to the 'phone, and the rest went to follow up the tracks. When I got back, Cramer went for the wagon."

McCabe's words came slowly. Sincere and undemonstrative grief lent the man a dignity he had never shown before.

"How many times was he shot?" asked the deputy.

"Just once. Right through the lungs. He fell behind those bushes yonder, where he couldn't be seen from the hill. I carried him over here, in the shade."

"Shouldn't have done that," said Windy. "You're supposed to leave the body where it was."

McCabe looked up. His eyes were stained with grief. "I don't give a damn about what I'm supposed not to do. I wouldn't have him layin' out there in the sun. . . . He was the only one of us worth hell-room. Tom was always mighty good to me."

"I hate to bother you any more, Mac, but there's things I have to know. Did you find any ca'tridge shells?"

"I don't know. Seems like they'd have said so, if they had. It was a thirty-forty, I think, the way the wound looks. I didn't go up. I was fixin' Tom up, decent. He was all doubled up."

Windy lifted Copeland's hat. The dead face was quiet and still, as in life. Windy had long felt a dim foreboding that this dead man and himself were destined to face each other in smoke, and he was glad it had chanced otherwise. Twisting the hat, his fingers felt a pronounced hump beneath the sweat-band! He felt again, stealthily. Two lumps! The deputy's iron face quivered, his hair tingled with a guess at the truth. "Over here, you said?" he questioned. Without waiting for a reply and still holding the hat, he walked across to the clump of bushes where Copeland had fallen. With his back turned, he drew something from beneath the sweat-band. It was a yellow bill, folded twice and again. He unfolded it. A hundred-dollar bill — and on it, in sprawling red letters, he read a single word. . . . *Slagle.*

His fingers trembled as he unfolded the second bill. The letters were feebler, uncertain, staggered; the blood had spread and blotted. But the word was clear. . . . *K P safe.*

Windy Bill's head rose in pride. This had been a man! In his death agony as the world dimmed to his dying eyes, he had written this message with a twig dipped in his own blood, had found a way to destroy his assassin while that assassin still floundered on the hillside. And the murderer had not climbed down that steep and thorny hill merely to view his handiwork, or even to make certain that his victim was dead. Nelson knew the story now. Knowing the men, and with these bloodstained bills to guide him, he knew why the murderer had sought out the body. There had been other bills like these . . . Except for the one fact that Copeland had renounced the fellowship and was leaving the country, Windy learned nothing later that he had not guessed. He refolded the bills and replaced them as they were; he went back and laid the hat over the dead man's face.

"Leave your horses, you fellows, and we'll go take a look," said Windy. They climbed that painful hill, leaving the dead man with his only mourner.

It was long before they came back; not until they saw the wagon coming, far up the cañon.

"Copeland was your friend, Mac?" said Windy.

McCabe hesitated. "Am I the sort that makes friends? Did you ever see a stray dog? Some is kind and some kicks 'em. He was always kind to me. All I want is to see the man hang that killed him."

"He'll hang. Copeland left word." Windy lifted the hat and handed it to McCabe. "Feel under the sweat-leather and see what you find there."

McCabe spread out the bills. He leaped up with a strangling shout. "Slagle? That sot?"

"Yes. He passed Copeland and laid in wait for him."

McCabe broke out in a torrent of black imprecations, not to be set down here.

"Did Slagle ride a gray horse?" Windy held out a few gray hairs from a horse's mane. "These was hung in a bush up the ridge. One man came that way and went back the same way. The bunch rode down the ridge. Of course, there was never no track there to follow. They was fixin' to fool me. You, too. They didn't take you in on the play. Leary of you. Leave Slagle to us," said Windy. "This other bill, now. What is it about the K P safe? You might as well tell me. We'll find out anyhow."

"Find out, then," said McCabe. "That's your business. I'm not talking. Tom always said you'd get us, sooner or later. You've got us. I don't give a damn. Glad of it, more than not, after what they done to Tom. But I'm not talking. Cramer'll talk."

"Cramer will not get the chance. We don't need him. We didn't need you either, but I thought — "

"I get you. Much obliged, but I'm not talking. Tom would like it better this way. Say, don't you want my gun?"

"It might look better," said Windy Bill, gravely.

"I want your gun, Cramer," said Windy. "You're pinched. And covered. Don't act foolish."

"What for? What do you want me for?"

"Oh, I just got a hunch. You see your lawyer. You may be able to get big damages out of me. Kirby to home?"

"Go and see, damn you!"

"I'll do that. Leastwise, I'll send. H'm! Let's see, now. Ten miles to the K P? maybe twelve; twenty to Shard. Six of us, two prisoners to guard, dead man to carry all the way 'round by the wagon road, Kirby to arrest — "

"McCabe talked!" snarled Cramer. He shot a murderous glance at his fellow.

"McCabe didn't talk and you won't be let. Shut up. I'm thinking. One more yelp and I'll gag you with a prickly pear. . . . Kirby to arrest, five K P men — let me count. Slagle, Ames, Blackie Wilcox, Davis — "

"And Butch Whitaker," said Sooner.

"And Whitaker. Five K P men squandering around at random. All this to do immediate, with six men — and no answer in the back of the book! Bud, you take your waddy and drag it for K P. Get Kirby, get what's in that safe, whatever it is, take it with you, take Kirby, round up all the saddle horses in that pasture, light out across the hills to your place, and keep two of your men on guard. Come on in tomorrow with the lot. Them K P peelers will go to Shard, go somewhere else, or come back home. If they come home, they have nothing but badly worn out horses to ride, and they can't go far. If they're in town, we got 'em. If they've gone elsewhere, we'll get 'em!"

"Well, so long!" said Bud. Windy looked at the blacksmith. "Storrs, I guess you're elected to drive the wagon. We're riding hard, full chisel, and you're not used to it."

McCabe rose up beside his friend's body. "Nelson," he said. "I want you to get Slagle. If you feel like taking a chance, I'll drive Tom to town. That'll leave you one more man. I'll take him in, too."

"By God, I believe you'll do it!" said Windy. "This will make one hell of a talk, but she goes as she lays. Lift him in boys. Gently!"

Mac, you find Rosy and get him to let you in the jail. Cramer will
ride your horse. Myers, you keep an eye on Cramer. If he makes a
false move, fill him full of lead. . . . Come on, boys. Getting late.
This is sure going to be hell on horses!"

7

"He had to be killed," said Slagle, "or else we were all set for a
noose or a life term. He said as much when he had us stuck up."

Blackie Wilcox confirmed this, lying smoothly. "Copeland aimed
to hide up safe. God knows where. He was always harpin' and
speculating around about the Argentine, off and on, for the last two
years. Then when he was all hunky a little letter to John Law, and
we'd be fixed proper. He didn't say so, right out, but he hinted. He
went sour on us. Nothing else to do."

"Suits me," said Butch Whitaker. He laughed brutally. "Only you
don't want to let that sap McCabe get wise to you. Tom was his
little tin god."

The K P men made a huddled clump on the winding ridge. In
the deep cañon, small and far below, Cramer and McCabe stood by
the dead man. As they looked, McCabe mounted and rode up the
hill on the north side of the cañon.

Davis spat. "There he goes now, makin' for the telephone. The
poor damned fool! He believed every word of it."

"Cramer's on," said Ames. "He sized up your horses, mighty fish-
eyed. Shape they was in was a dead giveaway to anybody but a nut
like McCabe. That guy, gentlemen, is the stupidest one man I ever
saw. He can shoot, at that."

"Something might happen to McCabe, maybe," said Wilcox. "He
might come to remember, later on, how sweaty and jammed up our
horses was, mine and Slagle's. The only reason I didn't put a slug in
Copeland myself, is that I was about five miles back. Couldn't keep
up with Slagle, in the roughs. Chi doesn't give a guy training for no
such hell-on-end country as this. I'm no damned brush-popper!"

"Well, let's go," said Slagle. "We got to make a bluff. We ride
down this ridge a ways and turn south till we come to the wagon
road from the C A P ranch. Make a noise like we was trackin' down
the murderer, see? After he struck the road, he followed it down,
and his track got mussed up with all the other tracks, see? After
we ride down the same road, nobody'll ever know any different.
Plain straight story. Murderer made a clean getaway. Why not?"

"You're missing one small bet," said Davis. "What did you two do
with your rifles?"

"Dumped 'em up the line, in a safe place," said Slagle. "We was out working. Not natural for us to have rifles. Copeland was killed with a thirty-forty, and we've got nothing but our six shooters."

"But what if somebody found 'em?"

"Who? These hicks? That boob sheriff?" Wilcox laughed scornfully. "I should worry! Pooh hoo, and pish-tush — likewise ha-ha! We'll get these rifles back to the K P later, after the dust settles. Come on, let's track down this desperado of ours."

An hour later, Slagle, in the lead, wheeled swiftly at a hill top, and turned back. The others reined up. Slagle leaped off and crawled back to the crest, where he peered through a bush. His face lit up with a fiendish joy. "Better and better! By God, we've overtaken the murderer! I never expected that. Here's that fresh guy, Early, whistlin' down the road alone. That leaves us in the clear. We turn back and follow this draw, hell-for-leather, leave our horses in'the gulch, and wait for him where the road cuts through the cedar brakes."

"Snuff him out?"

"Hell, no! After following his tracks all this way? We got to make this look good. We hold him up and take him in to Shard for killing Copeland."

"Killed Copeland, did he?" said Ben Hill. His eyes lit up with malicious mirth. "Think of that, now! Well, I'm not surprised, not one bit. This man Early acted real quarrelsome, right from the start." He leered at the captive.

The K P men shouted with laughter. A few ancient and wrecked Hell's Benders, who had followed from curiosity and for the chance of free drinks, tittered a feeble echo.

Taken by surprise as he rode past a low cedar into the muzzles of five cocked guns, and with no guess as to what was intended, Eddie had offered no resistance. His hands were tightly tied behind his back. His lips were swollen and a livid bruise showed on his cheek; a bruise made since that binding. Since that bruise, he had held grimly silent, wasting no breath in defense or denial.

Ben Hill mopped the bar with a towel. "Too bad everyone's off to the fire. I bet you boys is tired, and here you have to stand guard on your prisoner. You gotta be careful, or somebody'll be takin' him away from you and stretchin' his neck under that old mulberry out in front. Have another drink, boys. Early, he ain't in on this, Slagle. He's particular who he drinks with. This one's on me. How about it, Slagle? Ain't you a little afraid of a lynchin'?"

"Huh? Say, that's an idea!" said Slagle. "We got this guy with the

goods. Why should we give him a chance to get off if he gets him
a smart lawyer? What say, boys? Here's five of us to pull on the
rope."

A blear-eyed old prospector scrambled up from a chair, his legs
a-tremble from drink. "Hey, we won't stand for no lynching!" he
piped.

Ames struck the old man's mouth with the full swing of a back
hand blow. In that same blink of time, Eddie Early leaned his shoulders to the wall; his booted foot caught Ames in the belly and catapulted him against the bar. He caromed and fell; clutching, howling
with agony.

"That leaves four to pull on a rope," said Eddie Early. The barrel
of Slagle's forty-five struck his head a glancing blow. He staggered
back. Blood gushed along his bright hair.

"We'll have this trial right now," said Slagle. "Get a rope, Ben. . . .
Wilcox, you're the first witness."

It was nearing supper time when Eva and Skid reached the Jensen
gate. The girl ran up the winding walk. Skid led Wisenose and Jig
down a lane to the corral and unsaddled them. To him there came
Rosenthal, puffing and breathless.

"Hello, Rosy! Where's everybody? Town's empty."

"Woods afire!" gasped Rosy. "Me and Bauer, my clerk, Pete Jensen
and old Jamison — we are all. And your friend Early — up at the
Bend — they're fixin' to lynch him — for killing Copeland. One of
the Benders just came and told us."

"Copeland dead?" The saddle went again to Jig's back. Skid drew
the cinches swiftly.

"Didn't I say so? Are we talking? Go on, you young man with
a horse. Hold 'em till we come and, by God, what four old men
can do, we'll do."

Skid swung into the saddle. Eva came running to the fence. Every
vestige of color was drained from her face. "Skid! They're lynchin'
Eddie at the Bend!"

Jig flashed down the lane, a hand waved and Skid Jackson thundered down the empty street of Shard.

He wheeled up over the hill and came to the First Chance by the
rear door. He tiptoed, swiftly and noiselessly, through the empty
saloon. Slagle was on the high platform with Ben Hill. They were
holding Eddie — Eddie, silent, with bound hands and a noose to his
neck. Skid's gun pressed at Slagle's ear. The K P men were in the
road below with a few of the baser Benders.

"Hold everything! . . . Hill, you untie those hands. . . . Careful, men. Slagle would never regret it if you made a break. . . . Beat it, Eddie. Take Slagle's gun. Hop your Cry Baby and beat it back to Bud's place. Be with you in the morning."

"I'll stick it out with you," said Eddie, mumbling through puffed and bleeding lips.

"It's you they're after, simple! Get to hell out of here! Make a dust. They don't want me. I've got 'em. Do your stuff."

Cry Baby clattered up the stony hill. "The next number," said Skid, holding firmly to Slagle's coat collar, "will be for Ben Hill to collect the K P guns, real careful. . . . Don't you try it, Wilcox!"

Wilcox dived and drew. A cold wind passed by Skid's ear and Wilcox fell on his face in the dust, to shriek his life away. As Skid fired, Slagle tried to jerk free. The heavy gun barrel crashed down above his ear, and Slagle fell, stunned, rolling from the porch. A mighty dust whirled from the bend above, a black bulk charging down upon them. Wisenose! Eva! She heard the shots, she saw those writhing shapes. Wisenose slid and checked by the saloon porch. Skid was behind the saddle; Wisenose leaped again, his mighty muscles bunched in a last desperate effort. Bullets puffed beneath them, whined beside them, left them untouched. His arms were about her, her head upon his heart. They passed from sight beyond the curving hill, on their way to the far-off world.

Penalosa

PEÑALOSA

(A NARRATIVE)

OF THE VISITORS to this planet three centuries ago were two men who were half a lifetime apart and half a world: a Catalán and a Spaniard of Peru. They met once only, in Santa Fé of New Mexico, City Royal of the Holy Faith of Saint Francis; and that hour changed the tale of history.

The world was Spain's when blue-eyed Baltazar Fuentes was born in an old gray town, close nipped between the Pyrenees and the tideless midland sea: Cadaquez, in Catalonia. The Second Philip was yet king.

At fifteen years, the manling Fuentes went down to the lowlands, seeking fortune. Barcelona knew him for a space, and Tortosa. There were sea-ventures befitting a Catalán. Then he turned inland, followed the Ebro to Zaragoza, found fortune there and friends, and good repute, won him a fair young wife from the strong family of Caldas. So peace and love and home and pleasant years were Baltazar's; one strong son at last to crown his joy. The Third Philip died, and the Fourth took the crown: Olivarez the favorite ruled Spain, and Spain the world.

The world was breaking free when Baltazar Fuentes fled from walled Zaragoza with a king's wrath at his back. His wife rode by his side, loyal and brave; he carried before him in the saddle Timoteo, their son. Behind him in the cool, sweet dawn, something huddled and lay still in a pleasant glade by Zaragoza wall: something which of late had been a man, alive and breathing, arrogant and daring: the young Marquis of Calahorra, "fortunate Calahorra," darling of the court, right hand of the king's favorite. There had been a sneering word, glancing at Baltazar's young wife; swords; this.

The blood hate of Olivarez clung close upon their track. They fled westward, through Soria, Segovia, Valladolid, haunted Zamora, Orense; took ship at Vigo; to see gray Cadaquez no more, or green valley of the Ebro.

Their sail was yet white in the sea-road when a weary troop drew rein upon the whispering shore, and a cadet of Calahorra, his horse-hoofs in the foam and the flung spume salt upon his cheek, stared down the sun-lane to the west and shook his fist at the unconquered sea. And the sad mists rose, and night, and blotted out that sail.

Spain knew those fugitives no more. The New World swallowed them up. Olivarez fell in 1643. On a later year, when news of that fall came slowly to him, Fuentes came from the silent places of his hiding and took house in the City of Mexico. That brave wife was dead; Baltazar was a silent man, grave and thoughtful; turned fifty now. The boy Timoteo became a man in the city, married there, died there; leaving two sons.

Baltazar Fuentes became a Franciscan, "Of the Strict Observance." When he was sent out to the northern marches to serve his order, he had talk with the mate of his dead son and took with him into the north his youngest grandson, another Timoteo; the year 1656 brought him to Santa Fé: De Mendizaval was Governor and Captain-General of New Mexico.

The man I am to speak of now was born to splendor, apprenticed to greatness. Lima was his birthplace, 1624 the year.

Don Diego Dionisio de Peñalosa was descended from the famous houses of Peñalosa and Brizeño, Ocampo, Verdugo and Cordova: by the mother's side, from Dávila, Arias de Anaya, Valdivia, Cabrera, and Bobadilla. He was close and doubly kin to the Dukes of Sessa and Escalona, the Counts of Pietro en Rostro and to the Marquises of Maya: his wife was granddaughter to Fernan Cortéz, "the ever victorious."

We smile at this Hidalgo, "Son of Someone." But if we knew any man from our own stock clear in descent at once from Percy and Neville, Douglas and Graeme, Clifford and Talbot, Sidney, Raleigh and Drake, Howard and Gordon and Glendower, Clive, Hastings, Charnock and Wolfe — we would not smile.

Don Diego became early a man of mark. Family gave him opportunity; he used it greatly. For the man himself, he was in no way lacking: no unworthy "great-grandson of the three greatest knights":

a swift, alert man, fiery-daring, hardy, resolute, adroit, indomitable — and fortunate. He had need for the last two qualities: his ventures ranged through five thousand miles of hardship, toil and danger: brilliant and skillful soldier, wise and shifty administrator. One great and rarest virtue was his, a kindly tolerant, sympathetic patience with inferiors and with the copper children of the New World: one rank vice, an overgrown pride in his dealings with those of his own kidney: arrogant and stiff-necked pride, fiery, violent and overbearing.

A youth of war, pathmaking, building: this was a man in love with joy, and one who loved better to build than to war, and the long road more than either: "Lord of the cities of Gaurina and Farara, and of its eleven towns: Feudatory Commendatory Knight of the City of La Paz, and Perpetual Regidor therein, and in the Five Provinces of its District . . . making his house more illustrious by his sword with titles of Marquis and Count of fair cities which he has founded from the cornerstones." His list of titles may yet be found, poor Peñalosa, Brizeño y Verdugo, Ocampo y Valdivia: a double triangle worthy of an emperor; "Count of Valdivia in Chile, Viscount of La Ymperial, Marquis of Aranco and of Oristán, Governor and Captain-General of New Mexico, Adelantado (First-Man, Foregoer) of Chile and of the Gran Quivira in the west of this New World of America" — Dust that was Diego, how deep you drank of life!

A marked man: it was whispered, echoed in New World corridors that here was one fitted to carry on the great traditions of the Conquistadores. But our Diego took one wrong turning, at an unconsidered milestone; became tacit partisan of Saint Francis against Saint Dominic; and met his first setback when he quarreled with the brother of the Count of Salvatierra, Viceroy of Peru: quarrel patched up to peace by authority: smoldering.

Because of this quarrel and his desire of seeing Spain, Peñalosa embarked at Calloa in 1652. The ship foundered within sight of Payta Port: Don Diego lost forty thousand crowns thereby, saving some twelve thousand in pearls and precious stones. He proceeded to Panama: promptly found an uncle, Don Alonzo Brizeño, Bishop of Nicaragua: visited him. From here, after another shipwreck, he went to Mexico, capital of New Spain, where he awaited news and money from Peru.

Albuquerque was Viceroy of New Spain: dusky-brilliant Peñalosa pleased him well: found employment. He led reinforcements to Montalegre, holding Vera Cruz against Cromwell's fleet of sixty-eight men-of-war. The fleet captured Jamaica for England; Peñalosa bore himself well in that losing fight: was sent posthaste to periled Havana with his seasoned infantry: married there the granddaughter of

Cortéz. On his return, high in favor, he became governor of Xiquilpa, of Chilcota, Lieutenant-General in those provinces.

The Duke of Albuquerque passed, the Marquis-Count of Baños succeeded — "Great complaints were made to him against Don Bernardo Lopez de Mendizaval, Governor of New Mexico, whose greatest fault was his falling out with the inquisitors and their partisans. Nevertheless, he was recalled and the Count of Peñalosa was selected to command in his stead and to appease the troubles ordinary to that country" — This was the hour of his desire: New Mexico was on the very marches and bounds of empire: he would follow the path of Cabeça de Vaca, Coronado, Espejo, Juan de Oñate: outgo them. He received his commission as Governor and Captain-General at the close of the year 1660, and set forth at once. Yet he made no speed of that journey; lingered in Zacatecas for two months, another in Parral. Our Diego was Dionysius too: there is an offshoot house of "Peñalosa" in Zacatecas to this day, claiming descent from him.

Now all things prospered to Peñalosa's hand. "He defeated the hostile Indians called Apaches and compelled them to sue for peace. He founded two new cities, erected several public buildings and discovered new countries." He proved and armed his *dorados* — Golden Ones — "a very brilliant company of eighty Spaniards, among whom were some foreigners married in these parts," and he established the first American press agent, "Father Friar Nicolas de Freytas, of the Order of St. Francis, Preacher, Commissary Visitor of the Third Order, and Guardian of the Convent of San Yldefonso in this kingdom, and Chaplain to His Most Illustrious Lordship."

Freytas it was who wrote the "vague, bombastic and curious" account of the discovery by Peñalosa, in 1662, of the City and country of Quivira. "So glorious an enterprise, giving treasures to the crown of Spain to dominate the globe, for the Glory of God, in whose mighty hands are all things past, present, and to come, and of His Blessed Mother, the Virgin Mary, Our Lady, conceived without stain of original sin."

Those statistics are mixed. If you read that sentence carefully, you will get some hint of the confused whirling mind of Nicolas de Freytas — who was author also of a "Memorial of the Señor Adelantado," designed for the eye of Spanish Majesty: and of a sufficiently naïve "Account" of a previous expedition of Saldivar in 1618 to the far lands "fifteen days beyond the last of Moq" (Moqui) to the River of Good Hope, or del Tison — (Gila): wherein, on their turning back, one Father Friar Lazaras cried out "in a loud voice with wonderful grief," and eloquent eulogy of our Don Diego Dionisio de Peñalosa, and a judicious recital of his merits: although, at that time, our Diego would not be born for six years to come. This prenatal circumstance lends a saffron touch to the "Account," deepened by a broad hint near the end that the unborn Peñalosa "aspires to that [title] of Duke to become as illustrious of himself as the most excellent of his glorious progenitors, to whose titles of Marquis, Count and Viscount he is lawful heir, as of their zeal in honoring and patronizing our Seraphic order, as so Christian a knight and our Brother by Letters Patent."

The story trusts that the passage is sufficiently clear. Or the final paragraph of the "note" to the "Account":

"May our Lord in His infinite mercy grant that our Governor and Captain-General may by his valor and skill remove all the difficulties raised by those who are not accustomed to overcome the impossible, as his Lordship is, for whom Divine Providence has reserved it in its secret bosom from all time."

The Freytas record of the journey "through the country of the Escanxaques to the large river which they call Mischipi" is fearfully and wonderfully made. Nevertheless, it seems probable that Peñalosa reached the Missouri near where Omaha now stands: certain that he marched from Santa Fé three months northeast into the buffalo country. The description of rivers, soil, vegetation, fish, animals, are circumstantial and tally exactly to the last detail with our knowledge, bird and flower, shrub and tree; even to the Indian's proverb "To ten Hiroquees four of the Tuft, and to these two of the Escanxaques, and to ten Escanxaques one Apache." Also the sons of Peñalosa's *dorados* live in New Mexico today, Duran and Chavez, Lucero and Godoy: their twilight tales keep him Foregoer yet, hold him last of the Conquistadores.

Shifty-fortunate Peñalosa brought his *dorados* safely back to Santa Fé, not one lost on that long expedition, to Quivira, (Quebira, Great Land); he dreamed of map-making and Dukeships. There was also a sweet woman-child, born in Santa Fé at about this time, born to his love but not to his name, of whom he had much pride and joy. — The granddaughter of Cortéz had died young, and before Zacatecas.

Then, upon a day, planning new exploits, dreaming great things, Peñalosa looked forth from his window in the Adobe Palace and saw in the courtyard a gray friar, unknown to him: who shook a chiding finger at a young Indian boy, and, as Diego gathered, admonished him for some boyish failing. The boy was Popé, a lad of the Teguas; the friar was Father Baltazar Fuentes.

On the heels of this there was a prodigious tumult in the guard room:

black-gowned Huelva stormed in upon Don Diego; dark Huelva,
Commissary-General of the Inquisition; herding before him gray friar
and Indian boy of the courtyard, and Father Michael Guevera, Guardian of the Convent of Santa Fé. Huelva was flaming, Guevera cowed;
the lad stolid; the stranger friar unfluttered, eyes downcast, quiet.
Huelva's words came in a torrent.

"Things go from bad to worse here, there is no discipline, no
order: the spread of our holy religion is neglected, while we give ourselves to idleness and music, picture-making, joyance, and all disorder. Here is heathen idolatry flourishing in your capital, tolerated.
Punishment for the offenders! I demand instant justice!"

Peñalosa dandled his child. "Disorder is indeed rife, Holy Father,"
he said. "That is best proven by yourself. I think Your Paternity
takes a strange way of seeking order, when you so far forget your
station and mine that you break unannounced and blustering upon
your Governor, more like a tipsy soldier reeling to barracks than one
headman seeking counsel with another for the good of the state. If
you have cause of complaint against these three, set it forth in clear
words. I will see justice done."

Huelva quivered. He sought to control himself. Three words or
four he spoke calmly; then hate seized him, he shook with that passion. "Lashes for this red child of hell! — Lashes once and again for
this faithless Priest! Penance" — he whirled on Guevera — "penance
and discipline for the slothful shepherd!"

"Now, that may very well be," said Peñalosa, arching his silken
brows. "But I must remind Your Paternity that it is the custom of all
lands to know and name the crime before sentence is meted; and, in
this new world at least, we sometimes require proof to the accusation.
Again, if I may point it out, it is the part of the accuser to bear witness: it is for the judge to weigh, to give sentence or withhold it. And
it is my thought," said Peñalosa, evenly, "that Your Commissary-ship
has forgotten — again — who is Judge and Governor in Santa Fé."

"Do you bait me, then?" gritted Huelva.

"Not in the least, Reverend Father. I but mention, with admiration,
that humility to which you are sworn. I point out the seemly bearing
which befits a witness, seeking — justice, I believe you said? No more
than that. I await your leisure. You have charges to prefer?"

"Heresy! blasphemy! idolatry! This Popé of Tegua," cried Huelva,
pointing, "serves the devil his father! He was seen and heard at sunrise of this morning, practising the hellish rites of sun-worship; this
Franciscan Fuentes, unprofitable servant of God, lukewarm, rebuked
him with pleasant words, almost smiling — I saw and heard! — while

this Franciscan Guevera, Head of his Order here, looked on, consent-
ing, complacent."

Peñalosa considered. He spoke to the unknown friar:

"I have not seen you before, I think?"

Fuentes raised his eyes. "No, Señor Governor. I have been afield
since your coming: first in the village of the Pecos, lately in Acoma
and Zia. I am Father Fuentes."

"Baltazar Fuentes? Yes? I have heard another tale of you than this
— an old tale. But is this one true?"

"It is, Señor Governor. I found the lad in sun-worship, even as
Father Huelva has stated. The boy did as his fathers taught him:
made no concealment, thought no wrong. I instructed him to wor-
ship not the sun, but the Maker of suns."

"You hear?" cried Huelva in great voice. "They confess! The lash
for this smooth-spoken priest: the lash for the heretic redskin, death
if he bow himself before hell again."

"I have no great relish for these lashes of yours, Father," quoth
Peñalosa. "I hold that Father Fuentes erred greatly in that he did not
stress the enormity of the offense: that is his business. I recommend
him to the discipline of his Order. And I think," said Peñalosa smoothly, "that this is a fitting time to point out to Your Paternity a circumstance which seems to have escaped your notice: that the servants of
Saint Francis make no demand on those of Saint Dominic (already
overburdened) when they have need to correct a sinful brother."

Huelva glowered: was mute.

"For the boy, I would remind you that we are few: a handful of
Spaniards, cast down in a wilderness of savage nations, cut off from
any succor by a great journey and waste places. If it were policy
alone, it sorts well with our wisdom to be plainly just in the eyes of
these barbarous savages: even to smooth justice with mercy. It is a
rule that has served me well."

"You are yourself lax in the faith, long suspected," growled Huelva,
taken aback at this turning.

"I will make an end of suspicion then," said Don Diego, eyes
a-dance. "If I have been lax aforetime, I will be lax still. The boy
shall be warned and instructed in our true and holy faith: no hurt
shall fall to him. Why, 'tis but a child! Bethink you, Father, our Lord
Christ loved children." Peñalosa looked down at that brown-winsome
small daughter of his; summoning the nurse, he gave the child to
her keeping; dismissed the boy Popé, with grave monition; turned his
mocking eye on dark Huelva.

"Worshipped the sun, did he, the rascal? Well, I do not blame

him greatly. Holy Father, that sun, more like your hell than any place
I know, is yet visible Source and Giver of Life; small wonder if the
savages bow down to it."

Fanatic rage surged to Huelva's brow. "Blasphemer!" he thundered.
"You shall burn for this!" Guevera trembled. Baltazar eyed his new
governor with interest.

"It may be as you say," said Diego carelessly. "But in the meantime I am lord of this province, answerable for safety and upkeep:
my will is peace and not war. To the better keeping of that peace I
think it altogether needful to check your meddling tyranny and usur-
pations. We are at the world's edge here; I could name one who
stands in more peril than Peñalosa."

"I will break you for this insolence — *criollo!*"

Diego sat still under the insult: laughed aloud. "Breaking after
burning, Father? Come, you grow reasonable; my poor ashes could
bear that. It pleases me to see your arrogance dwindle; you move in
the right direction; I mean to teach you more reason still. Man, I
know your inches, your letters and plots! You harried de Mendizaval,
you were millstone to his neck. You would dispose sovereignly of all
things, make your lord and governor your puppet. You have med-
dled with affairs of mine from the first; conspired against me: tampered with my *dorados*, who told me straightway. Meddler and
marplot, they laugh at you; would cast you into prison at my word."

Huelva thrust out his chin. "Not one would dare lay hand on the
minister of our Most Holy Office! I defy you — creole!"

"Now, that may be true," said Peñalosa, softly, "though I think you
do some injustice to their daring. Yet the anger of the Holy Inquisition is a thing to be feared; you may be right after all. I shall not
put them to the test. The rather, because I know one whose daring
has never failed me: a *criollo!*" He flashed upon Huelva, hand on
throat, dagger to heart. "I arrest you as danger to the state!"

"*Baseborn — !*" gurgled Huelva. Diego's hand gripped his wind-
pipe, the keen steel drew back. Guevera started forward in horror:
Fuentes laid a large hand to Guevera's breast. Diego's hand loosed its
clutch a little.

"You were saying — ?" said Diego, waiting.

Huelva saw death glitter at his eyes. "An angry word," he muttered.

"Which you regret, doubtless?"

Guevera's knees shook with terror. Huelva's desperate eye rolled
to him, to calm-eyed Fuentes.

"Which you regret?"

"Which I regret," mumbled Huelva.

"And you yield yourself prisoner?"

"Yes."

Peñalosa plucked off his hand; the Inquisitor drew sweet air into his lungs with a deep breath, sweetest of his life. "Come, we grow acquainted," said Peñalosa. "You shall lie under lock and key in the next room until you make submission; with fair bread and water to purge your pride."

"And yet," said stubborn Huelva, "you have not called your guard."

"You speak a wise word there," laughed Peñalosa. "You are shrewd and stubborn, you shall be of use to me yet. This is a perilous matter: my golden ones shall not lay finger to it, nor know it. I will hold you prisoner in my own room; we will converse together; you shall meditate. You shall be help to me yet, not hindrance. To that end, I will have you turn your thoughts more to the spread of our Holy Gospel, and to defence, garrison, treaties, agriculture, commerce: with less talk of lashings, burnings and breakings. Take my arm, reverend sir; you shall seem to go as an honored guest, in friendly talk, lest rumor — perhaps laughter — glance upon your authority."

"Which friendly talk and seeming of guest," returned Huelva steadily, "safeguards your own authority as well as mine."

"You shall have the last word, too," said Peñalosa gaily. "You do not lack for brains, I find. These two will hold tongue between teeth, both for our sakes and their own. Will you not visit your room, reverend Father?"

Peñalosa came back at once. He pulled a long face and looked aslant on Fuentes, ignoring Guevera: Guevera says it, he tells the tale. Yet Guevera was of the grandees, Fuentes peasant-born: Peñalosa knew to judge a man.

"Here is a goodly coil!" says Diego.

"My fault, and I ask pardon for it," says Fuentes. "I was too mild with the boy, too stiff with the Dominican."

"No fault of yours," says Don Diego. "This affair was to be settled. It has been drawing to a head this year. The colony is in no posture to thrive under two masters. As for mildness and easy dealing with the heathen, that is root and branch of my policy, I stand or fall by that: I will not have the colony thrust into needless hazard: this clash was bound to come, tomorrow or today. Yet it is my poor thought that two of us three are greatly jeopardized. Saint Dominic carries all: if I cannot tame and master yonder hooded-crow, the Holy Office will make but one mouthful of the two of us." He considered for a brief silence. "I think we two have made history this day," said Peñalosa laughing lightly. "I think we are the first, in the New World at least, to raise finger against the Holy Office. It might be a wise choice, Father Fuentes, should you elect to ply your labors at our further outposts. Peñalosa might weather the storm, if storm there comes. Time will show." So says Guevera.

Huelva made submission, being prisoner seven days. It is certain that Don Diego put himself out to ingratiate himself, to captivate his captive; it is like that Huelva fell under his charm, in spite of fear, humiliation, fanatic hate. From that time, Diego heaped his late foe with high employment and honors. Governor and Commissary-General worked hand-in-glove; and all things went well with the colony. That was the golden age of New Mexico.

In 1664, Peñalosa returned to Mexico. Three months and a half he loitered in Parral, "in order to propose to the Viceroy the conquest of those countries which he had discovered." That loitering was his bane. In Mexico City, the Holy Office, "which never pardons anything done against its supreme authority," had him arrested: pounced upon him as he dismounted at the Viceroy's door.

In the north, wavering Guevera, himself a Catalán, gave Fuentes warning of the coming storm. Baltazar Fuentes took up his grandson Timoteo and fled away into the wilderness: wandered from tribe to tribe, befriended. He passed southward in a long valley between unknown mountains, met and companied a wandering family of the Moqui; turned eastward across a high mountain to the haunted valley of the Witch Hills, where the Moqui rode swiftly, with incantations: found thereby a fair high table-land walled by a long, red cliff, in which was a cleft pass a bare lance-length in width, with a creek of sweet water therein: for a day's journey on either side there was no other passway.

Then Father Fuentes lifted up his eyes, and saw that the wilderness was very great and he was very small, weak and stricken with years. He tarried at that red pass and there laid a trap for souls. Since the redskins were scattered far, since he could no longer seek them in his age, they should come to him in this gateway: seeking those pools of sweet water, they should find the water of life.

The Moqui aided him in his desire. In the narrow mouth of that red pass he built a roof of hewn cedar into the living rock, where it overhung and closed together: a floor of cedar logs, high above the floodway; rude wall and door, a high stairway to that door, a gate at the water-way: and there, on the eleventh of June, the day of Saint Barnabas the Apostle, he founded a church and named it for Saint Barnabas.

A far word had gone forth of Fuentes; the Sign of the Left Breast, "Goodheart," Father, was his to all the wandering tribes. His house of God became a Place of Truce, and he preached there a God mighty and merciful.

In the year 1680, driven by exaction and outrage, the tribes of New Mexico arose and exterminated the Spaniards, root and branch. A young chief of the Teguas was leader; his name, Popé. It was a well-planned rising: the blow was struck in all places at the same hour, sudden and swift. A scant few — civilians, soldiers, priests, women and children — outlived the first butcher-work, and fled south with Governor Otermin. Where the mission of Socorro, Our Lady of Succor, was once built for thankfulness, they were joined by other fugitives, a strong party from the Pecos; made a stand, made good their retreat to where El Paso now stands.

Of those left behind but two were spared by the savages: Timoteo the grandson of dead Fuentes; and Elena, daughter of Peñalosa. These two were wedded on a later year: housed themselves at a great spring under that red cliff, not far from the church Fuentes builded. For one fourth of a thousand years their descendants have dwelt under those forgotten skies: christened, wedded, buried by the Church of San Barnabe.

The Inquisition kept Peñalosa in prison for thirty-two months, "made inquiry into all his actions and all his words." It stripped him of his offices and declared him incapable of holding any office in New Spain. It sold his property (to itself) for eighty-six thousand crowns — worth three hundred thousand, says Peñalosa: fined him fifty-one thousand of those crowns, and kept the other thirty-five thousand.

Here is an account by an eye witness, of a "special" Auto de Fé celebrated at the convent of Santo Domingo on the third of February, 1668. It is from the diary of Antonio de Robles, a Pepys of Mexico.

"There also came forth in the said Auto de Fé, Diego de Peñalosa, governor of New Mexico, for unrestrained language (*sueltos da lengua*, leaps of the tongue) against priests and lords inquisitors, and some absurdities which bordered on blasphemy. He came out in a shirt, which was very fine; dress of black velvet; his hair (which was his own and long) well dressed; his stockings wrinkled; very large hand-ruffles of Flemish point-lace, then used, so that apparently he attired himself on purpose, without cloak or hat, with a green candle in his hand. He excited much compassion."

You may judge how Peñalosa was little like to stomach all this. You are to consider that the man had seen greatness at his finger-tips. The truth is, he liked it not at all: vowed revenge.

Discredited, penniless, friendless, without employment: poor antagonist for the all-powerful Inquisition! Where to begin? Letters to Peru were unanswered: Bishop-uncle was coy. Friends, of the Grandee sort, ignored him, and all men feared the wrath of the Holy Office: this man, guilty of the first press-agent, was also victim of the first blacklist.

Haughty-stubborn Peñalosa took sneer and slight of silken Grandees in very ill part. There were forbidden duels; tough Peñalosa victor; punishment not pushed home. We may hope that this unlooked-for clemency was in some part due to grudging admiration for the man, respect for unmerited misfortune: it is certain that once his vanquished antagonist pleaded for him. And authority shrank from any irrevocable affront to the powerful families of our Diego's kinsmen, who had drawn together to a sinister and sullen faction, during the months of his imprisonment. Even the all-powerful Inquisition had not quite dared Diego's death. In fact, they were lenient with him — as Inquisitors go. At that same very special Auto which condemned Diego, a lesser offender and of a less formidable family, one Ferdinand de Tolosa, received four hundred lashes on the installment plan, and was banished to the Philippine Islands. As reverse and offset to this, sullen Valdivias, Ocampos, Mayas, feared to offend the Inquisition; his life safe, they reached no aid to their blacksheep kinsman.

It would be shameful to tell you to what shifts Diego was driven to keep bare life: Bishop-uncle remaining shy. It was the bounty of an old foot-soldier of his that paid for passage to Havana, in 1669. Havana, once saved by him, received him but coldly: the terror of the Inquisition stalked abroad. Yet he contrived to live: lingered there for many months, awaited letters from Peru: none coming.

He took sail at last in a Canary Island vessel which took him to the Island of Teneriffe. The governor was Diego's cousin, and a bigot. He received his broken kinsman kindly enough but would further no voyage to Spain. Bearded sea captains, at Peñalosa's askings, looked aslant at him, whispered, shook their heads.

Peñalosa was resolved for Spain and justice. It was a time of truce: he took ship under an English heretic: landed in London. He gained favor with the English king and the Duke of York, who were keen to hear of that great river of his, the Mischipi or Paliçada, and the rich country of Quivira. But the Marquis de Fresno and the Count de Molina, Spanish Ambassadors, threw discredit upon him, gave him cold looks; told King James that this was a contumacious rebel, a man not allowed to set foot in Spain: Spanish justice! Diego saw at last how useless it was to seek redress of Spain.

Each rebuff and insult made deeper his haughty-stubborn hate, firmer his purpose; at each fresh wrong, Peñalosa tightened his belt and set his grim face to his task. He held that "leaping" tongue of his in leash now, pondered deeply on New World maps, probed Spain for the weak joint in her armor. He was American-born; to his death-day he never put foot to Spanish soil. The ambassadors persecuted him afresh, intrigued against him, sought his life by the hands of secret bravos — luckless! — heaped infamy upon him, quite cast down his credit at the court; drove him out at last.

He proceeded to France, threw himself "upon the protection of the greatest king in the world." Spanish ambassadors, Marquis de Los Balazes and others, looked upon him coldly, expressed "distrust of his stay in France."

By this time, Peñalosa's purpose was shaped and hardened. Taking a hint from the English king, who had shown so much interest in that river of Mischipi, he set himself to turn France to that great river, to throw France against Spain in the New World. He made it his life-work — and he succeeded.

By now he knew himself to be a marked man; knew that he was to mix no more at first hand with the affairs of the great. He accepted that fact, humbled himself, drew into the background. He sought for his middleman: found him in the young Sieur de La Salle, an adventurer whose imagination was fired by a storied river he was to follow from the Great Lakes for an eight months' journey to the Gulf of California — Road to China!

Peñalosa threw himself into La Salle's party, pushed La Salle's fortunes with all his genius. More especially he bent his intrigues to tempt the cupidity and ambition of the Grand Monarch with the richness of the *Gran Quivira*.

From this time, Peñalosa becomes a thin and shadowy figure. There is a glimpse of him at the house of one M. Morel, where he dined in company with La Salle and Beaujeu. He knew shallows and miseries. Rumor makes him fencing master — a good one — under the assumed name of Pinito Pino. And, year after year, trackless rumors of Quivira swell cumulative, beat on the ear of King and court and France, turn all eyes that way; La Salle is listened to, applauded, encouraged; gets his chance: France is committed to the "Mischipi."

Peñalosa, or a thin ghost of him, haunts the antechambers of the Tuileries: patient now, this son of the Conquistadores; that leaping tongue of his schooled to silence. There is a "Memorial" of his, "On the Affairs of America," given to Monsieur de Seignelai, Minister of the Marine: it sets forth the facility with which New Biscay may be conquered, a colony established: "an enterprise more ruinous to the Spanish monarchy than in any other place where his majesty can attack." There are alternative plans, with details. French "Fribustiers" from Santo Domingo are to make the attack, under their own chief, Grammont; Peñalosa is to be guide.

"He believes that he cannot give better pledges of his fidelity than by putting himself, without a single other countryman of his own, among a thousand or twelve hundred warlike Frenchmen, and at the discretion of the French commander, who is to lead them with him, and to whom he says orders may be given to hang him on the first tree, if he fails in any promise he makes."

Other "Memorials," too many: one, "touching the establishment of a new colony at the mouth of the river called Rio Bravo" — a project carried out somewhat later, by Philip Nolan and others.

At last — victory! French Government consents; La Salle's foray to New Biscay, Peñalosa's to Panuco, are mutually to support each other: La Salle's to go first. It is 1684: Peñalosa is sixty years old: La Salle sails from La Rochelle in July. Alas! A luckless expedition, and bungled; the Spaniards are alert, energetic; La Salle proves unfit: French Government loses heart, abandons both La Salle in Texas and Peñalosa in France. Beaujeu and the Abbe Cavelier record how eagerly they awaited the reinforcements under Peñalosa till the end of 1686. Peñalosa died in Paris on almost the same day that La Salle perished in Texas.

On this tormented planet perhaps there has been no man, missing greatness, who came so near that frantic blame and praise which men call Fame, and prize so strangely, as this baffled Peñalosa. He set a bound to the empire of Spain, that dim adventurer; his dream became Louisiana; his hand was first in America to strike a blow for freedom, first to dare the Inquisition: be that his epitaph. Our Bancroft terms him imposter, perhaps because the Inquisition indicted him as *"embustero."* I prefer the testimony of Popé the Tegua, who knew the man and spared his love-child. — It is so long ago! — the word cannot harm her now.

Say Now Shibboleth

=|||=

SAY NOW SHIBBOLETH

(AN ESSAY)

A BIT OF WORDLY WISDOM

I will not tell you where he lived; too much
Already has been said: it would be spiteful.
Many unkind remarks are made by such
As live in places far, far less delightful
Be this enough: it may be plainly stated,
His mind was very highly cultivated.

WHILE YET a small boy I was persuaded to earnest and painstaking study of language by hearing a report of a memorable examination. Some of you may have seen it:

And the Gileadites took the passages of Jordan before the Ephraimites; and it was so, that when those Ephraimites which were escaped said, Let me go over; that the men of Gilead said unto him, Art thou an Ephraimite? If he said, Nay: Then they said unto him, Say now Shibboleth; and he said Sibboleth; for he could not frame to pronounce it right. Then they took him, and slew him at the passages of Jordan.

They were purists, I take it.

Forty-and-two thousand failed to pass. The Gileadites were a strong and vigorous stock. Their spiritual descendants still keep sleepless watch at the passes of Jordan. True, they do not now hold to the strict letter of the olden penalty for lingual error, but they observe the spirit of it. It is still so.

There will be need now for care to avoid misconstruction of the few and heartfelt ensuing remarks. Take the "shortened Italian a" for example — our old friend "ă." For my single self, I like that sound. One of my earliest ambitions was to have graven upon my tombstone this epitaph: "Păss, traveler, nor åsk who lies beneath the gråss."

I do not foolishly dote upon either "ä" or its variant "å," you understand; but it seems to me that either of them is intrinsically a more pleasing sound than the flat "ă" — as in this same word "flat." There are many who use this "Italian a" sound naturally. Also properly. In such cases it is good hearing. But when its use — or misuse — requires visible effort by the speaker and its delivery leaves him with a startled air — makes him gâsp, in fact — the effect is spoiled. It has become a mincing affectation. And, in any case, I must and do hereby respectfully but firmly decline to consider that, if a man should ask me for a flask,[1] when he might say "flâsk," he is thereby branded by either moral turpitude or social impossibility. Nor will the reverse hold true. Yet we have seen the statement that "when a man speaks of a băth it may properly be inferred that he seldom uses a bâth." — And he said Sibboleth. And they slew him. — You hear just such inferences every day, based on similar premises.

It cannot be set forth too plainly, too early or too often, that the grievance which some of us hold against the Gileadite is not for what he says, but for the — objectionable — way he says it. He is frequently right in his contention. But wanton and offensive sneers do not precisely warm our heart to him or yet lead us to mend our ways. Just resentment for the precisian's contemptuous treatment of the erring but too often fosters a fond attachment for the error. I think these passwords will wither, most of them; not because they deserve to perish, but because their proponents, with a singular want of tact, urge them by heaping vituperation, abuse and insult upon the luckless tribesmen. There is an old injunction that we must "hate the sin and not the sinner." I fear we are in danger of reversing this by hating the virtue as well as the virtuous. We are joined to our idols; let us alone.

True, it is only a small minority of educated people that exhibits this Gileaditish spirit — else we uncultivated would grease the loud tumbrel and burn the colleges forthwith. But it is a voluble minority — a minority that loves to speak of itself as "cultured." The disdain of this paroxysmal minority is not here exaggerated. It can hardly be exaggerated. Before we go on to consider some other test words, commonly propounded at the passes of Jordan, let me prove to you that this arrogance is past exaggeration.

On my desk are three books. They are there by chance and not chosen to edge this feeble remonstrance. On the contrary, a careful second reading of them convinced me that it was high time someone rose to a point of order, like Abner Dean, of Angel's. For these books are typical of the Gileadite. If there were no more of their kind they

---

[1] Ammonia: for snakebite.

might be attributed to personal misfortune. But there are thousands of the kind; and the kind is recklessly mischievous.

The three authors are scholars and gentlemen of repute — one, at least, a name of nation-wide distinction. The books, one and all, are full of valuable and interesting matter, ably set forth; one and all, they are marred by unbelievable narrowness, by malignant rancor, by a haughty intolerance — not only for verbal error, be it marked, but for any usage differing from their own and for any mode of life not conforming to their habits. One book deals with English, severely; one with Words; and the third is a Life of Lincoln. Let us now take a worm's-eye view of the Essays on English, by the chiefest among these three.

You are at once struck by the frequent recurrence of "this sort of person" — our sort — and "enlightened" — his sort; in fact, he writes "Enlightened" with a capital after he gets well warmed to his work; "The Enlightened," who have a "sixth sense . . . and that sublimated taste which makes of its possessors a very special class."

"This sort of person is almost as low as the one . . . with whom men and women are always ladies and gentlemen." He explains about ladies and gentlemen, then, adding naïvely that these are matters that "the unenlightened will not understand, even after they have been explained." So there's no need of puzzling our poor heads over it. There is one phrase that seems pretty plain, however: "Whereas, if a man says that he was lunching with a 'woman,' there is a dangerous little implication which could not exist did he use the word 'lady' instead."

There is another little implication that might be made; but let it pass. I must say, however, that some of us judge a man by his character as much as by his words; and when a man's character cannot stand the strain of lunching with a "woman," he is in a parlous state.

He has tolerant spells, however. "The slang of the clubs and of university men is also quite consistent with good taste." It may be mentioned — but perhaps you have already guessed it — that he is notably a university man and a clubman.

Just so. The metaphorical use of the phrases "to cross swords" and "to parry a thrust" are elegant, reminiscent of the days when homicide was a fashionable recreation. But the metaphorical use of "bed-rock," "rolling-hitch," "cinch" and "balance" carry with them low suggestions — of work. I do not wish to misrepresent our author or to garble his words. So I hasten to state that the distinctions made in this paragraph are quoted from another writer and that our own author may not approve of them. Judge for yourself.

Here is a little extract in his happiest manner — and by this foot you may know Hercules.

"A slight provincial touch is given by the frequent use of 'minister' instead of 'clergyman,' and when one refers to a clergyman as a 'preacher,' the case is hopeless." Nothing provincial about that, is there? Yet if one, hearing this single sentence and having no knowledge of the author save that sentence, could not go to the ten-acre map in the Pennsylvania Station and put his unhesitating finger within one inch of that author's home, one's case would then be hopeless indeed.

"There is another provincial usage out of which it is to be hoped the American people will, in the course of time, be educated." — Did you get that? The usage of the American people is provincial; the use of an insular or peninsular corner of America is not provincial. The part is greater than the whole. — "They" — newspaper men — "spoke of his wife, of course, as 'Mrs. McKinley,' but they always mentioned his aged mother as 'Mother McKinley.' This was provincial and disgusting to a degree; and it is surprising that no one ever reverted to the dignified New England usage, which would have mentioned the dowager as 'Madam McKinley.'"

There! He told you himself! I was afraid he would. Anyhow, I didn't tell. And we have gained one advantage. After this, we can have no doubt as to the exact meaning of the word "provincial." Anything is "provincial" that does not conform to New England usage. We have it from his own mouth. We are on firm ground now.

"I should hardly have thought it necessary to recall this detestable bit of social ignorance," he proceeds, "had not President McKinley himself been guilty of it during a journey of his through the South. . . . Now this form of speech is not only crude and wholly alien to the little touches which give distinction, but its mental suggestions are unpleasant, since it is a form of speech that suggests Mother Goose and Mother Bunch, and brings to mind some wrinkled, blear-eyed beldam — a wizened crone, a raucous hag."

These be wild and whirling words, my masters! It doesn't matter so much about us. You and I are no better than we should be, and our shoulders are broad. But Uncle John, and Aunt Mary, and Mother Anderson, who helped us when little Jimmie died — to have them and their speech held up to contempt and derision — it hurts, I tell you! It rankles. They were kind and good and loving; they are not "disgusting" to our memories. Nor is Mother Goose, for that matter.

If it is not long since clear that I, now remonstrating, am but a rude, crude, rough, low and brutal person, unmistakably plebeian — just a plain, provincial American of no sublimated, very special caste — the fact is now expressly declared. I will also here state and proclaim that, if any healthy and sane he-Gileadite, between the ages of twenty and fifty, not more than ten pounds lighter or over forty pounds heavier than myself, shall, in my presence, venture to direct his insolence at these kindly, dim-eyed Ephraimite kindred of mine, I'm going to hit him once. That's the sort of person I am. If I subsequently have to say "Good mawnin', Judge!" or "Doctor, how long do you s'pose it'll be before I can get around again?" — why, I'll try to say it cheerfully.

Yes, sir. Not going to make any little declamation before I rebuke him, either. Folks that use that kind of wit should expect fitting repartee. He may strut and swell all he wants to, he may abuse me as long as it amuses him; but those "blear eyes" are faded with tears, those wrinkles are scars of Armageddon fight: he must teach his tongue to speak respectfully of them, or teach his hands to keep his head. It doesn't matter about the rest of us. Curiously enough, however much a person of this sort looks down on us, we never look up to him; it doesn't occur to us.

"Mother" called out all his rancor. Here is some more about it. Mr. McKinley said "mother" himself — "Mother" Hobson. "And when Mr. McKinley adopted it, it was so out of keeping . . . as to resemble the speech of one whose evenings in early youth were spent in some small, backwoods country 'store,' in the society of those who pendulously dangle their loutish legs over the sides of an empty cracker barrel."

Let us get back to earth. It may be well to remember that in just such a small country store Abraham Lincoln was wont to pendulously dangle his loutish legs; and that the work well done for their country and for all humanity by those who, in their early youth so dangled — pendulously dangled — their loutish legs in just such detestable places, so far outweighs anything done by dilettantes, pendulously dangling their loutish legs from easy chairs in any club or any university, that none — not even themselves — have ever felt the necessity of comparison.

By-the-way, how could one dangle his or her loutish legs except pendulously? I have pendulously dangled my loutish legs frequently, both from easy chairs and cracker barrels, empty or full — full cracker barrels, I mean — in large stores and small; but never, to my knowledge, have I dangled my loutish legs like a steeple, for instance, or a yardarm, or a nebular hypothesis. I must try it sometime. Always to dangle one's loutish legs pendulously shows deplorable lack of initiative.

This saddens one. It is enough to sadden a dozen. If the net result of a college education is to have erected, by the toil of years, and possibly by the self-denial of one's father and mother — of one's paternal and maternal ancestors — a tall, giddy and tolerably useless pedestal, whereon one is to sit for the remainder of one's life in close observation of one's personal pulchritude, like an introspective bronze Buddha, then, if sending our boys to college leads to such self-loving attitude, in Heaven's name let's not send 'em! No — that would be a cowardly evasion. Foolish, too, remembering the millions of kindly folk who remain kindly, fair-minded, considerate and just, though educated. Rather let us club together, we rough men, to endow in every school Chairs of Common Sense and of The Relative Proportion of Things — and get the best men to fill them.

The junior editor, reading this MS. as he dangles his loutish legs from the window-seat, says that I am all wrong; that the critic doesn't object to the word "mother," save as applied to dowagers, in lieu of "madam." But I maintain that there is not and never can be anything "disgusting" in any use of the word mother; that it is the noblest and sweetest word in the language. "Mother is growing old," says a man of his wife; or, to her, "Mother, how long is it since Charley Hilman went West?" So misused, the word is the final endearment.

It is even conceivable that a general — a general who protected his soldiers against embalmed meats and pasteboard shoes and their own weaknesses, for example — might be called "mother" by campfires; just as certain lewd fellows of the baser sort, who stood with Thomas at Chickamauga, spoke of that gallant soldier as "Pap" Thomas. You would infer, in such a case, that "mother" was a symbol of trust and affection — not of disgust or belittlement. But, if the general were called "Madam" . . . ?

"A person who addresses a physician affably as 'Doc,' and who . . . will speak of him as being 'raised' in such-and-such a place — this is the sort of person who also . . . wears a celluloid collar and eats peas with a knife."

Missed me that time! I never eat peas. But, if a man who wears celluloid collars addresses a physician affably as "Doc," what would a man who wears a flannel shirt be affably apt to call him? Sawbones, maybe. Yet the best-loved man of this generation said, as he lay dying: "Pull up the curtain, Doc; I'm afraid to go home in the dark."

"The unenlightened" — (and uncapitalized) — "person . . . may use the expression 'Between you and I,' just as he may, if he is very benighted, say 'You was.' These slips are to be expected from those . . . who describe a housemaid as 'the girl,' which is, of course, not quite so bad as to speak of her as 'the help,' but is, nevertheless, the linguistic earmark of a class — the class that splits its infinitives and thinks that

Fonetik Refawm is scholarly." This is respectfully referred to the Fonetik Refawmers, with the query whether a "help" is really a housemaid unless she wears a cap as a sort of badge of servility.

"The Enlightened person may, however, speak of 'those sort of things.'" Here follows a list of things that an enlightened person may say, ending with: "when very colloquial indeed, 'It is me!'" I judge that he does these permissible things himself, maybe.

"A vulgarism, '-hä-ouse-,' which, when they use it in the presence of a cultivated Englishman, ranks them at once in his mind with the caddish and the ignorant." Caddishness and ignorance are one and inseparable, it seems. We had not known this.

"Persons of this sort present as pathetic a spectacle to the Enlightened as do those who, in employing the broad 'a' because it is so English, introduce it ignorantly into words where the English never use it; saying, for example, 'fawncy' for 'fancy,' in which the educated Englishman always sounds the 'a' as flatly as any Philadelphian." Philadelphia is provincial, you see. Pretty much all the United States is provincial, south and west of a given point. As you now note, that point is north of Philadelphia. My own idea is that the given point lies somewhere between Stepleton and St. George — or at the Statute of Liberty, maybe. That would be a good place to fix it. Even so, there would be many unrefined people within the pale.

"To receive a letter containing such words as 'Xmas,' 'tho,' 'photo' and 'rec'd' affects one" — It affects one very badly indeed. I spare you the unpleasant details. Such letters "are usually written by the sort of men who sign their names in such abbreviated forms as 'Geo.,' 'Wm.,' 'Chas.,' 'Jas.' and 'Jno.'"

This is the method of Lady Grove, to quote Mr. Chesterton: "To terrify people from doing quite harmless things by telling them that if they do they are the kind of people who would do other things, equally harmless."

Let us look into this. I find, from the volume nearest at hand — and I mean by that the first and only work consulted — that of the fifty-five who pledged their lives, their fortunes and their sacred honor to the Declaration of Independence, no less than thirty signed with just such atrocious and detestable contractions. That is the sort of persons they were. Jefferson signed "Th.," Franklin wrote it "Benja." Of the Constitution framers, the immortal Geo. did not even stop at Geo. He signed it "Go." — just like that! Seventeen of the thirty-nine followed his noxious example by other low abbreviations. One even stooped to "Dan'l."

We are reminded of the devil demanding credentials from Tomlinson — and that is another pathetic spectacle:

"'You have read, you have heard, you
      have thought' quoth he.
      'God's mercy! what ha' y' *done?*'"

You see plainly, Jas., that our author was trying to impose upon
us merely his personal preference about "Wm." and "Chas." It is not
a matter of good taste or poor taste; it is only a matter of his taste
or your taste. It is not always so easy to see that such is the case as in
this instance; but that is about what he aims at all along. Even when
he is right, his ferocity defeats his purpose — if his purpose were
indeed to better our speech, which is hereby doubted. Take this
paper, for instance — which might have been the most limpid
Addisonian English, had it not been — were it not — only he got me
all roiled up.

Another little footprint. He says:

"I have always felt a genuine admiration for those among my cor-
respondents who write everything out in full; as, for example, 'January the twenty-eighth,' 'Seven hundred and sixty-three, Albermarle
Avenue,' and so on. There is a certain aristocratic suggestion of
leisure about this sort of thing that appeals to me and that is thoroughly consistent."

You see? Nobility and gentry — that sort of thing. People of
leisure, uncontaminated by work.

I don't think I am unfair to this man. This book of his — which
might otherwise have been valuable — is stained throughout by like
narrowness and intolerance.

Here is a bit of unconscious autobiography:

"But who among us would not be willing to spend three hours a
day in dining properly *chez Voisin*, rather than to save two hours
and fifty-five minutes of that time by furtively gobbling a plate of
corned-beef hash in a John Street beanery?"

He spells it out in full, you notice — even John Street. There is a
certain air of aristocratic leisure about this sort of thing that appeals
to one — doesn't it? John Street, I gather, is a very low place indeed.
People work there, possibly. Don't turn away, Wm. . . . Look me in
the eye. I trust you have never furtively gobbled a plate of corned-
beef hash in a Jno. St. beanery. I never have. But I will. If ever I
find out where Jno. St. is — information is hereby requested — I will
hie me to a beanery, pendulously dangle my loutish legs from a stool,
and furtively gobble a plate of corned-beef hash. Just to preserve my
self-respect. I do not like corned-beef hash.

"Very likely there are members of the American Philological Association who habitually eat peas with their knives and perhaps drink

out of finger bowls; but their example will hardly result in the establishment of a new social canon."

You mustn't cross him; he was raised a pet. He does not wait to find out your name, your station, your dwelling place or your destination — or even if you are a real person. A purely supposititious person who supposititiously fails to agree with his notions on any subject, however unimportant, is at once questioned as to motives, breeding, morals, family and color, and becomes the target for the cheap and easy satire which belittles its object less than it degrades the user; and that displays precisely so much wit as is shown withal by pressing the tip of one's thumb to the tip of one's nose and wiggling one's derisive fingers with a certain aristocratic suggestion of leisure.

He doesn't like this Philological Association. On questions of taste, he says, it is "entitled to speak with no more weight than the Ancient Order of Hibernians or the Knights of Labor." To prove it he tells this anecdote:

"Some time ago one of our most distinguished classical professors was asked why he never attended the meetings of the American Philological Association; and he replied, with an air of unutterable boredom: 'Oh, because, if I go, I shall have to meet so many persons who wear black trousers!' "

This is conclusive. We may now pass on to settle other vexed subjects.

"I used to open it and put it aside under the impression that it was a publication in the Magyar or Polish or Czechish tongue, brought out for the benefit of those interesting aliens who inhabit that portion of the country; and who, when they are not engaged in organizing strikes, amuse themselves by assassinating one another — a most laudable occupation, in which I am sure no judicious person would ever be anxious to discourage them."

It was *not* a publication in any of these tongues, mind you. That was merely his impression. He was not discussing Magyars, Poles or Czechs. He was discussing simplified spelling. But he was not one to let his light be hidden under a bushel. Accordingly he abandoned his discourse to give us his profound and well-considered views on those aliens and upon the labor question.

And yet, Thos., there are times when I realize how this sort of person feels, and sympathize with him. There is a Spanish adjective, "bronco," meaning rough, coarse, crusty, crabbed, rude — and also hoarse, harsh to the ear. On the English tongue it becomes a noun, meaning a horse; a rough, coarse, crusty, crabbed, rude and boisterous horse — a horse of no refinement. And there is a sort of person who spells it "broncho." There are some ninety-nine millions of such persons in this country alone. Probably the secondary meaning of the word, of hoarse, or harsh, deceived them. They seem to think that a bronco is a horse afflicted with bronchitis, hay fever, or phth — oh, well, asthma, then. It is very annoying to me that this obstinate, unreasonable ninety-nine million will persist in this provincial and disgusting usage, instead of conforming to the New Mexican standard. I do not hesitate to infer, believe and affirm that this sort of person eats peas with his knife; wears a celluloid collar and black trousers; is guilty of perjury, piracy on the high seas, bribery and corruption; does not write out his name, date and address in full; beats the hotels and his wife; tips his glass but not the waiter; gambles, wins; quotes Mother Goose; pendulously dangles his legs and furtively gobbles a plate of corned-beef hash in a John Street beanery — and works, maybe!

If one turns one's eyes from the Astors and the little asteroids to consider carefully in what desert corner of the universe our petty provincial system wanders darkling on the dim frontier of chaos, a fleeting spark for one brief split-second of Eternity — one would hardly think it worth one's while to be such an insufferable, unmitigated, complicated and complacent ass as I am about that "bronco" word — would one? For consider, that in the worlds beyond Aldebaran and Antares they may not use the word bronco at all. Or madam, either.

The book on Words is written in a more tolerant spirit. It is fair to believe that the writer's honest purpose was to help his readers to better usage. But inherent superiority cannot be completely suppressed. It peeps out: "Abominable"; "execrable"; "ignoramus"; "no one but a low fellow will say that"; "a vulgar colloquialism befitting a clodhopper."

A clodhopper is one who hops clods — in plowing. The term seems to be a euphemism for "farmer." That he who hops a clod is necessarily a low and despicable fellow is, for many, not the least of those truths which they hold to be self-evident. I think the inference is hasty. I think that never to have hopped a clod is but a negative virtue at best. I have known men who hopped clods with nimbleness and precision, but who, nevertheless, were estimable men, who personally knew what their own thoughts and opinions were without consulting the authorities or looking in the morning paper.

His instruction is right in the main, but he slips sometimes. "Viewpoint is the correct and elegant expression, unless we would countenance such vulgar words as washtub, cookstove and the like." He does not give us the elegant word for washtub. I wish he had supplied it. I would like to get one.

"The masses. This expression is thought by some to be as vulgar as the object it describes."

Let us pass over the implausibility of such reference to some one hundred and nine and a half millions — some say more — of our people, as "the object," or even "objects." For a question arises in our minds — if an object may be said to have a mind — whether this wholesale scorn is not at least as disrespectful to the Creator of that object, or objects, as to the object, or objects, which He created? Either this sweeping disdain is unjustified or He erred in not calling expert advice before creating this object, or objects. He might have heard of something to His advantage.

On the whole, I believe "objects" is the better word. It seems to concede to us a certain amount of personal identity.

Paste this in your hat, please. "Vulgar" means "of or pertaining to the mass or multitude of the people: common, general, ordinary, public; hence, in general use: vernacular." The evil meaning attached to the word has been forced upon it by such scornful patricians as have felt it needful systematically to advise the world that *they* were not common or ordinary. That a word or a man is vulgar is no more proof that such word or man is vile than that a vulgar fraction is vile. A vulgar man may be objectionable — but not because he is one of a multitude of people. That is not a criminal matter. It is not even a matter for sorrow. When you meet a man overgiven to the use of "vulgar," in its deprecating sense, shun him. He is a Gileadite; he will slay you. If it is not feasible to avoid him, at least let him do all the talking. Keep your mouth shut. You are safe then — unless you wear black trousers.

"He married his wife in Honolulu. Well, such a man is only fit to live on some far sea-island." Far from — er — where? I wonder. What has the place where a man lives to do with his fitness? Where is the moral Meridian of Greenwich? Honolulu is no farther away from any place whatever — *and I make no exceptions* — than any place whatever is from Honolulu. I say it deliberately; and I will maintain it with my life. I seem to have a dim remembrance of a parable wherein it is said: "I have married a wife, and therefore I cannot come." But the Giver of that parable lived in a far land Himself.

Surely this is literalism gone mad. To "marry" originally meant to take a husband; true. It means to wed, now — and has meant just that any time these four centuries. There is no such thing as the "sanctity" of language: a word means what it means, not what is once meant or what it might mean. So cruelly to exile a man, or even a person, for using a word in its universally accepted sense throws a strong sidelight on the animus of the hyper-critic. True, in the strictest literal sense a man who marries a wife thereby assists her to commit bigamy. A bride is not a wife until she is married. Theoretically, a man marries a maid, widow or divorcee; in practice we may say "he marries a wife" just as we say "he takes a wife." "Thou shalt not take a wife of the daughters of Canaan." No misunderstanding results. It seems hard to be consigned to outer darkness for using a term so convenient and so unambiguous.

The Life of Lincoln, which we now take up, is in many respects a valuable work. Its usefulness is heavily discounted by the opening pages, which are given to indiscriminating attack upon the threefold nature of the early settlers of Illinois and Indiana. The author imputes to them the lowest motives; he puts the worst possible construction on their every act. Lincoln himself does not escape rough handling; and as for his family, they are pursued with fire and sword — no city of refuge avails them.

That the pioneers built log huts before building palaces is a shameful thing; the forest was their personal misdemeanor; the privations of the foregoer are his reproach. Decency, cleanliness, morality, truthfulness, honor, common honesty, the author denies to them, directly or by implication. Indeed, of all possible virtues he grants them only two: "an ignoble physical courage" and "a sort of bastard contempt for hardship." These are his prudent words. For myself, I think that sort of bastard contempt for hardship would do nearly as well in a pinch as a legitimate contempt for hardship, with a church register rampant tattooed on its torso. Honestly, don't you think he went out of his way to be offensive?

What sticks in his gizzard most, however, was that these men were migratory. He doesn't approve of that. He rings all the changes on this theme: "restless"; "shiftless vagrants"; "the natural idler"; "nomads"; "rovers"; "waifs and strays from civilized communities"; "adventurers," forever "moving on." He intimates pretty strongly that they "moved on" to avoid paying their debts. He does not explain how they could have settled the West if they had stayed at home. He evidently thinks they might have been better employed. It is a pity. He blames them severely. "Wretched"; "brutal"; "squalid"; "frontier ruffians of the familiar type"; "uncouth"; "coarse"; "vulgarity"; "utter lack of barriers establishing strata of society" — these are but a few expressions culled from a dozen pages.

I want to do a little inferring now. I feel that I have a right to infer a little. My inference is that this author has lived too long among the noble oaks and the solid citizens, many of whom have never left their native parish, that he has acquired a wrong notion of this matter. I do not know his birthplace. I do not here hazard a guess. But I think I could find him if I had to.

There! I have done the man an injustice. He *does* credit these people with another virtue — a notable one. He says: "Finding life hard, they helped each other with a general kindliness which is impracticable among the complexities of elaborate social organizations."

We have noticed that. Our sort of objects seldom receive help or kindliness from really cultured people — or politeness, either. They invite us to say Shibboleth, generally. Then they slay us.

The question naturally arises: Is a stratified society that finds kindliness and helpfulness impracticable, really superior to a society in which kindliness and helpfulness are spontaneous and inevitable? (Cries of "Good!" "Good!")

"Troughs served for washtubs when washtubs were used." Exactly. It is difficult to imagine troughs serving for washtubs when washtubs were not used. That would have been a useless extravagance — as he would realize if he had never hollowed out a log with an adze. But perhaps he meant that they did not wash their clothes. On examination, it is likely that such was indeed his meaning. People living so far away commonly do not wash their clothes. That is well known.

"If a woman wanted a looking-glass she scoured a tin pan, but the temptation to inspect one's self must have been feeble."

I think it is your turn to infer a little while, Thos. If, speaking of these thousands of brave dead women, he could not keep his puny malice from this bitterest sneer, how much mercy do you think he showed the men? He had never seen these women, remember. And they are dead now. To be so ugly that the temptation to inspect one's self was feeble — and one a woman, mind you! — that is abnormal. It crushes one. Desecration can no further go.

They were our grandmothers. Thos; we hold that they were brave and pure and fair; their sons saved this nation. Let no one dream that we are gratified at this wanton insult. We will not say his grandam was but withered. It would not be the speech of a gentleman. And we do not know. Let us confine ourselves to the facts and to the living. We will say of him that he is the sort of person who would say that sort of thing. That squares it up, I fancy.

For myself, I deem and say that this stock was as good as any that ever came over in the Mayflower, loaded mast-high with Chippendale and Sheraton — well, furniture, anyhow. Maybe it was Cloisonné and Valenciennes. I don't really know about furniture. Chippendale and Sheraton are lovely words, so I used them.

The trouble with this sort of people is that they are that sort of people. They are puffed up with vainglory and presumption. A little astonished at themselves, too. They ignore the fact that language is a tool, made by those who use it — made by that use — and that it changes. They make no allowance for the growth of idiom, or for the modifications of a living tongue. Language is changed by modifying — never otherwise. Like other man-made instruments, language was at first more complicated than was needful. We have outgrown most of the cumbrous and clumsy inflections now; we are simplifying the spelling in our slow, easy-going way, and have been simplifying it for centuries: I think we shall simplify our pronunciation in time. The Greeks, when two letters came together in a word to make an ugly sound, systematically changed or dropped one of them to make a smooth and flowing sound. They had a beautiful and sonorous word for this euphonic process, too. I wish I could remember it. It is a bully word. Never mind — we are going to do the same thing. We are doing it. The dictionaries haven't caught up with us yet — that's all.

Cultured people give the words oil, noise and boy, as ô-ĭl, nô-ĭse and bô-ĭ, with a fur-lined mouth and the accent on the first sound — not exactly in two syllables, but, say, a syllable and a half; ice, mine and by are rendered ä-ēēce, mä-ēēne, bä-ēe′, with a pinched nose; the more carefully sheltered of them pronounce out, bound and now as thus: ä-ōōt, bä-ōō-nd, nä-ōō, with the lips closed — accent as above.

I think these elaborate pronunciations will die out after a while — not because they are not proper but because it is not convenient to frame to utter them. The last has now but few devoted adherents.

The next to go, as I judge, will be the Norman "u" — except as an initial sound and in some of the easier combinations. We can all pronounce "amusing" rightly enough. Lute, except as "loot," is too hard for us. This is a relic of the attempt to foist Norman-French upon England. The old aristocratic flavor still clings to it. Duke, lute, new, as dĭ-ōōk, lĭ-ōōt, nĭ-ōōw, serve as social insignia, verbal strawberry leaves. But the most enthusiastic practitioners of this admirable sound find it a difficult accomplishment. It will have to go, I think. We, the Ephraimites, the masses, the bourgeoisie, *hoi polloi*, the plebeians — the workers, in fact — desire it. We cannot frame to utter these distinguished words. — Good word that, bourgeoisie — eh? A bit difficult to frame it, however. A bourgeois, I gather, is one who supports himself by his own exertions and doesn't put on airs.

When a person approaches you with one of these linguistic feats, observe him closely. If he is pale, breathless, astonied, shun him. It is fair to say that many excellent people use any or all of these sounds — naturally, unconsciously and without consternation. This warning — and these comments — are not for them.

Fictionists will lose a valuable asset when the Norman "u" sound is abandoned. It is an old standby. You seldom read a story by a young writer without hitting upon "literachoor" or "literatoor." The thing interests him and he has but lately learned how one in his station in life should pronounce the word. "Brootal," too. Brootal seldom fails to win a smile. "Noo York" is another mirthmaker. And there is unfailing merriment in "calling" the midday meal "dinner."

Some novelists and story-tellers are offensive in their dialect writing. Others use precisely the same phonetics without hurting anyone. It depends upon the spirit in which the spelling is done. If the context is marked by haughty superiority, pride, disdain, arrogance and contempt, it is probable that no kindness is meant by the dialect. James Whitcomb Riley has grieved no Indiana heart by his loving mockery.

(Just a word of digression, boys and girls of literatoor: When your illiterate writes a letter, and you print it in your text, please do not permit him to keep up that dialect in that letter with a proper apostrophe in each fitting place. It isn't consistent; it isn't sensible; it isn't artistic. It is a blemish. We've all seen this done — too often. Manage to have him misspell without his own knowledge of it — surreptitiously, as it were.)

We'll skip three or four French and German sounds, produced by holding the vocal organs rigidly in position for the sound of one letter and then trying to give the sound of some other letter — not any other letter, you understand; some particular letter. The resultant disaster will be the required sound — perhaps. Let us hurry on.

There are place-Shibboleths over which there is much ink shed. Such a word is "gallery." Why is "gallery" taboo? It is of good and direct lineage, French and Spanish; brought here by French and Spanish settlers in Louisiana. Why are porch, portico, piazza and the Dutch "stoop" admitted, while "gallery" is so rigorously barred? Answer: It is the "favor of makers." It is because New Orleans has produced few lexicographers.

One more, and we are done. "Creek" is, I believe, pronounced "creak" in lexicographerland. I am entirely willing to pronounce it that way. Most of our millions, however, pronounce it "crik." That does not prove that this is a better way to pronounce it; it only proves that it is pronounced that way. Also, that it will probably continue to be pronounced that way. "Been" was once pronounced "bean." It is not, now. Why? Because the dictionaries changed, I rede you, Nay. The dictionaries changed for that a perverse and stiff-necked generation provincially pronounced it "bin" — because they wanted to, maybe; or perhaps because it is a little easier to say. That is a way dictionaries have. A dictionary does not create; it records. It is not a master; it is a tool. When we seriously decide that we want to have a tool changed, we change that tool.

So let us not be unduly hurt or angered by these continual little slurs and slings at our manners and our hopes and our people, Thos. Tonight, as we furtively gobble our plates of corned-beef hash, let us laugh over it. We have had our little say; we are just a trifle sheepish over our own blatant vindictiveness — a little ashamed of the childish perversity with which we cling to our sins.

We can afford to smile. The future is ours — yes, and the present, too. "The real language of a people is the spoken word, not the written." We can forgive even the Gileadite, if he will only show a little respect for helpless age and for the dead. For us — the living — let him scold. Poor fellow, he is beaten. He is conscious, too, that his class has never done that part of the world's work for which it has been fitted by its splendid opportunities. His class has been too much engrossed hitherto. But I think it will do its part and do it nobly, sometime. I think that time is drawing near. Heaven speed the day!

Have I any "constructive program"? I have; a simple one — not, I think, unreasonable; but it is not new. When pointing out to us our verbal faults, our teachers are under no bond to make and publish morose inferences as to our complexion, age, clothes, weight, height, disposition or ultimate destination. In noteworthy books dealing with the subject — and they are needed, for our errors are *not* right and our deficiencies are *not* accomplishments — you may find such phrases as these: This term is better than that one; This word is incorrect; That is not the preferred usage; Avoid this error. And for more emphasis: This blunder is only too common, but it cannot be justified; This usage is indefensible — care should be taken to avoid it. The authors of such books make no mention of our vices, our sins, our crimes, our bad manners or our clothes — judging, possibly, that we are sufficiently informed on those subjects. They confine themselves to the use or misuse of words and leave us to adjust those other matters with our God and our tailor.

The Hired Man
on Horseback

THE HIRED MAN ON HORSEBACK

(With apologies to G. K. Chesterton and Don Juan of Austria)

The typical cowboy is . . . simply a riding farmhand.
— James Stephens; *International Book Review*

The cowboy, after all, was never anything more than a hired man on horseback.
— Editorial Page; *Minneapolis Tribune, San Francisco Chronicle*

Harp and flute and violin, throbbing through the night,
Merry eyes and tender eyes, dark head and bright;
Moon shadow on the sundial to mark the moments fleet,
The magic and enchanted hours where moonlight lovers meet;
And the harp notes come all brokenly by night winds stirred —
But the hired man on horseback is singing to the herd!

(Whoopie-ti-yo-o-o! Hi yo-o, my little dogies!)

Doggerel upon his lips and valor in his heart,
Not to flinch and not to fail, not to shirk his part;
Wearily and wearily he sees the stars wheel by,
And he knows his guard is nearly done by the great clock in the sky.
He hears the Last Guard coming and he hears their song begun,
A foolish song he will forget when he forgets the sun.

(Whoopie-ti-yo-o-o! Hi yo-o, my little dogies!)

'We got 'em now, you sleepy men, so pull your freight to bed
And pound your ear an hour or two before the east is red.'
If to his dreams a face may come? Ah, turn your eyes away,
Nor guess what face may come by dream that never comes by day.
Red dawn breaking through the desert murk;
The hired man on horseback goes laughing to his work.

The broker's in his office before the stroke of ten,
He buys and smiles and he sells and smiles at the word of other men;
But he gets his little commission flat, whether they buy or sell,
So be it drouth or storm or flood, the broker's crops do well.
They are short of Katy Common, they are long on Zinc Preferred —
But the hired man on horseback is swimming with the herd!

White horns gleaming where the flood rolls brown
Lefty fighting the lower point as the current sweeps them down.
Lefty fighting the stubborn steers that will not turn or slow,
They press beside him, they swim below him — 'Come out, and let them go!'
But Lefty does not leave them and Lefty tries once more,
He is swinging the wild leaders in toward the northern shore;
'He'll do to ride the river with!' (Bridging the years between,
Men shall use those words again — and wonder what they mean.)
He is back to turn the stragglers in to follow the leaders through
When a cottonwood snag comes twisting down and cuts the herd in two;
When a whirling snag comes twisting down with long arms lashing fate,
On wearied horse and wearied man — and they see it come, too late!
— A brown hand lifted in the splashing spray;
Sun upon a golden head that never will be gray;
A low mound bare until new grass is grown —
But the Palo Pinto trail herd has crossed the Cimarron!

A little midnight supper when the play is done,
Glancing lights and sparkling eyes — the night is just begun.
Beauteous night, O night of love! Youth and joy are met.
Shine on our enchantment still! 'Sweet, your eyes are wet.'
'Dear, they sing for us alone!' Such the lover's creed.
— But the hired man on horseback is off with the stampede!

There is no star in the pit-black night, there is none to know or blame,
And a hundred yards to left or right, there is safety there — and shame!
A stone throw out on either side, with none to guess or tell —
But the hired man on horseback has raised the rebel yell!
He has turned to loosen his saddle strings, he has fumbled his slicker free,
He whirls it high and snaps it wide wherever the foremost be.
He slaps it into a longhorn's eyes till he falters in his stride —
An oath and a shot, a laugh and a shot, and his wild mates race beside;
A pony stumbles — no, he is up, unhurt and running still;
'Turn 'em, turn 'em, turn 'em, Charlie! Good boy, Bill!'
They are crashing through the cedar mottes, they are skating the rim-rock
    slick,
They are thundering through the cactus flats where the badger holes are
    thick;
Day is breaking, clouds are lifting, leaders turn to mill —
'Hold 'em cowboys! Turn 'em, Charlie! — *God! Where's Bill?*'

The proud Young Intellectuals, a cultured folk are these,
They scorn the lowly Babbitts and their hearts are overseas;
They turn their backs upon us, and if we ask them why
They smile like jesting Pilate, and they stay for no reply;
They smile at faith and honor, and they smile at shame and crime —
But the old Palo Pinto man is calling for his time.

For he heard old voices and he heard hoofs beat,
Songs that long ago were gay to time with drumming feet;
Bent back straightens and dim eyes grow bright —
The last man on horseback rides on into the night!

Cossack and Saracen
Shout their wild welcome then,
Ragged proud Conquistadores claim him kind and kin,
And the wild Beggars of the Sea leap up to swell the din;
And Hector leans upon the wall, and David bends to scan
This new brown comrade for the old brown clan,
The great-hearted gentlemen who guard the outer wall,
Black with sin and stained with blood — and faithful through it all;
Still wearing for all ornament the scars they won below —
And the Lord God of Out-of-Doors, He cannot let them go!
They have halted the hired horseman beyond the outer gate,
But the gentlemen adventurers cry shame that he should wait;
And the sour saints soften, with a puzzled grin,
As Esau and Ishmael press to let their brother in.
Hat tip-tilted and his head held high,
Brave spurs jingling as he passes by —
Gray hair tousled and his lips a-quirk —
To the Master of the Workmen, with the tally of his work!

RHODES'S EPITAPH
WRITTEN FOR HIMSELF

Now hushed at last the murmur of his mirth,
Here he lies quiet in the quiet earth.
—When the last trumpet sounds on land and sea
He will arise then, chatting cheerfully,
And, blandly interrupting Gabriel,
He will go sauntering down the road to hell.
He will pause loitering at the infernal gate
Advising Satan on affairs of state,
Complaining loudly that the roads are bad,
and bragging what a jolly grave he had!